D0034789

JOHN GRIMES
LIEUTENANT OF THE SURVEY SERVICE

Books by A. Bertram Chandler

John Grimes (series)

The Road to the Rim (1967)
To Prime the Pump (1971)
The Hard Way Up (1972)
Spartan Planet (1968)
The Inheritors (1972)
The Broken Cycle (1975)
The Big Black Mark (1975)
The Far Traveller (1977)
Star Courier (1977)
To Keep the Ship (1978)
Matilda's Stepchildren (1979)
Star Loot (1980)
The Anarch Lords (1981)
The Last Amazon (1984)
The Wild Ones (1984)
Catch the Star Winds (1969)
Into the Alternate Universe (1964)
Contraband from Other-Space (1967)
The Rim Gods (1969)
The Dark Dimensions (1971)
Alternate Orbits (1971)
The Gateway to Never (1972)
The Way Back (1976)

Derek Calver (series)

The Rim of Space (1961)
The Ship from Outside (1963)

Christopher Wilkinson (series)

The Coils of Time (1964)
The Alternate Martians (1965)

Empress (series)

Empress of Outer Space (1965)
Space Mercenaries (1965)
Nebula Alert (1967)

Other Novels

Bring Back Yesterday (1961)
Rendezvous on a Lost World (1961)
The Hamelin Plague (1963)
Beyond the Galactic Rim (1963)
Glory Planet (1964)
The Deep Reaches of Space (1964)
The Sea Beasts (1971)
The Bitter Pill (1974)
Kelly Country (1983)
To Rule the Refugees (1983)
Frontier of the Dark (1984)
Find the Lady (1984)

Short Fiction

Up to the Sky in Ships (1982)
From Sea to Shining Star (1990)

JOHN GRIMES LIEUTENANT OF THE SURVEY SERVICE

The Road to the Rim

To Prime the Pump

The Hard Way Up

Spartan Planet

The Inheritors

A. BERTRAM CHANDLER

This is a work of fiction. All the characters and events portrayed in these novels are either fictitious or are used fictitiously.

First SFBC Science Fiction Printing: December 2000.

Published by arrangement with the author's estate, via JABberwocky Literary Agency, P.O. Box 4558
Sunnyside, NY 11104-0558

Visit The SFBC at *http://www.sfbc.com*

ISBN 0-7394-1486-0

PRINTED IN THE UNITED STATES OF AMERICA.

Contents

THE ROAD TO THE RIM 1

TO PRIME THE PUMP 101

THE HARD WAY UP 227

SPARTAN PLANET 357

THE INHERITORS 485

The Road to the Rim

For Admiral Lord Hornblower, R.N.

— 1 —

HIS UNIFORM WAS new, too new, all knife-edged creases, and the braid and buttons as yet undimmed by time. It sat awkwardly upon his chunky body—and even more awkwardly his big ears protruded from under the cap that was set too squarely upon his head. Beneath the shiny visor his eyes were gray (but not yet hard), and his face, for all its promise of strength, was as yet unlined, had yet to lose its immature softness. He stood at the foot of the ramp by which he had disembarked from the transport that had carried him from the Antarctic Base to Port Woomera, looking across the silver towers that were the ships, interplanetary and interstellar, gleaming in the desert. The westering sun was hot on his back, but he did not notice the discomfort. There were the ships, the *real* ships—not obsolescent puddle-jumpers like the decrepit cruiser in which he, with the other midshipmen of his class, had made the training cruise to the moons of Saturn. There were the ships, the star ships, that span their web of commerce from Earth to the Centaurian planets, to the Cluster Worlds, to the Empire of Waverley, to the Shakespearian Sector and beyond.

(But they're only merchantmen, he thought, with a young man's snobbery.)

He wondered in which one of the vessels he would be taking passage. Merchantman or not, that big ship, the one that stood out from her neighbors like a city skyscraper among village church steeples, looked a likely enough craft. He pulled the folder containing his orders from his inside breast pocket, opened it, read (not for the second time, even), the relevant page.

. . . you are to report on board the Interstellar Transport Commission's Delta Orionis . . .

He was not a spaceman yet, in spite of his uniform, but he knew the Commission's system of nomenclature. There was the *Alpha* class, and the *Beta* class, and there were the *Gamma* and *Delta* classes. He grinned wryly. His ship was one of the smaller ones. Well, at least he would not be traveling to Lindisfarne Base in an *Epsilon* class tramp.

Ensign John Grimes, Federation Survey Service, shrugged his broad shoulders and stepped into the ground car waiting to carry him and his baggage from the airport to the spaceport.

2

GRIMES LOOKED AT the officer standing just inside *Delta Orionis*' airlock, and she looked at him. He felt the beginnings of a flush spreading over his face, a prickling of the roots of his close-cropped hair, and felt all the more embarrassed by this public display of his embarrassment. But spaceborn female officers, at this time, were almost as scarce as hens' teeth in the Survey Service—and such few as he had met all looked as though they shared a common equine ancestry. It was all wrong, thought Grimes. It was unfair that this girl (this attractive girl) should already be a veteran of interstellar voyages while he, for all his uniform and commission, should be embarking upon his first, his very first trip outside the bounds of the Solar System. He let his glance fall from her face (but not without reluctance), to the braid on her shoulderboards. Gold on a white facing. So it wasn't too bad. She was only some sort of paymaster—or, to use Merchant Service terminology, only some sort of purser.

She said, her clear, high voice almost serious, "Welcome aboard the *Delia O'Ryan*, Admiral."

"Ensign," corrected Grimes stiffly. "Ensign Grimes . . ."

". . . of the Federation Survey Service," she finished for him. "But you are all potential admirals." There was the faintest of smiles flickering upon her full lips, a barely discernible crinkling at the corners of her eyes. *Her brown eyes,* thought Grimes. *Brown eyes, and what I can see of her hair under that cap seems to be auburn . . .*

She glanced at her wristwatch. She told him, her voice now crisp and businesslike, "We lift ship in precisely ten minutes' time, Ensign."

"Then I'd better get my gear along to my cabin, Miss . . . ?"

"I'll look after that, Mr. Grimes. Meanwhile, Captain Craven sends his compliments and invites you to the Control Room."

"Thank you." Grimes looked past and around the girl, trying to discover for himself the door that gave access to the ship's axial shaft. He was determined not to ask.

"It's labeled," she told him with a faint smile. "And the cage is waiting at this level. Just take it up as far as it goes, then walk the rest. Or do you want a pilot?"

"I can manage," he replied more coldly than he had intended, adding, "thank you." He could see the sign over the door now. It was plain enough. AXIAL SHAFT. So was the button that he had to press to open the door—but the girl pressed it for him. He thanked her, again—and this time his coldness was fully intentional—and stepped into the cage. The door slid shut behind him. The uppermost of the studs on the elevator's control panel was marked CAPTAIN'S DECK. He pushed it, then stood there and watched the lights flashing on the panel as he was swiftly lifted to the nose of the ship.

When he was carried no further he got out, found himself on a circular walk surrounding the upper extremity of the axial shaft. On the outside of the shaft itself there was a ladder. After a second's hesitation he climbed it, emerged through a hatch into the control room.

It was like the control room of the cruiser in which he had made his training cruise—and yet subtly (or not so subtly), unlike it. Everything—but so had it been aboard the Survey Service vessel—was functional, but there was an absence of high polish, of polishing for polishing's sake. Instruments gleamed—but it was the dull gleam that comes from long and continual use, and matched the dull gleam of the buttons and rank marks on the uniforms of the officers already seated at their stations, the spacemen to whom, after all, a uniform was no more (and no less), than an obligatory working rig.

The big man with the four gold bars on each shoulder half turned his head as Grimes came up through the hatch. "Glad to have you aboard, Ensign," he said perfunctorily. "Grab yourself a seat—there's a spare one alongside the Mate's. Sorry, there's no time for introductions right now. We're due to get upstairs."

"Here!" grunted one of the officers.

Grimes made his way to the vacant acceleration chair, dropped into it, strapped himself in. While he was so doing he heard the Captain ask, "All secure, Mr. Kennedy?"

"No, sir."

"Then why the hell not?"

"I'm still waiting for the purser's report, sir."

"Are you?" Then, with a long-suffering sigh, "I suppose she's still tucking some passenger into her—or *his*—bunk. . . ."

"She could still be stowing some passenger's gear, sir," contributed Grimes. "Mine," he added.

"Indeed?" The Captain's voice was cold and elaborately uninterested.

Over the intercom came a female voice. "Purser to Control. All secure below."

"And bloody well time," grumbled the shipmaster. Then, to the officer at the transceiver, "Mr. Digby, kindly obtain clearance."

"Obtain clearance, sir," acknowledged that young man brightly. Then, into his microphone, "*Delta Orionis* to Port Control. Request clearance to lift ship. Over."

"Port Control to *Delta Orionis*. You may lift. Bon voyage. Over."

"Thank you, Port Control. Over and out."

Then the ship was throbbing to the rhythmic beat of her Inertial Drive, and Grimes felt that odd sense of buoyancy, of near weightlessness, that persisted until the vessel broke contact with the ground—and then the still gentle acceleration induced the reverse effect. He looked out through the nearest viewport. Already the ocher surface of the desert, streaked by the long, black shadows of ships and spaceport buildings, was far below them, with the vessels and the immobile constructions looking like toys, and one or two surface vehicles like scurrying insects. Far to the north, dull-ruddy against the blue of the sky, there was a sandstorm. *If that sky were darker,* thought Grimes, *this would look like Mars,* and the mental comparison reminded him that he, too, was a spaceman, that he, too, had been around (although only within the bounds of Sol's planetary system). Even so, he was Survey Service, and these others with him in Control were only merchant officers, fetchers and carriers, interstellar coach and truck drivers. (But he envied them their quiet competency.)

Still the ship lifted, and the spaceport below her dwindled, and the land horizon to the north and the now visible sea horizon to the south began to display the beginnings of curvature. Still she lifted, and overhead the sky was dark, and the first bright stars, Sirius and Canopus, Alpha and Beta Centauri, were sparkling there, beckoning, as they had beckoned for ages immemorial before the first clumsy rocket clambered heavenward up the ladder of its own fiery exhaust, before the first airplane spread its flimsy wings, before the first balloon was lifted by the hot, expanding gases from its airborne furnace. . . .

"Mr. Grimes," said the Captain suddenly, his voice neither friendly nor unfriendly.

"Sir?"

"We lift on I.D. until we're clear of the Van Allens."

"I know, sir," said Grimes—then wished that he could unsay the words. But it was too late. He was conscious of the shipmaster's hostile silence, of the amused contempt of the merchant officers. He shrank into his chair, tried to make himself as inconspicuous as possible. The ship's people talked among themselves in low voices, ignoring him. They allowed themselves a period of relaxation, producing and lighting cigarettes. Nobody offered the Ensign one.

Sulkily he fumbled for his pipe, filled it, lighted it. The Chief Officer coughed with quite unnecessary vigor. The Captain growled, "Put that out, please," and muttered something about stinking out the control room. He, himself, was puffing at a villainous black cigar.

The ship lifted, and below her the Earth was now a great sphere, three-quarters in darkness, the line of the terminator drawn across land masses, cloud formations and oceans. City lights twinkled in the gloom like star clusters, like nebulae. In a quiet voice an officer was calling readings from the radar altimeter.

To the throbbing of the Inertial Drive was added the humming, shrilling to a whine, of the directional gyroscopes as the ship turned about her short axis hunting the target star. The pseudogravity of centrifugal force was at an odd angle to that of acceleration—and the resultant was at an odder angle still. Grimes began to feel sick—and was actually thankful that the Captain had made him put his pipe out. Alarm bells sounded, and then somebody was saying over the intercom. "Prepare for acceleration. Prepare for acceleration. Listen for the countdown."

The countdown. Part of the long tradition of space travel, a hangover from the days of the first, unreliable rockets. Spaceships still used rockets—but only as auxiliaries, as a means of delivering thrust in a hurry, of building up acceleration in a short time.

At the word *Zero!* the Inertial Drive was cut and, simultaneously, the Reaction Drive flared into violent life. The giant hand of acceleration bore down heavily upon all in the ship—then, suddenly, at a curt order from the Captain, lifted.

Grimes became aware of a thin, high keening, the song of the ever-precessing gyroscopes of the Mannschenn Drive. He knew the theory of it—as what spaceman did not?—although the mathematics of it were beyond the comprehension of all but a handful of men and women. He knew what was happening, knew that the ship, now that speed had been built up, was, as one of his instructors had put it, going ahead in space and astern in time. He felt, as he had been told that he would feel, the uncanny sensation of *déja vu,* and watched the outlines of the control room and of every person and instrument in the compartment shift and shimmer, the colors sagging down the spectrum.

Ahead, the stars were pulsating spirals of opalescence, astern, Earth and Moon were frighteningly distorted, uncanny compromises between the sphere and the tesseract. But this was no more than the merest subliminal glimpse; in the twinkling of an eye the Home Planet and her daughter were no more than dust motes whirling down the dark dimensions.

The Captain lit a fresh cigar. "Mr. Kennedy," he said, "you may set normal Deep Space watches." He turned to Grimes. His full beard almost hid his expression, that of one performing a social duty with no enthusiasm. "Will you join me in my day cabin, Ensign?"

"It will be my pleasure, sir," lied Grimes.

3

HANDLING HIS BIG BODY with easy grace in the Free Fall conditions, the Captain led the way from the control room. Grimes followed slowly and clumsily, but with a feeling of great thankfulness that after his training cruise he was no longer subject to spacesickness. There were drugs, of course, and passengers used them, but a spaceman was expected to be independent of pharmaceutical aids. Even so, the absence of any proper "up" or "down" bothered him more than he cared to admit.

The shipmaster slid open the door to his accommodation, motioned to Grimes to enter, murmuring sardonically, "Now you see how the poor live." The so-called poor, thought Grimes, didn't do at all badly. This Deep Space sitting room was considerably larger than the day cabin of the Survey Service cruiser's Captain had been. True, it was also shabbier—but it was far more comfortable. Its decorations would never have been approved aboard a warship, were obviously the private property of the Master. There were a full dozen holograms on the bulkhead, all of them widely differing but all of them covering the same subject matter. Not that the subject matter was covered.

"My harem," grunted the Captain. "That one there, the redhead, I met on Caribbea. Quite a stopover that was. The green-haired wench—and you can see that it's not a dye job, although I've often wondered why women can't be *thorough*—isn't human, of course. But indubitably humanoid, and indubitably mammalian. Belongs to Brrrooonooorrrooo—one of the worlds of the Shaara Empire. The local Queen Mother offered to sell Lalia—that's her name—to me for a case of Scotch. And I was tempted . . ." He sighed. "But you Service Survey types aren't the only ones who have to live by Regulations."

Grimes said nothing, tried to hide his interest in the art gallery.

"But take a pew, Ensign. Spit on the mat and call the cat a bastard—this is Liberty Hall."

Grimes pulled himself to one of the comfortable chairs, strapped himself in. He said lamely, "I don't see any cat, sir."

"A figure of speech," growled the Captain, seating himself next to what looked like a drink cabinet. "Well, Mr. Grimes, your Commandant at the Academy, Commodore Bradshaw, is an old friend and shipmate of mine. He said that you were a very promising young officer"—like a balloon in a comic strip the unspoken words, "God knows why," hung between them—"and asked me to keep an eye on you. But I have already gained the impression that there is very little that a mere merchant skipper such as myself will be able to teach you."

Grimes looked at the bulky figure seated opposite him, at the radiation-darkened skin of the face above the black, silver-streaked beard, at the fiercely jutting nose, at the faded but bright and intelligent blue eyes, the eyes that were regarding him with more than a hint of amused contempt. He blushed miserably as he recalled his brash, "I know, sir," in this man's own control room. He said, with an effort, "This is my first Deep Space voyage, sir."

"I know." Surprisingly the Captain chuckled—and as though to celebrate this minor scoring over his guest opened the liquor cabinet. "Pity to have to suck this excellent Manzanila out of a bulb—but that's one of the hardships of Free Fall. Here!" He tossed a little pear-shaped container to Grimes, kept one for himself. "Your health, Ensign!"

"And yours, sir."

The wine was too dry for Grimes' taste, but he made a pretense of enjoying it. He was thankful that he was not asked to have a second drink. Meanwhile, his host had pulled a typewritten sheet from a drawer of his desk and was looking at it. "Let me see, now . . . You're in cabin 15, on D Deck. You'll be able to find your own way down, won't you?"

Grimes said that he would and unbuckled his lapstrap. It was obvious that the party was over.

"Good. Now, as an officer of the Survey Service you have the freedom of the control room and the engine rooms. . . ."

"Thank you, sir."

"Just don't abuse the privilege, that's all."

After that, thought Grimes, *I'm not likely to take advantage of it, let alone abuse it.* He let himself float up from his chair, said, "Thank you, sir." (For the drink, or for the admonition? What did it matter?) "I'll be getting down to my cabin, sir. I've some unpacking to do."

"As you please, Mr. Grimes."

The Captain, his social duty discharged, had obviously lost interest in his guest. Grimes let himself out of the cabin and made his way, not without difficulty, to the door in the axial shaft. He was surprised at the extent to which one not very large drink had interfered with the control of his body in Free Fall. Emerging from the elevator cage on D Deck he stumbled, literally, into the purser. "Let go of me," she ordered, "or I shall holler rape!"

That, he thought, *is all I need to make this trip a really happy one.*

She disengaged herself, moved back from him, her slim, sandaled feet, magnetically shod, maintaining contact with the steel decking, but gracefully, with a dancing motion. She laughed. "I take it that you've just come from a home truth session with B.B."

"B.B.?"

"The Bearded Bastard. But don't take it too much to heart. He's that way with all junior officers. The fact that you're Survey Service is only incidental."

"Thank you for telling me."

"His trouble," she went on. "His *real* trouble is that he's painfully shy."

He's not the only one, thought Grimes, looking at the girl. She seemed even more attractive than on the occasion of their first meeting. She had changed into shorts-and-shirt shipboard uniform—and she was one of the rare women who could wear such a rig without looking lumpy and clumpy. There was no cap now to hide her hair—smooth, lustrous, with coppery glints, with a straight white part bisecting the crown of her finely shaped head.

She was well aware of his scrutiny. She said, "You must excuse me, Ensign. I have to look after the other customers. They aren't seasoned spacemen like you."

Suddenly bold, he said, "But before you go, what is your name?"

She smiled dazzlingly. "You'll find a list of all ship's personnel posted in your cabin. I'm included." Then she was gone, gliding rapidly around the curve of the alleyway.

He looked at the numbers over the cabin doors, outboard from the axial shaft, making a full circuit of that hollow pillar before he realized that this was only the inner ring, that he would have to follow one of the radial alleyways to reach his own accommodation. He finally found No. 15 and let himself in.

His first action was to inspect the framed notices on the bulkhead.

I.S.S. Delta Orionis, he read.

Captain J. Craven, O.G.S., S.S.R.

So the Old Man held a Reserve commission. And the Order of the Golden Star was awarded for something more than good attendance.

Mr. P. Kennedy, Chief Officer.

He ignored the other names on the list while he searched for one he wanted. Ah, here it was.

Miss Jane Pentecost, Purser.

He repeated the name to himself, thinking that, despite the old play on words, this Jane was not plain. (But Janes rarely are.) *Jane Pentecost* . . . Then, feeling that he should be showing some professional interest, he acquainted himself with the names of the other members of the ship's crew. He was intrigued by the manning scale, amazed that such a large vessel, relatively speaking, could be run by such a small number of people. But this was not a warship; there were no weapons to be manned, there would never be the need to put a landing party ashore on the surface of a hostile planet. The Merchant Service could afford to automate, to employ machinery in lieu of ratings. The Survey Service could not.

Virtuously he studied the notices dealing with emergency procedures, ship's routine, recreational facilities and all the rest of it, examined with care the detailed plan of the ship. Attached to this was a card, signed by the Master, requesting passengers to refrain, as much as possible, from using the elevator in the axial shaft, going on to say that it was essential, for the good of their physical health, that they miss no opportunity for taking exercise. (In a naval vessel, thought Grimes, with a slight sneer, that would not be a request—it would be an order. And, in any case, there would be compulsory calisthenics for all hands.)

He studied the plan again and toyed with the idea of visiting the bar before dinner. He decided against it; he was still feeling the effects of the drink that the Captain had given him. So, to pass the time, he unpacked slowly and carefully, methodically stowing his effects in the drawers under the bunk. Then, but not without reluctance, he changed from his uniform into his one formal civilian suit. One of the officer-instructors at the Academy had advised this. "Always wear civvies when you're traveling as passenger. If you're in uniform, some old duck's sure to take you for one of the ship's officers and ask you all sorts of technical questions to which you don't know the answers."

While he was adjusting his frilled cravat in front of the mirror the sonorous notes of a gong boomed from the intercom.

4

THE DINING SALOON was much more ornate than the gunroom of that training cruiser had been, and more ornate than her wardroom. The essentials were the same, of course, as they are in any ship—tables and chairs secured to the deck, each seat fitted with its strap so that the comforting pressure of buttocks on padding could give an illusion of gravity. Each table was covered with a gaily colored cloth—but beneath the fabric there was the inevitable stainless steel to which the stainless steel service would be held by its own magnetic fields. But what impressed Grimes was the care that had been taken, the ingenuity that had been exercised to make this compartment look like anything but part of a ship.

The great circular pillar of the axial shaft was camouflaged by trelliswork, and the trelliswork itself almost hidden by the luxuriance of some broad-leaf climbing plant that he could not identify. Smaller pillars were similarly covered, and there was a further efflorescence of living decoration all around the circular outer wall—the wall that must be the inner skin of the ship. And there were windows in this wall. No, Grimes decided, not windows, but holograms. The glowing, three dimensional pictures presented and maintained the illusion that this was a hall set in the middle of some great park. But on what world? Grimes could not say. Trees, bushes and flowers were unfamiliar, and the color of the sky subtly strange.

He looked around him at his fellow diners, at the dozen passengers and the ship's officers, most of whom were already seated. The officers were in neat undress uniform. About half the male passengers were, like himself, formally attired; the others were sloppy in shorts and shirts. But this was the first night out and some laxity was allowable. The women, however, all seemed to have decided to outshine the glowing flowers that flamed outside the windows that were not windows.

There was the Captain, unmistakable with his beard and the shimmering rainbow of ribbons on the left breast of his blouse. There were the passengers at his table—the men inclined to portliness and pomposity, their women sleek and slim and expensive looking. Grimes was relieved to see that there was no vacant place—and yet, at the same time, rather hurt. He knew that he was only an Ensign, a one-ringer, and a very new Ensign at that—but, after all, the Survey Service was the Survey Service.

He realized that somebody was addressing him. It was a girl, a small, rather chubby blonde. She was in uniform—a white shirt with black shoulderboards, each bearing a narrow white stripe, sharply creased slacks, and black, highly polished shoes. Grimes assumed, correctly, that she was a junior member of the purser's staff. "Mr. Grimes," she said, "will you follow me, please? You're at Miss Pentecost's table."

Willingly he followed the girl. She led him around the axial shaft to a table for four at which the purser with two passengers, a man and a woman, was already seated. Jane Pentecost was attired as was his guide, the severity of her gold-trimmed black and white in pleasing contrast to the pink and blue frills and flounces that clad the other woman, her slenderness in still more pleasing contrast to the other's untidy plumpness.

She smiled and said pleasantly, "Be seated, Admiral."

"Admiral?" asked the man at her left, unpleasantly incredulous. He had, obviously, been drinking. He was a rough looking customer, in spite of the attempt that he had made to dress for dinner. He was twice the Ensign's age, perhaps, although the heavily lined face under the scanty sandy hair made him look older. "Admiral?" He laughed, revealing irregular yellow teeth. "In what? The Space Scouts?"

Jane Pentecost firmly took control. She said, "Allow me to introduce Ensign Grimes, of the Survey Service . . ."

"Survey Service . . . Space Scouts . . . S.S. . . . What's the difference?"

"Plenty!" answered Grimes hotly.

The purser ignored the exchange. "Ensign, this is Mrs. Baxter. . . ."

"Pleased to meet you, I'm sure," simpered the woman.

"And Mr. Baxter."

Baxter extended his hand reluctantly and Grimes took it reluctantly. The amenities observed, he pulled himself into his seat and adjusted his lapstrap. He was facing Jane Pentecost. The man was on his right, the woman on his left. He glanced first at her, then at her husband, wondering how to start and to maintain a conversation. But this was the purser's table, and this was her responsibility.

She accepted it. "Now you're seeing how the poor live, Admiral," she remarked lightly.

Grimes, taking a tentative sip from his bulb of consomme, did not think that the self-styled poor did at all badly, and said as much. The girl grinned and told him that the first night out was too early to draw conclusions. "We're still on shoreside meat and vegetables," she told him, "and you'll not be getting your first taste of our instant table wine until tomorrow. Tonight we wallow in the unwonted luxury of a quite presentable Montrachet. When we start living on the produce of our own so-called farm, washing it down with our own reconstituted plonk, you'll see the difference."

The Ensign replied that, in his experience, it didn't matter if food came from tissue-culture vats or the green fields of Earth—what *was* important was the cook.

"Wide experience, Admiral?" she asked sweetly.

"Not very," he admitted. "But the gunroom cook in my last ship couldn't boil water without burning it."

Baxter, noisily enjoying his dinner, said that this preoccupation with food and drink was symptomatic of the decadence of Earth. As he spoke his knife grated unpleasantly on the steel spines that secured his charcoal broiled steak to the surface of his plate.

Grimes considered inquiring if the man thought that good table manners were also a symptom of decadence, then thought better of it. After all, this was not *his* table. Instead, he asked, "And where are you from, Mr. Baxter?"

"The Rim Worlds, Mr. Grimes. Where we're left to sink or swim—so we've no time for much else than keeping ourselves afloat." He sucked noisily from his bulb of wine. "Things might be a little easier for us if your precious Survey Service did something about keeping the trade routes open."

"That is our job," said Grimes stiffly. "And we do it."

"Like hell! There's not a pirate in the Galaxy but can run rings around you!"

"Practically every pirate has been hunted down and destroyed," Grimes told him coldly.

"Practically every pirate, the man says! A few small-time bunglers, he means!"

"Even the notorious Black Bart," persisted Grimes.

"Black Bart!" Baxter, spluttering through his full mouth, gestured with his laden fork at Grimes. "Black Bart! He wasn't much. Once he and that popsy of his split brass rags he was all washed up. I'm talkin' about the *real* pirates, the ones whose ships wear national colors, instead o' the Jolly Roger, the ones that your precious Survey Service daren't say boo to. The ones who do the dirty work for the Federation."

"Such as?" asked Grimes rigidly.

"So now you're playin' the bleedin' innocent. Never heard o' the Duchy o' Waldegren, Mr. Ensign Grimes?"

"Of course. Autonomous, but they and the Federation have signed what's called a Pact of Perpetual Amity."

"Pretty words, ain't they? Suppose we analyze them. Suppose we analyze by analogy. D'yer know much about animals, Mr. Ensign Grimes?"

"Animals?" Grimes was puzzled. "Well, I suppose I do know something. I've taken the usual courses in xenobiology. . . ."

"Never mind that. You're a Terry. Let's confine ourselves to a selection of yer own Terran four-footed friends."

"What the hell are you driving at?" flared Grimes, losing his temper. He threw an apologetic glance in Jane Pentecost's direction, saw that she was more amused than shocked.

"Just think about a Pact of Perpetual Amity between an elephant and a tom cat," said Baxter. "A fat an' lazy elephant. A lean, scrawny, vicious tom cat. If the elephant wanted to he could convert that cat into a fur bedside rug just by steppin' on him. But he doesn't want to. He leaves the cat alone, just because the cat is useful to him. He does more than just leave him alone. He an' this feline pull out their pens from wherever they keep 'em an' sign their famous Pact.

"In case you haven't worked it out for yourself, the elephant's the Federation, and the tom cat's the Duchy of Waldegren."

"But why?" asked Grimes. *"Why?"*

"Don't they teach you puppies any interstellar politics? Or are those courses reserved for the top brass? Well, Mr. Grimes, I'll tell you. There's one animal that has the elephant *really* worried. Believe it or not, he's scared o' mice. An' there're quite a few mice inside the Federation, mice that make the elephant nervous by their rustlings an' scurryings an' their squeaky demands for full autonomy. That's where the cat comes in. By his free use of his teeth an' claws, by his very presence, he keeps the mice quiet."

"And just who are these famous mice, Mr. Baxter?" asked Grimes.

"Don't they teach you nothin' in your bleedin' Academy? Well, I'll tell you. In *our* neck o' the woods, the mice are the Rim Worlds, an' the tom cat, as I've already made clear, is the Duchy o' Waldegren. The Duchy gets away with murder—murder an' piracy. But accordin' to the

Duchy, an' accordin' to your big, stupid elephant of a Federation, it's not piracy. It's—now, lemme see, what fancy words have been used o' late? Contraband Control. Suppression of Espionage. Violation of the Three Million Mile Limit. Every time that there's an act of piracy there's some quote legal unquote excuse for it, an' it's upheld by the Federation's tame legal eagles, an' you Survey Service sissies just sit there on your big, fat backsides, an' don't lift a pinkie against your dear, murderous pals, the Waldegrenese. If you did, they send you screaming back to Base, where some dear old daddy of an Admiral'd spank your little plump bottoms for you."

"Please, Mr. Baxter!" admonished Jane Pentecost.

"Sorry, Miss. I got sort of carried away. But my young brother was Third Reaction Drive Engineer of the old *Bunyip* when she went missing. Nothin' was ever proved—but the Waldegrenese Navy was holdin' fleet maneuvers in the sector she was passin' through when last heard from. Oh, they're cunnin' bastards. They'll never go for one o' these ships, or one of the Trans-Galactic Clippers; it'll always be some poor little tramp that nobody'll ever miss but the friends an' relatives o' the crew. And, I suppose, the underwriters—but Lloyds makes such a packet out o' the ships that don't get lost that they can well afford to shell out now an' again. Come to that, it must suit 'em. As long as there're a few 'overdues' an' 'missings' they can keep the premiums up."

"But I still can't see how piracy can possibly pay," protested Grimes.

"O' course it pays. Your friend Black Bart made it pay. An' if you're goin' to all the expense of building and maintaining a war fleet it might just as well earn its keep. Even your famous Survey Service might show a profit if you were allowed to pounce on every fat merchantman who came within range o' your guns."

"But for the Federation to condone piracy, as you're trying to make out . . . That's utterly fantastic."

"If you lived on the Rim, you might think different," snarled Baxter.

And Jane Pentecost contributed, "Not piracy. Confrontation."

5

AS SOON AS the meal was finished the Baxters left rather hastily to make their way to the bar, leaving Grimes and Jane Pentecost to the leisurely enjoyment of their coffee. When the couple was out of earshot Grimes remarked, "So those are Rim Worlders. They're the first I've met."

"They're not, you know," the girl told him.

"But they are. Oh, there are one or two in the Survey Service, but I've never run across them. Now I don't particularly want to."

"But you did meet one Rim Worlder before you met the Baxters."

"The Captain?"

She laughed. "Don't let him hear you say that—not unless you want to take a space walk without a suit!"

"Then who?"

"Who could it be, Admiral? Whom have you actually met, to talk to, so far in this ship? Use your crust."

He stared at her incredulously. "Not you?"

"Who else?" She laughed again, but with a touch of bitterness. "We aren't all like our late manger companions, you know. Or should know. Even so, you'd count yourself lucky to have Jim Baxter by your side in any real jam. It boils down to this. Some of us have acquired veneer. Some of us haven't. Period."

"But how did you . . . ?" He groped for words that would not be offensive to conclude the sentence.

"How did I get into this galley? Easily enough. I started my space-faring career as a not very competent Catering Officer in *Jumbuk,* one of the Sundowner Line's more ancient and decrepit tramps. I got sick in Elsinore. Could have been my own cooking that put me in the hospital. Anyhow, I was just about recovered when the Commission's *Epsilon Serpentis* blew in—and she landed *her* purser with a slightly broken leg. She'd learned the hard way that the Golden Rule—*stop whatever you're doing and secure everything when the acceleration warning sounds*—is meant to be observed. The Doctor was luckier. She broke his fall. . . ."

Grimes was about to ask what the Doctor and the purser had been doing, then was thankful that he had not done so. He was acutely conscious of the crimson blush that burned the skin of his face.

"You must realize," said the girl dryly, "that merchant vessels with mixed crews are not monastic institutions. But where was I? Oh, yes. On Elsinore. Persuading the Master of the *Snaky Eppy* that I was a fit and proper person to take over his pursering. I managed to convince him that I was at least proper—I still can't see what my predecessor saw in that lecherous old goat of a quack, although the Second Mate had something. . . ." Grimes felt a sudden twinge of jealousy. "Anyhow, he signed me on, as soon as I agreed to waive repatriation.

"It was a long voyage; as you know, the *Epsilon* class ships are little better than tramps themselves. It was a long voyage, but I enjoyed it—seeing all the worlds that I'd read about and heard about and always wanted to visit. The Sundowner Line doesn't venture far afield—just the four Rim Worlds, and now and again the Shakespearian Sector, and once in a blue moon one of the drearier planets of the Empire of Waverley. The Commission's tramps, of course, run *everywhere.*

"Anyhow, we finally berthed at Woomera. The Old Man must have put in a good report about me, because I was called before the Local Superintending Purser and offered a berth, as a junior, in one of the *Alpha* class liners. *Alpha Centauri,* if you must know. She was on the Sol-Sirius service. Nothing very glamorous in the way of ports of call, but she was a fine ship, beautifully kept, efficiently run. A couple of years there knocked most of the sharp comers off me. After that—a spell as Assistant Purser of *Beta Geminorum.* Atlanta, Caribbea Carinthia and the Cluster Worlds. And then my first ship as Chief Purser. This one."

One of Jane's girls brought them fresh bulbs of coffee and ampuls of a sweet, potent liqueur. When she was gone Grimes asked, "Tell me, what are the Rim Worlds like?"

She waited until he had applied the flame of his lighter to the tip of her long, thin cigar, then answered, "Cold. Dark Lonely. But . . . they have something. The feeling of being on a frontier. *The* frontier. The last frontier."

"The frontier of the dark . . ." murmured Grimes.

"Yes. The frontier of the dark. And the names of our planets. They have something too. A . . . poetry? Yes, that's the word. Lorn, Ultimo, Faraway and Thule . . . And there's that night sky of ours, especially at some times of the year. There's the Galaxy—a great, dim-glowing lenticulate nebula, and the rest is darkness. At other times of the year there's only the darkness, the blackness that's made even more intense by the sparse, faint stars that are the other Rim Suns, by the few, faint luminosities that are the distant island universes that we shall never reach. . . ."

She shivered almost imperceptibly. "And always there's that sense of being on the very edge of things, of hanging on by our fingernails with the abyss of the eternal night gaping beneath us. The Rim Worlders aren't a spacefaring people; only a very few of us ever get the urge. It's analogous, perhaps, to your Maoris—I spent a leave once in New Zealand and got interested in the history of the country. The Maoris come of seafaring stock. Their ancestors made an epic voyage from their homeland paradise to those rather grim and dreary little islands hanging there, all by themselves, in the cold and stormy Southern Ocean, lashed by frigid gales sweeping up from the Antarctic. And something—the isolation? the climate?—killed the wanderlust that was an essential part of the makeup of their race. You'll find very few Maoris at sea—or in space—although there's no dearth of Polynesians from the home archipelagoes aboard the surface ships serving the ports of the Pacific. And there are quite a few, too, in the Commission's ships. . . ."

"We have our share in Survey Service," said Grimes. "But tell me, how do you man your vessels? This Sundowner Line of yours . . ."

"There are always the drifters, the no-hopers, the castoffs from the Interstellar Transport Commission, and Trans-Galactic Clippers, and Waverley Royal Mail and all the rest of them."

"And from the Survey Service?"

The question lifted her out of her sombre mood. "No," she replied with a smile. "Not yet."

"Not ever," said Grimes.

6

ONCE HIS INITIAL shyness had worn off—and with it much of his Academy-induced snobbery—Grimes began to enjoy the voyage. After all, Survey Service or no Survey Service, this was a ship and he was a spaceman. He managed to accept the fact that most of the ship's officers, even the most junior of them, were far more experienced spacemen than he was. Than he was *now*, he often reminded himself. At the back of his mind lurked the smug knowledge that, for all of them, a captaincy was the very limit of promotion, whereas he, one day, would be addressed in all seriousness as Jane Pentecost now addressed him in jest.

He was a frequent visitor to the control room but, remembering the Master's admonition, was careful not to get in the way. The watch officers accepted him almost as one of themselves and were willing to initiate him into the tricky procedure of obtaining a fix with the interstellar drive in operation—an art, he was told, rather than a science.

Having obtained the permission of the Chief Engineers he prowled through the vessel's machinery spaces, trying to supplement his theoretical knowledge of reaction, inertial and interstellar drives with something more practical. The first two, of course, were idle, and would be until the ship emerged from her warped Space-Time back into the normal continuum—but there was the Pile, the radioactive heart of the ship, and there was the auxiliary machinery that, in this tiny, man-made planet, did the work that on a natural world is performed by winds, rivers, sunlight and gravity.

There was the Mannschenn Drive Room—and, inside this holy of holies, no man need fear to admit that he was scared by the uncanny complexity of ever-precessing gyroscopes. He stared at the tumbling rotors, the gleaming wheels that seemed always on the verge of vanishing into nothingness, that rolled down the dark dimensions, dragging the ship and all aboard her with them. He stared, hypnotized, lost in a vague, disturbing dream in which Past and Present and Future were inextricably mingled—and the Chief Interstellar Drive Engineer took him firmly by the arm and led him from the compartment. "Look at the time-twister too long," he growled, "and you'll be meeting yourself coming back!"

There was the "farm"—the deck of yeast and tissue-culture vats—which was no more (and no less), than a highly efficient protein factory, and the deck where stood the great, transparent globes in which algae converted the ship's organic waste and sewage back into usable form (processed as nutriment for the yeasts and the tissue-cultures and as fertilizer for the hydroponic tanks, the biochemist was careful to explain), and the deck where luxuriant vegetation spilled over from the trays and almost barricaded the inspection walks, the source of vitamins and of flowers for the saloon tables and, at the same time, the ship's main air-conditioning unit.

Grimes said to Jane Pentecost, who had accompanied him on this tour of inspection, "You know, I envy your Captain."

"From you, Admiral," she scoffed, "that *is* something. But why?"

"How can I put it? You people do the natural way what we do with chemicals and machinery. The Captain of a warship is Captain of a warship. Period. But your Captain Craven is absolute monarch of a little world."

"A warship," she told him, "is supposed to be able to go on functioning as such even with every compartment holed. A warship cannot afford to depend for the survival of her crew upon the survival of hosts of other air-breathing organisms."

"Straight from the book," he said. Then, puzzled, "But for a . . ." He hesitated.

"But for a woman, or for a purser, or for a mere merchant officer I know too much," she finished for him. "But I can read, you know. And when I was in the Sundowner Line, I, as well as all the other officers, was supposed to keep up with all the latest Survey Service publications."

"But why?" he asked.

"But why not? We'll have a Navy of our own, one day. Just stick around, Admiral."

"Secession?" he inquired, making it sound like a dirty word.

"Once again—why not?"

"It'd never work," he told her.

"The history of Earth is full of secessions that did work. So is the history of Interstellar Man. The Empire of Waverley, for example. The Duchy of Waldegren, for another—although that's one that should have come to grief. We should all of us be a great deal happier if it had."

"Federation policy . . ." he began.

"Policy, shmolicy! Don't let's be unkind to the Waldegrenese, because as long as they're in being they exercise a restraining influence upon the Empire of Waverley and the Rim Worlds . . ." Her pace slackened. Grimes noticed that they were passing through the alleyway in which she and her staff were accommodated. She went on, "But all this talking politics is thirsty work. Come in for a couple of drinks before lunch."

"Thank you. But, Jane"—she didn't seem to have noticed the use of her given name—"I don't think that either of us is qualified to criticize the handling of foreign and colonial affairs."

"Spoken like a nice, young, well-drug-up future admiral. Oh, I know, I know. You people are trained to be the musclemen of the Federation. Yours not to reason why, yours but to do and die, and all the rest of it. But I'm a Rim Worlder—and out on the Rim you learn to think for yourself." She slid her door open. "Come on in. This is Liberty Hall—you can spit on the mat and call the cat a bastard."

Her accommodation was a suite rather than a mere cabin. It was neither as large nor as well fitted as the Captain's, but it was better than the Chief Officer's quarters, in which Grimes had already been a guest. He looked with interest at the holograms on the bulkhead of the sitting room. They were—but in an altogether different way—as eye-catching as Captain Craven's had been. There was one that was almost physically chilling, that induced the feeling of utter cold and darkness and loneliness. It was the night sky of some planet—a range of dimly seen yet sharply serrated peaks bisecting a great, pallidly glowing, lenticulate nebula. "Home, sweet home," murmured the girl, seeing what he was looking at. "The Desolation Mountains on Faraway, with the Galactic Lens in the background."

"And you feel homesick for *that?*"

"Darn right I do. Oh, not all the time. I like warmth and comfort as well as the next woman. But . . ." She laughed. "Don't stand around gawking—you make the place look untidy. Pull yourself into a chair and belay the buttocks."

He did so, watching her as she busied herself at the liquor cabinet. Suddenly, in these conditions of privacy, he was acutely conscious of the womanliness of her. The rather right and rather short shorts, as she bent away from him, left very little to the imagination. And her legs, although slender, were full where they should be full, with the muscles working smoothly under the golden skin. He felt the urge, which he sternly suppressed, to plant a kiss in the delectable hollow behind each knee. She turned suddenly. "Here! Catch!" He managed to grab the bulb that was hurtling toward his face, but a little of the wine spurted from the nipple and struck him in the right eye. When his vision cleared he saw that she was seated opposite him, was laughing (at or with him?). At, he suspected. A real demonstration of sympathy would have consisted of tears, not laughter. Her face grew momentarily severe. "Not the mess," she said reprovingly. "But the waste."

Grimes examined the bulb. "I didn't waste much. Only an eyeful."

She raised her drink in ritual greeting. "Here's mud in your eye," adding, "for a change."

"And in yours."

In the sudden silence that followed they sat looking at each other. There was a tension, some odd resultant of centrifugal and centripitel forces. They were on the brink of something, and both of them knew it, and there was the compulsion to go forward countered by the urge to go back.

She asked tartly, "Haven't you ever seen a woman's legs before?"

He shifted his regard to her face, to the eyes that, somehow, were brown no longer but held the depth and the darkness of the night through which the ship was plunging.

She said, "I think you'd better finish your drink and go."

He said, "Perhaps you're right."

"You better believe I'm right." She managed a smile. "I'm not an idler, like some people. I've work to do."

"See you at lunch, then. And thank you."

"Don't thank me. It was on the house, as the little dog said. Off with you, Admiral."

He unbuckled his lapstrap, got out of the chair and made his way to the door. When he was out of her room he did not go to his own cabin but to the bar, where he joined the Baxters. They, rather to his surprise, greeted him in a friendly manner. Rim Worlders, Grimes decided, had their good points.

It was after lunch when one of the purserettes told him that the Captain wished to see him. *What have I done now?* wondered Grimes—and answered his own question with the words, *Nothing. Unfortunately.*

Craven's manner, when he admitted Grimes into his dayroom, was severe. "Come in, Ensign. Be seated."

"Thank you, sir."

"You may smoke if you wish."

"Thank you, sir."

Grimes filled and lighted his pipe; the Captain ignited one of his pungent cigars, studied the eddying coils of smoke as though they were writing a vitally important message in some strange language.

"Er, Mr. Grimes, I believe that you have been seeing a great deal of my purser, Miss Pentecost."

"Not a great deal, sir. I'm at her table, of course."

"I am told that she has entertained you in her quarters."

"Just one bulb of sherry, sir. I had no idea that we were breaking ship's regulations."

"You were not. All the same, Mr. Grimes, I have to warn you."

"I assure you, sir, that nothing occurred between us."

Craven permitted himself a brief, cold smile. "A ship is not a Sunday school outing—especially a ship under my command. Some Masters, I know, do expect their officers to comport themselves like Sunday school pupils, with the Captain as the principal—but *I* expect *my* senior officers to behave like intelligent and responsible adults. Miss Pentecost is quite capable of looking after herself. It is you that I'm worried about."

"There's no need to be worried, sir."

The Captain laughed. "I'm not worried about your morals, Mr. Grimes. In fact, I have formed the opinion that a roll in the hay would do you far more good than harm. But Miss Pentecost is a dangerous woman. Before lifting ship, very shortly before lifting ship, I received a confidential report concerning her activities. She's an efficient purser, a highly efficient purser, in fact, but she's even more than that. Much more." Again he studied the smoke from his cigar. "Unfortunately there's no *real* proof, otherwise she'd not be sailing with us. Had I insisted upon her discharge I'd have been up against the Interstellar Clerical and Supply Officers' Guild."

"Surely not," murmured Grimes.

Craven snorted. "You people are lucky. You haven't a mess of Guilds to deal with, each and every one of which is all too ready to rush to the defense of a Guild member, no matter what he or she is supposed to have done. As a Survey Service Captain you'll never have to face a suit for wrongful dismissal. You'll never be accused of victimization."

"But what has Miss Pentecost done, sir?" asked Grimes.

"Nothing—or too damn much. You know where she comes from, don't you? The Rim Worlds. The planets of the misfits, the rebels, the nonconformists. There's been talk of secession of late—but even those irresponsible anarchists know full well that secession will never succeed unless they build up their own space power. There's the Duchy of Waldegren, which would pounce as soon as the Federation withdrew its protection. And even the Empire of Waverley might be tempted to extend its boundaries. So . . .

"They have a merchant fleet of sorts, these Rim Worlders. The Sundowner Line. I've heard rumors that it's about to be nationalized. But they have no fighting navy."

"But what's all this to do with Miss Pentecost, sir?"

"If what's more than just hinted at in that confidential report is true—plenty. She's a recruiting sergeant, no less. Any officer with whom she's shipmates who's disgruntled, on the verge of throwing his hand in—or on the verge of being emptied out—she'll turn on the womanly sympathy for, and tell him that there'll always be a job waiting out on the Rim, that the Sundowner Line is shortly going to expand, so there'll be quick promotion and all the rest of it."

"And what's that to do with *me*, Captain?"

"Are all Survey Service ensigns as innocent as you, Mr. Grimes? Merchant officers the Rim Worlds want, and badly. Naval officers they'll want more badly still once the balloon goes up."

Grimes permitted himself a superior smile. "It's extremely unlikely, sir, that I shall ever want to leave the Survey Service."

"Unlikely perhaps—but not impossible. So bear in mind what I've told you. I think that you'll be able to look after yourself now that you know the score."

"I think so too," Grimes told him firmly. He thought, *The old bastard's been reading too many spy stories.*

7

THEY WERE DANCING.

Tables and chairs had been cleared from the ship's saloon, and from the big, ornate playmaster throbbed the music of an orchestra so famous that even Grimes had heard of it—The Singing Drums.

They were dancing.

Some couples shuffled a sedate measure, never losing the contact between their magnetically shod feet and the polished deck. Others—daring or foolhardy—cavorted in Nul-G, gamboled fantastically but rarely gracefully in Free Fall.

They were dancing.

Ensign Grimes was trying to dance.

It was not the fault of his partner that he was making such a sorry mess of it. She, Jane Pentecost, proved the truth of the oft-made statement that spacemen and spacewomen are expert at this form of exercise. He, John Grimes, was the exception that proves the rule. He was sweating, and his feet felt at least six times their normal size. Only the fact that he was holding Jane, and closely, saved him from absolute misery.

There was a pause in the music. As it resumed Jane said, "Let's sit this one out, Admiral."

"If you wish to," he replied, trying not to sound too grateful.

"That's right I wish to. I don't mind losing a little toenail varnish, but I think we'll call it a day while I still have a full set of toenails."

"I'm sorry," he said.

"So am I." But the flicker of a smile robbed the words of their sting.

She led the way to the bar. It was deserted save for the bored and sulky girl behind the gleaming counter. "All right, Sue," Jane told her. "You can join the revels. The Admiral and I will mind the shop."

"*Thank* you, Miss Pentecost." Sue let herself out from her little cage, vanished gracefully and rapidly in the direction of the saloon. Jane took her place.

"I *like* being a barmaid," she told the ensign, taking two frosted bulbs out of the cooler.

"I'll sign for these," offered Grimes.

"You will not. This comes under the heading of entertaining influential customers."

"But I'm not. Influential, I mean."

"But you will be." She went on dreamily. "I can see it. I can just see it. The poor old *Delia O'Ryan,* even more decrepit that she is now, and her poor old purser, about to undergo a fate worse than death at the hands of bloody pirates from the next Galaxy but three. . . . But all is not lost. There, light years distant, is big, fat, Grand Admiral Grimes aboard his flagship, busting a gut, to say nothing of his Mannschenn Drive unit, to rush to the rescue of his erstwhile girlfriend. 'Dammitall,' I can hear him muttering into his beard. 'Dammitall. That girl used to give me free drinks when I was a snotty nosed ensign. I will repay. Full speed ahead, Gridley, and damn the torpedoes!' "

Grimes laughed—then asked sharply, "Admiral in which service?"

"What do you mean, John?" She eyed, him warily.

"*You* know what I mean."

"So . . ." she murmured. "So . . . I know that you had another home truth session with the Bearded Bastard. I can guess what it was about."

"And is it true?" demanded Grimes.

"Am I Olga Popovsky, the Beautiful Spy? Is that what you mean?"

"More or less."

"Come off it, John. How the hell can I be a secret agent for a nonexistent government?"

"You can be a secret agent for a subversive organization."

"What *is* this? Is it a hangover from some halfbaked and half-understood course in counterespionage?"

"There was a course of sorts," he admitted. "I didn't take much interest in it. At the time."

"And now you wish that you had. Poor John."

"But it wasn't espionage that the Old Man had against you. He had some sort of story about your acting as a sort of recruiting sergeant, luring officers away from the Commission's ships to that crumby little rabble of star tramps calling itself the Sundowner Line. . . ."

She didn't seem to be listening to him, but was giving her attention instead to the music that drifted from the saloon. It was one of the old, Twentieth Century melodies that were enjoying a revival. She began to sing in time to it.

"Goodbye, I'll run
To seek another sun
Where I
May find
There are hearts more kind
Than the ones left behind . . ."

She smiled somberly and asked, "Does that answer your question?"

"Don't talk in riddles," he said roughly.

"Riddles? Perhaps—but not very hard ones. That, John, is a sort of song of farewell from a very old comic opera. As I recall it, the guy singing it was going to shoot through and join the French Foreign Legion. (But there's no French Foreign Legion anymore. . . .) We, out on the Rim, have tacked our own words on to it. It's become almost a national anthem to the Rim Runners, as the people who man our ships—such as they are—are already calling themselves.

"There's no French Foreign Legion anymore—but the misfits and the failures have to have somewhere to go. I haven't *lured* anybody away from this service—but now and again I've shipped with officers who've been on the point of getting out, or being emptied out, and when they've cried into my beer I've given them advice. Of course, I've a certain natural bias in favor of my own home world. If I were Sirian born I'd be singing the praises of the Dog Star Line."

"Even so," he persisted, "your conduct seems to have been somewhat suspect."

"Has it? And how? To begin with, *you* are not an officer in this employ. And if you were, I should challenge you to find anything in the Commission's regulations forbidding me to act as I have been doing."

"Captain Craven warned me," said Grimes.

"Did he, now? That's *his* privilege. I suppose that he thinks that it's also his duty. I suppose he has the idea that I offered you admiral's rank in the Rim Worlds Navy as soon as we secede. *If* we had our own Navy—which we don't—we might just take you in an Ensign, Acting, Probationary."

"Thank you."

She put her elbows on the bar counter, propping her face between her hands, somehow conveying the illusion of gravitational pull, looking up at him. "I'll be frank with you, John. I admit that we do take the no-hopers, the drunks and the drifters into our merchant fleet. I know far better than you what a helluva difference there is between those rustbuckets, and the well-found, well-run ships of the Commission and, come to that, Trans-Galactic Clippers and Waverley Royal Mail. But when we do start some kind of a Navy we shall want better material. Much better. We shall want highly competent officers who yet, somehow, will have the Rim World outlook. The first batch, of course, will have to be outsiders, to tide us over until our own training program is well under way."

"And I don't qualify?" he asked stiffly.

"Frankly, no. I've been watching you. You're too much of a stickler for rules and regulations, especially the more stupid ones. Look at the way you're dressed now, for example. Evening wear, civilian, junior officers, for the use of. No individuality. You might as well be in uniform. Better, in fact. There'd be some touch of brightness."

"Go on."

"And the way you comport yourself with women. Stiff. Starchy. Correct. And you're all too conscious of the fact that I, even though I'm a mere merchant officer, and a clerical branch at that, put up more gold braid than you do. I noticed that especially when we were dancing. I was having to lead all the time."

He said defensively, "I'm not a very good dancer."

"You can say that again." She smiled briefly. "So there you have it, John. You can tell the Bearded Bastard, when you see him again, that you're quite safe from my wiles. I've no doubt that you'll go far in your own Service—but you just aren't Rim Worlds material."

"I shouldn't have felt all that flattered if you'd said that I was," he told her bluntly—but he knew that he was lying.

8

"YES?" JANE WAS saying. "Yes, Mr. Letourneau?"

Grimes realized that she was not looking at him, that she was looking past him and addressing a newcomer. He turned around to see who it was. He found—somehow the name hadn't registered—that it was the Psionic Radio Officer, a tall, pale, untidily put together young man in a slovenly uniform. He looked scared—but that was his habitual expression, Grimes remembered. They were an odd breed, these trained telepaths with their Rhine Institute diplomas, and they were not popular, but they were the only means whereby ships and shore stations could communicate instantaneously over the long light years. In the Survey Service they were referred to, slightingly, as Commissioned Teacup Readers. In the Survey Service and in the Merchant Service they were referred to as Snoopers. But they were a very necessary evil.

"Yes, Mr. Letourneau?"

"Where's the Old Man? He's not in his quarters."

"The Master"—Jane emphasized the title—"is in the saloon." Then, a little maliciously, "Couldn't you have used your crystal ball?"

Letourneau flushed. "You know very well, Miss Pentecost, that we have to take an oath that we will always respect the mental privacy of our shipmates. . . . But I must find him. Quickly."

"Help yourself. He's treading the light fantastic in there." When he was gone she said, "Typical. Just typical. If it were a real emergency he could get B.B. on the intercom. But no. Not him. He has to parade his distrust of anything electronic and, at the same time, make it quite clear that he's not breaking his precious oath. . . . Tell me, how do you people handle your spaceborne espers?"

He grinned. "We've still one big stick that you people haven't. A court martial followed by a firing party. Not that I've ever seen it used."

"Hardly, considering that you've only been in Space a dog watch." Her face froze suddenly. "Yes, Sue?"

It was the girl whom Jane had relieved in the bar. "Miss Pentecost, will you report to the Captain in Control, please. At once."

"What have I done now?"

"It's some sort of emergency, Miss Pentecost. The Chief Officer's up there with him, and he's sent for the Doctor and the two Chief Engineers."

"Then I must away, John. Look after the bar again, Sue. Don't let the Admiral have too many free drinks."

She moved fast and gracefully, was gone before Grimes could think of any suitable repartee. He said to the girl, "What *is* happening, Sue?"

"I don't know, Ad—" She flushed. "Sorry, Ensign. And, in any case, I'm not supposed to talk to the passengers about it."

"But I'm not a real passenger," he said—and asked himself, *Am I a* real *anything?*

"No, I suppose you're not, Mr. Grimes. But you're not on duty."

"An officer of the Survey Service is *always* on duty," he told her, with some degree of truth. "Whatever happens on the spacelanes is our concern." It sounded good.

"Yes," she agreed hesitantly. "That's what my fiancé—he's a Lieutenant J.G.—is always telling me."

"So what's all the flap about?"

"Promise not to tell anybody?"

"Of course."

"Mr. Letourneau came wandering into the Saloon. He just stood there staring about, the way he does, then he spotted the Captain. He was actually dancing with me at the time. . . ." She smiled reminiscently, and added, "He's a very good dancer."

"He would be. But go on."

"He came charging across the dance floor—Mr. Letourneau, I mean. He didn't care whose toes he trod on or who he tripped over. I couldn't help overhearing when he started babbling away to Captain Craven. It's a distress call. From one of our ships—*Epsilon Sextans.*" Her voice dropped to a whisper. "And it's piracy."

"Piracy? Impossible."

"But, Mr. Grimes, it's what he said."

"Psionic Radio Officers have been known to go around the bend before now," Grimes told her, "and to send false alarm calls. And to receive non-existent ones."

"But the *Sexy Eppy*—sorry, *Epsilon Sextans*—has a cargo that'd be worth pirating. Or so I heard. The first big shipment of Antigeriatridine to Waverly. . . ."

Antigeriatridine, the so-called Immortality Serum. Manufactured in limited, but increasing quantities only on Marina (often called by its colonists Submarina), a cold, unpleasantly watery world in orbit about Alpha Crucis. The fishlike creatures from which the drug was obtained bred and flourished only in the seas of their own world.

But piracy . . .

But the old legends were full of stories of men who had sold their souls for eternal youth.

The telephone behind the bar buzzed sharply. Sue answered it. She said, "It's for you, Mr. Grimes."

Grimes took the instrument. "That you, Ensign?" It was Captain Craven's voice. "Thought I'd find you there. Come up to Control, will you?" It was an order rather than a request.

All the ship's executive officers were in the Control Room, and the Doctor, the purser and the two Chief Engineers. As Grimes emerged from the hatch he heard Kennedy, the Mate, say, "Here's the Ensign now."

"Good. Then dog down, Mr. Kennedy, so we get some privacy." Craven turned to Grimes. "You're on the Active List of the Survey Service, Mister, so I suppose you're entitled to know what's going on. The situation is this. *Epsilon Sextans,* Marina to Waverley with a shipment of Antigeriatridine, has been pirated." Grimes managed, with an effort, to refrain from saying "I know." Craven went on. "Her esper is among the survivors. He says that the pirates were two frigates of the Waldegren Navy. Anyhow, the Interstellar Drive Engineers aboard *Epsilon Sextans* managed to put their box of tricks on random precession, and they got away. But not in one piece. . . ."

"Not in one piece?" echoed Grimes stupidly.

"What the hell do you expect when an unarmed merchantman is fired upon, without warning, by two warships? The esper says that their Control has had it, and all the accommodation spaces. By some miracle the Psionic Radio Officer's shack wasn't holed, and neither was the Mannschenn Drive Room."

"But even one missile . . ." muttered Grimes.

"If you want to capture a ship and her cargo more or less intact," snapped Craven, "you don't use missiles. You use laser. It's an ideal weapon if you aren't fussy about how many people you kill."

"Knowing the Waldegrenese as *we* do," said Jane Pentecost bitterly, "there wouldn't have been any survivors anyhow."

"Be quiet!" roared Craven. Grimes was puzzled by his outburst. It was out of character. True, he could hardly expect a shipmaster to react to the news of a vicious piracy with equanimity—but this shipmaster was an officer of the Reserve, had seen service in warships and had been highly decorated for outstanding bravery in battle.

Craven had control of himself again. "The situation is this. There are people still living aboard *Epsilon Sextans.* Even though all her navigators have been killed I think that I shall be able to find her in time. Furthermore, she has a very valuable cargo and, in any case, cannot be written off as a total loss. There is little damage that cannot be repaired by welded patches. I have already sent a message to Head Office requesting a free hand. I have salvage in mind. I see no reason why the ship and her cargo should not be taken on to Waverley."

"A prize crew, sir?"

"If you care to put it that way. This will mean cutting down the number of officers aboard my own vessel—but I am sure, Mr. Grimes, that you will be willing to gain some practical watchkeeping experience. All that's required is your autograph on the ship's Articles of Agreement."

"Thank you, sir."

"Don't thank me. I may be thanking you before the job's over and done." He turned to his Chief Officer. "Mr. Kennedy, keep in touch with Mr. Letourneau and let me know if anything further comes through either from *Epsilon Sextans* or from Head Office. The rest of you—keep this to yourselves. No sense in alarming the passengers. I'm sure that the Doctor and Miss Pentecost between them can concoct some soothing story to account for this officers' conference."

"Captain Craven," said Jane Pentecost.

"Well?"

'The other man at my table, Mr. Baxter. I knew him out on the Rim. He holds Chief Reaction Drive Engineer's papers."

"Don't tell him anything yet. But I'll keep him in mind. Now, Mr. Grimes, will you join me in my day cabin?"

9

THE HOLOGRAMS WERE all gone from the bulkheads of Captain Craven's cabin. To replace them there was just one picture—of a woman, not young, but with the facial bone structure that defies age and time. She was in uniform, and on her shoulderboards were the two and a half stripes of a Senior Purser. The shipmaster noticed Grimes' interest and said briefly and bitterly. "She was too senior for an *Epsilon* class ship—but she cut her leave short, just to oblige, when the regular purser went sick. She should have been back on Earth at the same time as me, though. Then we were going to get married. . . ."

Grimes said nothing. He thought, *Too senior for an* Epsilon *class ship?* Epsilon Sextans, *for example?* What could he say?

"And that," said Craven savagely, "*was* that."

"I'm sorry, sir," blurted Grimes, conscious of the inadequacy of his words. Then, foolishly, "But there are survivors, sir."

"Don't you think that I haven't got Letourneau and his opposite number checking? And have *you* ever seen the aftermath of a Deep Space battle, Mister? Have you ever boarded a ship that's been slashed and stabbed to death with laser beams?" He seemed to require no answer; he pulled himself into the chair by his desk, strapped himself in and motioned to Grimes to be seated. Then he pulled out from a drawer a large sheet of paper, which he unfolded. It was a cargo plan. "Current voyage," he grunted. "And we're carrying more to Lindisfarne than one brand-new ensign."

"Such as, sir?" ventured Grimes.

"Naval stores. I don't mind admitting that I'm more than a little rusty insofar as Survey Service procedure is concerned, even though I still hold my Reserve Commission. You're more familiar with fancy abbreviations than I am. Twenty cases RERAT, for example. . . ."

"Reserve rations, sir. Canned and dehydrated."

"Good. And ATREG?"

"Atmospheric regeneration units, complete."

"So if *Epsilon Sextans'* 'farm' has been killed we shall be able to manage?"

"Yes, sir."

"Do you think you'd be able to install an ATREG unit?"

"Of course, sir. They're very simple, as you know. Just synthetic chlorophyl and a UV source. . . . In any case, there are full instructions inside every container."

"And this? A double M, Mark XV?"

"Anti-Missile Missile."

"And ALGE?"

"Anti-Laser Gas Emitter."

"The things they do think of. I feel more at home with these AVMs—although I see that they've got as far as Mark XVII now."

"Anti-Vessel Missiles," said Grimes. A slight enthusiasm crept into his voice. "The XVII's a real honey."

"What does it do?"

"I'm sorry, sir. Even though you are a Reserve Officer, I can't tell you."

"But they're effective?"

"Yes. Very."

"And I think you're Gunnery Branch, Mr. Grimes, aren't you?"

"I am sir." He added hastily, "But I'm still quite capable of carrying out a watch officer's duties aboard this vessel should the need arise."

"The main thing is, you're familiar with naval stores and equipment. When we find and board *Epsilon Sextans* I shall be transshipping certain items of cargo . . ."

"RERAT and ATREG, sir?"

"Yes. And the others."

"But, sir, I can't allow it. Not unless I have authority from the Flag Officer commanding Lindisfarne Base. As soon as your Mr. Letourneau can be spared I'll get him to try and raise the station there."

"I'm afraid that's out of the question, Mr. Grimes. In view of the rather peculiar political situation, I think that the answer would be No. Even it it were Yes, you know as well as I how sluggishly the tide flows through official channels. Furthermore, just in case it has escaped your notice, *I* am the Master."

"And I, sir, represent the Survey Service. As the only commissioned officer aboard this vessel *I* am responsible for Survey Service cargo."

"As a Reserve Officer, Mr. Grimes, I rank you."

"Only when you have been recalled to Active Service. Sir."

Craven said, "I was rather afraid that you'd take this attitude. That's why I decided to get this interview over and done with, just so we all know where we stand." He put away the cargo plan, swiveled his chair so that he could reach out to his liquor cabinet. He pulled out two bulbs, tossed one to Grimes. "No toasts. If we drank to Law and Order we should mean different things. So just drink. And listen.

"To begin with, *Epsilon Sextans* doesn't know where she is. But Letourneau is one of the rare telepaths with the direction finding talent, and as soon as he's able to get lined up we shall alter course to home on the wreck. That's what he's trying to do now.

"When we find her, we shall synchronize and board, of course. The first thing will be medical aid to the survivors. Then we patch the ship up. And then we arm her. And then, with a prize crew under myself, we put ourselves on the trajectory for Waverley—hoping that those Waldegrenese frigates come back for another nibble."

"They'd never dare, sir."

"Wouldn't they? The original piracy they'll try to laugh off by saying that it was by *real* pirates—no, that's, not quite right, but you know what I mean—wearing Waldegren colors. The second piracy—they'll make sure that there are no survivors."

"But I still can't see how they can hope to get away with it. It's always been an accepted fact that the main weapon against piracy has been psionic radio."

"And so it was—until some genius developed a jamming technique. *Epsilon Sextans* wasn't able to get any messages out until her crazy random precession pulled her well clear."

"And you hope, sir, that they *do* attack you?"

"I do, Mr. Grimes. I had hoped that I should have a good gunnery officer under me, but"—he shrugged his massive shoulders—"I think that I shall be able to manage."

"And you hope that you'll have your weapons," persisted Grimes.

"I see no reason why I should not, Ensign."

"There is one very good reason, sir. That is that I, a commissioned officer of the Survey Service, am aboard your vessel. I insist that you leave the tracking down and destruction of the pirates to the proper authorities. I insist, too, that no Survey Service stores be discharged from this ship without my written authority."

For the first time the hint of a smile relieved the somberness of

Craven's face. "And to think that I believed that Jane Pentecost could recruit *you*," he murmured. Then, in a louder voice, "And what if I just go ahead without your written authority, Ensign?"

Grimes had the answer ready. "Then, sir, I shall be obliged to order your officers not to obey your unlawful commands. If necessary, I shall call upon the male passengers to assist me in any action that is necessary."

Craven's bushy eyebrows went up and stayed up. "Mr. Grimes," he said in a gritty voice, "it is indeed lucky for you that I have firsthand experience of the typical Survey Service mentality. Some Masters I know would, in these circumstances, send you out on a spacewalk without a suit. But, before I take drastic action, I'll give you one more chance to cooperate." His tone softened. "You noticed the portrait I've put up instead of all the temporary popsies. Every man, no matter how much he plays around, has one woman who is *the* woman. Gillian was *the* woman as far as I was concerned—as far as I *am* concerned. I've a chance to bring her murderers under my guns—and, by God, I'm taking that chance, no matter what it means either to my career or to the somewhat odd foreign policy of the Federation. I used to be annoyed by Jane Pentecost's outbursts on that subject—but now I see that she's right. And she's right, too, when it comes to the Survey Service's reluctance to take action against Waldegren.

"So I, Mr. Grimes, am taking action."

"Sir, I forbid you . . ."

"*You* forbid *me*? Ensign, you forget yourself. Perhaps this will help you remember."

This was a Minetti automatic that had appeared suddenly in the Captain's hand. In his hairy fist the little, glittering weapon looked no more than a toy but Grimes knew his firearms, knew that at the slightest pressure of Craven's finger the needle-like projectiles would stitch him from crown to crotch.

"I'm sorry about this, Mr. Grimes." As he spoke, Craven pressed a button set in his desk with his free hand. "I'm sorry about this. But I realize that I was expecting rather too much of you. After all, you have your career to consider. . . . Time was," he went on, "when a naval officer could put his telescope to his blind eye as an excuse for ignoring orders—and get away with it. But the politicians had less power in those days. We've come a long way—and a wrong way—since Nelson."

Grimes heard the door behind him slide open. He didn't bother to look around, not even when hard hands were laid on his shoulders.

"Mr. Kennedy," said Craven, "things turned out as I feared that they would. Will you and Mr. Ludovic take the Ensign along to the Detention Cell?"

"I'll see you on trial for piracy, Captain!" flared Grimes.

"An interesting legal point, Ensign—especially since you are being entered in my Official Log as a mutineer."

10

THE DETENTION CELL was not uncomfortable, but it was depressing. It was a padded cell—passengers in spacecraft have been known to exhibit the more violent symptoms of mania—which detracted from its already inconsiderable cheerfulness if not from its comfort. However, Grimes was not mad—not in the medical sense, that is—and so was considered able to attend to his own bodily needs. The little toilet was open to him, and at regular intervals a bell would sound and a container of food would appear in a hatch recessed into the bulkhead of the living cabin. There was reading matter too—such as it was. The Ensign suspected that Jane Pentecost was the donor. It consisted of pamphlets published by some organization calling itself The Rim Worlds Secessionist Party. The almost hysterical calls to arms were bad enough—but the ones consisting mainly of columns of statistics were worse. Economics had never been Grimes' strong point.

He slept, he fed at the appointed times, he made a lengthy ritual of keeping himself clean, he tried to read—and, all the time, with only sounds and sensations as clues, he endeavored to maintain a running plot of the ship's maneuvers.

Quite early there had been the shutting down of the Mannschenn Drive, and the consequent fleeting sensation of temporal disorientation. This had been followed by the acceleration warning—the cell had an intercom speaker recessed in the padding—and Grimes, although it seemed rather pointless in his sponge rubber environment, had strapped himself into his couch. He heard the directional gyroscopes start up, felt the effects of centrifugal force as the ship came around to her new heading. Then there was the pseudo-gravity of acceleration, accompanied by the muffled thunder of the reaction drive. It was obvious, thought the Ensign, that Captain Craven was expending his reaction mass in a manner that, in other circumstances, would have been considered reckless.

Suddenly—silence and Free Fall, and almost immediately the off-key keening of the Mannschenn Drive. Its note was higher, much higher, than Grimes remembered it, and the queasy feeling of temporal disorientation lasted much longer than it had on previous occasions.

And that, for a long time, was all.

Meals came, and were eaten. Every morning—according to his watch—the prisoner showered and applied depilatory cream to his face. He tried to exercise—but to exercise in a padded cell, with no apparatus, in Free Fall, is hard. He tried to read—but the literature available was hardly more interesting to him than a telephone directory would have been. And, even though he never had been gregarious, the lack of anybody to talk to was wearing him down.

It was a welcome break from the monotony when he realized that, once again, the ship was maneuvering. This time there was no use of the directional gyroscopes; there were no rocket blasts, but there was a variation of the whine of the Drive as it hunted, hunted, as the temporal precession rate was adjusted by tens of seconds, by seconds, by microseconds.

And then it locked.

The ship shuddered slightly—once, twice.

Grimes envisaged the firing of the two mooring rockets, one from the bow and one from the stern, each with the powerful electromagnet in its nose, each trailing its fathoms of fine but enormously strong cable. Merchant vessels, he knew, carried this equipment, but unlike naval ships rarely used it. But Craven, as a Reservist, would have seen and taken part in enough drills.

The ship shuddered again—heavily.

So the rendezvous had been made. So *Delta Orionis* and *Epsilon Sextans,* their Drives synchronized, bound together by the rescue ship's cables, were now falling as one unit through the dark immensities.

So the rendezvous had been made—and already the survivors of the wreck were being brought aboard the *Delia O'Ryan,* were being helped out of their stinking spacesuits, were blurting out their story to Craven and his officers. Grimes could visualize it all, almost as clearly as though he were actually watching it. He could visualize, too, the engineers swarming over the wreck, the flare of their burning and welding torches, the cannibalizing of nonessential plating from the ship's structure for hull patches. It was all laid down in the Survey Service's

Damage Control Manual—and Captain Craven, at least, would know that book as thoroughly as did Grimes.

And what of the cargo, the Survey Service stores, *Grimes'* stores? A trembling in the ship's structure, a barely felt vibration, told him that gantries and conveyor belts were being brought into operation. There would be no great handling problems. Lindisfarne was *Delta Orionis'* first port of call, and the Survey Service consignment would be top stowage. But there was nothing that Grimes could do about it—not a thing. In fact, he was beginning to doubt the legality of the stand he had made against the Master. And he was the small frog in this small puddle, while Captain Craven had made it quite clear that he was the big frog. Grimes wished that he was better versed in astronautical law—although a professional lawyer's knowledge would be of no use to him in his present situation.

So, with some hazy idea that he might need all his strength, both mental and physical, for what was to befall him (but *what?*), in the near future, he strapped himself into his bunk and did his best to forget his worries in sleep. He was well enough acquainted with the psychiatrists' jargon to know that this was no more than a return to the womb but, before dropping off into a shallow slumber, shrugged, *So what*?

He jerked into sudden wakefulness.

Jane Pentecost was there by his bunk, looking down at him.

"Come in," he said. "Don't bother to knock. Now you see how the poor live. This is Liberty Hall; you can spit on the mat and call the cat a bastard."

She said, "That's not very funny."

"I know it's not. Even the first time that I heard it aboard this blasted ship I was able to refrain from rolling in the aisles."

She said, "There's no need to be so bitchy, John."

"Isn't there? Wouldn't you be bitchy if you'd been thrown into this padded cell?"

"I suppose I would be. But you asked for it, didn't you?"

"If doing my duty—or trying to do my duty—is asking for it, I suppose that I did. Well—and has our pirate Captain cast off yet, armed to the teeth with the weapons he's stolen?"

"No. The weapons are still being mounted. But let's not argue legalities, John. There's not enough time. I . . . I just wanted to say goodbye."

"Goodbye?" he echoed.

"Yes. Somebody has to do the cooking aboard *Epsilon Sextans*—and I volunteered."

"You?"

"And why the hell not?" she flared. "Captain Craven has been pushed over to *our* side of the fence, and it'd be a pretty poor show if we Rim Worlders weren't prepared to stand by him. Baxter's gone across to take over as Reaction Drive Engineer; the only survivor in that department was the Fourth, and he's only a dog watch in Space."

"And who else?"

"Nobody. The *Sexy Eppy's* Chief, Second and Third Interstellar Drive Engineers survived, and they're willing—anxious, in fact, now that their ship's being armed—to stay on. And the Psionic Radio Officer came through, and is staying on. All of our executive officers volunteered, of course, but the Old Man turned them down. He said that, after all, he could not hazard the safety of this ship by stripping her of her trained personnel. Especially since we carry passengers."

"That's his worry," said Grimes without much sympathy. "But how does he hope to fight his ship if those frigates pounce again?"

"He thinks he'll be able to manage—with remote controls for every weapon brought to his main control panel."

"Possible," admitted Grimes, his professional interest stirred. "But not very efficient. In a naval action the Captain has his hands full just handling the ship alone, without trying to control her weaponry."

"And you'd know, of course."

"Yes."

"Yes, you've read the books. And Captain Craven commanded a light cruiser during that trouble with the Dring, so he knows nothing."

"He still hasn't got four hands and two heads."

"Oh, let's stop talking rubbish," she cried. "I probably shan't see you again, John and . . . and . . . oh, hell, I want to say goodbye properly, and I don't want you to think too badly about either the Old Man or . . . or myself."

"So what are we supposed to do about it?"

"Damn you, Grimes, you snotty-nosed, stuck-up spacepuppy! Look after yourself!"

Suddenly she bent down to kiss him. It was intended to be no more than a light brushing of lips, but Grimes was suddenly aware, with his entire body, of the closeness of her, of the warmth and, the scent of her, and almost without volition his arms went about her, drawing her closer still to him. She tried to break away, but it was, only a halfhearted effort. He heard her murmur, in an odd, sardonic whisper, "wotthehell, wotthehell," and then, "toujours gai." It made no sense at the time but, years later, when he made the acquaintance of the Twentieth Century poets, he was to remember and to understand. What was important now was that her own arms were about him.

Somehow the buttons of her uniform shirt had come undone, and her nipples were taut against Grimes' bare chest. Somehow her shorts had been peeled away from her. hips—unzippered by whom? and how?—and somehow Grimes' own garments were no longer the last barrier between them.

He was familiar enough with female nudity; he was one of the great majority who frequented the naked beaches in preference to those upon which bathing costumes were compulsory. He knew what a naked woman looked like—but this was different. It was not the first time that he had kissed a woman—but it was the first time that he had kissed, and been kissed by, an unclothed one. It was the first time that he had been alone with one.

What was happening he had read about often enough—and, like most young men, he had seen his share of pornographic films. But this was different. This was happening to *him.*

And for the first time.

When it was over, when, still clasped in each others' arms they drifted in the center of the little cabin, impelled there by some odd resultant of forces, their discarded clothing drifting with them, veiling their perspiration-moist bodies, Grimes was reluctant to let her go.

Gently, Jane tried to disengage herself.

She whispered, "That was a warmer goodbye than I intended. But I'm not sorry. No. I'm not sorry. . . ."

Then, barely audibly, "It was the first time for you, wasn't it?"

"Yes."

"Then I'm all the more glad it happened. But this *is* goodbye."

"No."

"Don't be a fool, John. You can't keep me here."

"But I can come with you."

She pushed him from her. Somehow he landed back on the bed. Before he could bounce he automatically snapped one of the confining straps about his middle. Somehow—she was still wearing her sandals but nothing else—she finished up standing on the deck, held there by the contact between the magnetic soles and the ferrous fibers in the padding. She put out a long, graceful arm and caught her shirt. She said harshly, "*I'm* getting dressed and out of here. *You* stay put. Damn you, Grimes, for thinking that I was trying to lure you aboard the *Sexy Eppy* with the body beautiful. I told you before that I am not, repeat not, Olga Popovsky, the Beautiful Spy. And I'm not a prostitute. There's one thing

I wouldn't *sell* if I were offered the services of the finest Gunnery Officer (which you aren't) in the whole bloody Galaxy in payment!"

"You're beautiful when you flare up like that," said Grimes sincerely. "But you're *always* beautiful." Then, in a louder voice, "Jane, I love you."

"Puppy love," she sneered. "And I'm old enough to be your . . ." A faint smile softened her mouth. "Your maiden aunt."

"Let me finish. All right, it's only puppy love—*you* say. But it's still love. But"—he was extemporizing—convincingly, he hoped—"but my real reason for wanting to come with you is this. I can appreciate now what Captain Craven lost when *Epsilon Sextans* was pirated. I can see—I can *feel*—why he's willing to risk his life and his career to get his revenge. And I think that it's worth it. And I want to help him."

She stood there, her shirt half on, eying him suspiciously. "You mean that? You really mean that?"

"Yes."

"Then you're a liar, Grimes."

"No," he said slowly. "No. Not altogether. I want to help the Old Man—and I want to help *you*. This piracy has convinced me that you Rim Worlders *are* getting the dirty end of the stick. I may not be the finest Gunnery Officer in the whole Galaxy—but I'm better acquainted with the new stuff than Captain Craven is."

Her grin was openly derisive. "First it's fellow-feeling for another spaceman, then it's international politics. What next?"

"Where we started. I *do* love you, Jane. And if there's going to be any shooting, I want to be on hand to do the shooting back on your behalf. I'll admit that . . . that what's happened has influenced my decision. But you didn't buy me, or bribe me. Don't think that. Don't ever think that." There was a note of pleading in his voice. "Be realistic, Jane. With another officer along, especially an officer with recent gunnery training, you stand a damn sight better chance than you would otherwise."

"I . . . I suppose so. But I still don't like it."

"You don't have to. But why look a gift horse in the mouth?"

"All right. You win. Get your clothes on and come and see the Old Man."

11

JANE PENTECOST LED Grimes to the airlock. The ship seemed oddly deserted, and he remarked on this. The girl explained that the passengers had been requested to remain in their accommodations, and that most of *Delta Orionis'* personnel were employed in work aboard *Epsilon Sextans.*

"So I haven't been the only one to be kept under lock and key," commented Grimes sardonically.

"You're the only one," retorted the girl, "who's been compensated for his imprisonment."

There was no answer to that, so the Ensign remained silent. Saying nothing, he inspected with interest the temporary tunnel that had been rigged between the airlocks of the two ships. So *Epsilon Sextans'* pressure hull had been made good, her atmosphere restored. That meant that the work of installing the armament had been completed. He hoped that he would not have to insist upon modifications.

The wreck—although she was a wreck no longer—bore her scars. The worst damage had been repaired, but holes and slashes that did not impair her structural strength were untouched, and spatters of once molten metal still made crazy patterns on beams and frames, stanchions and bulkheads. And there were the scars made by Craven's engineers—the raw, bright cicatrices of new welding.

Forward they made their way, deck after deck. The elevator in the axial shaft was not yet working, so Grimes had time and opportunity to appreciate the extent of the damage. They passed though the wreckage of the "farm"—the burst algae tanks, the ruptured vats in which yeast and tissue cultures were black and dead, frostbitten and dehydrated.

They brushed through alleyways choked with the brittle fronds of creeping plants killed by the ultimate winter.

And then they were passing through the accommodation levels. Bulkheads had been slashed through, destroying the privacy of the cabins that they had once enclosed. Destroying the privacy—and the occupants. There were no longer any bodies; for this Grimes was deeply thankful. (He learned later that Craven's first action had been to order and conduct a funeral service.) There were no bodies—but there were still stains. Men and women die quickly in hard vacuum—quickly and messily.

Captain Craven was alone in the Control Room. He was working, rather slowly and clumsily, wiring up an obviously makeshift panel that was additional to the original one installed before the Master's acceleration chair. It was obvious what it was—the remote controls for the newly fitted weaponry. Grimes said quickly, "There's no need for that, sir."

Craven started, let go of his screwdriver, made a fumbling grab for it as it drifted away from him. He stared at Grimes, then growled, "So it's *you*, is it?" Then, to Jane, "What the hell do you mean by letting this puppy out of his kennel?"

"Captain Craven," she told him quietly, "Mr. Grimes wants to come with us."

"*What?* I warn you, Miss Pentecost, I'm in no mood for silly jokes."

"This is not a silly joke, Captain," said Grimes. "I've had time to think things over. I feel, I really feel, that you have a far better chance if there's a qualified officer along to handle the gunnery."

Craven looked at them, from the girl to Grimes, then back again. He said, "Ensign, didn't I warn you?"

"It's not that way at all, sir," Grimes told him, flushing. "In fact, Miss Pentecost has been trying hard to dissuade me."

"*Oh?*"

"It's true," said Jane. "But he told me that we couldn't afford to look a gift horse in the mouth."

"I don't know what's been happening," rasped Craven. "I don't want to know what's been happening between the pair of you. This change of mind, this change of heart is rather . . . sudden. No matter. One volunteer, they say, is worth ten pressed men." He glared coldly at the Ensign. "And you volunteer?"

"Yes, Captain."

"I believe you. I have no choice in the matter. But you realize the consequences?"

"I do."

"Well, I *may* be able to do something to clear your yardarm. I've still to make my last entries in the Official Log of *Delta Orionis,* before I hand over to Captain Kennedy. And when it comes to such documentation, nobody cares to accuse a shipmaster of being a liar. Not out loud." He paused, thinking. "How does this sound, Miss Pentecost? Date, Time, Position, etc., etc. Mr. John Grimes, passenger, holding the rank of Ensign in the Federation Survey Service, removed by force from this vessel to *Epsilon Sextans,* there to supervise the installation and mounting of the armament, Survey Service property, discharged on my orders from No. 1 hold, also to advise upon the use of same in the subsequent event of an action's being fought. Signed, etc., etc. And witnessed."

"Rather long-winded, sir. But it seems to cover the ground."

"I intend to do more than advise!" flared Grimes.

"Pipe down. Or, if you must say it, make sure that there aren't any witnesses around when you say it. Now, when it comes to the original supervision, you see what I'm trying to do. Will it work?"

"After a fashion, sir. But it will work much better if the fire control panel is entirely separate from maneuvering control."

"You don't think that I could handle both at once?"

"You *could.* But not with optimum efficiency. No humanoid could. This setup of yours might just work if we were Shaara, or any of the other multilimbed arthropods. But even the Shaara, in their warships, don't expect the Queen-Captain to handle her ship *and* her guns simultaneously."

"You're the expert. I just want to be sure that you're prepared to, quote, advise, unquote, with your little pink paws on the actual keyboard of your battle organ."

"That's just the way that I propose to advise."

"Good. Fix it up to suit yourself, then. I should be able to let you have a mechanic shortly to give you a hand."

"Before we go any further, sir, I'd like to make an inspection of the weapons themselves. Just in case . . ."

"Just in case I've made some fantastic bollix, eh?" Craven was almost cheerful. "Very good. But try to make it snappy. It's time we were on our way."

"Yes," said Jane, and it seemed that the Captain's discarded somberness was hanging about her like a cloud. "It's time."

12

AT ONE TIME, before differentiation between the mercantile and the fighting vessel became pronounced, merchant vessels were built to carry a quite considerable armament. Today, the mounting of weapons on a merchantman presents its problems. After his tour of inspection Grimes was obliged to admit that Captain Craven had made cunning use of whatever spaces were available—but Craven, of course, was a very experienced officer, with long years of service in all classes of spacecraft. Too—and perhaps, luckily—there had been no cannon among the Survey Service ordnance that had been requisitioned, so recoil had not been among the problems.

When he was finished, Grimes returned to the Control Room. Craven was still there, and with him was Jane Pentecost. They had, obviously, been discussing something. They could, perhaps, have been quarreling; the girl's face was flushed and her expression sullen.

"Yes?" snapped the Captain.

"You've done a good job, sir. She's no cruiser, but she should be able to defend herself."

"Thank you. Then we'll be on our way."

"Not so fast, sir. I'd like to wire up my control panel properly before we shove off."

Craven laughed. "You'll have time, Mr. Grimes. I still have a few last duties to discharge aboard *Delta Orionis*. But be as quick as you can."

He left the compartment, followed by Jane Pentecost. She said, over her shoulder, "I'll send Mr. Baxter to help you, John."

The Rim Worlder must have been somewhere handy; in a matter of seconds he was by Grimes' side, an already open tool satchel at his belt. As he worked, assisting deftly and then taking over as soon as he was sure of what was required, he talked. He said, "Mum wanted to come along, but I soon put the damper on that. But I was bloody amazed to find *you* here."

"Were you?" asked Grimes coldly.

"You bet I was. Never thought you were cut out to be a bloody pirate." He cursed briefly as a spatter of hot metal from his sizzling soldering iron stung his hand. "A cold weld'd be better, but it'd take too much time. But where was I? Oh, yes. The shock to me system when I saw you comin' aboard this wagon."

"I have my quite valid reasons," Grimes told him stiffly.

"You're tellin' me. Just as my missus had quite valid reasons for wantin' to come with me. But she ain't a gunnery expert." He added piously, "Thank Gawd."

"And I am one," said the Ensign, trying to change the drift of the conversation before he lost his temper. "Yes. that's right. Just stick to the color code. The blue wiring's the ALGE . . ."

"I know," Baxter told him. "Tell me, is it any good?"

"Yes. Of course, if an enemy held us in her beams for any prolonged period we should all be cooked, but as far as it goes it's effective enough."

"Hope you're right." He made the last connections, then replaced the panel on the open shallow box. "Here's yer magic cabinet, Professor. All we have ter see now is what rabbits yer can pull outer the hat."

"Plenty, I hope," said Captain Craven, who had returned to Control. "And are you ready now, Mr. Grimes?"

"Yes, sir."

"Good. Then we'll make it stations. If you will take the copilot's chair, while Mr. Baxter goes along to look after his rockets."

"Will do, Skipper," said the engineer, packing away his tools as he pulled himself toward the exit hatch.

The ship's intercom came to life, in Jane Pentecost's voice. "Connection between vessels severed. Airlock door closed."

"We're still connected," grumbled Craven. "*Delia O'Ryan* still has her magnetic grapnels out." He spoke into the transceiver microphone: "*Epsilon Sextans* to *Delta Orionis*. Cast off, please. Over."

"*Delta Orionis* to *Epsilon Sextans*. Casting off." Through a viewport Grimes could see one of the bright mooring wires, snaking back into its recess. "All clear, Captain."

"Thank you, *Captain* Kennedy." And in a softer voice, "And I hope you keep that handle to your name, Bill."

"Thank you, sir. And all the best, Captain, from all of us, to all of you. And good hunting."

"Thanks. And look after the old *Delia,* Captain. And yourself. Over—and out."

"*Delia Orionis* to *Epsilon Sextans.* Over and out."

(There was something very final, thought Grimes, about those outs.)

He was aware that the ships were drifting slowly apart. Now he could see all of *Delta Orionis* from his viewport. He could not help recalling the day on which he had first seen her, at the Woomera spaceport. So much had happened since that day. (And so much was still to happen—he hoped.) He heard Craven say into the intercom, "Stand by for temporal precession. We're desynchronizing." Then, there was the giddiness, and the off-beat whine of the Mannschenn Drive that pierced his eardrums painfully, and beyond the viewports the great, shining shape of the other ship shimmered eerily and was suddenly warped into the likeness of a monstrous Klein flash—then vanished. Where she had been (where she still was, in space but not in time) shone the distant stars, the stars that in this distorted continuum were pulsing spirals of iridescence.

"Mannschenn Drive. *Cut*!"

The thin, high keening died abruptly. Outside, the stars were glittering points of light, piercingly bright against the blackness.

"Mr. Grimes!" Craven's voice was sharp. "I hope that you take more interest in gunnery than you do in ship handling. In case it has escaped your notice, I would remind you that you are second in command of this vessel, and in full charge in the event of my demise."

"Sorry, sir," stammered Grimes. Then, suddenly bold, "But I'm not your second in command, sir. I've signed no Articles."

Surprisingly, Craven laughed. "A spacelawyer, yet! Well, Mr. Grimes, as soon as we get this vessel on course we'll attend to the legal formalities. Meanwhile, may I request your close attention to what I am doing?"

"You may, sir."

Thereafter he watched and listened carefully. He admired the skill with which Craven turned the ship on her directional gyroscopes until the red-glowing target star was centered exactly in the cartwheel sight. He noted that the Captain used his reaction drive at a longer period and at a higher rate of acceleration than usual, and said as much. He was told, the words falling slowly and heavily in the pseudo-gravity, "They . . . will . . . expect . . . us . . . to . . . be . . . in . . . a . . . hurry. We must . . . not . . . disappoint . . . them."

Speed built up, fast—but it was a velocity that, in the context of the interstellar distances to be traversed, was no more than a snail's crawl. Then—and the sudden silence was like a physical blow—the thunder of the rockets ceased. The screaming roar had died, but the ship was not quiet. The whine of the Mannschenn Drive pervaded her every compartment, vibrated through every member of her structure. She was falling, falling through space and time, plunging through the warped continuum to her rendezvous with Death. . . .

And whose death? wondered Grimes.

He said, "I should have asked before, sir. But how are . . . how are *they* going to find us?"

"I don't know," said Craven. "I don't know. But they've found other ships when they've wanted to. They've never used the old pirate's technique of lying in wait at breaking-out points. A Mass Proximity Indicator? Could be. It's theoretically possible. It could be for a ship under Mannschenn Drive what radar is for a ship in normal space-time. Or some means of homing on a temporal precession field? That's more like it, I think, as this vessel was able to escape when she went random.

"But if they want us—and they will—they'll find us. And then"—he looked at Grimes, his blue gaze intense—"and then it's up to you, Ensign."

"To all of us," said Grimes.

13

SHE WAS UNDERMANNED, this *Epsilon Sextans,* but she functioned quite efficiently. Craven kept a Control Room watch himself, and the other two watchkeepers were Grimes and Jane Pentecost. Four on and eight off were their hours of duty—but there was plenty of work to be done in the off duty periods. The Captain, of course, was in over-all charge, and was trying to bring his command to the pitch of efficiency necessary for a fighting ship. Jane Pentecost was responsible for meals—although these, involving little more than the opening of cans, did not take up too much of her time. She had also taken over biochemist's duties, but called now and again upon Grimes to help her with the ATREG unit. Its operation was simple enough, but it was inclined to be tempermental and, now and again, allowed the carbon dioxide concentration to reach a dangerous level. Grimes' main concern was his armament. He could not indulge in a practice shot—the expulsion of mass by a ship running under interstellar drive is suicidal; even the employment of laser weapons is dangerous. But there were tests that he could make; there was, in the ship's stores, a spare chart tank that he was able to convert to a battle simulator.

Craven helped him, and set up targets in the tank, glowing points of light that were destroyed by the other sparks that represented Grimes' missiles. After one such drill he said, "You seem to know your stuff, Ensign. Now, what's your grasp of the tactical side of it?"

Grimes considered his words before speaking. "Well, sir, we *could* use laser with the Drive in operation—but we haven't got laser. The pirates have. They can synchronize and just carve us up at leisure. This time, I think they'll go for the interstellar drive engine room first, so that we can't get away by the use of random precession."

"Yes. That's what they'll do. That's why I have that compartment literally sealed in a cocoon of insulation. Oh, I know it's not effective, but it will give us a second or so of grace. No more."

"We can't use our reflective vapor," went on Grimes. "That'd be almost as bad, from our viewpoint, as loosing off a salvo of missiles. But, sir, when this ship was first attacked there must have been a considerable loss of mass when the atmosphere was expelled through the rents in the shell plating . . . the Drive was running. How was it that the ship wasn't flung into some other space-time?"

"Come, come, Mr. Grimes. You should know the answer to that one. She was held by the powerful temporal precession fields of the drive units of the two pirates. And then, of course, when the engineers managed to set up their random precession there was no mass left to be expelled."

"H'm. I see. Or I think I see. Then, in that case, why shouldn't I use my ALGE as soon as we're attacked?"

"No. Better not. Something might just go wrong—and I don't want to become one of my own ancestors."

"Then . . . ?"

"You tell me, Mr. Grimes."

"Cut our Drive . . . ? Break out into the normal continuum? Yes . . . it could work." He was becoming enthusiastic. "And then we shall be waiting for them, with our missile batteries, when *they* break out."

"We'll make an admiral of you yet, young Grimes."

With watchkeeping and with off-watch duties time was fully occupied. And yet there was something missing. There was, Grimes said to himself, one hell of a lot missing. Jane Pentecost had her own watch to keep, and her own jobs to do when she was not in the control room—but she and Grimes had some free time to share. But they did not share it.

He broached the subject when he was running a test on the artificial chlorophyl in the ATREG. "Jane, I was hoping I'd see more of you."

"You're seeing plenty of me."

"But not enough."

"Don't be tiresome," she snapped. Then, in a slightly softer voice, "Don't . . ."

". . . spoil everything?" he finished for her sardonically.

"You know what I mean," she told him coldly.

"Do I?" He groped for words. "Jane . . . Damn it all, I hoped . . . After what happened aboard the *Delia D'Ryan* . . ."

"That," she said, "was different." Her face flushed. "I tell you this, Grimes, if I'd known that you were coming along with us it never would have happened."

"No?"

"NO!"

"Even so . . . I don't see any reason why we shouldn't . . ."

"Why we shouldn't what? Oh, all right, all right. I know what you mean. But it's out of the question., I'll tell you why, in words of one syllable. In a ship such as *Delta Orionis* discreet fun and games were permissible, even desirable. No shortage of women—both crew and passengers. Here, I'm the only female. Your friend Mr. Baxter has been sniffing after me. And Mr. Wolverton, the Interstellar Chief. *And* his Second. And even, bereaved though he is, the Bearded Bastard. *He* might get away with it—the privileges of rank and all that. But nobody else would—most certainly not yourself. How long would it remain a secret if we went to bed together?"

"I suppose you're right, but . . ."

"But what? Oh John, John, you *are* a stubborn cow."

"Cow?"

"Sorry. Just Rimworldsese. Applicable to both sexes."

"Talking of sex . . ."

"Oh, shut *up*!"

"I'll not." She looked desirable standing there. A small smudge of grease on her flushed cheek was like a beauty spot. "I'll not," he said again. She was close to him, and he was acutely conscious that beneath the thin uniform shirt and the short shorts there was only Jane. He had only to reach out. He did so. At first she did not resist—and then exploded into a frenzy of activity. Before he could let go of her a hard, rough hand closed on his shirt collar and yanked him backwards.

"Keep yer dirty paws off her!" snarled a voice. It was Baxter's. "Keep yer dirty paws off her! If we didn't want yer ter let off the fireworks I'd do yer, here an' now."

"And keep *your* dirty paws off me!" yelped Grimes. It was meant to be an authentic quarterdeck bark, but it didn't come out that way.

"Let him go, Mr. Baxter," said Jane, adding, "please."

"Oh, orl right. If yer says so. But I still think we should run him up ter the Old Man."

"No. Better not." She addressed Grimes, "Thank you for your help on the ATREG, Mr. Grimes. And thank *you*, Mr. Baxter, for your help. It's time that I started looking after the next meal."

She left, not hastily, but not taking her time about it either. When she was gone Baxter released Grimes. Clumsily the Ensign turned himself around, with a wild flailing motion. Unarmed combat had never been his specialty, especially unarmed combat in Free Fall conditions. But he knew that he had to fight, and the rage and the humiliation boiling up in him made it certain that he would do some damage.

But Baxter was laughing, showing all his ugly, yellow teeth. "Come orf it, Admiral! An' if we must have a set-to—not in here. Just smash the UV projector—an' bang goes our air conditioning! Simmer down, mate. Simmer down!"

Grimes simmered down, slowly. "But I thought you were out for my blood, Mr. Baxter."

"Have ter put on a show for the Sheilas now an' again. Shouldn't mind puttin' on another kind o' show, *with* her. But not in public—like you was goin' to. It just won't do—not until the shootin' is over, anyhow. An' even then. . . . So, Admiral, it's paws off as far as you're concerned. An' as far as I'm concerned—*an'* the Chief Time Twister an' his sidekick. But, if, yer can spare the time, I propose we continue the conversation in my palatial dogbox."

Grimes should have felt uneasy as he followed the engineer to his accommodation but, oddly enough, he did not. The rough friendliness just could not be the prelude to a beating up. And it wasn't.

"Come in," said Baxter, pulling his sliding door to one side. "Now yer see how the poor live. This is . . ."

"No," protested Grimes. "No."

"Why? I was only goin' to say that this is me 'umble 'umpy. An' I'd like yer to meet a coupla friends o' mine—and there's more where they came from."

The "friends" were two drinking bulbs. Each bore proudly no less than four stars on its label. The brandy was smooth, smooth and potent. Grimes sipped appreciatively. "I didn't know that we had any of *this* aboard *Delia O'Ryan.*"

"An' nor did we. You'll not find this tipple in the bar stores of any merchantman, nor aboard any of yer precious Survey Service wagons. Space stock for the Emperor's yacht, this is. So here's ter the Waverley taxpayers!"

"But where did you get this from, Mr. Baxter?"

"Where d'yer think? I've had a good fossick around the holds o' this old bitch, an' there's quite a few things too good to let fall inter the hands o' those bloody Waldegrenese."

"But that's pillage."

"It's common sense. Mind yer, I doubt if Captain Craven would approve, so yer'd better chew some dry tea—that's in the cargo too—before yer see the Old Man again. All the bleedin' same—it's no worse than him borrowing your Survey Service stores an' weapons from *his* cargo."

"I suppose it's not," admitted Grimes. All the same, he still felt guilty when he was offered a second bulb of the luxurious spirit. But he did not refuse it.

14

HE WAS A good fossicker, was Baxter.

Two days later, as measured by the ship's chronometer, he was waiting for Grimes as he came off watch. "Ensign," he announced without preamble, "I've found somethin' in the cargo."

"Something new, you mean?" asked Grimes coldly. He still did not approve of pillage, although he had shared the spoils.

"Somethin' that shouldn't be there. Somethin' that's up *your* alley, I think."

"There's no reason why equipment for the Waverley Navy shouldn't be among the cargo."

"True enough. But it wouldn't be in a case with *Beluga Caviar* stenciled all over it. I thought I'd found somethin' to go with the vodka I half inched, but it won't."

"Then what is it?"

"Come and see."

"All right." Briefly Grimes wondered if he should tell Craven, who had relieved the watch, then decided against it. The Old Man would probably insist on making an investigation in person, in which case Grimes would have to pass another boring hour or so in the Control Room.

The two men made their way aft until they came to the forward bulkhead of the cargo spaces. Normally these would have been pressurized, but, when *Epsilon Sextans'* atmosphere had been replenished from *Delta Orionis'* emergency cylinders, it had seemed pointless to waste precious oxygen. So access was through an airlock that had a locker outside, in which suits, ready for immediate use, were stowed.

Grimes and Baxter suited up, helping each other as required. Then the engineer put out his gloved hand to the airlock controls. Grimes stopped him, bent forward to touch helmets. He said, "Hang on. If we open the door it'll register on the panel in Control."

"Like hell it will!" came the reply. "Most of the wiring was slashed through during the piracy. I fixed the hold lights—but damn all else." Grimes, through the transparency of the visors, saw the other's grin. "For obvious reasons."

Grimes shrugged, released Baxter. Everything was so irregular that one more, relatively minor irregularity hardly mattered. He squeezed with the engineer into the small airlock, waited until the atmosphere it held had been pumped back into the body of the ship, then himself pushed the button that actuated the mechanism of the inner valve.

This was not the first time that he had been in the cargo spaces. Some of the weapons "borrowed" from *Delta Orionis'* cargo had been mounted in the holds. When he had made his inspections it had never occurred to him that the opening and closing of the airlock door had not registered in Control.

He stood back and let Baxter lead the way. The engineer pulled himself to one of the bins in which he had been foraging. The door to it was still open, and crates and cartons disturbed by the pillager floated untidily around the opening.

"You'll have to get all this restowed," said Grimes sharply. "If we have to accelerate there'll be damage." But he might as well have been speaking to himself. The suit radios had not been switched on and, in any case, there was no air to carry sound waves, however faintly.

Baxter had scrambled into the open bin. Grimes followed him, saw him standing by the case, its top prized open, that carried the lettering, BELUGA CAVIAR. PRODUCE OF THE RUSSIAN SOCIAL DEMOCRATIC REPUBLIC. Baxter beckoned. Grimes edged his way past the drifting packages to join him.

There was something in the case—but it was not jars or cans of salted sturgeons' eggs. It looked at first like a glittering, complex piece of mobile statuary, although it was motionless. It was a metal mismating of gyroscope and Moëbius Strip. It did not look wrong—nothing functional ever does—but it did look *odd.*

Grimes was standing hard against Baxter now. Their helmets were touching. He asked, "What . . . what is it?"

"I was hopin' you'd be able ter tell me, Admiral." Then, as Grimes extended a cautious hand into the case, "Careful! Don't touch nothin'!"

"Why not?"

"'Cause this bloody lot was booby-trapped, that's why. See that busted spring? An' see that cylinder in the corner? That's a thermite bomb, or somethin' worse. Shoulda gone orf when I pried the lid up—but luckily I buggered the firin' mechanism with me bar when I stuck it inter just the right crack. But I think the bastard's deloused now."

"It looks as though it—whatever it is—is hooked up to one of the electrical circuits."

"Yair. An' it's not the lightin' circuit. Must be the airlock indicators."

"Must be." As a weapons expert, Grimes could see the thermite bomb—if that was what it was—had been rendered ineffective. It hadn't been an elaborate trap, merely a device that would destroy the—the *thing* if the case housing it were tampered with. Baxter had been lucky—and, presumably, those who had planted the—what the hell was it?—unlucky.

With a cautious finger he nudged the rotor.

It turned—and he was reminded of those other rotors, the ever-precessing gyroscopes of the Mannschenn Drive.

He remembered, then. He remembered a series of lectures at the Academy on future weapons and navigational devices. Having decided upon his specialty he had been really interested only in the weapons. But there had been talk of a man called Carlotti, who was trying to develop a device that would induce temporal precession in radio signals, so that instantaneous communications would be possible throughout the Galaxy without ships and shore stations having to rely upon the temperamental and unreliable telepaths. And beacons, employing the same principle, could be used for navigation by ships under interstellar drive. . . .

So this could be one of Signor Carlotti's gadgets. Perhaps the Empire of Waverley had offered him a higher price than had the Federation. But why the BELUGA CAVIAR? To deter and confuse industrial spies? But *Epsilon Sextans* possessed excellent strong rooms for the carriage of special cargo.

And why was the thing wired up?

Suddenly it was obvious. Somehow, the Duchy of Waldegren possessed Carlotti equipment. This . . . this beacon had been transmitting, unknown to anybody aboard the ship, during the voyage. The frigates had homed upon her. When, inadvertently, its power supply had been shut off, the victim, using random precession, had been able to make her escape.

So, if the pirates were to make a second attack it would have to be reactivated.

"We'd better throw this lot on to the Old Man's plate," said Grimes.

Captain Craven listened intently as Grimes and Baxter told their story. They feared that he was going to lose his temper when told of the engineer's cargo pillaging, but he only remarked, in a dry voice, "I guess that the consignees can afford to compensate us for our time and trouble. Even so, Mr. Baxter, I insist that this practice must cease forthwith." And then, when Grimes described the device, he said, "Yes, I have heard of Carlotti's work. But I didn't think that he'd got as far as a working model. But the thing could have been developed by Waldegrenese scientists from the data in his published papers."

"So you agree, sir, that it is some kind of beacon upon which the pirates can home?"

"What else can it be? Now, gentlemen, we find ourselves upon the horns of a dilemma. If we don't reactivate the bloody thing, the chances are that we shall deliver the ship and cargo intact, at no great risk to ourselves, and to the joy of the underwriters. If we *do* reactivate it—then the chances are that we shall have to fight our way through. And there's no guarantee that we shall be on the winning side."

"I was shanghaied away here as a gunnery officer," said Grimes.

"Shanghaied—or press-ganged?" queried Craven.

"The technique was more that of the shanghai," Grimes told him.

"Indeed?" Craven's voice was cold. "But no matter. You're here, and you're one of my senior officers. What course of action do *you* recommend?"

Grimes replied slowly and carefully. "Legally speaking, what we're involved in isn't a war. But it *is* a war, of sorts. And a just war. And, in any case, the Master of a merchant vessel has the legal right to resist illegal seizure or destruction by force of arms. Of course, we have to consider the illegal circumstances attending the arming of this ship. . . ."

"Let's not get bogged down in legalities and illegalities," said Craven, with a touch of impatience. "The lawyers can sort it all out eventually. Do we reactivate?"

"Yes," said Grimes.

"And you, Mr. Baxter. What do you say?"

"We Rim Worlders just don't like Waldegren. I'll not pass up a chance ter kick the bastards in the teeth. Reactivate, Skipper."

"Good. And how long will it take you to make good the circuit the beacon's spliced in to?"

"Twenty minutes. No more. But d' yer think we oughter put the whole thing to the vote first?"

"No. Everybody here was under the impression that we should be fighting. With one possible exception, they're all volunteers."

"But I did volunteer, sir," objected Grimes.

"Make your mind up, Ensign. You were telling me just now that you'd been shanghaied. All right. Everybody is a volunteer. So we just rebait the trap without any more yapping about it. Let me know as soon as you're ready, Mr. Baxter. Will you require assistance?"

"I'll manage, Skipper."

When he was gone Craven turned to Grimes. "You realize, Ensign, that this puts me in rather a jam. Let me put it this way. Am I justified in risking the lives of all my officers to carry out a private act of vengeance?"

"I think that you can take Mr. Baxter and myself as being representative, sir. As for the others—Miss Pentecost's a Rim Worlder, and her views will coincide with Baxter's. And the original crew members—they're just as entitled to vengeance as you are. I know that if I'd been an officer of this ship at the time of the original piracy I'd welcome the chance of hitting back."

"*You* would. Yes. Even if, as now, an alternative suddenly presented itself. But . . ."

"I honestly don't see what you're worrying about, sir."

"You wouldn't. It's a matter of training. But, for all my Reserve commission, I'm a merchant officer. Oh, I know that any military commander is as responsible for the lives of his men as I am—but he also knows that those lives, like his own, are expendable."

"It's a pity that Baxter found the beacon," said Grimes.

"It is—and it isn't. If he hadn't found it, I shouldn't be soliloquizing like a spacefaring Hamlet. And we should have brought the ship in intact and, like as not, all been awarded Lloyd's Medals. On the other hand—if he hadn't found it we—or I?—should have lost our chance of getting back at the pirates."

"You aren't Hamlet, sir." Grimes spoke with the assurance of the very young, but in later years he was to remember his words, and to feel neither shame nor embarrassment, but only a twinge of envy and regret. "You aren't Hamlet. You're Captain Craven, Master under God. Please, sir, for once in your life do something you want to do, and argue it out later with the Almighty if you must."

"And with my owners?" Grimes couldn't be sure, but he thought he saw something like a smile beneath Craven's full beard. "And with my owners?"

"Master Astronauts' certificates aren't all that common, sir. If worst comes to worst, there's always the Rim Worlds. The Sundowner Line, isn't it?"

"I'd already thought of that." There was no doubt about it. Craven was smiling. "After all that you've been saying to me, I'm surprised that *you* don't join forces with our Miss Pentecost."

"Go out to the Rim, sir? Hardly."

"Don't be so sure, young Grimes. Anyhow, you'd better get Miss Pentecost up here now so that we can see how friend Baxter is getting on. There's always the risk that he'll find a few more things among the cargo that aren't nailed down."

15

GRIMES CALLED JANE Pentecost on the intercom; after a minute or so she made her appearance in Control. Craven told her what Baxter had discovered and what he, Craven, intended doing about it. She nodded in emphatic agreement. "Yes," she said. "The thing's here to be used—and to be used the way that *we* want to use it. But I don't think that we should make it public."

"Why not, Miss Pentecost?"

"I could be wrong, Captain, but in my opinion there are quite a few people in this ship who'd welcome the chance of wriggling out of being the cheese in the mousetrap. When there's no alternative they're brave enough. When there's a face-saving alternative . . ."

Baxter's voice came from the intercom speaker. "Chief Reaction Drive Engineer to Control. Repairs completed. Please check your panel."

Yes, the circuit had been restored. The buzzer sounded, and on the board a glowing red light showed that the outer door to the cargo hold airlock was open. How much of the failure of the indicators was due to battle damage and how much to Baxter's sabotage would never be known. Craven's heavy eyebrows lifted ironically as he looked at Grimes, and Grimes shrugged in reply.

Then, the watch handed over to the girl, the two men made their way aft from the Control Room. Outside the airlock they found Baxter, already suited up save for his helmet. There had been only two suits in the locker, and the engineer had brought another one along for the Captain from somewhere.

The little compartment would take only two men at a time. Craven and Grimes went through first, then were joined by Baxter. There was no longer any need for secrecy, so the suit radios were switched on. The only person likely to be listening in was Jane Pentecost in Control.

Grimes heard Craven muttering angrily as they passed packages that obviously had been opened and pillaged, but the Captain did no more than mutter. He possessed the sense of proportion so essential to his rank—and a few bulbs of looted liquor were, after all, relatively unimportant.

They came to the bin in which the case allegedly containing caviar had been stowed, in which some secret agent of Waldegren had tapped the circuit supplying power to the beacon. Inside the box the gleaming machine was still motionless. Craven said, "I thought you told me the current was on."

"It, is, Skipper." Baxter's voice was pained. "But I switched it off before I fixed the wiring." He extended a gloved finger, pressed a little toggle switch.

And nothing happened.

"Just a nudge." whispered the engineer.

The oddly convoluted rotor turned easily enough, and as it rotated it seemed almost to vanish in a mist of its own generating—a mist that was no more than an optical illusion.

It rotated, slowed—and stopped.

Baxter cast aspersions upon the legitimacy of its parenthood. Then, still grumbling, he produced a volt-meter. Any doubt that power was being delivered to the machine was soon dispelled. Power was being delivered—but it was not being used.

"Well, Mr. Baxter?" demanded Craven.

"I'm a fair mechanic, Skipper—but I'm no physicist."

"Mr. Grimes?"

"I specialized in gunnery, sir."

Craven snorted, the sound unpleasantly loud in the helmet phones. He said sarcastically, "I'm only the Captain, but I have some smatterings of Mannschenn Drive maintenance and operation. This thing isn't a Mannschenn Drive unit—but it's first cousin to one. As I recall it, some of the earlier models couldn't be started without the employment of a small, temporal precession field initiator. Furthermore, these initiators, although there is no longer any need for them, are still carried as engine room spares in the Commission's ships."

"And that gadget'll start *this* little time-twister, Skipper?" asked the engineer.

"It might, Mr. Baxter. It might. So, Mr. Grimes, will you go along to the Mannschenn Drive room and ask Mr. Wolverton for his initiator? No need to tell him what it's for."

Wolverton was in the Mannschenn Drive room, staring moodily at the gleaming complexity of precessing rotors. Grimes hastily averted his eyes from the machine. It frightened him, and he didn't mind admitting it. And there was something about the engineer that frightened him, too. The tall, cadaverous man, with the thin strands of black hair drawn over his gleaming skull, looked more like a seer than a ship's officer, looked like a fortune-teller peering into the depths of an uncannily mobile crystal ball. He was mumbling, his voice a low, guttural muttering against the thin, high keening of his tumbling gyroscopes. The Ensign, at last was able to make out the words.

"Divergent tracks. . . . To be, or not to be, that is the question—"

Grimes thought, *This ship should be renamed the* State of Denmark. *There's something rotten here. . . .* He said sharply, "Mr. Wolverton!"

Slowly the Chief Interstellar Drive Engineer turned his head, stared at Grimes unseeingly at first. His eyes came into focus. He whispered, "It's you."

"Who else, Chief? Captain's compliments, and he'd like to borrow your temporal precession field initiator."

"He would, would he? And why?"

"An—an experiment." said Grimes, with partial truth. The fewer people who knew the whole truth the better.

"An experiment?"

"Yes. If you wouldn't mind letting me have it now, Chief . . ."

"But it's engine room stores. It's the Commission's stores. It's a *very* delicate instrument. It is against the Commission's regulations to issue it to unqualified personnel."

"But Mr. Baxter is helping with the . . . experiment."

"Mr. Baxter! That letter-off of cheap fireworks. That . . . *Rim Runner!* No. No. Mr. Baxter is not qualified personnel."

"Then perhaps you could lend us one of your juniors."

"No. No, I would not trust them. Why do you think that I am here, Mr. Grimes? Why do you think that I have been tied to my gyroscopes? Literally tied, almost. If I had not been here, keeping my own watch, when the pirates struck, this ship would have been utterly destroyed. I *know* the Drive, Mr. Grimes." He seized the Ensign's arm, turned him so that he was facing the gleaming, spinning rotors, endlessly precessing, endlessly tumbling down the dark dimensions, shimmering on the very verge of invisibility. Grimes wanted to close his eyes, but could not. "I *know* the Drive, Mr. Grimes. It talks to me. It shows me things.

It warned me, that time, that Death was waiting for this ship and all in her. And now it warns me again. But there is a . . . a divergence. . . ."

"Mr. Wolverton, please! There is not much time."

"But what is Time, Mr. Grimes? What *is* Time? What do you know of the forking World Lines, the Worlds of If? I've lived with this machine, Mr. Grimes. It's part of me—or am I part of *it?* Let me show you. . . ." His grip on the Ensign's arm was painful. "Let me show you. Look. Look into the machine. What do you see?"

Grimes saw only shadowy, shimmering wheels and a formless darkness.

"I see you, Mr. Grimes," almost sang the engineer. "I see you—but not as you *will* be. But as you might be. I see you on the bridge of your flagship, your uniform gold-encrusted and medal-bedecked, with commodores and captains saluting you and calling you 'sir' . . . but I see you, too, in the control room of a shabby little ship, a single ship, in shabby clothes, and the badge on your cap is one that I have never seen, is one that does not yet exist. . . ."

"Mr. Wolverton! That initiator. *Please*!"

"But there is no hurry, Mr. Grimes. There is no hurry. There is time enough for everything—for everything that is, that has been, that will be and that might be. There is time to decide, Mr. Grimes. There is time to decide whether or not we make our second rendezvous with Death. The initiator is part of it all, Mr. Grimes, is it not? The initiator is the signpost that stands at the forking of the track. You weren't here, Mr. Grimes, when the pirates stuck. You did not hear the screams, you did not smell the stench of burning flesh. You're young and foolhardy; all that you want is the chance to play with your toys. And all that I want, now that I know that alternatives exist, is the chance to bring this ship to her destination with no further loss of life."

"Mr. Wolverton . . ."

"Mr. Grimes!" It was Captain Craven's voice, and he was in a vile temper. "What the hell do you think you're playing at?"

"Captain," said Wolverton. "I can no more than guess at what you intend to do—but I have decided not to help you to do it."

"Then give us the initiator. We'll work it ourselves."

"No, Captain."

"Give me the initiator, Mr. Wolverton. That's an order."

"A *lawful* command, Captain? As lawful as those commands of yours that armed this ship?"

"Hold him, Grimes!" (*And who's supposed to be holding whom?* wondered the Ensign. Wolverton's grip was still tight and painful on his arm.) "Hold him, while I look in the storeroom!"

"Captain! Get away from the door! You've no right . . ."

Wolverton relinquished his hold on Grimes who, twisting with an agility that surprised himself, contrived to get both arms about the engineer's waist. In the scuffle the contact between their magnetic shoe soles and the deck was broken. They hung there; helpless, with no solidity within reach of their flailing limbs to give them purchase. They hung there, clinging to each other, but more in hate than in love. Wolverton's back was to the machine; he could not see, as could Grimes, that there was an indraught of air into the spinning, shimmering complexity. Grimes felt the beginnings of panic, more than the mere beginnings. There were no guardrails; he had read somewhere why this was so, but the abstruse physics involved did not matter—all that mattered was that there was nothing to prevent him and Wolverton from being drawn into the dimension-twisting field of the thing.

He freed, somehow, his right hand, and with an effort that sprained his shoulder brought it around in a sweeping, clumsy and brutal blow to the engineer's face. Wolverton screamed and his grip relaxed. Violently, Grimes shoved away. To the action there was reaction.

Craven emerged from the storeroom, carrying something that looked like a child's toy gyroscope in a transparent box. He looked around for Grimes and Wolverton at deck level and then, his face puzzled, looked up. He did not, as Grimes had been doing for some seconds, vomit—but his face, behind the beard went chalk-white. He put out his free hand and, not ungently, pulled Grimes to the deck.

He said, his voice little more than a whisper, "There's nothing we can do. Nothing—except to get a pistol and finish him off. . . ."

Grimes forced himself to look again at the slimy, bloody obscenity that was a man turned, literally, inside-out—heart (if it was the heart) still beating, intestines still writhing.

16

IT WAS GRIMES who went for a pistol, fetching a Minetti from the weapons rack that he, himself, had fitted up in the Control Room. He told Jane Pentecost what he wanted it for. He made no secret of either his horror or his self blame.

She said, "But this is a war, even if it's an undeclared one. And in a war you must expect casualties."

"Yes, yes. I know. But *I* pushed him into the field."

"It was an accident. It could easily have been you instead of him. And I'm glad that it wasn't."

"But you haven't seen . . ."

"And I don't want to." Her voice hardened. "Meanwhile, get the hell out of here and back to the Mannschenn Drive room. If you're so sorry for the poor bastard, do something about putting him out of his misery."

"But . . ."

"Don't be such a bloody coward, Grimes."

The words hurt—mainly because there was so much truth in them. Grimes was dreading having to see again the twisted obscenity that had once been a man, was dreading having to breathe again the atmosphere of that compartment, heavy with the reek of hot oil, blood and fecal matter. But, with the exception of Craven, he was the only person in the ship trained in the arts of war. He recalled the words of a surgeon-commander who had lectured the midshipmen of his course on the handling of battle casualties—and recalled, too, how afterward the young gentlemen had sneered at the bloodthirstiness of one who was supposed to be a professional healer. *"When one of your shipmates has really had it, even if he's your best friend, don't hesitate a moment about finishing him off. You'll be doing him a kindness. Finish him off—and get him out of sight. Shockingly wounded men are bad for morale."*

"What are you waiting for?" demanded Jane Pentecost. "Do you want *me* to do it?"

Grimes said nothing, just hurried out of the Control Room.

Craven was still in the Mannschenn Drive room when Grimes got back there. With him were two of the interstellar drive engineers—the Second and the Third. Their faces were deathly white, and the Second's prominent Adam's apple was working spasmodically, but about them there was an air of grim resolution. The Third—how could he bear to touch that slimy, reeking mess?—had hold of its shoulders (white, fantastically contorted bone gleaming pallidly among red convolutions of flesh), while the Second, a heavy spanner in his hand, was trying to decide where to strike.

The Captain saw Grimes. "Give me that!" he snapped, and snatched the pistol from the Ensign's hand. Then, to the engineers, "Stand back!"

The little weapon rattled sharply and viciously. To the other smells was added the acridity of burned propellant. What had been Wolverton was driven to the deck by the impact of the tiny projectiles, and adhered there. There was surprisingly little blood, but the body had stopped twitching.

Craven handed the empty pistol back to the Ensign. He ordered, "You stay here, Mr. Grimes, and organize the disposal of the body." He went to the locker where he had put the initiator, took out the little instrument and, carrying it carefully, left the Mannschenn Drive room. Neither of the engineers, still staring with horrified fascination at their dead Chief, noticed.

"How . . . how did it happen?" asked the Second, after a long silence.

"He fell into the field," said Grimes.

"But how? How? He was always getting on us about being careless, and telling us what was liable to happen to us, and now it's happened to him—"

"That's the way of it," contributed the Third, with a certain glum satisfaction. "Don't do as I do, do as I say."

"Have you a box?" asked Grimes.

"A box?" echoed the Second.

"Yes. A box." Now that he was doing something, doing something useful, Grimes was beginning to feel a little better. "We can't have a funeral while we're running under interstellar drive. We have to . . . to put him somewhere." *Out of sight*, he mentally added.

"That chest of spares?" muttered the Second.

"Just the right size," agreed the Third.

"Then get it," ordered Grimes.

The chest, once the spares and their packing had been removed and stowed elsewhere, was just the right size. Its dimensions were almost those of a coffin. It was made of steel, its bottom magnetized, and remained where placed on the deck while the three men, fighting down their recurring nausea, handled the body into it. All of them sighed audibly in relief when, at last, the close-fitting lid covered the remains. Finally, the Third ran a welding torch around the joint. As he was doing so the lights flickered.

Was it because of the torch? wondered Grimes. Or was it because the beacon in the hold had been reactivated?

Somehow he could not feel any real interest.

Cleaned up after a fashion, but still feeling physically ill, he was back in the Control Room. Craven was there, and Baxter was with him. Jane Pentecost had been relieved so that she could attend to her duties in the galley. "Not that *I* feel like a meal," the Captain had said. "And I doubt very much that Mr. Grimes does either."

"Takes a lot ter put *me* off me tucker," the engineer declared cheerfully as he worked on the airlock door telltale panel.

"You didn't see Mr. Wolverton, Mr. Baxter," said Craven grimly.

"No, Skipper. An' I'm not sorry I didn't." He paused in his work to rummage in his tool bag. He produced bulbs of brandy. "But I thought you an' the Ensign might need some o' this."

Craven started to say something about cargo pillage, then changed his mind. He accepted the liquor without further quibbling. The three men sipped in silence.

Baxter carelessly tossed his squeezed empty bulb aside, continued with what he had been doing. The Captain said to Grimes, "Yes. We got the thing started again. And we've improved upon it."

"Improved upon it, sir? How?"

"It's no longer only a beacon. It's also an alarm. As soon as it picks up the radiation from the similar pieces of apparatus aboard the enemy frigates, the buzzer that Mr. Baxter is fitting up will sound, the red light will flash. We shall have ample warning. . . ."

"She'll be right, Skipper," said the engineer.

"Thank you, Mr. Baxter. And now; if you don't mind, I'd like a few words in private with Mr. Grimes."

"Don't be too hard on him, Skipper."

Baxter winked cheerfully at Grimes and left the control room.

"Mr. Grimes," Craven's voice was grave. "Mr. Grimes, today, early in your career, you have learned a lesson that some of us never have to learn. You have killed a man—yes, yes, I know that it was not intentional—and you have been privileged to see the end result of your actions.

"There are many of us who are, who have been, killers. There are many of us who have pushed buttons but who have never seen what happens at the other end of the trajectory. Perhaps people slaughtered by explosion or laser beam do not look quite so horrible as Wolverton—but, I assure you, they often look horrible enough, and often die as slowly and as agonizingly. You know, now, what violent death looks like, Mr. Grimes. So tell me, are you still willing to push your buttons, to play pretty tunes on your battle organ?"

"And what did the bodies in this ship look like, Captain?" asked Grimes. Then, remembering that one of the bodies had belonged to the woman whom Craven had loved, he bitterly regretted having asked the question.

"Not pretty," whispered Captain Craven. "Not at all pretty."

"I'll push your buttons for you," Grimes told him.

And for Jane Pentecost, he thought. *And for the others. And for myself? The worst of it all is that I haven't got the excuse of saying that it's what I'm paid for. . . .*

17

DOWN THE DARK dimensions fell *Epsilon Sextans,* falling free through the warped continuum. But aboard the ship time still possessed meaning, the master chronometer still ticked away the seconds, minutes and hours; the little man-made world was still faithful to that puissant god of scientific intelligences everywhere in the universe—the Clock. Watch succeeded watch in Control Room and engine room. Meals were prepared and served on time. There was even, toward the end, a revival of off-duty social activities: a chess set was discovered and brought into use, playing cards were produced and a bridge school formed.

But there was one social activity that, to Grimes' disappointment was not resumed—the oldest social activity of them all. More than once he pleaded with Jane—and every time she laughed away his pleas. He insisted—and that made matters worse. He was (as he said), the donkey who had been allowed one nibble of the carrot and who could not understand why the carrot had been snatched away. He was (she said), a donkey. Period.

He should have guessed what was happening, but he did not. He was young, and inexperienced in the ways of women—of men *and* women. He just could not imagine that Jane would spare more than a casual glance for any of the engineers or for the flabby, pasty youth who was the psionic radio officer—and in this he was right.

Epsilon Sextans was, for a ship of her class, very well equipped. In addition to the usual intercom system she was fitted with closed circuit television. In the event of emergency the Captain or watch officer, by the flip of a switch, could see what was happening in any compartment of the vessel. Over the control panel, in big, red letters, were the words: EMERGENCY USE ONLY. Grimes did not know what was the penalty for improper use of the apparatus in the Merchant Navy—but he did know that in the Survey Service officers had been cashiered and given an ignominious discharge for this offense. The more cramped and crowded the conditions in which men—and women—work and live, the more precious is privacy.

It was Grimes' watch.

When he had taken over, all the indications were that it would be as boring as all the previous watches. All that was required of the watch-keeper was that he stay awake. Grimes stayed awake. He had brought a book with him into Control, hiding it inside his uniform shirt, and it held his attention for a while. Then, following the example of generations of watch officers, he set up a game of three dimensional tic-tac-toe in the chart tank and played, right hand against left. The left hand was doing remarkably well when a buzzer sounded. The Ensign immediately cleared the tank and looked at the airlock indicator panel. But there were no lights on the board, and he realized that it was the inter-com telephone.

"Control," he said into his microphone.

"'P.R.O. here. I . . . I'm not happy, Mr. Grimes. . . ."

"Who is?" quipped Grimes.

"I . . . I feel . . . smothered."

"Something wrong with the ventilation in your shack?"

"No. NO. It's like . . . it's like a heavy blanket soaked in ice-cold water. . . . You can't move . . . you can't shout . . . you can't *hear*. . . . *It's like it was before*. . . ."

"Before what?" snapped Grimes—and then as the other buzzer sounded, as the additional red light flashed on the telltale panel, he realized the stupidity of his question.

At once he pressed the alarm button. This was it, at last. Action Stations! Throughout the ship the bells were shrilling, the klaxons squawking. Hastily Grimes vacated the pilot's chair, slipped into the one from which he could control his weapons—and from which he could reach out to other controls. But where was the Old Man? Where was Captain Craven? This was the moment that he had longed for, this was the consummation toward which all his illegalities had been directed. Damn it all, *where was he?*

Perhaps he was floating stunned in his quarters—starting up hurriedly from sleep he could have struck his head upon some projection, knocked himself out. If this were the case he, Grimes, would have to call Jane from her own battle station in Sick Bay to render first aid. But there was no time to lose.

The Ensign reached out, flipped the switches that would give him the picture of the interior of the Captain's accommodation. The screen brightened, came alive. Grimes stared at the luminous presentation in sick horror. Luminous it was—with that peculiar luminosity of naked female flesh. Jane was dressing herself with almost ludicrous haste. Of the Captain there was no sign—*on the screen.*

Craven snarled, with cold ferocity, "You damned, sneaking, prurient puppy!" Then, in a louder voice, "Switch that damn thing off! I'll deal with you when this is over."

"But, sir . . ."

"Switch it off, I say!"

Cheeks burning, Grimes obeyed. Then he sat staring at his armament controls, fighting down his nausea, his physical sickness. Somehow, he found time to think bitterly, *So I was the knight, all set and ready to stay dragons for his lady. And all the time, she . . .* He did not finish the thought.

He heard a voice calling over the intercom, one of the engineers. "Captain, they're trying to lock on! Same as last time. Random precession, sir?"

"No. Cut the Drive!"

"Cut the Drive?" Incredulously.

"You heard me. *Cut!*" Then, to Grimes, "And what the hell are *you* waiting for?"

The Ensign knew what he had to do; he had rehearsed it often enough. He did it. From the nozzles that pierced the outer shell spouted the cloud of reflective vapor, just in time, just as the enemy's lasers lashed out at their target. It seemed that the ship's internal temperature rose suddenly and sharply—although that could have been illusion, fostered by the sight of the fiery fog glimpsed through the viewports before the armored shutters slammed home.

There were targets now on Grimes' fire control screen, two of them, but he could not loose a missile until the tumbling rotors of the Drive had ceased to spin, to precess. The use of the anti-laser vapor screen had been risky enough. Abruptly the screens went blank—which signified that the temporal precession rates of hunted and hunters were no longer in synchronization, that the fields of the pirates had failed to lock on. In normal spacetime there would be no need to synchronize—and then the hunters would discover that their quarry had claws and teeth.

Aboard *Epsilon Sextans* the keening note of the Drive died to a whisper, a barely audible murmur, fading to silence. There was the inevitable second or so of utter disorientation when, as soon as it was safe, the engineers braked the gyroscopes.

Craven acted without hesitation, giving his ship headway and acceleration with Inertial Drive. He was not running—although this was the impression that he wished to convey. He was inviting rather than evading combat—but if the Waldegren captains chose to assume that *Epsilon Sextans* was, as she had been, an unarmed merchantman (after all, the anti-laser screen could have been jury rigged from normal ship's stores and equipment), taking evasive action, that was *their* error of judgment.

Grimes watched his screens intently. Suddenly the two blips reappeared, astern, all of a hundred kilos distant, but closing. This he reported.

"Stand by for acceleration!" ordered Craven. "Reaction Drive—stand by!"

It was all part of the pattern—a last, frantic squandering of reaction mass that could do no more than delay the inevitable. It would look good from the enemy control rooms.

"Reaction Drive ready!" reported Baxter over the intercom.

"Thank you. Captain to all hands, there will be no countdown. *Fire!*"

From the corner of his eye Grimes saw Craven's hand slam down on the key. Acceleration slammed him brutally back into his chair. There was a roar that was more like an explosion than a normal rocket firing, a shock that jarred and rattled every fitting in the Control Room.

Craven remarked quietly. "That must have looked convincing enough—but I hope that Baxter didn't really blow a chamber."

There was only the Inertial Drive now, and the two blips that, very briefly, had fallen astern, were now creeping up again, closing the range.

"Anti-laser," ordered Craven briefly.

"But, sir, it'll just be wasting it. They'll not be using laser outside twenty kilometers."

"They'll not be expecting a gunnery specialist aboard this wagon, either."

Once again the nozzles spouted, pouring out a cloud that fell rapidly astern of the running ship, dissipating uselessly.

Craven looked at his own reens, frowned, muttered, "They're taking their sweet time about it . . . probably low on reaction mass themselves." He turned to Grimes. "I think a slight breakdown of the I.D.'s in order."

"As you say, sir." The Ensign could not forget having been called a damned, sneaking, prurient puppy. Let Craven make his own decisions.

"Stand by for Free Fall," ordered the Captain quietly. The steady throbbing of the Inertial Drive faltered, faltered and ceased. There were two long minutes of weightlessness, and then, for five minutes, the Drive came back into operation. *A breakdown,* the enemy must be thinking. *A breakdown, and the engineers sweating and striving to get the ship under way again.* A breakdown—it would not be surprising after the mauling she had endured at the first encounter.

She hung there, and although her actual speed could be measured in kilometers a second she was, insofar as her accelerating pursuers were concerned, relatively motionless. Grimes wondered why the warships did not use their radio, did not demand surrender—*Epsilon Sextans'* transceiver was switched on, but no sound issued from the speaker but the hiss and crackle of interstellar static. He voiced his puzzlement to Craven.

Craven laughed grimly. "They know who *we* are—or they think that they know. And they know that we know who *they* are. After what happened before, why should we expect mercy? All that we can do now—they think—is to get the Mannschenn Drive going again. But with that comic beacon of theirs working away merrily they'll be able to home on us, no matter how random our precession." He laughed again. "They haven't a care in the world, bless their little black hearts."

Grimes watched his screens. Forty kilometers—thirty—"Sir, the ALGE?" he asked.

"Yes. It's your party now."

For the third time reflective vapor gushed from the nozzles, surrounding the ship with a dense cloud. Craven, who had been watching the dials of the external temperature thermometers, remarked quietly, "They've opened fire. The shell plating's heating up. Fast."

And in the Control Room it felt hot—and hotter, Grimes pressed the button that unmasked his batteries. The gas screen, as well as affording protection from laser, hid the ship from visual observation. The enemy would not be expecting defense by force of arms.

He loosed his first salvo, felt the ship tremble as the missiles ejected themselves from their launching racks. There they were on the screens—six tiny sparks, six moronic mechanical intelligences programmed to home upon and destroy, capable of countering evasive action so long as their propellant held out. There they were on the screens—six of them, then four, then one. This last missile almost reached its target—then it, too, blinked out. The Waldegren frigates were now using their laser for defense, not attack.

"I don't think," remarked Craven quietly, "that they'll use missiles. Not yet, anyhow. They want our cargo intact." He chuckled softly. "But we've got them worried."

Grimes didn't bother to reply. The telltale lights on his panel told him that the six AVM launchers were reloaded. The AMMs—the anti-missile missiles—had not yet been fired. Dare he risk their use against big targets? He carried in his magazines stock sufficient for three full salvos only—and with no laser for anti-missile work dare he deplete his supply of this ammunition?

He had heard the AMMs described as "vicious little brutes." They were to the Anti-Vessel Missiles as terriers are to mastiffs. Their warheads were small, but this was compensated for by their greater endurance. They were, perhaps, a little more "intelligent" than the larger rockets—and Grimes, vaguely foreseeing this present contingency, had made certain modifications to their "brains."

He pushed the button that actuated his modifications, that overrode the original programming. He depressed the firing stud. He felt the vibration as the war-rockets streaked away from the ship, and on his screens watched the tiny points of light closing the range between themselves and the two big blips that were the targets. They were fast, and they were erratic. One was picked off by laser within the first ten seconds, but the others carried on, spurting and swerving, but always boring toward their objectives. Grimes could imagine the enemy gunnery officers flailing their lasers like men, armed only with sticks, defending themselves against a horde of small, savage animals. There was, of course, one sure defense—to start up the Mannschenn Drive and to slip back into the warped continuum where the missiles could not follow. But, in all probability, the Waldegren captains had yet to accept the fact, emotionally, that this helpless merchantman had somehow acquired the wherewithal to strike back.

Two of the AMMs were gone now, picked off by the enemy laser. Three were still closing on the target on *Epsilon Sextans'* port quarter, and only one of target abaft the starboard beam. Grimes loosed his second flight of AMMs, followed it with a full salvo of AVMs. Then, knowing that the protective vapor screen must have been thinned and shredded by his rocketry, he sent out a replenishing gush of reflective gas.

He heard Craven cry out in exultation. The three AMMs of the first flight had hit their target, the three sparks had fused with the blip that represented the raider to port. The three sparks that were the second flight were almost there, and overtaking them were the larger and brighter sparks of the second AVM salvo. The Anti-Missile Missiles would cause only minor damage to a ship—but, in all probability, they would throw fire control out of kilter, might even destroy laser projectors. In theory, one AVM would suffice to destroy a frigate; a hit by three at once would make destruction a certainty.

And so it was.

Seen only on the radar screen, as a picture lacking in detail painted on a fluorescent surface by an electron brush, it was anticlimactic. The blips, the large one, the three small ones and the three not so small, merged. And then there was an oddly shaped blob of luminescence that slowly broke up into a cluster of glowing fragments, a gradually expanding cluster, a leisurely burgeoning flower of pale fire.

Said Craven viciously, "The other bastard's got cold feet. . . ."

And so it was. Where she had been on the screen was only darkness, a darkness in which the sparks that were missiles and anti-missiles milled about aimlessly. They would not turn upon each other—that would have been contrary to their programming. They would not, in theory, use their remaining fuel to home upon the only worthwhile target remaining—*Epsilon Sextans* herself. But, as Craven knew and as Grimes knew, theory and practice do not always coincide. Ships have been destroyed by their own missiles.

With reluctance Grimes pushed the DESTRUCT button. He said to the Captain, gesturing toward the wreckage depicted on the screen, "Pick up survivors sir? If there are any."

"If there are any," snarled Craven, "that's their bad luck. No—we give chase to the other swine!"

18

GIVE CHASE . . .

It was easier said than done. The surviving frigate had restarted her Mannschenn Drive, had slipped back into the warped continuum where, unless synchronization of precession rates was achieved and held, contact between vessels would be impossible. The Carlotti Beacon in *Epsilon Sextans'* hold was worse than useless; it had been designed to be homed upon, not to be a direction finding instrument. (In any case, it could function as such only if the beacon aboard the Waldegren ship were working.) Neither Craven nor Grimes knew enough about the device to effect the necessary modifications. The interstellar drive engineers thought that they could do it, but their estimates as to the time required ranged from days to weeks. Obviously, as long as it was operating it would be of value to the enemy only.

So it was switched off.

There was only one method available to Craven to carry out the pursuit—psionic tracking. He sent for his Psionic Radio Officer, explained the situation. The telepath was a young man, pasty faced, unhealthy looking, but not unintelligent. He said at once, "Do you think, Captain, that the other officers and myself are willing to carry on the fight? After all, we've made our point. Wouldn't it be wisest to carry on, now, for Waverley?"

"Speaking for meself," put in Baxter, who had accompanied Jane Pentecost to Control, "an' fer any other Rim Worlders present, I say that now the bastards are on the run it's the best time ter smack 'em again. An' hard. An' the tame time-twisters think the same as we do. I've already had words with 'em." He glared at the telepath. "Our snoopin' little friend here should know very well what the general consensus of opinion is."

"We do not pry," said the communications officer stiffly. "But I am willing to abide by the will of the majority."

"And don't the orders of the Master come into it?" asked Craven, more in amusement than anger.

"Lawful commands, sir?" asked Grimes who, until now, had been silent.

"Shut up!" snapped Jane Pentecost.

"Unluckily, sir," the young man went on, "I do not possess the direction-finding talent. It is, as you know, quite rare."

"Then what *can* you do?" demanded Craven.

"Sir, let me finish, please. The psionic damping device—I don't know what it was, but I suspect that it was the brain of some animal with which I am unfamiliar—was in the ship that was destroyed. The other vessel carries only a normal operator, with normal equipment—himself and some sort of organic amplifier. He is still within range, and I can maintain a listening watch—"

"And suppose *he* listens to you?" asked the Captain. "Even if you transmit nothing—as you will not do, unless ordered by myself—there could be stray thoughts. And that, I suppose, applies to all of us."

The telepath smiled smugly. "Direction-finding is not the only talent. I'm something of a damper myself—although not in the same class as the one that was blown up. I give you my word, sir, that this vessel is psionically silent." He raised his hand as Craven was about to say something. "Now, sir, I shall be able to find out where the other ship is heading. I know already that her Mannschenn Drive unit is not working at full capacity; it sustained damage of some kind during the action. I'm not a navigator, sir, but it seems to me that we could be waiting for her when she reemerges into the normal continuum."

"You're not a navigator," agreed Craven, "and you're neither a tactician nor a strategist. We should look rather silly, shouldn't we, hanging in full view over a heavily fortified naval base, a sitting duck. Even so . . ." His big right hand stroked his beard. "Meanwhile, I'll assume that our little friends are headed in the general direction of Waldegren, and set course accordingly. If Mr. Grimes will be so good as to hunt up the target star in the Directory . . ."

Grimes did as he was told. He had made his protest, such as it was, and, he had to admit, he was in favor of continuing the battle. It was a matter of simple justice. Why should one shipload of murderers be destroyed, and the other shipload escape unscathed? He was still more than a little dubious of the legality of it all, but he did not let it worry him.

He helped Craven to line the ship up on the target star, a yellow, fifth magnitude spark. He manned the intercom while the Captain poured on the acceleration and then, with the ship again falling free, cut in the Mannschenn Drive. When the vessel was on course he expected that the Old Man would give the usual order—"Normal Deep Space routine, Mr. Grimes,"—but this was not forthcoming.

"Now," said Craven ominously.

"Now *what*, sir?"

"You have a short memory, Ensign. A conveniently short memory, if I may say so. Mind you, I was favorably impressed by the way you handled your armament, but that has no bearing upon what happened before."

Grimes blushed miserably. He knew what the Captain was driving at. But, playing for time, he asked, "What do you mean, sir?"

Craven exploded. "What do I mean? You have the crust to sit there and ask me that! Your snooping, sir. Your violation of privacy. Even worse, your violation of the Master's privacy! I shall not tell Miss Pentecost; it would be unkind to embarrass her. But . . ."

Grimes refrained from saying that he had seen Miss Pentecost wearing even less than when, inadvertently, he had spied upon her. He muttered, "I can explain, sir."

"You'd better. Out with it."

"Well, sir, it was like this. I knew that we'd stumbled on the enemy—or that the enemy had stumbled upon us. I'd sounded Action Stations. And when you were a long time coming up to Control I thought that you must have hurt yourself, somehow . . . there have been such cases, as you know. So I thought I'd better check—"

"You thought . . . *you* thought. I'll not say that you aren't paid to think—because that's just what an officer *is* paid for. But you didn't think hard enough, or along the right lines." Grimes could see that Craven had accepted his explanation and that all would be well. The Captain's full beard could not hide the beginnings of a smile. "Did you ever hear of Sir Francis Drake, Ensign?"

"No, sir."

"He was an admiral—one of Queen Elizabeth's admirals. The first Elizabeth, of course. When the Spanish Armada was sighted he did not rush down to his flagship yelling 'Action Stations!' He knew that there was time to spare, and so he quietly finished what he was doing before setting sail."

"And what was he doing, sir?" asked Grimes innocently.

Craven glared at him, then snapped, "Playing bowls."

Then, suddenly, the tension was broken and both men collapsed in helpless laughter. In part it was reaction to the strain of battle—but in greater part it was that freemasonry that exists only between members of the same sex, the acknowledgment of shared secrets and shared experiences.

Grimes knew that Jane Pentecost was not for him—and wished Craven joy of her and she of the Captain. Perhaps they had achieved a permanent relationship, perhaps not—but, either way, his best wishes were with them.

Craven unbuckled his seat strap.

"Deep Space routine, Mr. Grimes. It is your watch, I believe."

"Deep Space routine it is, sir."

Yes, it was still his watch (although so much had happened). It was still his watch, although there were barely fifteen minutes to go before relief. He was tired, more tired than he had ever been in his life before. He was tired, but not unhappy. He knew that the fact that he had killed men should be weighing heavily upon his conscience—but it did not. They, themselves, had been killers—and they had had a far better chance then any of their own victims had enjoyed.

He would shed no tears for them.

19

CRAVEN CAME BACK to the Control Room at the change of watch, when Grimes was handing over to Jane Pentecost. He waited until the routine had been completed, then said, "We know where our friends are headed. They were, like us, running for Waldegren—but they're having to change course." He laughed harshly. "There must be all hell let loose on their home planet."

"Why? What's happened?" asked Grimes.

"I'll tell you later. But, first of all, we have an alteration of course ourselves. Look up Dartura in the Directory, will you, while I get the Drive shut down."

Epsilon Sextans was falling free through normal spacetime before Grimes had found the necessary information. And then there was the hunt for and the final identification of the target star, followed by the lining up by the use of the directional gyroscopes. There was the brief burst of acceleration and then, finally, the interstellar drive was cut in once more.

The Captain made a business of selecting and lighting a cigar. When the pungent combustion was well under way he said, "Our young Mr. Summers is a good snooper. Not as good as some people I know, perhaps." Grimes flushed and Jane Pentecost looked puzzled. "He's a supersensitive. He let me have a full transcript of all the signals, out and in. It took us a little time to get them sorted out—but not too long, considering. *Adler*—that's the name of the surviving frigate—*was* running for home. Her Captain sent a rather heavily edited report of the action to his Admiral. It seems that *Adler* and the unfortunate *Albatross* were set upon and beaten up by a heavily armed Survey Service cruiser masquerading as an innocent merchantman. The Admiral, oddly enough, doesn't want a squadron of Survey Service battlewagons laying nuclear eggs on his base. So *Adler* has been told to run away and lose herself until the flap's over. . . ."

"And did they send all that *en clair?*" demanded Grimes. "They must be mad!"

"No, they aren't mad. The signal's weren't *en clair.*"

"But . . ."

"Reliable merchant captains," said Craven, "are often entrusted with highly confidential naval documents. There were some such in my safe aboard *Delta Orionis,* consigned to the Commanding Officer of Lindisfarne Base. The officer who delivered them to me is an old friend and shipmate of mine, and he told me that among there was the complete psionic code used by the Waldegren Navy. Well, when I had decided to take over this ship, I'd have been a bloody fool not to have photostatted the whole damned issue.

"So that's the way of it. Herr Kapitan von Leidnitz thinks he can say what he likes to his superiors without anybody else knowing what he's saying. And all the while . . ." Craven grinned wolfishly. "It seems that there's a minor base, of sorts, on Dartura. Little more than repair yards, although I suppose that there'll be a few batteries for their protection. I can imagine the sort of personnel they have running the show—passed-over commanders and the like, not overly bright. By the time that we get there we shall have concocted a convincing story—convincing enough to let us hang off in orbit until *Adler* appears on the scene. After all, we have their precious code. Why should they suspect us?"

"Why shouldn't *we* be *Adler?*" asked Grimes.

"What do you mean, Ensign?"

"The Waldegren Navy's frigates are almost identical, in silhouette, with the Commission's *Epsilon* class freighters. We could disguise this ship a little by masking the dissimilarities by a rough patching of plating. After all, *Adler* was in action and sustained some damage—"

"Complicated," mused the Captain. "Too complicated. And two *Adlers*—each, presumably, in encoded psionic communication with both Waldegren and Dartura. . . . You've a fine, devious mind, young Grimes—but I'm afraid you've out-fixed yourself on that one."

"Let me talk, sir. Let me think out loud. To begin with—a ship running on Mannschenn Drive *can* put herself into orbit about a planet, but it's not, repeat not, recommended."

"Damn right it's not."

"But we have the heels of *Adler?* Yes? Then we could afford a slight delay to carry out the modifications—the disguise—that I've suggested. After all, forty odd light years is quite a long way."

"But what do we gain, Mr. Grimes?"

"The element of confusion, sir. Let me work it out. We disguise ourselves as well as we can. We find out, from intercepted and decoded signals, *Adler*'s ETA—*and* the coordinates of her breakthrough into the normal continuum. We contrive matters to be more or less in the same place at exactly the same time. And when the shore batteries and the guardships see no less than two *Adlers* slugging it out, each of them yelling for help in the secret code, they won't know which of us to open fire on."

"Grimes," said Craven slowly, "I didn't know you had it in you. All I can say is that I'm glad that you're on *our* side."

"Am I?" asked Grimes wonderingly, suddenly deflated. He looked at the Captain who, after all, was little better than a pirate, whose accomplice he had become. He looked at the girl, but for whom he would not be here. "Am I? Damn it all, whose side *am* I on?"

"You'd better go below," Craven told him gently. "Go below and get some sleep. You need it. You've earned it."

"Jeremy," said Jane Pentecost to Craven, "would you mind looking after the shop for half an hour or so? I'll go with John."

"As you please, my dear. As you please."

It was the assurance in the Captain's voice that hurt. *It won't make any difference to us,* it implied. *It can't make any difference. Sure, Jane, go ahead. Throw the nice little doggie a bone . . . we can spare it.*

"No thank you," said Grimes coldly, and left the Control Room.

But he couldn't hate these people.

20

AFTER A LONG sleep Grimes felt better. After a meal he felt better still. It was a good meal, even though the solid portion of it came from tins. Craven's standards were slipping, thought the Ensign. He was reasonably sure that such items as caviar, escargots, paté de foie gras, Virginia ham, Brie, and remarkably alcoholic cherries were not included in the Commission's inventory of emergency stores. And neither would be the quite reasonable Montrachet, although it had lost a little by being decanted from its original bottles into standard squeeze bulbs. But if the Captain had decided that the laborer was worthy of his hire, with the consignees of the cargo making their contribution toward that hire, that was his privilege . . . ? Responsibility?—call it what you will.

Jane Pentecost watched him eat. As he was finishing his coffee she said, "Now that our young lion has fed, he is required in the Control Room."

He looked at her both gratefully and warily. "What have I done now?"

"Nothing, my dear. It is to discuss what you—we—will do. Next."

He followed her to Control. Craven was there, of course, and so were Baxter and Summers. The Captain was enjoying one of his rank cigars, and a limp, roll-your-own cigarette dangled from the engineer's lower lip. The telepath coughed pointedly every time that acrid smoke expelled by either man drifted his way. Neither paid any attention to him, and neither did Grimes when he filled and lighted his own pipe.

Craven said, "I've been giving that scheme of yours some thought. It's a good one."

"Thank you, sir."

"Don't thank me. I should thank you. Mr. Summers, here, has been maintaining a careful listening watch. *Adler*'s ETA is such that we can afford to shut down the Drive to make the modifications that you suggest. To begin with, we'll fake patching plates with plastic sheets—we can't afford to cannibalize any more of the ship's structure—so as to obscure our name and identification letters. We'll use more plastic to simulate missile launchers and laser projectors—luckily there's plenty of it in the cargo."

"We found more than plastic while we were lookin' for it," said the engineer, licking his lips.

"That will do, Mr. Baxter. Never, in normal circumstances, should I have condoned . . ."

"These circumstances ain't normal, Skipper, an' we all bloody well know it."

"That will do, I say." Craven inhaled deeply, then filled the air of the Control Room with a cloud of smoke that, thought Grimes, would have reflected laser even at close range. Summers almost choked, and Jane snapped, "Jeremy!"

"This, my dear, happens to be *my* Control Room." He turned again to the Ensign. "It will not be necessary, Mr. Grimes, to relocate the real weapons. They functioned quite efficiently where they are and, no doubt, will do so again. And now, as soon as I have shut down the Drive, I shall hand the watch over to you. You are well rested and refreshed."

"Come on," said Jane to Baxter. "Let's get suited up and get that sheeting out of the airlock."

"Couldn't Miss Pentecost hold the fort, sir?" asked Grimes. He added, "I've been through the camouflage course at the Academy."

"And so have I, Mr. Grimes. Furthermore, Miss Pentecost has had experience in working outside, but I don't think that you have."

"No, sir. But . . ."

"That will be all, Mr. Grimes."

At Craven's orders the Drive was shut down, and outside the viewports the sparse stars became stars again, were no longer pulsing spirals of multi-colored light. Then, alone in Control, Grimes actuated his scanners so that he could watch the progress of the work outside the hull, and switched on the transceiver that worked on the spacesuit frequency.

This time he ran no risk of being accused of being a Peeping Tom.

He had to admire the competence with which his shipmates worked. The plastic sheeting had no mass to speak of, but it was awkward stuff to handle. Torches glowed redly as it was cut, and radiated invisibly in the infrared as it was shaped and welded. The workers, in their bulky, clumsy suits, moved with a grace that was in startling contrast to their attire—a Deep Space ballet, thought Grimes, pleasurably surprised at his own way with words. From the speaker of the transceiver came Craven's curt orders, the brief replies of the others. *"This way a little . . . that's it." "She'll do, Skipper." "No she won't. Look at the bend on it!"* Then Jane's laughing voice. *"Our secret weapon, Jeremy. A laser that fires around corners!" "That will do, Miss Pentecost. Straighten it, will you?" "Ay, ay, sir. Captain, sir."* The two interstellar drive engineers were working in silence, but with efficiency. Aboard the ship were only Grimes and Summers, the telepath.

Grimes felt out of it, but somebody had to mind the shop, he supposed. But the likelihood of any customers was remote.

Then he stiffened in his chair. One of the spacesuited figures was falling away from the vessel, drifting out and away, a tiny, glittering satellite reflecting the harsh glare of the working floods, a little, luminous butterfly pinned to the black velvet of the Ultimate Night. Who was it? He didn't know for certain, but thought that it was Jane. The ship's interplanetary drives—reaction and inertial—were on remote control, but reaction drive was out; before employing it he would have to swing to the desired heading by use of the directional gyroscopes. But the inertial drive was versatile.

He spoke into the microphone of the transceiver. "Secure yourselves. I am proceeding to rescue."

At once Craven's voice snapped back, "Hold it, Grimes. Hold it! There's no danger."

"But, sir . . ."

"Hold it!"

Grimes could see the distant figure now from a viewport, but it did not seem to be receding any longer. Hastily he checked with the radar. Range and bearing were not changing. Then, with relative bearing unaltered, the range was closing. He heard Jane call out, "Got it! I'm on the way back!"

Craven replied, "Make it snappy—otherwise young Grimes'll be chasing you all over the Universe!"

Grimes could see, now, the luminous flicker of a suit reaction unit from the lonely figure.

Later, he and the others examined the photographs that Jane had taken.

Epsilon Sextans looked as she was supposed to look—like a badly battle-scarred frigate of the Waldegren Navy.

21

IN TERMS OF space and of time there was not much longer to go.

The two ships—one knowing and one unknowing—raced toward their rendezvous. Had they been plunging through the normal continuum there would have been, toward the finish, hardly the thickness of a coat of paint between them, the adjustment of a microsecond in temporal precession rates would have brought inevitable collision. Craven knew this from the results of his own observations and from the encoded position reports, sent at six hourly intervals, by *Adler*. Worried, he allowed himself to fall astern, a mere half kilometer. It would be enough—and, too, it would mean that the frigate would mask him from the fire of planet-based batteries.

Summers maintained his listening watch. Apart from the position reports he had little of interest to tell the Captain. *Adler,* once or twice, had tried to get in contact with the Main Base on Waldegren—but, other than from a curt directive to proceed as ordered there were no signals from the planet to the ship. Dartura Base was more talkative. That was understandable. There was no colony on the planet and the Base personnel must be bored, must be pining for the sight of fresh faces, the sound of fresh voices. They would have their excitement soon enough, promised Craven grimly.

Through the warped continuum fell the two ships, and ahead the pulsating spiral that was the Dartura sun loomed ever brighter, ever larger. There were light years yet to go, but the Drive-induced distortions made it seem that tentacles of incandescent gas were already reaching out to clutch them, to drag them into the atomic furnace at the heart of the star.

In both Control Rooms watch succeeded watch—but the thoughts and the anticipations of the watchkeepers were not the same. Aboard *Adler* there was the longing for rest, for relaxation—although *Adler*'s Captain must have been busy with the composition of a report that would clear him (if possible) of blame for his defeat. Aboard *Epsilon Sextans* there was the anticipation of revenge—insofar as Craven, Baxter, Jane Pentecost and the survivors of the ship's original personnel were concerned. Grimes? As the hour of reckoning approached he was more and more dubious. He did not know what to think, what to feel. There was the strong personal loyalty to Craven—and, even now, to Jane Pentecost. There was the friendship and mutual respect that had come into being between himself and Baxter. There was the knowledge that *Adler*'s crew were no better than pirates, were murderers beyond rehabilitation. There was the pride he felt in his own skill as a gunnery officer. (But, as such, was he, himself, any better than a pirate, a murderer? The exercise of his craft aboard a warship would be legal—but here, aboard a merchantman, and a disguised merchantman at that, the legality was doubtful. What had his motives been when he volunteered—and as a commissioned officer of the Survey Service he had had no right to do so—and what were his motives now?)

He, Grimes, was not happy. He had far too much time to ponder the implications. He was an accessory before, during and after the fact. He had started off correctly enough, when he had tried to prevent Craven from requisitioning the Survey Service cargo aboard *Delta Orionis,* but after that . . . after he and Jane . . . (that, he admitted, was a memory that he wanted to keep, always, just as that other memory, of the bright picture of naked female flesh on the screen, he wished he could lose forever.)

He had started of correctly enough—and then, not only had he helped install the purloined armament but had used it. (*And used it well,* he told himself with a brief resurgence of pride.) Furthermore, the disguise of *Epsilon Sextans* had been his idea.

Oh, he was in it, all right. He was in up to his neck. What the final outcome of it all would be he did not care to contemplate.

But it would soon be over. He had no fears as to the outcome of the battle. The element of surprise would be worth at least a dozen missile launchers. *Adler* would never have the chance to use her laser.

Adler, reported Summers, had shut down her Mannschenn Drive and emerged briefly into normal spacetime to make her final course adjustment. She was now headed not for the Dartura Sun but for the planet itself—or where the planet would be at the time of her final—and fatal—reemergence into the continuum. The last ETA was sent, together with the coordinates of her planetfall. *Epsilon Sextans* made her own course adjustment—simultaneity in time and a half kilometer's divergence in space being Craven's objective. It was finicky work, even with the use of the ship's computer, but the Captain seemed satisfied.

The race—the race that would culminate in a dead heat—continued. Aboard the frigate there was, reported Summers, a lessening of tension, the loosening up that comes when a voyage is almost over. Aboard the merchantman the tension increased. The interstellar drive engineers, Grimes knew, were no happier about it all than he was—but they could no more back out than he could. Craven was calm and confident, and Baxter was beginning to gloat. Jane Pentecost assumed the air of dedication that in women can be so infuriating. Grimes glumly checked and rechecked his weaponry. It passed the time.

Dartura itself was visible now—not as tiny disk of light but as a glowing annulus about its distorted primary. The thin ring of luminescence broadened, broadened. The time to go dwindled to a week, to days, to a day, and then to hours . . .

To minutes . . .

To seconds . . .

Craven and Grimes were in the Control Room; the others were at their various stations. From the intercom came the telepath's voice, "He's cutting the Drive—"

"Cut the Drive!" ordered the Captain.

In the Mannschenn Drive room the spinning, precessing gyroscopes slowed, slowed, ceased their endless tumbling, assumed the solidity that they exhibited only when at rest. For perhaps two seconds there was temporal confusion in the minds of all on board as the precession field died, and past, present and future inextricably mingled. Then there was a sun glaring through the viewports, bright in spite of the polarization—a sun, and, directly ahead, a great, green-orange planet. There was a ship. . . .

There were ships—ahead of them, astern, on all sides.

There were ships—and, booming from the intership transceiver, the transceiver that was neither tuned nor switched on (but navies could afford induction transmitters with their fantastic power consumption), came the authorative voice: "*Inflexible* to *Adler!* Heave to for search and seizure! Do not attempt to escape—our massed fields will hold you!"

The effect was rather spoiled when the same voice added, in bewilderment, "Must be seeing double . . . there's two of the bastards."

The bewilderment did not last long. "*Inflexible* to *Adler* and to unidentified vessel. Heave to for search and seizure!"

"Hold your fire, Mr. Grimes," ordered Craven, quietly and bitterly. "It's the Survey Service."

"'I know," replied Grimes—and pressed the button.

22

HE NEVER KNEW just why he had done so.

Talking it over afterward, thinking about it, he was able to evolve a theory that fitted the facts. During the brief period immediately after the shutting down of the Drive, during the short session of temporal disorientation, there had been prescience, of a sort. He had known that *Adler,* come what may, would attempt one last act of defiance and revenge, just as *Adler*'s Captain or Gunnery Officer must have known, in that last split second, that Nemesis was treading close upon his heels.

He pushed the button—and from the nozzles in the shell plating poured the reflective vapor, the protective screen that glowed ruddily as *Adler*'s lasers slashed out at it.

From the speaker of the dead transceiver, the transceiver that should have been dead, roared the voice of the Survey Service Admiral. "*Adler!* Cease fire! Cease fire, damn you!" There was a pause, then: "You've asked for it!"

She had asked for it—and now she got it. Suddenly the blip on Grimes' screen that represented the Waldegren frigate became two smaller blips, and then four. The rolling fog outside *Epsilon Sextans'* viewports lost its luminosity, faded suddenly to drab grayness. The voice from the transceiver said coldly, "And now *you*, whoever you are, had better identify yourself. And fast."

Craven switched on the communications equipment. He spoke quietly into the microphone.

"Interstellar Transport Commission's *Epsilon Sextans.* Bound Waverly, with general cargo . . ."

"Bound Waverley? Then what the hell are you doing here? And what's that armament you're mounting?"

"Plastic," replied the Captain. "Plastic dummies."

"And I suppose your ALGE is plastic, too. Come off it, Jerry. We've already boarded your old ship, and although your ex-Mate was most reluctant to talk we got a story of sorts from him."

"I thought I recognized your voice, Bill. May I congratulate you upon your belated efforts to stamp out piracy?"

"And may I deplore your determination to take the law into your own hands? Stand by for the boarding party."

Grimes looked at Craven, who was slumped in his seat. The Master's full beard effectively masked his expression. "Sir," asked the Ensign. "What can they do? What will they do?"

"You're the space lawyer, Grimes. You're the expert on Survey Service rules and regulations. What will it be, do you think? A medal—or a firing squad? Praise or blame?"

"You know the Admiral, sir?"

"Yes. I know the Admiral. We're old shipmates."

"Then you should be safe."

"Safe? I suppose so. Safe from the firing squad—but not safe from my employers. I'm a merchant captain, Grimes, and merchant captains aren't supposed to range the spacelanes looking for trouble. I don't think they'll dare fire me—but I know that I can never expect command of anything better than *Delta* class ships, on the drearier runs." Grimes saw that Craven was smiling. "But there're still the Rim Worlds. There's still the Sundowner Line, and the chance of high rank in the Rim Worlds Navy when and if there is such a service."

"You have . . . inducements, sir?"

"Yes. There are . . . inducements. Now."

"I thought, once," said Grimes, "that I could say the same. But not now. Not any longer. Even so . . . I'm Survey Service, sir, and I should be proud of my service. But in this ship, this merchant vessel, with her makeshift armament, we fought against heavy odds, and won. And, just now, we saved ourselves. It wasn't the Survey Service that saved us."

"Don't be disloyal," admonished Craven.

"I'm not being disloyal, sir. But . . . or, shall we say, I'm being loyal. You're the first captain under whom I served under fire. If you're going out to the Rim Worlds I'd like to come with you."

"Your commission, Grimes. You know that you must put in ten years' service before resignation is possible."

"But I'm dead."

"Dead?"

"Yes. Don't you remember? I was snooping around in the Mannschenn Drive room and I got caught in the temporal precession field.

My body still awaits burial; it's in a sealed metal box in the deep freeze. It can never be identified."

Craven laughed. "I'll say this for you. You're ingenious. But how do we account for the absence of the late Mr. Wolverton? And your presence aboard this ship?"

"I can hide, sir, and . . ."

"And while you're hiding you'll concoct some story that will explain everything. Oh Grimes, Grimes—you're an officer I wish I could always have with me. But I'll not stand in the way of your career. All I can do, all I will do, is smooth things over on your behalf with the Admiral. I should be able to manage that."

Jane Pentecost emerged from the hatch in the Control Room deck. Addressing Craven she said formally, "Admiral Williams, sir." She moved to one side to make way for the flag officer.

"Jerry, you bloody pirate!" boomed Williams, a squat, rugged man the left breast of whose shirt was ablaze with ribbons. He advanced with outstretched hand.

"Glad to have you aboard, Bill. This is Liberty Hall—you can spit on the mat and call the cat a bastard!"

"Not again!" groaned Grimes.

"And who is this young man?" asked the Admiral.

"I owe you—or your Service—an apology, Bill. This is Ensign Grimes, who was a passenger aboard *Delta Orionis.* I'm afraid that I . . . er . . . press-ganged him into my service. But he has been most . . . cooperative? Uncooperative? Which way do you want it?"

"As we are at war with Waldegren—I'd say cooperative with reservations. Was it he, by the way, who used the ALGE? Just as well for you all that he did."

"At war with Waldegren?" demanded Jane Pentecost. "So you people have pulled your fingers out at last."

The Admiral raised his eyebrows.

"One of my Rim Worlders," explained Craven. "But I shall be a Rim Worlder myself shortly."

"You're wise, Jerry. I've got the buzz that the Commission is taking a very dim view of your piracy or privateering or whatever it was, and my own lords and masters are far from pleased with you. You'd better get the hell out before the lawyers have decided just what crimes you are guilty of."

"As bad as that?"

"As bad as that."

"And young Grimes, here?"

"We'll take him back. Six months' strict discipline aboard my flagship will undo all the damage that you and your ideas have done to him. And now, Jerry, I'd like your full report."

"In my cabin, Bill. Talking is thirsty work."

"Then lead on. It's your ship."

"And it's your watch, Mr. Grimes. She'll come to no harm on this trajectory while we get things sorted out."

Grimes sat with Jane Pentecost in the Control Room. Through the ports, had he so desired, he could have watched the rescue teams extricating the survivors from the wreckage of *Adler*; he could have stared out at the looming bulk of Dartura on the beam. But he did not do so, and neither did he look at his instruments.

He looked at Jane. There was so much about her that he wanted to remember—and, after all, so very little that he was determined to forget.

The intercom buzzed. "Mr. Grimes, will you pack whatever gear you have and prepare to transfer with Admiral Williams to the flagship? Hand the watch over to Miss Pentecost."

"But you'll be shorthanded, sir."

"The Admiral is lending me a couple of officers for the rest of the voyage."

"Very good, sir."

Grimes made no move. He looked at Jane—a somehow older, a tireder, a more human Jane than the girl he had first met. He said, "I'd have liked to have come out to the Rim with you. . . ."

She said, "It's impossible, John."

"I know. But . . ."

"You'd better get packed."

He unbuckled his seat belt, went to where she was sitting. He kissed her. She responded, but it was only the merest flicker of a response.

He said, "Goodbye."

She said, "Not goodbye. We'll see you out on the Rim, sometime."

With a bitterness that he was always to regret he replied, "Not very likely."

To Prime the Pump

1

GRIMES—LIEUTENANT JOHN GRIMES, Federation Survey Service, to give him his full name and title—had the watch. Slowly, careful not to break the contact of the magnetized soles of his shoes with the deck, he shuffled backwards and forwards in the narrow confines of the control room. Captain Daintree, commanding officer of the cruiser *Aries*, was a martinet, and one of the many things that he would not tolerate was a watchkeeper spending his spell of duty lounging in an acceleration chair, not even in (as now) Free Fall conditions. Not that Grimes really minded. He was a young and vigorous man and still not used to the enforced inactivity that is an inescapable part of spacefaring. This regulation pacing was exercise of a sort, was better than nothing.

He was a stocky young man, this Grimes, and the stiff material of his uniform shirt did little to hide the muscular development of his body. His face was too craggy for conventional handsomeness, but women, he already had learned, considered him good-looking enough. On the rare occasions that he thought about it he admitted that he was not dissatisfied with his overall appearance, even his protuberant ears had their uses, having more than once served as convenient handles by which his face could be pulled down to a waiting and expectant female face below. To complete the inventory, his close-cropped hair was darkly brown and his eyes, startlingly pale in his space-tanned face, were gray, at times a very bleak gray.

So this was Lieutenant John Grimes, presently officer-of-the-watch of the Survey Service cruiser *Aries*, slowly shuffling back and forth between the consoles, the banked instruments, alert for any information that might suddenly be displayed on dials or screens. He was not expecting any; the ship was in deep space, falling free through the warped continum induced by her Mannschenn Drive through regions well clear of the heavily frequented trade routes. There was only one human colony, Grimes knew, in this sector of the Galaxy, the world that had been named, not very originally but aptly, *El Dorado*; and two ships a standard year served the needs of that fabulous planet.

El Dorado . . .

Idly—but a watch officer has to think about something—Grimes wondered what it was really like there. There were stories, of course, but they were no more than rumors, exaggerated rumors, like as not. The El Doradans did not encourage visitors, and the two ships that handled their small trade—precious ores outwards, luxury goods inwards—were owned and manned by themselves, not that the vessels, space-borne miracles of automation, required more than two men, captain and engineer, apiece.

Grimes looked out through the viewports, roughly to where El Dorado should be. He did not see it, of course, nor did he expect to do so. He saw only warped Space, suns near and far that had been twisted to the semblance of pulsating, multicolored spirals, blackness between the suns that had been contorted into its own vast convolutions, sensed (but with what sense?) rather than seen. It was, as always, a fascinating spectacle; it was, as always, a frightening one. It was not good to look at it for too long.

Grimes turned his attention to the orderly universe in miniature displayed in the chart tank.

"Mr. Grimes!"

"Sir!" The Lieutenant started. He hadn't heard the old bastard come into the control room. He looked up to the tall, spare figure of Captain Daintree, to the cold blue eyes under the mane of white hair. "Sir?"

"Warn the engine room that we shall be requiring Inertial Drive shortly. And then, I believe that you're qualified in navigation, you may work out the trajectory for El Dorado."

2

LIEUTENANT COMMANDER COOPER, the Navigating Officer of *Aries,* was in a bad mood, a sulky expression on his plump, swarthy face, his reedy voice petulant. "Damn it all," he was saying. "Damn it all, what am *I* supposed to be here for? An emergency alteration of trajectory comes up and am I called for? Oh, no, that'd be far too simple. So young Grimes has to fumble his way through the sums that *I* should be doing, and the first that *I* know is when somebody condescends to sound the acceleration alarm . . ."

"Was there anything wrong with my trajectory, *sir?*" asked Grimes coldly.

"No, Mr. Grimes. Nothing at all wrong, although *I* was brought up to adhere to the principle that interstellar dust clouds should be avoided . . ."

"With the Mannschenn Drive in operation there's no risk."

"Isn't there? A little knowledge is a dangerous thing, Mr. Grimes. Inside some of these dark nebulae the Continuum is dangerously warped."

"But CCD736 can hardly be classed as a nebula . . ."

"Even so, the first principle of all navigation should be caution, and it's high time that you learned that."

Doctor Rassifern, the Senior Medical Officer, broke in. "Come off it, Pilot. Young Grimes *is* learning, and this idea of the Old Man's that every officer in the ship should be able to take over from the specialists is a very sound one . . ."

"Ha! It might be an idea if some of us were encouraged to take over *your* job, Doc!"

A flush darkened Passifern's already ruddy face. He growled, "That's not the same and you know it."

"Isn't it? Oh, I know that ever since the dawn of history you pill peddlers have made a sacred mystery of your technology . . ."

Grimes got to his feet, said, "What about some more coffee?" He collected the three mugs from the table, walked to the espresso machine that stood in a corner of the comfortable wardroom. He found it rather embarrassing when his seniors quarreled—the long-standing feud between the Navigator and the Doctor was more than good-natured bickering—and thought that a pause for refreshment would bring the opportunity for a change of subject. As he filled the mugs he remarked brightly, "At least this acceleration allows us to enjoy our drinks. I hate having to sip out of a bulb."

"Do you?" asked Cooper nastily. "I'd have thought that one of your tender years would enjoy a regression to the well-remembered and well-beloved feeding bottle."

Grimes ignored this. He set the mugs down on the low table, then dropped ungracefully into his easy chair. He said to Passifern, "But what *is* the hurry, Doc? I know that I'm only the small boy around here and that I'm not supposed to be told anything, but would you be breaking any vows of secrecy if you told us the nature of the emergency on El Dorado?"

"I don't know myself, Grimes. All I know is that there shouldn't be one. Those filthy rich El Doradans have the finest practitioners and specialists in the known Universe in residence; and they, by this time, must be almost as filthy rich as their patients! All *I* know is that *they* knew that we were in the vicinity of their planet, and requested a second opinion on something or other . . ."

"And our Lord and Master," contributed Cooper, "decided that it was a good excuse to give the Inertial Drive a gallop. He doesn't like Free Fall." He obliged with a surprisingly good imitation of Captain Daintree's deep voice: "Too much Free Fall makes officers soft."

"He could be right," said Passifern.

Cooper ignored this. "What puzzles me," he said, "is why these outstanding practitioners and specialists should call in a humble ship's quack . . ."

"As a major vessel of the Survey Service," Passifern told him coldly, "we carry a highly qualified and expert team of physicians, surgeons and technicians. And our hospital and research facilities would be the envy of many a planet. Furthermore, *we* have the benefit of experience denied to any planet-bound doctor . . ."

"And wouldn't *you* just love to be planet-bound on a world like El Dorado?" asked Cooper.

Before the Doctor could make an angry reply, Grimes turned to the Navigator. "And what *is* El Dorado like, sir? I was going to look it up, but the Old Man's taken the Pilot Book covering it out of the control room."

"Doing his homework," said Cooper. "Luckily it's not everybody who has to rush to the books when the necessity for an unscheduled landing crops up. We specialists, unlike the jacks-of-all-trades, do tend to be reasonably expert in our own fields." He took a noisy gulp of coffee. "All right. El Dorado. An essentially Earth-type planet in orbit about a Sol-type primary. A very ordinary sort of world, you might say. But it's not. And it wasn't."

It was Passifern who broke the silence. "What's so different about it?"

"Don't you know, Doc? You were hankering for its fleshpots only a minute ago. I suppose you have some sort of idea of what it's like now, but not how it got that way. Well, to begin with, it was an extraordinary world. It was one of those planets upon which life—life-as-we-know-it or any other kind of life—had never taken hold. There it was, for millions upon millions of years, just a sterile ball of rock and mud and water.

"And then it was purchased from the Federation by the so-called El Dorado Corporation.

"Even you, young Grimes, must know something of history. Even you must know how, on world after world, the trend has been towards socialism. Some societies have gone the whole hog, preaching and practicing the Gospel According to St. Marx. Some have contented themselves with State control of the means of production and supply, with ruinous taxation of the very well-to-do thrown in. There have been levelling up processes and levelling down processes, and these have hurt the aristocracies of birth and breeding as much as they have hurt the aristocracies of Big Business and industry.

"And so the Corporation was formed. Somehow its members managed to get most of their wealth out of their home worlds, and much of it was used for the terraforming of El Dorado. Terraforming? Landscape gardening would be a better phrase. Yes, that world's no more, and no less, than a huge, beautiful park, with KEEP OFF THE GRASS signs posted insofar as the common herd is concerned."

"What about servants? Technicians?" asked Grimes.

"The answer to that problem, my boy, was automation, automation and still more automation. Automation to an extent that would not have been practical on a world where the economics of it had to be considered. And on the rare occasions that the machines do need attention there are a few El Doradans to whom mechanics, electronics and the like are amusing and quite fascinating hobbies. And there will be others, of course, who enjoy playing around at gardening, or even farming."

"A world, in fact, that's just a rich man's toy," said Grimes.

"And don't forget the rich bitches," Cooper told him.

"I don't think I'd like it," went on Grimes.

"And I don't think that the El Doradans would like you," Cooper remarked. "Or any of us. As far as they're concerned, we're just snotty-nosed ragamuffins from the wrong side of the tracks."

"Still," said Passifern smugly, "they requested *my* services."

"God knows why," sneered Cooper.

There was silence while the Doctor tried to think of a scathing rejoinder. It was broken by Grimes. "Ah, here's Mr. Bose. Perhaps he can tell us."

"Our commissioned teacup reader," grunted the Navigator sardonically. "Singing and dancing."

Mr. Bose, the cruiser's Psionic Radio Officer, did not look the sort of man who would ever be heard or seen indulging in such activities. He was short and fat, and the expression of his shiny, chocolate-colored face was one of unrelieved gloom. On the occasions when a shipmate would tell him, for the love of all the odd gods of the Galaxy, to cheer up, he would reply portentiously, "But I *know* too much." What he knew of what went on in the minds of his shipmates he would never divulge; insofar as they were concerned, he always observed and respected the oath of secrecy taken by all graduates of the Rhine Institute. Now and again, however, he seemed to consider outsiders fair game and would pass on to his fellow officers what he had learned by telepathic eavesdropping.

"What cooks on El Dorado, Bosey Boy?" demanded Cooper.

"What cooks, Commander, sir? The flesh of animals. They are a godless people and partake of unclean foods."

"The same as we do, in this ship. But you know what I mean."

Surprisingly, the telepath laughed, a high-pitched giggle. "Yes, I know what you mean, Commander, sir."

"Of course you do, you damned snooper. But what cooks?"

"I . . . I cannot understand. I have tried to . . . to tune in on the thoughts of all the people. From their Psionic Radio officers I have learned nothing, nothing at all. They are experts, highly trained, with their minds impenetrably screened. But the dreams, the secret thoughts of the ordinary people are vague, confused. There is unease and there is fear, but it is not the fear of an immediate danger. But it is a very real fear . . ."

"Probably just an increasing incidence of tinea," laughed Cooper. "Right up your alley, Doc."

Passifern was not amused.

3

ARIES WAS IN orbit about El Dorado.

It was very quiet in the control room where Captain Daintree and his officers looked out, through the wide viewports, to the green, blue and golden, cloud-girdled planet that the slip was circling. The absence of the familiar, shipboard noises—the thin, high keening of the Mannschenn Drive, the odd, irregular throbbing of the inertial drive—engendered a feeling of tension, a taut expectancy. And this was more than just a routine planetfall. El Dorado was a new world to all of *Aries'* people. True, they had landed on new worlds before, worlds upon which they had been the first humans to set foot; but this fabled planet was—different. Grimes thought of the Moslem paradise with its timeless *houris* and grinned wryly. Such beauties would never confer their favours on—how had Cooper put it?—on a snotty-nosed ragamuffin from the wrong side of the tracks.

"And what do you find so amusing, Mr. Grimes?" asked Daintree coldly. "Perhaps you will share the joke with us."

"I . . . I was thinking, sir." Grimes felt his prominent ears redden.

"You aren't paid to think," came the age-old, automatic reply, the illogical rejoinder that has persisted through millenia. Grimes was tempted to point out that officers *are* paid to think, but thought better of it.

Commander Griffin, the Executive Officer, broke the silence. "The pinnace is all cleared away, sir, for the advance party."

"The *pinnace,* Commander? By whose orders?"

"I . . . I thought, sir . . ."

Another one! Grimes chuckled inwardly, permitted himself a slight grin as he looked at the embarrassed Griffin. Griffin looked back at him in a way that boded ill for the Lieutenant.

Daintree said, "I admit, Commander, that you are permitted to think. Even so, you should think to more purpose. How long is it since the rocket re-entry boat was exercised? Did you not consider that this would be an ideal opportunity to give the craft a test and training flight?"

"Why, yes, sir. It would be an ideal opportunity."

"Then have it cleared away, Commander. At once. Oh, which of your young gentlemen are you thinking of sending?"

"Doctor Passifern has arranged for Surgeon Lieutenant Kravisky to go with the advance party, sir."

"Never mind that. Who will be the pilot?"

"Er . . . Mr. Grimes, sir."

"Mr. Grimes." The captain switched his attention from the Commander to the Lieutenant. "Mr. Grimes, what experience have you had in the handling of rocket-powered craft?"

"At the Academy, sir. And during my first training cruise."

"And never since. You're like all the rest of the officers aboard this ship, far too used to riding around in comfort with an inertial drive unit tucked away under your backside. Very well, this will be an ideal opportunity for you to gain some experience of *real* spacefaring."

"Yes, sir. See to the boat, sir?"

"Not yet. Commander Griffin is quite capable of that." He walked to the chart desk, beckoned Grimes to follow him. The Navigator had already spread a chart on the flat surface, securing it with spring clips. "This," said Daintree, "was transmitted to us by whatever or whoever passes for Port Control on El Dorado. Mercator's Projection. Here is the spaceport"—his thin, bony fingers jabbed downwards—"by this lake . . ."

"Will the spaceport be suitable for the landing of the rocket boat, sir?" asked Grimes. "After all, if it was designed only to handle inertial drive vessels . . ."

"I've already thought of that point, Mr. Grimes. But our rocket boat is designed to land on water if needs be."

"But . . . but will they be ready for us, sir?"

"This vessel has established electronic radio communication with El Dorado, Mr. Grimes. I shall tell them to be ready for you. After all, we are visiting their planet at their request."

"Yes sir."

"Very good, then. You may study the chart until it is time for you to take the boat away."

"Yes, sir."

Grimes looked down at the new, as yet unmarked plan of the spaceport and its environs. He would far sooner have spent the time studying the Manual of Spacemanship, with special attention to that section devoted to the handling of rocket-powered re-entry vehicles. But, after all, he was qualified as an atmosphere pilot and had, for some time, been drawing the extra pay to which his certificate entitled him.

As he studied the chart he overheard Captain Daintree talking over the transceiver to somebody, presumably Port Control, on the planet below. "Yes, you heard me correctly. I am sending the advance party down in one of my rocket boats." Came the reply, "But, Captain, our spaceport is not suitable for the reception of such a craft." The voice was as arrogant as Daintree's own but in a different way. It was the arrogance that comes with money (too much money), with inherited titles, with a bloodline traced back to some uncouth robber baron who happened to be a more efficient thief and murderer than his rivals.

"*I* am sending away my rocket boat." One almost expected the acridity of ozone to accompany that quarterdeck snap and crackle.

"I am sorry, Captain—" Port Control didn't sound very sorry—"but that is impossible."

"Do you want our help, or don't you?"

There was a brief silence, then a reluctant "Yes."

"Your spaceport is on the northern shore of Lake Bluewater isn't it?"

"You have the chart that we transmitted to you, Captain."

"My rocket boat can be put down on water."

"You don't understand, Captain. Lake Bluewater is a very popular resort."

"Isn't that just too bad? Get your kids with their pails and spades and plastic animals off the beaches and out of the water."

Again the silence and then in a voice that shed none of its cold venom over the thousands of miles, "Very well, Captain. But please understand that we shall not be responsible for any accidents to your boat and your personnel."

"And *I*," said Daintree harshly, "refuse to accept responsibility for any picnic or paddling parties who happen to get in the way. The officer in charge of the re-entry vehicle will be using the same frequency as we are using now. He will keep you and me informed of his movements. Over."

"Roger," came the supercilious reply. "Roger. Over and standing by."

"Rocket boat cleared away and ready, sir," said Commander Griffin, who had returned to the control room.

"Very good, Commander. Man and launch. Mr. Grimes, you should have memorized that chart by now, and, in any case, there will be another copy in the boat."

"Yes, sir." Grimes followed the Commander from the control room.

Surgeon Lieutenant Kravisky, his slender body already pressure-suited, his thin, dark face behind the open face plate of his helmet wearing an anxious expression, was already waiting by the boat blister. In each hand he carried a briefcase: one containing ship's papers and the other his uniform. Disgustedly, Grimes stripped to his briefs. If he'd been allowed to take the pinnace instead of this relic from the bad old days, there would have been no need to dress up like a refugee from historical space opera. A rating helped him into his suit, another man neatly folded his shorts and shirt and stowed them, together with his shoes and stockings, into a small case. Being on the Advance Party had its advantages after all, Grimes decided. At least he would be spared the discomfort of full dress—frock coat, cocked hat and sword—which would be rig of the day when the big ship came in.

"Are you sure that you can drive this thing, John?" asked Kravisky.

"I don't know. I've never tried before." Then, before Commander Griffin could issue a scathing reprimand, he added. "Not this particular one, I mean. But I am qualified."

"That will do, Mr. Grimes," said Griffin. "You know the drill, I hope. After you're down, present yourself to Port Control and make the necessary arrangements for the reception of *Aries*. Don't forget that *you* represent the ship. Comport yourself accordingly. And try to refrain from misguided attempts at humor."

"Ay, ay, sir."

"Then board the boat. Procedure as per Regulations. Bo's'n!"

"Sir!" snapped the petty officer.

"Carry on!"

"Ay, ay, sir."

The inner door to the blister opened, revealing a small airlock. Grimes entered it first, followed by Kravisky, snapping shut his faceplate as he did so. He heard the sighing of the pumps as the air was exhausted from the chamber, watched the needle of the pressure dial drop to Zero. The red light came on. The outer door opened.

Beyond it was the graceless form of the rocket boat, a stubby, flattened dart with a venturi and control surfaces; and visible beyond it was black, star-flecked sky and a great, glowing arc that was the limb of El

Dorado. Grimes shuffled toward it on his magnetized soles, saw that the cabin door was already open, pulled himself into the vehicle. Then, while Kravisky was stowing the cases in a locker abaft the seats, he pushed the button that shut the door and another that pressurized the compartment. He looked at the dials and meters on the console, saw that the firing chamber had been warmed up and that all was ready for the launch. He strapped himself into his seat and waited until the Surgeon Lieutenant had done likewise. He opened the faceplate of his helmet. The air was breathable enough but carried a stale, canned flavor.

"All systems *Go!*" he said, feeling that the archaic spacemanese matched the archaic means of transportation.

"What was that?" snapped Griffin's voice from the speaker. Then, tiredly, "Oh, all right, Mr. Grimes. Five second count-down. Five . . . four . . . three . . . two . . . one . . . *fire!*"

Smoothly and efficiently the launching catapult threw the rocket boat away and clear from the cruiser. Not very smoothly, but efficiently enough, Grimes actuated the reaction drive, felt the giant hand of acceleration push him back into the padding of his seat.

"Mr. Grimes!" This time it was Captain Daintree's voice that came from the speaker. "Mr. Grimes, you should have been able to fall free all the way to the exosphere. You have no fuel to waste on astrobatics."

"Bloody back-seat drivers!" muttered Grimes, but he held his hand over the microphone as he did so.

4

NONETHELESS HE WAS having his fun, was young Mr. Grimes.

Once he had the feel of his unhandy craft, once he had stopped resenting having to worry about such matters as skin temperature, angle of attack, drag, and the rest of the aeronautical esoticera, he began to enjoy himself, to thrill to the sensation of speed as the first wisps of high altitude cirrus whipped by. This was better, after all, than making a slow, dignified descent in the pinnace, with its inertial drive, or in one of the other rocket boats—old-fashioned but not so downright archaic as this re-entry vehicle—in which he had now and again ridden, that cautiously shinnied down, stern first, the incandescent columns of their exhaust gases. He felt confident enough to withdraw his attention from his instruments, to risk a sidewise glance at his companion.

Grimes was happy but Kravisky was not. The Surgeon Lieutenant's face had paled to a peculiar, pale green. He seemed to be swallowing something. *Physician, heal thyself,* thought Grimes sardonically. "I . . . I wish you'd look where you're going," mumbled the young doctor.

"Beautiful view, isn't it?" Grimes glanced through the ports, then at his console. There was nothing to worry about. He had a hemisphere to play around in. By the time he was down, the terminator would be just short of Lake Bluewater. It would be a daylight landing, to save these very casual locals in Port Control the trouble of setting out a flare path. There would be the radio beacon to home upon and at least twenty miles of smooth water for his runway. It was—he searched his memory for the expression used by long ago and faraway pilots of the Royal Air Force; history, especially the history of the ships of Earth's seas and air oceans, was his favorite reading—it was a piece of cake.

"Isn't it . . . isn't it hot in here?" Why couldn't Kravisky relax?

"Not especially. After all, we're sitting in a hotmonococque."

"What's that?" Then, with a feeble attempt at humor,"The remedy sounds worse than the disease . . ."

"Just an airborne thermos flask."

"Oh."

"Like a park, isn't it?" said Grimes. "Even from up here, like a park. Green. No industrial haze. No smog . . ."

"Too . . . tame," said Kravisky, taking a reluctant interest.

"No, I don't think so. They have mountains, and high ones, too. They have seas that must be rough sometimes, even with weather control. If they want to risk life and limb, there'll be plenty of mountaineering and sailing . . ."

"And other sports . . ."

"Yeah." The radio compass seemed to be functioning properly, as were air speed indicator and radio altimeter. The note of the distant beacon was a steady hum. No doubt the El Doradans possessed far more advanced systems than were used by their own aircraft, but the reentry vehicle was not equipped to make use of them. "Yeah," said Grimes again. "Such as?"

"I'm a reservist, you know. But I'm also a ship's doctor in civil life. My last voyage before I was called up for my drill was in the Commission's *Alpha Cepheus* . . . A cruise to Caribbea. Passengers stinking with money and far too much time on their hands . . ."

"What's that to do with sports?"

"You'd be surprised. Or would you?"

No, thought Grimes, he wouldn't. His first Deep Space voyage had been as a passenger, and Jane Pentecost, the vessel's purser, had been very attractive. Where was she now? he wondered. Still in the Commission's ships, or back home, on the Rim?

Damn Jane Pentecost and damn the Rim Worlds. But this planet was nothing like Lorn, Faraway, Ultimo or Thule. He had never been to any of those dreary colonies (and never would go there, he told himself) but he had heard enough about them. Too much.

The air was denser now, and the control column that Grimes had been holding rather negligently was developing a life of its own. Abruptly the steady note of the beacon changed to a morse A—dot dash, dot dash. Grimes tried to get the re-entry vehicle back on course, overcompensated. It was N now—dash dot, dash dot. The Lieutenant was sweating inside his suit when he had the boat under control again. Flying these antique crates was far too much like work. But he could afford another glance at the scenery.

There were wide fields, some green and some golden-glowing in the light of the afternoon sun, and in these latter worked great, glittering machines, obviously automatic harvesters. There were dense clumps of darker green—the forests which, on this world, had been grown for aesthetic reasons, not as a source of cellulose for industry. But the El Doradans, on the income from their mines alone, could well afford to import anything they needed. Or wanted. And only the odd gods of the galaxy knew how many billions they had stashed away in the Federation Central Bank on Earth, to say nothing of other banks on other planets.

There were the wide fields and the forests, and towering up at the rim of the world the jagged blue mountains, the dazzlingly white-capped peaks. Rather too dazzling, but that was the glare of the late-afternoon sun, broad on the starboard bow of the rocket boat. Grimes adjusted the viewport polarizer. He could see houses now, large dwellings, even from this altitude, each miles distant from its nearest neighbor, each blending rather than contrasting with the landscape. He could see houses and beyond the huge, gleaming, azure oval that was Lake Bluewater, there were the tall towers of Spaceport Control and the intense, winking red light that was the beacon. Beyond the port again, but distant, shimmered the lofty spires of the city.

All very nice, but what's the air speed? Too high, too bloody high. Cut the rocket drive? Yes. Drag'll slow her down nicely, and there're always the parachute brakes and, in an emergency, the retro-rockets. Still on the beam, according to the beacon. In any case, I can see it plainly enough. Just keel it dead ahead . . .

Getting bumpy now, and mushy . . . What else, in such an abortion of an aircraft? But not to worry. Coming in bloody nicely, though I say it as shouldn't.

Looks like pine trees just inland from the beach. Cleared them all right. Must say that those supercilious drongoes in Port Control might have made some sort of stab at talking me in. All they said, "You may land." Didn't quite say, "Use the servants' entrance . . ."

Parachute brakes? No. Make a big bloody splash in their bloody lake and play hell with their bloody goldfish . . .

Kravisky shouted, screamed almost, and then Grimes, whose attention had been divided between the beacon and the altimeter, saw, cutting across the rocket boat's course, a small surface craft, a scarlet hull skittering over the water in its own, self-generated, double plume of snowy spray. But it would pass clear.

But that slim, golden figure, gracefully poised on a single water ski, would not.

With a curse Grimes released the parachute brakes and, at the same time, yanked back on his control column. He knew that the parachutes would not take hold in time, that before the rocket boat stalled it would crash into the woman. Yet—he was thinking fast, desperately fast—he dared not use either his main rocket drive to lift the boat up and clear, or his retro-rockets. Better for her, whoever she was, to run the risk of being crushed than to face the certainty of being incinerated.

Then there were birds (birds?), great birds that flew headlong at the control cabin, birds whose suicidal impact was enough to slow the boat sufficiently, barely sufficiently, to tip her so that forward motion was transformed to upward motion. The drogues took hold of the water, and that was that. She fell, soggily, ungracefully, blunt stern first, and as she did so Grimes stared stupidly at a broken wing, a broken *metal* wing that had been skewered by the forward antenna.

5

NEITHER GRIMES NOR Kravisky was hurt—seat padding and safety belts protected them from serious damage—but they were badly shaken. Grimes wondered, as the re-entry craft plunged below the churning surface of the lake, how deep it would sink before it rose again. And then he realized that it would not rise again, ever, or would not do so without the aid of salvage equipment. Aft there was an ominous gurgling that told its own story. Aft? That noise was now in the cabin itself. He looked down. The water was already about his ankles.

"Button up!" he snapped to the Surgeon Lieutenant.

"But what . . . ?" the words trailed off into silence.

"The ejection gear. I hope it works under water."

"But . . ." Kravisky, his faceplate still open, made as though to unsnap his seat belt. "The papers. Our uniforms. I must get them out of the locker . . ."

"Like hell you will. *Button up!*"

Sullenly, Kravisky checked that his belt was still tight, then sealed his helmet. Grimes followed suit. His hand hesitated over the big, red button on the control panel, then slammed down decisively. Even through the thick, resilient padding of his seat he felt the violent kick of the catapulting explosion. He cringed, expecting the skull-crushing impact of his head with the roof of the cabin, the last thing that he would ever feel. But it did not come, although he was faintly aware of the lightest of taps on his shoulder. And then he and the Surgeon Lieutenant, still strapped in their buoyant chairs, were shooting upwards, the sundered shell of the control cabin falling away beneath and below them, soaring to the surface in the midst of a huge bubble of air and other gases. Somehow he found time to look about him. The water was very blue and very clear. And there was a great, goggle-eyed fish staring at them from outside the bubble. It did not look especially carnivorous. Grimes hoped that it wasn't.

The two chairs broke surface simultaneously, bobbing and gyrating. Slowly, their motion ceased. They floated in the middle of a widening circle of discolored water, a spiralling swirl of iridescent oil slicks. And there were more than a few dead fish. Grimes could not repress a chuckle when he saw that they were golden carp. About five hundred yards away, its engine stopped, lay the scarlet power boat. But there was something in the water between it and the astronauts, something that was approaching at a speed that, to the spacemen should have been painfully slow and yet, in this environment, was amazingly fast.

There was a sleek head in a golden helmet—no, decided Grimes, it was hair, not an artificial covering—and there were two slim, golden-brown arms that alternately flashed up and swept down and back. And there was the rest of her, slim and golden-brown all over. Somehow it was suddenly important to Grimes that he see her face. He hoped that it would match what he could already see.

As she neared the floating chairs she reverted to a breaststroke and then, finally, came to a standstill, hanging there, a yard or so distant, just treading water. The spacemen could not help staring at her body through the shimmering transparency, her naked body. It was beautiful. With a sudden start of embarrassment Grimes forced his gaze to slide upwards to her face. It was thin, the cheekbones pronounced, the planes of the cheeks flat. Her mouth was a wide, scarlet slash, parted to reveal perfect white teeth. The eyes were an intense blue, an angry blue. She was saying something, and it was obvious that she was not whispering.

Grimes put up his hand, opened the faceplate of his helmet.

". . . offworld yahoos!" he heard. "My two favorite watchbirds destroyed, thanks to your unspacemanlike antics!" Her voice was not loud but it carried well. It could best be described as an icy soprano.

"Madam," Grimes said coldly. It didn't sound quite right but it would have to do. "Madam, I venture to suggest that the loss of my own boat is of rather greater consequence than the destruction of your . . . pets." (Pets? Watchbirds? That obviously metallic wing skewered on the antenna?) He went on, "Our Captain expressly requested that this lake be cleared as a landing area."

"Your *Captain?*" She made it sound as though the commanding officer of a Zodiac Class cruiser ranked with but below the butler.

"Look here, young woman . . ."

"*What* did you call me?"

"If you aren't a young woman," contributed Kravisky,"you look remarkably like one."

In her fury the girl forgot to tread water. She went down, came up spluttering. Only one word was intelligible and that was "Insolence!" She reached out a long, slender arm, caught hold of a projection at the edge of Grimes' chair. She floated there, maintaining her distance, glaring up at him.

"Now, young lady . . ."

She was mollified but only slightly. "Don't call me that, either," she snapped.

"Then what . . . ?"

"I am the Princess Marlene Von Stolzberg. You may call me 'Your Highness'."

"Very well, Your Highness," said Grimes stiffly. "It may interest Your Highness to know that I intend to register a strong complaint with Spaceport Control. Your Highness's lack of ordinary commonsense put Your Highness's life as well as ours in hazard and resulted in the probable total loss of a piece of valuable Survey Service equipment."

"Commonsense?" she sneered. "And what about your own lack of that quality, to say nothing of your appalling spacemanship? You saw me. You must have seen me. And yet *you,* you . . . offworlder, assumed that *you* had the right to disturb my afternoon's recreation!" She made an explosive, spitting noise.

"Let us be reasonable, Your Highness," persisted Grimes. It cost nothing to play along. "No doubt there was some misunderstanding . . ."

"Misunderstanding?" Her fine eyebrows arced in incredulity. "Misunderstanding? I'll say there was. You come blundering in here like . . . like . . ."

"Like snotty-nosed ragamuffins from the wrong side of the tracks?" asked Grimes sardonically.

Surprisingly, she laughed, tinkling merriment that was not altogether malicious. "How well you put it, my man."

Now was the time to take advantage of her change of mood. "Do you think, Your Highness, that you could call to your friend in the boat so that he can pick us up?"

She laughed again. "My friend in the boat? But I am by myself." She turned her head toward the bright scarlet craft. She called softly,"Ilse! To me, Ilse! "

There was a sudden turbulence at the thing's stern. It turned until it was stem on to the astronauts and the princess. It came in slowly and steadily, turned again until it was broadside on to the girl, brought itself to a smooth halt by an exact application of stern power. A short ladder with handrails extruded itself with a muted click. The Princess Marlene let go of Grimes' chair; two graceful strokes took her to her mechanical servitor. As she climbed on board Grimes saw that she was one of those rare women whose nudity is even more beautiful out of the water than in it; the surprisingly full breasts, deprived of their fluid support, did not sag, and there were no minor blemishes to have been veiled by ripples. He felt a stab of disappointment as she reached down for a robe of spotless white towelling and threw it about her. Still watching her, he made to unsnap his seat belt.

"Not so fast, my man!" she called coldly. "Not so fast. You are not riding in with me. But I shall tow you in." Expertly, she threw the end of a nylon line to Grimes. Not so expertly he caught it in his gloved hand.

"Thank you, Your Highness," he said as nastily as he dared.

The Port Control building, into which the girl finally led them, was deserted. She did not seem to be surprised. "After all," she condescended to explain,"Henri set up the beacon for you and gave you preliminary instructions. He assumed, wrongly, as it turned out, that you were good enough spacemen to find your way in by yourselves. After all, he has better things to do than to sit in this office all day."

"Such as?" asked Grimes. He added hastily,"Your Highness."

"Polo, of course."

"But, damn it all, we have to see *somebody.* We have to arrange for the landing and reception of the ship. We lost our uniforms when the boat went down, so we'd like a change of clothing. Spacesuits aren't very comfortable wear. Your Highness."

"Then take them off. I don't mind."

You wouldn't, thought Grimes. *The aristocrat naked before the serfs, the serfs naked before the aristocrat, what does it matter to the aristocrat?* He said,"The sun is down and it's getting chilly."

"Then keep them on."

"Please, Your Highness . . ." Grimes hated having to beg. He would far sooner have shaken some sense into this infuriating minx. But he was in enough trouble already. He was not looking forward explaining to Captain Daintree the loss of the re-entry vehicle. "Please, Your Highness, can't you help us?"

"Oh, all right. Although why you outworlders have to be so *helpless* is beyond me. Aren't you used to servants on your planets? I suppose not." She walked gracefully, her golden sandals faintly tapping on the polished floor, to what seemed to be, and was, a telephone booth. But there were neither dials nor buttons. She ordered, in her high, clear voice, "Get me the Comte de Messigny."

There was a brief delay, and then the screen on the rear wall of the booth swirled into glowing, three dimensional life. The man looking out from it was tall, clad in white helmet, shirt, riding breeches, and highly polished black boots. He lifted a slim, brown hand to the peak of his headgear in salute. A dazzling grin split the darkly tanned face under the pencil line of the mustache.

"Marlene!"

"Henri. Sorry to trouble you, but I've two lost sheep of spacemen here. They came blundering down in some sort of fire-breathing monstrosity—a dynosoar, would it be?—and cracked up in the lake . . ."

"I did warn you, Marlene."

"There was no risk to me, Henri, although it did cost me my two best watchbirds. But these offworlders, I suppose you'd better do something about them . . ."

"I suppose so. Put them on, please, Marlene."

"Stand where I was standing," the girl said to Grimes. Then, in a voice utterly devoid of interest, "Good evening to you." Then she was gone.

Grimes was conscious of being examined by the unwinking, dark eyes of the man in the screen who, at last, demanded, "Well?"

"Lieutenant Grimes," he replied, adding "sir" to be on the safe side. "Of *Aries.* And this is Surgeon Lieutenant Kravisky. We are the advance landing party . . ."

"You've landed, haven't you?"

"Sir . . ." It hurt to bow and scrape to these civilians, with their absurd, unearned titles. "Sir, we wish to report our arrival. We wish to report, too, that we are in a condition of some distress. Our re-entry vehicle was wrecked and we were badly shaken up. We are unable to establish radio contact with *Aries* so that we may tell our Captain what has happened. Our uniforms were lost in the wreck. We request clothing and food and accommodations." *And a good, stiff drink,* he thought.

"I shall inform your Captain that you are here," said de Messigny. "Meanwhile, the automatic servitors in the hostel have been instructed to obey all reasonable orders. You will find that provisions have been made for your reception and comfort on the floor above the one where you are presently situated."

"Thank you, sir. But when shall we make arrangements for the berthing and reception of *Aries?*"

"Tomorrow, Lieutenant. I shall see you some time tomorrow. Good evening to you."

The screen went blank.

Grimes looked at Kravisky, and Kravisky looked at Grimes. Then they looked around the huge, gleaming hall, beautifully proportioned, opulent in its fittings and furnishings; but, like this entire planet, cold, cold.

6

IF THERE WERE elevators to the upper floors they must be, thought Grimes, very well concealed. Tiredly, acutely conscious of the discomfort of his clammy spacesuit, he trudged toward the ornamental spiral staircase that rose, gracefully from the center of the iridescent, patterned floor. The Surgeon Lieutenant followed him, muttering something that sounded like, and probably was,"Inhospitable bastards!"

But the staircase was more than it seemed. As Grimes put his weight on the first of the treads, there was a subdued humming of machinery, almost inaudible, and he felt himself being lifted. The thing was, in fact, an escalator. For a few seconds Grimes' exhausted brain tried to grapple with the engineering problems involved in the construction of a moving stairway of this design, then gave up. It worked, didn't it? So what?

At the level of the next floor the treads flattened to a track, slid him gently on to the brightly colored mosaic of the landing. He waited there until he was joined by Kravisky. There was a sudden silence as the murmur of machinery ceased. The two men looked around. They were standing in a relatively small hallway, partly occupied by another staircase ascending to yet another level. The walls, covered with what looked like a silken fabric, were featureless. Suddenly a disembodied voice, cultured yet characterless, almost sexless yet male rather than female, spoke. "This way, please."

A sliding door had opened. Beyond it was a room, plainly furnished but comfortable enough, with two beds, chairs and a table. Apart from its size it could have been a ship's cabin. "Toilet facilities are on your right as you enter," the voice said. "Please leave soiled clothing in the receptacle provided."

"Perhaps a drink first . . ." suggested Kravisky.

"Toilet facilities are on your right as you enter. Please leave soiled clothing in the receptacle provided."

"I never did like arguing with robots," said Grimes. He walked slowly through the open doorway, then through the other door into the bathroom. As he turned, he saw that the main door had slid shut behind Kravisky. There did not seem to be any way of opening it from the inside, but, come to that, neither had there been any way of opening it from the outside. This should have seemed important, but right now the only matter of moment was shucking his stinking suit, clambering out of his sweat-soaked underwear. He pulled off his gloves, then clumsily fumbled with the fastenings of his armour. The protective clothing, fabric and metal with plastic and metal attachments, fell to the floor with an audible clank and rattle. He stepped out of the boots, peeled off his underpants. Kravisky, he saw, was managing quite well and would require no assistance. He started toward one of the two shower stalls.

"Please leave soiled clothing in the receptacle provided," said the annoying voice.

Yes, there was a receptacle, but it had not been designed to accommodate such bulky accoutrements as spacesuits. The underpants went through the hinged flap easily enough, but it was obvious that a full suit of space armour would be beyond its capabilities. In any case, such items of equipment were supposed to be surrendered only to the ship's Armourer for servicing.

"Please leave . . ."

"It won't go in," stated Grimes.

"Please . . ." There was a pause, and then a new voice issued from the concealed speaker. It was still a mechanical one but somehow possessed a definite personality. "Please dispose of your smaller articles of clothing and leave your suits on the floor. They will be collected for dehydration and deodorization later."

By whom? wondered Grimes. *Or by what?* But he could, at least, enjoy his shower now without being badgered. Naked, he stepped into the stall. Before he could raise a hand the curtain slid across the opening, before he could look for controls a fine spray of warm, soapy water came at him from all directions. This was succeeded, after a few minutes, by water with no added detergent and, finally, by a steady blast of hot air. When he was dry, the curtain slid back and, greatly refreshed, he walked out into the main bathroom. He noticed at once that the spacesuits were gone. He shrugged; after all, he had already lost a re-entry vehicle. He noticed, too, that two plain, blue robes were hanging inside the door and under each of them, on the floor, was a pair of slippers. He pulled one of the garments on to his muscular body, slid his feet into the soft leather footwear. They fitted as though they had been made for him. He went through into the bed-sitting room, waited for Kravisky. The subtly annoying voice asked, "Would you care for a drink before dinner?"

"Yes," answered Grimes. "We would. Two pink gins, please. Large. With ice."

A faint clicking noise drew his attention. He saw that an aperture had appeared in the center of the polished table top, realized that the stout pillar that was the only support of the piece of furniture must be a supply chute. There was another click and the panel was back in place, and on it were two misted goblets.

"Gin!" complained Kravisky. "Are you mad, John? We could have that aboard the ship. Now's our chance to live it up." He added,"*I* would have ordered Manzanilla."

"Sorry, Doc. I was forgetting that you have personal experience of how the filthy rich live. You can order dinner."

He dropped into one of the chairs at the table, picked up and sipped his drink with appreciation. After all, it wasn't bad gin.

"Please order your meal," said the voice.

Grimes looked at the Surgeon Lieutenant over what remained of his second gin—obviously they were to be allowed no more—and said, "Go ahead, Doc."

Kravisky licked his full lips a little too obviously. "Well . . ." he murmured. "Well . . ." He stared at the ceiling. "Of course, John, I'm a rather old-fashioned type. To my mind there's nothing like good, Terran food, properly cooked, and Terran wines. On a Terraformed planet such as this it must be available."

"Such as?" asked Grimes, knowing, from his own experience, that the foods indigenous to the overcrowded and urbanized home planet were among the most expensive in the Man-colonized Galaxy.

"Please order your meal," said the voice.

"Now . . . Let me see . . . Caviar, I think. Beluga, of course. With *very* thin toast. And unsalted butter. And to follow? I think, John, that after the caviar we can skip a fish course, although Dover sole or blue trout would be good . . . Yes, blue trout. And then? Pheasant under glass, perhaps, with new potatoes and *petit pois.* Then Crêpes Suzette. Then fruit—peaches and strawberries should do. Coffee, of course, with Napoleon brandy. And something *good* in the way of an Havana cigar apiece . . ."

"Rather shaky there, aren't you?" commented Grimes.

"In the cruise ships the tucker was for free but the cigars weren't, and even duty free they were rather expensive. But I haven't finished yet. To drink *with* the meal . . . With the caviar, make it vodka. Wolfschmidt. Well chilled. And then a magnum of Pommery . . ."

"I hope that they don't send the bill to Captain Daintree," said Grimes.

The center panel of the table sank from sight. After a very brief delay it rose again. On it were two full plates, two glasses, a carafe of red wine, cutlery and disposable napkins.

"What . . . what's *this?*" almost shouted Kravisky, picking up his fork and prodding the meat on his plate with it. "Steak!" he complained.

"We were instructed to obey all *reasonable* orders," said the mechanical voice coldly.

"But . . ."

"We were instructed to obey all reasonable orders."

"Looks like it's all we're getting," said Grimes philosophically. "Better start getting used to life in the servants' hall, Doc." He pulled his plate to him, cut off and sampled a piece of the meat. "And, after all, this is not at all bad."

It was, in fact, far better than anything from *Aries'* tissue culture vats and, furthermore, had not been ruined in the cooking by the cruiser's galley staff. Grimes, chewing stolidly, admitted that he was enjoying it more than he would have done the fancy meal that the Doctor had ordered.

Even so, their contemptuous treatment by the robot servitors, and by the robots' masters, rankled.

7

THE TWO MEN slept well in their comfortable beds, the quite sound brandy that had been served with their after-dinner coffee cancelling out the effects of nervous and physical overexhaustion and the strangeness of an environment from which all the noises, of human and mechanical origin, that are so much the manifestation of the life of a ship were missing. It seemed to Grimes that he had been asleep only for minutes when an annoyingly cheerful voice was chanting, "Rise and shine! Rise and shine!" Nonetheless, he was alert at once, opening his eyes to see that the soft, concealed lighting had come back on. He looked at his wrist watch, which he had set to the Zone Time of the spaceport, adjusting it at the same time to the mean rotation of Eldorado before leaving the cruiser. 0700 hours. It was high time that he was up and doing something about everything.

He slid out of the bed. Kravisky, in his own couch, was still huddled under the covers, moaning unhappily, the voice, louder now, was still chanting, "Rise and shine!"

There was a silver tea service on the table. Grimes went to it, poured himself a cup of tea, added milk and plenty of sugar. He sipped it appreciatively. He called to the Surgeon Lieutenant, "Show a leg, you lazy bastard. Come and have your tea while it's hot."

The doctor's rumpled head emerged from under the sheet. "I *never* have tea first thing in the morning," he complained. "I always have coffee."

"You should have made your wishes known before you retired last night," said the robot voice reprovingly. *At least,* thought Grimes, *this was a change from that irritating sing-song.*

"Oh, all right. *All* right." Kravisky got out of bed, pulled his robe about his thin body, joined Grimes at the table. He slopped tea from the pot into the thin, porcelain cup, slopping much of it into the saucer. He grimaced at the first mouthful. Then he asked, "What now, John?"

"Get ourselves cleaned up. The fleet's in port, or soon will be, and not a whore in the house washed."

"How can you be so bloody cheerful?"

"I always wake up this way."

Grimes set down his empty cup, went through to the bathroom. On the shelf under the mirror were two new toothbrushes, toothpaste, a tube of depilatory cream. *Service,* he thought. *But, so far, without a smile.* By the time that he was in the shower the Surgeon Lieutenant was commencing his own ablutions, was still showering when Grimes walked back into the bedroom. The beds, he saw, had been remade. He had heard nothing, decided that they must have been removed and replaced in the same way that the table service operated. On each tautly spread coverlet was fresh clothing: underwear, a shirt, a pair of shorts, sandals. Very gay the apparel looked against the dark, matte blue of the bedspreads—the shirts an almost fluorescent orange, the shorts a rich emerald green.

He said aloud,"Uniform would have been better."

The disembodied voice replied,"We have not the facilities."

"*You* won't have to explain to the Old Man why you aren't wearing the rig of the day," remarked Grimes.

There was silence. Haughty? Hurt? But it was better than some mechanical wisecrack.

"Breakfast," said Kravisky, who had come in from the bathroom.

It was standing there on the table—a coffeepot and cups, cream, sugar, two halves of grapefruit, toast, butter, honey and two covered plates. The Surgeon Lieutenant lifted one of the covers. "The spaceman's delight," he complained. "Ham and eggs."

"What's wrong with that?"

"Nothing. But I would have preferred kidneys and bacon."

"We are not telepathic," said the smug voice.

Breakfast over, the two men dressed. They looked at each other dubiously. "And do we have to face the Old Man like this?" asked Kravisky. "You should have let me save our uniforms, John."

"There wasn't time, Doc. It was all we could do to save ourselves."

"Look. The door's opening."

"Take the escalator to the next upper floor," ordered the robot voice. "You will find the Princess von Stolzberg and the Comte de Messigny awaiting you."

"And wipe the egg off your face," said Grimes to Kravisky.

There was an office on the next floor that, judging by the equipment along two of its walls, was also the spaceport control tower. In one of the big screens swam the image of *Aries,* a silvery, vaned spindle gleaming against the interstellar dark. It was the sight of his ship that first caught Grimes' attention but did not hold it for long. Inevitably his regard shifted to the woman who stood to one side of the screen, the tall woman with her hair braided into a golden coronet, sparkling with jewels, clad in a flowing white tunic of some diaphanous material that barely concealed the lines of her body. He smiled at her but her blue eyes, as she looked back at him, were cold. To her right was the tall man to whom they had talked the previous evening. He was in uniform, black and gold, with four gold bands on the cuffs of his superbly tailored tunic, a stylized, winged rocket gleaming on the left breast. So appareled he was obviously a spaceman, although, as Grimes well knew, it takes far more than gold braid and brass buttons to make an astronaut.

"Henri," said the girl quietly, "these are the two . . . gentlemen from the *Aries.* Mr. Grimes, this is Captain de Messigny."

De Messigny extended his hand without enthusiasm. Grimes shook it. It was like handling a dead fish. Kravisky shook it. The Comte said in a bored voice, "Of course, I am, as it were, only the Acting Harbourmaster. As the senior Master of our own small merchant fleet I was requested to make the arrangements for the landing of your ship." He waved a hand and a hitherto dull screen lit up, displaying what was obviously a plan of the spaceport. "But what is there to arrange? As you see, we can accommodate a squadron. Our own vessels are in their underground hangars, so the apron is absolutely clear. All that your Captain has to do is to set down *Aries* anywhere within the landing area."

"If he's as good a ship-handler as certain of his officers . . ." sneered the girl.

"Now, Marlene, that was quite uncalled for. You did make a small contribution to their crack-up, you know." He waved his hand again, and a triangle of bright red flashing lights appeared on the plan. "Still, I have actuated the beacons. They will serve as a guide."

"Has Captain Daintree been informed, sir?" asked Grimes.

"Of course."

"Has he been informed of the . . . er . . . circumstances of our landing?"

De Messigny smiled. "Not yet, Lieutenant. I told him last night that you were unable to get into direct radio contact with your ship, but no more than that. It will be better if you make your own report on the loss of the re-entry vehicle."

"Yes . . ." agreed Grimes unhappily.

"Very well, then." The tall man made casual gestures with his right hand. Some sort of visual code? wondered Grimes. Or did the controls of this fantastic communications equipment possess built-in psionic capabilities? Anyhow, de Messigny waved his hand and another screen came alive. It depicted the familiar interior of the control room of *Aries* and, in the foreground, the face of the Senior Communications Officer. His eyes lit up with recognition; it was obvious that he could see as well as be seen.

"Captain Daintree," snapped de Messigny. It was more of an order than a request.

"Yes, sir. In a moment."

And then the Old Man was glaring out of the screen. "Mr. Grimes! Mr. Kravisky! Why are you not in uniform?"

"We . . . we lost our uniforms, sir."

"You *lost* your uniforms?" Daintree's voice dropped to a menacing growl. "I am well aware, Mr. Grimes, that things seem to happen to you that happen to no other officer in the ship but, even so . . . Perhaps you will be so good as to explain how you mislaid the not inexpensive clothing with which the Survey Service, in a moment of misguided altruism, saw fit to cover your repulsive nakedness."

"We . . . we lost the re-entry vehicle, sir."

There was a long silence, during which Grimes waited for his commanding officer to reach critical mass. But, surprisingly, when Daintree spoke, his voice was almost gentle.

"But you didn't lose yourselves. Oh, no. That would be too much to hope for. But I shall have to make some sort of report to my Lords Commissioners, Mr. Grimes, and you may care to assist me in this duty by explaining. If you can."

"Well, sir, we were coming in to a landing on the surface of Lake Bluewater. As instructed."

"Yes. Go on."

Grimes looked at the girl, thought that he was damned if he was going to hide behind a woman's skirts. She returned his gaze coldly. He shrugged, no more than a twitch of his broad shoulders. He faced the screen again, saying, "I made an error of judgment, sir."

"An expensive one, Mr. Grimes, both to the Service and to yourself."

And then the Princess Marlene von Stolzberg was standing beside the Lieutenant. "Captain Daintree," she said haughtily, "your officer was not responsible for the loss of your dynosoar. If anybody was, it was I."

Daintree's heavy eyebrows lifted. "*You,* Madam?"

"Yes. It was my hour for water-skiing on the lake, and I saw no reason to cancel my evening recreation because of the proposed landing. I did not think, of course, that any Captain in his right senses would send his advance party down to a planetary surface in such an archaic, unhandy contraption as a dynosoar. Your Mr. Grimes was obliged to take violent evasive action as soon as he saw me cutting across his path. Furthermore, my two watchbirds, seeing that I was in danger, attacked the re-entry vehicle which, in consequence, crashed."

"Oh. Captain de Messigny, is this lady's story true?"

"It is, Captain Daintree."

"Thank you. And may I make a humble request, Captain?"

"You may, Captain."

"Just refrain, if you can, from holding tennis tournaments on the landing field or from converting the apron into a rollerskating rink when I'm on *my* way down. Over," he concluded viciously, "and *out!*"

8

THEY WATCHED *ARIES* come in—de Messigny, the Princess and, a little to one side, Grimes and Kravisky. Grimes had thought it strange that the spaceport control tower should be left unmanned at this juncture, but the two El Doradans, coldly and amusedly, had informed him that the electronic intelligences housed therein were quite capable of handling any normal landing without any human interference. Grimes did not like the way that the Comte slightly stressed the word "normal."

They stood there, the four of them, on the edge of the apron, well clear of the triangle of red lights. Above them, on gleaming wings, wheeled and hovered a quartet of flying things that looked like birds, that must be four of the watchbirds about which Grimes had already heard, which, in fact, he had already encountered. (*And,* he thought glumly, *there was still the enquiry into the loss of the re-entry vehicle to face.*)

The two El Doradans ignored their mechanical guardians. The Lieutenant could not, wondering what would happen should he make some inadvertent move that would be construed by the electronic brains as an act of hostility. He started to edge a little further away from Marlene von Stolzberg and de Messigny, then, with an audible grunt, stood his ground.

They saw the ship before they heard her—at first a glittering speck in the cloudless, morning sky and then, after only a few seconds, a gleaming spindle. She was well in sight when there drifted down to them the odd, irregular throbbing of an inertial drive unit in operation, no more than an uneasy mutter to begin with but swelling to an ominous, intermittent thunder, the voice of the power that had hurled men out among the stars.

But this was all wrong. On any civilized world, or on any civilized world other than this, there would have been an honor guard, ranks of soldiers, in ceremonial uniform, drawn to rigid attention. There would have been antique cannon with black powder charges to fire a salute to the Captain of a major Terran war vessel. There would have been flags and ceremonial. But here, here there was only one man—and his uniform, after all, was a mercantile one—and one woman. A self-styled Princess, perhaps, but even so . . . *And,* thought Grimes, *there's also Kravisky and myself, but dressed like beach boys.*

Lower dropped the ship, and lower, the noise of her Drive deafening now, every protrusion, every mast, turret and sponson that broke the smooth lines of her hull visible to the naked eye. From a staff just abaft her sharp stem the ensign of the Survey Service—a golden S on a black field, with the green, blue and gold globe of Earth in the upper canton—was broken out, streamed vertically upwards. Grimes did not have to turn to see that there was no bunting displayed from the masts of the spaceport administration buildings. Perhaps, he thought, there were in the Universe aristocrats sufficiently courteous to put out more flags to celebrate the arrival of snotty-nosed ragamuffins from the wrong side of the tracks, but the only aristocratic quality to be found in abundance on El Dorado was arrogance.

She was down at last, a shining, metallic tower poised between the buttresses of her tripedal landing gear. She was down and until the moment that Captain Daintree cut the Drive, an egg trapped between one of the huge pads and the concrete of the apron would have remained unbroken. And then the sudden silence as the machinery slowed to a halt was broken by the almost inaudible hissings and creakings as the ship's enormous mass adjusted itself to the gravitational field of the planet.

There were other soft noises behind the original reception party. Grimes turned. Three air cars of graceful, almost fragile design were coming in to a smooth landing, each attended by its pair of hovering watchbirds. From the first stepped a fat, bald, yellow-skinned man, his gross body draped in a dark blue robe. From the second emerged a tall, thin individual, black coated, gray trousered, wearing on his head a black hat of antique design. The occupant of the third car was a superbly made Negro, clad in a leopard skin flung carelessly about his body.

Grimes turned again, stiffening to attention, as he heard the bugles. *Aries* had her ramp out now, extending to the ground from the after airlock door. Stiffly, the two Marine buglers marched down it and as they set foot on the apron, raised their gleaming instruments to their lips and sounded another call. Twenty Marines came next, under their

Major, and formed two ranks on either side of the foot of the ramp. Then Captain Daintree appeared in the circular doorway, all black and gold and starched white linen, his cocked hat on his head, his ceremonial sword at his side, his decorations gleaming on his breast. He was followed by Surgeon Commander Passifern, looking a little (but only a little) ill at ease in his full dress finery. Marlene von Stolzberg whispered something to her companions and giggled.

Slowly, more like a humanoid robot than a man, Captain Daintree marched towards the waiting group, Passifern keeping step behind him. He glared at Grimes and Kravisky, standing there in their gaudy civilian clothes. His glance flickered over the others. Grimes could almost hear him thinking; who was in authority? Somehow he contrived a salute that included all of them. De Messigny answered it with a casual flip of his hand toward the gold-crusted peak of his cap, then stepped forward. He said,"We have already met at long range, Captain Daintree."

"Yes, M'sieur le Comte."

"Allow me to introduce the Princess Marlene von Stolzberg . . ." Daintree bowed slightly. "And Lord Tarlton of Dunwich, our Physician in Residence . . ." The tall, thin man in the black coat extended a pale hand; Daintree gripped it briefly. "And the Baron Takada . . ." The fat Oriental hissed and bobbed. "And Hereditary Chief Lobenga . . ." The big Negro's handshake made Daintree wince visibly. But his voice was cold and formal as he said, "To complete the introductions, this is Surgeon Commander Passifern, my Senior Medical Officer."

There was a long silence, broken by Daintree. He stated, "You asked for our assistance. Might I suggest that this is hardly the place to discuss the details. Perhaps Her Highness and you . . . er . . . gentlemen would care to step aboard my ship. I take it that you are representative of your government."

"We have no government, Captain Daintree, such as you understand the word," said de Messigny. "But it was decided that this little group here was best qualified to meet you. Will it be possible for you and Commander Passifern to come with us to the city? We shall provide transport."

"Very well," said Daintree. He looked at Grimes as he added, "I assume that your own atmosphere fliers are not harassed by careless sportsmen and sportswomen."

Grimes flushed as he heard Marlene von Stolzberg laugh softly.

9

CAPTAIN DAINTREE COULD not spare the time for an interview with the two officers of the advance party; he, with Dr. Passifern, was making his preparations and arrangements for the trip to the city, on which he and the Surgeon Commander would be accompanied by the Paymaster Lieutenant who was Daintree's secretary and by the Lieutenant of Marines. But Commander Griffin had time to spare. No sooner had Grimes and Kravisky mounted to the head of the ramp than the public address speakers were blatting their names, ordering them to report at once to the Commander's office.

They would have liked to have changed into more suitable attire, and Kravisky, in fact, did suggest that they do so. But that 'at once' at the end of the announcement had a nasty, peremptory ring to it, and Grimes knew Griffin far better than did the Surgeon Lieutenant. So they hurried through the ship, acutely conscious of the amused glances directed at them by the officers and ratings they encountered in the alleyways. Grimes heard one man mutter to his companion, "These officers don't half have it good! Looks like they've been on a bleeding holiday . . ."

And now the holiday, such as it it had been, was over. Griffin, seated behind his tidy desk, regarded them coldly, his fat face sullen under the sandy hair.

"So," he said. "So." There was an uneasy silence. "So you lose an expensive re-entry vehicle. Even if it can be salvaged, there will be repairs. So you rejoin the ship looking like a pair of beach bums." His podgy hands shuffled papers. "There will have to be an official report, you know. Or didn't that occur to you?"

"It had occurred to me, sir," replied Grimes.

"I am pleased to hear it, although I was far from pleased with the verbal report you made to the Captain. There is one important thing that you must learn, Mr. Grimes, and that is that although an officer is automatically a gentleman he should not, repeat not, allow chivalry to interfere with his duty. If that woman had not admitted that she was to blame for the loss of the dynosoar, the consequences to you could have been extremely serious, affecting most adversely your future career in this Service. As it is . . ." He grinned suddenly, relaxed visibly. "As it is, I hope that they never salvage that archaic contraption. It's always been a pain in the neck to me. Sit down, both of you." He pushed a box of cigarettes across his desk. "Smoke. And now, before you go away to start putting things down on paper in your best officialese, tell me in your own words just what has been happening to you."

Grimes told the Commander the full story, omitting nothing. Griffin was amused but, at the same time, annoyed. He said,"I gain the impression that everybody on this bloody planet has a title, except the butler. And he's a robot."

"That's the very impression that we gained," Grimes told him. "And even their robot servitors are snobs."

"You can say that again," declared Kravisky, and told again the story of the superb meal that he had ordered but not received.

"And yet they want our help . . ." mused the Commander. "It must have hurt their pride to have to call in outsiders. Whatever sort of a jam they're in, it must be a serious one."

"Have you any idea what it is, sir?" asked Grimes.

"Haven't a clue. Oh, it's something medical, we all know that much. But a world like this must be healthy. This Lord Tarlton of Dunwich, he used to be *the* physician on the planet of that name, although then he was plain Dr. Tarlton. He was the head of their College of Medicine, and we all know how highly a Dunwich degree is regarded throughout the Galaxy. As a diagnostician, he was a recognized genius. It seems incredible that he should be incapable of handling this emergency, whatever it is. What do you think, Kravisky? As a doctor, I mean."

"I think the same as you do, sir."

"And these others . . . I've been doing my homework in the microfiled Encyclopedia Galactica Year Books. Baron Takada. A multimillionaire on his planet of birth, Kobe. Flew the coop when the local income tax collectors got too avaricious. But known as much for his metaphysical researches as for his wealth. Hereditary Chief Lobenga, onetime native, and ruler, of New Katanga. Stinking rich, of course, but made his own world too hot to hold him by his dabbling in the more unsavory varieties of black magic."

"And the Princess?" asked Grimes.

Griffin chuckled. "She seems to have made quite an impression on you. Just a spoiled popsy from Thuringia. Too much money and didn't like to have to plough any of it back into the welfare of the miners and factory hands. Sold out at a pretty profit and bought her way into the El Dorado Corporation. De Messigny? Not even a millionaire but had a name as a space yachtsman and freelance explorer. I suppose that these people wanted somebody who was more or less their breed of cat to captain their merchant ships."

"All these titles . . ." said Kravisky.

"Fair dinkum, most of 'em. I often think that all these stories about effete aristocrats are put out by the aristocrats themselves. After all, *they* have practiced selective breeding for centuries . . ." He leaned back in his chair. "Money snobbery, snobbery of birth . . . It makes a pretty picture, doesn't it? And you two were in the picture. I suppose that we all are, now." His manner stiffened. "But if there's to be any shore leave, which I doubt, I shall impress upon every bastard aboard this ship, every officer, every rating, that he is to wear his uniform with *pride.*

"And, talking of uniforms . . ."

"We'd better get changed, sir," said Grimes.

"You'd better," said Griffin.

10

CAPTAIN DAINTREE AND the officers who had accompanied him returned from the city the following morning, delivered back to the spaceport by one of the graceful flying cars. The captain went straight to his own quarters, accompanied by Griffin, who had received him at the airlock. Dr. Passifern went straight to the ship's well-equipped laboratory, where his own staff was awaiting him. Paymaster Lieutenant Hodge and Lieutenant Lamont, of the Marine Corps, made their way to the wardroom, where all the off-duty officers, including Grimes, were already gathered.

"And what have you to say for yourself, Purser?" demanded Lieutenant Commander Cooper.

Hodge, a slight, clerkly young man, made a major production of drawing a cup of coffee from the dispenser. He sipped it, made a grimace. He complained, "*They* serve much better espresso than this . . ."

"You did more than drink coffee," stated Cooper.

"We did," said the Marine, stroking the luxuriant mustache that was supposed to give him a martial appearance. "We did. We sat around trying to look intelligent while our lords and masters conferred with all the counts and barons and princes and whatever."

"Any princesses?" asked somebody.

"Yes. There was one, come to think of it. A quite tasty blonde piece. Which reminds me, she gave me a letter for you, young Grimes."

"Never mind Mr. Grime's love life," said Cooper a little jealously. "That can wait. Why were we asked to call here? Or is that classified?"

"It is," Hodge told him primly. "No doubt the Captain will release such information as he sees fit when he feels like it."

"But we weren't told to say nothing of what we *saw*," pointed out Lamont.

"Can I have my letter?" asked Grimes.

"Later, later. It will keep."

"Mr. Grimes!" snapped Cooper, "I will not have the wardroom turned into a bear garden. You will please refrain from laying hands upon the brutal and licentious soldiery. Please continue, Mr. Lamont."

"Well, Pilot, we were taken to the city, as you know. That air car was really posh. Some sort of Inertial Drive but fully automated. There was a girl in charge of it, a Lady Jane Kennelly, one of those really snooty redheads, and she never laid so much as a pinky on the controls, just said in a bored voice, 'Head Office,' and the thing replied—there was a speaker on the console—'Head Office, your ladyship. Certainly, your ladyship.' I felt like saying, 'Home, James, and don't spare the horses,' but the Old Man gave me such a dirty look that I thought better of it.

"She, this Lady Jane, wasn't in a conversational mood and neither was the Old Man, so *nobody* talked. It was only a short flight, anyhow. We passed over what looked like farms, but more like gardens than farms, if you know what I mean. We saw big, specialized machines working in the fields, but never a human being.

"Then we came to the city. Oh, I know that we've all seen it from the air, but you have to be flying through it, below the level of the towers, really to appreciate it. Just towers, spires, rather, and each of them standing in its own park. Not many people around, and nobody looking to be in any sort of a hurry. Quite a few machines like oversized beetles pottering around in the gardens. My own interest in botany doesn't go beyond things you eat and drink, like cauliflowers and hops, but even I could see that just about every species of flower in the whole damn Galaxy must have been in full bloom in those beds.

"We dropped down on to a lawn in front of the really big tower, so tall that the big, golden standard flying from its peak was half-obscured by a wisp of low cloud. And it's not one of those flimsy, reinforced plastic jobs, either. Solid granite, it looked like. Solid granite, and polished, with a bit of gold trim here and there. Not at all gaudy. Like a huge tombstone, a, multimillionaire's tombstone, in good taste.

"Lady Jane said, in her cool voice, 'This is the end of the penny section.' She made it quite clear that she'd done her job and that what happened next was none of her concern. The door of the car opened and we got out. The Old Man first, then Doc, then the Pusser's pup, then myself. We were hardly clear of the car when the door shut and it lifted and went wiffling off down the avenue. So we stood there, sort of shuffling our feet and coughing politely. Shuffling our feet? That grass felt good. I'd have loved to have kicked off my boots and walked on it barefooted.

"By this time the Old Man was looking more than somewhat thunderous. He was just about to say something when I saw a big door opening at the base of the tower. And one of those damned mechanical voices that seemed to be coming from nowhere, or everywhere, said, very politely, 'Please to enter, gentlemen.'

"So we entered."

"And then?" pressed Cooper. "And then?"

"I think that's as far as we can take you," Hodge told him severely. "I think we've told you too much already."

"What about my letter?" asked Grimes.

"Shut up!" snarled the Navigator. He turned again to the Marine and Paymaster Lieutenant. "But you must know what it's all about."

"Yes, we know," Hodge told him smugly. "But until we have the Captain's permission we cannot tell you."

Lamont looked at the clerical officer with some distaste. Obviously he disliked having his story spoiled by this over-meticulous observance of regulations. He said, "I don't think that I'm contravening the Official Secrets Act or its Survey Service equivalent if I tell you that, although we saw quite a few people in the city, we didn't see a single child. Neither did we see in any of the parks and gardens we flew over anything that looked like a children's playground . . ."

There was a silence while those in the wardroom pondered the implications of Lamont's statement. It was broken by Grimes. "And now can I have my letter, Lamont?"

"What a one-track mind!" said Cooper, almost admiringly.

"Perhaps it's the right track," Grimes told him.

"Do you think *they* haven't tried it, lover boy?" sneered the Lieutenant Commander.

11

AS SOON AS he was able Grimes got away from the wardroom, hurried to his spartan dogbox of a cabin. He looked at the letter for quite a long while before he opened it. The envelope was pale blue and conveyed, by appearance and texture, an impression of expensiveness and quality. The address, Grimes decided at last, was typewritten, although he had never either seen or heard of a machine with Gothic characters. He grinned faintly. With that type, *Herr Leutnant* would have looked so much better than the plain, ordinary *Lieutenant.*

There was a tiny tab on the back of the envelope that made for easier opening. Grimes pulled it and the flap fell away. Immediately he was conscious of a hint of perfume, remembered it as the scent that the princess had worn at the time of their last meeting. He began to feel even more impatient, extracted the sheet of paper and unfolded it. It, too, was pale blue, deckle-edged, luxurious to sight and touch. The letter, apart from the firm, decisive signature, had been written by the same machine as the address. *Dear Mr. Grimes,* he read. *Having met and talked with your Captain I now realize how thoughtless and selfish my behavior was on the occasion of your landing on Lake Bluewater. On this world we are prone to forget that the mores of other planets are different from our own. Perhaps, when Captain Daintree grants shore leave, you would care to be my guest.*

Marlene.

He pursed his lips and whistled softly. *But it means nothing,* he told himself. *Just* noblesse oblige. *Or throw the good doggie a nice bone.* The Universe was full of people who said,"But you must stay with us . . ." And then were surprised and pained when you turned up their front doorstep, suitcase in hand. In any case, it yet remained to be seen whether or not Daintree would allow planet liberty.

The bulkhead speaker burped, then announced, "Attention all! Attention all! This is the Captain speaking. It is my pleasure to announce that the local authorities have agreed to permit shore leave. Arrangements will be made for sightseeing trips and the like. Details will be promulgated by Heads of Departments." There was a pause, then Daintree added, "Mr. Grimes to report to me at once."

So he can tell me that my leave is stopped, thought Grimes glumly.

"Sit down, Grimes." Captain Daintree was almost affable.

Grimes sat down.

"Ah, yes, Mr. Grimes. This business of the loss of the re-entry vehicle . . ."

"Sir?"

Surprisingly, the Old Man grinned. "There was a film made of the whole sorry business. One of those damned robots in Spaceport Control records, as a matter of routine, every spaceship arrival and departure. I saw the film." He grinned again. "I must admit that the spectacle of the Princess attired in a single water ski was, shall we say, distracting. An odd woman, Her Highness. But attractive, very attractive . . ."

Come to the point, you old goat, thought Grimes.

"Yes, very attractive and very frank. She freely admits that she was to blame for the bungled landing. Not that I altogether agree with her, but even so . . . As I've already said, an odd woman. With odd tastes. Very odd. Believe it or not, she wants to be your hostess during this vessel's stay on El Dorado." Daintree paused. Grimes decided not to say anything. Daintree went on, "I told her, of course, that your duties toward the ship come first. You have still to write the report on the loss of the dynosoar. You have still to oversee and carry out salvage operations; I declined Comte de Messigny's offer of equipment and robot submarine workers. Then you have to write the report upon the salvage."

"Of course, sir."

"I'm glad that you show some sense of responsibility. But when all these tasks have been completed to my satisfaction, *and not before,* you will be granted leave until the vessel's departure. This Princess von Stolzberg appears to be one of the rulers of this planet, insofar as they have rulers, so it might be advisable to, as it were, humor her."

"Thank you, sir."

"Don't thank me, Mr. Grimes. Thank Her Highness. *When* you get around to meeting her again."

If I ever do, thought Grimes.

Daintree, who had his telepathic moments, laughed. "You will, Mr. Grimes. You will. This medical emergency, I suppose that it could be called that, of theirs is more serious and less straightforward than an epidemic of measles. If *their* quacks can't come up with an answer, I can't see our Dr. Passifern and his aides getting to the bottom of the problem in five seconds flat . . ." He opened the box on his desk. "Smoke, Grimes?"

"My pipe if I may, sir."

"Suit yourself." Daintree tapped the end of his cigarette on his thumbnail to ignite the tobacco, looked thoughtfully at the thin, rising spiral of smoke. "Yes, quite a problem they have, these El Doradans. It all goes to show that money cannot buy happiness . . ."

"But with it, sir," pointed out Grimes, "you can, at least, be miserable in comfort."

"Ha! Very good. I must remember that. But it is a most peculiar situation. As you know, they bought this planet and then, at enormous expense, terraformed it. With improvements. They stocked with all the flora and fauna necessary for sport as well as food. Insofar as the animal and plant kingdoms are concerned the normal cycle of birth, procreation, death has been in operation from the very start. Insofar as the humans are concerned, there are no births. No, that's not quite correct. Some of the women were pregnant when they came here. The youngest of the children born on El Dorado is now a girl of seventeen."

"Something in the air, or the water, sir?"

"Could be, Grimes. Could be. But I'm a spaceman, not a quack. I wouldn't know. If it is, it must be something remarkably subtle. And you'd think that such an . . . agent? would affect the plants and the livestock as well as the people."

Grimes, flattered by the honor of a conversation with the normally unapproachable Captain, ventured another opinion. "Do you think, sir, that they called us in so that we could . . . ? How can I put it? A sort of artificial insemination by donor? Only not so artificial."

"Mr. Grimes!" Daintree at once reverted to his normal manner. "I ask, no, I order, you to put such ideas out of your alleged mind at once. These people, and never forget it, are in their own estimation the aristocrats of the Galaxy. They want children to inherit their wealth, their titles. But they made it quite clear to me that such children must be sired by themselves, not by mongrel outsiders." His face darkened. "I don't mind telling you, Mr. Grimes, that I was furious when I heard that term used. But, bear this in mind, if there are any incidents during this vessel's stay on El Dorado it will go hard, very hard indeed, with those responsible. You will learn, Mr. Grimes, that a senior officer has very often, too often, to subordinate his own true feelings to the well-being of his Service. We are not, repeat not, a drunken, roistering crew of merchant spacemen. We are Survey Service, and every man, from myself to the lowest mess boy, will comport himself like a gentleman."

And one definition of a gentleman, thought Grimes, *is a man who takes his weight on his elbows . . .*

"And this offer of hospitality by the Princess von Stolzberg, it's no more than her way of apologizing to you and to the Survey Service. You'd better not get any false ideas."

"I won't, sir."

"Very well. That will do. See the Commander and ask him for the necessary men and equipment for the salvage of the re-entry vehicle. I have already told him that the entire operation is to be directly under your charge."

"Very good, sir."

Grimes got to his feet, stiffened to attention in salute, turned about smartly and marched towards the door. Daintree's snarl halted him abruptly.

"Mr. Grimes!"

"Sir?"

"I know that I'm only the Captain, but may I point out that it is not correct to take official leave of a senior officer with a pipe stuck in the middle of your cretinous face?"

"Sorry, sir."

"And, Mr. Grimes, may I request that you watch your manners when you are mingling with the aristocracy?"

"I'll do my best, sir."

"Your best, on far too many occasions, has not been good enough. Get out!"

Ears burning, Grimes got out.

12

THE FOLLOWING MORNING, Grimes started the salvage operations.

As a unit of the Survey Service fleet, *Aries* was rich in all manner of equipment. She was a fighting ship but, officially at least, her prime function was exploration and survey, and a newly discovered watery world cannot be properly surveyed without underwater gear. Insofar as the raising of the dynosoar was concerned, the engineers' workshop was able to supply, at short notice, what little extra was needed.

Commander Griffin had let Grimes have one of the work boats, a powerful little brute fitted with inertial drive, aboard which the engineers had installed a powerful air compressor. There were coils of tough, plastic hose, together with the necessary valves and connections. There was a submarine welding outfit and a good supply of metal plates of various shapes and sizes. There were scuba outfits for Grimes and for the men who would be working with him.

Shortly after dawn, the airlock high on *Aries'* side opened and the work boat, muttering to itself, slid out, wobbled a little in midair and then, with Grimes at the controls, set course for the further end of Lake Bluewater, from the surface of which a light mist, golden in the almost level rays of the morning sun, was lazily rising. The Lieutenant was already in his skin-tight suit, as was the remainder of the working party, but had yet to put on his helmet and flippers. The interior of the boat was crowded with men and gear, and there would have been little room to undress and dress. By his side, similarly attired, sat Chief Petty Officer Anderson, a big man, grossly fat until you looked at him more closely and realized that the fat was solid muscle. Baldheaded, baby-faced, he was peering intently at the submerged metal indicator that had been installed on the work boat's control console. He looked up from the instrument, said, "If I were you, Mr. Grimes, I'd run to the end of the lake and then come back in short sweeps." It was a suggestion, not an order, but when a C.P.O. suggests to even a senior officer the words carry weight.

Grimes replied, cheerfully enough, "I'll do just that, Chief."

He reduced thrust, lost altitude as he approached the beach, so that the boat would make its run barely clear of the surface of the water.

"If I were you, Mr. Grimes, I'd keep her up. That way we get a better spread on the detector beam. Once we've found the wreck we can come down for finer location."

"All right, Chief." *And,* thought Grimes, *what the hell do we have officers for? To carry the can back, that's all.*

Slowly, steadily, the boat grumbled its way out over Lake Bluewater. There were not, Grimes was relieved to see, any early morning swimmers or water-skiers. An audience he could do without, especially when such an audience would have with it a horde of watchbirds. He had good reason to dislike those robotic guardian angels.

To the end of the lake flew Grimes, toward the clump of screw pines that backed the sandy beach. "Anything yet, Chief?" he asked Anderson.

"No, sir." Then, in a reproachful voice, "You should have released the marker buoy, Mr. Grimes."

"I didn't know that we had one."

"I installed it myself, Mr Grimes." Anderson was the ship's expert, rated and paid as such, in submarine operations.

"Why wasn't it an automatic release?" demanded the Lieutenant.

"Come, sir. You know better than that." The intonation made it quite clear that in the speaker's opinion Grimes didn't. "What if you make a crash landing on some hostile planet, in the sea, and don't want to give the potential enemy a chance to pinpoint your position? And hadn't you better watch those trees, sir?"

"I am watching them." Slowly Grimes turned the boat, started his sweeps back and forth across the width of the lake.

"Now!" exclaimed Anderson. "That's it, sir, I think. Bring her down, if you don't mind . . . Stop her. Now, back a little. Slowly, sir, slowly. Right a little . . . Stop her again. Cut the drive."

Gently, making only the slightest of splashes, the work boat settled to the surface. With the drive shut down it was suddenly very quiet. The air drifting in through the open windows carried a faint, refreshing tang of early morning mist. One of the ratings in the after compartment muttered, "This is a bit of all right. We should have brought fishing tackle."

Anderson turned his head. "You'll have all the fishing you want, Jones. It's a big, tin fish we've come to catch."

The men who knew what was good for them laughed.

"There are goldfish in the lake," contributed Grimes. His remark was received in silence. He shrugged. "All right, Chief. I'll go down to make the preliminary inspection. I'll let you know when I need help."

"Have you had your antibend shot, sir?" asked Anderson in a way that implied that all officers have to be wet-nursed, junior officers especially.

"Yes, Chief. Now, if somebody will help me on with my helmet..."

Anderson himself picked up the transparent sphere, lowered it carefully over Grimes' head, connected up the air pipes to the shoulder tank. The speaker inside the helmet said tinnily, "Testing, sir. Testing. Can you read me?"

"Loud and clear." The Lieutenant eased himself up from his chair, sat on the ledge of the open window, his back to the water. "Flippers," he said.

He saw Anderson speaking into the microphone that somebody had handed him. "If I were you, sir, I'd go down on the line."

"Just what I am doing, Chief. But I'll wear my flippers just the same."

Anderson strapped the large fins on to his bare feet, then made a thumbs-up gesture. Grimes replied in kind, leaned far back and then let himself fall. He knew that this unorthodox method of entering the water would not please the C.P.O. and, even as he hit the surface with a noisy splash, heard, through his helmet speaker, Anderson admonish the men, "Just because an officer does it that way you're not to. See?" The failure to place a hand over the microphone was probably deliberate.

He hit the water and, at once, started to sink. With his equipment and the disposable weights at his belt he had negative buoyancy. He looked up at the shimmering mirror that was the surface, broken by the black hull of the boat. Using his hands and feet he turned about his short axis until he was upright, saw the weighted line, pale-gleaming in the blueness. One tentative kick took him toward it. He grasped the rough-textured cord with one hand and hung there for a little while to get his bearings, to become acclimatized.

"Are you all right, Mr. Grimes?" It was Anderson, giving his famous imitation of a mother hen.

"Of course I'm all right, Chief."

The water was cool, but far from cold. And there was the exhilarating sensation of weightlessness. It was like being Outside in Free Fall but better, much better. There was the weightlessness but not the pressing loneliness, the dreadful emptiness. And the skin-tight suit was almost as good as nudity, did not, as did space armour, induce the beginnings of claustrophobia.

Grimes looked down.

Yes, there was the wreck, her canopy gaping open like the shell of some monstrous bivalve. Grimes hoped that it was not too badly damaged by the ejection; if it were not so, the task of sealing the ruptured hull would be much easier. Up through the gaping opening drifted a school of gleaming, golden fish. And that was a good sign; it meant that nothing larger and dangerous, even to Man, had taken up residence.

He relaxed his grip on the cord, felt it slide through his hand as he dropped slowly. Then, raising a flurry of fine silt, his flippered feet were on the bottom. He was about three yards from the sunken dynosoar.

"Calling C.P.O. Anderson," he said into the built-in microphone. "Making preliminary inspection." He heard the acknowledgement.

Clumsily at first, he swam the short distance. For several minutes he checked the canopy. Yes, it could be forced back into place and, where too badly buckled, welded over. If necessary, lines could be sent down from the boat to lift the valves to an upright position before their closure. Satisfied, he swam aft, closely inspecting the fuselage as he did so. He could find no damage on the upper surface; the damaged skin must be on the underside, buried in the silt. An air hose to blow the muck clear? Yes, but would it be necessary? After all, when expelled from the hull by air under pressure the water would have to have somewhere to go to, somewhere to get out from, and whatever holes there were in the plating could have been designed for that very purpose.

"Chief!"

"Yes, Mr. Grimes?"

"Tell your men to have the welding gear and the compressor and hoses ready. Then come down yourself as soon as you can."

"Coming, sir."

Something made Grimes look up. The big C.P.O. was already on his way, falling like a stone, weighted by the gear that he was grasping in both of his huge hands. Behind him trailed two of the air hoses and another cable, the power line of the welding equipment. Using his flippered feet only he controlled his descent, made a remarkably graceful landing not far from where Grimes was standing.

"And what do you have in mind, Mr. Grimes?" he asked.

"Get the canopy shut and sealed, Chief. Might run an air hose in at that point. Then blow her out, and up she comes."

"Up she comes you hope, sir. Or she'll blow up, with the internal pressure. Explode, I mean."

"There are holes in the fuselage aft, the holes through which the water entered in the first place."

"Then we have to seal them, Mr. Grimes."

"That shouldn't be necessary, Chief. As far as I can see, they're on the bottom of the hull."

"Very good, sir. But what if she topples? If I were you, I'd seal those holes and fit 'em with non-return valves."

"You arcn't mc. And don't forget that the brute was designed to fly this way up. Surely she'll *float* this way up."

Stiffly, "I'm not qualified in aerodynamics, sir."

"But you are in hydrodynamics. All right, then. Do you think she'll topple once she starts to lift?"

Anderson, leaving the tool case and the weighted ends of the hoses with Grimes, swam slowly around the wreck. "No," he admitted when he returned. "She shouldn't topple." He stayed by the fore end of the dynosoar, stood in the silt and tried to lift one of the parts of the open canopy. It moved but with extreme reluctance. Grimes heard the man, a massive, black-glistening giant in his suit, grunt with effort.

"I thought of running lines down from the boat," he said.

"And pull the boat over, or under? No, sir. That wouldn't do at all."

No, thought Grimes. It wouldn't. Not if he hoped to get any shore leave on this planet.

"We'll have to cut the flaps and then weld them back into place."

"Now you're talking, sir. With your permission?" he asked, then paused.

"Of course. Carry on, Chief."

"Jones, Willoughby, Antonetti. Down here, on the double. Bring the cutting torches, a bundle of sheeting and that bundle of metal strip. Jump to it! "

"And a spear gun," added Grimes. "If we have one." He had a feeling that the knife at his belt would be inadequate. Helplessly, he looked at the huge, silvery torpedo shape that was approaching them, that was staring at them from glassy eyes as big as dinner plates.

Then, even through his helmet, he heard the muffled whirring of machinery and laughed. "Don't worry, Chief," he said. "Just remember what the Captain told us all and comport yourself like a gentleman. You're on camera."

13

AFTER A WHILE Grimes decided to leave the frogmen to it. It was obvious that Anderson and his team knew what they were doing. The Lieutenant had tried to lend a hand; he had realized quite soon that any attempt at supervision by himself would lead only to confusion, but the C.P.O. had made it quite plain, without actually saying so, that he was just being a bloody nuisance. So he said, in his best offhand manner, "Carry on, Chief. I'll take a dekko at this submarine camera of theirs. Let me know if you want me."

"That'll be the sunny Friday!" he heard somebody mutter. He could not identify the voice.

He put the busy scene—the flaring torches, the exploding bubbles of steam, the roiling clouds of disturbed silt—behind him, swam slowly toward the robot midget submarine. And was it, he wondered, called a watchfish? At first he thought that the thing was ignoring him; its two big eyes remained fixed on the salvage operations. And then he noticed that a small auxiliary lens mounted on a flexible stalk was following his every movement. He thumbed his nose at it, the rude gesture giving him a childish satisfaction.

Then he swam on lazily. He should, he realized, have brought a camera with him. One of Anderson's team had one, he knew; but he knew, too, that all the footage of film would be devoted to the raising of the dynosoar. Shots of the underwater life of this lake would have made an interesting addition to *Aries'* film library. More than a score of worlds must have contributed their share of fresh water fauna. There were graceful shapes, and shapes that were grotesque, and all of them brightly colored. Some were fish and some were arthropods and some—he mentally christened them "magic carpets"—defied classification. And there were plants, too, a veritable subaqueous jungle that he was approaching, bulbous trunks, each crowned with a coronal of spiky branches. If they *were* plants. Grimes decided that he didn't like the look of them, changed course and paddled toward a grove of less menacing appearance, long green ribbons stretching from the muddy bottom to just below the silvery surface. Among the strands and fronds flashing gold and scarlet, emerald and blue, darted schools of the smaller fishes. And there was something larger, much larger, pale and glimmering, making its slow way through the shimmering curtains of waving water weed. The Lieutenant's right hand went to the knife at his belt.

It, whatever it was, was big. And dangerous? It wasn't a fish. It had limbs and was using them for swimming. It undulated gracefully through the last concealing screen of vegetation, swam towards Grimes.

It was a woman.

It was, he saw without surprise (now that the initial surprise had passed) Marlene von Stolzberg.

He looked at her. She was wearing a scuba outfit not unlike his own, with the exception of the skintight suit. Her own golden skin was covering enough. And she was carrying what looked like a spear gun, although it was much stubbier than the weapons of that kind with which he was vaguely familiar.

He said, "Dr. Livingstone, I presume . . ."

He save a frown darken her mobile features, clearly visible in the transparent helmet. From his own speaker came her voice, "That was neither original nor funny, Mr. Grimes." Then, as she saw his expression of astonishment, "It wasn't much trouble for us to find out what frequency you people are using."

"I suppose not. Your Highness."

"I hope, Mr. Grimes, that you don't mind my engaging in my usual activities. I promise to keep well clear of the salvage operations."

"It's your lake," he said. "And you don't seem to have any watchbirds with you this time."

"No," she agreed. "But . . ." She gestured with a slim arm. Grimes saw, then, that she was not alone, that she was attended by two things like miniature torpedoes. The analogy came into his mind, like a shark with pilot fish. But she was no shark, and pilot fish are mere scavengers.

They hung there in the water, silent for awhile. Grimes found that it was better for his peace of mind to concentrate his regard upon her face. She said at last, "Shouldn't you be looking after your men?"

"Frankly, Your Highness, they can manage better without me. Chief Petty Officer Anderson and his team are experts. I am not."

"You're not very expert in anything, Mr. Grimes, are you?" A grin rather than a smile robbed her words of maliciousness.

"I'm a fairish navigator and a better than average gunnery officer."

"I'll have to take your word for that. Well, Mr. Grimes, since the work seems to be going along very well without you, will you accompany me in a leisurely swim?"

"Cor stiffen the bleedin' crows, Chiefie," remarked an almost inaudible voice,"officers don't half have it good!"

"Watch your welding, Willoughby," came Anderson's reprimand. "That's all that *you're* good for."

There was a gusty sigh, and then, "Well, I suppose we can't *all* be fairish navigators and better than average gunnery officers . . ."

Grimes wished that he were wearing only a breathing mask and not a full helmet. The cool touch of water would have soothed his burning face. He heard the girl's light, tinkling laughter. But he knew that Anderson would deal with matters back at the wreck. And he knew, too, that the petty officer would never report to higher authority that Grimes had wandered away from the work in progress. What was it that he, Anderson, had said once? "You'll be a captain, and higher, while I'm still only a C.P.O. Why should I make enemies?" Then, when asked why he, himself, did not put in for a commission, he had replied,"I like things the way they are. I enjoy reasonable standards of comfort and authority without responsibility. A junior officer has responsibility without authority."

The Princess Marlene was swimming away now, slowly. She paused, made a beckoning gesture. Should he follow? Yes. To hell with it, he would. He said, "Chief Petty Officer Anderson."

"Sir?"

"One of the . . . er . . . local ladies has offered to take me on an inspection of the lake bottom. It could be useful. Let me know when you want me."

"Very good, sir."

As Grimes followed the girl it was not the lake bottom that he was inspecting.

He caught up with her. One of the silvery miniature torpedoes dashed toward him threateningly, then suddenly (in response to a telepathic command?) sheered away. He said, "You have vicious pets, Your Highness."

"Not vicious, Mr. Grimes. Just faithful."

"That's an odd word to use about machines."

"These, like our watchbirds, are more than mere machines. They have organic brains. These pilot fish of mine, for example, are essentially the small but highly intelligent cetaceans of Algol III with mechanical bodies." She must have read his expression. "Come, come, Lieutenant. There's no need to look so shocked. This is no worse than the dog's brains used by your Psionic Radio Officers as amplifiers. Not so bad, in fact. Our watchbirds and watchdogs and pilot fish have freedom to move about in bodies which, in fact, are rather superior to their original ones."

"It's . . . it's not the same."

She laughed scornfully. "That's what I've been telling you, my good man. One of your poodle's brains in aspic would sell its soul for the motility enjoyed by our guardians."

"Is that what you call them?"

"That is the general term. Yes."

"And their prime function is to protect their owners?"

"Their only function. Yes."

"So if I . . . tried to attack you?"

"It would be the last thing you ever did, Mr. Grimes."

He laughed grimly. "I don't think I'll try it out, Your Highness."

"You'd better not. But would you like a demonstration?"

"Not on me."

She stopped, holding herself stationary in the water with gentle movements of her long, graceful limbs. She pointed with the hand holding the gun. "Look! Do you see the rock ogre?"

"The *what?* I see something that looks like a slime-covered rock."

"That's it. Perhaps the only really dangerous denizen of these waters. Native to Australis. Excellent eating, properly prepared. That's why we introduced it."

"It looks innocent enough."

"But it's not. Keep well back and watch closely."

She swam toward the thing. Then, with explosive suddenness, three triangular flaps sprang back on the top of the rough shell and, uncoiling with lightning rapidity, a thick stalk shot out straight at the girl, a glistening limb tipped with a complexity of writhing tentacles and gnashing mandibles. Grimes cried out in horror and pulled his useless knife, but he was not fast enough, could never have been fast enough.

The pilot fish were there before him, flashing past him at a speed that, even under the water, produced a distinct whine. One of them dived into the orifice from which the stalk had been extruded, the other attacked the ogre's head. It was over almost as soon as it had been begun.

Mere flesh and blood, from whatever world, could not withstand the concerted onslaught of the little, armoured monsters. Only seconds had elapsed, and the girl was hanging there in the water, laughing, while the pilot fish frisked around her like dogs demanding an approbatory pat. An unpleasant, brownish mist was seeping up from the base of the stalk and from the debris of torn and severed tentacles, still feebly twitching, and broken mandibles at the head of it.

Grimes was sickened. It was not by the death of a dangerous (and, he had been told) edible creature, life owes its continuance to the destruction of life. It was by the genuine pleasure and amusement in the girl's high, clear laughter. But blood sports, he told himself dourly, have always been the favorite recreation of the so-called aristocracy.

He said, "I must be getting back to work. Your Highness."

He started off in what he thought was the right direction, but the water was heavily befogged by the ichor from the dying rock ogre. He did not see the other rock, the shell, rather, until he was almost on top of it. He screamed and made a frantic effort to avoid the terrifying head that shot out at him. He felt a sharp pain in his side as something grazed his body, heard a dull *thunk* followed by another. The rock ogre seemed to go mad, writhing violently. The thick stalk caught Grimes a flailing blow in the belly, knocking him well clear. He caught a glimpse, vivid, unforgettable, of Marlene, an underwater Artemis, with her gun raised for another shot.

And then the pilot fish swept in to finish the job.

14

HE SPRAWLED ON the muddy bottom, his hand pressed to the rent in his suit, the rent in his skin. He could feel the warmth of blood. He did not know how badly he was injured, but, at this moment, the imminence of suffocation was of far greater importance than loss of blood. He feared that the pipes from his liquid air tanks to his helmet had been buckled or severed and then, agonisingly, he was able to breathe again. It was the blow to the stomach that had knocked all the air out of his lungs.

She was hanging in the murky water looking at him, her stubby weapon pointing directly at him. A woman with a gun can be a frightening sight; a naked woman with a gun is always clothed in deadly menace.

Grimes whispered hoarsely, "Put that down!"

At first he thought that she had not heard him, then, slowly, she let her hand fall until the muzzle, from which protruded the lethal head of a new dart, was directed downward.

She muttered, "I'm sorry . . ."

Grimes tried to laugh. "What for? You saved my life."

"Yes." There was an odd note of astonishment in her voice. "Yes. I did, didn't I?" She made a swimming motion toward him. "Are you hurt?"

"I don't know how badly. That brute kicked like a mule. And one of your bolts grazed me. At least, I think it was only a graze."

"Mr. Grimes, sir," came Anderson's voice. "Mr. Grimes, what's been happening? Shall I send help?"

"Just a slight tussle with the local fauna, Chief. I got a little beaten up, but nothing serious. I'm on my way back to the wreck now."

"If I were you, sir, I'd surface and get back into the boat. I'll send Jones up to you. He's qualified in First Aid."

"Better do as the man says," advised the Princess. "I'll see you to your boat. Can you move?"

Grimes worked his arms and legs experimentally. "Yes. Nothing seems to be broken."

He detached the weights from his belt, let his buoyancy carry him upward. The girl floated alongside him. He could not help looking at her. She was beautiful in her nudity, and the few black trappings that she wore accentuated the golden luminosity of her skin. She was beautiful, but he shuddered as he remembered how she had appeared in her moment of bloodthirsty triumph, and how she had stared at him over her aimed weapon.

The silver mirror shattered into a myriad of glittering shards, and then Grimes' head was above the surface. He could not see the boat at first, turned slowly and clumsily in the water until she came into view. She was a long way off. He was, he knew, in no danger of drowning but doubted if he could swim that far in his weakened condition. And he did not know how much blood he was losing, or how fast.

She said softly, "Relax, Mr. Grimes. Let me see . . ."

He felt her alongside him, was conscious of her gently probing fingers, was aware that she had widened and lengthened the tear in his suit.

"Men are such babies," she remarked. "The skin's hardly broken."

He said stiffly, "I hope that your darts aren't poisoned."

"Of course not. And now, just follow me."

He followed her, thinking that it was the first time in his life that he had followed a girl, a naked girl at that, without a sense of pulse quickening anticipation.

He sat there glumly in the boat, dabbing the graze just below the ribs on his right side with antiseptic-soaked cotton wool. The Princess Marlene had helped him to mount the short ladder and then had left him, swimming away toward the further shore, a graceful, golden shape around which sported the two silver pilot fish. His self-administered first aid was interrupted by the man Jones, stocky, competent, revoltingly cheerful, who, as soon as he had clambered inboard, removed his helmet and tanks and then performed a like service for Grimes.

"Now, let's have a look at that, sir. Something bite you? Only a scratch, though. All the same, you'd better have an antibiotic shot. We don't know what microorganisms are in the water, do we? And perhaps whatever it was that attacked you didn't brush his or her teeth this morning. Ha, ha!"

"Ha, ha," echoed Grimes.

"No need to take your suit off for the shot, sir. I'll just pump it in where the fabric's already been torn away." He went to the first aid box and produced a syrette. "Now, sir, just stretch a little . . . Fine. Didn't feel a thing, sir, did you?"

"No," admitted Grimes.

"Then if you're all right, sir, I'll get aft and start the compressor." He reached across the Lieutenant and picked up the microphone. "Jones here, Chiefie. I've seen to Mr. Grimes; he's all right. O.K. to start pumping the air into her?"

"O.K.," came Anderson's voice. "She's all sealed and I think she'll hold. But stand by to stop the compressor at once if I give the word."

"Will do, Chiefie."

Jones left the seat by Grimes' side, made his way toward the stern. After a second or so came the steady throb of the machine; Grimes, looking overside, saw one of the heavy plastic hoses jerking rhythmically, as though alive. It reminded him unpleasantly of a rock ogre's trunk.

"She's holding," announced the Chief Petty Officer. Then, "Mr. Grimes, can I have a word with you, sir?"

"Yes, Chief?" replied Grimes into the microphone.

"She's holding all right. And, as you said, those holes aft are just made to order for blowing the water out of . . . I think she's starting to lift . . . Yes. May I suggest, sir, that you and Jones take in the hose as she comes up, in case she topples . . . Oh, yes, and tell Jones to stop the air pump. Now."

The compressor stopped. Grimes joined the rating where the hoses ran overside, helped him to bring the one that had been used inboard. It was heavy work, and soon both men were sweating uncomfortably under their skintight suits. Then Jones shouted, "There she blows!"

Yes, thought Grimes, she did look something like a whale as she broke surface, although she wasn't blowing. And then, around her, bobbed up the heads of Anderson and his men in their spherical helmets. The lieutenant saw the petty officer's mouth moving; it seemed odd that his voice should be coming from the speaker in the boat. "Jones! Throw us a line, will you?"

Jones picked up a coil of light nylon cord, with a padded weight spliced to the end, heaved it expertly—and even more expertly Anderson raised a hand to catch it. What followed was a pleasure to watch, was seamanship rather than spacemanship. A heavier line was passed, made fast to a ringbolt that had been welded to the dynosoar's nose, the other end of it taken by Jones to the towing bitts that had been installed at the boat's stern. And then, one by one, the Chief Petty Officer last of all, the salvage crew clambered back on board, stripping off their helmets and flippers, hauling to the surface their tools and other equipment. The competent Anderson insisted on checking every item before he was satisfied. Not until then did he lower his big frame into the seat beside Grimes.

"If I were you, sir, I'd tow her in and beach her by the spaceport."

"I'll do just that, Chief."

"Feel up to handling the boat yourself, sir?"

"Of course. It was only a scratch I got, and a few bruises."

"Right you are, then, Mr. Grimes."

Grimes started up the inertial drive, lifted the boat about a foot clear of the water. He turned her, slowly and carefully, avoiding the imposition of any sudden strain on the towline. He headed for the spaceport beacon inshore from the beach. He realized that he was scanning the water for any sign of the Princess Marlene. But either she had left the lake and gone home—wherever home was—or was still disporting herself in its depths. But she could look after herself, he thought grimly. She could look after herself very well indeed, she and her murderous pilot fish.

He heard Anderson mutter something uncomplimentary and concentrated on his steering; the boat, with that sluggish weight pulling her stern down, was behaving rather oddly. But he got the hang of it and beached the re-entry vehicle without incident.

He sat with Anderson in the boat while the men busied themselves about the stranded dynosoar.

"If I'd been you, sir," said the Chief Petty Officer, "do you know what I'd have done?"

About *what?* wondered Grimes. About the salvage? About the rock ogres? About Her Highness the Princess Marlene von Stolzberg?

"What would you have done?" he snapped.

"I'd have had the engineers waterproof an I.D. unit, complete with power cells, taken it down to the dynosoar, started it up—and Bob's your uncle!"

"He may be yours, Chief. But he's obviously not mine."

"But the way it was was all right, Mr. Grimes. It gave my boys some very useful training."

"Join the Interstellar Survey Service and see the bottom of the sea."

"I must remember that, sir. And that's the way that I wish it always was. But . . . Do you mind if I talk to you man to man, for a little?"

"Do just that."

"I know Captain Daintree. Well. He was an Ensign when I was a rating fourth class, before I started specializing. We've sailed together many a time."

"Go on."

"I won't talk. And the men won't talk. If they did, they'd know that all the Odd Gods of the Galaxy wouldn't be able to save 'em. From me. You officers think that you have power, but"—he slowly opened and then clenched a huge hand—"this is where the real power lies, in any Navy."

"Go on."

"Your report, sir. May I suggest that you tore your suit on a piece of jagged wreckage?"

"But why, Chief?"

"You were supposed to be in charge of the job, Mr. Grimes. The Captain won't like it if he hears that you went off with a girl." Anderson blushed incongruously. "A *naked* girl, at that."

"You've got a dirty mind, Chief."

"I haven't," said Anderson virtuously. "But the Old Man, I beg your pardon, sir, the Captain, and some of the other officers mightn't be so broadminded as me . . ."

Grimes chuckled.

"It's not funny, sir."

"Perhaps not. But your double entendre was."

"Yes, it was," admitted the C.P.O. complacently. "I must remember *that*, too . . . But what I'm getting at is that you should edit, or censor, your report on the operations rather carefully. The torn suit, for example; and the jagged projection . . ."

"Thank you, Chief. But no. I can't do it."

"If you knew the bloody liars that I've known that are Admirals now!"

"But they, Chief, didn't have a robot midget submarine sniffing around and recording everything. I've no doubt that whoever sent it will be willing to run the film for Captain Daintree. I'm afraid I have to tell the truth."

Anderson did not look happy. Grimes could imagine what was running through his mind. The petty officer, he knew, was concerned about him, but he would not be human if he were not also concerned about himself. Grimes could almost hear Daintree's voice. "And what were you thinking of, Chief Petty Officer Anderson, to allow a young, inexperienced officer to wander off alone in waters in which all sorts of dangerous creatures might have been—were, in fact—lurking? Not alone, you say? Even worse, then. In the company of a young lady who has already demonstrated her criminal irresponsibility."

"Yes," said Grimes. "I can edit my report."

"But this submarine camera you mentioned, sir . . ."

"We'd started work on the salvage, Chief, and then Her Highness came along and told me about the dangers on the lake bottom, such as the rock ogres. I thought that I'd better see one for myself so that I'd be able to identify them. Not only did she show me one but also persuaded it to give a demonstration of its capabilities. The demonstration was almost too effective . . ."

"Yes, Mr. Grimes. That should do, very nicely." He grinned. "You'll make Admiral yet."

"I hope so," said Grimes.

15

SHE CAME TO pick up Grimes the following afternoon, her blue and scarlet air car bringing itself down to a perfect landing hard by the main ramp of *Aries*. Daintree, rather to the Lieutenant's surprise, had granted him shore leave, but, at the same time, had made it quite clear that he was doing so only because Grimes had somehow—"and only the Odd Gods of the Galaxy know how!" swore the Captain—contrived to make powerful friends on this strange world. So Grimes, clad in the regulation go-ashore rig that was almost a uniform—slate gray shirt with the golden S embroidered on the breast, matching shorts and stockings, highly polished black shoes—marched down the gangway, a grip in either hand. In the bags, in addition to his toilet gear, he had packed changes of clothing, of some of which Daintree would not have approved. Too, he should have obtained official permission to take from the ship the deadly little Minetti automatic pistol which, together with spare clips of ammunition, was concealed among his shirts. Over his right shoulder was slung a camera, over his left shoulder a tape recorder. "The complete bloody tourist!" Lieutenant Commander Cooper had remarked when he encountered Grimes in the airlock.

But Grimes did not mind. He had decided a long time ago that, much as he liked ships, he did not like big ships. It would be good to get away from *Aries* for a few days or even, with luck, longer. It would be good to eat something better than the mediocre fare served up in the officers' mess. It would be good to be able to wear clothing not prescribed by regulations.

The door of the air car, a fragile-seeming, beautifully designed machine, a gay, mechanical dragonfly, adorned with nonfunctional fripperies, opened as Grimes approached it. The Princess Marlene raised a hand in casual greeting. She was dressed today in a flimsy green tunic, the hem of which came barely to mid-thigh. On her slender feet were rather ornate golden sandals. Her hair was pulled back to a casual (seemingly casual) pony tail. She smiled, said, "Hi!"

"Your Highness," replied Grimes formally.

"Throw your gear in the back, then get in beside me."

"Will your watchbirds mind, Your Highness?" asked Grimes, looking up, rather apprehensively, to the two circling guardian angels.

"Not to worry, Mr. Grimes. They've been told that you're a member of the family, acting, temporary . . ."

"Unpaid?"

She smiled again. "That all depends, doesn't it? But jump in."

Grimes didn't jump in. This contraption seemed of very light construction compared to the ugly, mechanized beetles to which he was accustomed. He got in, watching carefully where he put his feet. He lowered himself cautiously into the cushioned seat. The door slid shut.

"Home," ordered Marlene.

There was a murmur of machinery and the thing lifted, took a wide sweep around the ship, then headed in a direction away from the distant city.

"And now," said the girl, "what do they call you?"

"What do you mean, Your Highness?"

"To begin with, Lieutenant, you can drop the title, as long as you're my guest. And I want to be able to drop yours." In spite of the friendliness of her voice and manner, the "for what it's worth" was implied, although not spoken. "I don't know what planet you were born and dragged up on, but you must have some other name besides Grimes."

"John, Your . . ."

"You may call me Marlene, John. But don't go getting ideas."

I've already got them, thought Grimes. *I got them a long time ago. But I have no desire to be the guest of honor at a lynching party.*

"Cat got your tongue, John?"

"No. I was . . . er . . . thinking."

"Then don't. Too much of it is bad for you. Just relax. You're away from your bloody ship, and all the stiffness and starchiness that are inevitable when the common herd puts on gold braid and brass buttons."

You snobbish bitch! thought Grimes angrily.

"Sorry," she said casually. "But you have to remember that we, on El Dorado, regard ourselves as rather special people."

"That reminds me," said Grimes, "of two famous Twentieth Century writers. Hemingway and Scott Fitzgerald. Fitzgerald said to Hemingway, quite seriously, 'The rich are different from us.' Hemingway replied, 'Yes. They have more money.' "

"So you read, John. You actually read. A spacefaring intellectual. I didn't know that there were any such."

"There are quite a few of us, Marlene. But microfilmed editions aren't the same as *real* books."

"You'll find plenty of real books on this world. Every home has its library."

"You've room here, on this world."

"There's room on every planet but Earth for people to live as they should. But your average colonist, what does he do? He builds cities and huddles in almost exact replicas of Terran slums."

"You aren't average?"

"Too bloody right we're not. And we were determinded when we purchased El Dorado that overpopulation would never become one of our problems. But . . ."

"But?"

"But once people start dying that will be the start of the reverse process . . ." Then a laugh dispelled her sombre expression. "However did we get started on this morbid subject? And what sort of hostess am I?" Her voice suddenly became that of the guide of a conducted tour. "Slightly ahead, and to our right, you will see the Croesus Mines. They constitute the only fully automated mining operation in the Galaxy . . ."

Grimes looked. There was nothing to indicate the nature of the industrial process. There were no roads, no railways, no towering chimneys, no ugly pithead gear. There was only a low, spotlessly white building in a shallow green valley.

"Everything," the girl went on, "is subterranean, including the rail communication with our few factories and with the spaceport. We do not believe in ruining the scenery of our planet while there is ample space underground for industry. Now, coming up on our left, we see the Laredo Ranch. It is not as fully automated as it might be, but you must understand that Senator Crocker, the owner, enjoys the open air life. It irks him, he says, that he must use robot cowboys for his roundups; but that, on this world, is unavoidable . . ."

Grimes, looking out and down, saw a solitary horseman riding toward a herd of red-brown cattle. Crocker, he supposed, making do without his despised mechanical aides.

"Count Vitelli's vineyard. His wines are not bad, although they are only a hobby with him. There is some local consumption and considerable export. Most of *us*, of course, prefer imported vintages."

"You would," said Grimes sharply.

She looked at him in a rather hostile manner, then grinned. "And you, John, would say just that. But this is *our* world. We like it, and we can afford it."

"Money doesn't always bring happiness, Marlene."

"Perhaps not. But we can be miserable in comfort."

"Luxury, you mean."

"All right, luxury. And why the hell not?"

To this there was no answer. Grimes stared ahead, saw on a hilltop a grim, gray castle that was straight out of a book of Teutonic mythology. "Your *Schloss?*" he asked.

"My *what?*" She laughed. "Your pronunciation, my dear. You'd better stick to English. Yes, that is Castle Stolzberg, and in the forests around it I hunt the stag and the boar."

"Is that all you do?"

"Of course not. As you know very well I am fond of aquatic sports. And I am serving my term on the Committee of Management."

"And who lives there with you?"

"Nobody. I entertain sometimes, but at the moment I have no guests. With the exception, of course, of yourself."

"And you mean to tell me that that huge building is for *one* person?"

"Isn't it time that you started to lose your petty-bourgeois ideas, John? I warn you, if you start spouting Thorsten Veblen at me on the subject of conspicuous waste I shall lose my temper. And as for Marxism, there just isn't any exploited proletariat on El Dorado, with the exception of the lower deck ratings aboard *your* ship."

"They aren't exploited. Anyhow, what about the people on the other worlds who've contributed to your fantastically high standard of living?"

"They were happy enough to buy us out, and they're happy enough to buy our exports. And, anyhow, you're a spaceman, not a politician or an economist. Just relax, can't you? Just try to be good company while you're my guest, otherwise I'll return you to your transistorized sardine can."

"I'll try," said Grimes. "When in Rome, and all the rest of it. I shall endeavor to be the noblest Roman of them all."

"That's better," she told him.

Slowly, smoothly, the air car drifted down to a landing in the central courtyard, dropping past flagpoles from which snapped and fluttered heavy standards, past turrets and battlemented walls, down to the gray, rough flagstones. From somewhere came the baying of hounds. Then, as the doors slid open, there was a high, clear trumpet call, a flourish of drums.

"Welcome to Schloss Stolzberg," said the girl gravely.

16

"WELCOME TO SCHLOSS Stolzberg," she said, and suddenly, for no immediately apparent reason, Grimes remembered another girl (and where was she now?) who had told him, "This is Liberty Hall. You can spit on the mat and call the cat a bastard." He could not imagine the Princess Marlene using that expression, no matter how friendly she became. And Castle Stolzberg did not look, could never look like Liberty Hall. If there were no dungeons under the grim (or Grimm, he mentally punned) pile, there should have been.

He got out of his seat, stepped to the ground, then helped the girl down. Her hand was pleasantly warm and smooth in his. She thanked him politely and then turned her head to the car, saying, "We shan't be needing you again. You can put yourself to bed."

A gentle *toot* from somewhere in the vehicle's interior replied, and it lifted smoothly, flew toward a doorway that had suddenly and silently opened in the rough stone wall.

"My bags . . ." said Grimes.

"They will be taken to your room, John. Surely, by this time, you have come to learn how efficient our servitors are."

"Efficient, yes. But they've given *me* enough trouble, Marlene."

"They were doing the jobs for which they were designed. But come."

She put her hand in the crook of his left arm, guided him to a tall, arched doorway. The valves were of some dark timber, iron studded, and as they moved on their ponderous hinges they creaked loudly. Grimes permitted himself a smile. So the robots who ran this place weren't so efficient after all. Even a first trip deck boy would have known enough to use an oil can without being told.

Marlene read his expression and smiled in reply, a little maliciously. "The doors *should* creak," she said. "If they didn't, it would spoil the decor."

"Talking of noises . . . Those rowdy dogs we heard when we landed . . . Also part of the decor, I suppose. And was all that baying a recording?"

"Part of the decor, yes. As for the rest, real hounds in real kennels, I told you that hunting was one of my amusements."

"And where do you keep the vampire bats?"

"You improve with acquaintance, John. But this is not Transylvania."

They were in the main hall now, a huge barn of a place, thought Grimes. But he corrected himself. A barn, when empty, can be a little cheerless; when full its atmosphere is one of utilitarian warmth. This great room was cheerless enough, but far from empty: Only a little daylight stabbed through the high, narrow windows, and the flaring torches and the fire that blazed in the enormous fireplace did little more than cast a multiplicity of confused, flickering shadows. Ranged along the walls were what, at first glance, looked like armoured men standing to rigid attention. But it was not space armour; these suits, if they were genuine (and Grimes felt that they were), had been worn by men of Earth's Middle Ages. By men? By knights and barons and princes, rather; in those days the commonality had gone into battle with only thick leather (if that) as a partial protection. And then had come those equalizers—long bow and crossbow and the first, cumbersome firearms. Grimes wondered if any of this armour had been worn by Marlene's ancestors, and what they would think if they could watch their daughter being squired by a man who, in their day, would have been a humble tiller of the fields or, in battle, a fumbling pikeman fit only to be ridden down by a charge of iron-clad so-called chivalry. *Grimes, you're an inverted snob,* he told himself. He shivered involuntarily as he thought that he saw one of the dark figures move. But it was only the shifting fire and torchlight reflected from dull-gleaming panoply and broad-sword. But he looked away from it, nonetheless, to the antique weapons high on the walls, then to the dull, heavy folds of the ancient standards that sagged heavily from their shafts.

He said, "A homey little place you have here."

It was, of course, the wrong thing. Marlene did not think the remark at all funny. She said icily, "Please keep your petty bourgeois witticisms for your ship."

"I'm sorry."

She thawed slightly. "I suppose that the castle *is* home, but never forget that it is history. These stones were shipped from Earth, every one of them."

"I thought that you came from Thuringia."

"Yes, I did. But we're all Terrans, after all, if you go back far enough. And that's not very far."

"I suppose not."

She led him across the hall, past a long, heavy banqueting table with rows of high-backed chairs on either side. She took a seat at the head of it, occupied it as though it were the throne it looked like. In her scanty, flimsy attire she should have struck a note of utter incongruity, but she did not. She was part of the castle, and the castle was part of her. Like some wicked, beautiful queen out of ancient legend she seemed, or like some wicked, beautiful witch. The pale skin of her bare limbs was luminous in the semidarkness, and her body, scarcely veiled by the diaphanous material of her dress, only slightly less so.

She motioned Grimes to the chair at her right hand. He was amazed to find that it was extremely comfortable, although the wood, at first, was cold on the backs of his legs. He wondered what subtle modifications had been made to the archaic furniture, and at what expense. But he hadn't had to pay the bill. He saw that a decanter of heavy glass had been set out on the table, and with it two glittering, cut crystal goblets. Marlene poured the dark ruby wine with an oddly ceremonial gesture.

She said matter-of-factly, "Angel's blood, from Deneb VII. I hope you Like it."

"I've never tried it before." *(And that's not surprising,* he thought, *at the price they charge for it, even on its world of origin.)* "But does it . . . er . . . match the decor?"

Surprisingly she smiled. "Of course, John. In the old days, when the prince and his knights feasted here, there were delicacies from all over the then known world on this table . . ."

Salt beef and beer, thought Grimes dourly, remembering his Terran history.

"To . . ." she started, raising her glass. "To . . . to your stay on this world."

She sipped slowly and Grimes followed suit. The wine was good, although a little too sweet for his taste. It was good but not good enough to warrant a price of forty credits a bottle, Duty Free and with no freight charges.

Away from the gloomy main hall, the rest of the castle was a surprise. Spiral staircases that had been converted into escalators—rather a specialty of El Doradan architectural engineering—spacious apartments, light, color, luxury, all in the best of taste, all in the best of the tastes of at least five score of worlds. At last Marlene showed Grimes into the suite that was to be his. It was a masculine apartment, with no frills or flounces anywhere, almost severe in its furnishings but solidly comfortable. There was a bar, and a playmaster with well-stocked racks of spools and a long shelf with books, real books. Grimes went to it, took from its place one of a complete set of Ian Fleming's novels, handled it reverently. It was old, but dust jacket, cover, binding and pages had been treated with some preservative.

"Not a First Edition," the girl told him, "but, even so, quite authentic Twentieth Century."

"These must be worth a small fortune."

"What's money for if not to buy the things you like?"

There was no answer to that, or no answer that would not lead to a fruitless and annoying argument.

She said, "Make yourself at home. I have a few things to attend to before I change for dinner. We dine, by the way, at twenty hundred hours. In the banqueting hall."

"Where we had the wine?"

"Where else?" She paused in the doorway that had opened for her. "Dress, of course."

Of course, thought Grimes. He decided that in these surroundings his uniform mess dress would be the most suitable. He looked for his bags so that he could unpack. He could not find them anywhere. A disembodied voice said, "Lord, you will find your clothing in the wardrobe in your bedroom."

His clothing was there, hung neatly on hangers, folded away in drawers. But of the Minetti pistol and its ammunition there was no sign.

"Damn it!" he swore aloud, "where the hell's my gun?"

"It will be returned to you, Lord, when you leave the castle. Should Her Highness wish you to accompany her on a boar hunt, a *suitable* weapon will be provided."

Suitable? A Minetti, used intelligently, could kill almost any known life form.

"I'd like my own weapon back," snapped Grimes.

"For centuries, Lord, it has been the rule of this castle that guests surrender their weapons when accepting its hospitality. We are programmed to maintain the old traditions."

"It's a good story," said Grimes. "Stick to it."

In an atmosphere of mutually sulky silence he went to the bar and poured himself a Scotch on the rocks, without too many rocks.

17

SLOWLY, SAVORING ITS expensive aroma and smoothness, Grimes finished his Scotch. He poured himself a second glass, being more generous this time with the ice. He let it stand on the glass top of the bar, prowled through the apartment. He considered leaving it to explore the castle, but decided that this would be one sure and certain way of incurring the Princess Marlene's hostility. He found a window that had been concealed by heavy drapes, stared out through it. His quarters were high in the building, must be just under the battlemented roof, but as the casement could not be opened he was not able to stick his head out to confirm this. For long minutes he looked out at the scene—the wooded hills, the green valleys, the silvery streams, over which poured the golden light of the afternoon sun. Earth born and bred as he was, he found himself pining for the sight of another human habitation, of a road with vehicles in motion, of a gleaming airliner in the empty sky.

He returned to the sitting room, examined the catalogue of playmaster spools that stood by the machine. It was comprehensive, fantastically so, putting to shame the collection of taped entertainment available in *Aries'* wardroom, or in any of her recreation rooms. There were the very latest plays and operas, and there were recordings of films that dated bank to the dawn of cinematography. There was too much to choose from. Fleming, perhaps? A screened version of one of the 007 novels? Grimes had read them all during his course in English Literature at the Academy and, although his tastes had been considered somewhat odd by his fellow students, had enjoyed them. A title in the catalogue, CASINO ROYALE, caught his eye. He pressed the right sequence of buttons.

The playmaster hummed gently and its wide screen came to glowing life. Grimes stared at the procession of gaudy credits, then at the initial scene depicting the meeting of the two agents in the *pissoir*. Surely this was not James Bond as he had been described by the master storyteller, as he had been imagined by his reader. And then, a little later, there was Sir James Bond, dignified in his mansion with its lion-infested grounds. Grimes gave up, settled down to enjoy himself.

Suddenly, annoyingly, the screen went blank. It was just as Mata Bond had been snatched by the scarlet-uniformed Horse Guardsman, who had galloped with her up the ramp of an odd-looking spacecraft. Grimes got up from his chair to investigate. As he did so, that smug mechanical voice remarked, "Lord, I regret that there is no time for you to witness the end of this entertainment. If you are to perform your ablutions and attire yourself fittingly before escorting Her Highness to dinner, you must commence immediately."

Grimes sighed. After all, he had not become the Princess's guest to spend all his time watching films, no matter how fascinating. He went through to the bedroom, shed his clothing, and then into the bathroom. It operated on the same principle as the one in the spaceport's accommodation for transients. When he came out, he found that somebody (something?) had removed the clothes that he had intended to wear from the wardrobe, disposed them neatly on the bed. He resented it rather; why should some complication of printed circuits or whatever take it upon itself to decide that he, a man, would be correctly attired for the occasion only in gold braid, brass buttons and all the trimmings?

He shrugged, thought, *Better play along*. He got into his underwear, his stiff white shirt, his long, black, sharply creased trousers with the thin gold stripe along the outer seams. He carefully knotted the bow tie, wondering who, with the exception of officers in the various services, ever wore this archaic neckwear. The made-up variety lasted far longer and looked just as good, if not better. He put on his light, glistening black shoes. He got into his white waistcoat, with its tiny gilt buttons, and finally into the "bum-freezer" jacket, on the breast of which were three miniature medals. Two of them were for good attendance, the third one really meant something. ("It will be either a medal or a court martial," the Admiral had told him. "The medal is less trouble all round.")

There was a knock at the outer door of the apartment. "Come in!" he called. He was expecting the Princess; surely the mechanical servitors, whatever they looked like (he had imagined something multi-appendaged, like an oversized tin spider) would not knock. The door opened and a man entered. No, not a man. Humanoid, but nonhuman, nonorganic. No attempt had been made to disguise the dull sheen of metal that was obvious on the face and hands. He (it?) was attired in a livery even more archaic than Grimes' uniform: white stockings and knee breeches over silver-buckled shoes, a black, silver-buttoned claw-hammer coat, a froth of white lace at the throat. An elaborately curled white wig completed the ensemble. The face was as handsome as that of a marble statue, and as lifeless. The eyes were little glass beads set in pewter. Nonetheless, the gray lips moved. "Lord, Her Highness awaits you."

"Lead on, MacDuff."

"My name, Lord, is not MacDuff. It is Karl. Furthermore, Lord, the correct quotation is, 'Lay on, MacDuff.' "

"Lead on, anyhow."

"Very well, Lord. Please to follow."

It was like a maze, the interior of the castle. Finally the robot conducted Grimes along a gallery, the walls of which were covered with portraits of long dead and gone von Stolzbergs. Men in armour, men in uniform, they glowered at the spaceman; and those toward the end, those with the Crooked Cross among their insignia, seemed to stir and shift menacingly in their ornate frames. Grimes suddenly remembered his Jewish grandmother and could just imagine that proud old lady staring fiercely and contemptuously back at these arrogant murderers. And there were the von Stolzberg ladies. He didn't mind looking at them, and he had the feeling that they didn't mind looking at him. Although the earlier ones tended to plumpness, many of them had something of the Princess Marlene in their appearance, or she had something of them in hers.

A door at the end of the corridor silently opened. Karl stood to one side, bowing. Grimes went through.

The room beyond it was brightly lit, opulent, but in its furnishings there were glaring incongruities. Weapons, however beautifully designed and finished, look out of place on the satin-covered walls of a lady's *salon*. But they caught Grimes' attention. As a gunnery specialist he could not help looking at the firearms: the heavy projectile rifles, the lighter but possibly deadlier laser guns, the peculiar bell-mouthed weapons that, in a bad light, would have been antique blunderbusses but which, obviously, were not.

"I like to have my toys around me, John," said the Princess.

"Oh, yes. Of course." Grimes felt his ears burn. He turned to face her. "I . . . I must apologize, Marlene. My . . . er . . . professional interest was rather ill-mannered."

"It was, but understandable. Although not many people can appreciate the aesthetic qualities of well-made weaponry." She added, "I'm glad that you can, John."

"Thank you."

"Sit down, unless you would rather stand."

He sat down, looking at his hostess as he did so. She was different, far different, from the naked water nymph of his first acquaintance, but still the heavy folds of her brocaded, long-sleeved, high-necked gown could not quite conceal the fluid beauty of the limbs and body beneath the golden glowing fabric, Her pale hair, platinum rather than gold in this light, was piled high on her head, and in it rather than on it was a bejewelled coronet. Yes, those weapons were beautiful, but she, too, was beautiful.

And in the same way?

"Some sherry, John?"

Her slender hand went to the slim decanter that stood on the lustrous surface of the low table between them, removed the stopper. She poured the pale wine into two glittering, fragile glasses. She raised hers, smiled, inclined her head slightly. It was more of a formal bow than a mere nod.

Grimes did his best to follow suit. They both sipped.

"An excellent Tio Pepe," he commented gravely. She need never know that it was the only wine that he could identify easily.

"Yes," she agreed. "But why put up with second best when you can import the best?"

And was there some hidden meaning in this seemingly innocent remark? But she, of all people, would never admit that any inhabitant of El Dorado was inferior to any offworlder.

"Will you take a second glass with me, John?"

"I shall be pleased to, Marlene."

Again they drank, slowly, gravely. And then, when they were finished, she extended a long, elegant arm toward him. There was an uncomfortable lag until he realized the implication of the gesture. His ears (inevitably) reddening, he got hastily (but not, he congratulated himself too hastily) to his feet, assisted her from her deep chair. Saying nothing, moving with slow grace, she contrived to take charge of the situation. Grimes found himself advancing with her toward the door, her right hand resting in the crook of his left arm. Grimes was sorry that there was not a full-length mirror in which he could see his companion and himself. The doorway gaped open as they approached it. There stood the robot Karl, bowing deeply. There stood four other humanoid robots, in uniform rather than in livery, attired as foot soldiers from some period of Earth's barbaric past. Each of them held aloft a flaring torch. All the other lights in the long corridor had been extinguished.

Slowly, in time to a distant drumbeat, they marched along the gallery—Karl, then two of the torch-bearers, then Grimes and the Princess, then the remaining pair of robots. Past the portraits they marched, past the men in the uniform of the Thuringian Navy (a service that had been disbanded after Federation), past the men in the uniforms of the armed and punitive forces of the Third Reich, past the commanders of mercenaries and the robber barons. There was a sense of uneasy menace. How much of the personality of the sitter survived in the painted likeness? There was a sense of uneasy menace, but the von Holzberg women smiled encouragingly from within their frames.

They came to a wide stairway. Surely it had not been there before. They came to the broad flight of steps, with ornate wrought-iron balustrades that led down into the fire-lit, torch-lit hall. The drums were louder now, and there was a flourish of trumpets. It was a pity that this effective entrance was wasted on the handful of serving robots that stood to attention around the long table. Grimes wished that his shipmates could witness it.

They descended the stairs, Karl still in the lead, walked slowly to the massive board. Ceremonially, the major-domo saw to the seating of Marlene; one of the lesser serving robots pulled out a chair for Grimes at her right hand. Then, suddenly, all the torches were somehow extinguished, and the only light was that from the blazing fire and from the score of candles set in an elaborately Gothic wrought-iron holder.

There was more wine, poured by Karl.

There was a rich soup served in golden bowls.

"Bisque of rock ogre," said Marlene. "I hope you like it."

Grimes, remembering the monster that had almost killed him, was sure that he would not but, after telling himself that a lobster, or even a prawn, would be a horrendous monstrosity to a man reduced to the size of a mouse, decided to try it. It was good, the flavor not unlike that of crayfish, but different. A hint of squid, perhaps? Or, just possibly, turtle? And then there was a roast of wild boar, and to accompany it a more than merely adequate Montrachet. To conclude the meal there was fresh fruit and a platter of ripe cheeses, with a red wine from Portugal, from grapes grown on the banks of the Douro.

Marlene said, "I like a man who likes *real* food."

Grimes said, "I like a woman who likes *real* food."

The robot. Karl filled their coffee cups, offered a box of Panatellas to the Princess, who selected one carefully, and then to Grimes, who took the first one to hand. And then—it was a delightfully outre touch—a jet of intense white flame appeared at the end of Karl's right index finger. He carefully lit the Princess's cigar, and then the spaceman's.

"The brandy, Karl," said Marlene, through a cloud of fragrant smoke.

"The Napoleon, Your Highness?"

"You know as well as I do that it has no more connection with the Emperor of the French than . . . than Lieutenant Grimes has. But . . . Oh, very well, then. The Napoleon."

To Grimes it was just brandy, but he had no cause for complaint.

"And what would you like to do now?" asked the Princess.

Grimes did know but could not muster up the courage to state his desire.

"Oh, yes," said the girl after an uncomfortable pause. "I told you, I think, that I am a member of the Committee of Management. Would you be interested in finding out what that entails?"

"Yes . . ." answered Grimes dubiously.

18

BEFORE ITS FANTASTICALLY costly dismantling and transportation Schloss Stolzberg had been well equipped with what, in the Middle Ages, were regarded as the finest modern conveniences. Now not even a hole in the ground somewhere in Germany marked the site of these dungeons and torture chambers; where the Castle had once brooded stood a towering block of apartments. But still there were subterranean galleries and spaces: wine cellars, storerooms, and the Monitor Vault.

"It is our obligation as members of the Committee of Management," explained the Princess, "to watch. And we, even during our tenure of office, know that we can be watched . . ."

"You mean that there's no privacy?" asked Grimes, shocked.

"I suppose that you could put it that way."

"But . . . But I thought that this was a society of . . . aristocratic anarchists."

"That's a good way of putting it, John. And a true way." She lay back in the chair set before the huge screen, relaxed, but with her fine features thoughtful. "But, can't you see, neither the aristocrat nor the anarchist suffers from false shame. I can conceive of situations in which a petty bourgeois such as yourself would be agonizingly embarrassed if he knew that he was being watched. During copulation for example, or defecation. But *we* . . ." In spite of her almost supine position she managed a delicate shrug. "But *we* . . . We *know* that it doesn't matter."

"But why this body of elected, I suppose that you are elected, Big Brothers? And Big Sisters."

"El Dorado," she told him, "could be a Paradise. But there are snakes in every Eden. When such a snake is found, he is placed aboard a small, one-man spacecraft, with whatever personal possessions he can pack into two suitcases, and a Universal Letter of Credit that will allow him sufficient funds to make a fresh start elsewhere. He is then sent into exile."

"Have there been many such cases?"

"Since the foundation of the colony, several. About a dozen."

"I'm surprised that none of these deportees has talked. Their stories, sold to newspapers and magazines throughout the Galaxy, would bring in enough to maintain them in luxury for the rest of their lives."

She smiled. "Somebody must *know* what happens, but quite a few of us suspect. After all, not much engineering skill would be required to convert a perfectly functioning ship into a perfectly functioning time bomb."

"I suppose not. But tell me, Marlene, just what does anybody have to do to get slung off this, insofar as you all are concerned, perfect world?"

"There was one man who still lusted for power, direct, personal power. Working in secret he tried to form a Party, with himself as Leader, of course, on the same lines as the old fascist and Communist Parties . . ." She almost whispered, "I was lucky not to have been involved. Anyhow, *he* went. And there was another man . . . We still have the record. I'll show you."

She made a slight gesture with her right hand. There was the slightest of humming noises, a hesitant click, and then misty forms and colors swirled in the depths of the big screen, slowly coalesced. And there was sound, too, a woman's voice screaming, *"No! Please! No!"*

Horrified, yet obsessed by a fascination of which he was afterwards bitterly ashamed, Grimes stared at the picture. It showed the interior of a cellar, and there was a naked girl, her body dreadfully elongated, stretched out on a rack, and a pale, fat slug of a man, stripped to the waist, in the act of taking a white-hot iron from a glowing brazier.

Suddenly there was an ingress of men and women, all of them armed, one of them carrying a bell-mouthed pistol like the ones Grimes had seen in Mariene's room. The report, when it was fired, was no more than a soft *chuff.* At once the torturer was trapped, emmeshed in a net of metal strands that seemed to be alive, that working with a sort of mechanical intelligence bound his hands and arms and legs and feet, swiftly immobilizing him. He fell against his own brazier, and the others left him there while they attended to his victim. Grimes could see the smoke and the steam that rose from his burning body, could hear his wordless screams (until the net somehow gagged him), thought (although this could have been imagination) that he could smell charred flesh.

The screen went blank.

"And who was that?" asked Grimes, with feeble, cheap humor. "The Marquis de Sade?"

"No. Oddly enough, a Mr. Jones from New Detroit."

"And did he . . . die?"

"Probably. But not on El Dorado."

"And how did you suspect?"

"Oh we *knew*. But his first victims were collaborators more than martyrs, and he did them no permanent damage. And that girl, for example, was expecting nothing worse (or better?) than a mild, sexually stimulating whipping. However, the Monitor sees all, knows all, and gave the alarm, but on the rare occasions that arrests are necessary we prefer that they be made by ourselves, not by robots."

"But if your Monitor is so highly efficient, why the human Big Brothers?"

"We monitor the Monitor. That first man I told you about, the would-be dictator, almost succeeded in subverting it."

"I'm not sure that I'd like to live here, Marlene."

"I'm not sure that we'd have you, John, at least not until you've made your first billion or produced cast-iron documentary evidence of a family tree going back to Adam. Or both." But the words were spoken without malice. "And now, John, would you like to see how your lords and masters are behaving themselves?"

"No," he should have said.

"They are guests at the Duchess of Leckhampton's masked ball—the Captain and Surgeon Commander Passifern."

"That sounds innocuous enough," he said, disappointed.

Again there was the languid wave of her slim hand, again there was the coalescing swirl of light and form and color. Again there was sound, distorted at first, that reminded Grimes of Ravel's *Waltz Dream.* But it was not Ravel that poured from the concealed speakers when the picture clarified; it was Strauss, rich, creamy, sensual, unbearably sweet, and to it the dancers swayed and glided over the wide, wide expanse of mirror floor, and in the background there was red plush and gilt, and overhead blazed and sparkled the crystalline electroliers.

Grimes stared, shocked, incredulous.

Crinolines and hussars' uniforms would have added the final touch but not, relieved (accentuated) only by masks and sandals and jewellery, nudity.

And yet . . .

He shifted uneasily in his seat, acutely conscious of his telltale ears. He muttered, "Surely not the Old Man and the Chief Quack . . ."

And then, as though the Monitor had heard his words (perhaps it had), he was looking directly at Captain Daintree and Commander Passifern. The two officers were not among the naked dancers. They were seated at a table against the wall, stiff and incongruous in their dress uniforms. With them was a lady, elderly, elaborately clothed, one of the few people on this world of perpetual youth and near immortality showing her age and not ashamed of it. There was a silver ice bucket, bedewed with condensation; there were three goblets in which the wine sparkled.

Fascinated, Grimes stared at the faces of his superiors. Daintree—he would—was playing the part of the disapproving puritan, his mouth set in a grim line. But his eyes betrayed him, flickering avidly, almost in time to the music, as the nude men and women swirled past. Passifern was more honest, was making no pretence. A shiny film of perspiration covered his plump features. There was more than a suggestion of slobber about his thick lips.

"Your Grace," he muttered, "I . . . I almost wish that I could join them."

The old lady smiled, tapped the Doctor on the arm with her fan. "Naughty, naughty, Commander. You may look but you mustn't touch."

"I wish that I could . . ." sighed Passifern, while Daintree glared at him.

The scene shifted again to an overall view of the ballroom. The scene shifted and, once more, the music seemed to Grimes to carry the subtle discordancies of Ravel's distortion of the traditional Viennese waltz.

The scene faded.

"Decadent," whispered Grimes to himself. "Decadent . . ."

"Do you think so, John?" asked the Princess. She answered herself, "Yes, I suppose that it is. But erotic stimulation carried to extremes is one of the ways that we have tried to deal with our . . . problem. And there are other ways . . ."

Although the screen was still dark, from the speakers drifted a throb and grumble of little drums. Gradually there was light, faint at first then flaring to brilliant reds and oranges. It came from a fire and from torches held aloft by white-robed men and women. It grew steadily brighter, illuminating the clearing in the forest, in the jungle, rather. It shone on the altar, on the squatting, naked drummers, on the rough-hewn wooden cross that stood behind the altar, its arms thrust through the sleeves of a ragged black coat, a band of white cloth like a clerical collar, where a human neck would have been, the whole surmounted by a battered black hat.

Grimes was an agnostic, but this apparent blasphemy shocked him. He turned to look at the girl. "John!" she whispered, "if you could only see your face! That cross is the symbol of a religion at least as valid as any of the others. It represents Baron Samedi, the Lord of Graveyards. But watch!"

A huge man, black and glistening, was bowing before the altar, before the . . . the idol? He was bowing low before the altar and the frightening effigy of Baron Samedi. He straightened, and Grimes saw that he carried a long, gleaming knife in his right hand. He turned to face the celebrants. His eyes and his teeth were very white in his ebony face. Grimes recognized him, saw that it was the Hereditary Chief Lobenga. Lobenga, the exile from New Katanga, the dabbler in black magic, in voodoo.

The enormous Negro called, his voice a resonant baritone, "De woman! Bring out de woman! Prepare de sacrifice! "

"The woman!" a chords of voices echoed him. "The woman!"

And while the drums throbbed and muttered, a figure, wrapped in an all-enveloping black cloak and hood, was led to the altar by four of the white-robed worshippers. Their clothing made it impossible for Grimes to determine their sex, but he thought that two of them were men, two of them women. Lobenga faced the victim, towering over her. She seemed to cringe. His left hand went out to her throat, did something, and as the stuttering of the drums rose to a staccato roar, her cloak fell away from her. Beneath it she was naked, her flesh gleaming golden in the fire-lit darkness, her hair reflecting the ruddy flames.

She did not resist. As Lobenga moved to a position directly behind the altar, between it and the cross, she allowed herself to be led forward and then, quite willingly it seemed, lay down upon the dark, gold-embroidered altar cloth. She was beautiful of face, her body perfectly formed. Even in this supine posture her breasts did not sag. She was young, or was she? On this world, thought Grimes, she could be any age at all.

Lobenga had raised his knife. Above the now-muted drums rose the voices of the communicants. "The sacrifice! The sacrifice!"

Grimes was half out of his seat. "Marlene! What's your bloody Monitor doing about it? What are *you* doing?"

"Be quiet, damn you!" she snarled.

"The sacrifice!" cried the people on the screen.

And those about the altar laid hands upon the girl, one to each ankle, one to each wrist, spread-eagling her.

"The sacrifice!"

"De white goat!" shouted Lobenga, knife upraised.

The white goat . . . the goat without horns . . . "Marlene!" Grimes' hand was on her arm. "Marlene, we must *do* something. Now. Before it's too late."

She shook him off. "Be quiet!"

And suddenly there *was* a white goat, bleating, struggling. Two men threw the animal on its side to the ground, grasping its feet, lifting it. They set it down on the girl's naked body, its back to her breasts and belly, its head between her legs. The drums throbbed softly, insistently. The priest's knife swept down; the animal's cries ceased in mid-bleat, although its now released limbs kicked spasmodically. The girl, free herself from restraining hands, held the dying body to her.

The drums were clamorous now, ecstatic, yet maintaining a compelling rhythm. All over the clearing men and women were throwing aside their white robes, had begun to dance, to prance, rather, and there was no doubt as to what the outcome would be. Lobenga had lifted the blood-spattered woman off the altar, was carrying her into the darkness. The way that her arms were twined about his neck was proof of her willingness.

"I think," said Grimes, "that I'm going to be sick."

"Karl will escort you to your quarters," said Marlene.

As he walked unsteadily through the doorway of the Monitor Vault he looked back. The girl was still staring raptly into the screen.

19

NOT SURPRISINGLY HE dreamed that night, when at last he fell into an uneasy sleep.

There was the nightmare in which naked women and huge white goats, erect on their hind legs, danced to the music of Ravel's *Waltz Dream,* while across the mirror floor, scattering the dancers, stalked Baron Samedi.

There was that other dream, even more frightening.

It seemed that he half woke up but was unable to stir a muscle, to open his eyes more than the merest slit. There was a strange, acridly sweet smell in the air. There were low voices of a man and a woman. He could just see them, standing there by his bed. He thought that, in spite of the darkness, he could recognize them.

"Are you sure?" asked the woman.

"I am sure," replied the man. Although there was now no trace of accent, that deep, rolling baritone was unmistakable. "The white goat."

"The goat without horns." Then, "But I do not like it."

"It must be done."

"Then do it now. Get it over with."

"No. The . . . conditions must be right. You do know enough about these matters."

"After what I watched on the Monitor, I am not sure that I want to know any more than I know already."

"But you watched."

"Yes. I watched."

"Did he?"

"Some of it."

"Come." The larger of the two figures was already out of range of Grimes' vision.

"All right."

And then both of them were gone, and Grimes slept deeply until morning.

20

HE WAS AWAKENED by the inevitable disembodied voice calling softly at first, then louder, "Lord, it is time to arise . . ."

It took a considerable effort to force his gummy eyelids open. His head was fuzzy, his mouth dry and stale-tasting. The uneasy memory of that last nightmare persisted.

There was a condensation-clouded glass on the table beside his bed. He picked it up in a rather shaky hand, drained it gratefully. The chilled, unidentifiable fruit juice was tart and refreshing. After it he began to feel a little better.

"And what's on today, I wonder?" he muttered, more to himself than to any possible listener.

"You will perform your ablutions, Lord," replied the irritating unseen speaker. "Then you will partake of breakfast. And then you will join Her Highness at the hunt." There was a pause. "And would you care to place your order for the meal now?"

"What's on?" asked Grimes, feeling faint stirrings of appetite.

"Anything that you may desire, Lord."

"No stipulations about 'reasonable orders'?"

"Of course not, Lord." The voice was mildly reproachful. "As a guest of Schloss Stolzberg you may command what you will."

"As a Lord, acting, temporary, unpaid, you mean. It was a different story when I was a mere spaceman. But you wouldn't know about that, would you?"

There was the suggestion of a smirk in the reply. "Lord, to the Monitor all things are known."

"Are you part of the Monitor, then?"

"I am not permitted to answer that question, Lord."

"Oh, all right. Skip it. Now, breakfast. A pot of coffee, black, hot and strong. Sugar, but no milk or cream. Two four-minute eggs. Hens' eggs, that is. Plenty of toast. Butter. Honey."

"It will be awaiting you, Lord."

Grimes went through to the bathroom, performed his morning ritual. When he came out, in his dressing gown, he noted that clothing had been laid out on the already made bed. He looked at it curiously; it was nothing that he had brought with him, but he had no doubt that it would prove a perfect fit. His breakfast was waiting on the table in the bedroom, and with it a crisp newspaper. THE ELDORADO CHRONICLE he read as he picked it up. Curious, he skimmed through it over his first cup of coffee. It contained little more than social gossip, although its editor had condescended to notice the presence of *Aries* at the spaceport, and there were even some photographs of the ship's personnel. Grimes chuckled over one of Captain Daintree and Surgeon Commander Passifern at the Duchess of Leckhampton's masked ball, at another one that showed a conducted party of the ship's ratings, looking acutely uncomfortable in their uniforms, at an ocean beach on which the rig of the day was the only sensible one for swimming and sunbathing. He found a brief item which informed anybody who might be interested that Lieutenant Grimes was the house guest of the Princess Marlene von Stolzberg. On the back page there was Galactic news, but most of it was financial.

Grimes put the paper down and applied himself to his breakfast, which was excellent. After one last cup of coffee he went back to the bedroom and examined curiously the heavy shirt, the tough breeches, the thick stockings and the heavy boots before putting them on. A tweed cap completed the ensemble. He was admiring himself in the mirror when, unannounced, Marlene came in. He removed his hat, turned to look at her. She was dressed as he was, but on her the rough clothing looked extremely feminine.

He said, "Good morning, Marlene."

She said, "Good morning, John." Then, "I trust that you slept well."

"Yes," he lied.

"Good." Her mood seemed to be that of a small girl setting out on a long-promised outing. "Then shall we make a start? The woods are so much better in the morning."

"Your tin butler said something about a hunt."

"Yes. There is a boar, a great, cunning brute that I have promised myself the pleasure of despatching for many a day."

"I don't know anything about hunting."

"But you must. As an officer of an armed service you must, at times, have been a hunter—and, at times, the hunted."

"That's not quite the same."

"No. I suppose it's not. Didn't somebody say once that Man is the most dangerous game of all?"

"But I'm not sure that I approve of blood sports."

She was amusedly contemptuous. "John, John, you typical Terran petty bourgeois! You approved of that roast of wild boar at dinner last night. And that animal was killed by *me*, not in some sterile, allegedly humane abattoir. There is a big difference between killing for sport and mere butchering."

"You could be right."

"Of course I'm right. But come."

She led the way out of Grimes' quarters. He supposed that, given six months or so, he would eventually learn to find his way about this castle, but this morning he certainly needed a guide. At last, several corridors and a couple of escalators later, he followed her into a panelled room at ground level, against the walls of which were stacks of weapons: light and heavy firearms, longbows and, even, spears.

One of these latter she selected, a seven-foot shaft of some dull-gleaming timber, tipped with a wickedly sharp metal head. She tested the point of it on the ball of her thumb, said, "This will do. Select yours."

"A *spear*?" demanded Grimes, incredulous.

"Yes, a spear. What did you expect? A laser cannon? A guided missile with a fusion warhead? Wars were fought with these things, John, once upon a time. Fought and won."

"And fought and lost when the other side came up with bows and arrows."

"The boar only has his tusks. And hooves."

"And he knows how to use them." Grimes deliberately handled his spear clumsily, making it obvious that this was one weapon that *he* did not know how to use.

"Just stay with me," she told him. "You'll be quite safe."

Grimes flushed but said nothing, walked with her out of the castle into the open air.

It was a fine morning, the sun rising in a cloudless sky, the last of the dew still on the grass, the merest suggestion of a pleasantly cool breeze. Grimes found himself remembering the possibly mythical upper-class

Englishman who was supposed to have said, "It's a beautiful day. Let's go out and kill something." So it was a beautiful day for killing wild boars, and last night (that memory suddenly flooded back) had been a beautiful night for killing white goats. He shivered a little. A boar hunt would be clean, wholesome by comparison. And, he had to admit, there was a certain glamor about sport of this kind, cruel though some might consider it.

He looked at the hounds, their pelts boldly patterned in ruddy brown and white, streaming ahead of them in a loose pack. They were silent now, although they had belled lustily when released from their kennels. They were part of the countryside, part of this kind of life. And so was Marlene, striding mannishly (but not too mannishly) beside him. Even the two humanoid robots, tricked out in some sort of forester's livery, each carrying a bundle of spears and one of those bell-mouthed net-throwing pistols, were more part of the picture than he, Grimes, was. Even the inevitable pair of watchbirds, hovering and soaring overhead, looked like real birds, fitted in.

There was no need for a path over the grass, something had kept it cropped short. But as they approached the woods Grimes saw that there was a track through the trees, made either by human agency or by wild animals. But the hounds ignored it, split up, each making its own way into the green dimness. They gave voice again, a cacophonous baying that, thought Grimes uneasily, must surely infuriate rather than frighten any large and dangerous animal. But they seemed to know what they were doing, which was more than he did.

He remarked, "Intelligent animals, aren't they?"

"Within their limitations," she replied. "They have been told to find a wild boar, *the* wild boar, rather, and drive him toward us. And they have enough brains to keep out of trouble themselves."

"Which is more than I have."

"You can say that again. Hold your spear at the ready, like this. The way you're handling it he could be on you, ripping your guts out, before you got the point anywhere near him."

"If your watchbirds let him."

"They can't operate in a forest, John." She grinned. "But Fritz and Fredrik"—she made a slight gesture towards the robot foresters—"have very fast reactions."

"I'm pleased to hear that."

They were well into the woods now, on either side of them the ancient oaks (artificially aged? imported as full-grown trees?) and overhead the branches and thick foliage that shut out the blue of the sky. Things rustled in the underbrush. Something burst from the bushes and ran across their path. Instinctively, Grimes raised his spear, lowered it when he saw that the animal was only a rabbit.

"For *them*, John," remarked the Princess chidingly, "we have shotguns."

The baying of the hounds was distant now, muffled by the trees. Perhaps they wouldn't find the boar or, old and cunning as he was, he would not allow himself to be chivvied into the open. Grimes found himself sympathizing with the animal. As Marlene had surmised, he had been in his time both hunter and hunted. He knew (as she did not) what it was like to be at the receiving end.

The baying of the hounds was still distant but, it seemed, a little closer. "Stop," ordered the girl. "Wait here. Let him come to us."

I'd sooner not wait, thought Grimes. *I'd sooner get out of this blasted forest as though I had a Mark XIV missile up my tail.*

"Not long now," said the girl. The tip of her pink tongue moistened her scarlet lips. She looked happy. Grimes knew that he did not. He glanced at the foresters. They were standing there stolidly just behind the humans. They had not bothered to unholster their net-throwing guns. The spaceman muttered something about brass bastards too tired to pull a pistol. "Don't *worry* so, John," the Princess told him. "Relax."

The clamor of the pack was louder and growing louder all the time. It was the only sound in the forest. All the little disturbing rustlings and squeakings and twitterings had ceased. Then there was a new noise, or combination of noises. It was like a medium tank crashing through the undergrowth, squealing as it came. And there was no fear in that high-pitched, nasal screaming, only rage.

"Open up," ordered the Princess. "Give him a choice of targets. It will confuse him."

There was room for them to spread themselves out in the clearing in which they were standing. Marlene, on his right, moved away from him. He could hear, behind him, the feet of the robots shuffling over the dead leaves and coarse grass. He stayed where he was. A shift to the left would bring him too close to the bushes, out of which the enraged animal might emerge at any moment. He thought, *What am I doing here?* He was no stranger to action, but a fire fight at relatively long range is impersonal. This was getting to be too personal for comfort.

And then, ahead of them, the wild boar exploded into the clearing. He stood there for what seemed a long time (it could have been only a second, if that) glaring at them out of his little red eyes. Here was no fat and lazy piglet leading a contented life (but a short one) in the very shadow of the bacon factory. Here was a wild animal, a dangerous animal, one of those animals that are said to be wicked because they defend themselves. The tusks on him, transposed to the upper jaw, would not have been a discredit to a sabre-toothed tiger.

He made his decision, charged at the Princess like a runaway rocket torpedo. She stood her ground, spear extended and ready and then, with a motion as graceful as it was horrible, with the sharp point deftly flicked out the brute's left eye. He was blinded on that side and she had skipped away and clear. He was blind on that side, but his right eye was good, and he could see Grimes and, furthermore, another spear licked out, wielded by one of the robots, not to kill but with the intention of turning him toward the new pain, toward the spaceman.

Grimes wanted to run but knew that he would never be fast enough. (The girl could look after herself, or, if she could not, her faithful automatic servitors would protect her.) He wanted to run, but stubbornness more than any other quality made him remain rooted to the spot. And then—he never knew why—he *threw* his spear. It was not a javelin, was not designed to be used in this manner but, miraculously, sped straight and true, hitting the boar in the left shoulder, missing the bones, plunging through into the fiercely beating heart.

Even so, the animal almost reached him, finally collapsed at his very feet.

Slowly, Grimes turned to look at the others—at the Princess, at the robot foresters, at the grinning, tongue-lolling dogs. He felt betrayed, sensed that only his own luck (rather than skill) had saved him.

Marlene stared back, her eyes and wide mouth very vivid in her pale face. Then she made a tremulous attempt at a smile.

"Third time lucky," she said. "For you."

"What do you mean?"

"That I've shot *my* bolt. Somebody else can do the dirty work."

"What do you mean?"

"Never mind. Let us return to the castle."

In silence they walked back out from the dark woods.

21

THEY LAY, SUPINE and naked, on the velvet grass of the lawn that surrounded the swimming pool, soaking up the warmth and the radiation of the afternoon sun. Grimes raised himself on his shoulders, looked at the perfect body of the girl. He thought, *Yes, you may look, but you mustn't touch.* And he wanted to touch, badly. Hastily he turned over onto his belly.

"What's bothering you, John?" she asked, her voice lazy.

Can't you see? he did not dare to say. Instead, extemporizing, he said, "I'm still puzzled by what you said. After I killed the boar."

"What did I say?"

"Something about third time lucky. And about somebody else having to do the dirty work." He was silent for a little. "And, tell me, was the first time when I brought the dynosoar in to a landing? And was the second time when we had the difference of opinion with the rock ogre?"

"I don't know what you're talking about, John. I can't remember saying anything about third time lucky."

"Can't you?"

"No. You must have imagined it. You were rather badly shaken up." There was a touch of scorn in her voice. "Still, I suppose that it was the first time that you'd ever killed anything at short range."

"Never mind that. Here's another point. I gained the impression that your precious Fritz and Fredrik weren't busting their tin guts to get me out of the jam."

"You hardly gave them time, did you? Also, they are not supposed to intervene until the last possible moment. It's like . . . how shall I put it? It's like the amusement parks you have on most of the overcrowded planets. There are those affairs called . . . roller coasters? Big Dippers? Anyhow, they give their passengers the illusion of danger. We work on the same principle."

"So El Dorado is just one huge amusement park for the very rich?"

She laughed, but without warmth. "You could put it that way." She got up slowly, walked to the battlements. Grimes watched the play of the muscles under her smooth skin, the sway of her round buttocks. *Yes,* he thought, *a huge amusement park, with swimming pools on the roofs of Gothic castles, and the illusion of danger when you want it (and when you don't) and the illusion of glamorous sex. The real thing isn't for snotty-nosed ragamuffins from the wrong side of the tracks.*

She turned to face him. The sun was full on her. She was all golden, the slender length of her, save for the touches of contrasting color that were her eyes, her mouth, her taut nipples and the enameled nails of her fingers and toes.

She said, "You aren't happy here, John." There was regret in her voice.

He said, looking at her, "You're a marvellous hostess. But . . . But I can't help feeling an outsider."

"But you *are*," she stated simply. "All of you, from your almighty Captain down to the lowest rating, are. We can fraternise with you all, but only within limits."

"And who lays down those limits? Your precious Monitor?" She was shocked. "Of course not. *We* know what those limits are. Normally we just do not mix with those who are not our kind of people. But, as we called your ship in, we realize that we are under an obligation. In *your* case I am trying to make up for the trouble I got you into from the very start."

"And ever since," he said.

"That is not fair, John. You impressed me as being the type of young man who is quite capable of getting himself into trouble without much help or encouragement."

And this young woman has helped me enough, thought Grimes, *nonetheless. Young* woman? But was she? For all he knew she could be old enough to be his grandmother.

"Why are you staring at me, John?"

"A cat can look at a Queen," he quipped. "Or a Princess."

"And many a cat has lost all of its nine lives for doing just that."

Grimes transferred his attention to a tiny, jewelled beetle that was crawling over the grass just under his face.

She said, "If you aren't happy here, John, I'll take you back to your ship."

"Do you want me to go?"

"No," she said at last.

"All right. I'll stay, as long as you'll have me."

"That wasn't very gracious."

"I'm sorry. It was just my proletarian origins showing."

She told him, "Please don't let them show tonight. You must be on your best behavior. I, we, have guests."

"Oh. Anybody I know?"

"Yes. Henri, Comte de Messigny. Hereditary Chief Lobenga and his wife, the Lady Eulalia. The Duchess of Leckhampton. Those whom you have not already met you have seen."

"The Duchess? Yes. I remember now. On the Monitor, at the masked ball. But the Lady Eulalia?"

"At the voodoo ceremony. It was she on the altar."

"His *wife?*"

"Yes. Lobenga is a very moral man, moral, that is, by your somewhat outdated standards."

And that, thought Grimes, robbed the rites that he had witnessed of much of their sinful glamor. There had been, of course, that revolting business with the white goat but all over the Galaxy, with every passing second, animals were being slaughtered to serve the ends of Man. He, himself, had killed the boar and, quite possibly, sooner or later would enjoy its cooked flesh.

Suddenly he found himself pitying these people with their empty, sterile lives. Messigny, playing at being a spaceman, Lobenga and his wife playing at Black Magic, and the old Duchess casting herself in the role of Grande Dame. And the Princess? *There's nothing wrong with you,* he thought, *that a good roll in the hay wouldn't cure.* And yet, looking at her as she stood there, proud and naked, looking down at him, he knew that she would have to make the first move.

She said, "There is a slight chill in the air. Shall we go down?" She walked to the turret that housed the top of the escalator. He followed her. The robot Karl was awaiting them, helped the girl into a fleecy robe, knelt to slide golden sandals onto her slim feet. Grimes picked up his own robe from where he had left it, got into his footwear unassisted. He knew that had he waited a few seconds Karl would have served him as he served his mistress, but the spaceman was neither used to nor welcomed such attention.

The moving stairway took them down into the castle.

Grimes, tricked out once again in his dress uniform, sat watching the screen of the playmaster in his living room, awaiting the summons. He had decided to allow himself just one weak drink, and was sipping a pink gin. He was ready for the knock on the door when it came, drained what was left in his glass and then followed Karl through long corridors that were, once again, strange to him. Finally he was conducted into a room furnished with baroque splendor, in which Marlene and her guests were already seated.

They broke off their conversation as he came in, and the two men and the Princess got to their feet. "Your Grace," said Marlene formally, "may I introduce Lieutenant John Grimes, of *Aries?*" The Duchess looked him up and down. *If she smiles,* thought Grimes, *the paint will crack and the powder will flake off* . . . But smile she did, thinly, a final touch to the antique elegance already enhanced by an elaborate, white-powdered wig, black beauty spot on the left cheek of her face, black ribbon around the wrinkled neck, gently fluttering fan. She extended a withered hand. Rather to his own surprise, Grimes bowed from the waist to kiss it. She looked at him approvingly.

"Lady Eulalia, may I introduce . . . ?"

Grimes found it hard to believe that this was the naked woman whom he had seen stretched upon the altar, who had participated in the obscene sacrifice, who had been carried into the dark jungle by the giant Negro. She smiled sweetly, demurely almost, up at him. Her skin was hardly darker than Marlene's, and only a certain fullness of the lips betrayed her racial origin. Her auburn-glinting hair was piled high on her narrow head. Her splendid body was clad in a slim sheath of glowing scarlet. The effect was barbaric, and suddenly, credence restored, he could visualize her as she had appeared on the screen. He felt his ears burning.

"We have met before, young Grimes," said de Messigny, shaking his hand. Although the grip was firm, it was cold. The Comte was not in uniform tonight, was sombrely well-dressed in form-fitting black, with a froth of lace at throat and wrists. He, like the Duchess, seemed a survivor from some earlier, more courtly age.

"I remember seeing you at the spaceport, Lieutenant," rumbled Lobenga, a wide, dazzling smile splitting his broad, ebony face. The Hereditary Chief was wearing a white jacket over sharply creased black trousers and, under the white satin butterfly of his necktie, a double row of lustrous black pearls adorned his starched shirt front. "I am pleased with the opportunity to make your acquaintance properly." The hand that crushed Grimes' was the hand that had slain the sacrificial goat.

"Please be seated," ordered Marlene, resuming her own chair. She, tonight, was imperially robed in purple, and an ornate golden brooch—or was it some Order?—gleamed over her left breast. In her hair, as before, was the jewelled coronet. Grimes watched her as she sat down and was suddenly aware that de Messigny was watching him. Glancing sideways, he imagined that he detected jealousy on the tall man's face. *But you've nothing to be jealous of,* he thought.

And then the robot servitors were offering trays of drinks, and the conversation was light and desultory, normal—"And what do you really think of our world, Mr. Grimes?" "The most beautiful planet I've seen, your Grace"—platitudinous, but a welcome change from the platitudes bandied about in *Aries*' wardroom, and after a pleasant enough half hour or so, it was time to go down to dinner.

22

THEY PARTOOK OF food and wine in the great banqueting hall, waited upon by the silent, efficient serving robots. Grimes—a young man keenly appreciative of the pleasures of the table, although he had yet to acquire discrimination—could never afterwards remember what it was that they ate and drank. There was food and there was wine, and presumably both were palatable and satisfying, but those sitting around the board were of far greater importance than what was set upon it.

Opposite Grimes was Marlene. On her left, darkly glowering, was Lobenga, and to his left was the Duchess. To Grimes' right was the Lady Eulalia, with de Messigny beyond her. The table should have been a little oasis of light and warmth in the huge, dark hall, a splash of color in contrast to the ranged suits of dull-gleaming armour, the sombre folds of the standards that sagged from their inward pointing staffs. It should have been, but it was not. It could have been imagination, but it seemed to Grimes that the candle flames were burning blue, and the fire in the enormous hearth was no more than an ominous smoulder. Somewhere background music was playing, softly, too softly. It could have been the whispering of malign spirits.

De Messigny, speaking diagonally across the table, said abruptly, "And are the ghosts of your Teutonic ancestors walking tonight, Marlene?"

She stared back at him, her face grave, shadows under her high cheekbones, what little light there was reflected from the jewels in her coronet, an unhappy princess out of some old German fairy story. She said at last, "The ghosts of Schloss Stolzberg stayed on Earth, Henri."

"Unfortunately," added Lobenga, his low rumble barely audible.

"And was the Castle haunted?" asked Grimes, breaking the uneasy hush.

They all turned to stare at him—the Princess gravely, Lobenga sullenly, the Duchess with a birdlike maliciousness. On his right Eulalia laughed softly and coldly, and de Messigny glared at him down his long, thin nose.

"Yes," said Marlene at last. "It *was* haunted. There was the faithless Princess Magda, who used to run screaming through the corridors, the hilt of her husband's dagger still protruding from between her breasts. There was Butcher Hermann, who met his end in the torture chamber at the hands of his own bastard son. There was S.S. General von Stolzberg, roasted in this very fireplace by his slave-labor farm workers when the Third Reich collapsed . . ."

"We could do without *them*," de Messigny stated.

"Hermann and the General, perhaps," cackled the Duchess. "But Magda would have been at home here." As she said this she ceased to be the Grande Dame, looked more, thought Grimes, like the Madam of a whorehouse.

"Yes," agreed the Comte. "She would have been." Had he not looked so long and hard at Marlene as he said it, the remark would have been inoffensive.

Eulalia laughed again. "I have often wondered why some men persist in attaching such great importance to the supremely unimportant." She shrugged her slim, elegant shoulders. "But, of course, Lobenga has no cause to worry about me. Not even on this world. Perhaps, Henri, we could enroll you in a course of study in the so-called Black Arts."

"That filth!" exploded the Comte.

"Sir," the huge Negro told him gravely, "it is not filth. We have seen, on this planet, what happens when Man gets too far away from the mud and blood of his first beginnings. Every member of the Committee of Management, with the exception of Lord Tarlton . . ."

"That *materialist!*" interjected his wife.

". . . agrees that we are on the right track. There is disagreement regarding which method to employ. Her Grace, for example, pins her faith in supercivilized but decadent orgies . . ."

"Thank you, Lobenga," said the old woman sardonically.

"On the other hand, Her Highness concurs with me that a sacrifice is necessary."

"Then," put in de Messigny, "why were not such few criminals as we have discovered on El Dorado executed *here*, instead of being sent to their deaths somewhere in outer space?"

"You heard what was said about Hermann von Stolzberg and his descendant, the S.S. General. We can do without such raw material."

"Rubbish!" The Comte's normally pale face was flushed. "Marlene carries in her veins the blood of her murderous ancestors. We all of us carry in our veins the blood of ancestors guilty of every crime—yes, and of every sin—known to Man."

"There has been a certain refining process," the Duchess told him.

"Perhaps that's the trouble. Perhaps we are all too refined. Or perhaps we have culminated in a new species of Mankind that is sterile."

The Duchess cackled. "That from you, Henri? I recall, just the other day, that you were telling me about your illegitimate children on Caribbea and Austral." Then, maliciously, "but are you sure that they are yours?"

"There is a strong family resemblance," he snapped.

"And so, Henri, you alone on El Dorado are capable of the act of procreation. Why don't you . . ."

"I didn't mean it that way, Honoria."

"We have a guest," Marlene reminded the others.

"And so we have," agreed de Messigny, tossing down almost a full glass of wine. "Or so *you* have. But we must not offend Mr. Grimes' delicate susceptibilities, although I am sure that an officer of the Survey Service will be able to take the rough with the smooth." He managed to make the last word sound obscene.

"Henri. You know very well that that would be entirely contrary to the rules by which we live."

"You have always made your own rules, Marlene. As we all, at this table, know."

"As we all know," stated Lobenga.

"That is my privilege," she said. "As it is the privilege of all on El Dorado."

"But you told us," complained the Duchess, "that you would, for the good of us all, cooperate. Cooperate, did I say? As I recall it, you were to play a leading part in one of the schemes."

"I did," said Marlene. "I did. But we von Stolzbergs have a family tradition. Shall I tell you? Try to do something, and fail. Try a second time, and fail. Try a third time, and fail. Try a fourth time, and the consequences are unforeseen and disastrous."

"Superstition," growled the Hereditary Chief.

"This from *you*, Lobenga . . ." murmured the Princess.

"The Old Religion is *not* superstition!" flared Eulalia. "If we had been allowed to do things *our* way . . ."

"We still can," said her husband.

"But not," stated the Princess, "in Schloss Stolzberg. I am fully conscious of the obligations of a host."

"Mr. Grimes!" It was the Duchess of Leckhampton addressing him. Then, sharply, "Mr. Grimes!"

He turned to her, still bewildered by the conversation in which he had played no part, but of which he appeared to have been the subject. "Your Grace?"

She was very much the great lady again, and she spoke with hauteur. "Mr. Grimes, I shall apologize to you, even if these others will not. It must be embarrassing for an outsider to be the witness to what, in effect, is a family quarrel. Yes, we are a family here on El Dorado, even though we are of diverse races and origins. But I must commend you, Mr. Grimes, for having the good sense and the courtesy not to take sides."

He tried to make a joke of his reply. "I didn't know whose side to take, Your Grace."

"Didn't you, Mr. Grimes?" sneered de Messigny.

"No," said Grimes. He allowed his indignation to take charge. "Damn it all, you people are the upper crust of the entire bloody Galaxy, or think that you are. But I tell you that such squabbling at table would not be tolerated in the Fourth Class Ratings' messroom, let alone the wardroom of a ship."

"That will do, Grimes!" snapped the Count.

"That will do, Henri!" almost snarled the Princess. "John was right in what he said."

"*John?*" echoed de Messigny, with a sardonic lift of his black eyebrows. "But I was forgetting, Marlene. After all, you have Karl and Fritz and Fredrik and Augustin and Johann . . . Although John has the advantage of being flesh and blood, not metal."

"De Messigny . . ." Lobenga's voice was an ominous rumble. "De Messigny, you will be silent." His strange yellow eyes swept the table. "You will all of you be silent, until I have had my say." Then he addressed the Lieutenant directly. "Mr. Grimes, what has happened should never have happened. What has been said should never have been said. But there are forces loose tonight in this old castle. Perhaps, even though there are no ghosts, the centuries of bloodstained history that these walls have seen have left a record of some kind on the very stones. There has been a clash of personalities. There has been sexual jealousy, and so the record has been played back. It was in this very hall, I am told, that Her Highness's forebear, Magda, died of her wounds.

"Be that as it may, Mr. Grimes, too much has been said in your hearing. You know too much, and too little. But I, we, feel that you have the right to know more. Do we have your word, as an officer and a gentleman, that what we shall tell you will never be divulged?"

Grimes' head was buzzing. Could it have been the effects of too much wine, or of something in the wine? And those yellow eyes staring into his were strangely hypnotic.

"Do we have your word?" asked Lobenga.

"Yes," he whispered.

"Is this wise?" asked Eulalia.

"Shut yo' mouf, woman." The deliberate lapse into the archaic dialect was frightening rather than ludicrous. This was the High Priest speaking, not the cultured Negro gentleman. "Shut yo' mouf, all of yo', until Ah is done.

"Mr. Grimes," he went on, "I can tell you that you were to have been honored, greatly honored. But circumstances now are such that, after your stay here, you will be allowed to return to your ship."

"Honored?" asked Grimes. "How?"

"You were to have been the white goat, the goat without horns."

Grimes stared around the table in horror rather than in disbelief.

"It is true," said Marlene.

23

"YES," SAID LOBENGA, breaking the heavy silence, "you are entitled to an explanation."

"You can say that again," Grimes told him.

The Hereditary Chief ignored this. "You are aware, Mr. Grimes," he went on, "of the nature of our problem on this planet."

"Yes." The spaceman was deliberately flippant. "You miss the pitterpatter of little feet and all the rest of it."

"Crudely put, sir. Crudely put, but true. Even though our lives are enormously prolonged, even though our system of safeguards almost obviates the possibility of accidental death, or death by any kind of violence, we are not immortal. And what use is great wealth if you have nobody to whom to leave it? What comfort is a bloodline stretching back to antiquity if it dies out with yourself ?"

"Those," said Grimes, "are worries that I'm never likely to have."

"But you are not one of us," stated Marlene.

Lobenga continued. "All we ask, sir, is to be able to live our own kind of life on the planet of our choice. But for this one, but dreadfully important, factor we have no complaints. We are neither impotent nor frigid. Our sex lives are normal, better than normal. But we are sterile, even though our finest medical practitioners assure us that there are no physical abnormalities or deficiencies."

"I was told," said Grimes, "that the women who were already pregnant when they came here were successfully brought to term and that their children lived and are now adults."

"That is correct."

"And I learned tonight that Captain de Messigny has fathered offspring on other planets."

"So he tells us," said Lobenga, adding, before the Comte could flare up, "and I have no reason to doubt his word. Furthermore, the Comte de Messigny has, on occasion, acted as procurer, bringing young men of good family to El Dorado for a vacation. Women with wealth and family lines of their own entertained them. But even though de Messigny's friends could, like himself, offer proof of their capacity for parenthood, they achieved nothing here."

"And what is the explanation?" asked Grimes. "Something in the air, or the water? Some virus or radiation?"

"According to Lord Tarlton and his colleagues, no. And we adherents to the Old Religion, in its various forms, are in agreement with the materialists."

"Then have *you* a theory?"

"We have, sir. If you will be patient I shall try to explain it to you. But, first of all, I shall ask a question. What is life?"

"I . . . I don't know. Growth? But a crystal does that. Metabolism? Motility? The ability to reproduce? We have inorganic machines that can do all these things."

"Perhaps *soul* would be the correct word," said Lobenga. "Not used in its conventional sense but, nonetheless, soul. Something indefinable, intangible that makes the difference between the organic and the inorganic, between the warm, soupy primordial seas, the lifeless fluids rich in minerals held in solution, cloudy with suspended matter, and the first viruses. And with those humble and simple beginnings the cycle was started. How did the poet put it? *Birth, procreation, death—and there's an end to it.* But as long as there's death, there's no end to it."

"And somebody or something," cackled the Duchess, "has put a spoke in the wheel of the cycle."

"Yes, Your Grace," agreed Lobenga. "*We* have. We have interrupted the natural sequence."

"But how?" asked Grimes.

"Imagine, if you can," said the Negro, "a reservoir of soul-stuff, of life-essence on every inhabited planet. Imagine, too, that *soul* has evolved, just as physical form has evolved. Visualize the act of conception the coupling of humans, of dogs, cats, fishes, even the pollenization of a flower—and try to see that before the process of growth can commence there has to be a third factor involved, a priming of the pump, as it were. A drop has to be withdrawn from the reservoir and that reservoir is always kept topped up by the process of death."

"I begin to see."

"Good. Now this world, as you know, was utterly sterile when we purchased it, before we terraformed it, with improvements. We brought in our plant life, our animals, ourselves. Insofar as the plants and animals are concerned the normal cycle was resumed in a matter of months, at the outside. There were the inevitable deaths, the equally inevitable births. Insofar as *we* are concerned, the normal cycle has never been initiated."

"But it could have been," said Grimes. "That is, if your theory is correct."

"How, sir?"

"You, even you, have had criminals. I have seen pictures from the Monitor's memory bank. These criminals, I am informed, were arrested and sent into exile, although it was hinted that they would not survive to make planet fall on another world. If, Mr. Lobenga, these men had been executed on El Dorado, surely your pump would have been primed."

"Do you think that we have not thought of that?" asked Lobenga. "There are two valid reasons why this has never been done. To begin with, we have always taken great pains to impress upon the Monitor the sanctity of the lives of all members of the El Dorado Corporation, and have always striven to maintain the Master/Servant relationship, with ourselves, of course, as the Masters. Secondly, if you were going to top up a reservoir of any kind, would you use polluted fluids?"

"Our own souls were dipped out of dirty buckets," chuckled the Duchess of Leckhampton. "Marlene's not the only one here with a murky family past."

"But we have *evolved,*" Lobenga explained patiently.

"Hah!" exploded the old lady sardonically.

"Then," said Grimes, "there is another solution."

"You are a veritable mine of information, John," the Princess told him.

"I was taught," he said, "that spacemanship is only applied commonsense. And commonsense can be applied to more things than the handling of ships. All right. We *know* that women who had conceived before coming to El Dorado bore their children here. We have reason to believe that Captain de Messigny has fathered children on other worlds. Then why, *why*, WHY shouldn't all of you who feel the urge to parenthood do your breeding off-planet?"

"Because," said Lobenga sombrely, "we have too much to lose. Because we are cowards. Because we are like the rich men mentioned, time after time in the Christian Bible, who would not give up their worldly possessions for an assured place in the Kingdom of Heaven. There is always risk involved in travelling off-planet. On El Dorado the Monitor protects us from all possible harm. On other worlds we are liable to death from disease, accident, premeditated violence. Oh, there have been couples who have taken the risk. None of them have returned. The Bernsteins both drowned in a boating accident on Atlantia. Dom Pedro da Silva and his wife, *he* was executed on Waverley for the murder of her lover. She committed suicide. I could go on. It seems that a malign fate pursues us once we lift beyond the limits of our own atmosphere . . ." He paused. "It seems that all the risks that we avoid by living here accumulate, as it were, and once we are away from the protection of the Monitor topple, and crush us beneath their weight."

"Captain de Messigny is still with you," observed Grimes.

"Yes," said the Comte coldly. "I am still around. But before I became a member of the Corporation I led an adventurous life. And, furthermore, I could never remain planetbound for long. *That* would kill me, Monitor or no Monitor. But even I am reluctant to leave the safety of my ship in strange ports and, furthermore, do all my entertaining on board."

"Yet another solution," put forward Grimes happily. "Build a passenger vessel, with accommodation for fifty or a hundred couples. Make a landing on a world with a well-topped-up reservoir and then breed like rabbits."

"And do you think that we haven't tried it?" the Comte asked. "The ship was half-way back to El Dorado when, inexplicably, her micropile went critical. I need not tell you that there were no survivors."

"And so," asked Grimes, "where does the white goat come into it? Where do *I* come in?"

"We are a moral people," said Lobenga gravely. The Duchess snorted. "We are a moral people," he stated firmly. "It would have been relatively easy for us to have arranged an accident that would have destroyed your *Aries* and all her crew when she was coming in for a landing. But, apart from the question of morality, there would have been a full scale investigation by the Survey Service. In the same way, it would be possible to stage an accident that would wipe out one of the parties of sightseers from your ship presently touring our planet. But, once again, it would be a needless sacrifice of life and, furthermore, your Captain Daintree is no fool. Too, those of us who are practitioners of what are loosely called the Black Arts resorted to various methods of divination; even Her Grace is an expert manipulator of the Tarot pack. Each and every one of us came up with the same prognostication, the same conclusion. This was that the first off-worlder to make a landing would be the bringer of new life to El Dorado. And that first off-worlder was you."

"It is expedient for one man to die for the good of the people," quoted Grimes bitterly.

"Yes. And it would have been in an accident costing only one life, or, in the case of the crash-landing of your dynosoar, only two lives. There would have been no investigation."

"But why can't one of *you* prime the pump?" almost shouted Grimes. "You're always saying what a wonderful world you have here. Hasn't any one of you the guts to make a sacrifice for it?"

"Not *that* sacrifice. Mr. Grimes, I do not ask you for your sympathy, your pity, but I do ask for some measure of understanding. Only a man who has known great possessions knows how hard it is to give them up."

"And so you'd cheerfully slaughter an innocent outsider just so that you can enjoy a few more years in your sterile Eden."

"Not cheerfully, Mr. Grimes. Not cheerfully. And tell me, sir, have *you* ever slaughtered innocent outsiders?"

"No."

"Not yet, you should have said. As an officer of the armed forces of the Federation you will inevitably do so. You *will*, I said. Because, Mr. Grimes, you will live to take part in punitive expeditions, in raids upon commerce, in all the unsavory operations that are always fully justified by the historians of the winning side. We have reread the cards and the cups and the entrails, we have cast the bones. Your lifeline is a long one, but I shall not tell you the surprising turns that it will take.

"You have our word for it, Mr. Grimes. You are safe from us. Neither you nor anybody from your ship is destined to become the white goat, the goat without horns."

"You have our word," echoed the others solemnly.

He believed them. He almost said thank you, but why should he thank them for giving back to him what was not theirs to give, his life?

The Princess Marlene rose to her feet, and her guests followed suit. She said, "We are all tired. I suggest that we retire."

Robot servitors led the humans to their quarters. Grimes, entering his bedroom, saw something small and dull-gleaming in the center of the coverlet of his bed. It was his Minetti automatic pistol, and beside it was the carton of spare ammunition.

And now that I shan't need it, he thought, *they give it back to me.*

24

NONETHELESS, HE WAS not sorry to have the deadly little weapon back in his own possession. If there were to be any more hunting of large and dangerous animals, he would prefer to have something with which he was familiar to defend himself with. His successful use of that absurd spear against the wild boar had been nothing but luck, and he knew it.

He slept well, with the pistol under his pillow. Lobenga and the others had given their words that he was safe insofar as they were concerned, but what if they were not the only parties involved in the scheme to set the normal cycle of death and birth running on El Dorado? That gun of his own, loaded and ready to hand, gave him a sense of security that otherwise would have been lacking.

He was called in the morning in the usual manner. After he had freshened up, he found that clothing similar to that which he had worn for the boar hunt had been laid out on the remade bed. The Minetti slipped easily into the right-hand side pocket of the breeches. He practiced drawing. He would never be the Fastest Gun in the West or anywhere else, but he was sure that he would be able to defend himself adequately given only a little warning.

He enjoyed his breakfast of beautifully grilled kidneys, bacon and sausages, skimmed through the morning paper. As before, it was mainly social news and gossip. He noted that the Duchess of Leckhampton, the Comte de Messigny, the Hereditary Chief Lobenga and the Lady Eulalia were guests of the Princess von Stolzberg, as was, still, Lieutenant John Grimes. And Captain Daintree and Surgeon Commander Passifern, together with other officers, had been present at Count Vitelli's wine tasting. Passifern, at least, would have enjoyed himself.

Karl entered silently, made a metallic cough to attract Grimes' attention. "Lord, Her Highness awaits you in the gun room."

The gun room? It took a second or so for Grimes' mind to orient itself. Aboard a ship the gun room is to cadets and midshipmen (if such are carried) what the wardroom is to commissioned officers. *The gun room?* The robot must mean that panelled chamber with its racks of assorted weaponry.

"And what's on today?" asked the spaceman through a mouthful of buttered toast dripping with honey. "Another wild boar hunt? Or are we going out for tigers or rogue elephants?"

"None of them, Lord." (Robots are apt to be humorless.) "Today you are shooting Denebian fire pheasants." There was a touch of envy in the mechanical voice. "I am told that they are very good eating, as well as affording excellent sport."

"How so? Are they the size of corvettes, heavily armed and armoured, and vicious when aroused?"

"No, Lord. They are relatively small creatures, brilliantly plumaged, but when put up their flight is extremely fast and erratic."

"Then they should be safe enough from me."

"I was informed, Lord, that you are a gunnery specialist."

"Shooting at large targets, Karl, with a shipful of electronic aids to do all the work for me." He finished his coffee, patted his lips with the napkin (if the supercilious tin butler had not been watching, he would have wiped them) and followed the robot through the doorway.

Marlene was waiting in the gun room. With her were the Duchess, Lobenga and his wife, and the Comte de Messigny. Grimes noted that only the Princess was dressed for rough outdoor activities, the others were in light, comfortable attire, suitable for lounging about indoors or in the garden. They all seemed in a cheerful mood but for de Messigny, whose handsome features were darkened by what was almost a scowl.

"Good morning, John," the Princess greeted him. "It's a fine day for a shoot."

"I always think that it's a pity," said the Duchess, "to destroy those beautiful birds."

"You enjoy them when they appear on the table," Marlene told her.

"Yes, my dear. Yes. And you enjoy blasting them out of the sky, so each of us has her pleasures."

"Blood sports," said the Comte, "are primitive." He permitted himself a sneer. "No doubt they are very much to the taste of a Survey Service gunnery officer, although he may find a shotgun a little small after the weapons that he is used to."

"You are a spaceman yourself, Henri," said Marlene.

"Yes. And a good one. But I'm a merchant spaceman, and before that I was a yachtsman."

"And your ship, as you have said to me, packs the armament of a light cruiser."

"Defensive, Marlene. Defensive. It is the right of any shipmaster or of any man to use any and every means available to defend his own ship, property or whatever."

"I have never liked guns," stated Lobenga, more or less changing the subject. "A hunt in which spears are used—that is to my taste."

"Not to mine," said Grimes.

He took the weapon that Marlene handed him, examined it curiously. It was a shotgun, twin-barreled, light, but with just enough heft to it. Carefully keeping it pointed at the floor, he inspected the action, soon got the hang of it. "Two shots only," he commented, "and then you reload. Wouldn't an automatic weapon be better?"

"Yes," said the Princess, "if all you want to do is kill things. But it would take away the necessity for real skill, would destroy any element of sport."

"But I thought that the whole idea of hunting was to kill things."

"You, John," she told him, "are the sort of man who would use grenades in a trout stream."

"However did you guess?" he countered.

"Mr. Grimes," sneered de Messigny, "is obviously unacquainted with the *mystique* of huntin', shootin' and fishin'. But I have no doubt, Marlene, that under your expert tutelage he will acquire a smattering."

"No doubt," she agreed coldly. "Now, John, you have your gun. I shouldn't need to tell you about safety catches, pointing it at people and all the rest of it. Here's your bag of cartridges." Grimes took it, slung it over his shoulder. "A miniwagon will accompany us to bring in the game we shoot and will also carry our refreshments. Are you ready?"

"Yes," he said.

He followed her out of the gun room.

"Good huntin'!" called the Duchess ironically.

As before, it was a beautiful morning. They strode out over the dew-spangled grass, the sunlight warm on their faces, the grim pile of the castle behind them. To one side and a little back trundled the miniwagon, a vehicle little more than a rectangular box on balloon tired wheels. No doubt it possessed a rudimentary intelligence as well as hidden capabilities. Overhead soared the watchbirds, and ahead, trotting sedately, was a pair of beautiful dogs, red- rather than brown-coated, their plumed tails upraised and waving.

They left the relatively short grass of the fields for rougher ground, gently undulating, with outcroppings of chalky rock (but limestone, thought Grimes, could not exist on this planet), with clumps of golden-blossoming gorse, of purple-flowered heather. The warm air was full of spicy scent, and the stridulation of unseen insects was a pleasant monotone.

Suddenly the Princess stopped, broke her gun, snapped two cartridges into the breech, clicked the weapon into a state of readiness. A little clumsily, Grimes followed suit. Then Marlene gave an order in a language with which Grimes was not familiar, and both dogs yelped softly in acknowledgment. They were away then, running between the boulders and the gorse clumps, tails in a rigid line with their bodies. They were away, something almost serpentine in their smooth, fluid motion, vanishing up the hillside.

There was an outburst of yapping, a surprisingly loud clatter of wings. Two gaudy birds rocketed up, levelled off and flew toward Grimes and the Princess. They were fast, fantastically fast, and their line of flight was unpredictable. The butt of Marlene's gun was to her shoulder and the twin barrels twitched gently as she lined up, leading the birds. There was a report, dull rather than sharp, and, a microsecond later, another one. Two bundles of ruined feathers fell to the ground. The miniwagon rolled toward them, extended a long, thin tentacle, picked up the bodies and dropped them into a receptacle at its rear.

"Nice shooting," said Grimes. He felt that it was expected of him.

"Yes," she agreed, without false modesty. "With the next pair we shall see how you can do."

Again the dogs gave voice, and again a couple of fire pheasants took to the air. Grimes was used to taking snapshots with a pistol, but never with a weapon like the one that he was holding now. But it was so well designed and balanced that it was almost part of him. He let go with his left barrel, felt the satisfaction of seeing a little explosion of scarlet and orange feathers as the shot struck home. But he was too slow with his right, and the surviving bird was darting away and clear before he could pull the trigger.

But it was coming back, flying straight toward him, steadily this time. Grimes fired, was sure that he had scored a hit, but the thing still came on steadily. Hastily, but without fumbling, he ejected and reloaded, fired again, both barrels in quick succession.

Damn it! he thought, *the brute must be armour-plated!*

Again the ejection and the reloading but before he could bring the gun up to his shoulder, the Princess put out a hand to stop him.

"What the hell are you playing at?" she blazed. "First you smash my watchbirds with your bloody dynosoar, and now you try to shoot them!"

"A . . . a watchbird?"

"What else?"

Yes, it was one of the watchbirds; now that he was no longer looking into the sun Grimes could see that. It circled them, its machinery humming, a few feet above their heads, then hovered there. From it came a voice, and some humorist had endowed the thing with a psitacoid squawk.

"Your Highness," it began.

"Yes. What is it?"

"Danger, Your Highness. The Monitor has informed me that a new model of protective avian, still in the experimental stage, has gotten out of control and is heading this way. It is liable to kill any human being on sight."

The Princess laughed. "Yes. I have heard of this new model. A fire pheasant's brain has been incorporated and with it, perhaps, a certain resentment toward ourselves. But it will not be long before it is rounded up and destroyed."

"Hadn't we better return to the Castle?" asked Grimes.

"If you're afraid, yes."

"I am," he said frankly. "And shouldn't we ride in the miniwagon?"

"No. We can walk as fast and run, if we must, faster."

"Your Highness," screeched the watchbird. "It approaches. We go to intercept."

And then a metallic flash in the almost still air and it was gone. Marlene shrugged, whistled the dogs and then, when they came bounding up, told Grimes, "All right. We beat a retreat. But we'd better be ready to fight a rearguard action."

25

THEY WALKED BACK toward the castle in silence, the miniwagon trundling along to their right, the setters to heel. Somehow, it seemed to Grimes, there was a sudden chill in the air, although the climbing sun still shone brightly, although there was only the gentlest of breezes. *And the dogs,* he thought, *feel something too.* He looked back at the two animals. They were padding along in a cowed manner, their tails drooping.

Marlene said suddenly, angrily, "This is absurd!"

"How so?" asked Grimes.

"Running from a watchbird. They are designed to protect us, not to attack us."

"But you heard what *your* watchbird said. 'It is liable to kill any human being on sight'."

"Any offplanet human being it must have meant. Such as you." She shrugged. "Well, you are my guest, after all. I am responsible for you."

"I've managed to look after myself, so far."

"Thank you. A truly gracious guest."

"And I want to look after you," he said.

She looked full at him then. Momentarily, the harsh lines of her face softened and then she smiled. "I believe that you mean that, John. In any case, some of that incredible luck of yours might rub off on me . . ." She paused, then went on. "Yes, you are lucky. But how will it end? You recall that story I told you about our family superstition, the consequences that always ensued if something is tried, stubbornly, for a fourth time? Well, I was not quite truthful. The *third* attempt is the crucial one."

"It's that way with me and with most people."

"Is it? Anyhow, three times I tried to bring about your accidental death and failed. I'm glad I failed. But something is bound to happen to me now. With that third failure some cataclysmic sequence of events was set in motion."

"Don't be so bloody cheerful."

"This is a morbid conversation, isn't it? As for what's happening now, or what's liable to happen, I have no doubt that my own two watchbirds will be able to deal with the rogue."

Grimes wished that he could share her confidence. After all, he had been instrumental in destroying two of the things. On the other hand, there had been a certain disparity in size and weight, two relatively flimsy miniature flying machines against a re-entry vehicle.

One of the dogs whined. Grimes stopped, looked back and down. The animals had turned around, had stiffened in the classic pointing posture. He stared in the direction toward which they were staring, at first saw nothing. And then he could make out three distant specks in the clear sky, three dots apparently in frantic orbital motion about each other.

"Take these," said Marlene. She had got two pairs of binoculars from somewhere in the miniwagon, gave Grimes one of them. He slung his gun, lifted the high-powered glasses to his eyes. A mere touch of his finger sufficed to focus them.

It was like something from one of the History of Warfare films that the cadets had been shown at the Academy. It reminded him of an aerial dogfight over the battlefields of Flanders in the Kaiser's War. There was the rogue, larger than its assailants, brilliantly enameled in orange and scarlet. There were Marlene's two watchbirds, metallically glittering in the sunlight. They were diving and feinting, soaring up and away, diving again. All that was missing was the rattle of machine-gun fire. Contemptuously, the experimental model bore on, ignoring its smaller adversaries. And then one of them, coming up from below while its companion drove in from above, struck the rogue at the juncture of starboard wing with body, oversetting it. It fell out of control, almost to the ground, and then with a frantic fluttering of gaudy pinions somehow made a recovery. There was a burst of bright flame at its tail, a puff of smoke. It went up, almost vertically, like a rocket.

It was a rocket, a rocket with a brain and with the instincts of a bird of prey . . . and with the armament, miniaturized but still deadly, of a minor warship.

The two watchbirds, which had gained altitude, plunged to meet it. From the nose of the rogue came an almost invisible flicker, and the nearer of the airborne guardians burst at once into flames, exploded in blinding blue fire. The other one was hit, too, but only part of its tail was shorn away. It dived, racing its burning companion to the surface, recovered and came up again. The rogue spread its wings and turned in the air to meet the attack.

The watchbird climbed slowly, slowly, unsteadily. It must have been damaged more than superficially by the slashing blade of radiation that had almost missed it. But still it climbed, and the rogue just hung there, waiting, swinging about its short axes, deliberately sighting.

There was another flicker from the vicinity of its beak, and its crippled antagonist was no more (and no less) than a bundle of coruscating, smoking wreckage drifting groundwards.

"Laser . . ." whispered Grimes. "The bloody thing's got laser!"

"We must run!" For the first time there was fear in Marlene's voice, the fear of one who has seen her impregnable defences fall before superior, overwhelming fire power. Grimes knew how she must feel. He had felt the same way himself, as everybody has felt when faced with the failure of foolproof, *everything* proof mechanisms. "We must run!"

"Where to? That thing'll pick us off faster than you picked off the fire pheasants. He grabbed her arm before she could stumble away in panic flight. "Cover!" he shouted. "That's the answer."

"The miniwagon!" So she was thinking again.

"No." He could visualize the thing's machinery exploding as the mechanism of the watchbirds had exploded. He pulled her to one of the outcroppings of rock, about five feet high. It wasn't very good but it was better than nothing. He and the girl dropped behind it as the rogue screamed over, using its rocket drive, firing its laser gun. There was an explosion of smoke and dust and splinters from the top of the boulder.

"Quick!" cried Grimes. "Before it can turn!" He got to his feet, yanked the girl to hers, dragged her around to the other side of the outcropping. He unslung his gun. His pistol would not have been a better weapon, it didn't have the range or the spread. There was always the chance that the shotgun pellets would find some vital spot. It was a slim one, he knew, but . . .

The rogue seemed to be having trouble in turning. It came round at last, lined up for the natural fortification (such as it was). It drove in, its laser beam scoring a smouldering furrow in the turf. Unless it lifted its sights, Grimes knew that he was safe until the last moment, or he *hoped* that he was safe. He stood his ground.

Now!

A left and a right, the noise of the explosions deafening, and he dropped to the ground, his ears still ringing, but he was able to hear the sharp *crack* of riven rock, felt a gust of heat.

He scrambled to his feet. This time he did not have to help the girl up. Together they ran around the clump of weatherworn boulders. Grimes halftripped over something soft, which yelped. The dogs were still with them.

He stood there, reloading.

From the ground Marlene said, "You hit it, John."

"Yes. I hit it. Like hitting a dreadnaught with a peashooter. Keep down. Here comes the bastard again!"

It seemed to be slower this time and erratic in its flight. The wavering laser beam started a flaring, crackling fire in the gorse. But it straightened up toward the finish of its run, came in fast. Grimes let fly with both barrels at once and dropped hastily. The Princess snatched the smouldering cap off his head.

"John! John! Are you . . . ?"

"I'm all right. My brains are no more addled than usual. Come on!"

Like a game of musical chairs, he thought. *And somebody has to be the loser . . .*

This last time it came in slowly, using wings and not reaction drive. And its laser seemed to be out of action. It came in slowly, a mechanical bird of prey, climbing, finally hanging directly above the man and the girl and the two cringing dogs, high, but not too high to be a good target.

As we, thought Grimes, *are good targets for its bombs, if it carries any.*

Standing, he could not bring his gun to bear, so lay supine, the weapon aimed directly upwards. The air in the shallow hollow was blue with acrid smoke and the turf was littered with empty shells as Grimes fired again and again and again, as the Princess matched him shot for shot. Something hot stung his cheek; it was a pellet from his own gun or from Marlene's. They must be falling all over this circumscribed area like a metallic hail.

One of the dogs cried out sharply; it must have been hit and hurt by the fall of shot. Yelping, its tail between its legs, it dashed out from the barely adequate shelter of the outcropping. Its companion followed it. Then, screaming, the rogue dived. Grimes scrambled erect somehow, kept the butt of the shotgun to his shoulder, led the thing as it plunged and let it have both barrels.

Perhaps he hit again, perhaps he did not, but it made no difference. The killer bird swooped down upon the leading dog, and its long, straight beak (rapier as well as laser gun) skewered the hapless animal just behind the ribs, hooked it up from the ground, shrieking, and then with a peculiar midair twisting motion tossed it up and away. The body, its legs still running in nothingness, fell against a rock with an audible *crunch,* and then was still.

The other setter howled dismally, kept on running, but it could never be as fast as the rogue. It almost made the protection of a clump of gorse, and then the murderous machine was on it. This time it did not use its blood-dripping beak. It banked, like an old-fashioned aircraft, and the leading edge of one stiff wing slashed the animal across the hindquarters. Howling still, it tried to drag itself along with its forelegs.

Marlene was saying something. "I must go, John. I must put him out of his misery."

He caught her arm. "No. Don't be a fool."

She shook him off. "I *must.* Cover me."

She was running out over the uneven turf, slipping and staggering. Grimes dropped his shotgun, pulled the pistol from his pocket, started after her. The rogue reached her before he did. She screamed as the deadly beak grazed her shoulder, tearing a ragged square of fabric out of her shirt; she fell to her hands and knees. But she was up again, still staggering toward her dying dog, then knocked sprawling by buffeting metal wings. Again there was the thrust of the rapier beak, and this time most of the back of her upper garment was carried away on the point of it.

I must fire, thought Grimes, *before it gets too close to her. In case it blows up.* The rattle of the Minetti, set on full automatic, was startlingly loud, and the butt vibrated in the moist palm of his hand. The rogue, obligingly, was making a good target of itself (it *must* have been damaged by all the shotgun fire) slowly turning broadside on before coming in for another attack.

Grimes ejected the empty clip, put in a full one. He was firing more slowly and carefully now, in short bursts. Then, anticlimactically, the rogue fluttered slowly to the ground. There was no explosion, only a thin trickle of blue smoke. He watched it for a second, then hurried to Marlene. She was sitting up now, only a few shreds of ruined shirt clinging to her torso. There was a trickle of blood from her right shoulder.

She waved him away, pointing. "Bruno. First you must . . . do what is necessary for him . . ."

He did it. A single shot from the Minetti sufficed. Then he walked slowly back to her, fell on his knees beside her.

"Marlene! You're hurt . . ."

"Only a scratch. But for you I . . . I could have been killed."

And when you're a near-immortal, he thought, *death can be important.* But, for the first time perhaps, he could see her point of view, could feel with her and for her. Suddenly there was a warmth between them, a warmth that, until now, had been lacking. It could be that it was shared fear that brought them together, shared peril. It could be that, at last, there was the admission of a common humanity.

But her arms were about him and her face, grimy and tear-stained, was lifted to his, and his arms were about her, and her mouth on his was soft and warm and moist, and suddenly all barriers were down, scattered like the clothing that littered the turf around them, and the sun was warm on their naked bodies, although never as warm as the heat of their own mutual generating . . .

Almost, Grimes did not hear the sharp *plop.*

Almost he did not hear it, but he felt the metal strands writhing about his bare skin, biting into his limbs, binding himself and Marlene together in a ghastly parody, an obscene exhibition of physical love.

Into his limited range of vision, still further obscured by the tangle of the girl's blonde hair, stepped de Messigny. In his hand he held one of the bellmouthed net-throwing pistols.

"A pretty picture!" he sneered. "A very pretty picture." In spite of the deliberate coldness of his voice, it was obvious that he was struggling to contain his fury. "As for you, Marlene, you slut! An affair with one of us, I could have tolerated, but for you to give yourself to a lowbred outworlder!"

Her voice, in reply, was muffled. Grimes could feel her lips moving against his face. "I'm not property, Henri. I'm not *your* property."

"I would not want you now, you bitch."

Grimes saw that the man had pulled a knife from the sheath at his belt. He struggled to get his mouth clear, after an effort was able to mumble, "Put that thing away."

"Not yet, Mr. Grimes. Not yet."

"But this is not Marlene's fault, de Messigny."

"I have come here neither as judge nor as executioner, Mr. Grimes, although Marlene will be most appropriately punished for what *she* has done. I have come only to sacrifice Lobenga's white goat, and the white goat is *you.*"

Grimes waited for the descent of the blade. Stab or slash, what did it matter? Although a stab might be faster. And then de Messigny uttered a choking cry, seemed to be trying to contort himself so that he could strike with the blade at something behind him. Wound tightly about his neck there was a thin, metal tentacle. He was jerked out of sight.

Grimes heard the threshing sounds of the Comte's struggles slowly diminish. They finally ceased.

"The miniwagon . . ." whispered Marlene. "It's only a carryall but it has intelligence of sorts, and it's supposed to protect its mistress to the best of its ability. But it's slow. It was almost too slow . . ."

"It . . . it got here in time."

"Only . . . just."

She was close to him, even closer then she had been before de Messigny cast his net. Suddenly he was acutely conscious of her, all of her. And he had some freedom, not much, but a little, enough.

"Can you . . . ?" she murmured. Then, "After all, as the old saying has it, we might as well be hung for sheep as lambs . . ."

"I can . . ." he muttered.

He did.

And then, only then, did Marlene give careful orders to the dim-witted machine, telling it to pick up the pistol with its tentacle, telling it how to set the weapon so that a pulse of radiation would cause the net to loose its hold. Neither of them could see what was happening, and Grimes feared that the stupid thing would well-meaningly pick up and fire the Minetti at them.

But it did not, and each of them felt a brief tingling sensation, and then they were free. Marlene wept again over her slaughtered dogs, stared at the purple-faced, contorted body of de Messigny without expression. She resumed her clothing. Grimes resumed his.

They clambered into the miniwagon, let it carry them in silence back to the Castle.

26

THEY WERE WAITING for Grimes and Marlene in the castle courtyard—Lobenga, the Lady Eulalia, and the Duchess of Leckhampton. They were an oddly assorted trio: the Negro in his leopard skin, with a necklace of bones (animal? human?) and with a hide bag, containing who knew what disgusting relics slung at his waist; his wife robed in spotless white, with a gold circlet about her dark hair; the Duchess in gaudy finery, flounced skirt boldly striped in black and scarlet, sequined lemon-yellow blouse, a blue, polka dotted kerchief as a head covering. The clay pipe that she was smoking with obvious enjoyment should have been incongruous, but it suited her. Before them was a large box, a three dimensional viewing screen. To one side was the grim effigy of Baron Samedi, the wooden cross in its scarecrow clothing. It should have looked absurd in broad daylight, in these surroundings, but it did not.

Witch doctor, priestess and fortune teller . . . thought Grimes bewilderedly.

"What is this?" demanded Marlene. "What are you doing here?"

"We had to come outside, Princess," Lobenga told her. "There is magic soaked into the very stones of your castle, but it is the wrong sort of magic."

"Magic!" her voice was contemptuous, "That?" She gestured to the extension of the Monitor, in the screen of which the dead man, the dead dogs and the crumpled wreckage of the rogue were still visible. "Or *that?*" Her arm pointed rigidly at the clothed cross.

"Or both?" asked the Duchess quietly.

"You watched?"

"We watched," confirmed Lobenga.

"Everything?"

"Everything."

"And you did nothing to help?"

"It was all in the cards," said the Duchess.

"And you watched, everything. And you felt a vicarious thrill, just as you do at those famous masked balls of yours, Your Grace. There is nothing more despicable than a *voyeur*, especially one who spies upon her friends."

"We were obliged to watch," said Lobenga.

"By whom? By what?"

"The bones were cast," almost sang Eulalia, "the cards were read. But still there was the possibility of the unforeseen, the unforeseeable, some malign malfunction of the plan. We had to be ready to intervene."

"There were quite a few times when you could have intervened," growled the spaceman. "When you *should* have intervened."

"No," said Lobenga. "No, Mr. Grimes. The entire operation went as planned."

"What a world!" snarled the Lieutenant. "What a bloody world! I'm sorry, Marlene, but I can't stay in this castle a second longer. I don't like your friends. Call me a taxi, or whatever you do on this planet, so that I can get back to the ship. Tell that tin butler of yours to pack my bags."

"John!"

"I mean it, Marlene."

"Let him go," said Eulalia. "He has played his part."

"As I have," whispered the princess.

"Yes."

"As Henri did."

"Yes."

She flared, "What sort of monsters are you?"

"Not monsters, Marlene," said Lobenga gently. "Just servants of a higher power."

"Of the Monitor?" she sneered. "Or of Baron Samedi?"

"Or both?" asked Eulalia.

"Things went a little too far," said the Duchess.

"You mean Henri's death?" queried Marlene. "But somebody had to die."

"I do not mean Henri's death. I mean what happened afterwards. But it does not matter. After all, the English aristocracy has always welcomed an occasional infusion of fresh blood. And, my dear, in a way the child, if there is one, will be Henri's."

"That," said Marlene, her voice expressionless, "is a comforting thought."

"I'm glad that you see it that way." The Duchess sucked on her pipe, blew out a cloud of smoke that was acrid rather than fragrant. "You know, my dear, the cards were really uncanny. The Hanged Man kept turning up." For Grimes' benefit she explained, "That is one of the cards of ill-omen in the Tarot pack." She went on, "Of course, we were expecting a death, a violent death, but not in so literal a manner."

"Must we go into all this, Honoria?" asked Marlene.

"If you would rather not, my dear, we will not. But . . ."

"But *what?"*

"Poor Henri was addicted to the use of archaic slang but, oddly enough, only when he was talking to me. Just before he went out to play Vulcan to your Venus and Mars he said that he was going to fix your wagon." She deliberately took her time refilling and relighting her short pipe. "But your wagon fixed him."

"Let us leave these ghouls," said Marlene disgustedly. Grimes fell rather than jumped out of the miniwagon, then helped the girl to the ground. Together they walked into the castle.

"Yes, John," said Marlene. "It is better that you return to your ship. You have played your part, more than your part."

Grimes looked at the girl's grave face. There was nothing in it for him any more. He looked past her to the shining weapons incongruously displayed on the wall of her boudoir. He thought, *I know more about guns than women.*

He said, "I'm sorry it happened."

"Don't be a liar, John. You wanted me from the very first moment that you saw me, and you finally got me."

"Are you sorry it happened?"

For the first time since their return to the castle, she showed signs of emotion.

"That is a hard question to answer, John. But, no, I am not sorry that it happened. I am not even sorry that it happened the way that it did. What I am sorry about is the humiliation. And, of course, Henri's death." Her features suddenly contorted into a vicious mask. "But he deserved it!"

"And somebody, as everybody here has been telling me, had to die."

"And better, I suppose, one of us than one of you. It keeps it all in the family, doesn't it? Very neat, very tidy." There were the beginnings of hysteria in her voice.

"Marlene!"

"No. *Don't touch me!*"

"All right. But I thought . . ."

"Don't think. It's dangerous."

"Marlene, what about the child, if there is one?"

"What about it?"

"Well . . . it could be . . . embarrassing. Will you marry me?"

She laughed then but it was not hysterical laughter. It was not altogether contemptuous. "Oh, John, John . . . The perfect petty bourgeois to the very last. Offering to make an honest woman of me, *me*, and on a world which can boast the finest medical brains in the Galaxy. Not that our physicians have had much practice in terminating pregnancies. Marry *you*, John, a penniless Survey Service Lieutenant? Oh, I appreciate it, appreciate the offer, but it just wouldn't work out. You aren't our sort of people and we aren't yours. I'd sooner have married Henri, and he asked me often enough, with all his faults."

"We could marry," he pressed doggedly, "and then divorce."

"No. This is El Dorado, not some lower middle-class slum of a planet. And furthermore, John, I shall be a heroine. I shall go down in history. The first woman to conceive on this world."

"You don't know that you have."

"But I do. I . . . I *felt* it."

He got slowly to his feet. "I'll see if Karl has packed my bags."

She said, "You don't have to go."

He asked, "Do you want me to?"

Her expression softened almost imperceptibly. "What if I told you that Lobenga, Eulalia and the Duchess have already left the castle? They have done what they had to do."

"And have they? Left, I mean."

"Yes."

He felt the weakening of his resolution. Those other guests had witnessed what had happened between Marlene and himself but, as servants of the Monitor, there was much that they must have witnessed. Now that he would no longer be obliged to meet them socially . . .

"You will stay?" she asked.

"Why?" he queried bluntly.

"Because . . ."

"Because what?"

"Because I want to be sure."

"You told me that you were."

She quoted, "Only two things in life are certain, death and taxes. Death, John, not birth. But, together, we can bring some degree of certainty to the fact of conception."

He said, "You are a cold-blooded bitch."

"But I'm not, John, I'm not." She was on her feet, her body gleaming golden through the translucent green wrap that she had changed into, her slender arms slightly away from her sides. He took a step toward her, and another, until she was pressed against him. Her hands went up, clasped at the back of his neck, pulled his mouth down to hers.

There was a discreet, metallic cough.

The princess pulled away from Grimes, asked coldly, "Yes, Karl?"

"I must apologize, Your Highness. But a call has come through by way of the Monitor for all personnel of the cruiser *Aries*. It seems that the ship is urgently required to help quell an insurrection on Merganta, which world, as you know, is only two light years from El Dorado. Lieutenant Grimes' bags are already in the air car."

She said, "You have to go."

He said, "Yes."

"Goodbye."

"I'll be back."

"Will you?" she asked, her face suddenly hard. "Will you?" Her laugh was brittle. "Yes, John, come back when you have your first billion credits."

He could think of nothing more to say, turned abruptly on his heel and followed the robot to the waiting air car.

27

THERE WAS THE insurrection on Merganta, a bloody affair, in the suppression of which *Aries* did all that was demanded of her, but no more. Many of her officers and most of her crew felt more than a little sympathy for the rebels. It was Grimes, in command of one of the cruiser's armed pinnaces, who intervened to stop the mass executions of three hundred women, wives of leading insurgents, turning his weapons on the government machine gunners. For this he was reprimanded, officially, by Captain Daintree, who, later, in a stormy interview with the planetary president, used such phrases as "an overly zealous officer" and "mistaken identity," adding coldly that Lieutenant Grimes naturally assumed that it was not the forces of law and order who were about to commit cold-blooded murder.

There was the mutiny aboard the Dog Star Line's freighter *Corgi* and the long chase, almost clear out to the Rim, before the merchantman was overhauled and boarded. The mutineers did not put up a fight, for which Grimes, in charge of the boarding party, was profoundly thankful. He had seen enough of killing.

There was the earthquake that destroyed Ballantrae, the capital of Ayr, one of the planets of the Empire of Waverley. *Aries*, the only major vessel in the vicinity, hastened to the stricken city, performed nobly in the rescue work and then, from her generators, supplied power for essential services until the work of reconstruction was well under way.

All in all, it was an eventful voyage, and a long one, with the movements of the ship unpredictable. The married men, those who were pining for letters from home, were far from sorry when, at last, *Aries* was recalled to Lindisfarne Base.

Almost all the officers were in the wardroom when the mail came on board. They waited impatiently. Finally Hodge, the Paymaster Lieutenant, came in, followed by a rating carrying a large hamper of packages. "Gentlemen," he announced. "Cupid's messenger, in person. Sweethearts and wives, all in the same basket. What am I bid?"

"Cut the cackle, Hodge!" snarled Lieutenant Commander Cooper. "Deal 'em out, although mine'll be only bills and please explains as usual."

"As you say, sir, Lieutenant Commander, sir. Roll up, roll up, for the lucky dip!"

"Get on with it, Hodge!" snapped the Navigator. He was not the only one becoming impatient. Luckily the mail had already been sorted, so there was little delay in its distribution. Most of the officers, as soon as they had received their share, retired to the privacy of their own cabins to read it.

Grimes looked at his, recognizing handwriting, typescript styles, postage stamps. A letter from Faraway . . . From Jane? Nice of her to write after all these years. One from Caribbea. That would be from Susanna. And a parcel, a little, cubical parcel. The address typed, with oddly Gothic lettering. And the stamp in the likeness of a gold coin, and it probably was embossed goldleaf at that . . .

Surgeon Commander Passifern was demanding attention. "This is interesting," he declaimed. "This is *really* interesting. You remember how we we were called in to El Dorado so that I could help their top doctor, Lord Tarlton of Dunwich, with his problem. I worked with him and his people—they've some brilliant men there, too—quite closely. 'Diet,' I said to him. 'Diet, Tarlton, that's the answer. Cut out all this fancy, mucked-up food of yours, get back to the simple life. Don't overeat. Don't drink.' "

"Physician, heal thyself . . ." muttered Cooper.

Passifern ignored this. "and it worked. This—" he waved the sheet of expensive looking paper—"is a letter front Lord Tarlton. In it he thanks me—well, *us*, actually, but he's just being polite to the ship—for our help. Since we left there have been no fewer than four hundred and twenty-five births."

"Did he . . ." began Grimes, "did he say who the mothers were?"

"Hardly, young Grimes. Not in a short note."

"At least," put in Cooper, "we know that none of us were the fathers."

Grimes left the wardroom then. He found himself resenting the turn that the conversation had taken. He went to his cabin, shut the door behind him, then sat down on his bunk. He found the little tab on the seal of the parcel, pulled it sharply. The wrapping fell away.

Inside it was a solidograph. From its depths smiled a blonde woman, Marlene, a more mature Marlene, a matronly Marlene, looking down at the infant in her arms.

Grimes had been amused more than once by the gushing female friends of young mothers with their fatuous remarks: "Oh, he's got his mother's eyes," or "He's got his Uncle Fred's nose," or "He's got his Auntie Kate's mouth . . ."

But there was, he admitted now, something in it.

This child, indubitably, had his father's ears.

Suddenly he felt very sorry that he would never make that billion credits.

The Hard Way Up

With Good Intentions

PATHFINDER WAS NOT a happy ship.

Pathfinder's Captain was not a happy man, and made this glaringly obvious.

Young Lieutenant Grimes, newly appointed to the Survey Service cruiser, was also far from happy. During his few years in Space he had served under strict commanding officers as well as easy going ones, but never under one like Captain Tolliver.

"You must make allowances, John," Paymaster Lieutenant Beagle told him as the two young men were discussing matters over a couple or three drinks in Grimes's cabin.

"Make allowances?" echoed Grimes. "I don't know what's biting him—but I know what's biting me. Him, that's what."

"All the same, you should make allowances."

"It's all very well for you to talk, Peter—but you idlers can keep out of his way. We watchkeepers can't."

"But he's a Worrallian," said Beagle. "Didn't you know?"

"No," admitted Grimes. "I didn't."

He knew now. He knew, too, that there were only a hundred or so Worrallians throughout the entire Galaxy. Not so long ago the population of Worrall had been nudging the thirty million mark. Worrall had been a prosperous planet—also it had been among the few Man-colonised worlds of the Interstellar Federation upon which the concepts of race and nationality had been allowed to take hold and develop. "It makes for healthy competition," had been the claim of the Worrallian delegations—three of them—whenever the subject came up at the meetings of the Federation Grand Council. And so they had competed happily among themselves on their little ball of mud and rock and water—North Worrall, and South Worrall, and Equatorial Worrall—until all three nations laid simultaneous claim to a chain of hitherto worthless islands upon which flourished the stinkbird colonies. The stinkbird—it was more of a flying reptile really, although with certain mammalian characteristics—had always been regarded as more unpleasant than useful, and if anybody had wanted those barren, precipitous rocks lashed by the perpetually stormy seas the stinkbird would soon have gone the way of many another species unlucky enough to get in Man's way. The stinkbird—along with everything and everybody else on Worrall—finally was unlucky, this being when a bright young chemist discovered that a remarkably effective rejuvenating compound was secreted by certain glands in its body. Worrall, although a prosperous enough closed economy, had always been lacking, until this time, in exports that would fetch high prices on the interstellar market.

So there was a squabble—with words at first, and then with weapons. In its ultimate stage somebody pushed some sort of button—or, quite possibly, three buttons were pushed. The only Worrallians to survive were those who were elsewhere at the time of the button-pushing.

And Captain Tolliver was a Worrallian.

Grimes sighed. He felt sorry for the man. He could visualise, but dimly, what it must be like to have no place in the entire Galaxy to call home, to know that everything, but everything had been vaporised in one hellish blast of fusion flame—parents, friends, lovers, the house in which one was brought up, the school in which one was educated, the bars in which one used to drink. Grimes shuddered.

But he still felt sorry for himself.

Grimes realised that Captain Tolliver had come into the control room. But, as the commanding officer had not announced his presence, the young man went on with what he was doing—the midwatch check of the ship's position. Carefully, trying hard not to fumble, Grimes manipulated the Carlotti Direction Finder—an instrument with which he was not yet familiar—lining up the antenna, an elliptical Mobius Strip rotating about its long axis, with the Willishaven beacon, finally jotting down the angle relative to the fore-and-aft line of the ship. Then, still working slowly and carefully, he took a reading on Brownsworld and, finally, on Carlyon. By this time he was perspiring heavily and his shirt was sticking to his body, and his prominent ears were flushed and burning painfully. He swivelled his chair so that he could reach the chart tank, laid off the bearings. The three filaments of luminescence intersected nicely, exactly on the brighter filament that marked *Pathfinder*'s trajectory. Decisively Grimes punched the keys that caused the time of the observation, in tiny, glowing figures, to appear alongside the position.

"Hrrmph."

Grimes simulated a start of surprise, swung round in his chair to face the Captain. "Sir?"

Tolliver was a tall, gangling scarecrow of a man, and even though his uniform was clean and correct in every detail it hung on him like a penitent's sackcloth and ashes. He stared down at his officer from bleak grey eyes. He said coldly, "Mr. Grimes, I checked the time it took you to put a position in the tank. It was no less than eleven minutes, forty-three point five seconds. Objective speed is thirty-five point seven six lumes. Over what distance did this ship travel from start to finish of your painfully slow operations?"

"I can work it out, sir . . ." Grimes half got up from his chair to go to the control room computer.

"Don't bother, Mr. Grimes. Don't bother. I realise that watchkeepers have more important things with which to exercise their tiny minds than the boresome details of navigation—the girl in the last port, perhaps, or the girl you hope to meet in the next one . . ."

More than Grimes's ears was flushed now. A great proportion of his watch had been spent reminiscing over the details of his shore leave on New Capri.

"This cross of yours looks suspiciously good. I would have expected an inexpert navigator such as yourself to produce more of a cocked hat. I suppose you did allow for distance run between bearings?"

"Of course, sir."

"Hrrmph. Well, Mr. Grimes, we will assume that this fix of yours is reasonably accurate. Put down a D.R. from it for 1200 hours, then lay off a trajectory from there to Delta Sextans."

"Delta Sextans, sir?"

"You heard me."

"But aren't we bound for Carlyon?"

"We were bound for Carlyon, Mr. Grimes. But—although it may well have escaped your notice—the arm of our lords and masters in Admiralty House is a long one, extending over many multiples of light years. For your information, we have been ordered to conduct a survey of the planetary system of Delta Sextans."

"Will there be landings, sir?" asked Grimes hopefully.

"Should it concern you, Mr. Grimes, you will be informed when the time comes. Please lay off the trajectory."

Lieutenant Commander Wanger, the ship's Executive Officer, was more informative than the Captain had been. Convening off-duty officers in the wardroom he gave them a run-down on the situation. He said, "No matter what the biologists, sociologists and all the rest of 'em come up with, population keeps on exploding. And so we, as well as most of the other survey cruisers presently in commission, have been ordered to make more thorough inspections of habitable planets which, in the past, were filed away, as it were, for future reference.

"Delta Sextans has a planetary family of 10 worlds. Of these, only two—Delta Sextans IV and Delta Sextans V—could possibly meet our requirements. According to Captain Lovell's initial survey IV could be rather too hot, and V more than a little too cold. Both support oxygen-breathing life forms, although V, with its mineral wealth, has greater industrial potential than IV. In any case it is doubtful if IV will be selected as the site for the Delta Sextans colony; Captain Lovell said that in his opinion, and in that of his biologists, at least one of the indigenous species comes into the third category."

"And what is that?" asked a junior engineer.

"Any being in the third category," explained the Executive Officer, "is considered capable of evolving into the second category."

"And what is the second category?" persisted the engineer.

"The likes of us. And the first category is what we might become—or, if we're very unlucky, run into. Anyhow, the ruling is that third category beings may be observed, but not interfered with. And taking somebody else's world is classed as interference. Will somebody pour me some more coffee?"

Somebody did, and after lubricating his throat Wanger went on. "The drill will be this. We establish a camp of observers on IV—according to the initial surveys there's nothing there that could be at all dangerous to well-equipped humans—and then the ship shoves off for V to get on with the real work. There's no doubt that V will be selected for the new colony—but it will be as well if the colonists know something about their next-door neighbours."

"Any idea who'll be landed on IV?" asked Grimes.

"Haven't a clue, John. There'll be a team of biologists, ethologists, cartographers, geologists, and whatever. If the Old Man abides by Regulations—and he will—there'll be an officer of the military branch officially in charge of the camp. Frankly, it's not a job that I'd care for—I've had experience of it. Whoever goes with the boggins will soon find that he's no more than chief cook and bottle washer—quite literally."

Nonetheless, Grimes was pleased when he was told, some days later, that he was to be in charge of the landing party.

Pathfinder hung in orbit about Delta Sextans IV until the boat was safely down, until Grimes reported that the camp was established. To start with, Grimes enjoyed his authority and responsibility—then found that once the turbulent atmospheric approach had been negotiated and the landing craft was sitting solidly and safely on the bank of a river it was responsibility only. The scientists—not at all offensively—soon made it clear that once they were away from the ship gold braid and brass buttons meant less than nothing. When the stores and equipment were unloaded each of them was concerned only with his own treasures. They cooperated, after a fashion, in setting up the inflatable tents that were living quarters and laboratory. Reluctantly they agreed to defer their initial explorations until the following morning. (The boat, following the Survey Service's standard practice, had landed at local dawn, but by the time that Grimes had things organised to his liking the sun, a blur of light and heat heavily veiled by the overcast, was almost set.)

It was Grimes who cooked the evening meal—and even though the most important tool employed in its preparation was a can opener he rather resented it. Three of the six scientists were women, and if anybody had ever told them that a woman's place is in the kitchen they had promptly forgotten it. He resented it, too, when nobody showed any appreciation of his efforts. His charges gobbled their food without noticing what it was, intent upon their shop talk. The only remark addressed to Grimes was a casual suggestion that he have the flitters ready for use at first light.

The Lieutenant left the surveying party, still talking nineteen to the dozen, in the mess tent, hoping that they would eventually get around to stacking the dishes and washing up. (They didn't.) Outside it was almost dark and, in spite of the heat of the past day, there was a damp chill in the air. Something was howling in the forest of cabbagelike trees back from the river bank, and something else flapped overhead on wide, clattering wings. There were insects, too—or things analogous to insects. They did not bite, but they were a nuisance. They were attracted, Grimes decided, by his body heat. He muttered to himself, "If the bastards like warmth so much, why the hell can't they come out in the daytime?"

He decided to switch on the floods. With this perpetual overcast he might have trouble recharging the batteries during the hours of daylight, but they should hold out until *Pathfinder*'s return. He was able to work easily in the harsh glare and made a thorough check of the alarm system. Anything trying to get into the camp would either be electrocuted or get a nasty shock, according to size. (The same applied, of course, to anything or anybody trying to get out—but he had warned the scientists.) Finally he opened the boxes in which the flitters were stowed, started to assemble the first of the machines. He did not like them much himself—they were flimsy, one-person helicopters, with a gas bag for greater lift—but he doubted that he would get the chance to use one. Already he could see that he would be confined to camp for the duration of the party's stay on IV.

With the camp secure for the night and the flitters assembled he returned to the mess tent—to find that the scientists had retired to their sleeping tents and left him with all the washing up.

Came the dawn, such as it was, and Grimes was rudely awakened by Dr. Kortsoff, one of the biologists. "Hey, young Grimes," shouted the bearded, burly scientist. "Rise and shine! What about some breakfast? Some of us have to work for our livings, you know!"

"I know," grumbled Grimes, "That's what I was doing most of last night."

He extricated himself from his sleeping bag, pulled on yesterday's shirt and shorts (still stiff with dried sweat, but they would have to do until he got *himself* organised) and thrust his feet into sandals, stumbled out of his tent—and was surrounded by a mob of naked women. There were only three of them, as a matter of fact, but they were making enough noise for a mob. One of them, at least—the red-haired Dr. Margaret Lazenby—possessed the sort of good looks enhanced by anger, but Grimes was not in an appreciative mood.

"Mr. Grimes!" she snapped. "Do you want to *kill* us?"

"What do you mean, Dr. Lazenby?" he asked meekly.

"That bloody force field of yours, or whatever it is. When we were trying to go down to the river for our morning swim Jenny and I were nearly electrocuted. Turn the bloody thing off, will you?"

"I warned you last night that I'd set it up . . ."

"We never heard you. In any case, there aren't any dangerous animals here . . ."

"Never take anything for granted . . ." Grimes began.

"You can say that again, Grimes. Never take it for granted, for example, that everybody knows all about the odd things you do during the night when sensible people are sleeping. Setting up force fields on a world where there's nothing more dangerous than a domestic cat!"

"What about some *coffee*, Mr. Grimes?" somebody else was yelling.

"I've only one pair of hands," muttered Grimes as he went to switch off the force field.

And so it went on throughout the day—fetch this, fix that, do this, don't do that, lend a hand here, there's a good fellow . . . Grimes remembered, during a very brief smoke, what Maggie Lazenby had told him once about the pecking order, claiming that what was true for barnyard fowls was also true for human beings. "There's the boss bird," she had said, "and she's entitled to peck everybody. There's the number two bird—and she's pecked by the boss, and pecks everybody else. And so on, down the line, until we come to the poor little bitch who's pecked by *everybody*."

"But that doesn't apply to humans," Grimes had demurred. "Doesn't it just, duckie! In schools, aboard ships . . . I've nothing to do with the administration of this wagon—thank all the Odd Gods of the Galaxy!—but even I can see now that poor Ordinary Spaceman Wilkes is bullied by everybody . . ."

Grimes had never, so far as he knew, bullied that hapless rating—but he found himself wishing that the man were here. As he was not, Grimes was bottom bird in the pecking order. There was no malice about it—or no conscious malice. It was just that Grimes was, by the standards of the scientific party, only semi-literate, his status that of a hewer of wood, a drawer of water. He was in an environment where his qualifications counted for little or nothing, where the specialists held sway. And these same specialists, Grimes realised, must have resented the very necessary discipline aboard the ship. Although they would never have admitted it to themselves they were dogs having their day.

The next day wasn't so bad. Six of the flitters were out—which meant that Grimes had the camp to himself. Two by two the scientists had lifted from the camp site, ascending into the murk like glittering, mechanical angels. Carrying a portable transceiver—and a projectile pistol, just in case—Grimes went for a stroll along the river bank. He felt a little guilty about deserting his post, but should any of his charges get into trouble and yell for help he would know at once. He decided that he would walk to the first bend in the wide stream, and then back.

Delta Sextans IV was not a pretty world. The sky was grey, with a paler blur that marked the passage of the hot sun across it. The river was grey. The fleshy-leaved vegetation was grey, with the merest hint of dull green. There was little distinction between blossom and foliage as far as a non-botanist like Grimes was concerned.

But it was good to get away from the camp, from that huddle of plastic igloos, and from the multitudinous chores. It was good to walk on the surface of a world unspoiled by Man, the first time that Grimes had done so. Captain Lovell's survey had been, after all, a very superficial effort and so, thought Grimes, there was a chance that he, even he, would find something, some plant or animal, that would be named after him. He grinned wryly. If any Latin tags were to be affixed to local fauna and flora his own name would be the last to be considered.

He came to the bend in the river, decided to carry on for just a few yards past it. *Well*, he thought with a glow of pleasure, *I have found* something—*something which the others, flapping around on their tin wings, have missed*... The something was an obvious game trail leading through the jungle to the water's edge. But why in this particular spot? Grimes investigated. Elsewhere the bank was steep—here there was a little bay, with a gently shelving beach. Here, too, growing in the shallow water, was a clump of odd-looking plants—straight, thick stems, each a few feet high, each topped by a cluster of globules varying in size from grape to orange. And here, too, something had died or been killed. Only the bones were left—yellowish, pallidly gleaming. There was a rib cage, which must have run the entire length of a cylindrical body. There was a skull, almost spherical. There were jaws, with teeth—the teeth of a herbivore, thought Grimes. The beast, obviously, had been a quadruped, and about the size of a Terran Shetland pony.

Suddenly Grimes stiffened. Something was coming along that trail through the jungle—something that rustled and chattered. As he backed away from the skeleton he pulled out his pistol, thumbed back the safety catch. He retreated to the bend of the river and waited there, ready to fight or run—but curious as to what sort of animal would appear.

There were more than one of them. They spilled out on to the river bank—about a dozen grey, shaggy brutes, almost humanoid. Mostly they walked upright, but now and again dropped to all fours. They chattered and gesticulated. They varied in size from that of a small man to that of a young child—but somehow Grimes got the idea that there were no children among them.

They had not come to drink. They went straight to the plants, started tearing the largest—the ripest?—fruit from the stems, stuffing them into their wide mouths, gobbling them greedily. There was plenty for all—but, inevitably, there was one who wasn't getting any. It was not that he was the smallest of the tribe—but neither was he the largest. Even so, his trouble seemed to be psychological rather than physical; he seemed to be hampered by a certain diffidence, a reluctance to join in the rough and tumble scramble.

At last, when all his mates were busy gorging themselves, he shambled slowly through the shallows to the fruit plants. Glancing timorously around to see that nobody was watching he put out a hand, wrenched one of the spheroids from its stem. He was not allowed to even taste it. A hairy paw landed on the side of his head with a loud *hunk,* knocking him sprawling into the muddy water. The brute who had attacked him snatched the fruit from his hand, bit into it, spat and grimaced and threw it out into the river. No less than three times there was a roughly similar sequence of events—and then, as though in response to some inaudible signal, the troop scampered back into the jungle, the victim of the bullies looking back wistfully to the fruit that he had not so much as tasted.

That evening Grimes told the scientists about his own minor exploration, but none of them was interested. Each was too engrossed in his own project—the deposit of rich, radioactive ores, the herds of food animals, the villages of the simian-like creatures. Maggie Lazenby did say that she would accompany Grimes as soon as she had a spare five minutes—but that would not be until her real work had been tidied up. And then, after dinner, Grimes was left with the washing up as usual.

That night he set an alarm to wake him just before sunrise, so that he was able to switch off the force fields to allow the women to leave the camp for their morning swim, to make coffee and get breakfast preparations under way. After the meals he was left to himself again.

He was feeling a certain kinship with the native who was bottom bird in the pecking order. He thought smugly: "If Maggie were right, I'd kick him around myself. But I'm civilised." This time he took with him a stun-gun instead of a projectile pistol, setting the control for mini minimum effect.

The natives had not yet arrived at the little bay when he got there. He pulled off his shoes and stockings, waded out through the shallow water to where the fruit-bearing plants were growing. He plucked two of the largest, ripest-seeming globes. He didn't know whether or not they would be dangerous to the human metabolism, and was not tempted to find out. Even with their tough skins intact they stank. Then he retired a few yards from the end of the trail, sat down to wait.

At almost exactly the same time the gibbering, gesticulating troop debouched from the jungle. As before, the timid member hung back, hovering on the outskirts of the scrum, awaiting his chance—his slim chance—to get some fruit for himself. Grimes got slowly to his feet. The primitive humanoids ignored him, save for the timorous one—but even he stood his ground. Grimes walked carefully forward, the two ripe fruit extended in his left hand. He saw a flicker of interest, of greed, in the creature's yellow eyes, the glisten of saliva at the corners of the wide, thin-lipped mouth. And then, warily, the thing was shambling towards him. "Come and get it," whispered Grimes. "Come and get it."

Was the native telepathic? As soon as he was within snatching distance of the spaceman he snatched, his long nails tearing the skin of Grimes's left hand. Were his fellows telepathic? Growling, the leader of the troop dropped the fruit that he had been guzzling, scampered through the shallows and up the bank towards the recipient of Grimes's gift. That miserable being whined and cringed, extended the fruit towards the bully in a placatory gesture.

Grimes growled too. His stun-gun was ready, and aiming it was a matter of microseconds. He pressed the stud. The bully gasped, dropped to the ground, twitching. "Eat your bloody fruit, damn you!" snarled Grimes. This time the timorous one managed a couple of bites before another bully—number two in the pecking order?—tried to steal his meal. By the time the fruit were finished no less than half a dozen bodies were strewn on the mosslike ground-covering growth. They were not dead, Grimes noted with some relief. As he watched the first two scrambled unsteadily to their feet, stared at him reproachfully and then shambled away to feed on what few ripe fruit were left. Characteristically they did not pluck these for themselves but snatched them from the weaker members of the troop. Oddly enough they made no attempt to revenge themselves on Grimes's protégé.

The next day Grimes continued his experiment. As before, he plucked two tempting—but not to him—fruit. As before, he presented them to Snuffy. (It was as good a name as any.) This time, however, he was obliged to use his stun-gun only once. Grimes thought that it was the troop leader—again—who was least capable of learning by experience. The third day he did not have to use the weapon at all, and Snuffy allowed him to pat him, and patted him back. The fourth day he did not think that he would be using the gun—and then one of the smaller humanoids, one who had taken Snuffy's place as tribal butt, screamed angrily and flew at Snuffy, all claws and teeth. Snuffy dropped his fruit and tried to run—and then the whole troop was on him, gibbering and hitting and kicking. Grimes—the gun set on wide beam, shocked them all into unconsciousness. When they recovered all of them scampered back into the jungle.

On the fifth day Grimes was all ready for the next stage of his experiment. He was glad that the scientists were still fully occupied with their own games; he suspected that they—especially Maggie Lazenby—would want to interfere, would want things done their way, would complicate an essentially simple situation. It was all so glaringly obvious to the young Lieutenant. Snuffy would have to be taught to defend himself, to protect his own rights.

He picked the two fruits as usual. He used the stun-gun to deter the bullies—and then he used the weapon on Snuffy, giving him another shock every time that he showed signs of regaining consciousness. He realised that the creature—as he had hoped would be the case—was not popular with his troop fellows; when the time came for them to return to their village or whatever it was they vanished into the jungle without a backward glance. Grimes lifted Snuffy—he wasn't very heavy—and carried him to where the skeleton of the horse-like animal lay on the bank like the bones of a wrecked and stranded ship. He felt a tickling on his skin under his shirt, was thankful that he had thought to make a liberal application of insect-repellent before leaving the camp. He deposited the hairy body on the thick moss, then went to work on the skeleton. Using his knife to sever the dry, tough ligaments he was able to detach the two thigh bones. They made good clubs—a little too short and too light for a man's use, but just right for a being of Snuffy's size. Finally he picked some more fruit—there were a few ripe ones that had been missed by the troop.

At last Snuffy came round, making his characteristic snuffling sound. He stared at Grimes. Grimes looked calmly back, offered him what he had come to think of as a stink-apple. Snuffy accepted it, bit into it. He belched. Grimes regretted that he was not wearing a respirator. While the humanoid was happily munching. Grimes juggled with one of the thigh bones. Snuffy finally condescended to notice what he was doing, to evince some interest. With a sharp *crack* Grimes brought his club down on the skeleton's rib cage. Two of the ribs were broken cleanly in two.

Snuffy extended his hands toward the club. Grimes gave it to him, picking up the other one.

The native was a good pupil. Finally, without any prompting from the spaceman, he was flailing away at the skull of the dead animal, at last cracking it. Grimes looked guiltily at his watch. It was time that he was getting back to the camp to get the preparations for the evening meal under way. Still feeling guilty, he wondered how Snuffy would make it back to his own living place, what his reception would be. But he was armed now, would be able to look after himself—Grimes hoped.

And then it became obvious that the native had no intention of going home by himself. Still carrying his bone club he shambled along at Grimes's side, uttering an occasional plaintive *eek.* He would not be chased off, and Grimes was reluctant to use the stun-gun on him. But there was a spare tent that would be used eventually for the storage of specimens. Snuffy would have to sleep there.

To Grimes's surprise and relief the native did not seem to mind when he was taken into the plastic igloo. He accepted a bowl of water, burying his wrinkled face in it and slurping loudly. Rather dubiously he took a stick of candy, but once he had sampled it it soon disappeared. (Grimes had learned from the scientists that anything eaten by the life form of Delta Sextans IV could be handled by the human metabolism; it was logical to suppose that a native of IV could eat human food with safety.) More water, and more candy—and Snuffy looked ready to retire for the night, curling up on the floor of the tent in a foetal posture. Grimes left him to it.

He did not sleep at all well himself. He was afraid that his . . . guest? prisoner? would awake during the hours of darkness, would awaken the whole camp by howling or other anti-social conduct. Grimes was beginning to have an uneasy suspicion that the scientists would not approve of his experiments. But the night was as silent as night on Delta Sextans IV ever was, and after their usual early breakfast the scientific party flapped off on its various occasions.

Grimes went to the spare tent, opened the flap. The stench that gusted out made him retch, although Snuffy did not seem to be worried by it. The native shambled into the open on all fours, and then, rising to an approximately erect posture, went back inside for his previous club. With his free hand he patted Grimes on the arm, grimacing up at him and whining. Grimes led him to where a bucket of water was standing ready, and beside it two candy bars.

The spaceman, fighting down his nausea, cleaned up the interior of the tent. It had been bad enough washing up after the scientists—but this was too much. From now on Snuffy would have to look after himself. He had no occasion to change his mind as the aborigine followed him around while he coped with the camp chores. The humanoid displayed an uncanny genius for getting in the way.

At last, at long last, it was time to get down to the river. Grimes strode along smartly, Snuffy shuffling along beside him, winging his club. Their arrival at the little bay coincided with that of the troop of humanoids. Snuffy did not hang back. He got to the fruit before the others did. The troop leader advanced on him menacingly. For a moment it looked as though Snuffy were going to turn and run—then he stood his ground, seeming suddenly to gain inches in stature as he did so. Clumsily he raised his club, and even more clumsily brought it crashing down. More by luck than otherwise the blow fell on the bully's shoulder.

The second blow caught him squarely on the side of the head, felling him. Grimes saw the glisten of yellow blood in the grey, matted fur.

Snuffy screamed—but it was not a scream of fear. Brandishing the club he advanced on those who had been his tormentors. They broke and ran, most of them. The two who did not hastily retreated after each had felt the weight of the primitive weapon.

Grimes laughed shakily. "That's my boy," he murmured. "That's my boy . . ."

Snuffy ignored him. He was too busy stuffing himself with the pick of the ripe fruit.

When you have six people utterly engrossed in their own pursuits and a seventh person left to his own devices, it is easy for that seventh person to keep a secret. Not that Grimes even tried to do so. More than once he tried to tell the scientists about his own experiment in practical ethology, and each time he was brushed aside. Once Maggie Lazenby told him rather tartly, "You're only our bus driver, John. Keep to your astronautics and leave real science to us."

Then—the time of *Pathfinder*'s return from Delta Sextans V was fast approaching—Grimes was unable to spend much, if any, time on the river bank. The preliminaries to shutting up shop were well under way with specimens and records and unused stores to be packed, with the propulsion unit of the landing craft to be checked. Nonetheless, Grimes was able to check up now and again on Snuffy's progress, noted with satisfaction that the native was making out quite well.

In all too short a time the cruiser signalled that she was establishing herself in orbit about IV, also that the Captain himself would be coming down in the pinnace to inspect the camp. Grimes worked as he had never worked before. He received little help from the others—and the scientists were such untidy people. There should have been at least six general purpose robots to cope with the mess, but there was only one. Grimes. But he coped.

When the pinnace dropped down through the grey overcast the encampment was as near to being shipshape and Bristol fashion as it ever could be. Grimes barely had time to change into a clean uniform before the boat landed. He was standing to attention and saluting smartly when Captain Tolliver strode down the ramp.

Tolliver, after acknowledging the salute, actually smiled. He said, "You run a taut shore base, Mr. Grimes. I hope that when the time comes you will run a taut ship."

"Thank you, sir."

Grimes accompanied the Captain on his rounds of the encampment, the senior officer grunting his approval of the tidiness, the neatly stacked items all ready to be loaded into the landing craft and the pinnace in the correct order. And the scientists—thank the Odd Gods of the Galaxy!—were no longer their usual slovenly selves. Just as the camp was a credit to Grimes, so were they. Maggie Lazenby winked at him when Captain Tolliver was looking the other way. Grimes smiled back gratefully.

Said Tolliver, "I don't suppose that you've had time for any projects of your own, Mr. Grimes. Rather a pity . . ."

"But he has found time, sir," said the Ethologist.

"Indeed, Dr. Lazenby. What was it?"

"Er . . . We were busy ourselves, sir. But we gained the impression that Mr. Grimes was engaged upon research of some kind."

"Indeed? And what was it, Mr. Grimes?"

Grimes looked at his watch. It was almost time. He said, "I'll show you, sir. If you will come this way. Along the river . . ."

"Lead the way, Mr. Grimes," ordered Tolliver jovially. In his mind's eye Grimes saw the glimmer of that half ring of gold braid that would make him a Lieutenant Commander. Promotions in the Survey Service were the result of Captain's Reports rather than seniority.

Grimes guided Tolliver along the river bank to where the trail opened from the jungle to the little bay. "We wait here, sir," he said. He looked at his watch again. It shouldn't be long. And then, quite suddenly, Snuffy led the way out of the jungle. He was proudly carrying his bone club, holding it like a sceptre. He was flanked by two smaller humanoids, each carrying a crude bone weapon, followed by two more, also armed. He went to the fruit plants, tore at them greedily, wasted more than he ate. The others looked on hungrily. One tried to get past the guards, was clubbed down viciously. Grimes gulped. In a matter of only three days his experiment was getting out of hand.

"I have studied Captain Lovell's films of these beings," said Tolliver in a cold voice. "Are *you* responsible for this?"

"Yes, sir. But . . ."

"You will be wise to apply for a transfer, Mr. Grimes. Should you continue in the Service, which is doubtful, I sincerely hope that you discover the legendary fountain of youth."

"Why, sir?"

"Because it's a bloody pity that otherwise you won't be around to see the end results of what you started," said Tolliver bitterly.

The Subtracter

THE FEDERATION'S SURVEY Service Cruiser *Pathfinder* returned to Lindisfarne Base, and Lieutenant Grimes was one of the officers who was paid off there. He was glad to leave the ship; he had not gotten on at all well with Captain Tolliver. Yet he was far from happy. What was going to happen to him? Tolliver—who, for all his faults, was a just man—had shown Grimes part of the report that he had made on *Pathfinder*'s officers, and this part of the report was that referring to Grimes.

"Lieutenant Grimes shows initiative," Tolliver had written, "and has been known to be zealous. Unfortunately his initiative and zeal are invariably misdirected."

Grimes had decided not to make any protest. There had been occasions, he knew very well, when his initiative and zeal had not been misdirected—but never under Tolliver's command. But the Captain, as was his right—his duty—was reporting on Grimes as *he* had found him. His report was only one of many. Nonetheless Grimes was not a little worried, was wondering what his next appointment would be, what his future career in the Survey Service (if any) would be like.

Dr. Margaret Lazenby had also paid off *Pathfinder*, at the same time as Grimes. (Her Service rank was Lieutenant Commander, but she preferred the civilian title.) As old shipmates, with shared experiences, she and Grimes tended to knock about in each other's company whilst they were on Lindisfarne. In any case, the Lieutenant liked the handsome, red-haired ethologist, and was pleased that she liked him. With a little bit of luck the situation would develop favorably, he thought. Meanwhile, she was very good company, even though she would permit nothing more than the briefest goodnight kiss.

One night, after a drink too many in the almost deserted B.O.Q.

wardroom, he confided his troubles to her. He said, "I don't like it, Maggie . . ."

"What don't you like, John?"

"All this time here, and no word of an appointment. I told you that I'd seen Tolliver's report on me . . ."

"At least six times. But what of it?"

"It's all right for you, Maggie. For all your two and a half rings you're not a spacewoman. *You* don't have to worry about such sordid details as promotion. I do. I'm just a common working stiff of a spaceman, a trade school boy. Space is all I know."

"And I'm sure you know it well, duckie." She laughed. "But not to worry. Everything will come right in the end. Just take Auntie Maggie's word for it."

"Thank you for trying to cheer me up," he said. "But I can't help worrying. After all, it's *my* career."

She grinned at him, looking very attractive as she did so. "All right. I'll tell you. Your precious Captain Tolliver wasn't the only one to put in a report on your capabilities. Don't forget that the Delta Sextans IV survey was carried out by the Scientific Branch. You, as the spaceman, were officially in command, but actually it was *our* show. Dr. Kortsoff—or Commander Kortsoff if you'd rather call him that—was the real head of our little expedition. *He* reported on you too."

"I can imagine it," said Grimes. "I can just imagine it. This officer, with no scientific training whatsoever, took it upon himself to initiate a private experiment which, inevitably, will disastrously affect the ecology, ethology, zoology and biology of the planet. Have I missed any 'ologies' out?"

"We all liked you," said the girl. "I still like you, come to that. Just between ourselves, we all had a good laugh over your 'private experiment.' You might have given your friend Snuffy and his people a slight nudge on to the upward path—but no more than a slight nudge. Sooner or later—sooner rather than later, I think—they'd have discovered weapons by themselves. It was bound to happen.

"Do you want to know what Dr. Kortsoff said about you?"

"It can't be worse than what Captain Tolliver said."

" 'This officer,' " quoted Maggie Lazenby, " 'is very definitely command material.' "

"You're not kidding?" demanded Grimes.

"Most certainly not, John."

"Mphm. You've made me feel a little happier."

"I'm glad," she said.

And so Grimes, although he did not get promotion, got command. The Survey Service's Couriers, with their small crews, were invariably captained by two ringers, mere lieutenants. However, as the twentieth century poet Gertrude Stein might have said, "a captain is a captain is a captain . . ." The command course which Grimes went through prior to his appointment made this quite clear.

There was one fly in the ointment, a big one. His name was Damien, his rank was Commodore, his function was Officer Commanding Couriers. He knew all about Grimes; he made this quite clear at the first interview. Grimes suspected that he knew more about Grimes than he, Grimes, did himself.

He had said, toying with the bulky folder on the desk before him, "There are so many conflicting reports about you, Lieutenant. Some of your commanding officers are of the opinion that you'll finish up as the youngest Admiral ever in the Service, others have said that you aren't fit to be Third Mate in Rim Runners. And then we have the reports from high-ranking specialist officers, most of whom speak well of you. But these gentlemen are not spacemen.

"There's only one thing to do with people like you, Lieutenant. We give you a chance. We give you the command of something small and relatively unimportant—and see what sort of a mess you make of it. I'm letting you have *Adder*. To begin with you'll be just a galactic errand boy, but if you shape well, *if* you shape well, you will be entrusted with more important missions.

"Have I made myself clear?"

"Yes, sir."

"Then try to remember all that we've tried to teach you, and try to keep your nose clean. That's all."

Grimes stiffened to attention, saluted, and left Damien's office.

Grimes had come to love his first command, and was proud of her, even though she was only a little ship, a Serpent Class Courier, lightly armed and manned by a minimal crew. In addition to Grimes there were two watch-keeping officers, both Ensigns, an engineering officer, another one ringer, and two communications officers, Lieutenants both. One was in charge of the vessel's electronic equipment, but could he be called upon to stand a control room watch if required. The other was the psionic radio officer, a very important crew member, as *Adder* had yet to be fitted with the Carlotti Deep Space Communications and Direction Finding System. In addition to crew accommodation there was more than merely adequate passenger accommodation; one function of the Couriers is to get V.I.P.s from Point A to Point B in a hurry, as and when required.

"You will proceed," said Commodore Damien to Grimes, "from Lindisfarne Base to Doncaster at maximum speed, but considering at all times the safety of your vessel."

"And the comfort of my passenger, sir?" asked Grimes.

"That need not concern you, Lieutenant." Damien grinned, his big teeth yellow in his skull-like face. "Mr. Alberto is . . . tough. Tougher, I would say, than the average spaceman."

Grimes's prominent ears flushed. The Commodore had managed to imply that he, Grimes, was below average. "Very well, sir," he said. "I'll pile on the Gees and the Lumes."

"Just so as you arrive in one piece," growled Damien. "That's all that our masters ask of you. Or, to more exact, just so as Mr. Alberto arrives in one piece, and functioning." He lifted a heavily sealed envelope off his desk, handed it to Grimes. "Your Orders, to be opened after you're on trajectory. But I've already told you most of it." He grinned again. "On your bicycle, spaceman!"

Grimes got to his feet, put on his cap, came stiffly to attention. He saluted with his free right hand, turned about smartly and marched out of the Commodore's office.

This was his first Sealed Orders assignment.

Clear of the office, Grimes continued his march, striding in time to martial music audible only to himself. Then he paused, looking towards the docking area of the spaceport. There was his ship, already positioned on the pad, dwarfed by a huge *Constellation* Class cruiser to one side of her, a *Planet* Class transport to the other. But she stood there bravely enough on the apron, a metal spire so slender as to appear taller than she actually was, gleaming brightly in the almost level rays of the westering sun. And she was *his*. It did not matter that officers serving in larger vessels referred to the couriers as flying darning needles.

So he strode briskly to the ramp extruded from the after airlock of his flying darning needle, his stocky body erect in his smart—but not too smart—uniform. Ensign Beadle, his First Lieutenant, was there to greet him. The young man threw him a smart salute. Grimes returned it with just the right degree of sloppiness.

"All secure for lift off—Captain!"

"Thank you, Number One. Is the passenger aboard?"

"Yes, sir. And his baggage."

Grimes fought down the temptation to ask what he was like. Only when one is really senior can one unbend with one's juniors. "Very well, Number One." He looked at his watch. "My lift off is scheduled for 1930 hours. It is now 1917. I shall go straight to Control, Mr. Beadle . . ."

"Mr. von Tannenbaum and Mr. Slovotny are waiting for you there, sir, and Mr. McCloud is standing by in the engine room."

"Good. And Mr. Deane is tucked safely away with his poodle's brain in aspic?"

"He is, sir."

"Good. Then give Mr. Alberto my compliments, and ask him if he would like to join us in Control during lift off."

Grimes negotiated the ladder in the axial shaft rapidly, without losing breath. (The *Serpent* Class couriers were too small to run to an elevator.) He did not make a stop at his own quarters. (A courier captain was supposed to be able to proceed anywhere in the Galaxy, known or unknown, at a second's notice.) In the control room he found Ensign von Tannenbaum ("The blond beast") and Lieutenant Slovotny (just "Sparks") at their stations. He buckled himself into his own chair. He had just finished doing so when the plump, lugubrious Beadle pulled himself up through the hatch. He addressed Grimes. "I asked Mr. Alberto if he'd like to come up to the office, Captain . . ."

"And is he coming up, Number One?" Grimes looked pointedly at the clock on the bulkhead.

"No, Captain. He said . . ."

"Out with it man. It's time we were getting up them stairs."

"He said, 'You people look after your job, and I'll look after mine.' "

Grimes shrugged. As a courier captain he had learned to take V.I.P.s as they came. Some—a very few of them—he would have preferred to have left. He asked, "Are Mr. Alberto and Mr. Deane secured for lift off?"

"Yes, Captain, although Spooky's not happy about the shockproof mount for his amplifier . . ."

"He never is. Clearance, Sparks . . ."

"Clearance, Captain." The wiry little radio officer spoke quietly into his microphone. "Mission 7DKY to Tower. Request clearance."

"Tower to Mission 7DKY. You have clearance. Bon voyage."

"Thank him," said Grimes. He glanced rapidly around the little control room. All officers were strapped in their acceleration chairs. All tell-tale lights were green. "All systems *Go* . . ." he muttered, relishing the archaic expression.

He pushed the right buttons, and *went*.

It was a normal enough courier lift off. The inertial drive developed maximum thrust within microseconds of its being started. Once his radar told him that the ship was the minimum safe altitude above the port, Grimes cut in his auxiliary rockets. The craft was built to take stresses that, in larger vessels, would have been dangerous. Her personnel prided themselves on their toughness. And the one outsider, the passenger. Grimes would have grinned had it not been for the acceleration flattening his features. Commodore Damien had said that Mr. Alberto was tough—so Mr. Alberto would just have to take the Gs and like it.

The ship drove up through the last, high wisps of cirrus, into the darkling, purple sky, towards the sharply bright, unwinking stars. She plunged outward through the last, tenuous shreds of atmosphere, and the needles of instruments flickered briefly as she passed through the van Allens. She was out and clear now, out and clear, and Grimes cut both inertial and reaction drives, used his gyroscopes to swing the sharp prow of the ship on to the target star, the Doncaster sun, brought that far distant speck of luminosity into the exact center of his spiderweb sights. Von Tannenbaum, who was Navigator, gave him the corrections necessitated by Galactia Drift; it was essential to aim the vessel at where the star was *now,* not where it was some seventy-three years ago.

The Inertial Drive was restarted, and the ever-precessing rotors of the Mannschenn Drive were set in motion. There was the usual brief queasiness induced by the temporal precession field, the usual visual shock as colors sagged down the spectrum, as the hard, bright stars outside the viewports became iridescent nebulosities. Grimes remained in his chair a few minutes, satisfying himself that all was as it should be. Slowly and carefully he filled and lit his foul pipe, ignoring a dirty look from Beadle who, in the absence of a Bio-Chemist, was responsible for the ship's air-regeneration system.

Then, speaking through a swirl of acrid smoke, he ordered. "Set Deep Space watches, Number One. And tell Mr. Deane to report to Lindisfarne Base that we are on trajectory for Doncaster."

"E.T.A. Doncaster, Captain?" asked Beadle.

Grimes pulled the sealed envelope from the pouch at the side of his chair, looked at it. He thought, *For Your Eyes Only. Destroy By Fire Before Reading.* He said, "I'll let you know after I've skimmed through this bumf." After all, even in a small ship informality can be allowed to go only so far. He unbuckled himself, got up from his seat, then went down to his quarters to read the Orders.

There was little in them that he had not already been told by Commodore Damien. Insofar as the E.T.A. was concerned, this was left largely to his own discretion, although it was stressed that the courier was to arrive at Doncaster not later than April 23, Local Date. And how did the Doncastrian calendar tally with that used on Lindisfarne? Grimes, knowing that the Blond Beast was now on watch, called Control and threw the question on to von Tannenbaum's plate, knowing that within a very short time he would have an answer accurate to fourteen places of decimals, and that as soon as he, Grimes, made a decision regarding the time of arrival the necessary adjustment of velocity would be put in hand without delay. Von Tannenbaum called back. "April 23 on Doncaster coincides with November 8 on Lindisfarne. I can give you the exact correlation, Captain . . ."

"Don't bother, Pilot. My Orders allow me quite a bit of leeway. Now, suppose we get Mr. Alberto to his destination just three days before the deadline . . . It will give him time to settle in before he commences his duties, whatever they are, in the High Commissioner's office. As far as I can gather, we're supposed to stay on Doncaster until directed elsewhere—so an extra three days in port will do us no harm."

"It's a pleasant planet, I've heard, Captain." There was a pause, and Grimes could imagine the burly, flaxen-headed young man running problems through the control room computer, checking the results with his own slipstick. "This calls for a reduction of speed. Shall I do it by cutting down the temporal precession rate, or by reducing actual acceleration?"

"Two G *is* a little heavy," admitted Grimes.

"Very well, Captain. Reduce to 1.27?"

"That will balance?"

"It will balance."

"Then make it so."

Almost immediately the irregular throbbing of the Inertial Drive slowed. Grimes felt his weight pressing less heavily into the padding of his chair. He did not need to glance at the accelerometer mounted among the other tell-tale instruments on the bulkhead of his cabin. Von Tannenbaum was a good man, a good officer, a good navigator.

There was a sharp rap on his door.

"Come in," called Grimes, swivelling his seat so that he faced the caller. This, he realised, would be his passenger, anticipating the captain's invitation to an introductory drink and talk.

He was not a big man, this Mr. Alberto, and at first he gave an impression of plumpness, of softness. But it was obvious from the way that he moved that his bulk was solid muscle, not fat. He was clad in the dark grey that was almost a Civil Service uniform—and even Grimes, who knew little of the niceties of civilian tailoring, could see that both the material and the cut of Alberto's suit were superb. He had a broad yet very ordinary looking face; his hair was black and glossy, his eyes black and rather dull. His expression was petulant. He demanded rather than asked, "Why have we slowed down?"

Grimes bit back a sharp retort. After all, he was only a junior officer, in spite of his command, and his passenger probably piled on far more Gs than a mere lieutenant. He replied, "I have adjusted to a comfortable actual velocity, Mr. Alberto, so as to arrive three days, local, before the deadline. I trust that this suits your plans."

"Three days . . ." Alberto smiled—and his face was transformed abruptly from that of a sulky baby to that of a contented child. It was, Grimes realised, no more than a deliberate turning of charm—but, he admitted to himself, it was effective. "Three days . . . That will give me ample time to settle down, Captain, before I start work. And I know, as well as you do, that overly heavy acceleration can be tiring."

"Won't you sit down, Mr. Alberto? A drink, perhaps?"

"Thank you, Captain. A dry sherry, if I may . . ."

Grimes grinned apologetically. "I'm afraid that these Couriers haven't much of a cellar. I can offer you gin, scotch, brandy . . ."

"A gin and lime, then."

The Lieutenant busied himself at his little bar, mixed the drinks, gave Alberto his glass, raised his own in salute, "Here's to crime!"

Alberto smiled again. "Why do you say that, Captain?"

"It's just one of those toasts that's going the rounds in the Service. Not so long ago it was, 'Down the hatch!' Before that it was, 'Here's mud in yer eye . . .' "

"I see." Alberto sipped appreciatively. "Good gin, this."

"Not bad. We get it from Van Diemen's Planet." There was a brief silence. Then, "Will you be long on Doncaster, Mr. Alberto? I rather gained the impression that we're supposed to wait there until you've finished your . . . business."

"It shouldn't take long."

"Diplomatic?"

"You could call it that." Again the smile—but why should those white teeth look so carnivorous? *Imagination,* thought Grimes.

"Another drink?"

"Why, yes. I like to relax when I can."

"Yours is demanding work?"

"And so is yours, Captain."

The brassy music of a bugle drifted into the cabin through the intercom.

"Mess call," said Grimes.

"You do things in style, Captain."

Grimes shrugged. "We have a tape for all the calls in general use. As for the tucker . . ." He shrugged again. "We don't run to a cook in a ship of this class. Sparks—Mr. Slovotny—prepares the meals in space. As a chef he's a good radio officer . . ."

"Do you think he'd mind if I took over?" asked Alberto. "After all, I'm the only idler aboard this vessel."

"We'll think about it," said Grimes.

"You know what I think, Captain . . ." said Beadle.

"I'm not a telepath, Number One," said Grimes. "Tell me."

The two men were sitting at ease in the Courier's control room. Each of them was conscious of a certain tightness in the waistband of his uniform shorts. Grimes was suppressing a tendency to burp gently. Alberto, once he had been given a free hand in the galley, had speedily changed shipboard eating from a a necessity to a pleasure. (He insisted that somebody else always do the washing up, but this was a small price to pay.) This evening, for example, the officers had dined on *saltimbocca*, accompanied by a rehydrated rough red that the amateur chef had contrived, somehow, to make taste like real wine. Nonetheless he had apologised—actually apologised!—for the meal. "I should have used *prosciutto*, not any old ham. And *fresh* sage leaves, not dried sage . . ."

"I think," said Beadle, "that the standard of the High Commissioner's entertaining has been lousy. Alberto must be a *cordon bleu* chef, sent out to Doncaster to play merry hell in the High Commissioner's kitchen."

"Could be," said Grimes. He belched gently. "Could be. But I can't see our lords and masters laying on a ship, even a lowly *Serpent* Class Courier, for a cook, no matter how talented. There must be cooks on Doncaster just as good."

"There's one helluva difference between a chef and a cook."

"All right. There must be chefs on Doncaster."

"But Alberto is *good*. You admit that."

"Of course I admit it. But one can be good in quite a few fields and still retain one's amateur status. As a matter of fact, Alberto told me that he was a mathematician . . ."

"A mathematician?" Beadle was scornfully incredulous. "You know how the Blond Beast loves to show off his toys to anybody who'll evince the slightest interest. Well, Alberto was up in the control room during his watch; you'll recall that he said he'd fix the coffee maker. Our Mr. von Tannenbaum paraded his pets and made them do their tricks. He was in a very disgruntled mood when he handed over to me when I came on. How did he put it? 'I don't expect a very high level of intelligence in planetlubbers, but that Alberto is in a class by himself. I doubt if he could add two and two and get four twice running . . .' "

"Did he fix the machinetta?"

"As a matter of fact, yes. It makes beautiful coffee now."

"Then what are you complaining about, Number One?"

"I'm not complaining, Captain. I'm just curious."

And so am I, thought Grimes, *so am I.* And as the commanding officer of the ship he was in a position to be able to satisfy his curiosity. After Mr. Beadle had gone about his multifarious duties Grimes called Mr. Deane on the telephone. "Are you busy, Spooky?" he asked.

"I'm always busy, Captain," came the reply. This was true enough. Whether he wanted it or not, a psionic radio officer was on duty all the time, sleeping and waking, his mind open to the transmitted thoughts of other telepaths throughout the Galaxy. Some were powerful transmitters, others were not, some made use, as Deane did, of organic amplifiers, others made do with the unaided power of their own minds. And there was selection, of course. Just as a wireless operator in the early days of radio on Earth's seas could pick out his own ship's call sign from the babble and Babel of Morse, could focus all his attention on an S.O.S. or T.T.T., so the trained telepath could "listen" selectively. At short ranges he could, too, receive the thoughts of the non-telepaths about him—but, unless the circumstances were exceptional, he was supposed to maintain the utmost secrecy regarding them.

"Can you spare me a few minutes, Spooky? After all, you can maintain your listening watch anywhere in the ship, in my own quarters as well as in yours."

"Oh, all right, Captain. I'll be up. I already know what you're going to ask me."

You would, thought Grimes.

A minute or so later, Mr. Deane drifted into his day cabin. His nickname was an apt one. He was tall, fragile, so albinoid as to appear almost translucent. His white face was a featureless blob.

"Take a pew, Spooky," ordered Grimes. "A drink?"

"Mother's ruin, Captain."

Grimes poured gin for both of them. In his glass there was ice and a generous sprinkling of bitters. Mr. Deane preferred his gin straight, as colorless as he was himself.

The psionic radio officer sipped genteelly. Then: "I'm afraid that I can't oblige you, Captain."

"Why not, Spooky?"

"You know very well that we graduates of the Rhine Institute have to swear to respect privacy."

"There's no privacy aboard a ship, Spooky. There cannot be."

"There can be, Captain. There must be."

"Not when the safety of the ship is involved."

It was a familiar argument—and Grimes knew that after the third gin the telepath would weaken. He always did.

"We got odd passengers aboard this ship, Spooky. Surely you remember that Waldegren diplomat who had the crazy scheme of seizing her and turning her over to his Navy . . ."

"I remember, Captain." Deane extended his glass which, surprisingly, was empty. Grimes wondered, as he always did, if its contents had been teleported directly into the officer's stomach, but he refilled it.

"Mr. Alberto's another odd passenger," he went on.

"But a Federation citizen," Deane told him.

"How do we know? He could be a double agent. Do *you* know?"

"I don't." After only two gins Spooky was ready to spill the beans. This was unusual. "I don't know *anything*."

"What do you mean?"

"Usually, Captain, we have to shut our minds to the trivial, boring thoughts of you psionic morons. No offense intended, but that's the way we think of you. We get sick of visualisations of the girls you met in the last port and the girls you hope to meet in the next port." He screwed his face up in disgust, made it evident that he did, after all, possess features. "Bums, bellies and breasts! The Blond Beast's a tit man, and *you* have a thing about *legs* . . ."

Grimes's prominent ears reddened, but he said nothing.

"And the professional wishful thinking is even more nauseating. *When do I get my half ring? When do I get my brass hat? When shall I make Admiral?"*

"Ambition . . ." said Grimes.

"Ambition, shambition! And of late, of course, *I wonder what Alberto's putting on for breakfast? For lunch? For dinner?"*

"What *is* he putting on for dinner?" asked Grimes. "I've been rather wondering if our tissue culture chook could be used for *Chicken Cacciatore . . ."*

"I don't know."

"No, you're not a chef. As well we know, after the last time that you volunteered for galley duties."

"I mean, I don't know what the menus will be." It was Deane's turn to blush. "As a matter of fact, Captain, I *have* been trying to get previews. I have to watch my diet . . ."

Grimes tried not to think uncharitable thoughts. Like many painfully thin people, Deane enjoyed a voracious appetite.

He said, "You've been *trying* to eavesdrop?"

"Yes. But there are non-telepaths, you know, and Alberto's one of them. *True* non-telepaths, I mean. Most people transmit, although they can't receive. Alberto doesn't transmit."

"A useful qualification for a diplomat," said Grimes. "If he is a diplomat. But could he be using some sort of psionic jammer?"

"No. I'd know if he were."

Grimes couldn't ignore that suggestively held empty glass any longer. He supposed that Deane had earned his third gin.

The Courier broke through into normal space/time north of the plane of Doncaster's ecliptic. In those days, before the Carlotti Beacons made FTL position fixing simple, navigation was an art rather than a science—and von Tannenbaum was an artist. The little ship dropped into a transpolar orbit about the planet and then, as soon as permission to land had been granted by Aerospace Control, descended to Port Duncannon. It was, Grimes told himself smugly, one of his better landings. And so it should have been; conditions were little short of ideal. There was no cloud, no wind, not even any clear air turbulence at any level. The ship's instruments were working perfectly, and the Inertial Drive was responding to the controls with no time lag whatsoever. It was one of those occasions on which the Captain feels that his ship is no more—and no less—than a beautifully functioning extension of his own body. Finally, it was morning Local Time, with the sun just lifting over the verdant, rolling hills to the eastward, bringing out all the color of the sprawling city a few miles from the spaceport, making it look, from the air, like a huge handful of gems spilled carelessly on a green carpet.

Grimes set the vessel down in the exact center of the triangle marked by the blinkers, so gently that, until he cut the drive, a walnut under the vaned landing gear would not have been crushed. He said quietly, "Finished with engines."

"Receive boarders, Captain?" asked Beadle.

"Yes, Number One." Grimes looked out through the viewport to the ground cars that were making their way from the Administration Block. Port Health, Immigration, Customs . . . The Harbourmaster paying his respects to the Captain of a visiting Federation warship . . . And the third vehicle? He took a pair of binoculars from the rack, focused them on the flag fluttering from the bonnet of the car in the rear. It was dark blue, with a pattern of silver stars, the Federation's colours. So the High Commissioner himself had come out to see the ship berth. He wished that he and his officers had dressed more formally, but it was too late to do anything about it now. He went down to his quarters, was barely able to change the epaulettes of his shirt, with their deliberately tarnished braid, for a pair of shining new ones before the High Commissioner was at his door.

Mr. Beadle ushered in the important official with all the ceremony that he could muster at short notice. "Sir, this is the Captain, Lieutenant Grimes. Captain, may I introduce Sir William Willoughby, Federation High Commissioner on Doncaster?"

Willoughby extended a hand that, like the rest of him was plump. "Welcome aboard, Captain. Ha, ha. I hope you don't mind my borrowing one of the favorite expressions of you spacefaring types!"

"We don't own the copyright, sir."

"Ha, ha. Very good."

"Will you sit down, Sir William?"

"Thank you, Captain, thank you. But only for a couple of minutes. I shall be out of your hair as soon as Mr. Alberto has been cleared by Port Health, Immigration and all the rest of 'em. Then I'll whisk him off to the Residence." He paused, regarding Grimes with eyes that, in the surrounding fat, were sharp and bright. "How did you find him, Captain?"

"Mr. Alberto, sir?" What was the man getting at? "Er . . . He's a very good cook . . ."

"Glad to hear you say it, Captain. That's why I sent for him. I have to do a lot of entertaining, as you realise, and the incompetents I have in my kitchens couldn't boil water without burning it. It just won't do, Captain, it just won't do, not for a man in my position."

"So he *is* a chef, sir."

Again those sharp little eyes bored into Grimes's skull. "Of course. What else? What did you think he was?"

"Well, as a matter of fact we were having a yarn the other night, and he sort of hinted that he was some sort of a mathematician . . ."

"Did he?" Then Willoughby chuckled. "He was having you on. But, of course, a real chef *is* a mathematician. He has to get his equations just right—this quantity, that quantity, this factor, that factor . . ."

"That's one way of looking at it, Sir William."

Beadle was back then, followed by Alberto. "I must be off, now, Captain," said the passenger, shaking hands. "Thank you for a very pleasant voyage."

"Thank *you*," Grimes told him, adding, "We shall miss you."

"But you'll enjoy some more of his cooking," said the High Commissioner genially. "As officers of the only Federation warship on this world you'll have plenty of invitations—to the Residence as well as elsewhere. Too, if Mr. Alberto manages to train my permanent staff in not too long a time you may be taking him back with you."

"We hope so," said Grimes and Beadle simultaneously.

"Good day to you, then. Come on, Mr. Alberto—it's time you started to show my glorified scullions how to boil an egg!"

He was gone, and then the Harbourmaster was at the door. He was invited in, took a seat, accepted coffee. "Your first visit to Doncaster," he announced rather than asked.

"Yes, Captain Tarran. It looks a very pleasant planet."

"Hphm." That could have meant either "yes" or "no."

"Tell me, sir, *is* the cooking in the High Commissioner's Residence as bad as he makes out?"

"I wouldn't know, Captain. I'm just a merchant skipper in a shore job, I don't get asked to all the posh parties, like you people." The sudden white grin in the dark, lean face took the rancor out of the words. "And I thank all the Odd Gods of the Galaxy for that!"

"I concur with your sentiments, Captain Tarran. One never seems to meet any *real* people at the official bunstruggle . . . it's all stiff collars and best behavior and being nice to nongs and drongoes whom normally you'd run a mile to avoid . . ."

"Still," said Mr. Beadle, "the High Commissioner seems to have the common touch . . ."

"How so?" asked Grimes.

"Well, coming out to the spaceport in person to pick up his chef . . ."

"Cupboard love," Grimes told him. "Cupboard love."

There were official parties, and there were unofficial ones. Tarran may not have been a member of the planet's snobocracy, but he knew people in all walks of life, in all trades and professions, and the gatherings to which, through him, Grimes was invited were far more entertaining affairs than the official functions which, now and again, Grimes was obliged to attend. It was at an informal supper given by Professor Tolliver, who held the Chair of Political Science at Duncannon University, that he met Selma Madigan.

With the exception of Tarran and Grimes and his officers all the guests were university people, students as well as instructors. Some were human and some were not. Much to his surprise Grimes found that he was getting along famously with a Shaara Princess, especially since he had cordially detested a Shaara Queen to whom he had been introduced at a reception in the Mayor's Palace. ("And there I was," he had complained afterwards to Beadle, "having to say nice things to a bedraggled old oversized bumblebee loaded down with more precious stones than this ship could lift . . . and with all that tonnage of diamonds and the like she couldn't afford a decent voice box; it sounded like a scratched platter and a worn-out needle on one of those antique record players . . .") This Shreen was—beautiful. It was an inhuman beauty (of course), that of a glittering, intricate mobile. By chance or design—design thought Grimes—her voice box produced a pleasant, almost seductive contralto, with faintly buzzing undertones. She was an arthroped, but there could be no doubt about the fact that she was an attractively female member of her race.

She was saying, "I find you humans so fascinating, Captain. There is so much similarity between yourselves and ourselves, and such great differences. But I have enjoyed my stay on this planet . . ."

"And will you be here much longer, Your Highness?"

"Call me Shreen, Captain," she told him.

"Thank you, Shreen. My name is John. I shall feel honored if you call me that." He laughed. "In any case, my real rank is only Lieutenant."

"Very well, Lieutenant John. But to answer your question. I fear that I shall return to my own world as soon as I have gained my degree in Socio-Economics. Our Queen-Mother decided that this will be a useful qualification for a future ruler. The winds of change blow through our hives, and we must trim our wings to them."

And very pretty wings, too, thought Grimes.

But Shreen was impossibly alien, and the girl who approached gracefully over the polished floor was indubitably human. She was slender, and tall for a woman, and her gleaming auburn hair was piled high in an intricate coronal. Her mouth was too wide for conventional prettiness, the planes of her thin face too well defined. Her eyes were definitely green. Her smile, as she spoke, made her beautiful.

"Another conquest, Shreen?" she asked.

"I wish it were, Selma," replied the Princess. "I wish that Lieutenant John were an arthroped like myself."

"In that case," grinned Grimes, "I'd be a drone."

"From what I can gather," retorted the human girl, "that's all that spaceship captains are anyhow."

"Have you met Selma?" asked Shreen. Then she performed the introductions.

"And are you enjoying the party, Mr. Grimes?" inquired Selma Madigan.

"Yes, Miss Madigan, It's a very pleasant change from the usual official function—but don't tell anybody that I said so."

"I'm glad you like us. We try to get away from that ghastly Outposts of Empire atmosphere. Quite a number of our students are like Shreen here, quote aliens unquote . . ."

"On *my* world *you* would be the aliens."

"I know, my dear, and I'm sure that Mr. Grimes does too. But all intelligent beings can make valuable contributions to each other's cultures. No one race has a sacred mission to civilise the Galaxy. . . ."

"I wish you wouldn't *preach*, Selma." It was amazing how much expression the Princess could get out of her mechanical voice box. "But if you must, perhaps you can make a convert out of Lieutenant John." She waved a thin, gracefully articulated fore limb and was away, gliding off to join a group composed of two human men, a young Hallichek and a gaudy pseudo-saurian from Dekkovar.

Selma Madigan looked directly at Grimes. "And what do you think of our policy of integration?" she asked.

"It has to come, I suppose."

"It has to come," she mimicked. "You brassbound types are all the same. You get along famously with somebody like Shreen, because she's a real, live Princess. But the Shaara royalty isn't royalty as we understand it. The Queens are females who've reached the egg-laying stage, the Princesses are females who are not yet sexually developed. Still—Shreen's a Princess. You have far less in common with her, biologically speaking, than you have with Oona—but you gave Oona the brush-off and fawned all over Shreen."

Grimes flushed. "Oona's a rather smelly and scruffy little thing like a Terran chimpanzee. Shreen's—beautiful."

"Oona has a brilliant mind. Her one weakness is that she thinks that Terrans in pretty, gold-braided uniforms are wonderful. You snubbed her. Shreen noticed. I noticed."

"As far as I'm concerned," said Grimes, "Oona can be Her Imperial

Highness on whatever world she comes from, but I don't *have* to like her."

Professor Tolliver, casually clad in a rather grubby toga, smoking a pipe even fouler than Grimes's, joined the discussion. He remarked, "Young Grimes has a point . . ."

"Too right I have," agreed Grimes. "As far as I'm concerned, people are people—it doesn't matter a damn if they're humanoid, arachnoid, saurian or purple octopi from the next galaxy but three. If they're our sort of people, I like 'em. If they ain't—I don't."

"Oona's our sort of people," insisted Selma.

"She doesn't smell like it."

The girl laughed. "And how do you think *she* enjoys the stink of your pipe—and, come to that, Peter's pipe?"

"Perhaps she does enjoy it," suggested Grimes.

"As a matter of fact she does," said Professor Tolliver.

"*Men* . . ." muttered Selma Madigan disgustedly.

Tolliver drifted off then, and Grimes walked with the girl to the table on which stood a huge punchbowl. He ladled out drinks for each of them. He raised his own glass in a toast. "Here's to integration!"

"I wish that you really meant that."

"Perhaps I do . . ." murmured Grimes, a little doubtfully. "Perhaps I do. After all, we've only one Universe, and we all have to live in it. It's not so long that blacks and whites and yellows were at each other's throats on the Home Planet—to say nothing of the various subdivisions within each color groups. Von Tannenbaum—that's him over there, the Blond Beast we call him. He's an excellent officer, a first class shipmate, and a very good friend. But *his* ancestors were very unkind to mine, on my mother's side. And mine had quite a long record of being unkind to other people. I could be wrong—but I think that much of Earth's bloody history was no more—and no less—than xenophobia carried to extremes . . ."

"Quite a speech, John." She sipped at her drink. "It's a pity that the regulations of your Service forbid you to play any active part in politics."

"Why?"

"You'd make a very good recruit for the new Party we're starting. LL . . ."

"LL . . . ?"

"The obvious abbreviation. The League of Life. You were talking just now of Terran history. Even when Earth's nations were at war there were organisations—religions, political parties, even fraternal orders—

with pan-national and pan-racial memberships. The aim of the League of Life is to build up a membership of all intelligent species."

"Quite an undertaking."

"But a necessary one. Doncaster could be said to be either unfortunately situated, or otherwise, according to the viewpoint. Here we are, one Man-colonised planet on the borders of no less than two . . . yes, I'll use that word, much as I dislike it . . . no less than two alien empires. The Hallichek Hegemony, the Shaara Super-Hive. We know that Imperial Earth is already thinking of establishing Fortress Doncaster, converting this world into the equivalent of a colossal, impregnably armored and fantastically armed dreadnought with its guns trained upon both avian and arthroped, holding the balance of power, playing one side off against the other and all the rest of it. But there are those of us who would sooner live in peace and friendship with our neighbours. That's why Duncannon University has always tried to attract non-Terran students—and that's why the League of Life was brought into being." She smiled. "You could, I suppose call it enlightened self-interest."

"Enlightened," agreed Grimes.

He liked this girl. She was one of those women whose physical charm is vastly enhanced by enthusiasm. She did far more to him, for him, than the sort of female equally pretty or prettier, whom he usually met.

She said, "I've some literature at home, if you'd like to read it."

"I should—Selma."

She took the use of her given name for granted. Was that a good sign, or not?

"That's splendid—John. We could pick it up now. The party can get along without us."

"Don't you . . . er . . . live on the premises?"

"No. But it's only a short walk from here. I have an apartment in Heathcliff Street."

When Grimes had collected his boat cloak and cap from the cloakroom she was waiting for him. She had wrapped herself in a green academic gown that went well with her hair, matched her eyes. Together they walked out into the misty night. There was just enough chill in the air to make them glad of their outer garments, to make them walk closer together than they would, otherwise—perhaps—have done. As they strode over the damp-gleaming cobblestones Grimes was conscious of the movements of her body against his. *Political literature,* he thought with an attempt at cynicism. *It makes a change from etchings.* But he could not remain cynical for long. He had already recognised in her qualities of leadership, had no doubt in his mind that she would achieve high political rank on the world of her birth. Nonetheless, this night things could happen between them, probably would happen between them, and he, most certainly, would not attempt to stem the course of Nature. Neither of them would be the poorer; both of them, in fact, would be the richer. Meanwhile, it was good to walk with her through the soft darkness, to let one's mind dwell pleasurably on what lay ahead at the end of the walk.

"Here we are John," she said suddenly.

The door of the apartment house was a hazy, golden-glowing rectangle in the dimness. There was nobody in the hallway—not that it mattered. There was an elevator that bore them swiftly upwards, its door finally opening on a richly carpeted corridor. There was another door—one that, Grimes noted, was opened with an old-fashioned metal key. He remembered, then, that voice-actuated locks were not very common on Doncaster.

The furnishing of her living room was austere but comfortable. Grimes, at her invitation, removed his cloak and cap, gave them to her to hang up somewhere with her own gown, sat down on a well-sprung divan. He watched her walk to the window that ran all along one wall, press the switch that drew the heavy drapes aside, press another switch that caused the wide panes to sink into their housing.

She said, "The view of the city is good from here—especially on a misty night. And I like it when you can smell the clean tang of fog in the air . . ."

"You're lucky to get a clean fog," said Grimes, Earth-born and Earth-raised.

He got up and went to stand with her. His arm went about her waist. She made no attempt to disengage it. Nonetheless, he could still appreciate the view. It was superb; it was like looking down at a star cluster enmeshed in a gaseous nebula . . .

"Smell the mist . . ." whispered Selma.

Dutifully, Grimes inhaled. *Where did that taint of garlic come from?* It was the first time that he had smelled it since Alberto ceased to officiate in the ship's galley. *It must come from a source in the room with them . . .*

Grimes could act fast when he had to. He sensed rather than saw that somebody was rushing at him and the girl from behind. He let go of her, pushed her violently to one side. Instinctively he fell into a crouch, felt a heavy body thud painfully into his back. He dropped still lower, his arms and the upper part of his torso hanging down over the windowsill. What followed was the result of luck rather than of any skill on the spaceman's part—good luck for Grimes, the worst of bad luck for his assailant. The assassin slithered over Grimes's back, head down, in an ungraceful dive. The heel of a shoe almost took one of the Lieutenant's prominent ears with it. And then he was staring down, watching the dark figure that fell into the luminous mist with agonising slowness, twisting and turning as it plunged, screaming. The scream was cut short by a horridly fluid *thud.*

Frantically, Selma pulled Grimes back to safety.

He stood there, trembling uncontrollably. The reek of garlic was still strong in the air. He broke away from her, went back to the window and was violently sick.

"There are lessons," said Commodore Damien drily, "that a junior officer must learn if he wishes to rise in the Service. One of them is that it is unwise to throw a monkey wrench into the machinations of our masters."

"How was I to know, sir?" complained Grimes. He flushed. "In any case, I'd do it again!"

"I'm sure that you would, Mr. Grimes. No man in his right senses submits willingly to defenstration—and no gentleman stands by and does nothing while his companion of the evening is subjected to the same fate. Even so . . ." He drummed on his desk top with his skeletal fingers. "Even so, I propose to put you in the picture, albeit somewhat belatedly.

"To begin with, the late Mr. Alberto was criminally careless. Rather a neat play on words, don't you think? Apparently he officiated as usual in the High Commissioner's kitchen on the night in question, and Sir William had, earlier in the day, expressed a wish for *pasta* with one of the more redolent sauces. As a good chef should, Alberto tasted, and tasted, and tasted. As a member of his *real* profession he should have deodorised his breath before proceeding to Miss Madigan's apartment—where, I understand, he concealed himself in the bathroom, waiting until she returned to go through her evening ritual of opening the window of her living room. He was not, I think, expecting her to have company—not that it would have worried him if he had . . ."

"What happened served the bastard right," muttered Grimes.

"I'm inclined to agree with you, Lieutenant. But we are all of us no more than pawns insofar as Federation policy is concerned. Or, perhaps, Alberto was a knight—in the chess sense of the word, although the German name for that piece, *springer,* would suit him better.

"Alberto was employed by the Department of Socio-Economic Science, and directly responsible only to its head, Dr. Barratin. Dr. Barratin is something of a mathematical genius, and uses a building full of computers to extrapolate from the current trends on all the worlds in which the Federation is interested. Doncaster, I need hardly tell you, is such a world, and the League of Life is a current trend. According to the learned Doctor's calculations, this same League of Life will almost certainly gain considerable influence, even power, in that sector of the Galaxy, under the leadership of your Miss Madigan . . ."

"She's not *my* Miss Madigan, sir. Unfortunately."

"My heart fair bleeds for you. But, to continue. To Dr. Barratin the foreign and colonial policies of the Federation can all be worked out in advance like a series of equations. As you will know, however, equations are apt, at times, to hold undesirable factors. Alberto was employed to remove such factors, ensuring thereby that the good Doctor's sums came out. He was known to his employers as the Subtracter . . ."

"Very funny," said Grimes. "Very funny. Sir."

"Isn't it?" Damien was laughing unashamedly. "But when things went so very badly wrong on Doncaster, Barratin couldn't see the joke, even after I explained it to him. You see, Grimes, that *you* were a factor that wasn't allowed for in the equation. Alberto travelled to Doncaster in *your* ship, a Serpent Class Courier. *You* were with Miss Madigan when Alberto tried to . . . subtract her.

"And you were captain of the *Adder!*"

The Tin Messiah

"I'M AFRAID, LIEUTENANT," said Commodore Damien, "that your passenger, this trip, won't be able to help out in the galley."

"As long as he's not another assassin, he'll do me," said Grimes. "But I've found, sir, that anybody who likes to eat also likes now, and again, to prepare his own favorite dishes . . ."

"This one does. All the time."

Grimes looked at his superior dubiously. He suspected the Commodore's sense of humor. The older man's skull-like face was stiffly immobile, but there was a sardonic glint in the pale grey eyes.

"If he wants galley privileges, sir, it's only fair that he shares, now and again, what he hashes up for himself."

Damien sighed. "I've never known officers so concerned about their bellies as you people in the *Adder*. All you think about is adding to your weight . . ." Grimes winced—as much because of the unfairness of the imputation as in reaction to the pun. The Couriers—little, very fast ships—did not carry cooks, so their officers, obliged to cook for themselves, were more than usually food-conscious. *Adder*'s crew was no exception to this rule. Damien went on, "I've no doubt that Mr. Adam would be willing to share his . . . er . . . nutriment with you, but I don't think that any of you, catholic as your tastes may be, would find it palatable. Or, come to that, nourishing. But who started this particularly futile discussion?"

"You did, sir," said Grimes.

"You'll never make a diplomat, Lieutenant. It is doubtful that you'll ever reach flag rank in this Service, rough and tough spacemen though we be, blunt and outspoken to a fault, the glint of honest iron showing through the work-worn fabric of our velvet gloves . . . H'm. Yes. Where was I?"

"Talking about iron fists in velvet gloves, sir."

"Before you side-tracked me, I mean. Yes, your passenger. He is to be transported from Lindisfarne Base to Delacron. You just dump him there, then return to Base forthwith." The Commodore's bony hand picked up the heavily sealed envelope from his desk, extended it. "Your Orders."

"Thank you, sir. Will that be all, sir?"

"Yes. Scramble!"

Grimes didn't exactly scramble; nonetheless he walked briskly enough to where his ship, the Serpent Class Courier *Adder,* was berthed. Dwarfed as she was by the bigger vessels about her she still stood there, tall, proud and gleaming. Grimes knew that she and her kind were referred to, disparagingly, as "flying darning needles," but he loved the slenderness of her lines, would not have swapped her for a hulking dreadnought. (In a dreadnought, of course, he would have been no more than one of many junior officers.) She was *his.*

Ensign Beadle, his First Lieutenant, met him at the airlock ramp, saluted. He reported mournfully (nobody had ever heard Beadle laugh, and he smiled but rarely), "All secure for lift off, Captain."

"Thank you, Number One."

"The . . . The passenger's aboard . . ."

"Good. I suppose we'd better extend the usual courtesy. Ask him if he'd like the spare seat in Control when we shake the dust of Base off our tail vanes."

"I've already done so, Captain. It says that it'll be pleased to accept the invitation."

"*It,* Number One. *It*? Adam is a good Terran name."

Beadle actually smiled. "Technically speaking, Captain, one could not say that Mr. Adam is of Terran birth. But he is of Terran manufacture."

"And what does he eat?" asked Grimes, remembering the Commodore's veiled references to the passenger's diet. "A.C. or D.C.? Washed down with a noggin of light lubricating oil?"

"How did you guess, Captain?"

"The Old Man told me, in a roundabout sort of way. But . . . A passenger, not cargo . . . There must be some mistake."

"There's not, Captain. It's intelligent, all right, and it has a personality. I've checked its papers, and officially it's a citizen of the Interstellar Federation, with all rights, privileges and obligations."

"I suppose that our masters know best," said Grimes resignedly.

It was intelligent, and it had a personality, and Grimes found it quite impossible to think of Mr. Adam as "it." This robot was representative of a type of which Grimes had heard rumors, but it was the first one that he had ever seen. There were only a very few of them in all the worlds of the Federation—and most of that few were of Earth itself. To begin with, they were fantastically expensive. Secondly, their creators were scared of them, were plagued by nightmares in which they saw themselves as latter day Frankensteins. Intelligent robots were not a rarity—but intelligent robots with imagination, intuition, and initiative were. They had been developed mainly for research and exploration, and could survive in environments that would be almost immediately lethal to even the most heavily and elaborately armored man.

Mr. Adam sat in the spare chair in the control room. There was no need for him to sit, but he did so, in an astonishingly human posture. Perhaps, thought Grimes, he could sense that his hosts would feel more comfortable if something that looked like an attenuated knight in armor were not looming tall behind them, peering over their shoulders. His face was expressionless—it was a dull-gleaming ovid with no features to be expressive with—but it seemed to Grimes that there was the faintest flicker of luminosity behind the eye lenses that could betoken interest. His voice, when he spoke, came from a diaphragm set in his throat.

He was speaking now. "This has been very interesting, Captain. And now, I take it, we are on trajectory for Delacron." His voice was a pleasant enough baritone, not quite mechanical.

"Yes, Mr. Adam. That is the Delacron sun there, at three o'clock from the center of the cartwheel sight."

"And that odd distortion, of course, is the resultant of the temporal precession field of your Drive . . ." He hummed quietly to himself for a few seconds. "Interesting."

"You must have seen the same sort of thing on your way out to Lindisfarne from Earth."

"No, Captain. I was not a guest, ever, in the control room of the cruiser in which I was transported." The shrug of his gleaming, metal shoulders was almost human. "I . . . I don't think that Captain Grisby trusted me."

That, thought Grimes, was rather an odd way of putting it. But he knew Grisby, had served under him. Grisby, as a naval officer of an earlier age, on Earth's seas, would have pined for the good old days of sail, of wooden ships and iron men—and by "iron men" he would not have meant anything like this Mr. Adam . . .

"Yes," the robot went on musingly, "I find this not only interesting, but amazing . . ."

"How so?" asked Grimes.

"It could all be done—the lift off, the setting of trajectory, the delicate balance between acceleration and temporal precession—so much . . . faster by one like myself . . ."

You mean "better" rather than faster, thought Grimes, *but you're too courteous to say it.*

"And yet . . . and yet . . . You're flesh and blood creatures, Captain, evolved to suit the conditions of just one world out of all the billions of planets. Space is not your natural environment."

"We carry our environment around with us, Mr. Adam." Grimes noticed that the other officers in Control—Ensign von Tannenbaum, the Navigator, Ensign Beadle, the First Lieutenant, and Lieutenant Slovotny, the radio officer—were following the conversation closely and expectantly. He would have to be careful. Nonetheless, he had to keep his end up. He grinned. "And don't forget," he said, "that Man, himself, is a quite rugged, self-maintaining, self-reproducing, all-purpose robot."

"There are more ways than one of reproducing," said Mr. Adam quietly.

"I'll settle for the old-fashioned way!" broke in von Tannenbaum.

Grimes glared at the burly, flaxen-headed young man—but too late to stop Slovotny's laughter. Even Beadle smiled.

John Grimes allowed himself a severely rationed chuckle. Then: "The show's on the road, gentlemen. I'll leave her in your capable hands. Number One. Set Deep Space watches. Mr. Adam, it is usual at this juncture for me to invite any guests to my quarters for a drink and a yarn . . ."

Mr. Adam laughed. "Like yourself, Captain, I feel the occasional need for a lubricant. But I do not make a ritual of its application. I shall, however, be very pleased to talk with you while you drink."

"I'll lead the way," said Grimes resignedly.

In a small ship passengers can make their contribution to the quiet pleasures of the voyage, or they can be a pain in the neck. Mr. Adam, at first, seemed pathetically eager to prove that he could be a good shipmate. He could talk—and he did talk, on anything and everything. Mr. Beadle remarked about him that he must have swallowed an encyclopedia. Mr. McCloud, the Engineering Officer, corrected this statement, saying that he must have been built around one. And Mr. Adam could listen. That was worse than his talking—one always had the impression of invisible wheels whirring inside that featureless head, of information either being discarded as valueless or added to the robot's data bank. He could play chess (of course)—and on the rare occasions that he lost a game it was strongly suspected that he had done so out of politeness. It was the same with any card game.

Grimes sent for Spooky Deane, the psionic communications officer. He had the bottle and the glasses ready when the tall, fragile young man seeped in through the doorway of his day cabin, looking like a wisp of ectoplasm decked out in Survey Service uniform. He sat down when invited, accepted the tumbler of neat gin that his captain poured for him.

"Here's looking up your kilt," toasted Grimes coarsely.

"A *physical* violation of privacy, Captain," murmured Deane. "I see nothing objectionable in that."

"And just what are you hinting at, Mr. Deane?"

"I know, Captain, that you are about to ask me to break the Rhine Institute's Privacy Oath. And this knowledge has nothing to do with my being a telepath. Every time that we carry passengers it's the same. You always want me to pry into their minds to see what makes them tick."

"Only when I feel that the safety of the ship might be at stake." Grimes refilled Deane's glass, the contents of which had somehow vanished.

"You are . . . frightened of our passenger?"

Grimes frowned. "Frightened" was a strong word. And yet mankind has always feared the robot, the automaton, the artificial man. A premonitory dread? Or was the robot only a symbol of the machines—the *mindless* machines—that with every passing year were becoming more and more dominant in human affairs?

Deane said quietly, "Mr. Adam is not a mindless machine."

Grimes glared at him. He almost snarled, "How the hell do you know what I'm thinking?"—then thought better of it. Not that it made any difference.

The telepath went on, "Mr. Adam has a mind, as well as a brain."

"That's what I was wondering."

"Yes. He broadcasts, Captain, as all of you do. The trouble is that I haven't quite got his . . . frequency."

"Any . . . hostility towards us? Towards humans?"

Deane extended his empty glass. Grimes refilled it. The telepath sipped daintily, then said, "I . . . I don't think so, but, as I've already told you, his mind is not human. Is it contempt he feels? No . . . Not quite. Pity? Yes, it could be. A sort of amused affection? Yes . . ."

"The sort of feelings that we'd have towards—say—a dog capable of coherent speech?"

"Yes."

"Anything else?"

"I could be wrong, Captain. I most probably am. This is the first time that I've eavesdropped on a non-organic mind. There seems to be a strong sense of . . . mission . . ."

"Mission?"

"Yes. It reminds me of that priest we carried a few trips back—the one who was going out to convert the heathen Tarvarkens . . ."

"A dirty business," commented Grimes. "Wean the natives away from their own, quite satisfactory local gods so that they stop lobbing missiles at the trading post, which was established without their consent anyhow . . ."

"Father Cleary didn't look at it that way."

"Good for him. I wonder what happened to the poor bastard?"

"Should you be talking like this, Captain?"

"I shouldn't. But with you it doesn't matter. You know what I'm thinking, anyhow. But this Mr. Adam, Spooky. A missionary? It doesn't make sense."

"That's just the *feeling* I get."

Grimes ignored this. "Or, perhaps, it does make sense. The robots of Mr. Adam's class are designed to be able to go where Man himself cannot go. In our own planetary system, for example, they've carried out explorations on Mercury, Jupiter, and Saturn. A robot missionary on Tarvark would have made sense, being impervious to poisoned arrows, spears, and the like. But on Delacron, an Earth colony? No."

"But I still get that *feeling,*" insisted Deane.

"There are feelings *and* feelings," Grimes told him. "Don't forget that this is non-organic mind that you're prying into. Perhaps you don't know the code, the language . . ."

"Codes and languages don't matter to a telepath." Deane contrived to make his empty glass obvious. Grimes refilled it. "Don't forget, Captain, that there are machines on Delacron, *intelligent* machines. Not a very high order of intelligence, I admit, but . . . And you must have heard of the squabble between Delacron and its nearest neighbour, Muldoon . . ."

Grimes had heard of it. Roughly midway between the two planetary systems was a sun with only one world in close orbit about it—and that solitary planet was a fantastic treasure house of radioactive ores. Both

Delacron and Muldoon had laid claim to it. Delacron wanted the rare metals for its own industries, the less highly industrialized Muldoon wanted them for export to other worlds of the Federation.

And Mr. Adam? Where did he come into it? Officially, according to his papers, he was a programmer, on loan from the Federation's Grand Council to the Government of Delacron. A programmer . . . A teacher of machines . . . An intelligent machine to teach other intelligent machines . . . To teach other intelligent machines *what?*

And who had programmed *him*—or had he just, as it were, happened?

A familiar pattern—vague, indistinct, but nonetheless there—was beginning to emerge. It had all been done before, this shipping of revolutionaries into the places in which they could do the most harm by governments absolutely unsympathetic towards their aspirations. . . .

"Even if Mr. Adam had a beard," said Deane, "he wouldn't *look* much like Lenin . . ."

And Grimes wondered if the driver who brought that train into the Finland Station knew what he was doing.

Grimes was just the engine driver, and Mr. Adams was the passenger, and Grimes was tied down as much by the Regulations of his Service as was that long ago railwayman by the tracks upon which his locomotive ran. Grimes was blessed—or cursed—with both imagination and a conscience, and a conscience is too expensive a luxury for a junior officer. Those who can afford such a luxury all too often decide that they can do quite nicely without it.

Grimes actually wished that in some way Mr. Adam was endangering the ship. Then he, Grimes, could take action, drastic action if necessary. But the robot was less trouble than the average human passenger. There were no complaints about monotonous food, stale air and all the rest of it. About the only thing that could be said against him was that he was far too good a chess player, but just about the time that Grimes was trying to find excuses for not playing with him he made what appeared to be a genuine friendship, and preferred the company of Mr. McCloud to that of any the other officers.

"Of course, Captain," said Beadle, "they belong to the same clan."

"What the hell do you mean, Number One?"

Deadpan, Beadle replied, "The Clan MacHinery."

Grimes groaned, then, with reluctance, laughed. He said, "It makes sense. A machine will have more in common with our Engineering

Officer than the rest of us. Their shop talk must be fascinating." He tried to initiate McCloud's accent. "An' tell me, Mr. Adam, whit sorrt o' lubricant d'ye use on yon ankle joint?"

Beadle, having made his own joke, was not visibly amused. "Something suitable for heavy duty I should imagine, Captain."

"Mphm. Well, if Mac keeps him happy, he's out of our hair for the rest of the trip."

"He'll keep Mac happy, too, Captain. He's always moaning that he should have an assistant."

"Set a thief to catch a thief," cracked Grimes. "Set a machine to . . . to . . ."

"Work a machine?" suggested Beadle.

Those words would do, thought Grimes, but after the First Lieutenant had left him he began to consider the implications of what had been discussed. McCloud was a good engineer—but the better the engineer, the worse the psychological shortcomings. The Machine had been developed to be Man's slave—but ever since the twentieth century a peculiar breed of Man had proliferated that was all too ready and willing to become the Machine's servants, far too prone to sacrifice human values on the altar of Efficiency. Instead of machines being modified to suit their operators, men were being modified to suit the machines. And McCloud? He would have been happier in industry than in the Survey Service, with its emphasis on officer-like qualities and all the rest of it. As it was, he was far too prone to regard the ship merely as the platform that carried his precious engines.

Grimes sighed. He didn't like what he was going to do. It was all very well to snoop on passengers, on outsiders—but to pry into the minds of his own people was not gentlemanly.

He got out the gin bottle and called for Mr. Deane.

"Yes, Captain?" asked the telepath.

"You know what I want you for, Spooky."

"Of course. But I don't like it."

"Neither do I." Grimes poured the drinks, handed the larger one to Deane. The psionic communications officer sipped in an absurdly genteel manner, the little finger of his right hand extended. The level of the transparent fluid in his glass sank rapidly.

Deane said, his speech ever so slightly slurred, "And you think that the safety of the ship is jeopardised?"

"I do." Grimes poured more gin—but not for himself.

"If I have your assurance, Captain, that such is the case . . ."

"You have."

Deane was silent for a few seconds, looking through rather than at Grimes, staring at something . . . elsewhere. Then: "They're in the computer room. Mr. Adam and the Chief. I can't pick up Adam's thoughts—but I feel a sense of . . . rightness? But I can get into Mac's mind . . ." On his almost featureless visage the grimace of extreme distaste was startling. "I . . . I don't understand . . ."

"You don't understand what, Spooky?"

"How a man, a human being, can regard a hunk of animated ironmongery with such reverence . . ."

"You're not a very good psychologist, Spooky, but go on."

"I . . . I'm looking at Adam through Mac's eyes. He's bigger, somehow, and he seems to be self-luminous, and there's a sort of circle of golden light around his head . . ."

"That's the way that Mac sees him?"

"Yes. And his voice. Adam's voice. It's not the way that *we* hear it. It's more like the beat of some great engine . . . And he's saying, 'You believe, and you will serve.' And Mac has just answered, 'Yes, Master. I believe, and I will serve.' "

"What are they *doing?*" demanded Grimes urgently.

"Mac's opening up the computer. The memory bank, I think it is. He's turned to look at Adam again, and a panel over Adam's chest is sliding away and down, and there's some sort of storage bin in there, with rows and rows of pigeonholes. Adam has taken something out of one of them . . . A ball of greyish metal or plastic, with connections all over its surface. He's telling Mac where to put it in the memory bank, and how to hook it up . . ."

Grimes, his glass clattering unheeded to the deck, was out of his chair, pausing briefly at his desk to fling open a drawer and to take from it his .50 automatic. He snapped at Deane, "Get on the intercom. Tell every officer off duty to come to the computer room, armed if possible." He ran through the door out into the alleyway, then fell rather than clambered down the ladder to the next deck, and to the next one, and the next. At some stage of his descent he twisted his ankle, painfully, but kept on going.

The door to the computer room was locked, from the inside—but Grimes, as Captain, carried always on his person the ship's master key. With his left hand—the pistol was in his right—he inserted the convoluted sliver of metal into the slot, twisted it. The panel slid open.

McCloud and Adam stared at him, at the weapon in his hand. He stared back. He allowed his gaze to wander, but briefly. The cover plate had been replaced over the memory bank—but surely that heavily insulted cable leading to and through it was something that had been added, was an additional supply of power, too much power, to the ship's electronic bookkeeper.

McCloud smiled—a vague sort of smile, yet somehow exalted, that looked odd on his rough-hewn features. He said, "You and your kind are finished, Captain. You'd better tell the dinosaurs, Neanderthal Man, the dodo, the great auk, and all the others to move over to make room for you."

"Mr. McCloud," ordered Grimes, his voice (not without effort on his part) steady, "switch off the computer, then undo whatever it is that you have done."

It was Adam who replied. "I am sorry, genuinely sorry, Mr. Grimes, but it is too late. As Mr. McCloud implied, you are on the point of becoming extinct."

Grimes was conscious of the others behind him in the alleyway. "Mr. Beadle?"

"Yes, Captain?"

"Take Mr. Slovotny with you down to the engine room. Cut off all power to this section of the ship."

"You can try," said Mr. Adam. "But you will not be allowed. I give notice now; I am the Master."

"You are the Master," echoed McCloud.

"Mutiny," stated Grimes.

"Mutiny?" repeated Adam, iron and irony in his voice. He stepped towards the Captain, one long, metallic arm upraised.

Grimes fired. He might as well have been using a pea-shooter. He fired again, and again. The bullets splashed like pellets of wet clay on the robot's armor. He realised that it was too late for him to turn and run; he awaited the crushing impact of the steel fist that would end everything.

There was a voice saying, "No . . . *No* . . ."

Was it his own? Dimly, he realised that it was not.

There was the voice saying, "*No*!"

Surprisingly Adam hesitated—but only for a second. Again he advanced—and then, seemingly from the computer itself, arced a crackling discharge, a dreadful, blinding lightning. Grimes, in the fleeting instant before his eyelids snapped shut, saw the automaton standing there, arms outstretched rigidly from his sides, black amid the electric fire that played about his body. Then, as he toppled to the deck, there was a metallic crash.

When, at long last, Grimes regained his eyesight he looked around the computer room. McCloud was unharmed—physically. The engineer was huddled in a corner, his arms over his head, in a foetal position. The computer, to judge from the wisps of smoke still trickling from cracks in its panels, was a total write-off. And Adam, literally welded to the deck, still in that attitude of crucifixion, was dead.

Dead . . . thought Grimes numbly. *Dead* . . . Had he ever been alive, in the real sense of the word?

But the ship, he knew, had been briefly alive, had been aware, conscious, after that machine which would be God had kindled the spark of life in her electronic brain. And a ship, unlike other machines, always has personality, a pseudo-life derived from her crew, from the men who live and work, hope and dream within her metal body.

This vessel had known her brief minutes of full awareness, but her old virtues had persisted, among them loyalty to her rightful captain.

Grimes wondered if he would dare to put all this in the report that he would have to make. It would be a pity not to give credit where credit was due.

The Sleeping Beauty

COMMODORE DAMIEN, OFFICER Commanding Couriers, was not in a very good mood. This was not unusual—especially on the occasions when Lieutenant Grimes, captain of the Serpent Class Courier *Adder,* happened to be on the carpet.

"Mr. Grimes . . ." said the Commodore in a tired voice.

"Sir!" responded Grimes smartly.

"Mr. Grimes, you've been and gone and done it *again.*"

The Lieutenant's prominent ears reddened. "I did what I could to save my ship and my people, sir."

"You destroyed a *very* expensive piece of equipment, as well as playing merry hell with the Federation's colonial policy. My masters—who, incidentally, are also *your* masters—are not, repeat not, amused."

"I saved my ship," repeated Grimes stubbornly.

The Commodore looked down at the report on his desk. A grim smile did little, if anything, to soften the harsh planes of his bony face. "It says here that your ship saved you."

"She did," admitted Grimes. "It was sort of mutual . . ."

"And it was your ship that killed—I suppose that 'kill' is the right word to use regarding a highly intelligent robot—-Mr. Adam . . . H'm. A *slightly* extenuating circumstance. Nonetheless, Grimes, were it not for the fact that you're a better than average spaceman you'd be O-U-bloody-T, trying to get a job as Third Mate in Rim Runners or some such outfit." He made a steeple of his skeletal fingers, glared at the Lieutenant coldly over the bony erection. "So, in the interests of all concerned, I've decided that your *Adder* will not be carrying any more passengers for a while—at least, not with you in command of her. Even so, I'm afraid that you'll not have much time to enjoy the social life—such as it is—of Base . . ."

Grimes sighed audibly. Although a certain Dr. Margaret Lazenby was his senior in rank he was beginning to get on well with her.

"As soon as repairs and routine maintenance are completed, Mr. Grimes, you will get the hell off this planet."

"What about my officers, sir? Mr. Beadle is overdue for Leave . . ."

"My heart fair bleeds for him."

"And Mr. McCloud is in hospital . . ."

"Ensign Vitelli, your new Engineering Officer, was ordered to report to your vessel as soon as possible, if not before. The work of fitting a replacement computer to *Adder* is already well in hand." The Commodore looked at his watch. "It is now 1435. At 1800 hours you will lift ship."

"My Orders, sir . . ."

"Oh, yes, Grimes. Your Orders. A matter of minor importance, actually. As long as you get out of *my* hair that's all that matters to me. But I suppose I have to put you in the picture. The Shaara are passing through a phase of being nice to humans, and we, of the Federation, are reciprocating. There's a small parcel of *very* important cargo to be lifted from Droomoor to Brooum, and for some reason or other our arthropedal allies haven't a fast ship of their own handy. Lindisfarne Base is only a week from Droomoor by Serpent Class Courier. So . . ."

So Viper, Asp *and* Cobra *have all been in port for weeks,* thought Grimes bitterly, *but* I *get the job.*

The Commodore had his telepathic moments. He smiled again, and this time there was a hint of sympathy. He said, "I want you off Lindisfarne, young Grimes, before there's too much of a stink raised over this Mr. Adam affair. You're too honest. I can bend the truth better than you can."

"Thank you, sir," said Grimes, meaning it.

"Off you go, now. Don't forget these." Grimes took the heavily sealed envelope. "And try not to make too much of a balls of this assignment."

"I'll try, sir."

Grimes saluted, marched smartly out of the Commodore's office, strode across the apron to where his "flying darning needle," not yet shifted to a lay-up berth (not that she would be now), was awaiting him.

Mr. Beadle met him at the airlock. He rarely smiled—but he did so, rather smugly, when he saw the Orders in Grimes's hand. He asked casually, "Any word of my relief, Captain?"

"Yes. You're not getting it, Number One," Grimes told him, rather hating himself for the pleasure he derived from being the bearer of bad tidings. "And we're to lift off at 1800 hours. Is the new engineer aboard yet?"

Beadle's face had resumed its normal lugubrious case. "Yes," he said. "But stores, Captain . . . Repairs . . . Maintenance . . ."

"Are they in hand?"

"Yes, but . . ."

"Then if we aren't ready for space, it won't be our fault." But Grimes knew—and it made him feel as unhappy as his first lieutenant looked—that the ship would be ready.

Adder lifted at precisely 1800 hours. Grimes, sulking hard—he had not been able to see Maggie Lazenby—did not employ his customary, spectacular getting-upstairs-in-a-hurry technique, kept his fingers off the auxiliary reaction drive controls. The ship drifted up and out under inertial drive only, seemingly sharing the reluctance to part of her officer. Beadle was slumped gloomily in his chair, von Tannenbaum, the navigator, stared at his instruments with an elaborate lack of interest, Slovotny, the electronic communications officer, snarled every time that he had occasion to hold converse with Aerospace Control.

And yet, once the vessel was clear of the atmosphere, Grimes began to feel almost happy. *Growl you may,* he thought, *but go you must.* He had gone. He was on his way. He was back in what he regarded as his natural element. Quite cheerfully he went through the motions of lining *Adder* up on the target star, was pleased to note that von Tannenbaum was cooperating in his usual highly efficient manner. And then, once trajectory had been set, the Mannschenn Drive was put into operation and the little ship was falling at a fantastic speed through the warped Continuum, with yet another mission to be accomplished.

The captain made the usual minor ritual of lighting his pipe. He said, "Normal Deep Space routine, Number One."

"Normal Deep Space routine, sir."

"Who has the watch?"

"Mr. von Tannenbaum, Captain."

"Good. Then come to see me as soon as you're free."

When Beadle knocked at his door Grimes had the envelope of instructions open. He motioned the first lieutenant to a chair, said, "Fix us drinks, Number One, while I see what's in this bumf . . ." He extended a hand for the glass that the officer put into it, sipped the pink gin, continued reading. "Mphm. Well, we're bound for Droomoor, as you know . . ."

"As well I know." Beadle then muttered something about communistic bumblebees.

"Come, come, Mr. Beadle. The Shaara are our brave allies. And they aren't at all bad when you get to know them."

"I don't want to get to know them. If I couldn't have my leave I could have been sent on a mission to a world with real human girls and a few bright lights . . ."

"Mr. Beadle, you shock me. By your xenophobia as well as by your low tastes. However, as I was saying, we are to proceed to Droomoor at maximum velocity consistent with safety. There we are to pick up a small parcel of very important cargo, the loading of which is to be strictly supervised by the local authorities. As soon as possible thereafter we are to proceed to Brooum at maximum velocity &c &c."

"Just delivery boys," grumbled Beadle. "That's us."

"Oh, well," Grimes told him philosophically, "it's a change from being coach drivers. And after the trouble we've had with passengers of late it should be a welcome one."

Droomoor is an Earth-type planet, with the usual seas, continents, polar icecaps and all the rest of it. Evolution did not produce any life-forms deviating to any marked degree from the standard pattern; neither did it come up with any fire-making, tool-using animals. If human beings had been the first to discover it, it would have become a Terran colony. But it was a Shaara ship that made the first landing, so it was colonised by the Shaara, as was Brooum, a very similar world.

Grimes brought *Adder* in to Port Sherr with his usual competence, receiving the usual cooperation from the Shaara version of Aerospace Control. Apart from that, things were not so usual. He and his officers were interested to note that the aerial traffic which they sighted during their passage through the atmosphere consisted of semi-rigid airships rather than heavier-than-air machines. And the buildings surrounding the landing apron at the spaceport were featureless, mud-coloured domes rather than angular constructions of glass and metal. Beadle mumbled something about a huddle of bloody beehives, but Grimes paid no attention. As a reasonably efficient captain he was interested in the layout of the port, was trying to form some idea of what facilities were available. A ship is a ship is a ship, no matter by whom built or by whom manned—but a mammal is a mammal and an arthroped is an arthroped, and each has its own separate requirements.

"Looks like the Port Officials on their way out to us," remarked von Tannenbaum.

A party of Shaara had emerged from a circular opening near the top of the nearer dome. They flew slowly towards the ship, their gauzy wings almost invisible in the sunlight. Grimes focused his binoculars on them. In the lead was a Princess, larger than the others, her body more slender, glittering with the jeweled insignia of her rank. She was followed by two drones, so hung about with precious stones and metal that it was a wonder that they were able to stay airborne. Four upper caste workers, less gaudily caparisoned than the drones, but with sufficient ornamentation to differentiate them from the common herd, completed the party.

"Number One," said Grimes, "attend the airlock, please. I shall receive the boarding party in my day cabin."

He went down from the control room to his quarters, got out the whisky—three bottles, he decided, should be sufficient, although the Shaara drones were notorious for their capacity.

The Princess was hard, businesslike. She refused to take a drink herself, and under her glittering, many-faceted eyes the workers dare not accept Grimes's hospitality, and even the drones limited themselves to a single small glass apiece. She stood there like a gleaming, metallic piece of abstract statuary, motionless, and the voice that issued from the box strapped to her thorax was that of a machine rather than of a living being.

She said, "This is an important mission, Captain. You will come with me, at once, to the Queen-Mother, for instructions."

Grimes didn't like being ordered around, especially aboard his own ship, but was well aware that it is foolish to antagonise planetary rulers. He said:

"Certainly, Your Highness. But first I must give instructions to my officers. And before I can do so I must have some information. To begin with, how long a stay do we have on your world?"

"You will lift ship as soon as the consignment has been loaded." She consulted the jewelled watch that she wore strapped to a forelimb. "The underworkers will be on their way out to your vessel now." She pointed towards the four upper caste working Shaara. "These will supervise stowage. Please inform your officers of the arrangements."

Grimes called Beadle on the intercom, asked him to come up to his cabin. Then, as soon as the First Lieutenant put in an appearance, he told him that he was to place himself at the disposal of the supervisors and to ensure that *Adder* was in readiness for instant departure. He then went through into his bedroom to change into a dress uniform, was pulling off his shirt when he realised that the Princess had followed him.

"'What are you doing?" she asked coldly.

"Putting on something more suitable, Your Highness," he told her.

"That will not be necessary, Captain. You will be the only human in the presence of Her Majesty, and everybody will know who and what you are."

Resignedly Grimes shrugged himself back into his uniform shirt, unadorned save for shoulder boards. He felt that he should be allowed to make more of a showing, especially among beings all dressed up like Christmas trees themselves, but his orders had been to cooperate fully with the Shaara authorities. And, in any case, shorts and shirt were far more comfortable than long trousers, frock coat, collar and tie, fore-and-aft hat and that ridiculous ceremonial sword. He hung his personal communicator over his shoulder, put on his cap and said, "I'm ready, Your Highness."

"What is that?" she asked suspiciously. "A weapon?"

"No, Your Highness! A radio transceiver. I must remain in touch with my ship at all times."

"I suppose it's all right," she said grudgingly.

When Grimes walked down the ramp, following the Princess and her escorting drones, he saw that a wheeled truck had drawn up alongside *Adder* and that a winch mounted on the vehicle was reeling in a small airship, a bloated gasbag from which was slung a flimsy car, at the after end of which a huge, two-bladed propeller was still lazily turning. Workers were scurrying about on the ground and buzzing between the blimp and the truck.

"Your cargo," said the Princess. "And your transport from the spaceport to the palace."

The car of the airship was now only a foot above the winch. From it the workers lifted carefully a white cylinder, apparently made from some plastic, about four feet long and one foot in diameter. Set into its smooth surface were dials, and an indicator light that glowed vividly green even in the bright sunlight. An insulated lead ran from it to the airship's engine compartment where, thought Grimes, there must be either a battery or a generator. Yes, a battery it was. Two workers, their wings a shimmering transparency, brought it out and set it down on the concrete beside the cylinder.

"You will embark," the Princess stated.

Grimes stood back and assessed the situation. It would be easy enough to get on to the truck, to clamber on top of the winch and from there into the car—but it would be impossible to do so without getting his white shorts, shirt and stockings filthy. Insofar as machinery was concerned the Shaara believed in lubrication, and plenty of it.

"I am waiting," said the Princess.

"Yes, Your Highness, but . . ."

Grimes did not hear the order given—the Shaara communicated among themselves telepathically—so was somewhat taken aback when two of the workers approached him, buzzing loudly. He flinched when their claws penetrated the thin fabric of his clothing and scratched his skin. He managed to refrain from crying out when he was lifted from the ground, carried the short distance to the airship and dumped, sprawling, on to the deck of the open car. The main hurt was to his dignity. Looking up at his own vessel he could see the grinning faces of von Tannenbaum and Slovotny at the control room viewports.

He scrambled somehow to his feet, wondering if the fragile decking would stand his weight. And then the Princess was with him, and the escorting drones, and the upper caste worker in command of the blimp had taken her place at the simple controls and the frail contraption was ballooning swiftly upwards as the winch brake was released. Grimes, looking down, saw the end of the cable whip off the barrel. He wondered what would happen if the dangling wire fouled something on the ground below, then decided that it was none of his business. These people had been playing around with airships for quite some years and must know what they were about.

The Princess was not in a communicative mood, and obviously the drones and the workers talked only when talked to—by her—although all of them wore voice boxes. Grimes was quite content with the way that things were. He had decided that the Shaaran was a bossy female, and he did not like bossy females, mammalian, arthropedal or whatever. He settled down to enjoy the trip, appreciating the leisurely—by his standards—flight over the lush countryside. There were the green, rolling hills, the great banks of flowering shrubs, huge splashes of colour that were vivid without being gaudy. Thousands of workers were busily employed about the enormous blossoms. There was almost no machinery in evidence—but in a culture such as this there would be little need for the machine, workers of the lower grades being no more than flesh-and-blood robots.

Ahead of them loomed the city.

Just a huddle of domes it was, some large, some small, with the greatest of all of them roughly in the center. This one, Grimes saw as they approached it, had a flattened top, and there was machinery there—a winch, he decided.

The airship came in high, but losing altitude slowly, finally hovering over the palace, its propeller just turning over to keep it stemming the light breeze. Two workers flew up from the platform, caught the end of the dangling cable, snapped it on to the end of another cable brought up from the winch drum. The winch was started and, creaking in protest, the blimp was drawn rapidly down. A set of wheeled steps was pushed into position, its upper part hooked on to the gunwale of the swaying car. The Princess and her escort ignored this facility, fluttering out and down in a flurry of gauzy wings. Grimes used the ladder, of course, feeling grateful that somebody had bothered to remember that he was a wingless biped.

"Follow me," snapped the Princess.

The spaceman followed her, through a circular hatch in the platform. The ramp down which she led him was steep and he had difficulty in maintaining his balance, was unable to gain more than a confused impression of the interior of the huge building. There was plenty of light, luckily, a green-blue radiance emanating from clusters of luminescent insects hanging at intervals from the roof of the corridor. The air was warm, and bore an acrid but not unpleasant tang. It carried very few sounds, however, only a continuous, faintly sinister rustling noise. Grimes missed the murmur of machinery. Surely—apart from anything else—a vast structure such as this would need mechanical ventilation. In any case, there was an appreciable air flow. And then, at a junction of four corridors, he saw a group of workers, their feet hooked into rings set in the smooth floor, their wings beating slowly, maintaining the circulation of the atmosphere.

Down they went, and down, through corridors that were deserted save for themselves, through other corridors that were busy streets, with hordes of workers scurrying on mysterious errands. But they were never jostled; the lower caste Shaara always gave the Princess and her party a respectfully wide berth. Even so, there seemed to be little, if any curiosity; only the occasional drone would stop to stare at the Earthman with interest.

Down they went, and down . . .

They came, at last, to the end of a long passageway, closed off by a grilled door, the first that Grimes had seen in the hive. On the farther side of it were six workers, hung about with metal accoutrements. Workers? No, Grimes decided, soldiers, Amazons. Did they, he wondered, have stings, like their Terran counterparts? Perhaps they did—but the laser pistols that they held would be far more effective.

"Who comes?" asked one of them in the sort of voice that Grimes associated with sergeant-majors.

"The Princess Shrla, with Drones Brrynn and Drryhr, and Earth-Drone-Captain Grrimes."

"Enter, Princess Shrla, Enter, Earth-Drone-Captain Grrimes."

The grille slid silently aside, admitting Grimes and the Princess, shutting again, leaving the two drones on its further side. Two soldiers led the way along a tunnel that, by the Earthman's standards, was very poorly illuminated, two more brought up the rear. Grimes was pleased to note that the Princess seemed to have lost most of her arrogance.

They came, then, into a vast chamber, a blue-lit dimness about which the shapes of the Queen-Mother's attendants rustled, scurried and crept. Slowly they walked over the smooth, soft floor—under Grimes's shoes it felt unpleasantly organic—to the raised platform on which lay a huge, pale shape. Ranged around the platform were screens upon which moved pictures of scenes all over the planet—one of them showed the spaceport, with *Adder* standing tall slim and gleaming on the apron—and banks of dials and meters. Throne-room this enormous vault was, and nursery, and the control room of a world.

Grimes's eyes were becoming accustomed to the near-darkness. He looked with pity at the flabby, grossly distended body with its ineffectual limbs, its useless stubs of wings. He did not, oddly enough, consider obscene the slowly moving belt that ran under the platform, upon which, at regular intervals, a glistening, pearly egg was deposited, neither was he repelled by the spectacle of the worker whose swollen body visibly shrank as she regurgitated nutriment into the mouth of the Shaara Queen—but he was taken aback when that being spoke to him while feeding was still in progress. He should not have been, knowing as he did that the artificial voice boxes worn by the Shaara have no connection with their organs of ingestion.

"Welcome, Captain Grimes," she said in deep, almost masculine tones.

"I am honored, Your Majesty," he stammered.

"You do us a great service, Captain Grimes."

"That is a pleasure as well as an honor, Your Majesty."

"So . . . But, Captain Grimes, I must, as you Earthmen say, put you in the picture." There was a short silence. "On Brooum there is crisis. Disease has taken its toll among the hives, a virus, a mutated virus. A cure was found—but too late. The Brooum Queen-Mother is dead. All Princesses not beyond fertilisation age are dead. Even the royal eggs, larvae and pupae were destroyed by the disease.

"We, of course, are best able to afford help to our daughters and sisters on Brooum. We offered to send a fertilisable Princess to become Queen-Mother, but the Council of Princesses which now rules the colony insists that their new monarch be born, as it were, on the planet. So, then, we are dispatching, by your vessel, a royal pupa. She will tear the silken sheath and emerge, as an imago, into the world over which she will reign."

"Mphm . . ." grunted Grimes absentmindedly. "Your Majesty," he added hastily.

The Queen-Mother turned her attention to the television screens. "If we are not mistaken," she said, "the loading of the refrigerated cannister containing the pupa has been completed. Princess Shrla will take you back to your ship. You will lift and proceed as soon as is practicable." Again she paused, then went on. "We need not tell you, Captain Grimes, that we Shaara have great respect for Terran spacemen. We are confident that you will carry out your mission successfully. We shall be pleased, on your return to our planet, to confer upon you the Order of the Golden Honeyflower.

"On your bicycle, spaceman!"

Grimes looked at the recumbent Queen dubiously. Where had she picked up *that* expression? But he had heard it said—and was inclined to agree—that the Shaara were more human than many of the humanoids throughout the Galaxy.

He bowed low—then, following the Princess, escorted by the soldiers, made his way out of the throne-room.

It is just three weeks, Terran Standard, from Droomoor to Brooum as the Serpent Class Courier flies. That, of course, is assuming that all systems are Go aboard the said Courier. All systems were not Go insofar as *Adder* was concerned. This was the result of an unfortunate combination of circumstances. The ship had been fitted with a new computer at Lindisfarne Base, a new Engineering Officer—all of whose previous experience had been as a junior in a Constellation Class cruiser—had been appointed to her, and she had not been allowed to stay in port long enough for any real maintenance to be carried out.

The trouble started one evening, ship's time, when Grimes was discussing matters with Spooky Deane, the psionic communications officer. The telepath was, as usual, getting outside a large, undiluted gin. His captain was sipping a glass of the same fluid, but with ice cubes and bitters as additives.

"Well, Spooky," said Grimes, "I don't think that we shall have any trouble with *this* passenger. She stays in her cocoons—the home-grown one and the plastic outer casing—safe and snug and hard-frozen, and thawing her out will be up to her loyal subjects. By that time we shall be well on our way . . ."

"She's alive, you know," said Deane.

"Of course she's alive."

"She's conscious, I mean. I'm getting more and more attuned to her thoughts, her feelings. It's always been said that it's practically impossible for there to be any real contact of minds between human and Shaara telepaths, but when you're cooped up in the same ship as a Shaara, a little ship at that . . ."

"Tell me more," ordered Grimes.

"It's . . . fascinating. You know, of course, that race memory plays a big part in the Shaara culture. The princess, when she emerges as an imago, will *know* just what her duties are, and what the duties of those about her are. She *knows* that her two main functions will be to rule and to breed. Workers exist only to serve her, and every drone is a potential father to her people . . ."

"Mphm. And is she aware of *us*?"

"Dimly, Captain. She doesn't know, of course, who or what we are. As far as she's concerned we're just some of her subjects, in close attendance upon her . . ."

"Drones or workers?"

Spooky Deane laughed. "If she were more fully conscious, she'd be rather confused on that point. Males are drones, and drones don't work . . ."

Grimes was about to make some unkind remarks about his officers when the lights flickered. When they flickered a second time he was already on his feet. When they went out he was halfway through the door of his day cabin, hurrying towards the control room. The police lights came on, fed from the emergency batteries—but the sudden cessation of the noise of pumps and fans, the cutting off in mid-beat of the irregular throbbing of the inertial drive, was frightening. The thin, high whine of the Mannschenn Drive Unit deepened as the spinning, precessing gyroscopes slowed to a halt, and as they did so there came the nauseating dizziness of temporal disorientation.

Grimes kept going, although—as he put it, later—he didn't know if it was Christmas Day or last Thursday. The ship was in Free Fall now, and he pulled himself rapidly along the guide rail, was practically swimming in air as he dived through the hatch into Control.

Von Tannenbaum had the watch. He was busy at the auxiliary machinery control panel. A fan restarted somewhere, but a warning buzzer began to sound. The navigator cursed. The fan motor slowed down and the buzzer ceased.

"What's happened, Pilot?" demanded Grimes.

"The Phoenix jennie I *think,* Captain. Vitelli hasn't reported yet . . ."

Then the engineer's shrill, excited voice sounded from the intercom speaker. "Auxiliary engine room to Control! I have to report a leakage of deuterium!"

"What pressure is there in the tank?" Grimes asked.

"The gauges still show 20,000 units. But . . ."

"But what?" Grimes snapped.

"Captain, the tank is empty."

Grimes pulled himself to his chair, strapped himself in. He looked out through the viewports at the star-begemmed blackness, each point of light hard and sharp, no longer distorted by the temporal precession fields of the Drive, each distant sun lifetimes away with the ship in her present condition. Then he turned to face his officers—Beadle, looking no more (but no less) glum than usual, von Tannenbaum, whose normally ruddy face was now as pale as his hair, Slovotny, whose dark complexion now had a greenish cast, and Deane, ectoplasmic as always. They were joined by Vitelli, a very ordinary looking young man who was, at the moment, more than ordinarily frightened.

"Mr. Vitelli," Grimes asked him. "This leakage—is it into our atmosphere or outside the hull?"

"Outside, sir."

"Good. In that case . . ." Grimes made a major production of filling and lighting his battered pipe. "Now I can think. Mphm. Luckily I've not used any reaction mass this trip, so we have ample fuel for the emergency generator. Got your slipstick ready, Pilot? Assuming that the tanks are full, do we have enough to run the inertial and interstellar drives from here to Brooum?"

"I'll have to use the computer, Captain."

"Then use it. Meanwhile, Sparks and Spooky, can either of you gentlemen tell me what ships are in the vicinity?"

"The Dog Star Line's *Basset,*" Slovotny told him. "The cruiser *Draconis,*" added Deane.

"Mphm." It would be humiliating for a Courier Service Captain to have to call for help, but *Draconis* would be the lesser of two evils. "Mphm. Get in touch with both vessels, Mr. Deane. I'm not sure that we can spare power for the Carlotti, Mr. Slovotny. Get in touch with both vessels, ask their positions and tell them ours. But don't tell them anything else."

"*Our* position, sir, is . . . ?"

Grimes swivelled his chair so that he could see the chart tank, rattled off the coordinates, adding, "Near enough, until we get an accurate fix . . ."

"I can take one now, Captain," von Tannenbaum told him.

"Thank you, Pilot. Finished your sums?"

"Yes." The navigator's beefy face was expressionless. "To begin with, we have enough chemical fuel to maintain all essential services for a period of seventy-three Standard days. *But* we do not have enough fuel to carry us to Brooum, even using Mannschenn Drive only. We could, however, make for 2X1797—sol-type, with one Earth-type planet, habitable but currently uninhabited by intelligent life forms . . ."

Grimes considered the situation. If he were going to call for help he would be better off staying where he was, in reasonable comfort.

"Mr. Vitelli," he said, "you can start up the emergency generator. Mr. Deane, as soon as Mr. van Tannenbaum has a fix you can get a message out to *Basset* and *Draconis* . . ."

"But she's properly awake," Deane muttered. "She's torn upon the silk cocoon, and the outer cannister is opening . . ."

"What the hell are you talking about?" barked Grimes.

"The Princess. When the power went off the refrigeration unit stopped. She . . ." The telepath's face assumed an expression of rapt devotion. "We must go to her . . ."

"We must go to her . . ." echoed Vitelli.

"The emergency generator!" almost yelled Grimes. But he, too, could feel that command *inside* his brain, the imperious demand for attention, for . . . love. Here, at last, was something, somebody whom he could serve with all the devotion of which he was, of which he ever would be capable. And yet a last, tattered shred of sanity persisted.

He said gently, "We must start the emergency generator. *She* must not be cold or hungry."

Beadle agreed. "We must start the emergency generator. For *her.*"

They started the emergency generator and the ship came back to life—of a sort. She was a small bubble of light and warmth and life drifting down and through the black immensities.

The worst part of it all, Grimes said afterwards, was *knowing* what was happening but not having the willpower to do anything about it. And then he would add, "But it was educational. You can't deny that. I always used to wonder how the Establishment gets away with so much. Now I know. If you're a member of the Establishment you have that inborn . . . arrogance? No, not arrogance. That's not the right word. You have the calm certainty that everybody will do just what you want. With *our* Establishment it could be largely the result of training, of education. With the Shaara Establishment no education or training is necessary.

"Too, the Princess had it easy—almost as easy as she would have done had she broken out of her cocoon in the proper place at the proper time. Here she was in a little ship, manned by junior officers, people used to saluting and obeying officers with more gold braid on their sleeves. For her to impose her will was child's play. Literally child's play in this case. There was a communication problem, of course, but it wasn't a serious one. Even if she couldn't actually speak, telepathically, to the rest of us, there was Spooky Deane. With him she could dot the i's and cross the t's.

"And she did."

And she did.

Adder's officers gathered in the cargo compartment that was now the throne-room. A table had been set up, covered with a cloth that was, in actuality, a new Federation ensign from the ship's flag locker. To it the Princess—the Queen, rather—clung with her four posterior legs. She was a beautiful creature, slim, all the colors of her body undimmed by age. She was a glittering, bejeweled piece of abstract statuary, but she was alive, very much alive. With her great, faceted eyes she regarded the men who hovered about her. She was demanding something. Grimes knew that, as all of them did. She was demanding something—quietly at first, then more and more insistently.

But what?

Veneration? Worship?

"She hungers," stated Deane.

She hungers . . . thought Grimes. His memory was still functioning, and he tried to recall what he knew of the Shaara.

He said, "Tell her that her needs will be satisfied."

Reluctantly yet willingly he left the cargo compartment, making his way to the galley. It did not take him long to find what he wanted, a squeeze bottle of syrup. He hurried back with it.

It did not occur to him to hand the container to the Queen. With his feet in contact with the deck he was able to stand before her, holding the bottle in his two hands, squeezing out the viscous fluid, drop by drop, into the waiting mouth. Normally he would have found that complexity of moving parts rather frightening, repulsive even—but now they seemed to possess an essential rightness that was altogether lacking from the clumsy masticatory apparatus of a human being. Slowly, carefully he squeezed, until a voice said in his mind, *Enough. Enough.*

"She would rest now," said Deane.

"She shall rest," stated Grimes.

He led the way from the cargo compartment to the little wardroom.

In a bigger ship, with a larger crew, with a senior officer in command who, by virtue of his rank, was a member of the Establishment himself, the spell might soon have been broken. But this was only a little vessel, and of her personnel only Grimes was potentially a rebel. The time would come when this potentiality would be realised—just as, later, the time of compromise would come—but it was not yet. He had been trained to obedience—and now there was aboard *Adder* somebody whom he obeyed without question, just as he would have obeyed an Admiral.

In the wardroom the officers disposed of a meal of sorts, and when it was over Grimes, from force of habit, pulled his pipe from his pocket, began to fill it.

Deane admonished him, saying, "*She* wouldn't like it. It taints the air."

"Of course," agreed Grimes, putting his pipe away.

Then they sat there, in silence, but uneasily, guiltily. They should have been working. There was so much to be done about the Hive. Von Tannenbaum at last unbuckled himself from his chair and, finding a soft rag, began, unnecessarily, to polish a bulkhead. Vitelli muttered something about cleaning up the engineroom and drifted away, and Slovotny, saying that he would need help, followed him. Beadle took the dirty plates into the pantry—normally he was one of those who washes the dishes *before* a meal.

"She is hungry," announced Deane.

Grimes went to the galley for another bottle of syrup.

So it went on, for day after day, with the Queen gaining strength and, if it were possible, even greater authority over her subjects. And she was learning. Deane's mind was open to her, as were the minds of the others, but to a lesser degree. But it was only through Deane that she could speak.

"She knows," said the telepath, "that supplies in the Hive are limited, that sooner or later, sooner rather than later, we shall be without heat, without air or food. She knows that there is a planet within reach. She orders us to proceed there, so that a greater Hive may be established on its surface."

"Then let us proceed," agreed Grimes.

He knew, as they all knew, that a general distress call would bring help—but somehow was incapable of ordering it made. He knew that the establishment of a Hive, a colony on a planet of ZX1797 would be utterly impossible—but that was what *she* wanted.

So *Adder* awoke from her sleeping state, vibrating to the irregular rhythm of the inertial drive and, had there been an outside observer, flickered into invisibility as the gyroscopes of the Mannschenn Drive unit precessed and tumbled, falling down and through the warped continuum, pulling the structure of the ship with them.

Ahead was ZX1797, a writhing, mufti-hued spiral, expanding with every passing hour.

It was von Tannenbaum who now held effective command of the ship—Grimes had become the Queen's personal attendant, although it was still Deane who made her detailed wishes known. It was Grimes who fed her, who cleansed her, who sat with her hour after hour in wordless communion. A part of him rebelled, a part of him screamed soundlessly and envisaged hard fists smashing those great, faceted eyes, heavy boots crashing through fragile chitin. A part of him rebelled—but was powerless—and *she* knew it. She was female and he was male and the tensions were inevitable, and enjoyable to one if not to the other.

And then Deane said to him, "She is tiring of her tasteless food."

She would be, thought Grimes dully. And then there was the urge to placate, to please. Although he had never made a deep study of the arthropedal race he knew, as did all.spacemen, which Terran luxuries were appreciated by the Shaara. He went up to his quarters, found what he was looking for. He decanted the fluid from its own glass container into a squeeze bottle. Had it been intended for human consumption this would not have been necessary, now that the ship was accelerating, but Shaara queens do not, ever, feed themselves.

He went back to the throne-room. Deane and the huge arthroped watched him. The Queen's eyes were even brighter than usual. She lifted her forelimbs as though to take the bottle from Grimes, then let them fall to her side. Her gauzy wings were quivering in anticipation.

Grimes approached her slowly. He knelt before her, holding the bottle before him. He raised it carefully, the nippled end towards the working mandibles. He squeezed, and a thin, amber stream shot out. Its odor was rich and heavy in the almost still air of the compartment.

More! the word formed itself in his mind. *More!*

He went on squeezing.

But . . . You are not a worker . . . You are a drone . . .

And that word "drone" denoted masculinity, not idleness.

You are a drone . . . You shall be the first father of the new Hive . . .

"Candy is dandy, but liquor is quicker . . ." muttered Deane, struggling to maintain a straight face.

Grimes glared at the telepath. What was so funny about this? He was feeling, strongly, the stirrings of desire. *She* was female, wasn't she? She was female, and she was beautiful, and he was male. She was female—and in his mind's eye those flimsy wings were transparent draperies enhancing, not concealing, the symmetry of the form of a lovely woman—slim, with high, firm breasts, with long, slender legs. She wanted him to be her mate, her consort.

She wanted him.

She . . .

Suddenly the vision flickered out.

This was no woman spread in alluring, naked abandon.

This was no more than a repulsive insect sprawled in drunken untidiness, desecrating the flag that had been spread over the table that served it for a bed. The wings were crumpled, a dull film was over the faceted eyes. A yellowish ichor oozed from among the still-working mandibles.

Grimes retched violently. To think that he had almost . . .

"Captain!" Deane's voice was urgent. "She's out like a light! She's drunk as a fiddler's bitch!"

"And we must keep her that way!" snapped Grimes. He was himself again. He strode to the nearest bulkhead pick-up. "Attention, all hands! This is the Captain speaking. Shut down inertial and interstellar drive units. Energise Carlotti transceiver. Contact any and all shipping in the vicinity, and request aid as soon as possible. Say that we are drifting, with main engines inoperable due to fuel shortage." He turned to Deane. "I'm leaving you in charge, Spooky. If she shows signs of breaking surface, you know what to do." He looked sternly at the telepath. "I suppose I can trust you . . ."

"You can," the psionic communications officer assured him. "You can. Indeed you can, captain. I wasn't looking forward at all, at all, to ending my days as a worker in some *peculiar* Terran-Shaara Hive!" He stared at Grimes thoughtfully. "I wonder if the union *would* have been fertile?"

"That will do, Mr Deane," growled Grimes.

"Fantastic," breathed Commodore Damien. "Fantastic. Almost, Mr. Grimes, I feel a certain envy. The things you get up to . . ."

The aroma of good Scotch whisky hung heavily in the air of the Commodore's office. Damien, although not an abstainer, never touched the stuff. Grimes's tastes were catholic—but on an occasion such as this he preferred to be stone cold sober.

"It is more than fantastic," snarled the Shaara Queen-Emissary, the special envoy of the Empress herself. Had she not been using a voice-box her words would have been slurred. "It is . . . disgusting. Reprehensible. This officer *forced* liquor down the throat of a member of *our* Royal family. He . . ."

"He twisted her arm?" suggested the Commodore.

"I do not understand. But she is now Queen-Mother of Brooum. A drunken, even alcoholic Queen-Mother."

"I saved my ship and my people," stated Grimes woodenly.

Damien grinned unpleasantly. "Isn't this where we came in, Lieutenant? But no matter. There are affairs of far more pressing urgency. Not only do I have to cope with a direct complaint from the personal representative of Her Imperial Majesty . . ."

Even though she was wearing a voice-box, the Queen-Emissary contrived to hiccough. And all this, Grimes knew, was going down on tape. It was unlikely that he would ever wear the ribbon of the Order of the Golden Honeyflower, but it was equally unlikely that he would be butchered to make a Shaara holiday.

"He *weaned* her on Scotch . . ." persisted the Queen-Emissary.

"Aren't you, perhaps, a little jealous?" suggested Damien. He switched his attention back to Grimes. "Meanwhile, Lieutenant, I am being literally bombarded with Carlottigrams from Her not-so-Imperial Majesty on Brooum demanding that I despatch to her, as soon as possible if not before, the only drone in the Galaxy with whom she would dream of mating . . ."

"No!" protested Grimes. "*NO!*"

"Yes, mister. Yes. For two pins I'd accede to her demands." He sighed regretfully. "But I suppose that one must draw some sort of a line somewhere . . ." He sighed again—then, "Get out, you *drone!*" he almost shouted. It was a pity that he had to spoil the effect by laughing.

"We are not amused," said the Shaara Queen.

The Wandering Buoy

IT SHOULDN'T HAVE been there.

Nothing at all should have been there, save for the sparse drift of hydrogen atoms that did nothing at all to mitigate the hard vacuum of interstellar space, and save for the Courier *Adder,* proceeding on her lawful occasions.

It shouldn't have been there, but it was, and Grimes and his officers were pleased rather than otherwise that something had happened to break the monotony of the long voyage.

"A definite contact, Captain," said von Tannenbaum, peering into the monotony of the long voyage.

"A definite contact, Captain," said von Tannenbaum, peering into the spherical screen of the mass proximity indicator.

"Mphm . . ." grunted Grimes. Then, to the Electronic Communications Officer. "You're quite sure that there's no traffic around, Sparks?"

"Quite sure, Captain," replied Slovotny. "Nothing within a thousand light years."

"Then get Spooky on the intercom, and ask him if *he's* been in touch with anybody—or anything."

"Very good, Captain," said Slovotny rather sulkily. There was always rivalry, sometimes far from friendly, between electronic and psionic communications officers.

Grimes looked over the Navigator's shoulder into the velvety blackness of the screen, at the tiny, blue-green spark that lay a little to one side of the glowing filament that was the ship's extrapolated trajectory. Von Tannenbaum had set up the range and bearing markers, was quietly reading aloud the figures. He said, "At our present velocity we shall be up to it in just over three hours."

"Spooky says that there's no psionic transmission at all from it, whatever it is," reported Slovotny.

"So if it's a ship, it's probably a derelict," murmured Grimes.

"Salvage . . ." muttered Beadle, looking almost happy.

"You've a low, commercial mind, Number One," Grimes told him. *As I have myself,* he thought. The captain's share of a fat salvage award would make a very nice addition to his far from generous pay. "Oh, well, since you've raised the point you can check towing gear, space-suits and all the rest of it. And you, Sparks, can raise Lindisfarne Base on the Carlotti. I'll have the preliminary report ready in a couple of seconds . . ." He added, speaking as much to himself as to the others, "I suppose I'd better ask permission to deviate, although the Galaxy won't grind to a halt if a dozen bags of mail are delayed in transit . . ."

He took the message pad that Slovotny handed him and wrote swiftly, *To Officer Commanding Couriers. Sighted unidentified object coordinates A1763.5 x ZU97.75 x J222.0 approx. Request authority investigate. Grimes.*

By the time that the reply came Grimes was on the point of shutting down his Mannschenn Drive and initiating the maneuvers that would match trajectory and speed with the drifting object.

It read, *authority granted, but please try to keep your nose clean for a change. Damien.*

"Well, Captain, we can *try,*" said Beadle, not too hopefully.

With the Mannschenn Drive shut down radar, which gave far more accurate readings than the mass proximity indicator, was operable. Von Tannenbaum was able to determine the elements of the object's trajectory relative to that of the ship, and after this had been done the task of closing it was easy.

At first it was no more than a brightening blip in the screen and then, at last, it could be seen visually as *Adder*'s probing searchlight caught it and held it. To begin with it was no more than just another star among the stars, but as the ship gained on it an appreciable disc was visible through the binoculars, and then with the naked eye.

Grimes studied it carefully through his powerful glasses. It was spherical, and appeared to be metallic. There were no projections on it anywhere, although there were markings that looked like painted letters or numerals. It was rotating slowly.

"It could be a mine . . ." said Beadle, who was standing with Grimes at the viewport.

"It could be . . ." agreed Grimes. "And it could be fitted with some sort of proximity fuse . . ." He turned to address von Tannenbaum. "You'd better maintain our present distance off, Pilot, until we know better what it is." He stared out through the port again. Space mines are a defensive rather than offensive weapon, and *Adder* carried six of the things in her own magazine. They are a dreadfully effective weapon when the conditions for their use are ideal—which they rarely are. Dropped from a vessel being pursued by an enemy they are an excellent deterrent—provided that the pursuer is not proceeding under interstellar drive. Unless there is temporal synchronisation there can be no physical contact.

Out here, thought Grimes, in a region of space where some sort of interstellar drive *must* be used, a mine just didn't make sense. On the other hand, it never hurt to be careful. He recalled the words of one of the Instructors at the Academy. "There are old spacemen, and there are bold spacemen, but there aren't any old, bold spacemen."

"A sounding rocket . . ." he said.

"All ready, Captain," replied Beadle.

"Thank you, Number One. After you launch it, maintain full control throughout its flight. Bring it to the buoy or the mine or whatever it is *very* gently—I don't want you punching holes in it. Circle the target a few times, if you can manage it, and then make careful contact." He paused. "Meanwhile, restart the Mannschenn Drive, but run it in neutral gear. If there is a big bang we might be able to start precessing before the shrapnel hits us." He paused again, then, "Have any of you gentlemen any bright ideas?"

"It might be an idea," contributed Slovotny, "to clear away the laser cannon. Just in case."

"Do so, Sparks. And you, Number One, don't launch your rocket until I give the word."

"Cannon trained on the target," announced Slovotny after only a few seconds.

"Good. All right, Number One. Now you can practise rocketship handling."

Beadle returned to the viewport, with binoculars strapped to his eyes and a portable control box in his hands. He pressed a button, and almost at once the sounding rocket swam into the field of view, a sleek, fishlike shape with a pale glimmer of fire at its tail, a ring of bright red lights mounted around its midsection to keep it visible at all times to the aimer. Slowly it drew away from the ship, heading towards the enigmatic ball that hung in the blaze of the searchlight. It veered to one side to pass the target at a respectable distance, circled it, went into orbit about it, a miniscule satellite about a tiny primary.

Grimes started to get impatient. He had learned that one of the hardest parts of a captain's job is to refrain from interfering—even so . . . "Number One," he said at last, "don't you think you could edge the rocket in a little closer?"

"I'm trying, sir," replied Beadle. "But the bloody thing won't answer the controls."

"Do you mind if I have a go?" asked Grimes.

"Of course not, Captain." Implied but not spoken was, "And you're bloody welcome!"

Grimes strapped a set of binoculars to his head, then took the control box. First of all he brought the sounding rocket back towards the ship, then put it in a tight turn to get the feel of it. Before long he was satisfied that he had it; it was as though a tiny extension of himself was sitting in a control room in the miniature spaceship. It wasn't so very different from a rocket-handling simulator.

He straightened out the trajectory of the sounding rocket, sent it back towards the mysterious globe and then, as Beadle had done, put it in orbit. So far, so good. He cut the drive and the thing, of course, continued circling the metallic sphere. A brief blast from a braking jet—that should do the trick. With its velocity drastically reduced the missile should fall gently towards its target. But it did not—as von Tannenbaum, manning the radar, reported.

There was something wrong here, thought Grimes. The thing had considerable mass, otherwise it would never have shown so strongly in the screen of the MPI. The greater the mass, the greater the gravitational field. But, he told himself, there are more ways than one of skinning a cat. He actuated the steering jets, tried to nudge the rocket in towards its objective. "How am I doing, Pilot?" he asked.

"What are you trying to do, Captain?" countered von Tahnenbaum. "The elements of the orbit are unchanged."

"Mphm." Perhaps more than a gentle nudge was required. Grimes gave more than a gentle nudge—and with no result whatsoever. He did not need to look at Beadle to know that the First Lieutenant was wearing his best I-told-you-so expression.

So . . .

So the situation called for brute strength and ignorance, a combination that usually gets results.

Grimes pulled the rocket away from the sphere, almost back to the ship. He turned it—and then, at full acceleration, sent it driving straight for the target. He hoped that he would be able to apply the braking jets before it came into damaging contact—but the main thing was to make contact, of any kind.

He need not have worried.

With its driving jet flaring ineffectually the rocket was streaking back towards *Adder,* tail first. The control box was useless. "Slovotny!" barked Grimes. "Fire!"

There was a blinding flare, and then only a cloud of incandescent but harmless gases, still drifting towards the ship.

"And what do we do now, Captain?" asked Beadle. "Might I suggest that we make a full report to Base and resume our voyage?"

"You might, Number One. There's no law against it. But we continue our investigations."

Grimes was in a stubborn mood. He was glad that *Adder* was not engaged upon a mission of real urgency. These bags of Fleet Mail were not important. Revised Regulations, Promotion Lists, Appointments . . . If they never reached their destination it would not matter. But a drifting menace to navigation was important. Perhaps, he thought, it would be named after him. Grimes's Folly . . . He grinned at the thought. There were better ways of achieving immortality.

But what to do?

Adder hung there, and the *thing* hung there, rates and directions of drift nicely synchronised, and in one thousand seven hundred and fifty-three Standard years they would fall into or around Algol, assuming that Grimes was willing to wait that long—which, of course, he was not. He looked at the faces of his officers, who were strapped into their chairs around the wardroom table. They looked back at him. Von Tannenbaum—the Blond Beast—grinned cheerfully. He remarked, "It's a tough nut to crack, Captain—but I'd just hate to shove off without cracking it." Slovotny, darkly serious, said, "I concur. And I'd like to find out how that repulsor field works." Vitelli, not yet quite a member of the family, said nothing. Deane complained, "If the thing had a mind that I could read it'd all be so much easier . . ." "Perhaps it's allergic to metal . . ." suggested von Tannenbaum. "We could try to bring the ship in towards it, to see what happens . . ."

"Not bloody likely, Pilot," growled Grimes. "Not yet, anyhow. Mphm . . . you might have something. It shouldn't be too hard to cook up, with our resources, a sounding rocket of all-plastic construction . . ."

"There has to be metal in the guidance system . . ." objected Slovotny.

"There won't be any guidance systems, Sparks. It will be a solid fuel affair, and we just aim it and fire it, and see what happens . . ."

"*Solid* fuel?" demurred Beadle. "Even if we had the formula we'd never be able to cook up a batch of cordite or anything similar . . ."

"There'd be no need to, Number One. We should be able to get enough from the cartridges for our projectile small arms. But I don't intend to do that."

"Then what do you intend, Captain?"

"We have graphite—and that's carbon. We've all sorts of fancy chemicals in our stores, especially those required for the maintenance of our hydroponics system. Charcoal, sulphur, saltpeter . . . Or we could use potassium chlorate instead of that . . ."

"It *could* work," admitted the First Lieutenant dubiously.

"Of course it will work," Grimes assured him.

It did work—although mixing gunpowder, especially in Free Fall conditions, wasn't as easy as Grimes had assumed that it would be. To begin with, graphite proved to be quite unsuitable, and the first small sample batch of powder burned slowly, with a vile sulphurous stench that lingered in spite of all the efforts of the air conditioner. But there were carbon water filters, and one of these was broken up and then pulverised in the galley food mixer—and when Grimes realised that the bulkheads of this compartment were rapidly acquiring a fine coating of soot he ordered that the inertial drive be restarted. With acceleration playing the part of gravity things were a little better.

Charcoal 13 percent, saltpeter 75 percent, sulphur 12 percent . . . That, thought Grimes, trying hard to remember the History of Gunnery lectures, was about right. They mixed a small amount dry, stirring it carefully with a wooden ladle. It was better than the first attempt, using graphite, had been—but not much. And it smelled as bad. Grimes concluded that there was insufficient space between the grains to allow the rapid passage of the flame.

"Spooky," he said in desperation. "Can you read my mind?"

"It's against Regulations," the telepath told him primly.

"Damn the Regulations. I sat through all those Gunnery Course lectures, and I'm sure that old Commander Dalquist went into the history of gunnery *very* thoroughly, but I never thought that the knowledge of how to make black powder would be of any use at all to a modern spaceman. But it's all there in my memory—if I could only drag it out!"

"Relax, Captain." Spooky Deane told him in a soothing voice. "Relax. Let your mind become a blank. You're tired, Captain. You're very tired. Don't fight it. Yes, sit down. Let every muscle go loose . . ."

Grimes lay back in the chair. Yes, he *was* tired . . . But he did not like the sensation of cold, clammy fingers probing about inside his brain. But he trusted Deane. He told himself very firmly that he *trusted* Deane . . .

"Let yourself go back in Time, Captain, to when you were a midshipman at the Academy . . . You're sitting there, on a hard bench, with the other midshipmen around you . . . And there, on his platform before the class, is old Commander Dalquist . . . I can see him, with his white hair and his white beard, and his faded blue eyes looking enormous behind the spectacles . . . And I can see all those lovely little models on the table before him . . . The culverin, the falcon, the carronade . . . He is droning on, and you are thinking, *How can he make anything so interesting so boring?* You are wondering, *What's on for dinner tonight?* You are hoping that it won't be boiled mutton *again* . . . Some of the other cadets are laughing. You half heard what the Commander was saying. It was that the early cannoneers, who mixed their own powder, maintained that the only possible fluid was a wine drinker's urine, their employer to supply the wine . . . And if the battle went badly, because of misfires the gunners could always say that it was due to the poor quality of the booze . . . But you are wondering now if you stand any chance with that pretty little Nurse . . . You've heard that she'll play. You don't know what it's like with a woman, but you want to find out . . ."

Grimes felt his prominent ears turning hot and scarlet. He snapped into full wakefulness. He said firmly, "That will do, Spooky. You've jogged my memory sufficiently. And if any of you gentlemen think I'm going to order a free wine issue, you're mistaken. We'll use plain water, just enough to make a sort of mud, thoroughly mixed, and then we'll dry it out. No, we'll not use heat, not inside the ship. Too risky. But the vacuum chamber should do the job quite well . . ."

"And then?" asked Beadle, becoming interested in spite of himself.

"Then we crush it into grains."

"Won't that be risky?"

"Yes. But we'll have a plastic bowl fitted to the food mixer, and the Chief can make some strong, plastic paddles. As long as we avoid the use of metal we should be safe enough."

They made a small batch of powder by the method that Grimes had outlined. Slovotny fitted a remote control switch to the food mixer in the galley, and they all retired from that compartment while the cake was being crushed and stirred. The bowlful of black, granular matter looked harmless enough—but a small portion of it transferred to a saucer—and taken well away from the larger amount remaining in the bowl—burned with a satisfying *whoof!* when ignited.

"We're in business!" gloated Grimes. "*Adder* Pyrotechnics, Unlimited!"

They were in business, and while Grimes, Beadle and von Tannenbaum manufactured a large supply of gunpowder Slovotny and Vitelli set about converting a half-dozen large, plastic bottles into rocket casings. They were made of thermoplastic, so it was easy enough to shape them as required, with throat and nozzle. To ensure that they would retain the shape after firing they were bound about with heavy insulating tape. After this was finished there was a rocket launcher to make—a tube of the correct diameter, with a blast shield and with the essential parts of a projectile pistol as the firing mechanism.

Then all hands joined forces in filling the rockets. Tubes of stiff paper, soaked in a saturated solution of saltpeter and allowed to dry, were inserted into the casing and centered as accurately as possible. The powder was poured around them, and well tamped home.

While this was being done Spooky Deane—who, until now, had played no part in the proceedings—made a suggestion. "Forgive me for butting in, Captain, but I remember—with *your* memory—the models and pictures that the Instructor showed the class. Those old chemical rockets had sticks or vanes to make them fly straight . . ."

For a moment this had Grimes worried. Then he laughed. "Those rockets, Spooky, were used in the atmosphere. Sticks or vanes would be utterly useless in a vacuum." But he couldn't help wondering if vanes set actually in the exhaust would help to keep the missiles on a straight trajectory. But unless he used metal there was no suitable material aboard the ship—and metal was out.

Grimes went outside, with von Tannenbaum, to do the actual firing. They stood there on the curved shell plating, held in place by the magnetic soles of their boots. Each of them, too, was secured by lifelines. Neither needed to be told that to every action there is an equal and opposite reaction. The backblast of the home-made rockets would be liable to sweep them from their footing.

Grimes held the clumsy bazooka while the Navigator loaded it, then he raised it slowly. A cartwheel sight had been etched into the transparent shield. Even though the weapon had no weight in Free Fall it still had inertia, and it was clumsy. By the time that he had the target, gleaming brightly in the beam of *Adder*'s searchlight, in the center of the cartwheel he was sweating copiously. He said into his helmet microphone, "Captain to *Adder.* I am about to open fire."

"*Adder* to Captain. Acknowledged," came Beadle's voice in reply.

Grimes's right thumb found the firing stud of the pistol. He recoiled involuntarily from the wash of the orange flame that swept over the blast shield—and then he was torn from his hold on the hull plating, slammed back to the full extent of the lifeline. He lost his grip on the rocket launcher, but it was secured to his body by stout, fireproof cords. Somehow he managed to keep his attention on the fiery flight of the rocket. It missed the target, but by a very little. To judge by the straight wake of it, it had not been deflected by any sort of repulsor field.

"It throws high . . ." commented Grimes.

He pulled himself back along the line to exactly where he had been standing before. Van Tannenbaum inserted another missile into the tube. This time, when he aimed, Grimes intended to bring the target to just above the center of the cartwheel. But there was more delay; the blast shield was befogged by smoke. Luckily this eventuality had been foreseen, and von Tannenbaum cleaned it off with a soft rag.

Grimes aimed, and fired.

Again the blast caught him—but this time he hung in an untidy tangle facing the wrong way, looking at nothingness. He heard somebody inside the ship say, "It's blown up!"

What had blown up?

Hastily Grimes got himself turned around. The mysterious globe was still there, but between it and *Adder* was an expanding cloud of smoke, a scatter of fragments, luminous in the searchlight's glare. So perhaps the nonmetallic missiles weren't going to work after all—or perhaps this missile would have blown up by itself, anyhow.

The third rocket was loaded into the bazooka. For the third time Grimes fired—and actually managed to stay on his feet. Straight and true streaked the missile. It hit, and exploded in an orange flare, a cloud of white smoke which slowly dissipated.

"Is there any damage?" asked Grimes at last. He could see none with his unaided vision, but those on the control room had powerful binoculars at hand.

"No," replied Beadle at last. "It doesn't seem to be scratched."

"Then stand by to let the Pilot and myself back into the ship. We have to decide what we do next."

What they did next was a matter of tailoring rather than engineering. *Adder* carried a couple of what were called "skin-divers' suits." These were, essentially, elasticised leotards, skin-tight but porous, maintaining the necessary pressure on the body without the need for cumbersome armor. They were ideal for working in or outside the ship, allowing absolute freedom of movement—but very few spacemen liked them. A man feels that he should be armored, well armored, against an absolutely hostile environment. Too, the conventional spacesuit has built-in facilities for the excretion of body wastes, has its little tank of water and its drinking tube, has its container of food and stimulant pellets. (Grimes, of course, always maintained that the ideal suit should make provision for the pipe smoker . . .) A conventional spacesuit is, in fact, a spaceship in miniature.

Now these two suits had to be modified. The radio transceivers, with their metallic parts, were removed from the helmets. Plastic air bottles were substituted for the original metal ones. Jointures and seals between helmet and shoulderpieces were removed, and replaced by plastic.

While this was going on Beadle asked, "Who are you sending, Captain?"

"I'm *sending* nobody, Number One. I shall be going myself, and if any one of you gentlemen cares to volunteer . . . No, not you. You're second in command. You must stay with the ship."

Surprisingly it was Deane who stepped forward. "I'll come with you, Captain."

"*You,* Spooky?" asked Grimes, not unkindly.

The telepath flushed. "I . . . I feel that I should. That . . . That *thing* out there is awakening. It was as though that rocket was a knock on the door . . ."

"Why didn't you tell us?"

"I . . . I wasn't sure. But the feeling's getting stronger. There's something there. Some sort of intelligence."

"Can't you get in touch with it?"

"I've been trying. But it's too vague, too weak. And I've the feeling that there has to be actual contact. Physical contact, I mean."

"Mphm."

"In any case, Captain, you *need* me with you."

"Why, Spooky?"

Deane jerked his head towards the watch on Grimes's wrist. "We'll not be allowed to take any metal with us. How shall we know when we've been away long enough, that we have to get back before our air runs out?"

"How shall we know if you're along?"

"Easy. Somebody will have to sit with Fido, and clockwatch all the time, really concentrating on it. At that short range Fido will pick up the thoughts even of a non-telepath quite clearly. I shall remain *en rapport* with Fido, of course."

"Mphm," grunted Grimes. Yes, he admitted to himself, the idea had its merits. He wondered whom he should tell off for the clock-watching detail. All spacemen except psionic radio officers hate the organic amplifiers, the so-called "dogs' brains in aspic," the obscenely naked masses of canine thinking apparatus floating in their spherical containers of circulating nutrient fluid.

Slovotny liked dogs. He'd be best for the job.

Slovotny was far from enthusiastic, but was told firmly that communications are communications, no matter how performed.

The Inertial Drive was restarted to make it easier for Grimes and Deane to get into their suits. Each, stripped to brief, supporting underwear, lay supine on his spread-out garment. Carefully they wriggled their hands into the tight-fitting gloves—the gloves that became tighter still once the fabric was in contact with the skin. They worked their feet into the bootees, aided by Beadle and von Tannenbaum, acting as dressers. Then, slowly and carefully, the First Lieutenant and the Navigator drew the fabric up and over arms and legs and bodies, smoothing it, pressing out the least wrinkle, trying to maintain an even, all-over pressure. To complete the job the seams were welded. Grimes wondered, as he had wondered before, what would happen if that fantastic adhesive came unstuck when the wearer of the suit was cavorting around in hard vacuum. It hadn't happened yet—as far as he knew—but there is always a first time.

"She'll do," said Beadle at last.

"She'd better do," said Grimes. He added, "If you're after promotion, Number One, there are less suspect ways of going about it."

Beadle looked hurt.

Grimes got to his feet, scowling. If one is engaged upon what might be a perilous enterprise armor is so much more appropriate than long underwear. He said, "All right. Shut down inertial drive as soon as we've got our helmets on. Then we'll be on our way."

They were on their way.

Each man carried, slung to his belt, a supply of little rockets—Roman candles, rather—insulated cardboard cylinders with friction fuses. They had flares, too, the chemical composition of such making them combustible even in a vacuum.

The Roman candles functioned quite efficiently, driving them across the gap between ship and sphere. Grimes handled himself well, Deane not so well. It was awkward having no suit radio; it was impossible to give the telepath any instructions. At the finish Grimes came in to a perfect landing, using a retro blast at the exact split second. Deane came in hard and clumsily. There was no air to transmit the *clang,* but Grimes felt the vibration all along and through his body.

He touched helmets. "Are you all right, Spooky?"

"Just . . . winded, Captain."

Grimes leading, the two men crawled over the surface of the sphere, the adhesive pads on gloves, knees, elbows and feet functioning quite well—rather too well, in fact. But it was essential that they maintain contact with the smooth metal. Close inspection confirmed distant observation. The 100-foot-diameter globe was utterly devoid of protuberances. The markings—they were no letters or numerals known to the Earthmen—could have been painted on, but Grimes decided that they were probably something along the lines of an integrated circuit. He stopped crawling, carefully made contact with his helmet and the seamless, rivetless plating. He listened. Yes, there was the faintest humming noise. Machinery?

He beckoned Deane to him, touched helmets. He said, "There's something working inside this thing, Spooky."

"I know, Captain, And there's something alive in there. A machine intelligence, I think. It's aware of us."

"How much time have we?"

Deane was silent for a few seconds, reaching out with his mind to his psionic amplifier aboard *Adder.* "Two hours and forty-five minutes."

"Good. If we could only find a way to get into this oversized beach ball . . ."

Deane jerked his head away from Grimes's. He was pointing with a rigid right arm. Grimes turned and looked. Coming into view in the glare of the searchlight, as the ball rotated, was a round hole, an aperture that expanded as they watched it. Then they were in shadow, but they crawled towards the opening. When they were in the light again they were almost on top of it. They touched helmets again. "Will you come into my parlor . . . ?" whispered Grimes.

"I . . . I feel that it's safe . . ." Deane told him.

"Good. Then we'll carry on. Is that an airlock, I wonder? There's only one way to find out . . ."

It was not an airlock. It was a doorway into cavernous blackness, in which loomed great, vague shapes, dimly visible in the reflected beam of *Adder*'s searchlight—then invisible as this hemisphere of the little, artificial world was swept into night. Grimes was falling; his gloves could get no grip on the smooth, slippery rim of the hole. He was falling, and cried out in alarm as something brushed against him. But it was only Deane. The telepath clutched him in an embrace that, had Deane been of the opposite sex, might have been enjoyable.

"Keep your paws off me, Spooky!" ordered Grimes irritably. Yet he, too, was afraid of the dark, was suffering the primordial fear. The door through which they had entered must be closed now, otherwise they would be getting some illumination from *Adder*'s searchlight. The dense blackness was stifling. Grimes fumbled at his belt, trying to find a flare by touch. The use of one of the little rockets in this confined space could be disastrous. But there had to be light. Grimes was not a religious man, otherwise he would have prayed for it.

Then, suddenly, there was light.

It was a soft, diffused illumination, emanating from no discernible source. It did not, at first, show much. The inner surface of the sphere was smooth, glassy, translucent rather than transparent. Behind it hulked the vague shapes that they had glimpsed before their entry. Some were moving slowly, some were stationary. None of them was like any machine or living being that either of the two men had ever seen.

Helmets touched.

"It's aware of us. It knows that we need light . . ." whispered Deane.

"What is It?"

"I . . . I dare not ask. It is too . . . big?"

And Grimes, although no telepath, was feeling it too, awe rather than fear, although he admitted to himself that he was dreadfully afraid. It was like his first space walk, the first time that he had been out from the frail bubble of light and warmth, one little man in the vastness of the emptiness between the worlds. He tried to take his mind off it by staring at the strange machinery—if it was machinery—beyond that glassy inner shell, tried to make out what these devices were, what they were doing. He focused his attention on what seemed to be a spinning wheel of rainbow luminescence. It was a mistake.

He felt himself being drawn into that radiant eddy—not physically, but psychically. He tried to resist. It was useless.

Then the pictures came—vivid, simple.

There was a naked, manlike being hunkered down in a sandy hollow among rocks. Manlike? It was Grimes himself. A flattish slab of wood was held firmly between his horny heels, projecting out and forward, away from him. In his two hands he gripped a stick, was sawing away with it, to and fro on the surface of the slab, in which the pointed end of it had already worn a groove. (Grimes could *feel* that stick in his hands, could feel the vibration as he worked it backwards and forwards.) There was a wisp of blue smoke from the groove, almost invisible at first, but becoming denser. There was a tiny red spark that brightened, expanded. Hastily Grimes let go of the fire stick, grabbed a handful of dried leaves and twigs, dropped them on top of the smoulder. Carefully he brought his head down, began to blow gently, fanning the beginnings of the fire with his breath. There was flame now—feeble, hesitant. There was flame, and a faintly heard crackle as the kindling caught. There was flame—and Grimes had to pull his head back hastily to avoid being scorched.

The picture changed.

It was night now—and Grimes and his family were squatting around the cheerful blaze. One part of his mind that had not succumbed to the hypnosis wondered who that woman was. He decided wryly that she—big-bellied, flabby-breasted—was not his cup of tea at all. But he *knew* that she was his mate, just as he *knew* that those almost simian brats were his children.

It was night, and from the darkness around the camp came the roars and snarls of the nocturnal predators. But they were afraid of fire. He, Grimes, had made fire. Therefore those beasts of prey should be afraid of him. He toyed with the glimmerings of an idea. He picked up a well-gnawed femur—that day he had been lucky enough to find a not-too-rotten carcass that had been abandoned by the original killer and not yet discovered by the other scavengers—and hefted it experimentally in his hand. It seemed to belong there. From curiosity rather than viciousness he brought it swinging around, so that the end of it struck the skull of the woman with a sharp *crack*. She squealed piteously. Grimes had no language with which to think, but he knew that a harder blow could have killed her. Dimly he realised that a hard blow could kill a tiger . . .

He . . .

He was outside the sphere, and Deane was with him. Coming towards him was a construction of blazing lights. He was afraid—and then he snapped back into the here-and-now. He was John Grimes, Lieutenant, Federation Survey Service, Captain of the courier *Adder*. That was his ship. His home. He must return to his home, followed by this Agent of the Old Ones, so that observation and assessment could be made, and plans for the further advancement of the race.

The ship was no longer approaching.

Grimes pulled a Roman candle from his belt, motioned to Deane to do likewise. He lit it, jetted swiftly towards *Adder.* He knew, without looking around, that the sphere was following.

Although blinded by the searchlight he managed to bring himself to the main airlock without mishap, followed by Deane. The two men pulled themselves into the little compartment. The outer door shut. Atmospheric pressure built up. Grimes removed the telepath's helmet, waited for Deane to perform a like service for him.

Deane's face was, if possible, even paler than usual. "Captain," he said, "we got back just in time. We've no more than a few minutes' air in our bottles . . ."

"Why didn't you tell me?"

Deane laughed shakily. "How could I? I was being . . . educated. If it's any use to me or to anybody else, I know how to make wheels out of sections of tree trunk . . ."

Beadle's voice crackled from an intercom bulkhead speaker. "Captain! Captain! Come up to Control! It's . . . vanished!"

"What's vanished?" demanded Grimes into the nearest pick-up.

"That . . . That sphere . . ."

"We're on our way," said Grimes.

Yes, the sphere had vanished. It had not flickered out like a snuffed candle; it had seemed to recede at a speed approaching that of light. It was gone, and no further investigation of its potentialities and capabilities would be possible.

It was Deane who was able to give an explanation of sorts. He said, "It was an emissary of the Old Ones. All intelligent races in this Galaxy share the legends—the gods who came down from the sky, bearing gifts of fire and weaponry, setting Man, or his local equivalent, on the upward path . . ."

"I played God myself once," said Grimes. "I wasn't very popular. But go on, Spooky."

"These Old Ones . . . Who were they? We shall never know. What were their motivations? Missionary zeal? Altruism? The long-term development of planets, by the indigenes, so that the Old Ones could, at some future date, take over?

"Anyhow, I wasn't entirely under Its control. I was seeing the things that It meant me to see, feeling the things that It meant me to feel—but, at the same time, I was picking up all sorts of outside impressions. It was one of many of Its kind, sent out—how long ago?—on a missionary voyage. It was a machine, and—as machines do—it malfunctioned. Its job was to make a landing on some likely world and to make contact with the primitive natives, and to initiate their education. It was programmed, too, to get the hell out if It landed on a planet whose natives already used fire, who were already metal workers. That was why It, although not yet awakened from Its long sleep, repelled our metallic sounding rocket. That was why you, Captain, got this odd hunch about a nonmetallic approach.

"Your plastic rocket woke It up properly. It assumed that we, with no metal about us, were not yet fire-making, tool-using animals. It did what It was built to do—taught us how to make fire, and tools and weapons. And then It followed us home. It was going to keep watch over us, from generation to generation, was going to give us an occasional nudge in the right direction. Possibly It had another function—to act as a sort of marker buoy for Its builders, so that They, in Their own good time, could find us, to take over.

"But even It, with Its limited intelligence, must have realised, at the finish, that we and It were in airless space and not on a planetary surface. It must have seen that we, using little rocket-propulsion units, were already sophisticated fire users. And then, when we entered an obviously metallic spaceship, the penny must finally have dropped, with a loud clang.

"Do you want to know what my last impression was, before It showed off?"

"Of course," said Grimes.

"It was one of hurt, of disillusion, of bewilderment. It was the realisation that It was at the receiving end of a joke. The thing was utterly humorless, of course—but It could still hate being laughed at."

There was a silence, broken by Beadle. "And Somewhere," he said piously, "at Some Time, Somebody must have asked, 'Where is my wandering buoy tonight?' "

"I sincerely hope," Grimes told him, "that this Somebody is not still around, and that He or It never tries to find out."

The Mountain Movers

OLGANA—EARTH-TYPE, REVOLVING around a Soltype primary—is a backwater planet. It is well off the main Galactic trade routes, although it gets by quite comfortably by exporting meat, butter, wool and the like to the neighbouring, highly industrialised Mekanika System. Olgana was a Lost Colony, one of those worlds stumbled upon quite by chance during the First Expansion, settled in a spirit of great thankfulness by the personnel of a hopelessly off-course, completely lost emigrant lodejammer. It was rediscovered—this time with no element of chance involved—by the Survey Service's *Trail Blazer,* before the colonists had drifted too far from the mainstream of human culture. Shortly thereafter there were legal proceedings against these same colonists, occupying a few argumentative weeks at the Federation's Court of Galactic Justice in Geneva, on Earth; had these been successful they would have been followed by an Eviction Order. Even in those days it was illegal for humans to establish themselves on any planet already supporting an intelligent life form. *But*—and the colonists' Learned Counsel made the most of it—that law had not been in existence when *Lode Jumbuk* lifted off from Port Woomera on what turned out to be her last voyage. It was only a legal quibble, but the aborigines, had no representation at Court—and, furthermore, Counsel for the Defense had hinted, in the right quarters, that if he lost this case he would bring suit on behalf of his clients against the Interstellar Transport Commission, holding that body fully responsible for the plights of *Lode Jumbuk*'s castaways and their descendants. ITC, fearing that a dangerous and expensive precedent might be established, brought behind-the-scenes pressure to bear and the case was dropped. Nobody asked the aborigines what they thought about it all.

There was no denying that the Olganan natives—if they were natives—were a backward race. They were humanoid—to outward appearances human. They did not, however, quite fit into the general biological pattern of their world, the fauna of which mainly comprised very primitive, egg-laying mammals. The aborigines were mammals as highly developed as Man himself; although along slightly different lines. There had been surprisingly little research into Olganan biology, however; the Colony's highly competent biologists seemed to be entirely lacking in the spirit of scientific curiosity. They were biological engineers rather than scientists, their main concern being to improve the strains of their meat-producing and wool-bearing animals, descended in the main from the spermatozoa and ova which *Lode Jumbuk*—as did all colonisation vessels of her period—had carried under refrigeration.

To Olgana came the Survey Service's Serpent Class Courier *Adder,* Lieutenant John Grimes commanding. She carried not-very-important dispatches for Commander Lewin, Officer-in-Charge of the small Federation Survey Service Base maintained on the planet. The dispatches were delivered and then, after the almost mandatory small talk, Grimes asked, "And would there be any Orders for me, Commander?"

Lewin—a small, dark, usually intense man—grinned. "Of a sort, Lieutenant. Of a sort. You must be in Commodore Damien's good books. When *I* was a skipper of a Courier it was always a case of getting from Point A to Point B as soon as possible, if not before, with stopovers cut down to the irreducible minimum . . . Well, since you ask, I received a Carlottigram from Officer Commanding Couriers just before you blew in. I am to inform you that there will be no employment for your vessel for a period of at least six weeks local. You and your officers are to put yourselves at my disposal . . ." The Commander grinned again. "I find it hard enough to find jobs enough to keep my own personnel as much as half busy. So . . . enjoy yourselves. Go your merry ways rejoicing, as long as you carry your personal transceivers at all times. See the sights, such as they are. Wallow in the fleshpots—such as *they* are." He paused. "I only wish that the Commodore had loved me as much as he seems to love you."

"Mphm," grunted Grimes, his prominent ears reddening. "I don't think that it's quite that way, sir." He was remembering his last interview with Damien. *Get out of my sight!* the Commodore had snarled. *Get out of my sight, and don't come back until I'm in a better temper, if ever . . .*

"Indeed?" with a sardonic lift of the eyebrows.

"It's this way, Commander. I don't think that I'm overly popular around Lindisfarne Base at the moment . . ."

Lewin laughed outright, "I'd guessed as much. Your fame, Lieutenant, has spread even to Olgana. Frankly, I don't want you in *my* hair, around *my* Base, humble though it be. The administration of this planet is none of my concern, luckily, so you and your officers can carouse to your hearts' content as long as it's not in *my* bailiwick."

"Have you any suggestions, sir?" asked Grimes stiffly.

"Why yes. There's the so-called Gold Coast. It got started after the Trans-Galactic Clippers started calling here on their cruises."

"Inflated prices," grumbled Grimes. "A tourist trap . . ."

"How right you are. But not every TG cruise passenger is a millionaire. I could recommend, perhaps, the coach tour of Nevernever. You probably saw it from Space on your way in—that whacking great island continent in the Southern Hemisphere."

"How did it get its name?"

"The natives call it that—or something that sounds almost like that. It's the only continent upon which the aborigines live, by the way. When *Lode Jumbuk* made her landing there was no intelligent life at all in the Northern Hemisphere."

"What's so attractive about this tour?"

"Nevernever is the only unspoiled hunk of real estate on the planet. It has been settled along the coastal fringe by humans, but the Outback—which means the Inland and most of the country north of Capricorn—is practically still the way it was when Men first came here. Oh there're sheep and cattle stations, and a bit of mining, but there won't be any real development, with irrigation and all the rest, until population pressure forces it. And the aborigines—well, most of them still live in the semi-desert the way they did before *Lode Jumbuk* came." Lewin was warming up. "Think of it, Lieutenant, an opportunity to explore a primitive world whilst enjoying all mod. cons.! You might never get such a chance again."

"I'll think about it," Grimes told him.

He thought about it. He discussed it with his officers. Mr. Beadle, the First Lieutenant, was not enthusiastic. In spite of his habitual lugubrious mien he had a passion for the bright lights, and made it quite clear that he had enjoyed of late so few opportunities to spend his pay that he could well afford a Gold Coast holiday. Von Tannenbaum, Navigator, Slovotny, Electronic Communications, and Vitelli, Engineer, sided with Beadle. Grimes did not try to persuade them—after all, he was getting no commission from the Olganan Tourist Bureau. Spooky Deane, the psionic communications officer, asked rather shyly if he could come along with the Captain. He was not the companion that Grimes would have chosen—but he was a telepath, and it was just possible that his gift would be useful.

Deane and Grimes took the rocket mail from Newer York to New Melbourne, and during the trip Grimes indulged in one of his favorite gripes, about the inability of the average colonist to come up with really original names for his cities. At New Melbourne—a drab, oversized village on the southern coast of Nevernever—they stayed at a hotel which, although recommended by Trans-Galactic Clippers, failed dismally to come up to Galactic standards, making no attempt whatsoever to cater for guests born and brought up on worlds with widely differing atmospheres, gravitational fields and dietary customs. Then there was a day's shopping, during which the two spacemen purchased such items of personal equipment as they had been told would be necessary by the office of Nevernever Tours. The following morning, early, they took a cab from their hotel to the Never-Never Coach Terminus. It was still dark, and it was cold, and it was raining.

They sat with the other passengers, all of whom were, like themselves, roughly dressed, in the chilly waiting room, waiting for something to happen. To pass the time Grimes sized up the others. Some were obviously outworlders—there was a TG Clipper in at the spaceport. Some—their accent made it obvious—were Olganans, taking the opportunity of seeing something of their own planet. None of them, on this dismal morning, looked very attractive. Grimes admitted that the same could be said about Deane and himself; the telepath conveyed the impression of a blob of ectoplasm roughly wrapped in a too gaudy poncho.

A heavy engine growled outside, and bright lights stabbed through the big windows. Deane got unsteadily to his feet. "Look at that, Captain!" he exclaimed. "Wheels, yet! I expected an inertial drive vehicle, or at least a hoverbus!"

"You should have read the brochure, Spooky. The idea of this tour is to see the country the same way as the first explorers did, to get the *feel* of it."

"I can get the feel of it as well from an aircraft as from that archaic contraption!"

"We aren't all telepaths . . ."

Two porters had come in and were picking up suitcases, carrying them outside. The tourists, holding their overnight grips, followed, watched their baggage being stowed in a locker at the rear of the coach.

From the p.a. system a voice was ordering, "All passengers will now embus! All passengers will now embus!"

The passengers embussed, and Grimes and Deane found themselves seated behind a young couple of obviously Terran origin, while across the aisle from them was a pair of youngish ladies who could be nothing other than schoolteachers. A fat, middle-aged man, dressed in a not very neat uniform of grey coveralls, eased himself into the driver's seat. "All aboard?" he asked. "Anybody who's not, sing out!" The coach lurched from the terminus on to the rain-wet street, was soon bowling north through the dreary suburbs of New Melbourne.

Northeast they ran at first, and then almost due north, following the coast. Here the land was rich, green, well-wooded, with apple orchards, vineyards, orange groves. Then there was sheep country, rolling downland speckled with the white shapes of the grazing animals. "It's wrong," Deane whispered to Grimes. "It's all wrong . . ."

"What's wrong, Spooky?"

"I can feel it—even if you can't. The . . . the resentment . . ."

"The aborigines, you mean?"

"Yes. But even stronger, the native animals, driven from their own pastures, hunted and destroyed to make room for the outsiders from beyond the stars. And the plants—what's left of the native flora in these parts. Weeds to be rooted out and burned, so that the grapes and grain and the oranges may flourish . . ."

"You must have felt the same on other colonised worlds, Spooky."

"Not as strongly as here. I can almost put it into words . . . *The First Ones* let us alone."

"Mphm," grunted Grimes. "Makes sense, I suppose. The original colonists, with only the resources of *Lode Jumbuk* to draw upon, couldn't have made much of an impression. But when they had all the resources of the Federation to draw upon . . ."

"I don't think it's quite that way . . ." murmured Deane doubtfully.

"Then what *do* you think?"

"I . . . I don't know Captain . . ."

But they had little further opportunity for private talk. Slowly at first, and then more rapidly, the coachload of assorted passengers was thawing out. The driver initiated this process—he was, Grimes realised, almost like the captain of a ship, responsible for the well-being, psychological as well as physical, of his personnel. Using a fixed microphone by his seat he delivered commentaries on the places of interest that they passed, and, when he judged that the time was ripe, had another microphone on a wandering lead passed among the passengers, the drill being that each would introduce himself by name, profession and place of residence.

Yes, they were a mixed bag, these tourists. About half of them were from Earth—they must be, thought Grimes, from the TG Clipper *Cutty Sark* presently berthed at the spaceport. Public Servants, lawyers, the inevitable Instructors from universities, both major and minor, improving their knowledge of the worlds of the Federation in a relatively inexpensive way. The Olganans were similarly diversified.

When it came to Grimes's turn he said, "John Grimes, spaceman. Last place of permanent residence St. Helier, Channel Islands, Earth."

Tanya Lancaster, the young and prettier of the two teachers across the aisle, turned to him. "I thought you were a Terry, John. You don't mind my using your given name, do you? It's supposed to be one of the rules on this tour . . ."

"I like it, Tanya."

"That's good. But you can't be from the *Cutty Sark*. I should know all the officers, at least by sight, by this time."

"And if I were one of *Cutty Sark*'s officers," said Grimes gallantly (after all, this Tanya wench was not at all bad looking, with her chestnut hair, green eyes and thin, intelligent face), "I should have known you by this time."

"Oh," she said, "you must be from the Base."

"Almost right."

"You are making things awkward. Ah, I have it. You're from that funny little destroyer or whatever it is that's berthed at the Survey Service's end of the spaceport."

"She's not a funny little destroyer," Grimes told her stiffly. "She's a Serpent Class Courier."

The girl laughed. "And she's *yours*. Yes, I overheard your friend calling you 'Captain' . . ."

"Yes. She's mine . . ."

"And now, folks," boomed the driver's amplified voice, "how about a little singsong to liven things up? Any volunteers?"

The microphone was passed along to a group of young Olganan students. After a brief consultation they burst into song.

"When the jolly *Jumbuk* lifted from Port Woomera
Out and away for Altair Three

Glad were we all to kiss the tired old Earth
good-bye—
Who'll come a-sailing in *Jumbuk* with me?

Sailing in *Jumbuk*, sailing in *Jumbuk,*
Who'll come a-sailing in *Jumbuk* with me?
Glad were we all to kiss the tired old Earth good-bye—
You'll come a-sailing in *Jumbuk* with me!

Then there was Storm, the Pile and all the engines dead—
Blown out to Hell and gone were we!
Lost in the Galaxy, falling free in sweet damn all—
Who'll come a-sailing *Jumbuk* with me?

Sailing in *Jumbuk,* sailing in *Jumbuk,*
Who'll come a-sailing in *Jumbuk* with me?
Lost in the Galaxy, falling free in sweet damn all—
You'll come a-sailing in *Jumbuk* with me!

Up jumped the Captain, shouted for his Engineer,
'Start me the diesels, one, two, three!
Give me the power to feed into the Ehrenhafts—
You'll come a-sailing in *Jumbuk* with me!' "

"But that's *ours!"* declared Tanya indignantly, her Australian accent suddenly very obvious. "It's our *Waltzing Matilda!"*

"*Waltzing Matilda* never was yours," Grimes told her. The words—yes, but the tune, no. Like many another song it's always having new verses tacked on to it."

"I suppose you're right. But these comic lyrics of theirs—what are they all about?"

"You've heard of the Ehrenhaft Drive, haven't you?"

"The first FTL Drive, wasn't it?"

"I suppose you could call it that. The Ehrenhaft generators converted the ship, the lodejammer, into what was, in effect, a huge magnetic particle. As long as she was on the right tramlines, the right line of magnetic force, she got to where she was supposed to get to in a relatively short time. But a magnetic storm, tangling the lines of force like a bowl of spaghetti, would throw her anywhere—or nowhere. And these storms also drained the micropile of all energy. In such circumstances, all that could be done was to start up the emergency diesel generators, to supply electric power to the Ehrenhaft generators. After this the ship would stooge along hopefully, trying to find a habitable planet before the fuel ran out . . ."

"H'm." She grinned suddenly. "I suppose it's more worthy of being immortalised in a song than our sheep-stealing Jolly Swagman. But I still prefer the original." And then aided by her friend, Moira Stevens—a fat and cheerful young woman—she sang what she still claimed was the original version. Grimes allowed himself to wonder what the ghost of the Jolly Swagman—still, presumably, haunting that faraway billabong—would have made of it all. . . .

That night they reached the first of their camping sites, a clearing in the bush, on the banks of a river that was little more than a trickle, but with quite adequate toilet facilities in plastic huts. The coach crew—there was a cook as well as the driver—laid out the pneumatic pup tents in three neat rows, swiftly inflated them with a hose from the coach's air compressor. Wood was collected for a fire, and folding grills laid across it. "The inevitable steak and billy tea," muttered somebody who had been on the tour before. "It's *always* steak and billy tea . . ."

But the food, although plain, was good, and the yarning around the fire was enjoyable and, finally, Grimes found that the air mattress in his tent was at least as comfortable as his bunk aboard *Adder*. He slept well, and awoke refreshed to the sound of the taped *Reveille*. He was among the first in the queue for the toilet facilities and, dressed and ready for what the day might bring, lined up for his eggs and bacon and mug of tea with a good appetite. Then there was the washing up, the deflation of mattresses and tents, the stowing away of these and the baggage—and, very shortly after the bright sun had appeared over the low hills to the eastward, the tour was on its way again.

On they drove, and on, through drought-stricken land that showed few signs of human occupancy, that was old, old long before the coming of Man. Through sun-parched plains they drove, where scrawny cattle foraged listlessly for scraps of sun-dried grass, where tumbleweed scurried across the roadway, where dust-devils raised their whirling columns of sand and light debris. But there was life, apart from the thirsty cattle, apart from the grey scrub that, with the first rains of the wet season, would put forth its brief, vivid greenery, its short-lived gaudy flowers. Once the coach stopped to let a herd of sausagekine across the track—low-slung, furry quadrupeds, wriggling like huge lizards on their almost rudimentary legs. There was a great clicking of cameras. "We're lucky, folks," said the driver. "These beast are almost extinct. They were classed as pests until only a couple of years ago—now they've been reclassed as protected fauna . . ." They rolled past an aboriginal encampment where gaunt, black figures, looking arachnoid rather than humanoid, stood immobile about their cooking fires. "Bad bastards those," announced the driver. "Most of the others will put on shows for us, will sell us curios—but not that tribe . . ."

Now and again there were other vehicles—diesel-engined tourist coaches like their own, large and small hovercraft and, in the cloudless sky, the occasional high-flying inertial drive aircraft. But, in the main, the land was empty, the long, straight road seeming to stretch to infinity ahead of them and behind them. The little settlements—pub, general store and a huddle of other buildings—were welcome every time that one was reached. There was a great consumption of cold beer at each stop, conversations with the locals, who gathered as though by magic, at each halt. There were the coach parks—concentration camps in the desert rather than oases, but with much appreciated hot showers and facilities for washing clothing.

On they drove, and on, and Grimes and Deane teamed up with Tanya and Moira. But there was no sharing of tents. The rather disgruntled Grimes gained the impression that the girl's mother had told her, at an early age, to beware of spacemen. Come to that, after the first two nights there were no tents. Now that they were in regions where it was certain that no rain would fall all hands slept in their sleeping bags only, under the stars.

And then they came to the Cragge Rock reserve. "Cragge Rock," said the driver into his microphone, "is named after Captain Cragge, Master of the *Lode Jumbuk*, just as the planet itself is named after his wife, Olga." He paused. "Perhaps somewhere in the Galaxy there's a mountain that will be called Grimes Rock—but with all due respect to the distinguished spaceman in our midst he'll have to try hard to find the equal to Cragge Rock! The Rock, folks is the largest monolith in the known Universe—just a solid hunk of granite. Five miles long, a mile across, half a mile high." He turned his attention to Tanya and Moira. "Bigger than *your* Ayers Rock, ladies!" He paused again for the slight outburst of chuckles. "And to the north, sixty miles distant, there's Mount Conway, a typical mesa. Twenty miles to the south there's Mount Sarah, named after Chief Officer Conway's wife. It's usually called 'the Sallies,' as it consists of five separate domes of red conglomerate. So you see that geologically Cragge Rock doesn't fit in. There're quite a few theories, folks. One is that there was a submarine volcanic eruption when this was all part of the ocean bed. The Rock was an extrusion of molten matter from the core of the planet. It has been further shaped by millions of years of erosion since the sea floor was lifted to become this island continent."

As he spoke, the Rock was lifting over the otherwise featureless horizon. It squatted there on the skyline, glowering red in the almost level rays of the westering sun, an enormous crimson slug. It possessed beauty of a sort—but the overall impression was one of strength.

"We spend five full days here, folks," went on the driver. "There's a hotel, and there's an aboo settlement, and most of the boos speak English. They'll be happy to tell you *their* legends about the Rock—Wuluru they call it. It's one of their sacred places, but they don't mind us coming here as long as we pay for the privilege. That, of course, is all taken care of by the Tourist Bureau, but if you want any curios you'll have to fork out for them . . . See the way that the Rock's changing color as the sun gets lower? And once the sun's down it'll slowly fade like a dying ember. . . ."

The Rock was close now, towering above them, a red wall against the darkening blue of the cloudless sky. Then they were in its shadow, and the sheer granite wall was purple, shading to cold blue . . . Sunlight again, like a sudden blow, and a last circuit of the time-pocked monolith, and a final stop on the eastern side of the stone mountain.

They got out of the coach, stood there, shivering a little, in the still, chilly air. "It has something . . ." whispered Tanya Lancaster. "It has something . . ." agreed Moira Stevens.

"Ancestral memory?" asked Deane, with unusual sharpness.

"You're prying!" snapped the fat girl.

"I'm not, Moira. But I couldn't help picking up the strong emanation from your minds."

Tanya laughed. "Like most modern Australians we're a mixed lot—and, in our fully integrated society, most of us have some aboriginal blood. But . . . Why should Moira and I feel so at home here, both at home and hopelessly lost?"

"If you let me probe . . ." suggested Deane gently.

"No," flared the girl. "No!"

Grimes sympathised with her. He knew, all too well, what it is like to have a trained telepath, no matter how high his ethical standards, around. But he said, "Spooky's to be trusted. I know."

"You might trust him, John. I don't know him well enough."

"He knows *us* too bloody well!" growled Moira.

"I smell steak," said Grimes, changing the subject.

The four of them walked to the open fire, where the evening meal was already cooking.

Dawn on the Rock was worth waking up early for. Grimes stood with the others, blanket-wrapped against the cold, and watched the great hulk flush gradually from blue to purple, from purple to pink. Over it and beyond it the sky was black, the stars very bright, almost as bright as in airless Space. Then the sun was up, and the Rock stood there, a red island in the sea of tawny sand, a surf of green brush breaking about its base. The show was over. The party went to the showers and toilets and then, dressed, assembled for breakfast.

After the meal they walked from the encampment to the Rock. Tanya and Moira stayed in the company of Grimes and Deane, but their manner towards the two spacemen was distinctly chilly; they were more interested in their guidebooks than in conversation. On their way they passed the aboriginal village. A huddle of crude shelters it was, constructed of natural materials and battered sheets of plastic. Fires were burning, and gobbets of unidentifiable meat were cooking over them. Women—naked, with straggling hair and pendulous breasts, yet human enough—looked up and around at the well-clothed, well-fed tourists with an odd, sly mixture of timidity and boldness. One of them pointed to a levelled camera and screamed, "First gibbit half dollar!"

"You'd better," advised the driver. "Very commercial minded, these people . . ."

Men were emerging from the primitive huts. One of them approached Grimes and his companions, his teeth startlingly white in his coal-black face. He was holding what looked like a crucifix. "Very good," he said, waving it in front of him. "Two dollar."

"I'm not religious . . ." Grimes began, to be cut short by Tanya's laugh.

"Don't be a fool, John," she told him. "It's a throwing weapon."

"A throwing weapon?"

"Yes. Like our boomerangs. Let me show you." She turned to the native, held out her hand. "Here. Please."

"You throw, missie?"

"Yes. I throw."

Watched by the tourists and the natives she held the thing by the end of its long arm, turned until she was facing about forty-five degrees away from the light, morning breeze, the flat surfaces of the cross at right angles to the wind. She raised her arm, then threw, with a peculiar flick of her wrist. The weapon left her hand, spinning, turned so that it was flying horizontally, like a miniature helicopter. It travelled about fifty yards, came round in a lazy arc, faltered, then fell in a flurry of fine sand.

"Not very good," complained the girl. "You got better? You got proper one?"

The savage grinned. "You know?"

"Yes. I know."

The man went back into his hut, returned with another weapon. This one was old, beautifully made, and lacking the crude designs that had been burned into the other with redhot wire. He handed it to Tanya, who hefted it approvingly. She threw it as she had thrown the first one—and the difference was immediately obvious. There was no clumsiness in its flight, no hesitation. Spinning, it flew, more like a living thing than a machine. Its arms turned more and more lazily as it came back—and Tanya, with a clapping motion, deftly caught it between her two hands. She stood admiring it—the smooth finish imparted by the most primitive of tools, the polish of age and of long use.

"How much?" she asked.

"No for sale, missie." Again the very white grin. "But I give."

"But you can't. You mustn't."

"You take."

"I shouldn't, but . . ."

"Take it, lady," said the driver. "This man is Najatira, the Chief of these people. Refusing his gift would offend him." Then, businesslike, "You guide, Najatira?"

"Yes. I guide." He barked a few words in his own language to his women, one of whom scuttled over the sand to retrieve the first fallen throwing weapon. Then, walking fast on his big, splayed feet he strode towards the Rock. Somehow the two girls had ranged themselves on either side of him. Grimes looked on disapprovingly. Who was it who had said that these natives were humanoid only? This naked savage, to judge by his external equipment, was all too human. Exchanging disapproving glances, the two spacemen took their places in the little procession.

"Cave," said Najatira, pointing. The orifice, curiously regular, was exactly at the tail of the slug-shaped monolith. "Called, by my people, the Hold of Winds. Story say, in Dream Time, wind come from there, wind move world . . . Before, world no move. No daytime, no nighttime . . ."

"Looks almost like a venturi, Captain," Deane marked to Grimes.

"Mphm. Certainly looks almost too regular to be natural. But erosion does odd things. Or it could have been made by a blast of gases from the thing's inside . . ."

"Precisely," said Deane.

"But you don't think . . . ? No. It would be impossible."

"I don't know what to think," admitted Deane.

Their native guide was leading them around the base of the Rock. "This Cave of Birth. Tonight ceremony. We show you . . . And there—

look up. What we call the fishing net. In Dream Time caught big fish . . ."

"A circuit . . ." muttered Grimes. "Exposed by millenia of weathering . . ." He laughed. "I'm getting as bad as you, Spooky. Nature comes up with the most remarkable imitations of Man-made things . . ."

So it went on, the trudge around the base of the monolith, under the hot sun, while their tireless guide pointed out this and that feature. As soon as the older members of the party began to show signs of distress the driver spoke into his wrist transceiver, and within a few minutes the coach came rumbling over the rough track and then, with its partial load, kept pace with those who were still walking. Grimes and Deane were among these hardy ones, but only because Tanya and Moira showed no signs of flagging, and because Grimes felt responsible for the women. After all, the Survey Service had been referred to as the Policemen of the Galaxy. It was unthinkable that two civilised human females should fall for this unwashed savage—but already he knew that civilised human females are apt to do the weirdest things.

At last the tour came to an end. Najatira, after bowing with surprising courtesy, strode of towards his own camp. The tourists clustered hungrily around the folding tables that had been set up, wolfed the thick sandwiches and gulped great draughts of hot, sweet tea.

During the afternoon there were flights over the Rock and the countryside for those who wished them, a large blimp having come in from the nearest airport for that purpose. This archaic transport was the occasion for surprise and incredulity, but it was explained that such aircraft were used by *Lode Jumbuk*'s people for their initial explorations.

"The bloody thing's not safe," complained Deane as soon as they were airborne.

Grimes ignored him. He was looking out and down through the big cabin windows. Yes, the Rock did look odd, out of place. It was part of the landscape—but it did not belong. It had been there for million of years—but still it did not belong. Mount Conway and Mount Sarah were natural enough geological formations—*but,* he thought, *Cragge Rock was just as natural.* He tried to envision what it must have looked like when that upwelling of molten rock thrust through the ocean bed.

"It wasn't like that, Captain," said Deane quietly.

"Damn you, Spooky! Get out of my mind."

"I'm sorry," the telepath told him, although he didn't sound it. "It's just that this locality is like a jigsaw puzzle. I'm trying to find the pieces, and to make them fit." He looked around to make sure that none of the others in the swaying, creaking cabin was listening. "Tanya and Moira . . . The kinship they feel with Najatira . . ."

"Why don't you ask them about it?" Grimes suggested, jerking his head towards the forward end of the car, where the two girls were sitting. "Is it kinship, or is it just the attraction that a woman on holiday feels for an exotic male?"

"It's more than that."

"So you're prying."

"I'm trying not to." He looked down without interest at Mount Conway, over which the airship was slowly flying. "But it's hard not to."

"You could get into trouble, Spooky. And you could get the ship into trouble . . ."

"And you, Captain."

"Yes. And me." Then Grimes allowed a slight smile to flicker over his face. "But I know you. You're on to something. And as we're on holiday from the ship I don't suppose that I can give you any direct orders . . ."

"I'm not a space-lawyer, so I'll take your word for that."

"Just be careful. And keep me informed."

While they talked the pilot of the blimp, his voice amplified, had been giving out statistics. The conversation had been private enough.

That night there was the dance.

Flaring fires had been built on the sand, in a semi-circle, the inner arc of which faced the mouth of the Cave of Birth. The tourists sat there, some on the ground and some on folding stools, the fires at their backs, waiting. Overhead the sky was black and clear, the stars bitterly bright.

From inside the Cave there was music—of a sort. There was a rhythmic wheezing of primitive trumpets, the staccato rapping of knocking sticks. There was a yelping male voice—Najatira's—that seemed to be giving orders rather than singing.

Grimes turned to say something to Tanya, but she was no longer in her place. Neither was Moira. The two girls must have gone together to the toilet block; they would be back shortly. He returned his attention to the black entrance to the Cave.

The first figure emerged from it, crouching, a stick held in his hands. Then the second, then the third . . . There was something oddly familiar about it, something that didn't make sense, or that made the wrong kind of sense. Grimes tried to remember what it was. Dimly he realised that Deane was helping him, that the telepath was trying to bring his memories to the conscious level.

Yes, that was it. That was the way that the Marines disembarked on the surface of an unexplored, possibly hostile planet, automatic weapons at the ready . . .

Twelve men were outside the Cave now, advancing in a dance-like step. The crude, tree-stem trumpets were still sounding, like the plaint of tired machinery, and the noise of the knocking sticks was that of the cooling metal. The leader paused, stood upright. With his fingers in his mouth he gave a piercing whistle.

The women emerged, carrying bundles, hesitantly, two steps forward, one step back. Grimes gasped his disbelief. Surely that was Tanya, as naked as the others—and there was no mistaking Moira. He jumped to his feet, ignoring the protests of those behind him, trying to shake off Deane's restraining hand.

"Let go!" he snarled.

"Don't interfere, Captain!" The telepath's voice was urgent. "Don't you see? They've gone native—no, that's not right. But they've reverted. And there's no law against it."

"I can still drag them out of this. They'll thank me after." He turned around and shouted, "Come on, all of you! We must put a stop to this vile performance!"

"Captain Grimes!" This was the coach driver, his voice angry. "Sit down, sir! This sort of thing has happened before, and it's nothing to worry about. The young ladies are in no danger!"

"It's happened before," agreed Deane, unexpectedly. "With neurotic exhibitionists, wanting to have their photographs taken among the savages. But not *this* way!"

Then, even more unexpectedly, it was Deane who was running out across the sand, and it was Najatira who advanced to meet him, not in hostility but in welcome. It was Grimes who, unheeded, yelled, "Come back, Spooky! Come back here!"

He didn't know what was happening, but he didn't like it. First of all those two silly bitches, and now one of his own officers. What the hell was getting into everybody? Followed by a half-dozen of the other men he ran towards the cave mouth. Their way was barred by a line of the tribesmen, holding their sticks now like spears (which they were)—not like make-believe guns. Najatira stood proudly behind the armed men, and on either side of him stood the two girls, a strange, arrogant pride in every line of their naked bodies. And there was Deane, a strange smile on his face. His face, too, was strange, seemed suddenly to have acquired lines of authority.

"Go back, John," he ordered. "There is nothing that you can do." He added softly, "But there is much that I can do."

"What the hell are you talking about, Spooky?"

"I'm an Australian, like Moira and Tanya here. Like them, I have the Old Blood in my veins. Unlike them, I'm a spaceman. Do you think that after all these years in the Service I, with my talent, haven't learned how to handle and navigate a ship, any ship? I shall take my people back to where they belong."

And then Grimes *knew*. The knowledge came flooding into his mind, from the mind of Deane, from the minds of the others, whose ancestral memories had been awakened by the telepath. But he was still responsible. He must still try to stop this craziness.

"Mr. Deane!" he snapped as he strode forward firmly. He brushed aside the point of the spear that was aimed at his chest. He saw Tanya throw something, and sneered as it missed his head by inches. He did not see the cruciform boomerang returning, was aware of it only as a crashing blow from behind, as a flash of crimson light, then darkness.

He recovered slowly. He was stretched out on the sand beside the coach. Two of the nurses among the passengers were with him.

He asked, as he tried to sit up, "What happened?"

"They all went back into the Cave," the girl said. "The rock . . . The rock closed behind them. And there were lights. And a voice, it was Mr. Deane's voice, but loud, loud, saying, 'Clear the field! Clear the field! Get back, everybody. Get well back. Get well away!' So we got well back."

"And what's happening now?" asked Grimes. The nurses helped him as he got groggily to his feet. He stared towards the distant Rock. He could hear the beat of mighty engines and the ground was trembling under the monolith. Even with the knowledge that Deane had fed into his mind he could not believe what he was seeing.

The Rock was lifting, its highest part suddenly eclipsing a bright constellation. It was lifting, and the skin of the planet protested as the vast ship, that for so long had been embedded in it, tore itself free. Tremors knocked the tourists from their feet, but somehow Grimes remained standing, oblivious to the shouts and screams. He heard the crash behind him as the coach was overturned, but did not look. At this moment it was only a minor distraction.

The Rock was lifting, had lifted. It was a deeper blackness against the blackness of the sky, a scattering of strange, impossible stars against the distant stars, a bright cluster (at first) that dimmed and diminished, that dwindled, faster and faster, and then was gone, leaving in its wake utter darkness and silence.

The silence was broken by the coach driver. He said slowly, "I've had to cope with vandalism in my time, but nothing like this. What the

Board will say when they hear that their biggest tourist attraction has gone I hate to think about . . ." He seemed to cheer up slightly. "But it was one of *your* officers, Captain Grimes, from *your* ship, that did it. I hope you enjoy explaining it!"

Grimes explained, as well as he was able, to Commander Lewin.

He said, "As we all know, sir, there are these odd races, human rather than humanoid, all through the Galaxy. It all ties in with the Common Origin of Mankind theories. I never used to have much time for them myself, but now . . ."

"Never mind that, Grimes. Get on with the washing."

"Well, Deane was decent enough to let loose a flood of knowledge into my mind just before that blasted Tanya clonked me with her boomerang. It seems that millions of years ago these stone spaceships, these hollowed out asteroids, were sent to explore this Galaxy. I got only a hazy idea of their propulsive machinery, but it was something on the lines of our Inertial Drive, and something on the lines of our Mannschenn Drive, with auxiliary rockets for maneuvering in orbit and so forth. They were never meant to land, but they could, if they had to. Their power? Derived from the conversion of matter, any matter, with the generators or converters ready to start up when the right button was pushed—but the button had to be pushed psionically. Get me?"

"Not very well. But go on."

"Something happened to the ship, to the crew and passengers of this ship. A disease, I think it was, wiping out almost all the adults, leaving only children and a handful of not very intelligent ratings. Somebody—it must have been one of the officers just before he died—got the ship down somehow. He set things so that it could not be re-entered until somebody with the right qualifications came along."

"The right qualifications?"

"Yes. Psionic talents, more than a smattering of astronautics, and descended from the Old People . . ."

"Like your Mr. Deane. But what about the two girls?"

"They had the old Blood. And they were highly educated. And they could have been latent telepaths . . ."

"Could be." Lewin smiled without much mirth. "Meanwhile, Lieutenant, I have to try to explain to the Olganan Government, with copies to Trans-Galactic Clippers *and* to our own masters, including *your* Commodore Damien. All in all, Grimes, it was a fine night's work. Apart from the Rock, there were two TG passengers *and* a Survey Service officer . . ."

"*And* the tribe . . ."

"The least of the Olganan Government's worries, and nothing at all to do with TG or ourselves. Even so . . ." This time his smile was tinged with genuine, but sardonic, humor.

"Even so?" echoed Grimes.

"What if those tribesmen and—women decided to liberate—I suppose that's the right word—those other tribespeople, the full-blooded ones who're still living in the vicinity of the other stone spaceship? What if the Australians realise, one sunny morning, that their precious Ayers Rock has up and left them?"

"I know who'll be blamed," said Grimes glumly.

"How right you are," concurred Lewin.

What You Know

LIEUTENANT JOHN GRIMES, captain of the Serpent Class Courier *Adder,* was in a bitter and twisted mood. He had his reasons. To begin with, he had just been hauled over the coals by Commodore Damien, Officer Commanding Couriers, and still resented being blamed for the disappearance of Cragge Rock from Olgana. Then he had been told that his ship's stay at Lindisfarne Base was to be a very short one—and Dr. Maggie Lazenby, with whom he hoped to achieve something warmer than mere friendship, was off planet and would not be returning until after his own departure. Finally, he had seen the latest Promotion List and had noted that officers junior to himself had been given their half rings, were now Lieutenant Commanders. And some of those same officers, in Grimes's words, wouldn't be capable of navigating a plastic duck across a bathtub.

Ensign Beadle, his first lieutenant, was sympathetic. He said, "But it isn't what you do, Captain. It isn't what you know, even. It's whom you know . . ."

"You could be right, Number One," admitted Grimes. "But in my case I'm afraid that it boils down to who knows me . . . Did you ever see that book, *How to Win Friends and Influence People?* I often think that I must have read the wrong half, the second half . . ."

Beadle made a noncommittal noise. Then, "We're ready to lift ship, Captain. Mechanically, that is, Mr. Hollister, the new psionic radio officer, has yet to join—and, of course, there are the passengers . . ." Grimes allowed himself a sardonic smile. "I wonder what the Commodore has against *them?*"

Beadle took the question literally. "We're the only Courier in port,

Captain, and it's essential that the Commissioner reaches Dhartana as soon as possible . . ."

". . . if not before," finished Grimes. "Mphm. All right, Number One. Is the V.I.P. suite swept and garnished?"

"I . . . I've been busy with the *important* preparations for space, Captain . . ."

Grimes scowled. "I sincerely hope, Number One, that Mrs. Commissioner Dalwood never hears you implying that she's unimportant. We'll make a tour of the accommodation *now*."

Followed by Beadle he strode up the ramp into the airlock of his little ship, his "flying darning needle." The V.I.P. suite took up almost the entire compartment below the officers' flat. As he passed through the sliding door into the sitting room Grimes's prominent ears reddened; with him it was a sign of anger as well as of embarrassment. "Damn it all, Number One," he exploded, "don't you realise that this woman is one of the civilian big wheels on the Board of Admiralty? You may not want promotion—but I do. Look at that table top! Drinking glass rings—and it must have been something sweet and sticky!—and bloody nearly an inch of cigarette ash! And the ashtrays! They haven't been emptied since Christ was a pup!"

"The suite hasn't been used since we carried Mr. Alberto . . ."

"I know that. Am I to suppose that you've kept it the way he left it in loving memory of him?"

"You did say, sir, that bearing in mind the circumstances of his death we should leave everything untouched in case his department wanted to make a thorough investigation . . ."

"And his department did check just to make sure that he'd left nothing of interest on board when he disembarked on Doncaster. But that was months ago. And this bedroom . . . The way it is now I wouldn't put a dog into it. Get on the blower at once to Maintenance, ask them? no, *tell* them—to send a cleaning detail here immediately."

Grimes became uncomfortably aware that there was somebody behind him. He turned slowly, reluctantly, looked into the hard, steel-grey eyes of the woman who was standing just inside the doorway. She returned his stare coldly. She was tall, and she was handsome, with short-cut platinum blonde hair, wearing a beautifully tailored grey costume that looked like a uniform but wasn't, that looked more like a uniform than a deliberately casual rig of the day affected by Grimes and Beadle in common with all Courier Service officers. Her figure seemed to be that of a girl—but her face, although unlined, was old. There were no physical marks of age, but it was somehow obvious that she had seen too much, experienced too much. Grimes thought, *If she smiles, something will crack.*

She didn't smile.

She said—and her voice, although well modulated, was hard as the rest of her—"Mr. Grimes . . ."

"Ma'am?"

"I am Commissioner Dalwood."

She did not extend her hand. Grimes bowed stiffly. "Honored to have you aboard, Ma'am."

"The honor is all yours, Mr. Grimes. Tell me, is the rest of your ship like this pigsty?"

"We're having the suite put to rights, Mrs. Dalwood."

"Pray do not put yourself out on my behalf, Mr. Grimes. My lady's maid and my two robot servants are at this moment bringing my baggage aboard. The robots are versatile. If you will let them have the necessary cleaning gear they will soon have these quarters fit for human occupancy."

"Mr. Beadle," ordered Grimes, "belay that call to Maintenance. See that Mrs. Dalwood's servants are issued with what they need."

"Very good, sir," replied Beadle smartly, glad of the chance to make his escape.

"And now, Mr. Grimes, if I may sit down somewhere in less squalid surroundings . . ."

"Certainly, Ma'am. If you will follow me . . ."

Grimes led the way out of the suite. The two humanoid robots, with expensive-looking baggage piled at their feet, stared at him impassively. The maid—small, plump, pert, and darkly brunette—allowed a flicker of sympathy to pass over her rosy face. Grimes thought that she winked, but couldn't be sure. On the way up to his own quarters Grimes was relieved to see that Beadle had kept the rest of the ship in a reasonably good state of cleanliness, although he did hear one or two disapproving sniffs from his passenger. His own day cabin was, he knew, untidy. He liked it that way. He was not surprised when Mrs. Dalwood said, "Your *desk,* Mr. Grimes. Surely some of those papers are of such a confidential nature that they should be in your safe."

Grimes said, "Nobody comes in here except by invitation. I trust my officers, Ma'am."

The Commissioner smiled thinly. Nothing cracked. She said, "What a child you are, Lieutenant. One of the first lessons I learned in politics was never to trust anybody."

"In space, aboard ship, you have to trust people, Ma'am."

She sat down in Grimes's easy chair, extending her long, elegant legs. Grimes suspected that she looked at her own limbs with brief admiration before returning her regard to him. Her laugh was brittle. "How touching, Lieutenant. And that is why ships are lost now and again."

"Can I offer you refreshment, Ma'am?" Grimes said, changing the subject.

"And do *you* drink, Lieutenant?"

I know damn well that I'm only a two ringer, Grimes thought, *but I do like being called* Captain *aboard my own ship . . .* He said, "Never on departure day, Mrs. Dalwood."

"Perhaps I shall be wise if I conform to the same rule. I must confess that I am not used to travelling in vessels of this class, and it is possible that I shall need all my wits about me during lift off. Might I ask for a cup of coffee?"

Grimes took from its rack the thermos container, which he had refilled from the galley coffee maker that morning. After he had removed the cap he realised that he had still to produce a cup, sugar bowl, spoon and milk. His tell-tale ears proclaiming his embarrassment, he replaced the container, conscious of the woman's coldly amused scrutiny. At last he had things ready, finally filling the jug from a carton of milk in his refrigerator.

She said, "The milk should be warmed."

"Yes, Mrs. Dalwood. Of course. If you wouldn't mind waiting . . ."

"If I took my coffee white I should mind. But I prefer it black, and unsweetened."

Grimes poured out, remembering that the coffee maker was long overdue for a thorough cleaning. *Adder*'s coffee had a tang of its own. Her people were accustomed to it. The Commissioner was not. After one cautious sip she put her cup down, hard. She asked, "And what is the food like aboard this ship?"

"Usually quite good, Ma'am. We carry no ratings or petty officers, so we take it by turns cooking. Mr. Beadle—he's my First Lieutenant—makes an excellent stew." Grimes babbled on. "It's a sort of a curry, actually, but not quite, if you know what I mean . . ."

"I don't, Lieutenant. Nor do I wish to. As I have already told you, my robots are versatile. Might I suggest that they take over galley duties, first of all thoroughly cleaning all vessels and implements, starting with your coffee maker? Apart from anything else it will mean that your officers will have more time to devote to their real duties."

"If you want it that way, Mrs. Dalwood . . ."

"I do want it that way."

To Grimes's intense relief the intercom phone buzzed. He said to the Commissioner, "Excuse me, Ma'am," and then into the speaker/microphone, "Captain here."

"First Lieutenant, Captain. Mr. Hollister, the new P.C.O., has just boarded. Shall I send him up to report to you?"

"Yes, Mr. Beadle. Tell him that I'll see him in the Control Room. Now." He turned to Mrs. Dalwood. "I'm afraid I must leave you for a few minutes, Ma'am. There are cigarettes in that box, and if you wish more coffee . . ."

"I most certainly do not. And, Mr. Grimes, don't you think that you had better put those papers away in your safe before you go about your pressing business?" She allowed herself another thin smile. "After all, you haven't asked yet to see *my* identification. For all you know I could be a spy."

And if you are, thought Grimes, *I hope I'm the officer commanding the firing squad.* He said, "You are very well known, Ma'am." He swept his desk clean, depositing the pile of official and private correspondence on the deck, then fumbled through the routine of opening his safe. As usual the door stuck. Finally he had the papers locked away. He bowed again to Mrs. Dalwood, who replied with a curt nod. He climbed the ladders to Control, glad to get to a part of the ship where, Commissioner or no Commissioner, he was king.

Beadle was awaiting him there with a tall, thin, pale young man who looked like a scarecrow rigged out in a cast-off Survey Service uniform. He announced, before Beadle could perform the introductions, "I don't like this ship. I am very sensitive to atmosphere. This is an unhappy ship."

"She didn't use to be," Grimes told him glumly.

Usually Grimes enjoyed shiphandling. Invariably he would invite his passengers to the control room during lift off, and most times this invitation would be accepted. He had extended the courtesy to Mrs. Dalwood, hoping that she would refuse the offer. But she did not. She sat there in the spare acceleration seat, saying nothing but noticing everything. It would almost have been better had she kept up a continual flow of Why-do-you-do-this? and Why-don't-you-do-that?

Her very presence made Grimes nervous. The irregular best of the inertial drive sounded wrong to him as *Adder* climbed slowly up and away from her pad. And, as soon as she was off the ground, the ship yawed badly, falling to an angle of seven degrees from the vertical. It must look bad, Grimes knew. It looked bad and it felt worse. The only thing to do about it was to get upstairs in a hurry before some sarcastic comment from Port Control came through the transceiver. Grimes picked his moment for turning on the auxiliary rockets, waiting until the tall, slender tower that was *Adder* was canted away from the wind. That way, he hoped, he could make it all look intentional, convey the impression that he was using the quite stiff north-wester to give him additional speed. He managed to turn in his seat in spite of the uncomfortable acceleration and said, forcing out the words, "Letting . . . the . . . wind . . . help . . . us . . ."

She—calm, unruffled—lifted her slender eyebrows and asked, with apparently genuine unconcern, "Really?"

"Time . . ." Grimes persisted, "Is . . . money . . ."

"So," she told him, "is reaction mass."

Flushing, Grimes returned to his controls. Apart from that annoying yaw the ship was handling well enough. Beadle, and von Tannenbaum, the navigator, and Slovotny, electronic communications, were quietly efficient at their stations. They were certainly quiet. There was none of the usual good-humoured banter.

Sulkily Grimes pushed *Adder* up through the last, high wisps of cirrus, into the purple twilight, towards the bright, unwinking stars. She screamed through the last tenuous shreds of atmosphere, and shortly thereafter von Tannenbaum reported that she was clear of the Van Allens. Grimes, still far too conscious of the Commissioner's cold regard, cut inertial and reaction drives, then slowly and carefully—far more slowly than was usual—used his directional gyroscopes to swing the sharp prow of the ship on to the target star. He applied correction for Galactic Drift—and then realized that he had put it on the wrong way. He mumbled something that sounded unconvincing even to himself about overcompensation and, after a few seconds that felt more like minutes, had the vessel headed in the right direction.

He wondered what would happen when he started the Mannschenn Drive—but nothing did; nothing, that is, worse than the familiar but always disquietening sense of *dejà vu.* He had a vision of himself as an old, old lieutenant with a long white beard—but this was nothing to do with the temporal precession field of the Drive, was induced rather by the psionic field generated by the Commissioner. He didn't like her and had a shrewd suspicion that she didn't like him.

She said, "Very educational, Mr. Grimes. Very educational."

She unstrapped herself from her chair. Slovotny and von Tannenbaum got up from their own seats, each determined courteously to assist her from hers. They collided, and von Tannenbaum tripped and fell, and Beadle fell over him.

"Very educational," repeated the Commissioner, gracefully extricating herself from her chair unaided. "Oh, Mr. Grimes, could you come to see me in ten minutes' time? We have to discuss the new galley routine."

"Certainly, Mrs. Dalwood." Grimes turned to his embarrassed officers. "Deep Space Routine, Mr. Beadle." Usually he said, "Normal Deep Space Routine," but had more than a suspicion that things would not be at all normal.

Things were not normal.

Usually *Adder*'s people were gourmands rather than gourmets, and a certain tightness of waistbands was an accepted fact of life. Even when whoever was doing the cooking produced an inedible mess bellies could be filled, and were filled, with sandwiches of the doorstep variety. But these relatively happy days were over.

As she had told Grimes, the Commissioner's robots were skilled cooks. To have called them chefs would not have been exaggerating. Insofar as subtlety of flavorings and attractiveness of presentation were concerned nobody could fault them. To the average spaceman, however, quantity is as important as quality. But there were no second helpings. The coldly efficient automatons must have calculated just how much nutriment each and every person aboard required to operate efficiently himself—and that was all that he ever got. Too, there was always at least one of the mechanical servitors doing something or other around the galley and storerooms, and Grimes and his officers knew that the partaking of snacks between meals would be reported at once to Mrs. Dalwood.

A real Captain, one with four gold bands on his shoulderboards and scrambled egg on the peak of his cap, would never have tolerated the situation. But Grimes, for all his authority and responsibility, was too junior an officer. He was only a Lieutenant, and a passed-over one at that, while the Commissioner, although a civilian, could tell Admirals to jump through the hoop.

But he was hungry.

One morning ship's time, he went down to the solarium for his daily exercises. This compartment could, more aptly, have been called the gymnasium, but since it was part of the "farm" it got its share of the ultra violet required for the hydroponics tanks. Mrs. Dalwood and her maid, Rosaleen, were still there, having their daily workout, when Grimes came in. Always he had timed his arrival until the two women had finished, but for some reason he was running late. It was not that he was prudish, and neither were they, but he had decided that the less he had to do with them the better.

As he came into the room he noticed their gowns hanging outside the sauna. He shrugged. *So what?* This was *his* ship. He took off his own robe and then, clad only in trunks, mounted the stationary bicycle. He began to pedal away almost happily, watching the clock as he did so.

From the corner of his eye he saw the door to the sauna open. The Commissioner, followed by her maid, came out. It was the first time that he had seen her naked. He almost whistled, then thought better of it. She was a bit of all right, he admitted, if you liked 'em lean and hungry. He inclined his head towards her courteously, carried on pedalling.

Rather to his surprise she stood there, looking him over. She said, "Mr. Grimes, there is a little improvement in your condition, but that probably is due to a properly balanced diet." She walked towards him, her feet slim and elegant on the carpeted deck, her breasts jouncing ever so slightly. "Get off that thing will you?"

Grimes did so, on the side away from her. She stooped, with fluid grace, and tested the pedals with her right hand.

"Mr. Grimes! How in Space do you hope to get any benefit from these exercises unless you do them properly?" Her hand went to the adjusting screw of the roller on top of the wheel, turned it clockwise. The muscles of her right arm stood out clearly under the smooth brown skin as she tested the pedals again. Then she actually smiled, saying, "On your bicycle, spaceman!"

Grimes remounted. He had to push, hard, to start the wheel rotating. He had to push, to keep it rotating. Now and again he had ridden on real bicycles, but almost always had dismounted rather than pedal up a steep hill. She stood there watching him. Until now he would have thought it impossible actively to dislike an attractive naked woman. But there has to be a first time for anything.

The Commissioner turned to her maid. "Rosaleen, you were last on the bicycle. Did you readjust it?"

The girl blushed guiltily over her entire body. "Yes, Ma'am."

"I see that I shall have to watch you too." The woman glanced at the watch that was her only article of clothing. "Unluckily I have some work to do. However, you may stay here for another thirty minutes. The bicycle again, the rowing machine, the horizontal bars. And you,

Mr. Grimes, will see to it that she does something about shedding that disgusting fat."

Grimes did not say what he was thinking. He had little breath to say anything. He managed to gasp, "Yes, Ma'am."

Mrs. Dalwood went to her gown, shrugged it on, thrust her feet into her sandals. She walked gracefully to the door. She did not look back at the man on the bicycle, the girl on the rowing machine.

As soon as the door had shut behind her Rosaleen stopped rowing. She said, "Phew!"

Grimes went on pedalling.

"Hey, Captain. Take five. Avast, or whatever you say."

Grimes stopped. He said, "You'd better carry on with your rowing."

The girl grinned. "We're quite safe, Captain. *She* is so used to having every order implicitly obeyed that she'd never dream of coming back to check up on us."

"You know her better than I do," admitted Grimes.

"I should." She got up from the sliding seat of the rowing machine, then flopped down on to the deck. She was, Grimes decided, at least as attractive as her mistress, and she had the advantage of youth. And there was so much more of her. The spaceman looked her over, studying her almost clinically. Yes, she had been losing weight. Her skin was not as taut as it should have been.

She noticed his look. She complained, "Yes, I'm starved . . ."

"You get the same as we do, Rosaleen."

"That's the trouble, Captain."

"But you have this sort of feeding all the time."

"Like hell I do. I have my nights off, you know, and then I can catch up on the pastries and candy, and the hot rolls with lots of butter, and the roast pork, with crackling . . ."

"Please stop," begged Grimes. "You're making me ravenous."

She went on, "But aboard your ship I have to toe the line. There's no escape."

"I suppose not."

"But surely *you* can do something. You've storerooms, with bread . . ."

"Yes, but . . ."

"You aren't scared of *her*, Captain?" She looked at him through her big, dark eyes. He had thought that they were black—now he saw that they were a very deep violet.

"Mphm." He allowed his glance to stray downwards, then hastily looked back at her face. There had been invitation in every line of her ample body. He was no snob, and the fact that her status was that of a servant weighed little with him. *But she was the Commissioner's servant.* A lady has no secrets from her lady's maid—is the converse true? Anyhow, they were both women, and no doubt happily prattled to each other, disparity of social status notwithstanding.

She said plaintively, "I'm hungry, Captain."

"So am I, Rosaleen."

"But you're the Captain."

Grimes got off the bicycle. He said, "It's time for my sauna." He threw his shorts in the general direction of the hook on which his robe was hanging, strode to the door of the hot room, opened it.

She followed him. He stretched out on one of the benches, she flopped on one opposite him. She said, "I'm hungry."

"It's those damned robots," complained Grimes. "Always hanging around the galley and storerooms."

"They won't be there tonight."

"How do you know?"

"They're much more than cooks. Even I don't know all the things they've been programmed for. This I do know. *She* has been working on a report, and tomorrow it will be encoded for transmission. The way that *she* does it is to give it to John—he's the one with the little gold knob on top of his head—to encode. And James decodes each sheet as John finishes it, to ensure that there are no errors."

"Are there ever any?"

"No. But *she* likes to be sure."

"*She* would." He wondered when he was going to start sweating. The girl was already perspiring profusely. "Tell me, when does this encoding decoding session take place?"

"After dinner."

"And there's no chance of her breaking it off?"

"None at all. When *she* starts something she likes to finish it."

"Mphm." The sweat was starting to stream out of Grimes's pores now. The girl got up, began to flick the skin of his back lightly with the birch twigs. He appreciated the attention. "Mphm. And are you free while all this Top Secret stuff is going on?"

"Yes."

"And she should have her nose stuck into it by 2000?"

"Yes, Captain."

"Then meet me outside the galley at, say, 2015 . . ."

"Yes!"

"Thick buttered toast . . ." murmured Grimes, deciding that talking about food took his mind off other things.

"*Lots* of butter . . ." she added.

"And sardines . . ."

"Fat, oily sardines . . ."

"With lemon wedges . . ."

"With mayonnaise . . ." she corrected.

"All right. Mayonnaise."

"And coffee. With sugar, and great dollops of cream . . ."

"I'll have beer, myself, even though it is fattening."

"We can have beer with, and coffee after . . ."

The door slid open and Hollister came in. Naked, the telepath looked more like a living skeleton than ever. Grimes regarded him with some distaste and wondered if the psionic radio officer had been eavesdropping. To do so would be contrary to the very strict code of the Rhine Institute—but espers, in spite of their occasional claims to superiority, are only humans.

He said, "I'm just about cooked, Rosaleen."

"So am I, Captain." She got up from her bench, the perspiration streaming down her still plump body, went through into the shower room. Through the closed door Grimes heard the hiss of the water, her little scream as its coldness hit her. There was the whine of the blowers as she dried off, and then she ran through the hot room on her way back into the solarium.

"Quite a dish, Captain," commented Hollister.

"We," Grimes told him coldly, "are neither kings nor peasants."

He took his own cold shower, and when he stepped out into the gymnasium Rosaleen was gone.

Dinner that night was as unsatisfying as usual. A clear soup, a small portion of delicious baked fish with a green salad, a raw apple for desert. Grimes, at the head of the table, tried to make conversation, but the Commissioner was in a thoughtful mood and hardly spoke at all. Beadle, Slovotny, Vitelli, and Hollister wolfed their portions as though eating were about to be made illegal, saying little. The four officers excused themselves as soon as they decently could—Slovotny going up to Control to relieve von Tannenbaum for *his* dinner, Beadle to have a look at the air circulatory system, Vitelli to check up on the Mannschenn Drive. Hollister didn't bother to invent an excuse. He just left. Von Tannenbaum came down, took his place at the table. He was starting to acquire a lean and hungry look that went well with his Nordic fairness. The Commissioner nodded to him, then patted her lips gently with her napkin. Grimes, interpreting the signs correctly, got up to help her from her chair. She managed to ignore the gesture.

She said, "You must excuse me, Mr. Grimes and Mr. von Tannenbaum. I am rather busy this evening."

"Can I, or my officers, be of any assistance?" asked Grimes politely.

She took her time replying, and he was afraid that she would take his offer. Then she said, "Thank you, Mr. Grimes. But it is very confidential work, and I don't think that you have Security clearance."

It may have been intended as a snub, but Grimes welcomed it.

"Good night, Ma'am."

"Good night, Mr. Grimes."

Von Tannenbaum turned to the serving robot which was waiting until he had finished his meal. "Any chance of another portion of fish, James?"

"No, sir," the thing replied in a metallic voice. "Her Excellency has instructed me that there are to be no second helpings, for anybody."

"Oh."

In sulky silence the navigator finished his meal. Grimes was tempted to include him in the supper party, but decided against it. The fewer people who knew about it the better.

The two men got up from the table, each going to his own quarters. In his day cabin Grimes mixed himself a drink, feeling absurdly guilty as he did so. "Damn it all," he muttered, "this is *my* ship. I'm captain of her, not that cast iron bitch!" Defiantly—but why *should* he feel defiant?—he finished what was in his glass, then poured another generous portion. But he made it last, looking frequently at his clock as he sipped.

2014 . . .

Near enough.

He got up, went out to the axial shaft, tried not to make too much noise going down the ladder. He paused briefly in the officers' flat, on the deck below and abaft his own. Faint music emanated from behind the door of von Tannenbaum's cabin—Wagner? It sounded like it—and loud snores from inside Beadle's room. His own air circulatory system could do with overhauling, thought Grimes. Slovotny was on watch, and Hollister, no doubt, was wordlessly communicating with his psionic amplifier, the poodle's brain in aspic. Vitelli could be anywhere, but was probably in the engineroom.

The V.I.P. suite was on the next deck down. As he passed the door Grimes could hear the Commissioner dictating something, one of the robots repeating her words. That took care of her. Another deck, with cabins for not very important people . . . He thought of tapping on Rosaleen's door, then decided against it. In any case, she was waiting for him outside the galley.

She whispered, "I was afraid you'd change your mind, Captain."

"Not bloody likely."

He led the way into the spotless—thanks to the industry of the robot servitors—galley. He was feeling oddly excited. It reminded him of his training cruise, when he had been a very new (and always hungry) cadet. But then there had been locks to pick . . .

He opened the door of the tinned food storeroom, ran his eye over the shelves. He heard Rosaleen gasp. "New Erin ham . . . Carinthian sausage . . ."

"You'll have Atlantan sardines, my girl, and like 'em . . . Ah, here we are . . . A can each?"

"*Two* cans."

"All right. Here you are. You can switch on the toaster while I rummage in the bread locker . . .

He thrust the cans into her eager hands, then collected bread, butter and seasonings. He tore open the wrapper of the loaf, then put the thick slices on the rack under the griller. The smell of the cooking toast was mouth-watering—too mouth-watering. He hoped that it would not be distributed throughout the ship by the ventilation system. But the Commissioner's overly efficient robots must, by this time, have put the air out-take filters to rights.

One side done . . . He turned the slices over. Rosaleen asked plaintively, "How *do* you work this opener?"

A metallic voice replied, "Like this, Miss Rosaleen—but I forbid you to use it."

"Take your claws off me, you tin bastard!"

Grimes turned fast. Behind him the toast smouldered unheeded. His hands went out to clamp on the wrists of the robot, whose own hands gripped the girl's arms. The automaton ignored him. If it could have sneered it would have done so.

"Mr. Grimes! Rosaleen!" The Commissioner's voice was hard as metal. In her all-grey costume she looked like a robot herself. "Mr. Grimes, please do not attempt to interfere with my servitor." She stood there, looking coldly at the little group. "All right, John, you may release Miss Rosaleen. But not until Mr. Grimes has taken his hands off you. And now, Mr. Grimes, what is the meaning of this? I seem to have interrupted a disgusting orgy. Oh, John, you might extinguish that minor conflagration and dispose of the charred remains."

"Supper," said Grimes at last.

"Supper?"

"Yes, Ma'am. Rosaleen and I were about to enjoy a light snack."

"A light snack? Don't you realise the trouble that went into working out suitable menus for this ship?" She paused, looking at Grimes with an expression of extreme distaste. "Legally, since your superiors, in a moment of aberration, saw fit to appoint you to command, you may do as you like aboard this vessel—within limits. The seduction of my maid is beyond those limits."

"Seduction?" This was too much. "I assure you that . . ."

"I was not using the word in its sexual sense. Come, Rosaleen, we will leave Mr. Grimes to his feast. He has to keep his strength up—although just for what I cannot say."

"Ma'am!" The girl's face was no longer soft, her voice held a compelling ring. "Since you use that word—it was I who seduced the captain."

"That hardly improves matters, Rosaleen. The commanding officer of a warship, even a very minor one, should not allow himself to be influenced by a woman passenger."

"You said it!" snapped Grimes. This could mean the ruin of his career, but he had been pushed too far. "You said it, Mrs. Dalwood. I should never have let myself be influenced by you. I should never have allowed your tin dieticians to run loose in *my* galley. I should have insisted, from the very start, on running *my* ship *my* way! Furthermore . . ." He was warming up nicely. "Furthermore, I doubt if even your fellow Commissioners will approve of your ordering an officer to spy on his captain."

"I don't know what you're talking about, Mr. Grimes."

"Don't you, Mrs. Dalwood? Who put you wise to this little party in the galley? Who would have known about it, who could have known about it but Hollister? I shouldn't like to be in your shoes when the Rhine Institute gets my report on my psionic radio officer. They're no respecters of admirals and their female equivalents."

"Have you quite finished, Mr. Grimes?" With the mounting flush on her cheeks the Commissioner was beginning to look human.

"For the time being."

"Then let me tell you, Lieutenant, that whatever secrets Lieutenant Hollister may have learned about you are still safely locked within his mind. If you had been reading up on the latest advances in robotics—which, obviously, you have not—you would have learned that already psionic robots, electronic telepaths, are in production. This has not been advertised—but neither is it a secret. Such automata can be recognised by the little gold knob on top of their skulls . . ."

The robot John inclined its head towards Grimes, and the golden embellishment seemed to wink at him sardonically.

"You tin fink!" snarled the spaceman.

"I am not a fink, sir. A fink is one who betrays his friend—and you were never a friend to me and my kind. Was it not in this very vessel, under your command, that Mr. Adam met his end?"

"That will do, John!" snapped the Commissioner.

"I still resent being spied upon!" almost shouted Grimes.

"That will do, Lieutenant!"

"Like hell it will. I give you notice that I have resigned from the Survey Service. I've had a bellyful of being treated like a child . . ."

"But that is all that you are."

"Captain," Rosaleen was pleading. "Please stop it. You're only making things worse. Mrs. Dalwood, it was my fault. I swear that it was . . ."

"Anything that happens aboard *my* ship is *my* fault," insisted Grimes.

"From your own mouth you condemn yourself, Lieutenant. I am tempted, as a Commissioner, to accept your resignation here and now, but I feel . . ." Her features sagged, the outlines of her body became hazy, the grey of her costume shimmered iridescently. "Leef I tub . . ." She was her normal self again. "But I feel . . ." Again the uncanny change. "Leef I tub . . ."

This is all I need . . . thought Grimes, listening to the sudden, irregular warbling of the Mannschenn Drive, recognising the symptoms of breakdown, time running backward and *dejà vu.* He had another vision—but this time he was not an elderly Survey Service Lieutenant; he was an even more elderly Rim Runners Third Mate. They'd be the only outfit in all the Galaxy that would dream of employing him—but even they would never promote him.

The thin, high keening of the Drive faded to a barely audible hum, then died as the tumbling, ever-precessing gyroscopes slowed to a halt. From the bulkhead speakers came Slovotny's voice—calm enough, but with more than a hint of urgency. "Captain to Control, please. Captain to Control . . ."

"On my way!" barked Grimes into the nearest speaker/microphone. "Carry on with emergency procedure."

"All hands secure for Free Fall. All hands secure for Free Fall. The inertial drive will be shut down in precisely thirty seconds."

"What is happening, Mr. Grimes?" demanded the Commissioner.

"It should be obvious, even to you."

"It is. Just what one could expect from this ship."

"It's not the ship's fault. She's had no proper maintenance for months!"

He pushed past the women and the robot, dived into the axial shaft. The greater part of his journey to Control was made in Free Fall conditions. He hoped maliciously that the Commissioner was being spacesick.

At least neither the Commissioner nor her robots had the gall to infest the control room. Grimes sat there, strapped into the command seat, surrounded by his officers. "Report, Mr. Vitelli," he said to the engineer, who had just come up from the engineroom.

"The Drive's had it, Captain," Vitelli told him. A greenish pallor showed through the engineer's dark skin, accentuated by a smear of black grease. "Not only the governor bearings, but the rotor bearings."

"We have spares, of course."

"We should have spares, but we don't. The ones we had were used by the shore gang during the last major overhaul, as far as I can gather from Mr. McCloud's records. They should have been replaced—but all that's in the boxes is waste and shavings."

"Could we cannibalise?" asked Grimes. "From the inertial drive generators?"

"We could—if we had a machine shop to turn the bearings down to size. But that wouldn't do us much good."

"Why not?"

"The main rotor's warped. Until it's replaced the Drive's unusable."

Beadle muttered something about not knowing if it was Christmas Day or last Thursday. Grimes ignored this—although, like all spacemen, he dreaded the temporal consequences of Mannschenn Drive malfunction.

"Sparks—is anybody within easy reach? I could ask for a tow."

"There's *Princess Helga,* Captain. Shall I give her a call?"

"Not until I tell you. Mr. Hollister, have you anything to add to what Mr. Slovotny has told me?"

"No, sir." The telepath's deep-set eyes were smouldering with resentment, and for a moment Grimes wondered why. Then he realised that the man must have eavesdropped on his quarrel with the Commissioner, had "heard" Grimes's assertion that he, Hollister, had carried tales to Mrs. Dalwood. *I'm sorry,* Grimes thought. *But how was I to know that that blasted robot was a mindreader?*

"I should have warned you, sir," admitted Hollister. The others looked at Grimes and Hollister curiously. Grimes could almost hear them thinking, *Should have warned him of what?*

"Princess Helga . . ." murmured Grimes.

"Light cruiser, Captain," Slovotny told him. "Royal Skandian Navy."

"And is the Federation on speaking terms with Skandia?" wondered Grimes audibly. He answered his own question. "Only just. Mphm. Well, there's no future—or too bloody much future!—in sitting here until somebody really friendly chances along. Get the *Princess* on the Carlotti, Sparks. Give her our coordinates. Ask her for assistance. Perhaps her engineers will be able to repair our Drive, otherwise they can tow us to the nearest port."

"Shouldn't we report first to Base, Captain?" asked Slovotny.

Yes, we should, thought Grimes. *But I'm not going to. I'll put out a call for assistance before Her Highness shoves her oar in. After that—* she *can have a natter to Base.* He said, "Get the signal away to *Princess Helga.* Tell her complete Mannschenn Drive breakdown. Request assistance. *You* know."

"Ay, Captain." Slovotny busied himself at his Carlotti transceiver. The pilot antenna, the elliptical Mobius strip rotating about its long axis, quivered, started to turn, hunting over the bearing along which the Skandian cruiser, invisible to optical instruments, unreachable by ordinary radio—which, in any case, would have had far too great a time lag—must lie.

"Locked on," announced the radio officer at last. He pushed the button that actuated the calling signal. Then he spoke into the microphone. "*Adder* to *Princess Helga. Adder* to *Princess Helga.* Can you read me? Come in, please."

There was the slightest of delays, and then the swirl of colors in the little glowing screen coalesced to form a picture. The young woman looking out at them could have been Princess Helga (whoever *she* was) herself. She was blue-eyed, and hefty, and her uniform cap did nothing to confine the tumbling masses of her yellow hair.

"*Princess Helga* to *Adder.* I read you loud and clear. Pass your message."

"Complete interstellar drive breakdown," said Slovotny. "Request assistance—repairs if possible, otherwise tow. Coordinates . . ." He rattled off a string of figures from the paper that von Tannenbaum handed him.

The girl was replaced by a man. He should have been wearing a horned helmet instead of a cap. His eyes were blue, his hair and beard were yellow. He grinned wolfishly. He demanded, "Your Captain, please."

Grimes released himself from his own chair, pulled himself into the one vacated by Slovotny. "Lieutenant Grimes here, Officer Commanding Courier Ship *Adder.*"

"Captain Olaf Andersen here, Lieutenant. What can I do for you?"

"Can your engineers repair my Drive?"

"I doubt it. They couldn't change a fuse."

"What about a tow to Dhartana?"

"Out of the question, Captain. But I can take you in to my own Base, on Skandia. The repair facilities there are excellent."

Grimes weighed matters carefully before answering. Skandia, one of the small, independent kingdoms, was only just on speaking terms with the Interstellar Federation. At the very best the Skandians would charge heavily for the two, would present a fantastically heavy bill for the repair work carried out by their yard. (But he, Grimes, would not be paying it.) At the worst, *Adder* and her people might be interned, could become the focus of a nasty little interstellar incident, a source of acute embarrassment to the Survey Service. *And so,* Grimes asked himself mutinously, *what?* That Promotion List had made him dangerously dissatisfied with his lot, the Commissioner had strained what loyalties remained to the breaking point.

The Commissioner . . .

"What exactly *is* going on here?" she asked coldly.

So she was getting in his hair again.

"I'm arranging a tow," Grimes told her. "The alternative is to hang here . . ." he gestured towards the viewports, to the outside blackness, to the sharp, bright, unwinking, distant stars . . . "in the middle of sweet damn all, thinking more and more seriously of cannibalism with every passing day."

"Very funny, Lieutenant." She stared at the screen. "Is that officer wearing *Skandian* uniform?"

"Of course, Madam," replied the Skandian Captain, who seemed to be very quick on the uptake. "Captain Olaf Andersen, at your service." He smiled happily. "And you, if I am not mistaken, are Mrs. Commissioner Dalwood, of the Federation's Board of Admiralty. According to our latest Intelligence reports you are *en route* to Dhartana." He smiled again. "Delete 'are.' Substitute 'were.' "

"Mr. Grimes, I forbid you to accept a tow from that vessel."

"Mrs. Dalwood, as commanding officer of this ship I must do all I can to ensure her safety, and that of her people."

"Mr. Slovotny, you will put through a call to Lindisfarne Base at once, demanding immediate assistance."

Slovotny looked appealingly at Grimes. Grimes nodded glumly. The grinning face of the Skandian faded from the screen, was replaced by a swirl of color as the pilot antenna swung away from its target. Sound came from the speaker—but it was a loud warbling note only. The radio officer worked desperately at the controls of the Carlotti transceiver. Then he looked up and announced, "They're jamming our signals; they have some very sophisticated equipment, and they're only light minutes, distant."

"Are you sure you can't get through?" demanded the Commissioner.

"Quite sure," Slovotny told her definitely.

She snorted, turned to Hollister. "Mr. Hollister, I'll have to rely on you."

"What about your own chrome-plated telepath?" Grimes asked her nastily.

She glared at him. "John's transmission and reception is only relatively short range. And he can't work with an organic amplifier, as your Mr. Hollister can."

"And *my* organic amplifier's on the blink," said Hollister.

"What do you mean?" demanded Grimes.

The telepath explained patiently. "There has to be a . . . relationship between a psionic communications officer and his amplifier. The amplifier, of course, is a living dog's brain . . ."

"I know, I know," the Commissioner snapped. "Get on with it."

Hollister would not be hurried. "The relationship is that which exists between a kind master and a faithful dog—but deeper, much deeper. Normally we carry our own, personal amplifiers with us, from ship to ship, but mine died recently, and so I inherited Mr. Deane's. I have been working hard, ever since I joined this ship, to win its trust, its affection. I was making headway, but I was unable to give it the feeling of security it needed when the temporal precession field of the Drive started to fluctuate. The experience can be terrifying enough to a human being who knows what is happening; it is even more terrifying to a dog. And so . . ."

"And so?" demanded the woman.

"And so the amplifier is useless, possibly permanently." He added brightly, "But I can get in touch with *Princess Helga* any time you want."

"You needn't bother," she snarled. Then, to Grimes, "Of all the ships in the Survey Service, why did I have to travel in this one?"

Why? echoed Grimes silently. *Why?*

Even the Commissioner was obliged to give Captain Andersen and his crew full marks for spacemanship. *Princess Helga* emerged into normal space/time only feet from the drifting *Adder.* At one moment there was nothing beyond the courier's viewports but the blackness of interstellar space, the bright, distant stars—at the next moment she was there, a vague outline at first, but solidifying rapidly. She hung there, a great spindle of gleaming plastic and metal, the sleekness of her lines marred by turrets and antennae. Another second—and the shape of her was obscured by the tough pneumatic fenders that inflated with almost explosive rapidity. Another second—and *Adder*'s people heard and felt the thump of the magnetic grapnels as they made contact.

Andersen's pleasant, slightly accented voice came from the transceiver. "I have you, Captain. Stand by for acceleration. Stand by for resumption of Mannschenn Drive."

"I suppose that your temporal precession field will cover us?" asked Grimes.

"Of course. In any case there is physical contact between your ship and mine."

"Where are you taking us?" demanded Mrs. Dalwood.

"To Kobenhaven, of course, Madam. Our Base on Skandia."

"I insist that you tow us to the nearest spaceport under Federation jurisdiction."

"You insist, Madam?" Grimes, looking at the screen, could see that Andersen was really enjoying himself. As long as somebody was . . . "I'm sorry, but I have my orders."

"This is piracy!" she flared.

"Piracy, Madam? The captain of your ship requested a tow, and a tow is what he's getting. Beggars can't be choosers. In any case, Space Law makes it quite plain that the choice of destination is up to the officer commanding the vessel towing, not the captain of the vessel towed."

She said, almost pleading but not quite, "In these circumstances the Federation could be generous."

Andersen lost his smile. He said, "I am a Skandian, Madam. My loyalty is to my own planet, my own Service. Stand by for acceleration."

The screen went blank. Acceleration pushed the group in *Adder*'s control room down into their chairs; Mrs. Dalwood was able to reach a spare seat just in time. Faintly, the vibration transmitted along the tow wires, they heard and felt the irregular throbbing of *Princess Helga*'s inertial drive—and almost coincidentally there was the brief period of temporal/spatial disorientation as the field of the cruiser's Mannschenn Drive encompassed both ships.

"You realise what this means to your career," said the Commissioner harshly.

"What was that?" asked Grimes. He had been trying to work out how it was that *Princess Helga* had been able to start up her inertial drive before the interstellar drive, how it was that there had been no prior lining up on a target star.

"You realise what this means to your career," repeated the woman.

"I haven't got one," said Grimes. "Not any longer."

And somehow it didn't matter.

The voyage to Kobenhaven was not a pleasant one.

The Commissioner made no attempt to conceal her feelings insofar as Grimes was concerned. Rosaleen, he knew, was on his side—but what could a mere lady's maid do to help him? She could have done quite a lot to make him less miserable, but her mistress made sure that there were no opportunities. The officers remained loyal—but not too loyal. They had their own careers to think about. As long as Grimes was captain they were obliged to take his orders, and the Commissioner knew it as well as they did. Oddly enough it was only Hollister, the newcomer, the misfit, who showed any sympathy. But he knew, more than any of the others, what had been going on, what was going on in Grimes's mind.

At last the two ships broke out into normal space/time just clear of Skandia's Van Allens. This Andersen, Grimes admitted glumly to himself, was a navigator and shiphandler of no mean order. He said as much into the transceiver. The little image of the Skandian captain in the screen grinned out at him cheerfully. "Just the normal standards of the Royal Skandian Navy, Captain. I'm casting you off, now. I'll follow you in. Home on the Kobenhaven Base beacon." He grinned again. "And don't try anything."

"What can I try?" countered Grimes, with a grin of his own.

"I don't know. But I've heard about you, Lieutenant Grimes. You have the reputation of being able to wriggle out of anything."

"I'm afraid I'm losing my reputation, Captain." Grimes, through the viewports, watched the magnetic grapnels withdrawn into their recesses in *Princess Helga*'s hull. Then, simultaneously, both he and Andersen applied lateral thrust. As the vessel surged apart the fenders were deflated, sucked back into their sockets.

Adder, obedient to her captain's will, commenced her descent towards the white and gold, green and blue sphere that was Skandia. She handled well, as well as Grimes had ever known her to do. But this was probably the last time that he would be handling this ship, any ship. The Commissioner would see to that. He shrugged. Well, he would make the most of it, would try to enjoy it. He saw that Beadle and von Tannenbaum and Slovotny were looking at him apprehensively. He laughed. He could guess what they were thinking.

"Don't worry," he told them. "I've no intention of going out in a blaze of glory. And now, Sparks, do you think you could lock on to that beacon for me?"

"Ay, Captain," Slovotny replied. And then, blushing absurdly, "It's a damn shame, sir."

"It will all come right in the end," said Grimes with a conviction that he did not feel. He shrugged again. At least that cast-iron bitch and her tin boyfriends weren't in Control to ruin the bittersweetness of what, all too probably, would be his last pilotage.

Adder fell straight and true, plunging into the atmosphere, countering every crosswind with just the right application of lateral thrust. Below her continents and seas expanded, features—rivers, forests, mountains, and cities—showed with increasing clarity.

And there was the spaceport, and there was the triangle of brilliant red winking lights in the center of which Grimes was to land his ship. He brought her down fast—and saw apprehension dawning again on the faces of his officers. He brought her down fast—and then, at almost the last possible second, fed the power into his inertial drive unit. She shuddered and hung there, scant inches above the concrete of the apron. And then the irregular throbbing slowed, and stopped, and *Adder* was down, with barely a complaint from the shock absorbers.

"Finished with engines," said Grimes quietly.

He looked out of the ports at the soldiers who had surrounded the ship.

"Are we under arrest, Captain?" asked von Tannenbaum.

"Just a guard of honor for the Commissioner," said Grimes tiredly.

Grimes's remark was not intended to be taken seriously—but it wasn't too far from the mark The soldiers were, actually, members of the Royal Bodyguard and they did, eventually, escort Mrs. Commissioner Dalwood to the Palace. But that was not until after the King himself had been received aboard *Adder* with all due courtesy, or such courtesy as could be mustered by Grimes and his officers after a hasty reading of *Dealings With Foreign Dignitaries. General Instructions.* Grimes, of course, could have appealed to the Commissioner for advice; she moved in diplomatic circles and he did not. He *could* have appealed to her. He thought, *As long as I'm Captain of this ship I'll stand on my own two feet.* Luckily the Port Authorities had given him warning that His Skandian Majesty would be making a personal call on board.

He was a big young man, this King Eric, heavily muscled, with ice-blue eyes, a flowing yellow moustache, long, wavy yellow hair. Over baggy white trousers that were thrust into boots of unpolished leather he wore a short-sleeved shirt of gleaming chain mail. On his head was a horned helmet. He carried a short battle-axe. The officers with him—with the exception of Captain Andersen, whose own ship was now down—were similarly uniformed, although the horns of their helmets were shorter, their ceremonial axes smaller. Andersen was in conventional enough space captain's dress rig.

Grimes's little day cabin was uncomfortably crowded. There was the King, with three of his high officers. There was Andersen. There was (of course) the Commissioner, and she had brought her faithful robot, John, with her. Only King Eric and Mrs. Dalwood were seated.

John, Grimes admitted, had his uses. He mixed and served drinks like a stage butler. He passed around cigarettes, cigarillos, and cigars. And Mrs. Dalwood had *her* uses. Grimes was not used to dealing with royalty, with human royalty, but she was. Her manner, as she spoke to the King, was kind but firm. Without being disrespectful she managed to convey the impression that she ranked with, but slightly above, the great-grandson of a piratical tramp skipper. At first Grimes feared (hoped) that one of those ceremonial but sharp axes would be brought into play—but, oddly enough, King Eric seemed to be enjoying the situation.

"So you see, Your Majesty," said the Commissioner, "that it is imperative that I resume my journey to Dhartana as soon as possible. I realise that this vessel will be delayed for some time until the necessary repairs have been effected, so I wonder if I could charter one of your ships." She added, "I have the necessary authority."

Eric blew silky fronds of moustache away from his thick lips. "We do not question that, Madam Commissioner. But you must realise that We take no action without due consultation with Our advisors. Furthermore . . ." he looked like a small boy screwing up his courage before being saucy to the schoolteacher . . . "We do not feel obliged to go out of Our way to render assistance to your Federation."

"The *Princess Ingaret* incident *was* rather unfortunate, Your Majesty . . ." admitted Mrs. Dalwood sweetly. "But I never thought that the Skandians were the sort of people to bear grudges . . ."

"I . . ." he corrected himself hastily . . . "We are not, Madam Commissioner. But a Monarch, these days, is servant to as well as leader of his people . . ."

Grimes saw the generals, or whatever they were, exchanging ironical glances with Captain Andersen.

"But, Your Majesty, it is to our common benefit that friendly relations between Skandia and the Federation be re-established."

Friendly relations? thought Grimes. *She looks as though she wants to take him to bed. And he knows it.*

"Let me suggest, Madam Commissioner, that you do me—Us—the honour of becoming Our guest? At the Palace you will be able to meet the Council of Earls as soon as it can be convened. I have no doubt—*We* have no doubt that such a conference will be to the lasting benefit of both Our realms."

"Thank you, Your Majesty. We are . . ." She saw Grimes looking at her sardonically and actually blushed. "I am honored."

"It should not be necessary for you to bring your aides, or your own servants," said King Eric.

"I shall bring John and James," she told him. "They are my robot servitors."

Eric, whose face had fallen, looked cheerful again. "Then We shall see that all is ready for you." He turned to one of his own officers. "General, please inform the Marshal of the Household that Madam Commissioner Dalwood is to be Our guest."

The general raised his wrist transceiver to his bearded lips, passed on the instructions.

"John," ordered the Commissioner, "tell Miss Rosaleen and James to pack for me. Miss Rosaleen will know what I shall require."

"Yes, Madam," replied the robot, standing there. He was not in telepathic communication with his metal brother—but UHF radio was as good.

"Oh, Your Majesty . . ."

"Yes, Madam Commissioner?"

"What arrangements are being made for Lieutenant Grimes and his officers, and for my lady's maid? Presumably this ship will be under repair shortly, and they will be unable to live aboard."

"Mrs. Dalwood!" Grimes did not try very hard to keep his rising resentment from showing. "May I remind you that I am captain of *Adder*? And may I remind you that Regulations insist that there must be a duty officer aboard at all times in foreign ports?"

"And may I remind you, Mr. Grimes, that an Admiral of the Fleet or a civilian officer of the Board of Admirality with equivalent rank can order the suspension of any or all of the Regulations? Furthermore, as such a civilian officer, *know* that nothing aboard your ship, armament, propulsive units or communications equipment, is on the Secret List. You need not fear that our hosts' technicians will learn anything at all to their advantage." She added, too sweetly, "Of course, you might learn from them . . ."

King Eric laughed gustily. "And that is why We must insist, Lieutenant, that neither you nor your officers are aboard while repairs are in progress. Captain Andersen, please make arrangements for the accommodation of the Terran officers."

"Ay, Your Majesty," replied Andersen smartly. He looked at Grimes and said without words, *I'm sorry, spaceman, but that's the way it has to be.*

Grimes and his officers were housed in the Base's Bachelor Officers' Quarters, and Rosaleen was accommodated in the barracks where the female petty officers lived. They weren't prisoners—quite. They were guests—but strictly supervised guests. They were not allowed near their own ship—and that hurt. They were not allowed near any of the ships—in addition to *Princess Helga* and *Adder* there were three destroyers, a transport and two tugs in port. Captain Andersen, who seemed to have been given the job of looking after them, was apologetic.

"But I have to remember that you're spacemen, Lieutenant. And I have to remember that *you* have the reputation of being a somewhat unconventional spaceman, with considerable initiative." He laughed shortly. "I shudder to think what would happen if you and your boys flew the coop in any of the wagons—yours or ours—that are berthed around the place."

Grimes sipped moodily from his beer—he and the Captain were having a drink and a chat in the well-appointed wardroom of the B.O.Q. He said, "There's not much chance of our doing that, sir. You must remember that the Commissioner is my passenger, and that I am responsible for her. I could not possibly leave without her."

"Much as you dislike her," grinned the other. "I think that she is quite capable of looking after herself."

"I know that she is, Captain. Even so . . ."

"If you're thinking of rescuing her . . ." said Andersen.

"I'm not," Grimes told him. He had seen the Palace from the outside, a grim, grey pile that looked as though it had been transported, through space and time, from Shakespeare's Elsinore. But there was nothing archaic about its defences, and it was patrolled by well-armed guards who looked at least as tough as the Federation's Marines. He went on, almost incuriously, "I suppose that she's being well-treated."

"I have heard that His Majesty is most hospitable."

"Mphm. Well, we certainly can't complain, apart from a certain lack of freedom. Mind you, Mr. Beadle is whining a bit. He finds your local wenches a bit too robust for his taste. He prefers small brunettes to great, strapping blondes . . . But your people have certainly put on some good parties for us. And Rosaleen was telling me that she's really enjoying herself—the P.O.s' mess serves all the fattening things she loves with every meal."

"Another satisfied customer," said Andersen.

"But *I'm* not satisfied, Captain. I know damn well that the repairs to my Mannschenn Drive took no more than a day. How long are we being held here?"

"That, Lieutenant, is a matter for my masters—and yours. We—and our ships—are no more than pawns on the board." The Captain looked at his watch. "Talking of ships, I have some business aboard *Princess Helga.* You must excuse me." He finished his beer and got to his feet. "Don't forget that after lunch you're all being taken for a sail on the Skaggerak . . ."

"I'll not forget, sir," Grimes informed him.

He was, in fact, looking forward to it. He enjoyed the sailing excursions in stout little wooden ships as much as any Skandian, already had proved himself capable of handling a schooner under a full press of canvas quite competently, was realising that seamanship and spacemanship, the skilled balancing of physical forces, have much in common.

He sat down again when Andersen had left the almost deserted wardroom, then saw Hollister coming towards him. The telepath said in a low voice, "I'm afraid you'll not be taking that sail, Captain."

Grimes was going to make some cutting remark about psionic snooping, then thought better of it. He asked, "Why not, Mr. Hollister?"

The psionic communications officer grinned wryly. "Yes, I've been snooping, Captain. I admit it. But not only on you. Not that it was really snooping. I've maintained contact of a sort with John . . ."

"The tin telepath . . ."

"You can call him that. He's very lonely in the Palace, and he's going to be lonelier . . ."

"What the hell are you talking about?"

"*She* has been getting on *very* well with the King. *She* has persuaded him to release us, even though the Council of Earls is not altogether in approval. We should get the word this afternoon, and we shall be on our way shortly afterwards. *Adder* is completely spaceworthy."

"I know. Captain Andersen's as good as told me. But why is John so lonely that he's spilling all these beans to you?"

"*She* wanted to make a farewell gift to His Majesty—and he, it seems, has always wanted a robot valet. Humanoid robots are not manufactured on Skandia, as you know."

"And so John's been sold down the river. My heart fair bleeds for him."

"No, Captain. Not John—James. John's 'brother.' They think of each other as brothers. They feel affection, a real affection, for each other . . ."

"Incredible."

"Is it, Captain? I've heard about the Mr. Adam affair, and how a mere machine was loyal to *you.*"

"Then not so incredible . . ."

One of the wall speakers crackled into life. "Will Lieutenant Grimes, captain of the Federation Survey Service Courier *Adder,* please come at once to telephone booth 14? Will Lieutenant Grimes, captain of the Federation Survey Service Courier *Adder,* please come at once to telephone booth 14?"

"Coming," grumbled Grimes. "Coming."

He was not surprised to see Andersen's face in the little screen, to hear him say, "Orders from the Palace, Lieutenant. You're to get your show on the road at 1500 hours Local. Mrs. Dalwood will board at 1430. You, your officers, and Miss Rosaleen Boyle will board at 1330. You will find all in order, all in readiness."

"Thank you, Captain."

Andersen grinned. "Don't thank me. Thank His Majesty—or Commissioner Dalwood."

Grimes returned to the table where he had left Hollister. He said, "You were right."

"Of course I was right. And now, if I may, I'll give you a warning."

"Go ahead."

"Watch John. Watch him very carefully. He's bitter, revengeful."

"Are you in touch with him now?"

"Yes." The telepath's face had the faraway expression that made it obvious that he was engaged in conversation with a distant entity. Suddenly he smiled. "It's all right. He has assured me that even though he feels that Mrs. Dalwood has betrayed him and his brother he is quite incapable of physically harming any human being. The built-in safe-guards are too strong for him to overcome."

"Then that's all right." Grimes knew that he should be worrying nonetheless, but the Commissioner was a big girl and could look after herself. And how could the robot harm her in any way but physically? "You've been snooping in its—his—mind, so you know how he ticks."

"Yes, Captain."

Grimes strode to the reception desk and asked the attractive, blonde petty offcer to have *Adder*'s crew paged.

Mrs. Dalwood looked well. She was softer, somehow, and she seemed to have put on a little weight!—although not as much as Rosaleen. She sat at ease in her day room, admiring the beautiful, jewel-encrusted watch that now adorned her left wrist. Grimes sat on the edge of his chair, watching her, waiting for her to speak. To one side stood the robot John, silent, immobile.

"Well, Lieutenant," she said, not too unpleasantly, "you managed to get us upstairs without any major catastrophes. I hope that we shall reach our destination in a reasonably intact condition. We should. As you must notice already, the work carried out by the Skandian technicians is of excellent quality . . . Like this watch . . ." She turned her wrist so that Grimes could see it properly. "It seems strange that a robust people such as the Skandians, space Vikings, should be such outstanding watchsmiths, but they are, as you probably know. His Majesty insisted that I accept this keepsake from him.

"Yes. Things *could* have been worse. Much worse, as it turned out. His Majesty and I reached an understanding. Together we accomplished more, much more, than the so-called diplomats . . ."

I can imagine it, thought Grimes—and to his surprise experienced a twinge of sexual jealousy.

Her manner stiffened. "But don't think, Mr. Grimes, that I shall not be putting in a full report on your conduct. It is my duty as a Commissioner to do so. I cannot forget that you gave me your resignation . . ."

Suddenly John spoke. He said tonelessly, "He is thinking of you."

The Commissioner seemed to forget that Grimes was present. Her face softened again. "He is? Tell me . . ."

"He misses you, Madam. He is thinking, *I really loved her. She reminded me so much of my dear old mother.*"

Grimes laughed. He couldn't help it. Mrs. Dalwood screamed furiously, "Be silent, John. I forbid you to speak, ever, unless spoken to by me."

"Yes, Madam."

"And as for you, Mr. Grimes, you heard nothing."

Grimes looked at her, into the eyes that were full of appeal. He remembered what he had heard of Mrs. Commissioner Dalwood before ever he had the misfortune to meet her. The beautiful Mrs. Dalwood, the proud Mrs. Dalwood, the so-called *femme fatale* of the Admiralty who could, and did, compete with much younger women on equal terms. In a less permissive society she could never have attained her high rank; in Earth's past she could have become a King's courtesan.

And in Skandia's present . . . ?

Grimes said softly, "Of course, King Eric's very young . . ."

"Mr. Grimes, you heard nothing . . ."

He could not resist the appeal in her voice, the very real charm. He thought, *I may not be an officer much longer, but I'll still try to be a gentleman.*

He said, "I heard nothing."

Commodore Damien looked at Grimes over his desk, over the skeletal fingers with which he had made the too-familiar steeple. He said, without regret, "So I shall be losing you, Grimes."

"Yes, sir."

"Frankly, I was surprised."

"Yes, sir."

"But not altogether pained."

Grimes wasn't sure how to take this, so said nothing.

"Tomorrow morning, Grimes, you hand over your command to Lieutenant Beadle. I think that he deserves his promotion."

"Yes, sir."

"But how did you do it, Grimes? Don't tell me that . . . ? No. She's not your type, nor you hers."

"You can say that again, sir."

"It can't be what you *do*. It can't be what you know. It must be *whom* you know . . ."

Or what you know about whom, thought Lieutenant Commander Grimes a little smugly.

Spartan Planet

For Susan, whose idea it was.

1

THERE WAS THAT sound again—thin, high, querulous, yet audible even above the rhythmic stamp and shuffle of the dance that beat out through the open windows of the Club. It sounded as though something were in pain. Something was.

Brasidus belched gently. He had taken too much wine, and he knew it. That was why he had come outside—to clear his head and, he hoped, to dispel the slight but definitely mounting waves of nausea. The night air was cool, but not too cool, on his naked body, and that helped a little. Even so, he did not wish to return inside just yet.

He said to Achron, "We may as well watch."

"No," replied his companion. "*No*. I don't want to. It's . . . dirty, somehow . . ." Then with a triumphant intonation he delivered the word for which he had been groping. "Obscene."

"It's not. It's . . . natural." The liquor had loosened Brasidus' tongue; otherwise he would never have dared to speak so freely, not even to one who was, after all, only a helot. "It's we who're being obscene by being unnatural. Can't you see that?"

"No, I can't!" snapped Achron pettishly. "And I don't want to. And I thank Zeus, and his priesthood, that *we* don't have to go through what that brute is going through."

"It's only a scavenger."

"But it's a sentient being."

"And so what? I'm going to watch, anyhow."

Brasidus walked briskly to where the sound was coming from, followed reluctantly by Achron. Yes, there was the scavenger, struggling in the center of the pool of yellow light cast by a streetlamp. The scavenger—or scavengers . . . Had either of the young men heard of Siamese twins, that would have been the analogy to occur to them—a pair of Siamese twins fighting to break apart. But the parallel would not have been exact, as one of the two linked beings was little more than half the size of the other.

Even in normal circumstances the scavengers were not pretty animals, although they looked functional enough. They were quadrupedal, with cylindrical bodies. At one end they were all voracious mouth, and from the other end protruded the organs of excretion and insemination. They were unlovely but useful, and had been encouraged to roam the streets of the cities from time immemorial.

Out on the hills and prairies and in the forests, their larger cousins were unlovely and dangerous, but they had acquired the taste for living garbage.

"So . . . messy," complained Achron.

"Not so messy as the streets would be if the beasts didn't reproduce themselves."

"There wouldn't be the same need for reproduction if you rough hoplites didn't use them as javelin targets. But you know what I'm getting at, Brasidus. It's just that I . . . it's just that some of us don't like to be reminded of our humble origins. How would *you* like to go through the budding process, and then have to *tear* your son away from yourself?"

"I wouldn't. But we don't have to, so why worry about it?"

"I'm not *worrying.*" Achron, slightly built, pale, blond, looked severely up into the rugged face of his dark, muscular friend. "But I really don't see why we have to watch these *disgusting* spectacles."

"You don't have to."

The larger of the scavengers, the parent, had succeeded in bringing one of its short hind legs up under its belly. Suddenly it kicked, and as it did so it screamed, and the smaller animal shrieked in unison. They were broken apart now, staggering over the cobbles in what was almost a parody of a human dance. They were apart, and on each of the rough, mottled flanks was a ragged circle of glistening, raw flesh, a wound that betrayed by its stench what was the usual diet of the lowly garbage eaters. The stink lingered even after the beasts, rapidly recovering from their ordeal, had scurried off, completing the fission process, in opposite directions.

That was the normal way of birth on Sparta.

2

THAT WAS THE normal way of birth on Sparta—but wherever in the universe there is intelligence there are also abnormalities.

Achron looked at his wristwatch, the instrument and ornament that marked him as something more than a common helot, as almost the social equal of the members of the military caste. He said, "I have to be getting along. I'm on duty at the crèche at 2400 hours."

"I hope you enjoy the diaper changing and the bottle feeding."

"But I do, Brasidus. You know that I do." His rather high voice dropped to a murmur. "I always feel that one or two of them might be . . . yours. There *are* a couple in this new generation that have your nose and eyes."

Brasidus put a large, investigatory and derisory hand to his face. "Impossible. I've still got them."

"Oh, you know what I mean."

"Why not keep a lookout for your own offspring, Achron?"

"It's not the *same*, Brasidus. In any case, it's not often I'm called upon to contribute . . ."

The two friends walked back to the Club House, but did not go farther inside than the cloakroom. Brasidus watched Achron slip into his tunic and sandals, then, on an impulse, Brasidus followed suit. Somehow he was no longer in the mood for the dance, and his prominent nose wrinkled a little at the acrid smell of perspiration, the sweet-sour reek of vomit and spilled wine that drifted into the anteroom from the main hall. The thudding of bare feet on the polished floor, in time to the drums and the screaming, brassy trumpets, usually excited him, but this night it failed to do so, as even did the confused shouting and scuffling that told him that the inevitable brawl had just broken out. On other occasions he had hurled himself gleefully into the press of struggling, sweating naked bodies—but this, too, had lost its attraction for him.

More and more he was feeling that there was something missing, just as there had been something missing when he had been a guest at Achron's club. He had thought, at the time, that it was the boisterous good fellowship, the hearty food and the strong, rough wine. Now he had sated himself with all of these, but was still unsatisfied.

He shrugged his heavy shoulders, then tugged the hem of his tunic down to its normal midthigh position. He said, "I'll stroll down to the crèche with you, Achron. I don't feel like going back to the barracks just yet. And, anyhow, tomorrow's my free day."

"Oh, thank you, Brasidus. But are you sure? Usually you hate to leave while there's any wine left in the jars."

"Just don't feel like any more drinking or dancing. Come on."

It was dark outside the building. The sky, although clear, was almost starless, and Sparta had no moons. The widely spaced streetlamps on their fluted columns seemed to accentuate the blackness rather than to relieve it, and the glimmering white pillars of street-fronting buildings appeared to be absorbing rather than reflecting what little light there was. In their shadows there was furtive movement, but it was no more than the scavengers going about their appointed tasks. Then, overhead, there was the drone of engines.

Brasidus stopped abruptly, laid a detaining hand on Achron's upper arm. He looked up, staring at the great, shadowy bulk that drove across the night sky, its course set for the blinking beacon atop the Acropolis, its tiers of ports strings of luminous beads, its ruby and emerald navigation lights pendants at the end of the necklace.

Achron said impatiently, "*Come* on. I don't want to be late clocking in. It's only the night mail from Helos. You must have seen it *dozens* of times."

"At least," agreed Brasidus. He fell into step again beside his companion. "But . . ."

"But you always wanted to join the Air Navy yourself, Brasidus. But you're too big, too heavy. A pity." There was a hint of spite in Achron's voice.

Brasidus recognized it, but ignored it. He murmured, "And there are even better things to be than an airman. I've often wondered why *we* didn't build any more spaceships after we colonized Latterhaven, why we allowed the Latterhaveneers to have the monopoly of the trade between the two worlds. We should own and operate our own spaceships."

Achron laughed unkindly. "And what chance do you think you'd have of being a spaceman? Two ships are *ample* for the trade, and the spice crop's only once a year. What would you do between voyages?"

"We could . . . explore."

"Explore?" Achron's slim arm described an arc against the almost empty sky. "Explore *what?* And on the other side of the world there's the Lens—and we all know that it's no more—or less—than a vast expanse of incandescent gases."

"So we've been told. But . . . I've managed an occasional talk with the Latterhaven spacemen when I've been on spaceport guard duty, and *they* don't think so."

"*They* wouldn't. Anyhow, you could be a lot worse things than a soldier—and in the Police Battalion of the Army at that. And as far as the possibility or otherwise of other worlds is concerned, I'd sooner listen to our own priests than to that atheistical bunch from Latterhaven."

They were almost at the crèche now, a huge, sprawling adjunct to the still huger temple. Its windows glowed with soft yellow light, and above the main doorway, in crimson neon, gleamed the insignia of the State Parenthood Service, the red circle from which, at an angle, a barbed arrow jutted up and out. Brasidus wondered, as he had wondered before, how the crèche had come to take for its own the symbol of Ares, the God of War. It was, he supposed, that the highest caste into which a child could grow was, after the priesthood, the military. Then he thought about his own alleged parenthood.

"These babies like me . . ." he said abruptly.

"Yes, Brasidus?"

"I . . . I think I'll come in with you, to see for myself."

"Why not? It's outside visiting hours—not that anybody does ever visit—but you're a police officer. Old Telemachus at the desk won't know if you're on duty or not."

Telemachus, bored by his night duty, welcomed the slight deviation from normal routine. He knew Brasidus slightly but, nonetheless, insisted that he produce his identity card. Then he asked, his wrinkled head protruding turtle-like from his robes, "And what is the purpose of your visit, Sergeant? Has some criminal taken refuge within our sacred precincts?"

"Achron tells me that two of his charges might be . . . mine."

"Ah. *Potential* criminals." The old man cackled at his own humor. "But seriously, Sergeant, it is a great pity that more of our citizens do not evince greater interest in their sons. Even though the direct physical link was abolished ages ago, there should still be responsibility. Yes.

Responsibility. Before I was asked to resign from the Council, I succeeded in having the system of regular visiting hours introduced—not that anybody has taken advantage of them . . ."

"Phillip will be waiting for his relief," broke in Achron sulkily.

"So he will. But it will not hurt that young man to be kept waiting. Do you know, at the 2200-hours feed he failed to ensure that the bottles were at the correct temperature! I could hear Doctor Heraklion carrying on, even out here. Luckily the Doctor came into the ward at just the right time." Telemachus added spitefully, "I honestly think that Phillip will make a better factory hand than a children's nurse."

"Is the correct temperature so important, sir?" asked Brasidus curiously. "After all, we can eat hot things and cold things, and it never seems to do us any harm."

"But we are fully developed, my dear boy. The children are not. Before the priests learned how to improve upon nature, a child, up to quite an advanced age, would be getting his nourishment directly from the father's bloodstream. So—can't you see?—these immature digestive organs must be coddled. They are not ready to handle what we should consider normal food and drink."

"Phillip will be in a bad temper," complained Achron. "I hate him when he's that way."

"All right then, you can relieve your precious Phillip. Are you sure you don't want to stay on for a talk, Brasidus?"

"No, thank you, Telemachus."

"Off you go, then. And try not to make any arrests."

Brasidus followed his friend through long corridors and then into the softly lighted ward where he was supposed to be on duty. They were met at the door by Phillip, a young man who, save for his dark coloring, was almost Achron's twin. He glowered at his relief. "So you've condescended to show up at last. I should give you something to help you to remember to get here on time."

"Do just that," said Brasidus roughly.

Phillip stared insolently at the Sergeant and sneered, "A pity you brought your *friend* with you. Well, I'm off, dearie. It's all yours, and you're welcome to it."

"What about the handover procedure?" demanded Achron sharply.

"What is there to hand over? Fifty brats, slumbering peacefully—until they all wake up together and start yelling their heads off. Thermostat in the dispenser's on the blink, so you'll have to check bottle temperatures before you break out rations for the little darlings. Clean nappy bin was replenished before the change of watch—or what *should* have been the change of watch. I'm off."

He went.

"Not really suitable for this profession, is he?" asked Achron softly. "I sometimes think that he doesn't *like* children." He gestured toward the double row of white cots. "But who couldn't love them?"

"Not you, obviously."

"But come with me, Brasidus. Leave your sandals by the door and walk softly. I don't want them woken." He tiptoed on bare feet over the polished floor. "Now," he whispered, "I'll show you. This is one of them." He paused at the foot of the crib, looked down lovingly.

And Brasidus looked down curiously. What he saw was just a bud, a baby, with a few strands of wispy black hair plastered across the overlarge skull, with unformed features. The eyes were closed, so he could not tell if there were any optical resemblance between himself and the child. The nose? That was no more than a blob of putty. He wondered, as he had often, how Achron and the other nurses ever told their charges apart. Not that it much mattered, not that it would matter until the boys were old enough for aptitude tests—and by that time all characteristics, psychological and physiological, would be well developed.

"Isn't he *like* you?" murmured Achron.

"Um. Yes."

"Don't you feel . . . proud?"

"Frankly, no."

"Oh, Brasidus, how *can* you be so insensitive?"

"It's a gift. It goes with *my* job."

"I don't believe you. Honestly, I don't. But quiet. Heraklion's just come in."

Brasidus looked up and saw the tall white-robed figure of the Doctor at the end of the aisle. He bowed stiffly, and the salutation was returned. Then Heraklion beckoned. Remembering to walk softly, the young man made his way between the rows of cots.

"Brasidus, isn't it?" asked Heraklion.

"Yes, Doctor."

"What are you doing here, Sergeant?"

"Just visiting, with Achron."

"I really don't approve, you know. Our charges are very . . . delicate. I shall appreciate it if you don't go wandering all over the building."

"I shan't be doing that, Doctor."

"Very well. Goodnight to you, Sergeant."

"Goodnight to you, Doctor."

And as he watched the tall, spare figure of Heraklion striding away along the corridor, Brasidus, the policeman in his makeup suddenly in the ascendant, asked himself, *What is* he *hiding?*

And then the first of the babies awoke, and almost immediately after the other forty-nine of them. Brasidus bade a hasty farewell to Achron and fled into the night.

3

THERE WAS AN odd, nagging suspicion at the back of Brasidus' mind as he walked slowly through the almost deserted streets to the police barracks. Normally he would have been attracted by the sounds of revelry that still roared from the occasional Club—but the mood that had descended upon him earlier still had not left him, and to it was added this new fretting surmise. Crime was not rare on Sparta, but it was usually of a violent nature and to cope with it required little in the way of detective ability. However, crime against the state was not unknown—and the criminals were, more often than not, highly placed officials, better educated and more intelligent than the commonalty. There was a certain smell about such malefactors—slight, subtle, but evident to the trained nose.

Brasidus possessed such an organ, and it had twitched at the odor that lingered about Doctor Heraklion.

Drugs? Could be—although the man himself did not appear to be an addict. But, in his position, he would have access to narcotics, and the peddlers had to get their supplies from *somebody.*

Even so, Brasidus was reluctant to pass his suspicions on to his superiors. To begin with, there was no proof. Secondly—and this was more important—he had witnessed what had happened, more than once, to overzealous officers who had contrived to trample on the toes of the influential. To present his captain with a *fait accompli,* with all the evidence (but of *what?*) against Heraklion neatly compiled, would be one thing, would almost certainly lead to promotion. To run to him with no more than the vaguest of suspicions, no more than a hunch, actually, could well result in permanent banishment to some dead-end hamlet in the bush.

Nonetheless, an investigation *could* bring rewards and, if carried out discreetly and on his own time, would not be too risky. After all, there was no law or regulation to debar any citizen from entry to the crèche. Now and again, at the instigation of members like Telemachus, the Council had attempted to encourage visits, although with little success. Perhaps a sudden access of parental feeling would look suspicious—but calling to see a friend, one of the children's nurses, would not. Too, Achron himself might have noticed something odd, might even be induced to remember and to talk about it.

"What's biting you, Sergeant?" asked the bored sentry on duty at the barracks gate.

Brasidus started. "Nothing," he said.

"Oh, come off it!" The man who had served with Brasidus for years and was shortly due for promotion himself, could be permitted liberties. "Anybody'd think you had a solid week's guard duty ahead of you, instead of your free day." The sentry yawned widely. "How was the dance, by the way? It's unlike you to be back so early, especially when you've a morning's lay-in for recuperation."

"So-so."

"Any good fights?"

"I don't know. There seemed to be one starting just as I left."

"And you didn't join in? You must be sickening for something. You'd better see a doctor."

"Maybe I'd better. Good night, Leonidas—or should it be good morning?"

"What does it matter to *you?* You'll soon be in your scratcher."

On his way to his sleeping quarters Brasidus had to pass the duty sergeant's desk. That official looked up as he approached. "Oh, Brasidus . . ."

"I'm off duty, Lysander."

"A policeman is *never* off duty—especially one who is familiar with the routine for spaceport guard duties." He consulted a pad on his desk. "You, with six constables, are to present yourself at the port at 0600 hours. The men have already been checked off for the duty, and arrangements have been made to have you all called. You'd better get some sleep."

"But there's no ship due. Not for *months.*"

"Sergeant Brasidus, you and I are policemen. Neither of us is an expert on astronautical matters. If the Latterhaveneers decide to send an unscheduled ship, and if the Council makes the usual arrangements for its reception, who are we to demand explanations?"

"It seems . . . odd."

"You're a creature of routine, Brasidus. That's your trouble. Off with you now, and get some sleep."

Once he had undressed and dropped onto the hard, narrow bed in his cubicle he did, rather to his surprise, fall almost at once into a dreamless slumber. And it seemed that only seconds had elapsed when an orderly called him at 0445 hours.

A cold shower completed the arousing process. He got into his black and silver uniform tunic, buckled on his heavy sandals and then, plumed helmet under his arm, made his way to the mess hall. He was the first one there. He looked with some distaste at the already laid table—the crusty bread, the joints of cold meat, the jugs of weak beer. But he was hungry, and pulled up a form and began his meal. As he was eating, the six constables of his detail came in. He nodded in greeting as they muttered sullenly, "Morning, Sergeant." Then, "Don't waste any time," he admonished. "They'll be waiting for us at the spaceport."

"Let 'em wait," growled one of the latecomers. He threw a gnawed bone in the general direction of the trash bucket, missed.

"That's enough from you, Hector. I hear that there's a vacancy for a village policeman at Euroka. Want me to recommend you?"

"No. Their beer's lousier even than this, and they can't make wine."

"Then watch your step, that's all."

The men got slowly to their feet, wiping their mouths on the back of their hands, halfheartedly dusting the crumbs from the fronts of their tunics. They took their helmets from the hooks on the wall, put them on, then filed slowly from the mess hall to the duty sergeant's desk. He was waiting for them, already had the armory door unlocked. From it he took, one by one, seven belts, each with two holsters. *So*, thought Brasidus, *this is an actual spaceship landing*. Staves and short swords were good enough for ordinary police duties. As the belts were being buckled on, the duty sergeant produced the weapons to go with them. "One stun gun," he muttered, passing them out. "One projectile pistol. To be used only in extreme urgency. But you know the drill, Sergeant."

"I know the drill, Sergeant," replied Brasidus.

"We should," grumbled Hector, "by this time."

"I'm telling you," explained the duty sergeant with ominous patience, "so that if you do something silly, which is all too possible, you won't be able to say that you weren't told not to do it." He came out from behind the desk, inspected the detail. "A fine body of men, Sergeant Brasidus," he declaimed sardonically. "A credit to the Army. I don't think. But you'll do, I suppose. There'll be nobody there to see you but a bunch of scruffy Latterhaven spacemen."

"What if they aren't from Latterhaven?" asked Brasidus. He was almost as surprised by his question as was the duty sergeant.

"Where else can they be from? Do you think that the gods have come all the way from Olympus to pay us a call?"

But if the gods came, it would be, presumably, on the wings of a supernal storm. It would not be a routine spaceship arrival—routine, that is, save for its unscheduled nature.

The men were silent during the ride to the spaceport.

Air-cushioned, the police transport sped smoothly over the cobbled streets of the city, the rough roads of the countryside. Dawn was not far off and already the harpies were uttering their raucous cries in the branches of the medusa trees. One of the birds, its wings whirring about its globular body, swept down from its perch and fluttered ahead of the driver's cab, squawking discordantly. The vehicle swerved. Hector cursed, pulled his projectile pistol, fired. The report was deafening in the still air. The harpy screamed for the last time and fell, a bloody tangle of membrane and cartilage, by the side of the road.

"Was that necessary, hoplite?" asked Brasidus coldly.

"You heard what Sergeant Lysander told us, Sergeant." The man leered. "This was an emergency."

Only a bird, thought Brasidus. *Only a stupid bird. Even so . . .* He asked himself, *Am I getting soft? But I can't be. Not in this job. And in all my relationships I'm the dominant partner.*

The spaceport was ahead now, its latticework control tower looming starkly against the brightening yellow of the eastern sky. Atop the signal mast there was flashing the intense green light that warned of incoming traffic. A ship was due. *Latterhaven Venus* or *Latterhaven Hera*? And what would either of them be doing here off season?

The car halted at the main gates, sitting there on the cloud of dust blown up and around it by its ducts. The guard on duty did not leave his box, merely actuated the mechanism that opened the gateway, waved the police through. As they drove to the Spaceport Security Office, Brasidus saw that the inner barrier was being erected on the concrete apron. He noticed, too, that only one conveyor belt had been rigged, indicating that there would be very little cargo either to load or to discharge. That, at this time of the year, made sense. But why should the ship be coming here at all?

They were outside the office now. The car stopped, subsided to the ground as its fans slowed to a halt. The constables jumped out, followed Brasidus into the building. To meet them there was Diomedes—corpulent, pallid, with a deceptively flabby appearance—the security captain. He returned Brasidus' smart salute with a casual wave of his pudgy hand. "Ah, yes. The guard detail. The usual drill, Sergeant. You're on duty until relieved. Nobody, Spartan or spaceman, to pass through the barrier either way without the Council's written authority." He glanced at the wall clock. "For your information, the ship is due at 0700 hours. You may stand down until 0650."

"Very good, sir. Thank you, sir," snapped Brasidus. "If I may ask, sir, which of the two ships is it?"

"You may ask, Sergeant. But I'm just Security. Nobody ever tells me anything." He relented slightly. "If you *must* know, it's neither of the two regular ships. It's some wagon with the most unlikely name of *Seeker III.*"

"Not like the Latterhaveneers to omit the name of their precious planet," muttered somebody.

"But, my dear fellow, the ship's not from Latterhaven. That's the trouble. And now, Sergeant, if you'll come with me I'll try to put you into the picture. It's a pity that nobody's put me into it first."

4

THE SHIP THAT was not from Latterhaven was no more than a glittering speck in the cloudless morning sky when Diomedes, followed by Brasidus and the six hoplites, marched out from the office onto the apron, to the wire mesh barrier that had been erected to define and enclose the strange vessel's landing place. It was no more than a speck, but it was expanding rapidly, and the rhythmic beat of the inertial drive, faint to begin with, was becoming steadily louder.

Old Cleon, the port master, was there, his long white hair streaming out in the breeze. With him were other officials, one of whom carried a portable transceiver. Brasidus could overhear both ends of the conversation. He learned little; it was no more than the exchange of messages to be expected with standard landing procedure. Cleon himself did not seem to be very interested. He turned to Diomedes. "Most unprecedented!" he complained. "Most unprecedented. Had it not been for the Council's direct orders I should have refused permission to land."

"It's not a very large ship," said Diomedes, squinting upwards.

"Large enough. Too large, for an intruder. Those rebels on Latterhaven might have let us know that they've discovered and colonized other habitable planets."

"They, too, must have a security service," said Diomedes.

"Secrets, secrets! How can I run a spaceport when nobody ever tells me anything? Answer me that, Captain!"

"Descending under full control, to area designated," reported the man with the transceiver.

Diomedes turned to his men. "I've told Sergeant Brasidus all that *I* know, and he's passed it on to you. So keep alert. We're not expecting any hostile action—but be ready for it. That's all."

Brasidus checked the freedom of his weapons in their holsters. The others followed his example.

Lower dropped the ship, lower. Even with nothing against which to measure her, it could be seen that she was small—only half the size, perhaps, of *Latterhaven Venus* or *Latterhaven Hera*. The gold letters embossed on her side were now readable. "*SEEKER III.*" (And what, wondered Brasidus, of *Seeker I* and *Seeker II*?) And above the name there was a most peculiar badge or symbol. A stylized harpy it looked like—a winged globe surmounted by a five-pointed star. It was nothing like the conventional golden rocker worn on Latterhaven uniforms.

The ship came at last between the waiting men and the rising sun, casting a long, chill shadow. The throbbing of its engines made speech impossible. And then, suddenly augmenting their beat, there was the drone of other machinery. Slowly, majestically, no less than six of the great airships of the Spartan Navy sailed over the spaceport and then, in line ahead, circled the landing field. Their arrival was clearly not fortuitous. Should *Seeker*'s crew attempt any hostile action they, and their ship, would be destroyed by a shower of high-explosive bombs—as would be, Brasidus realized, the military ground party and the port officials. The same thought must have occurred to Diomedes. The portly captain looked even unhappier than usual and muttered, "Nobody ever tells me *anything*."

With a crunch of metal on concrete the ship landed, an elongated ovoid quivering on her vaned landing gear, in spite of its bulk somehow conveying the impression that the slightest puff of wind could blow it away. Then, as the engines were shut down, it ceased to vibrate, settled down solidly. There was a loud *crack* and a jagged fissure appeared in the scarred concrete of the apron. But the strange vessel was not especially heavy. The initial damage had been caused by a clumsy landing of *Latterhaven Hera*, and Cleon, with months in which to make the necessary repairs, still hadn't gotten around to it.

Slowly an airlock door toward the stern of the ship opened. From it, tonguelike, an extensible ramp protruded, wavered, then sought and found the ground. There were beings standing in the airlock chamber. Were they human? Brasidus had read imaginative stories about odd, intelligent life-forms evolved on other planets—and, after all, this ship could be proof that there were more habitable planets than Sparta and Latterhaven in the universe. Yes, they seemed to be human. Nevertheless, the Sergeant's hands did not stray far from the butts of his holstered weapons.

Somebody was coming down the ramp, a man whose attire bore no resemblance to the carelessly informal rig of the Latterhaven spacemen.

There was gold on his visored cap, and a double row of gold buttons on his odd tunic, and bands of gold on the sleeves of it. His black trousers were not the shapeless coverings worn for warmth and protection in the hill country, but were shaped to his legs and sharply creased. His black, highly polished footwear afforded him complete coverage—*and must be*, thought Brasidus, wriggling his toes, *extremely uncomfortable*. He reached the ground, turned and made a gesture toward the open doorway. Another man came out of the airlock, followed the first one to the ground. He, although his uniform was similar, was dressed more sensibly, with a knee-length black kilt instead of the constricting trousers.

But was it a man, or was it some kind of alien? Brasidus once again recalled those imaginative stories, and the assumption made by some writers that natives of worlds with thin atmospheres would run to abnormal (by Spartan standards) lung development. This being, then, could be deformed, or a mutant, or an alien. Somebody muttered, "What an odd-looking creature!"

Walking with calm deliberation the two men approached the barrier. The one with the trousered legs called, "Anybody here speak English?" He turned to his companion and said, "That was a silly question to which I should get a silly answer. After all, we've been nattering to them on RT all the way in."

"We speak Greek," answered Diomedes.

The spaceman looked puzzled. "I'm afraid that I don't. But your English is very good. If you don't mind, it will have to do."

"But we have been speaking Greek all the time."

"Something odd here. But skip it. Allow me to introduce myself. I am Lieutenant Commander John Grimes, Interstellar Federation Survey Service. This lady is Doctor Margaret Lazenby, our ethologist . . ."

Lady, thought Brasidus. *Then he must be a member of some other race. The Ladies? I wonder where they come from. . . . And such odd names—Johngrimes, Margaretlazenby. But the Latterhaveneers go in for odd names, too.*

Diomedes was making his own self-introduction. "I am Diomedes, Captain of Spaceport Security. Please state your business, Johngrimes."

"I've already done so. And, as you must know, I received clearance to land."

"Then state your business again, Johngrimes."

"All right. We're carrying out the census in this sector of space. Of course, your cooperation isn't compulsory, but it will be appreciated."

"That is a matter for the King and his Council, Lieutenant Commander."

"We can wait. Meanwhile, I'd like to comply with all the usual regulations and clear my ship inwards. I'm ready to receive the officers from Port Health and Customs as soon as you like."

"We have no need for them here, Lieutenant Commander Johngrimes. My orders are that you and your crew stay on your side of the barrier until such time as you lift off."

The strange-looking man was talking to the spaceship commander in a high, angry voice. "But this is impossible, Commander. How can we carry out any sort of survey in these conditions? They distinctly told us that we could land—and now they turn their spaceport into a prison camp just for our benefit. *Do* something, Commander."

Brasidus saw the Captain's prominent ears redden. Nonetheless, he replied mildly enough, "But this is their world, Miss Lazenby. We're only guests."

"Guests? Prisoners, you mean. A wire barrier around us, and a fleet of antique gasbags cruising over us. Guests, you say!"

Strange, thought Brasidus, *how this peculiar-looking spaceman appears attractive when he's in a bad temper, while poor Achron and his like just get more and more repulsive. . . . And why do I compare him to Achron and the others? A finer bone structure, perhaps, and a more slender body—apart from that shocking deformity—and a higher voice?*

"Quiet, please!" The owner of the shocking deformity subsided. Johngrimes turned again to the barrier. "Captain Diomedes, I request that you get in touch with some higher authority. I am here on Federation business."

"What federation?" asked Diomedes.

"You don't know? You really don't know?"

"No. But, of course, I'm Security, so nobody ever tells me anything."

"What a bloody planet," murmured Margaretlazenby. "What a bloody planet!"

"That will do, Peggy," admonished Johngrimes.

And how many names do these people have? Brasidus asked himself. Through the wire mesh of the barrier he stared curiously at the Lady. *He must be some sort of alien*, he thought. And yet . . . Margaretlazenby, suddenly conscious of his stare, blushed, then returned his gaze in a cool, appraising manner that, fantastically, brought the blood flooding to the skin of his own face.

5

BRASIDUS FLUSHED AS he met the spaceman's appraising—and somehow approving—stare. He heard him murmur to his captain, "Buy that one for me, Daddy," and heard Johngrimes' reply, "Peggy, you're incorrigible. Get back on board at once."

"But I *am* the ethologist, John."

"No need to get wrapped up in your work. Get back on board."

"Yes, sir. Very good, sir. Aye, aye, sir."

He looked at Brasidus for a long, last time and then turned with a flounce of kilts. The movement of his hips and full buttocks as he mounted the ramp was disturbing.

"Now, perhaps," said the Commander, "we can get down to business. I may be old-fashioned, but I've never cared much for a mixed crew."

"So it's true, Lieutenant Commander," Diomedes said. "So you aren't from Latterhaven."

"Of course not. We shall be calling there after we've finished here. But tell me, what made the penny drop so suddenly?" He grinned. "Or should I have said 'obol'?"

"You speak strangely, Johngrimes. What do you mean?"

"Just a figure of speech. Don't you have automatic vendors? No? What I meant was this: Why should my mention of a mixed crew suddenly convince you that my claim that this is a Federal ship is correct?"

Diomedes did not answer at once. He glared around at Cleon and his aides, at Brasidus and his men. He growled, "You all of you have ears—unluckily. You all of you have heard far too much. But you will not speak of it. To anybody. I need not remind you of what has happened in the past to men who have breached Security." He turned back to the space captain. "Your arrival here, Lieutenant Commander, has rather upset our notions of cosmogony. It is now a matter for the Council—and for the Council only."

"But why *did* the penny drop?" persisted Johngrimes.

"Because you have brought evidence that there is more than one intelligent race in the universe. At first we thought that your Margaretlazenby was deformed—on this world, of course, he would have been exposed immediately after birth—and then you told us that you have a mixed crew."

The Commander stared at Diomedes incredulously. He said at last, "Of course, it has been said more than once, not altogether in jest, that they aren't really human. . . . But tell me, Captain Diomedes, do you actually mean what I think you mean? Haven't you anybody like her on your planet?"

"Like *what*, Lieutenant Commander?"

"Like her. Like Doctor Lazenby."

"Of course not. We are all human here. As we should be, Sparta being the birthplace of the human race."

"You really mean that?"

"Of course," replied Diomedes.

But does he? wondered Brasidus, who had worked with the Security Captain before.

"And you have no . . . ?" began the spaceman, then pulled himself up abruptly. Brasidus recognized the signs. *Find out all you can, but give nothing away yourself.*

"We have no what?" prompted Diomedes.

Johngrimes made a quick recovery. "No Immigration, no Customs, no Port Health?"

"I've already told you that, Lieutenant Commander. And I've already told you that you and your crew must remain confined to your ship."

"Then perhaps you would care to come aboard, Captain Diomedes, to talk things over."

"Not by myself—and not unarmed."

"You may bring one man with you," said Johngrimes slowly. "But both of you will leave your weapons this side of the barrier."

"We could board by force," said Diomedes.

"Could you? I think not. *Seeker* may be carrying out the Census, but she's still a frigate, with a frigate's armament. In a matter of seconds we could sweep this field—*and* the sky over the field—clear of life. This is not a threat, merely a statement of fact." The words carried conviction.

Diomedes hesitated. "Very well," he said at last. He looked up to the circling airships as though for reassurance, shook his head doubtfully. He addressed Cleon, "Port Master, please have your radioman inform the Flight Admiral of my movements." He turned to Brasidus, "Sergeant, you may come with me. Leave Leading Hoplite Hector in charge."

Brasidus got close enough to Diomedes so that he could speak in a low, urgent whisper. "But, sir, the standing orders . . . the passes, to be signed by a member of the Council . . ."

"And who do you think drew up those standing orders, Sergeant? *I* am Security." Diomedes unlocked the gate with a key from his belt pouch. "Come with me."

"Your weapons," reminded Johngrimes.

Diomedes sighed, unbuckled his belt with its two holstered pistols, passed it to one of the men. Brasidus followed suit. The Sergeant felt naked, far more so than when stripped for the dance or for field sports. He knew that he still retained one weapon in the use of which he was, as were all members of the police branch of the Army, superbly trained—his body. But he missed those smooth, polished wooden butts that fitted so snugly into his hands. Even a despised sword or spear would have been better than nothing.

Ahead of them, Johngrimes was walking briskly toward the open airlock door, toward the foot of the ramp. Diomedes and Brasidus followed. They could see, as they neared the vessel, that the odd excrescences on its skin were gun turrets, that from at least two of them slender barrels were trained upon them, following them, that from others heavier weapons tracked the circling airships.

Johngrimes was taking no chances.

Although he had been often enough on spaceport guard duties, this was the first time that Brasidus had been aboard a spaceship; usually it was only Diomedes who boarded visiting vessels. Mounting the ramp, the Sergeant eyed professionally the little group of officers waiting just inside the airlock. They all carried sidearms, and they all looked competent enough. *Even so*, thought Brasidus, *they'll not be able to use their pistols, for fear of hitting each other. The knee to the groin, the edge of the hand to the neck . . .*

"Better not," said Diomedes, reading his subordinate's face.

"Better not," said Johngrimes, turning back to look at the pair of them. "An incident could have unfortunate—for your planet—repercussions."

Better not, thought Brasidus.

Soldierlike, he approved the smartness with which the spacemen saluted their commander. And soldierlike, he did not like the feel of a deck under his feet instead of solid ground. Nonetheless, he looked about him curiously. He was disappointed. He had been expecting, vaguely, vistas of gleaming machines, all in fascinating motion, banks of fluorescing screens, assemblages of intricate instruments. But all that there was was a little metal-walled room, cubical except for the curvature of its outer side, and beyond that another little room, shaped like a wedge of pie with a bite out of its narrow end.

But there must be more to the ship than this.

An officer pressed a button on the far, inwardly curved wall of the inside room. A door slid aside, revealing yet another little compartment, cylindrical this time. Johngrimes motioned to his guests—*or hostages?* Diomedes (but he was familiar with spaceships) entered this third room without any hesitation. Apprehensively Brasidus followed him, with Johngrimes bringing up the rear.

"Don't worry," said Diomedes to Brasidus. "This is only an elevator."

"An . . . an elevator?"

"It elevates you. Is that correct, Lieutenant Commander?"

"It is, Captain Diomedes." Johngrimes turned to Brasidus. "At the moment, we are inside the axial shaft—a sort of hollow column running almost the full length of the ship. This cage that we've just entered will carry us up to my quarters. We never use it, of course, in free fall—only during acceleration or on a planetary surface."

"Do you have machines to do the work of your legs, sir?"

"Why not, Sergeant?"

"Isn't that . . . decadent?"

The spaceship commander laughed. "Men have been saying that ever since the first lazy *and* intelligent bastard invented the wheel. Tell me, did you march out from the city to the spaceport, or did you ride?"

"That's different, sir," said Brasidus lamely.

"Like hell it is." Johngrimes pressed a button. The door slid shut. And almost immediately Brasidus experienced an odd, sinking sensation in his stomach. He knew that the cage was in motion, felt that it was upward motion. Fascinated, he watched the lights flashing in succession on the panel by the door—and almost lost his balance when the elevator slowed to a stop.

The door slid open again, revealing a short stretch of alleyway. Still there were no machines, no instruments—but the air was alive with the subdued murmur of machinery.

Brasidus had likened the ship to a metallic tower, but this was not like being inside a building. It was like being inside a living organism.

6

"COME IN," SAID Johngrimes, pushing a button that opened another sliding door. "As a very dear friend of mine used to say, this is Liberty Hall. You can spit on the mat and call the cat a bastard."

"Cat?" asked Brasidus, ignoring an admonitory glare from Diomedes. "Bastard? What are they?" He added, "It's the second time you've used that last word, sir."

"You must forgive my Sergeant's unmannerly curiosity, Lieutenant Commander," said Diomedes.

"A healthy trait, Captain. After all, you are both policemen." He smiled rather grimly. "So am I, in a manner of speaking. . . . But sit down, both of you."

Brasidus remained standing until he received a grudging nod from his superior. Then he was amazed by the softness, by the comfort of the chair into which he lowered himself. On Sparta such luxury was reserved for the aged—and only for the highly placed aged at that, for Council members and the like. This lieutenant commander was not an old man, probably no older than Brasidus himself. Yet here he was, housed in quarters that the King might envy. The room in which Johngrimes was entertaining him and Diomedes was not large, but it was superbly appointed. There were the deep easy chairs, fitted with peculiar straps, there was a wall-to-wall carpet, indigo in color, with a deep pile, there were drapes, patterned blue, that obviously concealed other doorways, and there were pictures set on the polished paneling of the walls. They were like no paintings or photographs that Brasidus had ever seen. They glowed, seemingly, with a light of their own. They were three-dimensional. They were like little windows on to other worlds.

Brasidus could not help staring at the one nearest to him. It could have been a typical scene on his own Sparta—distant, snow-capped peaks in the background, blue water and yellow sand, then, in the foreground, the golden-brown bodies of naked athletes.

But . . .

Brasidus looked more closely. Roughly half of the figures were human—and the rest of them were like this mysterious Margaretlazenby. So that was what he must look like unclothed. The deformity of the upper part of the body was bad enough; that of the lower part was shocking.

"Arcadia," said Johngrimes. "A *very* pleasant planet. The people are enthusiastic nudists—but, of course, they have the climate for it."

"We," said Diomedes, turning his attention to the picture from the one that he had been studying, a bleak, mountain range in silhouette against a black sky, "exercise naked in all weathers."

"You would," replied Johngrimes lightly.

"So," went on Diomedes after a pause, "this Margaretlazenby of yours is an Arcadian." He got to his feet to study the hologram more closely. "H'm. How do they reproduce? Oddly enough, I have seen the same deformation on the bodies of some children who have been exposed. Coincidence, of course."

"You Spartans live up to your name," said Johngrimes coldly.

"I don't see what you mean, Lieutenant Commander. But no matter. I think I begin to understand. These Arcadians are a subject race—intelligent but nonhuman, good enough to serve in subordinate capacities, but temperamentally, at least, unqualified for full command."

"Doctor Lazenby was born on Arcadia. It's a good job she's not here to listen to you saying that."

"But it's true, isn't it? H'm. What amazes and disgusts me about this picture is the way in which humans are mingling with these . . . these aliens on terms of apparent equality."

"I suppose you could look at it that way."

"Here, even though we are all Men, we are careful not to be familiar with any but privileged helots. And these Arcadians are *aliens*."

"Some time," said Johngrimes, "I must make a careful study of your social history. It should be fascinating. Although that is really Peggy's job."

"Peggy?"

"Doctor Lazenby."

"And some time," said Diomedes, "*I* must make inquiries as to your system of nomenclature. I have heard you call this Margaretlazenby by his rank and profession, with the first part of his name missing. And I have heard you call him Peggy."

Johngrimes laughed. "I suppose that it is rather confusing to people who have only one name apiece. *We* have at least two—the surname, or family name . . ."

"But there is only one family. The State."

"On Sparta, perhaps. But let me finish, Captain Diomedes. We have the family name, which, with us, comes last, although some human races put it first. Then we have one, if not more, given name. Then we have nicknames. For example, Margaret, one word, Lazenby, one word. Peggy—which for some obscure reason is a corruption of Margaret. Of course, she could also be called Maggie or Meg. Or Peg. In my own case—John Grimes. But that 'John' can be changed to 'Jack' or 'Johnnie' by people who really know me."

"Like Theo for Theopompus," contributed Brasidus.

"Yes. Some of our nicknames are curtailments, like Margie or Margo for Margaret."

"How many names *has* that being got?" exploded Diomedes.

"I've heard her called other things—and called her them myself. But you wouldn't know what a bitch is, would you?"

"Doubtless some exotic beast you've run across on your travels. But, Lieutenant Commander, you keep on using these odd pronouns—'she' and 'her.' Are they confined to Arcadians?"

"You could say that." Grimes seemed to be amused by something. "Now, gentlemen, may I offer you refreshment? The sun's not yet over the yardarm, but a drop of alcohol won't kill us. Or would you rather have coffee?"

"Coffee? What's that?"

"Don't you have it here? Perhaps you would like to try some now."

"If you partake with us," said Diomedes cautiously.

"But of course." Grimes got to his feet, went to his desk, picked up a telephone. "Pantry? Captain here. I'd like my coffee now, please. Large pot, with all the trimmings. Three cups."

He took an oddly shaped wooden . . . instrument(?) off the desk top, stuffed a hollow bowl at the end of it with what looked like a dried brown weed, put the thin stem in his mouth, applied a flame from a little metal contraption to the open top of the bowl. He inhaled with apparent pleasure, then expelled from between his lips a cloud of fragrant fumes. "Sorry," he said, "do you smoke?" He opened an ornamental box, displaying rows of slim cylinders obviously rolled from the brown weed.

"I think that one strange luxury will be enough for one day, Lieutenant Commander," said Diomedes, to Brasidus' disappointment.

The door to the outside alleyway opened. A spaceman came in, by his uniform not an officer, carrying a large silver tray on which rested a steaming silver pot, a silver jug and a silver bowl filled with some white powder, and also three cups of gleaming, crested porcelain each standing in its own little plate. But it was not the tray at which Diomedes and Brasidus stared; it was at the bearer.

He was obviously yet another Arcadian.

Brasidus glanced from him to the picture, and back again. He realized that he was wondering what the spaceman would look like stripped of that severe, functional clothing.

"Milk, sir? Sugar?" the man was asking.

"I don't think that they have them on this planet, Sheila," said Grimes. "There's quite a lot that they don't have."

7

SLOWLY DIOMEDES AND Brasidus made their way down the ramp from the airlock. Both were silent, and the Sergeant, at least, was being hard put to sort and to evaluate the multitude of new impressions that had crowded upon him. The coffee—could it be a habit-forming drug? But it was good. And that burning weed the fumes of which Lieutenant Commander Grimes had inhaled with such enjoyment. And the un-Spartan luxury in which Grimes lived—luxury utterly unsuitable for a fighting man. And this Interstellar Federation, an officer of whose navy—although it was called the Survey Service—he claimed to be.

And those oddly disturbing Arcadians (if they were Arcadians)—the doctor Lazenby, the steward Sheila, and one or two more whom the Spartans had glimpsed on their way ashore . . .

They were out of earshot of the ship now, halfway between the airlock and the gate, outside which Hector and the other hoplites had stiffened to attention. Diomedes said, "Come to my office, Sergeant. I want to talk things over with you. There's a lot that I don't understand, but much of it strengthens my suspicions."

"Of whom, sir? This Lieutenant Commander Grimes?"

"No. He's just a spaceman, the same as Captain Bill and Captain Jim of the *Venus* and the *Hera*. If his service prefers to tack a double-barreled label on him, that's his worry. Oh, I want to find out where the ship *is* from and what's the *real* reason for its visit, but my main suspicions are much nearer home."

They passed through the gate, opened for them and locked after them by Hector. Old Cleon approached them, was brushed off by Diomedes. They continued their march to the office, although in the case of Diomedes it was more of a waddle.

"In my job," went on the Security Captain, buckling on his pistol belt as he walked, "I'm no respecter of persons. I shouldn't be earning my pay if I were." He gestured upwards. "Flight Admiral Ajax up there, for example. He holds his rank—and his life—only because I do not choose to act yet. When I do . . ." He closed his pudgy fist decisively and suggestively. "You're an ambitious man, Brasidus. And an intelligent one. I've had my eye on you for some time. I have been thinking of asking to have you transferred to Security. And when Diomedes *asks*, people hurry to oblige him."

"Thank you, sir."

"With promotion to lieutenant, of course."

"Thank you, sir."

"Think nothing of it. I need a young assistant for the . . . the legwork." He smiled, showing all his uneven, discolored teeth, obviously pleased with the expression that he had just coined. "The legwork," he repeated.

The two men entered the Spaceport Security Office, passed through into Diomedes' private room. At the Captain's order, Brasidus sat down. The chair was hard, comfortless, yet he felt far happier on it than he had felt in the luxury of Lieutenant Commander Grimes' day cabin. Diomedes produced a flagon of beer, two mugs. He poured. "To our . . . partnership," he said.

"To our partnership, sir."

"Now, *Lieutenant* Brasidus, what I am saying to you is strictly confidential. I need not remind you of the consequences to yourself if you abuse my confidence. To begin with, I played along with this man Grimes. I asked the silly questions that he'd assume that I would ask. But I formed my own conclusions."

"And what were they, sir?"

"Oh, I'm not telling you yet, young Brasidus. I could be wrong—and I want your mind to remain uninfluenced by any theories of mine. But they tie in, they tie in. They tie in with the most heinous crime of all—treason to the State. Now, tell me, who're the most powerful men on Sparta?"

"The most powerful man is the King, sir."

Diomedes' thin eyebrows lifted, arching over his muddy eyes. "Is he? But no matter. And I said 'the most powerful *men*.' "

"The Council, sir."

"H'm. Could be. *Could* be. But . . ."

"What are you driving at, sir?"

"What about the doctors, our precious medical priesthood? Don't they control the birth machines? Don't they decide who among the newly born is to live, and who, to die? Don't they conduct the fatherhood tests? Don't they say, in effect, that there shall be so many members of the military caste, so many helots—*and so many doctors?"*

"Yes. That's so, sir. But how could they be traitors?"

"Opportunity, dear boy. Opportunity. Opportunity for a betrayal of the principles upon which our State was founded. Frankly, although I have long harbored suspicions, I did not really think that it was possible until the man Grimes landed here with his ship and his mixed crew. Now I realize the evil spell that can be exerted by those . . . creatures."

"What creatures?" demanded Brasidus as impatiently as he dared.

"The Arcadians? Yes—that's as good a name as any." He refilled the mugs. "Now, I have to make my report and my recommendations to the Council. When Grimes made his first psionic contact with the spaceport authorities, before he reentered normal Space Time, he requested permission to land and to take a census, and also to carry out ecological and ethological surveys. Ethology, by the way, is the science of behavior. I learned that much, although I've been making use of its priciples for years. Later he confirmed this by normal radio—psionic reception at this end was rather garbled as our telepaths were completely unfamiliar with so many new concepts.

"As you well know, after your many spells of spaceport guard duty, it has always been contrary to Council policy to allow visiting spacemen to mingle with our population. But I shall recommend that in this case an exception be made, arguing that Grimes and his men are quite harmless, also that the Federation—yes, I'm afraid that there is one—is obviously powerful and might take offense if its servants are not hospitably received.

"My real reason for the recommendation I shall keep to myself."

"And what is it, sir?"

"When a pot boils, Brasidus, all sorts of scum come to the top. A few . . . Arcadians running around on Sparta might well bring the pot to the boil. And who will get scalded? *That* is the question."

"You don't like the doctors, Captain?"

"That I do not. I am hoping that those whom I suspect of treason will be forced to act—and to act rashly."

"There *is* something suspicious about them—or about some of them." Briefly, but omitting nothing, Brasidus told Diomedes of his encounter with Heraklion in the crèche. "He was hiding something," he concluded. "I am sure of that."

"And you're ideally situated to find out what it was, Brasidus." Diomedes was thoughtful. "This is the way that we shall play it. Officially you are still a sergeant in the Police Battalion. Your pay will be made up, however, to lieutenant's rates out of Security funds. You will be relieved of spaceport guard duties. You will discover, in fact, that your captain will be allowing you considerable free time—free insofar as *he* is concerned. As far as *I* am concerned, it will not be so free. Off duty, you will be able to visit your friend Achron at the crèche. I already knew of your friendship with him, as a matter of fact—that was one of the reasons why I was considering having you transferred to my Branch. One of the nurses might have been a better recruit—but their loyalties are so unreliable. On duty, you will act as escort to Lieutenant Commander Grimes and his officers.

"And you will report to me everything—and I mean *everything*—you learn."

"And what shall I learn, sir?"

"You'll be surprised. It could be that I shall be, too." He picked up the telephone on his desk, ordered his car brought round to the office. Then he said to Brasidus, "Give Hector his instructions. He can carry on until relieved. Then you can ride with me back to the city."

8

BACK IN THE city, Diomedes had his driver proceed directly to the police barracks. There, with no trouble, he obtained an interview with Brasidus' commanding officer. Brasidus, sitting on the hard bench outside the captain's office, wondered what was being said about him. Then the door opened and he was called in.

He looked at the two men confronting him—the squat, somehow squalid Diomedes, the tall, soldierly Lycurgus. Diomedes looked smugly satisfied, Lycurgus, resentful. There could be no doubt as to how things had gone—and, suddenly, Brasidus hoped that he would not regret this change of masters.

"Sergeant—or should I say Lieutenant?" growled Lycurgus. "I think that you already know of your transfer. Officially, however, you are still a sergeant and you are still working for me. Your real orders, however, will come from Captain Diomedes." He paused, then went on, "You are relieved from duty until 0800 hours tomorrow morning, at which time you are to report to the spaceport." He turned to Diomedes. "He's all yours, Diomedes."

"Thank you, Lycurgus. You may accompany me, Brasidus."

They left the office. Diomedes asked, "And when is your friend Achron on duty again, young man?"

"He has the midnight to 0600 shift for the rest of this week, sir."

"Good. Then I propose that you spend the rest of the day at leisure; after all, this was supposed to be your free time, wasn't it? Get some sleep this evening before midnight—you might visit Achron again then. Of course, you will report to me at the spaceport tomorrow morning. I have no doubt that I shall be able to persuade the Council to accede to

Lieutenant Commander Grimes' requests, so you will be required for escort duties."

"And when I visit Achron, sir? Am I to carry out any investigations?"

"Yes. But cautiously, cautiously. Find out what you can without sticking your neck out. But I must leave you now. I have to report to my lords and masters." His sardonic intonation left no doubt in Brasidus' mind as to who was the real lord and master.

Brasidus went to the mess hall for a late and solitary luncheon of bread, lukewarm stew and beer. Then, conscious of his new (but secret) rank and his new responsibilities, he decided to visit the library. There were books, of course, in the recreation hall of the barracks, but these were mainly works of fiction, including the imaginative thrillers that were his favorite reading. (But none of the writers had imagined monsters so fantastic as these Arcadians—fantastic because of similarities to as well as differences from normal humankind.) He was in uniform still, but that did not matter. However, there was his belt, with its holstered pistols. He went to the desk sergeant to turn it in.

"Keep it, Brasidus," he was told. "Captain Lycurgus said that you were on instant call as long as the spaceship's in port."

It made sense—just as the regulation forbidding the carrying of firearms when not on duty made sense; they might be used in a drunken brawl at one of the Clubs. However, Brasidus always felt happier when armed and so did not inquire further. He went out into the street, his iron-tipped sandals ringing on the cobbles. He stood on the sidewalk to watch a troop of armored cavalry pass, the tracks of the chariots striking sparks from the paving, the gay pennons whipping from the slender radio masts, the charioteers in their plumed helmets standing tall and proud in their turrets.

Cavalry in the city. The Council must be apprehensive.

Brasidus continued his walk when the chariots had gone by. He strode confidently up the wide stone steps to the white-pillared library entrance, but inside the cool building diffidence assailed him. An elderly man behind a big desk surveyed him disapprovingly, his gaze lingering on the weapons. "Yes, Sergeant?" he demanded coldly.

"I . . . I want to do some reading."

"Unless you've come here to make an arrest, that's obvious. What sort of reading? We do have a thriller section." He made "thriller" sound like a dirty word.

"No, not thrillers. We've plenty of those in our own recreation hall. History."

The bushy white eyebrows lifted. "Oh. Historical thrillers."

"No. Not thrillers." Brasidus was finding it hard to keep his temper. "History."

The old man did not get up from his seat, but turned and pointed. "Through there, Sergeant. That door. If you want to take a book out, you'll have to sign for it and pay a deposit, but there are tables and benches if you want to read on the premises."

"Thank you," said Brasidus.

He went through the door, noted the sign "HISTORICAL SECTION" above it. He stared at the book-lined walls, not knowing where to begin. He walked to the nearer shelves, just inside the doorway, the clatter of his uniform sandals on the marble floor drawing disapproving glares from the half dozen or so readers seated at the tables. But they were only helots, by the looks of them, and their feelings did not matter.

He scanned the row of titles. *A History of Sparta*, by Alcamenes. That would do to start with. He pulled it from its place on the shelf, carried it to a vacant table, sat down. He adjusted the reading lamp.

Yes, he had been lucky in his random choice. This seemed to be a very comprehensive history—starting, in fact, in prehistorical days. The story it told should not have been new to Brasidus. After all, he had been exposed to a normal education. But he had not paid much attention to his teachers; he had known that he was destined to be a soldier. So, apart from the study of past campaigns, of what value was education to him?

But here it all was. The evolution of a biped from a big-headed quadruped, with forelimbs modified to arms and hands. The slow, slow beginnings of civilization, of organized science. And then, at last, the invention of the birth machine by Lacedaemon, the perfection of the technique by which the father's seed could be brought to maturity apart from his body. No longer hampered by the process of budding, men went ahead by leaps and bounds. Aristodemus, the first King of Sparta, organized and drilled his army and navy, subjugated the other city-states, imposed the name of his capital upon the entire planet, although (even to this day, as Brasidus knew) there were occasional armed revolts.

And there were the scientific advancements. The mechanical branch of the priesthood advanced from aeronautics to astronautics and, under Admiral Latterus, a star fleet was launched, its object being the colonization of a relatively nearby planet. But Latterus was ambitious, set up his own kingdom, and with him he had taken the only priests who knew the secret of the interstellar drive. After many generations the people of Latterhaven—as Latterus' colony had been called—revisited Sparta. A trade agreement was drawn up and signed, complying with which the Latterhaveneers sent two ships every year, bringing various manufactured goods in exchange for shipments of the spices that grew only on Sparta.

Impatiently Brasidus turned to the index. Interstellar Federation. No. Not listed. Interstellar ships, interstellar drive, but no Federation. But that would have been too much to expect. Latterhaven had a history, but its people kept it to themselves. This Admiral Latterus had his ships and, no doubt, one planet had not been enough for him. He had his birth machines—and, even though Brasidus was no biologist, he was sure that it would be possible to accelerate production. The natural way—intercourse between two beings and, possibly, each one budding—was slow and wasteful. Suppose that *all* the seed were utilized. Then how long would it take to build up teeming populations on a dozen worlds?

Terra, for example.

And Arcadia?

No. Not Arcadia.

But *were* the Arcadians humans? Could they be the result of a malfunction of the birth machine set up on their planet? If this was the case, how could they, with their obvious physical deficiencies, reproduce?

Brasidus looked up Arcadia in the index. It was not, of course, listed.

He put Alcamenes' book back on the shelf, went out to see the old librarian. "Have you," he asked, "anything on the Interstellar Federation? Or on a world called Arcadia?"

"I told you," huffed the ancient man, "that it was fiction you wanted. Science fiction, at that."

"Suppose I told you that there *is* an Interstellar Federation? Suppose I told you that there are, at present, Arcadians on Sparta?"

"I'd say, young man, that you were quite mad—if it wasn't for your uniform. And it's not that I'm afraid of *that*, or of the guns you wear into my library. It's because that I know—as who doesn't?—that a strange unscheduled ship has made a landing at the spaceport. And you're a sergeant in the Police Battalion of the Army, so you know more about what's going on than we poor scholars." He cackled. "Go on, Sergeant. Tell me more. I am always willing to acquire new knowledge."

"What rumors have you heard?" asked Brasidus. After all, he was a Security officer now and might as well start acting like one.

"They say that this ship's a battleship—and, with the Air Navy hanging over the spaceport like a bad smell and the streets full of cavalry, it could well be. They say that the President of Latterhaven has demanded our instant surrender. They say, too, that the ship's not from Latterhaven at all, that it's manned by robots with twin turrets on their chests from which they shoot lethal rays."

"They must be functional . . ." mused Brasidus, "I suppose."

"What must be?" demanded the librarian.

"Those twin turrets. Good day to you."

He clanked out through the wide doorway, down the stone steps.

9

BRASIDUS WALKED BACK to his barracks, thinking over what he had read and what the librarian had told him. It all tied in—almost. But how did it tie in with Diomedes' suspicions of the medical priesthood? Perhaps tonight he would be able to find something out.

In the mess hall he partook of an early evening meal—and still his active brain was working. The spices exported to Latterhaven were a luxury, so much so that they were used but rarely in Spartan cookery. *And you can say that again*, Brasidus told himself, chewing viciously on his almost flavorless steak. Obviously they were also a luxury on the other planet; otherwise why should the Latterhaveneers find it worthwhile to send two ships every year for the annual shipment? But what *did* the Latterhaveneers bring in return for the spices? Manufactured goods. But *what* manufactured goods?

Brasidus, as a spaceport guard, had watched the Latterhaven ships discharging often enough. He had seen the unmarked wooden crates sliding down the conveyor belts into the waiting trucks, had vaguely wondered where these same trucks were bound when, escorted by police chariots, they had left the spaceport. He had made inquiries once, of one of the charioteers whom he knew slightly. "We just convey them into the city," the man had told him. "They're unloaded at that big warehouse—you know the one, not far from the crèche. Andronicus Imports."

And what did Andronicus import?

Diomedes might know.

Finishing his meal, Brasidus wandered into the recreation hall. He bought a mug of sweet wine from the steward on duty, sat down to watch television. There was the news first—but there was no mention of the landing of *Seeker III.* Fair enough. The Council had still to decide what to say about it as well as what to do about it. The main coverage was of the minor war in progress between Pharis and Messenia. Peisander, the Messenian general, was something of an innovator. Cleombrotus of Pharis was conservative, relying upon his hoplites to smash through the Messenian lines, and his casualties, under the heavy fire of the Messenian archers, were heavy. There were those who maintained that the bow should be classed as a firearm and its use forbidden to the ordinary soldiery, those not in the Police Battalion. Of course, if the hoplites, with their spears and swords, got loose among the archers, there would be slaughter. Against that, the archers, lightly armored, far less encumbered, could run much faster. The commentator, hovering above the battlefield, made this same comment, and Brasidus congratulated himself upon his grasp of military principles.

Following the news came a coverage of the games at Helos. Brasidus watched the wrestling bouts for a while, then got up and left the hall. After all, the games were no more than a substitute for war—and war, to every Spartan worth his salt, was the only sport for a man. Nonlethal sports were only for helots.

Finding the duty orderly, the Sergeant gave instructions to be called at 2330 hours.

He was almost at the crèche when he saw a slight form ahead of him. He quickened his pace, overtook the other pedestrian. As he had thought it would be, it was Achron.

The nurse was pleased to see him. He said, "I rang the barracks, Brasidus, and they told me that you were on duty all day."

"I was, but I'm off the hook now."

"You were at the spaceport, weren't you? Is it true that this ship is from *outside*, with a crew of monsters?"

"Just a ship," Brasidus told him.

"But the *monsters?*"

"What monsters?"

"Horribly deformed beings from outer space. *Mutants.*"

"Well, Diomedes and myself were entertained on board by the commander, and he's human enough."

"More than you can say for Diomedes," commented Achron spitefully. "I used to like him *once*, but not any more. Not after what he *did.*"

"What did he do?"

"I'll tell you sometime. Are you coming in, Brasidus?"

"Why not?"

"Telemachus will be pleased. He was saying to me what a fine example you are to the average Spartan."

"Back again, Sergeant?" the old man greeted him. "I shall soon think that you would welcome a return to the bad old days of budding."

"Hardly," said Brasidus, trying to visualize the difficulties that would be experienced in the use of weapons when encumbered by undetached offspring.

"And were you out at the spaceport today, Brasidus?"

"Yes."

"What are they *really* like, these monsters?"

"Captain Diomedes bound us all to secrecy."

"A pity. A pity. If you were to tell me what you saw, it would never go beyond the walls of this building."

"I'm sorry, Telemachus. You'll just have to wait until the news is released by the Council."

"The Council." The old man laughed bitterly. "In *my* day there were men of imagination serving on it. But now . . ." He looked up at the wall clock. "Well, in you go. Phillip is waiting for his relief. He was *most* unpleasant when he discovered that *I* had detained you this time yesterday."

Brasidus followed his friend to the ward where he was on duty. This time Phillip was in a better mood—and he, too, tried to pump the Sergeant about the day's events at the spaceport. Finally he gave up and left the two friends. As before, Brasidus allowed himself to be led to the sons who might be his own. Yet again he was unable to detect any real resemblance. And then—it was what he had been waiting for—all the babies awoke.

He retreated hastily, as any normal man would have done, leaving Achron to cope. But he did not go to the door by which he had entered, but to the farther doorway. He waited there for a minute or so, thinking that Doctor Heraklion or one of his colleagues might be attracted by the uproar—but, after all, such noises were common enough in the crèche.

But neither Heraklion nor anybody else appeared in the long, dimly lit corridor, and Brasidus decided to venture further afield. He was barefooted, so could walk silently. He was wearing a civilian tunic, which was advantageous. Should anybody who did not know him see him, his appearance would be less likely to cause alarm than if he was in uniform.

Cautiously he advanced along the corridor. His own was the only movement. If there were any sounds, he could not hear them for the bawling behind him. On either side of the corridor there were numbered doors. Storerooms? Laboratories? Cautiously he tried one. It was locked.

He continued his prowl. It was a long corridor, and he did not wish to get too far from the ward—yet this was a golden opportunity to find something out. He came to a cross passageway, hesitated. He saw that a chair was standing just inside the left-hand passage. Presumably it had just been evacuated—there was a book open, face down, on the seat, a flagon and a mug beside it. A guard? If so, not a very good one. No doubt he had some pressing reason for deserting his post—but he would never have done so, at no matter what cost to personal dignity, had he been a member of the military caste. A helot, then—or even a doctor? Heraklion? Brasidus did not know what the man's hours of duty were, but they could coincide with or overlap Achron's.

He picked up the book, looked at the title, *Galactic Spy*, by Delmar Brudd. Yet another of those odd double names. He turned to the title page, saw that the novel had been published by the Phoenix Press, Latterton, on the planet of Latterhaven. So this was a sample of the manufactured goods exported by that planet. But why should these books not be put into general circulation? If it were a question of freight, large editions could easily be printed here on Sparta.

He was suddenly aware that a door was opening. He heard someone say, "I must leave you, dear. After all, it *is* my turn for sentry duty."

A strange voice replied. It was too high-pitched, held an odd, throaty quality. Yet it was oddly familiar. What—*who*—did it remind Brasidus of? Even as he slid silently back around the corner—but not before he had replaced the book as he had found it—he had the answer. It sounded like the voice of the Arcadian, Margaret Lazenby. It was certainly not the voice of any native of Sparta.

Still, Brasidus was reluctant to retreat. He continued to peer around the corner, ready to jerk back in a split second. "I prefer you to the others, Heraklion," the Arcadian was saying.

"I'm flattered, Sally. But you shouldn't have come to me. It's very dangerous. If Orestes found that I'd deserted my post, there'd be all hell let loose. And besides . . ."

"Besides what?"

"Only last night—or, rather, yesterday morning—that revolting young pansy Achron had his boyfriend with him in the ward—and this same boyfriend is a police sergeant. A dumb one, luckily. Even so, we have to be careful."

"But why, Heraklion, why? You're priests as well as doctors. You control this planet. It would be easy for you to engineer a rough parity of the numbers of men and women—and then just let Nature take its course."

"You don't understand . . ."

"That's what you're always saying. But you saw to it that we were educated and drew some farfetched analogy between ourselves and the hetaerae of ancient Greece. I know that we're petted and pampered—but only within these walls. We've never seen outside them. Is that how women live on Latterhaven, on Terra, on all the Man-colonized planets?"

"You don't understand, Sally."

"No. Of course not. I'm only a woman. And it's obvious that you don't want me, so I'm getting back to my own quarters. To the *harem.*" This final word, dripping contempt, was strange to Brasidus.

"As you will."

"And the next time you come to *me,* I shall be busy."

The door opened properly, but still Brasidus did not withdraw his head. The couple who emerged from the storeroom or whatever it was had their backs to him. The shorter of the pair was dressed in a brief, black tunic woven from some transparent material. His lustrous, auburn hair hung to his smooth, gleaming shoulders and his rounded buttocks gleamed through the flimsy garment. He walked with a peculiarly provocative swing of the hips. Brasidus stared after him—and so, luckily, did Heraklion. Before the doctor could turn, Brasidus withdrew, hurried silently back along the corridor. There were no shouts, no pursuit. The only noise came from the ward, where Achron—*and what* was *a pansy?*—still had not pacified his charges.

Conquering his repugnance, Brasidus went in. "Can I help?" he asked the nurse.

"Oh, you're still here, Brasidus. I thought you'd have run away *ages* ago. Bring me some bottles from the dispenser, will you? You know how."

Brasidus obeyed. While he was so engaged, Doctor Heraklion strode through the doorway. "Really, Sergeant," he snapped, "I can't have this. This is the second time that you've come blundering in here, disturbing our charges. I shall have to complain to your superior."

"I'm sorry, Doctor."

"That isn't good enough, Sergeant. Leave, please. At once."

Brasidus left. He would gain nothing by staying any longer. And perhaps he should telephone Diomedes to tell him what he had learned. But what had he learned? That there was a nest of Arcadian spies already on Sparta? Spies—or infiltrators? Infiltrators—and the doctors working in collusion with them?

And how did that tie in with the visit of *Seeker III*, a vessel with Arcadians in its own crew?

Very well indeed, Brasidus told himself. *Very well indeed.*

He rang Diomedes from the first telephone booth he came to, but there was no answer. He rang again from the barracks, and there was still no answer. He looked at the time, shrugged his shoulders, went to his cubicle and turned in.

While he was having his breakfast, prior to going out to the spaceport, Captain Lycurgus sent for him. "Sergeant," he said, "I've received a complaint. About you. From Doctor Heraklion, at the crèche. In future, leave his nurses alone in duty hours."

"Very good, sir."

"And one more thing, Brasidus . . ."

"Yes, sir?"

"I shall pass the Doctor's complaint on to Captain Diomedes. I understand that he gives you your real orders these days."

10

DIOMEDES SENT HIS car round to the barracks in the morning to pick up Brasidus. It was another fine day, and the drive out to the spaceport was pleasant. The driver was not disposed to talk, which suited Brasidus. He was turning over and over in his mind what he would tell Diomedes and was wondering what conclusions Diomedes would draw from the events in the crèche. Meanwhile, there was the morning air to enjoy, still crisp, not yet tainted by the pungency from the spice fields on either side of the road.

Above the spaceport the ships of the Air Navy still circled and, as the car neared the final approaches, Brasidus noted that heavy motorized artillery as well as squadrons of armored cavalry had been brought up. Whatever John Grimes had in mind, the Police Battalion would be ready for him. But Brasidus did not regret that he had not, as a recruit, been posted to a mechanized unit. A hoplite such as himself was always fully employed, the armored cavalry, but rarely, the artillery, almost never.

The main gates opened as the car, without slackening speed, approached them. The duty guard saluted smartly—the vehicle rather than himself, Brasidus guessed. There was a spectacular halt in a column of swirling dust outside the Security office. Diomedes was standing in the doorway. He sneezed, glared at the driver, withdrew hastily into the building. Brasidus waited until the dust had subsided before getting out of the car.

"That Agis!" snarled the Captain as he sketchily acknowledged Brasidus' salute. "I'll have him transferred to the infantry!"

"I've seen him do the same when he's been driving you, sir."

"Hmph! That's different, young man. Well, he got you here in good time. Just as well, as I've instructions for you."

"And I've a report for you, sir."

"Already, Brasidus? You've wasted no time." He smiled greasily. "As a matter of fact, I've already had a call from Captain Lycurgus, passing on a complaint from Doctor Heraklion. What did you learn?"

Brasidus, who possessed a trained memory, told his superior what he had seen and heard. Diomedes listened intently. Then he asked, "And what do *you* think, Brasidus?"

"That Arcadians were already on Sparta before *Seeker* landed, sir."

"Arcadians? Oh, yes. The twin-turreted androids. Did you hear that rumor, too? And how do you think they got here?"

"There could have been secret landings, sir. Or they could have been smuggled in aboard *Latterhaven Venus* and *Latterhaven Hera.*"

"And neither of these theories throws Security in a very good light, does it? And the smuggling one rather reflects upon the spaceport guards."

"They needn't be smuggled in as adults, sir. Children could be hidden in some of those crates discharged by the Latterhaven ships. They could be drugged, too, so that they couldn't make any noise."

"Ingenious, Brasidus. Ingenious. But I've been aboard the *Venus* and the *Hera* often enough and, believe me, it would be impossible for either ship to carry more than her present complement. Not even children. They're no more than cargo boxes with a handful of cubicles, cells that we should consider inadequate for our criminals, perched on top of them."

"The cargo holds?"

"No. You can't have a man—or a child—living in any confined space without his leaving traces."

"But they didn't just . . . *happen,* sir. The Arcadians, I mean."

"Of course not. They either budded from their fathers or came out of a birth machine." Diomedes seemed to find this amusing. "No, they didn't just happen. They were either brought here or came here under their own power. But *why?*"

"Heraklion seemed to *like* the one that he was with last night. It was . . . unnatural."

"And what were *your* feelings toward him? Or *it?*"

Brasidus blushed. He muttered, "As you said yourself, sir, these beings possess a strange, evil power."

"So they do. So they do. That's why we must try to foil any plot in which they're engaged." He looked at his watch. "Meanwhile, my own original plan still stands. The Council has approved my suggestion that *Seeker*'s personnel be allowed to leave their ship. Today you will, using my car and driver, escort Lieutenant Commander Grimes and

Doctor Lazenby to the city, where an audience with the King and the Council has been arranged for them. You will act as guide as well as escort, and—you are armed—also as guard."

"To protect them, sir?"

"Yes. I suppose so. But mainly to protect the King. How do we know that when they are in his presence they will not pull a weapon of some kind? You will be with them; you will be situated to stop them at once. Of course, there will be plenty of my own men in the Council Chamber, but you would be able to act without delay if you had to."

"I see, sir."

"All right. Now we are to go aboard the ship to tell them that everything has been organized."

A junior officer met them in the airlock, escorted them up to the commander's quarters. Grimes was attired in what was obviously ceremonial uniform—*and very hot and uncomfortable it must be,* thought Brasidus. Professionally he ran his eye over the spaceman for any evidence of weapons. There was one, in full sight, but not a very dangerous one. It was a sword, its hilt gold-encrusted, in a gold-trimmed sheath at his left side. More for show than use, was Brasidus' conclusion.

John Grimes grinned at his two visitors. "I hate this rig," he confided, "but I suppose I have to show the flag. Doctor Lazenby is lucky. Nobody has ever gotten around to designing full dress for women officers."

There was a tap at the door and Margaret Lazenby entered. He was dressed as he had been the previous day, although the clothing itself, with its bright braid and buttons, was obviously an outfit that was worn only occasionally. He said pleasantly, "Good morning, Captain Diomedes. Good morning, Sergeant. Are *you* coming with us, Captain?"

"Unfortunately, no. I have urgent business here at the spaceport. But Brasidus will be your personal escort. Also, I have detailed two chariots to convoy you into the city."

"*Chariots?* Oh, you mean those light tanks that we've been watching from the control room."

"*Tanks?*" repeated Diomedes curiously. "A tank is something you keep fluids in."

"There are tanks *and* tanks. Where we come from, a tank can be an armored vehicle with caterpillar tracks."

"And what does 'caterpillar' mean?"

Grimes said, "Over the generations new words come into the language and old words drop out. Obviously there are no caterpillars on Sparta, and so the term is meaningless. However, Captain Diomedes, you are welcome to make use of our microfilm library; I would suggest the *Encyclopedia Galactica.*"

"Thank you, Lieutenant Commander." Diomedes looked at his watch. "But may I suggest that you and Doctor Lazenby proceed now to your audience?"

"And will the rest of my crew be allowed ashore?"

"That depends largely upon the impression that you make upon the King and his Council."

"Where's my fore-and-aft hat?" muttered Grimes. He got up, went through one of the curtained doorways. He emerged wearing an odd, gold-braided, black cloth helmet. He said, "Lead on, MacDuff."

"It should be 'Lay on, MacDuff,' " Margaret Lazenby told him.

"I know, I know."

"And who is MacDuff?" asked Diomedes.

"He's dead. He was the Thane of Cawdor."

"And where is Cawdor?"

Grimes sighed.

Brasidus, although he could not say why he did so, enjoyed the ride to the city. He, Grimes and Margaret Lazenby were in the back seat of the car, with the Arcadian (it was as good a label as any) sitting between the two humans. He was stirred by the close proximity of this strange being, almost uncomfortably so. When Margaret Lazenby leaned across him to look at a medusa tree swarming with harpies, he realized that those peculiar fleshy mounds, which even the severe uniform could not hide, were deliciously soft. So much for the built-in weapon theory. "What fantastic birds!" exclaimed the Arcadian.

"They are harpies," said Brasidus.

"Those round bodies do look like human heads, don't they? They could be straight out of Greek mythology."

"So you have already made a study of our legends?" asked Brasidus, interested.

"Of course." Margaret Lazenby smiled. (His lips against the white teeth were very red. Could it be natural?) "But they aren't just *your* legends. They belong to all Mankind."

"I suppose they do. Admiral Latterus must have carried well-stocked libraries aboard his ships."

"Admiral Latterus?" asked Margaret Lazenby curiously.

"The founder of Latterhaven. I am surprised that you have not heard of him. He was sent from Sparta to establish the colony, but he made himself King of the new world and never returned."

"What a beautiful history," murmured the Arcadian. "Carefully tailored to fit the facts. Tell me, Brasidus, did you ever hear of the Third Expansion, or of Captain John Latter, master of the early timejammer *Utah?* Come to that, did you ever hear of the First Expansion?"

"You talk in riddles, Margaret Lazenby."

"And you and your world are riddles that must be solved, Brasidus."

"Careful, Peggy," warned John Grimes.

The Arcadian turned to address his commander—and, as he did so, Brasidus was acutely conscious of the softness and resilience of the rump under the uniform kilt. "They'll have to be told the truth some time, John—and I'm sure that Brasidus will forgive me for using him as the guinea pig for the first experiment. But I am a little drunk, I guess. All this glorious fresh air after weeks of the canned variety. And look at those houses! With architecture like that, there should be *real* chariots escorting us, not these hunks of animated ironmongery. Still, apart from his sidearms, Brasidus is dressed properly."

"The ordinary hoplites," said Brasidus with some pride, "those belonging to the subject city-states, are armed only with swords and spears."

"They didn't have wristwatches in ancient Sparta," Grimes pointed out.

"Oh, be practical, John. He could hardly wear an hourglass or a sundial on his arm, could he?"

"It's . . . phony," grumbled Grimes.

"It should be as phony as all hell, but it's not," Margaret Lazenby told him. "I wish I'd known just how things are here, though. I'd have soaked up Hellenic history before we came here. . . . What are those animals, Brasidus? They look almost like a sort of hairless wolf."

"They are the scavengers. They keep the streets of the city clean. There is a larger variety, wild, out on the hills and plains. *They* are the wolves."

"But that one, there. Look! It's Siamese twins. It seems to be in pain. Why doesn't somebody *do* something about it?"

"But why? It's only budding. Don't *you* reproduce like us—or like we used to, before Lacedaemon invented the birth machine?" He paused. "But I suppose you have birth machines, too."

"We do," said Grimes—and Margaret Lazenby reddened. It was obviously a private joke of some kind.

"The glory that was Greece, the grandeur that was Rome," murmured the Arcadian after a long pause. "But this isn't—forgive me, Brasidus—quite as glorious as it should be. There's a certain . . . untidiness in your streets. And this absence of women seems . . . odd. As I recall it, the average Greek housewife was nothing much to write home about, but the hetaerae must have been ornamental."

"Did they have hetaerae in Sparta?" asked Grimes. "I thought that it was only in Athens."

We do have hetaerae in Sparta, Brasidus thought but did not say, recalling what he had seen and heard in the crèche. Sally (another queer name!) had admitted to being one. But what were hetaerae, anyhow?

"They had women," said Margaret Lazenby. "And some of them must have been reasonably good-looking, even by our standards. But Sparta was more under masculine domination than the other Greek states."

"Is that the palace ahead, Brasidus?" asked Grimes.

"It is, sir."

"Then be careful, Peggy. Watch your step—and your tongue."

"Aye, aye, Cap'n."

"And I suppose that you, Brasidus, will report everything that you've heard to Captain Diomedes?"

"Of course, sir."

"And so he should," Margaret Lazenby said. "When it gets around, these pseudo-Spartans might realize all that they are missing."

"And is the fact that they're missing it grounds for commiseration or congratulation?" asked Grimes quietly.

"Shut up!" snapped his officer mutinously.

11

IT WAS NOT the first time that Brasidus had been inside the palace, but, as always, he was awed (although he tried not to show it in front of the foreigners) by the long, colonnaded, high-ceilinged halls, each with its groups of heroic statuary, each with its vivid murals depicting scenes of warfare and the chase. He marched along beside his charges (who, he was pleased to note, had fallen into step), taking pride in the rhythmic, martial clank of the files of hoplites on either side of them, the heralds, long, brazen trumpets already upraised, ahead of them. Past the ranks of Royal Guards—stiff and immobile at attention, tiers of bright-headed spears in right alignment—they progressed. He realized, with disapproval, that John Grimes and Margaret Lazenby were talking in low voices.

"More anachronisms for you, Peggy. Those guards. Spears in hand—and projectile pistols at the belt . . ."

"And look at those murals, John. Pig-sticking—those animals aren't unlike boars—on motorcycles. But these people do have good painters and sculptors."

"I prefer my statues a little less aggressively masculine. In fact, I prefer them nonmasculine."

"You would. I find them a pleasant change from the simpering nymphs that are supposed to be decorative on most planets."

"You would."

Brasidus turned his head. "Quiet, please, sirs. We are approaching the throne."

There was a sharp command from the officer in charge of the escort. The party crashed to a halt. The heralds put the mouthpieces of their instruments to their lips, sounded a long, discordant blast, then another.

From a wide, pillared portal strode a glittering officer. "Who comes?" he demanded.

In unison the heralds chanted, "John Grimes, master of the star ship *Seeker*. Margaret Lazenby, one of his officers."

"Enter, John Grimes. Enter, Margaret Lazenby."

Again a command from the leader of the escort, and with a jangle of accouterments, the march resumed, although at a slower pace. Through the doorway they passed, halted again. There was another prolonged blast from the heralds' trumpets, a crash of grounded spear butts.

There was the King, resplendent in gold armor (which made the iron crown somehow incongruous), bearded (the only man on Sparta to be so adorned), seated erect on his high, black throne. There, ranged behind him on marble benches, was the Council—the doctors in their scarlet robes, the engineers in purple, the philosophers in black, the generals in brown and the admirals in blue. There was a small group of high-ranking helots—agronomists robed in green, industrialists in gray. All of them stared curiously at the men from the ship, from whom the guards had fallen away. But, Brasidus noted, there was more than curiosity on the faces of the scarlet-robed doctors as they regarded Margaret Lazenby. There was recognition, puzzlement and . . . guilt?

Grimes, at heel-clicking attention, saluted smartly.

"You may advance, Lieutenant Commander," said the King.

Grimes did so, once again drawing himself to attention when within two paces from the throne.

"You may relax, John Grimes. At ease." There was a long pause, then, "We have been told that you come from another world—another world, that is, beyond our polity of Sparta and Latterhaven. We have been told that you represent a government calling itself the Interstellar Federation. Assuming that there is such an entity, what is your business on Sparta?"

"Your Majesty, my mission is to conduct a census of the Man-colonized planets in this sector of space."

"The members of our Council concerned with such matters will be able to give you all the information you need. But we are told that you and your officers wish to set foot on this world—a privilege never accorded to the crews of Latterhaven ships. May we inquire as to your motives?"

"Your Majesty, in addition to the census, we are conducting a survey."

"A survey, Lieutenant Commander?"

"Yes, Your Majesty. There are worlds, such as yours, about which little is known. There are worlds—and yours is one of them—about which much more should be known."

"And this Federation of yours"—Brasidus, watching the King's face, could see that he had not been surprised by any of Grimes' answers, that he accepted the existence of worlds other than Sparta and Latterhaven without demur, that even the mention of this fantastic Federation had been no cause for amazement—"it has considerable military strength?"

"Considerable strength, Your Majesty. My ship, for example, is but a small and unimportant unit of our fleet."

"Indeed? And your whereabouts are known?"

"The movements of all vessels are plotted by Master Control."

"And so . . . and so, supposing that some unfortunate accident were to happen to your ship and your crew on Sparta, we might, just possibly, expect a visit from one or more of your big battleships?"

"That is so, Your Majesty."

"And we could deal with them, sire!" interpolated a portly, blue-robed Council member.

The King swiveled around in his throne. "Could we, Admiral Phileus? Could we? We wish that we possessed your assurance. But we do not. It does not matter how and by whom the planets of this Federation were colonized—what does matter is that they own spaceships, which we do not, and even space warships, which even Latterhaven does not. We, a mere monarch, hesitate to advise you upon naval tactics, but we remind you that a spaceship can hang in orbit, clear of the atmosphere—and therefore beyond reach of your airships—and, at the same time, release its shower of bombs upon our cities. Consider it, Phileus." He turned back to Grimes. "So, Lieutenant Commander, you seek permission for you and your men to range unhindered over the surface of our world?"

"I do, Your Majesty."

"Some of our ways and customs may be strange to you. You will not interfere. And you will impart new knowledge only to those best qualified to be its recipients."

"That is understood, Your Majesty."

"Sire!" This time it was one of the doctors. "I respectfully submit that permission to leave this outworld ship be extended only to *human* crew members."

"And what is your reason, Doctor? Let Margaret Lazenby advance so that we may inspect him."

The Arcadian walked slowly toward the King. Looking at his face, Brasidus could see that the being had lost some of his cockiness. But there was a certain defiance there still. *Should this attitude result in punishment ordered by the King,* thought Brasidus, *there will be a large measure of injustice involved.* The major portion of the blame would rest with Grimes who, after all, had so obviously failed to maintain proper disciplinary standards aboard his ship.

Cresphontes, King of All Sparta, looked long and curiously at the alien spaceman. He said at last, "They tell us that you are an Arcadian."

"That is so, Your Majesty."

"And you are a member of a space-faring race."

"Yes, Your Majesty."

"Turn around, please. Slowly."

Margaret Lazenby obeyed, his face flushing.

"So . . ." mused the King. "So . . ." He swiveled in his throne so that he faced the Council. "You have all seen. You have all seen that this Arcadian is smaller than a true man, is more slightly built. Do you think that he would be a match for one of our warriors, or even for a helot? A thousand of these creatures, armed, might be a menace. But . . ." He turned to address Grimes. "How many of them are there in your crew, Lieutenant Commander?"

"A dozen, Your Majesty."

"A mere dozen of these malformed weaklings, without arms. . . . No, there can be no danger. Obviously, since they are members of *Seeker*'s crew, they can coexist harmoniously with men. So, we repeat, there is no danger."

"Sire!" It was the doctor who had raised the objection. "You do not know these beings. You do not know how treacherous they can be."

"And do you, Doctor Pausanias? And if you do know, *how do you know?"*

The Councilman paled. He said, lamely, "We are experienced, sire, in judging who is to live and who is not to live among the newborn. There are signs, reliable signs. *She*"—he pointed an accusing finger at Margaret Lazenby—"exhibits them."

"Indeed, Doctor Pausanias? We admit that a child emerging from the birth machine with such a deformed chest would be among those exposed, but how is that deformity an indication of character?"

"It is written in her face, sire."

"In *her* face? Have you suddenly learned a new language, Doctor?"

"Sire, it was a slip of the tongue. *His* face."

"So . . . Face us, Margaret Lazenby. Look at us." The King's right hand went up to and stroked his short beard. "We read no treachery in your countenance. There is a softness, better suited to a children's nurse than to a warrior, but there is courage, and there is honesty."

"Sire!" Pausanius was becoming desperate. "Do not forget that sh—that he is an alien being. Do not forget that in these cases expression is meaningless. A woods boar, for example, will smile, but not from amiability. He smiles when at his most ferocious."

"And so do men at times." The King grinned, his teeth very white in his dark, bearded face. "We become ferocious, and we smile, when councilmen presume to tell us our business." He raised his voice. "Guards! Remove this man."

"But, sire . . ."

"Enough."

There was a scuffle at the back of the chamber as the doctor was hustled out by four hoplites. Brasidus noticed, with grim satisfaction, that none of the man's scarlet-robed colleagues made any move to defend him. He thought, *Crespontes knows where his real strength lies. With us, the military.*

"Lieutenant Commander Grimes!"

"Your Majesty?"

"We have decided that you may carry out your survey. You and your officers and men, both human and Arcadian, may leave your ship—but only as arranged with our Captain Diomedes, and only under escort. Is that quite clear?"

"Quite clear, Your Majesty. We shall see only what we are allowed to see."

"You have made a correct assessment of the situation. And now, as we have matters of import to discuss with our Council, you are dismissed."

Grimes saluted and then, slowly, he and Margaret Lazenby backed from the royal presence. Brasidus accompanied them. Beyond the door to the throne room the escort fell in about them.

As they marched out of the palace to the waiting car, Grimes asked, "Brasidus, what will happen to that doctor? The one who was dragged out of the chamber?"

"He will be beheaded, probably. But he is lucky."

"*Lucky?*"

"Yes. If he were not a doctor and a councilman, he could have his arms and legs lopped off before being exposed on the hillside with the defective children."

"You're joking, Brasidus!" exclaimed Margaret Lazenby.

"Joking? Of course not."

The Arcadian turned to Grimes. "John, can't we *do* something?"

Grimes shook his head. "Anything that we could do would mean the death of more than one man. Besides, our strict orders are not to interfere."

"It is expedient," said Margaret Lazenby bitterly, "that one man should die for the good of the people."

"Careful, Peggy. This place may be bugged. Remember that *we* aren't members of the Council."

"Spoken like a true naval officer of these decadent days. I often think that the era of gunboat diplomacy had much to recommend it."

12

THEY RODE BACK to the spaceport almost in silence. Brasidus realized that the two foreigners had been shocked when told of the probable fate of Pausanius. But why should they be? He could not understand it. Surely on their world, on any world, insolence toward the King himself must result in swift and drastic punishment. To make their reaction even stranger, the doctor had spoken against them, not for them.

They sped through the streets of the city, one chariot rattling ahead of the hovercar, the second astern of it. There were more people abroad now, more sightseers; word must have gotten around that aliens from the ship were at large. Citizen and helot, every man stared with avid curiosity at the Arcadian.

Margaret Lazenby shuddered. He muttered, "John, I don't like this planet at all, at all. I'd have said once that to be one woman in a world of men would be marvelous. But it's not. I'm being undressed by dozens of pairs of eyes. Do you know, I was afraid that the King was going to order me to strip."

"That shouldn't worry an Arcadian," John Grimes told him. "After all, you're all brought up as nudists."

"And I don't see why it should worry him," Brasidus put in, "unless he is ashamed of his deformities."

Margaret Lazenby flared, "To begin with, Sergeant, I'm not deformed. Secondly, the correct pronouns to use insofar as *I* am concerned are 'she' and 'her.' Got it?"

"And are those pronouns to be used when talking of the other spacemen who are similarly . . . malformed?" asked Brasidus.

"Yes. But, as a personal favor, will you, please, stop making remarks about the shape of my body?"

"All right." Then he said, meaning no offense, "On Sparta nobody is deformed."

"Not *physically*," remarked Margaret Lazenby nastily, and then it was the Sergeant's turn to lapse into a sulky silence, one that remained unbroken all the rest of the way to the ship.

Brasidus left the spacemen at the barrier, then reported to Spaceport Security. Diomedes was seated in his inner office, noisily enjoying his midday meal. He waved the Sergeant to a bench, gestured toward the food and drink on the table. "Help yourself, young man. And how did things go? Just the important details. I already know that the King has agreed to let Grimes carry out some sort of survey, and I've just received word that Pausanius has lost his head. But what were *your* impressions?"

Deliberately Brasidus filled a mug with beer. Officers were allowed stronger liquor than the lower-ranking hoplites, even those with the status of sergeant. He rather hoped that the day would soon come when he would be able to enjoy this tipple in public. He gulped pleasurably. Then he said, "It must be a funny world that they come from. To begin with, they didn't seem to have any real respect for the King. Oh, they were correct enough, but . . . I could sense, somehow, that they were rather looking down on him. And *then* . . . they were shocked, sir, really shocked when I told them what was going to happen to Pausanius. It's hard to credit."

"In my job I'm ready and willing to credit anything. But go on."

"This Margaret Lazenby, the Arcadian. She seems to have a terror of nudity."

"*She,* Brasidus?"

"Yes, sir. She told me to refer to her as 'she.' Do you know, it sounds and feels *right*, somehow."

"Go on."

"You'll remember, sir, that we saw a picture in Lieutenant Commander Grimes' cabin of what seemed to be a typical beach scene on Arcadia. Everybody was naked."

"H'm. But you will recall that in that picture humans and Arcadians were present in roughly equal numbers. To know that one is in all ways inferior is bad enough. To be inferior *and* in the minority—that's rather much. His—or her—attitude as far as this world is concerned makes sense, Brasidus. But how did it come up?"

"She said, when we were driving back through the city, that she felt as though she were being undressed by the eyes of all the people looking at her. (Why should she have that effect on humans? I'm always wondering myself what she is like under her uniform.) And she said that she was afraid that King Cresphontes was going to order her to strip in front of him and the Council."

"Men are afflicted by peculiar phobias, Brasidus. You've heard of Teleclus, of course?"

"The Lydian general, sir?"

"The same. A brave man, a very brave man, as his record shows. But let a harpy get into his tent and he's a glibbering coward." He picked up a meaty bone, gnawed on it meditatively. "So don't run away with the idea that this Arcadian is outrageously unhuman in his—or 'her'—reactions." He smiled greasily. "She may be more human than you dream."

"What are you getting at, sir? What do you *know?*"

Diomedes waved the bone playfully at Brasidus. "Only what my officers tell me. Apart from that—I'm Security, so nobody tells me anything. Which reminds me, there's something I must tell you. Your little friend Achron has been ringing this office all morning, trying to get hold of you." He frowned. "I don't want you to drop him like a hot cake now that you've acquired a new playmate."

"*What* new playmate, sir?"

"Oh, never mind, never mind. Just keep in with Achron, that's all. We still want to find out what's going on at the crèche, alien ships or no alien ships. As I've said—and I think you'll agree—it seems to tie in."

"But sir, wouldn't it be simple just to stage a raid?"

"I like my job, Brasidus—but I like the feel of my head on my shoulders much better. The doctors are the most powerful branch of the priesthood. This Pausanius, do you think that the King would have acted as he did if he hadn't known that he, Pausanius, was in bad with his own colleagues? All that happened was that he got himself a public execution instead of a very private one."

"It all seems very complicated, Captain."

"You can say that again, Brasidus." Diomedes tossed his bone into the trash basket. "Now . . ." He picked up a sheaf of crumpled, grease-stained papers from the untidy table. "We have to consider your future employment. You'll not be required for escort duties this afternoon. I shall be arranging his itinerary with Lieutenant Commander Grimes. And tomorrow the bold space commander and his Arcadian sidekick will not be escorted by yourself."

"And why not, sir?"

"Because you'll be working—working with your hands. You've

plainclothes experience. You can mix with helots as one of them and get away with it. This afternoon you pay a call on Alessis, who is both an engineer and—but let it go no further—on our payroll. Tomorrow Alessis with a gang of laborers will carry out the annual overhaul of the refrigerating machinery in the Andronicus warehouse. You will be one of the laborers."

"But I don't know anything about refrigeration, sir."

"Alessis should be able to teach you all that a common laborer should know this afternoon."

"But the other helots, sir. They'll know that I'm not a regular member of the gang."

"They won't. Alessis has just recruited green labor from at least half a dozen outlying villages. You'll be the one big-city boy in the crowd. Oh, this will please you. Your friend Heraklion will not be in the crèche. He has been called urgently to his estate. It seems that a fire of unknown origin destroyed his farm outbuildings."

"Unknown origin, sir?"

"Of course."

"But what has the Andronicus warehouse to do with the crèche?"

"I don't know yet. But I hope to find out."

Brasidus returned to the barracks in Diomedes' car, changed there into civilian clothes. He had been given the address of Alessis' office, walked there briskly. The engineer—a short, compact man in a purple-trimmed tunic—was expecting him. He said, "Be seated, Lieutenant. And I warn you now that tomorrow, on the job, I shall be addressing you as 'Hey, you!' "

"I'm used to plainclothes work, sir."

"As a helot?"

"Yes. As a helot."

"As a *stupid* helot?"

"If that is what's required."

"It will be. You're going to wander off by yourself and get lost. You'll be tracing the gas-supply main—that will be your story if anybody stumbles on you. I was supposed to be giving you an afternoon's tuition in refrigeration techniques, but that will not be necessary. All I ask of my helots is that they lift when I tell them to lift, put down when I tell them to put down, and so on and so forth. They're the brawn and I'm the brain. Get it?"

"Yes, sir."

"Good. Can you read a plan?"

"I can."

"Splendid." Alessis got up, opened a drawer of his desk and pulled out a large roll of tough paper. He flattened it out. "Now, this is the basement of the Andronicus warehouse. Power supply comes in *here*," his stubby forefinger jabbed, "through a conduit. Fans here, compressors here—all the usual. The odd chambers are all on the floor above—with the exception of this one. Deep freeze—very deep freeze, in fact."

"There's no reason why it shouldn't be in the basement."

"None at all. And there's no reason why it shouldn't be up one floor, with the other chambers. But it's not its location that's odd."

"Then what is?"

"It's got two doors, Brasidus. One opening into the basement, the other one right at the back. I found this second door, quite by chance, when I was checking the insulation."

"And where does it lead to?"

"That is the question. I think, although I am not sure, that there is a tunnel behind it. And I think that the tunnel runs to the crèche."

"But why?"

Alessis shrugged. "That's what our mutual friend Diomedes wants to find out."

13

A BLACK, WINDOWLESS cube, ugly, forbidding, the Andronicus warehouse stood across the cobbled street from the gracefully proportioned crèche complex. To its main door, a few minutes before 0800 hours, slouched the gang of workmen employed by Alessis, among them Brasidus. He was wearing dirty, ill-fitting coveralls, and he was careful not to walk with a military stride, proceeded with a helot's shamble.

The other men looked at him, and he looked at them. He saw a bunch of peasantry from the outlying villages, come to the city to (they vaguely hoped) better themselves. They saw a man like themselves, but a little cleaner, a little better fed, a little more intelligent. There were grunted self-introductions. Then, "You'll be the foreman?" asked one of the workmen.

"No," admitted Brasidus. "He'll be along with Alessis."

The engineer arrived in his hovercar, his foreman riding with him. They got out of the vehicle and the foreman went to the doorway, pressed the bell push set to one side of it. Then he said, "Jump to it. Get the tools out of the car." Brasidus—his years of training were not easily sloughed off—took the lead, swiftly formed an efficient little working party to unload spanners, hammers, gas cylinders and electrical equipment. He heard the foreman say to his employer, "Who's that new man, sir? We could use a few more like him."

Slowly the door opened. It was thick, Brasidus noted. It appeared to be armored. It looked capable of withstanding a chariot charge, or even the fire of medium artillery. It would have been more in keeping with a fortress than a commercial building. In it stood a man dressed in the gray tunic of an industrialist. That made him a helot, although one of a superior class. Nonetheless, his salutation of Alessis was not that of an inferior to a superior. There could even have been a hint of condescension.

The maintenance gang filed into the building—the engineer and his foreman unhampered, Brasidus and the others carrying the gear. So far there was little to be seen—just a long, straight corridor between featureless metal walls, terminating in yet another door. But it was all so clean, so sterile, impossibly so for Sparta. It reminded Brasidus of the interior of John Grimes' ship, but even that, by comparison, had a lived-in feel to it.

The farther door was heavily insulated. Beyond it was a huge room, crowded with machinery, the use of which Brasidus could only guess. Pumps, perhaps, and compressors, and dozens of white-faced gauges. Nothing was in motion; every needle rested at zero.

"Have you everything you want, Alessis?" asked the industrialist.

"I think so. Nothing's been giving any trouble since the last overhaul?"

"No. I need hardly tell you that the deep freeze is, as always, top priority. But *Hera*'s not due for another couple of months."

"Not to worry, what's the hurry?" quipped the engineer. Then, to his foreman, "O.K., Cimon, you can start taking the main compressor down. One of you"—he looked over his workmen carefully as though making a decision—"come with me to the basement to inspect the deep freeze. You'll do, fellow. Bring a hammer and a couple of screwdrivers. And a torch."

Brasidus opened the hatch in the floor for Alessis and then, as he followed the engineer down to the lower level, managed to shut it after himself. It was not difficult; the insulation, although thick, was light. In the basement there was more machinery seeming, thought Brasidus, to duplicate the engines on the floor above. It, too, was silent. And there was the huge, insulated door that he, as instructed by Alessis, opened.

The chamber beyond it was not cooled, but a residual chill seemed to linger in the still air. Physical or psychological? Or psychic? There was . . . something, some influence, some subtle emanation, that resulted in a slight, involuntary shudder, a sudden, prickly gooseflesh. It was as though there were a million voices—subsonic? supersonic? on the verge of audibility—crying out to be heard, striving, in vain, to impart a message. The voices of the dead? Brasidus must have spoken aloud, for Alessis said,"Or the not yet born."

"What do you mean?" demanded Brasidus. "What do you mean?"

"I . . . I don't know, Lieutenant. It seemed that the words were spoken to me by someone, by *something* outside."

"But this is only a deep-freeze chamber, sir."

"It is only a deep-freeze chamber—but it has too many doors."

"I can't see the second one."

"No. It is concealed. I found it only by accident. You see that panel? Take your screwdriver and remove the holding screws."

In spite of his unfamiliarity with power tools, with tools of any kind, Brasidus accomplished the job in a few seconds. Then, with Alessis' help, he pried the insulated panel out from the wall, lifted it to one side. There was a tunnel beyond it, high enough so that a tall man could walk without stooping, wide enough so that bulky burdens could be carried along it with ease. There were pipes and conduits on the roof of the tunnel, visible in the light of the torches.

"An alternative freezing system," explained Alessis. "Machinery in the crèche itself. I'm not supposed to know about it. The tunnel's insulated, too—and I've no doubt that when it's in use it can be brought down to well below zero."

"And what am I supposed to do?" Brasidus asked.

"You take your orders from Captain Diomedes, not from me. You're supposed to snoop—that's all that I know. And if you *are* caught, I risk my neck by providing you with some sort of a cover story. You thought—and I thought—that all these wires and pipes are supposed to be doing something. As, in fact, they are. Well, you'll find another door at the end, a proper one, and with dogs that can be operated from either side." His hand rested briefly on Brasidus' upper forearm. "I don't like this business. It's all too hasty; there's far too much last-minute improvisation. So be careful."

"I'll try," Brasidus told him. He stuck the hammer and the screwdriver into his belt—after all, he was supposed to be a workman, and if it came to any sort of showdown they would be better than no weapons at all—and, without a backward glance, set off along the tunnel.

The door at the far end was easy enough to open, and the screw clamps were well greased and silent. With the thick, insulated valve the slightest crack ajar, Brasidus listened. He could hear nothing. Probably there was nobody on the farther side. He hoped. The door opened away from him into whatever space there was on the other side. It was a pity, as anybody waiting there—the possibility still had not been ruled out—would be hidden from Brasidus as he emerged. But if the door were flung open violently, he would be not only hidden, but trapped.

Brasidus flung the door open violently, catching it just before it could thud noisily against the wall of the corridor.

So far, so good.

But what was there to see? Across the corridor there was yet another door, looking as though it, too, were insulated. And it was locked. To his left stretched a long, long passageway, soft ceiling lights reflected in the polished floor. To his right stretched a long, long passageway, similarly illuminated. On both sides there were doors, irregularly spaced, numbered.

Brasidus stood, silent and motionless, every sense tuned to a high pitch of sensitivity. There was the faintest hint of perfume in the air, merged with other hints—antiseptics, machinery, cooking—noticeable only by reason of its unusualness. A similar fragrance had lingered around Margaret Lazenby. And, remembered Brasidus, around that other Arcadian in this very building—Sally. And, oddly enough, around Heraklion. (Normally the only odors associated with doctors were those of the various spirits and lotions of their trade.)

So, he thought, *there are Arcadians here.*

So, he told himself, *I knew that already.*

So what?

His hearing was abnormally keen, and he willed himself to ignore the mutter of his own heartbeats, the susurus of his respiration. From somewhere, faint and faraway, drifted a murmur of machinery. There were voices, distant, and a barely heard tinkle of that silvery laughter he already associated with the Arcadians. There was a whisper of running water, evocative of a hillside rill rather than city plumbing.

He did not want to stray too far from the door, but realized that he would learn little, if anything, by remaining immobile. He turned to his left, mainly because that was the direction from which the Arcadian laughter and the faint splashing sounds were coming. He advanced slowly and cautiously, his hand hovering just clear of the haft of his hammer.

Suddenly a door opened. The man standing there was dressed in a long, soft, enveloping robe. He had long, blonde hair, and the fine features and the wide, red mouth of an Arcadian. There was about him—about *her*, Brasidus corrected himself—more than just a hint of that disturbing perfume. "Hello," she said in a high, pleasantly surprised voice. "Why, hello! A fresh face, as I live and breathe! And what are you doing in this abode of love?"

"I'm checking the refrigeration, sir."

"Sir!" There was the tinkling laughter, amused but not unkind. "Sir! That's a giveaway, fellow. You don't belong here, do you?"

"Why, sir, no."

The Arcadian sighed. "Such a handsome brute—and I have to chase you off. But it's getting on for the time when our learned lovers join us for . . . er . . . aquatic relaxation in the pool. And if *they* find you wandering around where you shouldn't be . . ." She drew the edge of her hand across her throat in an expressive gesture. "It's happened before—and, after all, who misses a helot? But where did you come from? Oh, yes, I see. You could be a refrigeration mechanic. . . . My advice to you is to get back into your hole and to pull it shut after you." Then she said, as Brasidus started to turn to retreat to the tunnel, "Not so fast, buster. Not so fast." A slim hand, with red-painted nails, caught his right shoulder to swing him so that he faced her; the other hand came up to rest upon his left shoulder. Her face was very close to his, the lips parted.

As though it were the most natural thing in the world, Brasidus kissed her. *Unnatural,* said a voice in his mind, flatly and coldly. *Unnatural, to mate with a monster from another world, even to contemplate such a sterile coupling. Unnatural. Unnatural.*

But his own arms were about her and he was returning her kiss—hotly, avidly, clumsily. That censor in his mind was, at the moment, talking only to itself. He felt the mounds of flesh on her chest pressing against him, was keenly aware of the softness of her thighs against his own.

Suddenly, somehow, her hands were between their upper bodies, pushing him away. With a twist of her head she disengaged her mouth. "Go, you fool!" she whispered urgently. "Go! If *they* find you, they'll kill you. Go. Don't worry—I'll say nothing. And if you have any sense, you'll not say anything either."

"But . . ."

"Go!"

Reluctantly, Brasidus went. Just as he closed the door he heard footsteps approaching along the alleyway.

But there was no alarm raised; his intrusion had been undetected.

Back in the deep-freeze chamber, Alessis looked at him curiously. "Have you been in a fight? Your mouth . . . there's blood."

Brasidus examined the back of his investigatory hand. "No," he said. "It's not blood. I don't know what it is."

"But what happened?"

"I don't know," replied Brasidus truthfully. Still he was not feeling the shame, the revulsion that should have been swamping him. "I don't know. In any case, I have to make my reports only to Captain Diomedes."

14

"SO IT WAS not the same one that you saw before?" asked Diomedes.

"No, Captain. At least, I don't think so. Her voice was different."

"H'm. There must be an absolute nest of Arcadians in that bloody crèche. . . . And all . . . she did was to talk to you and warn you to make yourself scarce before any of the doctors came on the scene?"

"That was all, Captain."

"You're lying, Brasidus."

"All right." Brasidus' voice was sullenly defiant. "I kissed him, her, it. And it—or she—kissed me back."

"You *what?*"

"You heard me, sir. Your very vague instructions to me were that I should find out all that I could. And that was one way of doing it."

"Indeed? And what did you find out?"

"That these Arcadians, as you have said, exercise a sort of hypnotic power, especially when there is physical contact."

"Hypnotic power? So the touch of mouth to mouth almost put you to sleep?"

"That wasn't the way I meant it, sir. But I did feel that, if I weren't very careful, I should be doing just what she wanted."

"And what did she want?"

"Do I have to spell it out for you, sir? Oh, I know that intercourse with an alien being must be *wrong*—but that was what she wanted."

"And you?"

"All right. I wanted it, too."

"Brasidus, Brasidus. . . . You know that what you have just told me could get you busted down to helot. Or worse. But in *our* job, as you are learning, we often have to break the law in order to enforce it."

"As a policeman, sir, I am reasonably familiar with the law. I cannot recall that it forbids intercourse with aliens."

"Not yet, Brasidus. Not yet. But you will recall that contact with the crews of visiting ships is prohibited. And I think that the preliminaries to making love may be construed as contact."

"But are these Arcadians in the crèche crew members of visiting ships?"

"What else can they be? They must have got here somehow." Diomedes looked long and hard at Brasidus, but there was no censure in his regard. "However, I am not displeased by the way in which things are turning out. You are getting to know something about these . . . *things*. These Arcadians. And I think that you are strong enough to resist their lure. . . . Now, what have we for you? This evening, I think, you will visit your friend Achron at the crèche. Keep your eyes and ears open, but don't stick your neck out. Tomorrow I have an assignment for you that you should find interesting. This Margaret Lazenby wishes to make a sightseeing trip, and she especially asked for you as her escort."

"Will Lieutenant Commander Grimes be along, sir?"

"No. He'll be consorting with the top brass. After all, he *is* the commander of *Seeker* and, to use spaceman's parlance, seems to pile on rather more Gs than the master of a merchantman. . . . Yes, Brasidus, have yourself a nice visit with your boyfriend, and then report to me here tomorrow morning at 0730 hours, washed behind the ears and with all your brasswork polished."

Brasidus spent the evening with Achron before the latter reported for duty. It was not the first time that he had been a guest at the nurse's Club—but it was the first time that he had felt uncomfortable there. Apart from his own feelings, it was no different from other occasions. There were the usual graceful, soft-spoken young men, proud and happy to play host to the hoplites who were their visitors. There was the usual food—far better cooked and more subtly seasoned than that served in the army messes. There was the usual wine—a little too sweet, perhaps, but chilled and sparkling. There was music and there was dancing—not the strident screaming of brass and the boom and rattle of drums, not the heavy thud of bare feet on the floor, but the rhythmic strumming of lutes and, to it, the slow gyrations of willowy bodies.

But . . .

But there was something lacking.

But what could be lacking?

"You are very thoughtful tonight, Brasidus," remarked Achron wistfully.

"Am I?"

"Yes. You . . . you're not with us, somehow."

"No?"

"Brasidus, I have to be on duty soon. Will you come with me to my room?"

The Sergeant looked at his friend. Achron was a pretty boy, prettier than most, but he was not, he could never be, an Arcadian. . . .

What am I thinking? he asked himself, shocked. *Why am I thinking it?*

He said, "Not tonight, Achron."

"But what is wrong with you, Brasidus? You never used to be like this." Then, with a sort of incredulous bitterness, "It can't be one of the men from the ship, can it? No, not possibly. Not one of those great, hairy brutes. As well consort with one of those malformed aliens they've brought with them!" Achron laughed at the absurdity of the idea.

"No," Brasidus told him. "Not one of the men from the ship."

"Then it's all right."

"Yes, it's all right. But I shall have a heavy day tomorrow."

"You poor dear. I suppose that the arrival of this absurd spaceship from some uncivilized world has thrown a lot of extra work on you."

"Yes. It has."

"But you'll walk with me to the crèche, won't you?"

"Yes. I'll do that."

"Oh, thank you. You can wait here while I get changed. There's plenty of wine left."

Yes, there was plenty of wine left, but Brasidus was in no mood for it. He sat in silence, watching the dancers, listening to the slow, sensuous thrumming. Did the Arcadians dance? And how would *they* look dancing, stripped for performance, the light gleaming on their smooth, golden skins? And why should the mere thought of it be so evocative of sensual imaginings?

Achron came back into the hall, dressed in his white working tunic. Brasidus got up from the bench, walked with him out into the night. The two friends made their way through the streets in silence at first, but it was not the companionable silence to which they had become used. Finally Brasidus spoke, trying to keep any display of real interest out of his voice.

"Wouldn't it be better if you nurses lived in at the crèche? The same as we do in the barracks."

"Then we shouldn't have these walks, Brasidus."

"You could visit me."

"But I don't *like* your barracks. And your Club's as bad."

"I suppose that the cooking could be improved in both. Just who *does* live in at the crèche?"

"All the doctors, of course. And there are some engineers who look after the machinery."

"No helots?"

"No. Of course not." Achron was shocked at the idea.

"Even *we*—but, after all, Brasidus, we are helots—have to live outside. But you know all that. Why are you asking me?"

That was a hard counterquestion to answer. At last Brasidus said, "There have been rumors . . ."

"Rumors of what?"

"Well, it's a very large building. Even allowing for the wards and the birth machine, there must be ample space inside. Do you think that the staff doctors and engineers could have . . . friends living with them?"

It was Achron's turn to hesitate. "You could be right, Brasidus. There are so many rules telling us that we must not stray away from our wards. Now that you raise the point, I can see that there has always been an atmosphere of . . . of secrecy . . ."

"And have you ever seen or heard anything?"

"No."

"And do the staff doctors and engineers have any friends among the nurses?"

"They wouldn't look at *us*." Resentment was all too evident in Achron's voice. "They're too high and mighty. Keep themselves to themselves, that's what *they* do. And their own accommodation, I've heard, the King himself might envy. They've a heated swimming pool, even. I've never seen it, but I've heard about it. And I've seen the food and the wine that come in. Oh, they do themselves well—far better than us, who do all the work."

"There might be inquiries being made," said Brasidus cautiously.

"There are always inquiries being made. That Captain Diomedes wanted me to work for him. But he's not . . . he's not a gentleman. We didn't get on. Why should I help him?"

"Would you help *me?*"

"And how can I, Brasidus?"

"Just look and listen. Let me know of anything out of the ordinary in the crèche."

"But the doctors can do no wrong," said Achron. "And even if they *did*, they *couldn't*. You know what I mean."

"In your eyes, you mean?"

"In my eyes," admitted the nurse. "But for you, and only for you, I'll . . . I'll look and listen. Does it mean promotion for you?"

"It does," said Brasidus.

"Are you coming in?" asked Achron as they reached the entrance to the crèche.

"No. I shall have a long and wearing day tomorrow."

"You . . . you don't give me much inducement to help you, do you? If I do, will things be the same between us again?"

"Yes," lied Brasidus.

15

BRASIDUS DROVE OUT to the spaceport in the car that had been placed at his disposal. He realized that he was looking forward to what he had told Achron would be a long and wearing day. He enjoyed the freshness of the morning air, looked up with appreciation at the Spartan Navy still, in perfect formation, circling the landing field. But now he did not, as he had done so many times in the past, envy the airmen. He was better off as he was. If he were up there, a crew member of one of the warships, even the captain of one of them, he would not be meeting the glamorous, exotic spacefarers—and most certainly would not, in the course of duty, be spending the entire day with one of them.

Margaret Lazenby was already ashore, was waiting in Diomedes' office, was engaged in conversation with the Security captain. Brasidus heard his superior say, "I'm sorry, Doctor Lazenby, but I cannot allow you to carry weapons. The cameras and recording equipment—yes. But not that pistol. Laser, isn't it?"

"It is. But, damn it all, Diomedes, on this cockeyed world of yours my going about unarmed degrades me to the status of a helot."

"And the Arcadians are not helots?"

"No. It should be obvious, even to a Security officer. Would a helot hold commissioned rank in the Federation's Survey Service?"

"Then if you possess warrior's status, your being let loose with a weapon of unknown potentialities is even worse insofar as we are concerned." The fat man, facing Margaret Lazenby's glare with equanimity, allowed himself to relent. "All right. Leave your pistol here, and I'll issue you with a stun gun."

"I shall not leave my weapon *here*. Will you be so good as to put me through to the ship so that I can tell the duty officer to send somebodv ashore to pick it up?"

"All right." Diomedes punched a few buttons on his board, picked up the handset, spoke into it briefly, then handed it to the Arcadian. He turned to Brasidus. "So you've arrived. Attention!" Brasidus obeyed with a military crash and jangle. "Let's look at you. H'm, brass not too bad, but your leatherwork could do with another polish. . . . But you're not going anywhere near the palace, so I don't suppose it matters. At ease! Stand easy! In fact, relax."

Meanwhile, Margaret Lazenby had finished speaking into the telephone. She returned the instrument to its rest. She stood there, looking down at the obese Diomedes sprawled in his chair—and Brasidus looked at her. She was not in uniform, but was wearing an open-necked shirt with a flaring collar cut from some soft, brown material, and below it a short kilt of the same color. Her legs were bare, and her slim feet were thrust into serviceable-looking sandals. At her belt was a holstered weapon of unfamiliar design. The cross straps from which depended her equipment—camera, sound recorder, binoculars—accentuated the outthrusting fleshy mounds on her chest that betrayed her alien nature.

She was, obviously, annoyed, and when she spoke it was equally obvious that she was ready and willing to transfer her annoyance to Brasidus. "Well, Brasidus," she demanded. "Seen enough? Or would you like me to go into a song and dance routine for you?"

"I . . . I was interested in that weapon of yours."

"Is *that* all?" For some obscure reason Brasidus' reply seemed to annoy her still further. And then a junior officer from *Seeker* came in, and Margaret Lazenby unbuckled the holstered pistol from her belt, handed it to the young spaceman. She accepted the stun gun from Diomedes, unholstered it, looked at it curiously. "Safety catch? Yes. Firing stud? H'm. We have similar weapons. Nonlethal, but effective enough. Oh, range?"

"Fifty feet," said Diomedes.

"Not very good. Better than nothing, I suppose." She clipped the weapon to her belt. "Come on, Brasidus. We'd better get out of here before he has me stripped to a peashooter and you polishing your belt and sandals."

"Your instructions, sir?" Brasidus asked Diomedes.

"Instructions? Oh, yes. Just act as guide and escort to Doctor Lazenby. Show her what you can of the workings of our economy—fields, factories. . . . You know. Answer her questions as long as there's no breach of security involved. And keep your own ears flapping."

"Very good, sir. Oh, expenses . . ."

"Expenses, Brasidus?"

"There may be meals, an occasional drink. . . ."

Diomedes sighed, pulled a bag of coins out of a drawer, dropped it with a clank on to the desk. "I know just how much is in this and I shall expect a detailed account of what you spend. Off with you. And, Doctor Lazenby, I expect you to bring Brasidus, here, back in good order and condition."

Brasidus saluted, then followed the spaceman out through the doorway.

She said, as soon as they were outside the building, "Expenses?"

"Yes, Doctor . . ."

"Call me Peggy."

"I have rations for the day in the car, Peggy, but I didn't think they were . . . suitable. Just bread and cold meat and a flagon of wine from the mess at the barracks."

"And so . . . and so you want to impress me with something better?"

"Why, yes," admitted Brasidus with a certain surprise. "Yes." (And it was strange, too, that he was looking forward to buying food and drink for this alien, even though the wherewithal to do so came out of the public purse. On Sparta every man was supposed to pay for his own entertainment, although not always in cash. In this case, obviously, there could be no reciprocation. *Or could there be?* But it did not matter.)

And then, with even greater surprise, Brasidus realized that he was helping Margaret Lazenby into the hovercar. Even burdened as she was, she did not need his assistance, but she accepted it as her due. Brasidus climbed in after her, took his seat behind the control column. "Where to?" he asked.

"That's up to you. I'd like a good tour. No, not the city—I shall be seeing plenty of that when I accompany John—Commander Grimes—on his official calls. What about the countryside and the outlying villages? Will that be in order?"

"It will, Peggy," Brasidus said. (And why should the use of that name be so pleasurable?)

"And if you'll explain things to me as you drive . . ."

The car lifted on its air cushion in a flurry of dust, moved forward, out through the main gateway, and for the first few miles headed toward the city.

"The spice fields," explained Brasidus with a wave of his hand. "It'll soon be harvest time, and then the two ships from Latterhaven will call for the crop."

"Rather . . . overpowering. The smell, I mean. Cinnamon, nutmeg, almond, but more so. . . . And a sort of mixture of sage and onion and garlic. But those men working in the fields with hoes and rakes, don't you have mechanical cultivators?"

"But why should we? I suppose that machines could be devised, but such mechanical tools would throw the helots out of employment."

"But you'd enjoy vastly increased production and would be able to afford a greater tonnage of imports from Latterhaven."

"But we are already self-sufficient."

"Then what *do* you import from Latterhaven?"

Brasidus creased his brows. "I . . . I don't know, Peggy," he admitted. "We are told that the ships bring manufactured goods."

"Such as?"

"I don't know." Then he recalled the strange book that he had seen in the crèche. "Books, perhaps."

"What sort of books?"

"I don't know, Peggy. The doctors keep them for themselves. But we turn off here. We detour the city and run through the vineyards."

The road that they were now following was little more than a track, running over and around the foothills, winding through the terraced vineyards on either side. As far as the eye could see the trellises were sagging under the weight of the great, golden fruit, each at least the size of a man's head, the broad, fleshy leaves. Brasidus remarked, "This has been a good year for grapes."

"*Grapes?* Are those things grapes?"

"What else could they be?" Brasidus stopped the car, got out, scrambled up the slope to the nearest vine. With his knife he hacked through a tough stem, then carried the ripe, glowing sphere back to Peggy. She took it, hefted it in her two hands, peered at it closely, sniffed it. "Whatever this is," she declared, "it ain't no grape—not even a grapefruit. Something indigenous, I suppose. Is it edible?"

"No. It has to be . . . processed. Skinned, trodden out, exposed to the air in open vats. It takes a long time, but it gets rid of the poison."

"Poison? I'll take your word for it." She handed the fruit back to Brasidus, who threw it onto the bank. "Oh, I should have kept that, to take to the ship for analysis."

"I'll get it again for you."

"Don't bother. Let the biochemist do his own fetching and carrying. But have you any of the . . . the finished product? You did say that you had brought a flagon of wine with you."

"Yes, Peggy." Brasidus reached into the back of the car, brought up the stone jug, pulled out the wooden stopper.

"No glasses?" she asked with a lift of the eyebrows.

"Glasses?"

"Cups, goblets, mugs—things you drink out of."

"I . . . I'm sorry. I never thought . . ."

"You have a lot to learn, my dear. But show me how you manage when you haven't any women around to exercise a civilizing influence."

"Women?"

"People like me. Go on, show me."

Brasidus grinned, lifted the flagon in his two hands, tilted it over his open mouth, clear of his lips. The wine was rough, tart rather than sweet, but refreshing. He gulped happily, then returned the jug to an upright position. He swallowed, then said, "Your turn, Peggy."

"You can't expect me to drink like that. You'll have to help me."

You wouldn't last five minutes on Sparta, thought Brasidus, not altogether derisively. He turned around in his seat, carefully elevated the wine flagon over Peggy's upturned face. He was suddenly very conscious of her red, parted lips, her white teeth. He tilted, allowing a thin trickle of the pale yellow fluid to emerge. She coughed and spluttered, shook her head violently. Then she gasped, "Haven't the knack of it—although I can manage a Spanish wineskin. Try again."

And now it was Brasidus who had to be careful, very careful. He was acutely aware of her physical proximity, her firm softness. "Ready?" he asked shakily.

"Yes. Fire at will."

This time the attempt was more successful. When at last she held up her hand to signal that she had had enough she must have disposed of at least a third of the flagon. From a pocket in her skirt she pulled a little square of white cloth, wiped her chin and dabbed at her lips with it. "That's not a bad drink," she stated. "Sort of dry sherry and ginger . . . but more-ish. No—that's enough. Didn't you ever hear the saying, 'Candy is dandy, but liquor is quicker'?"

"What is candy?" asked Brasidus. "And liquor is quicker for what?"

"Sorry, honey. I was forgetting that you have yet to learn the facts of life. Come to that, there're quite a few facts of life that I have to learn about this peculiar fatherland of yours. What is home without a mother?" She laughed. "Of course, you're lucky. You don't know *how* lucky. A pseudo-Hellenic culture and nary an Oedipus complex among the whole damn boiling of you!"

"Peggy, please speak Greek."

"Speak English, you mean. But I was using words and phrases that have dropped out of your version of our common tongue." She had slipped a little tablet into her mouth from a tube that she had extracted from her pocket. Suddenly her enunciation was less slurred. "Sorry, Brasidus, but this local tipple of yours is rather potent. Just as well that I brought along some soberer-uppers."

"But why do you need them? Surely one of the pleasures of drinking—*the* pleasure of drinking—is the effect; the . . . the loosening up."

"And the drunken brawl?"

"Yes," he said firmly.

"You mean that you'd like to . . . to brawl with me?"

Brasidus glimpsed a vivid mental picture of such an encounter and, with no hesitation, said, once again, "Yes."

"Drive on," she told him.

16

THEY DROVE ON, through and over the foothills, always climbing, the snowcapped peak of Olympus ever ahead, until, at last, Brasidus brought the car to a halt in the single street of a tiny village that clung precariously to the mountainside.

"Kilkis," he announced. "The tavern here could be worse. We halt here for our midday meal."

"Kilkis." The Arcadian repeated the name, gazed around her at the huddle of low but not ungraceful buildings, and then to the boulder-strewn slopes upon which grazed flocks of slow-moving, dun-colored beasts, many of them almost ready to reproduce by fission. "Kilkis," she repeated. "Ard how do the people here make a living? Do they take in each other's washing?"

"I don't understand, Peggy."

"Sorry, Brasidus. What are those animals?"

"Goats," he explained. "The major source of our meat supply." He went on, happy to be upon more familiar ground, "The only helots allowed to carry arms are the goatherds—see, there's one by that rock. He has a horn to summon assistance, and a sword, and a spear."

"Odd-looking goats. And why the weapons? Against rustlers?"

"Rustlers?"

"Cattle thieves. Or goat thieves."

"No. Goat raiding is classed as a military operation, and, in any case, none of the other city-states would dare to violate *our* borders. We have the Navy, of course, and firearms and armored chariots. They do not. But there're still the wolves, Peggy, and they're no respecters of frontiers."

"H'm. Then I think that you should allow your goatherds to carry at least a rifle. Is it a hazardous occupation?"

"It is, rather. But the schools maintain a steady flow of replacements, mainly from among those who have just failed to make the grade as hoplites."

"I see. Failed soldiers rather than passed veterinarians."

They got out of the car and walked slowly into the inn, into a long room with rush-strewn floor, tables and benches, low, raftered ceiling, and a not unpleasant smell of sour wine and cookery. At one end of the room there was an open fire, upon which simmered a huge iron cauldron. The half dozen or so customers—rough-looking fellows, leather-clad, wiry rather than muscular—got slowly to their feet at the sight of Brasidus' uniform, made reluctant and surly salutation. And then, as they got a proper look at his companion, there was more than a flicker of interest on their dark, seamed faces.

"You may be seated," Brasidus told them curtly.

"Thank you, Sergeant," replied one of them, his voice only just short of open insolence.

The taverner—fat, greasy, obsequious—waddled from the back of the room. "Your pleasure, lords?" he asked.

"A flagon of your best wine. And," added Brasidus, "two of your finest goblets to drink it from. What have you to eat?"

"Only the stew, lord. But it is made from a fine, fat young goat, just this very morning cast off from its father. Or we have sausage—well-ripened and well-seasoned."

"Peggy?" said Brasidus, with an interrogative intonation.

"The stew will do very nicely, I think. It smells good. And it's been boiled, so it should be safer . . ."

The innkeeper stared at her. "And may I be so impertinent as to inquire if the lord is from the strange spaceship?"

"You've already done so," Margaret Lazenby told him, then relented. "Yes. I am from the ship."

"You must find our world very beautiful, lord."

"Yes. It is beautiful. And interesting."

Roughly, Brasidus pulled out a bench from a vacant table, almost forced Peggy down onto the seat. "What about that wine?" he growled to the innkeeper.

"Yes, lord. Coming, lord. At once."

One of the goatherds whispered something to his companions, then chuckled softly. Brasidus glared at the men, ostentiously loosened the flap of the holster of his projectile pistol. There was an uneasy silence, and then, one by one, the goatherds rose to their feet and slouched out of the room. The Arcadian complained, "I had my recorder going." She did something to the controls of one of the instruments slung at her side. An amplified voice said loudly, "Since when has the Army been playing nurse to offworld monsters?"

"Insolent swine!"

"Don't be silly. They're entitled to their opinions."

"They're not. They insulted me." Then, as an afterthought, "And you."

"I've been called worse things than 'offworld monster' in my time. And you've ruined their lunchtime session, to say nothing of my chances of making a record of a typical tavern conversation."

Reluctantly, "I'm sorry."

"So you damn well should be."

The innkeeper arrived with a flagon and two goblets. They were mismatched, and they could have been cleaner, but they were of glass, not of earthenware or metal, and of a standard surprising in an establishment such as this. He placed them carefully on the rough surface of the table, then stood there, wine jug in hand, awaiting the word to pour.

"Just a minute," Margaret Lazenby said. She picked up one of the drinking vessels, examined it. "H'm. Just as I thought."

"And what did you think, Peggy?"

"Look," she said, and her pointed, polished fingernail traced the design of the crest etched into the surface of the glass. "A stylized Greek helmet. And under it, easy enough to read after all these years, 'I.T.T.S. DORIC.' "

"I.T.T.S.?"

"Interstellar Transport Commission's Ship."

"But I thought that your ship belonged to the Interstellar Federation's Survey Service."

"It does."

"But apart from the Latterhaven freighters, no ships but yours have ever called here."

"Somebody must have. But what about getting these . . . these antiques filled?"

Brasidus gestured to the innkeeper, who, after a second's hesitation, filled the Arcadian's glass first. One did not have to be a telepath to appreciate the man's indecision. Here was a sergeant—and a sergeant in the Police Battalion of the Army at that. Here was an alien, in what might be uniform and what might be civilian clothing. Who ranked whom?

Brasidus lifted his goblet. "To your good health, Peggy."

"And to yours." She sipped. "H'm. Not at all bad. Of course, in this setting it should be *retsina*, and there should be *feta* and black olives to nibble . . ."

"You will speak in riddles, Peggy."

"I'm sorry, Brasidus. It's just that you're so . . . so human in spite of everything that I keep forgetting that your world has been in isolation for centuries. But suppose we just enjoy the meal?"

And they did enjoy it. Brasidus realized that his own appreciation of it was enhanced by the Arcadian's obvious delight in the—to her—unfamiliar food and drink. They finished their stew, and then there were ripe, red, gleaming apples—"Like no apples that I've ever seen or tasted," commented Peggy, "but they'll do. Indeed they will"—and another flagon of wine. When they were done, save for the liquor remaining in the jug, Brasidus wiped his mouth on the back of his right hand, watched with tolerant amusement as his companion patted her lips with a little square of white cloth that she brought from one of her pockets.

She said, "That was *good*, Brasidus." From a packet that she produced from a shoulder pouch she half shook two slim brown cylinders. "Smoke?"

"Is this the same stuff that Commander Grimes was burning in that wooden thing like a little trumpet?"

"It is. Yours must be about the only Man-colonized world that hasn't tobacco. Commander Grimes likes his pipe; I prefer a cigarillo. See—this is the striking end. just a tap—so. Put the other end in your mouth." She showed him how, then remarked, as she exhaled a fragrant blue cloud, "I hope that the same doesn't happen to us as happened to Sir Walter Raleigh."

"And what did happen?" Brasidus inhaled, then coughed and spluttered violently. He hastily dropped the little cylinder onto his plate. Probably this Sir Walter Raleigh, whoever he was, had been violently ill.

"Sir Walter Raleigh was the Elizabethan explorer who first introduced tobacco into a country called England. He was enjoying his pipe after a meal in an inn, and the innkeeper thought that he was on fire and doused him with a bucket of water."

"This fat flunkey had better not try it on you!" growled Brasidus.

"I doubt if he'd dare. From what I've observed, a sergeant on this planet piles on more Gs than a mere knight in the days of Good Queen Bess." She laughed through the wreathing, aromatic fumes—then, suddenly serious, said, "We have company."

Brasidus swung round, his right hand on the butt of his pistol. But it was only the village corporal—a big man in slovenly uniform, his leather unpolished, his brass tarnished. His build, his broad, heavy face were indicative of slowness, both physical and mental, but the little gray eyes under the sandy thatch of the eyebrows were shrewd enough.

"Sergeant!" he barked, saluting and stiffening to attention.

"Corporal—at ease! Be seated."

"Thank you, Sergeant."

"Some wine, Corporal?"

The corporal reached out a long arm to one of the other tables, grabbed an earthenware mug, filled it from the flagon. "Thank you, Sergeant. Your health, Sergeant. And yours, sir." He drank deeply and noisily. "Ah, that was good. But, Sergeant, my apologies. I should have been on hand to welcome you and . . ." He stared curiously at the Arcadian. "You and your . . . guest?"

"Doctor Lazenby is one of the officers of the starship *Seeker*."

"I thought that, Sergeant. Even here there are stories." The man, Brasidus realized, was staring at the odd mounds of flesh that were very obvious beneath the thin shirt worn by the alien.

"They aren't concealed weapons," remarked the Arcadian wryly. "And, in the proper circumstances, they are quite functional."

The corporal flushed, looked away and addressed himself to his superior. "I was absent from the village, Sergeant, as today is Exposure Day. I had to supervise. But as soon as I was told of your arrival, I hastened back."

"Exposure Day?" asked Margaret Lazenby sharply.

"Yes," Brasidus told her. "One of the days on which the newly born—those newly born who are sickly or deformed, that is—are exposed on the mountainside."

"And what happens to them?"

"Usually the wolves finish them off. But without food or water they'd not last long."

"You're joking." It was an appeal rather than a statement or a question.

"But why should I joke, Peggy? The purity of the race must be maintained."

She turned to the corporal, her face white, her eyes blazing. "You. Had the wolves come when you left the . . . the Exposure?"

"No, sir. But they're never long in hearing the cries and winding the scent."

She was on her feet, pushing her bench away so violently that it toppled with a crash. "Get a move on, Brasidus. If we hurry, we may still be in time."

Brasidus was sickened by her reactions, by her words. Exposure was necessary, but it was not something to take pictures of, to make records of. As well join the scavengers in their filth-eating rounds of the city streets.

"Come *on!*" she flared.

"No," he said stubbornly. "I'll not help you to make a film that you and your shipmates can gloat over."

"Make a film?" Her voice was incredulous. "You fool. We may be in time to save them."

And then it was Brasidus' turn to experience a wave of incredulity.

17

"NO!" SAID BRASIDUS.

"Yes!" she contradicted him. But, incongruously, it was not the borrowed pistol that she was leveling at the two men, but a camera. Brasidus laughed—and then the slim hands holding the seemingly innocuous instrument twitched ever so slightly, and from the lens came an almost invisible flicker of light and, behind the policemen, something exploded. There was a sudden, acrid stench of flash-boiled wine, of burning wood.

That deadly lens was looking straight at Brasidus again.

"Laser," he muttered.

"Laser," she stated.

"But . . . but you were supposed to leave all your weapons behind."

"I'm not altogether a fool, honey. And, oddly enough, this *is* a camera, with flash attachment. Not a very good one, but multipurpose tools are rarely satisfactory. Now, are you going to drive me out to the Exposure?"

She'll have to bring along the corporal, thought Brasidus. *And the two of us should be able to deal with her.*

And now the deadly camera was in her left hand only, and the borrowed stun gun was out of its holster. She fired left-handed, and at this short range she could hardly miss. The corporal gasped, made one tottering step forward, then crashed untidily to the floor. The belled muzzle swung slightly and she fired again. There was the sound of another heavy fall behind Brasidus. That, he guessed, would be the innkeeper. There would be no telephone calls made to the city for several hours. The goatherds were notorious for their reluctance to assist the forces of law and order.

"Get into the car," she said. "I'll ride behind. And make it snappy."

He walked out of the inn, into the afternoon sunlight, deliberately not hurrying. He consoled himself with the thought that, even though he was falling down on the job as a sergeant of Police, he was earning his keep as a lieutenant of Security. He had been told to find out what made these aliens tick—and he was finding out. In any case, if the wolf packs were as ravenous as usual, there would be nothing left but a scatter of well-gnawed bones.

He climbed into the driver's seat, thought briefly about making a dash for it, then thought better of it. He could never get out of range in time. He heard her clambering in behind him. He wished that he knew which way that so-called camera was pointing—and then he succeeded in catching a glimpse of it in the rear mirror. If the firing stud were accidentally pressed, it would drill a neat, cauterized hole through his head. Or would the water content of his brains explode? In that case, it would not be so tidy.

"Get going," she said. And then, as an afterthought, "I suppose you know the way."

"I know the way," he admitted. The car lifted on its air cushion and proceeded.

"Faster. Faster."

"This is only a goat track," he grumbled. "And this isn't an armored chariot we're riding in."

Even so, deliberately taking the risk of fouling the fan casings on projecting stones, he managed to increase speed. Rather to his disappointment, the vehicle still rode easily, sped over the rough terrain without making any crippling contacts.

And then, ahead of them, seemingly from just over the next rise, sounded the ominous howling and snarling of the wolf pack, and with it, almost inaudible, a thin, high screaming.

"Hurry!" Margaret Lazenby was shouting. "Hurry!"

They were over the rise now. Once before, Brasidus had watched an Exposure, and the spectacle had sickened him, even though he had realized the necessity for it, and appreciated the essential justice of allowing Nature to erase its own mistakes in its own way. But to rescue one or more of these mewling, subhuman creatures—that was unthinkable.

The car was over the rise.

And then it was bearing down on the snarling, quarreling pack, on the carnivores too engrossed in their bloody business to notice the approach of potential enemies. But perhaps they heard the whine of the ducted fans and, even so, remembered that, on these occasions, Men never interfered with them.

The car was sweeping down the slope toward the melee, and Margaret Lazenby was firing. Brasidus could feel the heat of the discharges, cursed as the hair on the right side of his head crisped and smoldered. But he maintained a steady course nonetheless, and experienced the inevitable thrill of the hunt, the psychological legacy from Man's savage ancestors. Ahead there was a haze of vaporized blood; the stench of seared flesh was already evident. The howling of the pack rose to a frenzied crescendo but the animals stood their ground, red eyes glaring, slavering, crimsoned jaws agape. Then—an evil, gray, stormy tide—they began to surge up the hillside to meet their attackers.

Brasidus was shooting now, the control column grasped in his left hand, the bucking projectile pistol in his right. Between them, he and Margaret Lazenby cleared a path for their advance, although the car rocked and lurched as it passed over the huddle of dead and dying bodies. Then—"Stop!" she was crying. "Stop! There's a baby there! I saw it move!"

Yes, there among the ghastly litter of scattered bones and torn flesh, was a living child, eyes screwed tight shut, bawling mouth wide open. It would not be living much longer. Already two of the wolves, ignoring the slaughter of their companions, were facing each other over the tiny, feebly struggling body, their dreadful teeth bared as they snarled at each other.

Margaret Lazenby was out of the car before Brasidus could bring it to a halt. Inevitably she lost her balance and fell, rolling down the slope, almost to where the two carnivores were disputing over their prey. She struggled somehow to her knees just as they saw her, just as they abandoned what was no more than a toothsome morsel for a satisfying meal. Somehow, awkwardly, she managed to bring her camera-gun into firing position, but the weapon must have been damaged by her fall. She cried out and threw it from her, in a smoking, spark-spitting arc that culminated in the main body of the pack. Even as it exploded in a soundless flare of raw energy she was tugging the borrowed stun gun from its holster.

Once she fired, and once only, and one of the two wolves faltered in the very act of leaping, slumped to the ground. The other one completed its spring and was on her, teeth and taloned hind paws slashing. Brasidus was out of the car, running, a pistol in each hand. But he could not use his guns—animal and alien formed together a wildly threshing tangle, and to fire at one would almost certainly mean hitting the other. But the Arcadian was fighting desperately and well, as yet seemed to be undamaged. Her hands about the brute's neck were keeping those slavering jaws from her throat, and her knee in the wolf's belly was still keeping those slashing claws at a distance. But she was tiring. It would not be long before sharp fangs found her jugular or slashing talons opened her up from breastbone to groin.

Dropping his weapons, Brasidus jumped. From behind he got his own two hands around the furry throat, his own knee into the beast's back. He exerted all of his strength, simultaneously pulled and thrust. The animal whined, then was abruptly silent as the air supply to the laboring lungs was cut off. But it was still strong, was still resisting desperately, was striving to turn so that it could face this fresh enemy. Margaret Lazenby had fallen clear of the fight, was slowly crawling to where she had dropped her pistol.

She never had to use it. Brasidus brought his last reserves of strength into play, heard the sharp snap of broken vertebrae. The fight was over.

He got groggily to his feet, ready to face and to fight a fresh wave of carnivores. But, save for the Arcadian, the squalling child and himself, the hillside was bare of life. There were charred bodies, human and animal, where the laser weapon had exploded; the other wolves, such of them as had survived, must have fled. The stench of burning flesh was heavy in the air.

At a tottering run, Margaret Lazenby was hurrying to the child, the only survivor of the Exposure. More slowly, Brasidus followed, looked down at the little naked body. He said, "It would have been kinder to let it die. What sort of life can it expect with that deformity?"

"Deformity? What the hell do you mean?"

Wordlessly he pointed to the featureless scissure of the baby's thighs.

"Deformity? This, you fool, is a perfectly formed female child."

She got down to her knees and tenderly picked up the infant. And, as she did so, it became somehow obvious that the odd mounds of flesh on her chest, fully revealed now that her shirt had been torn away, were, after all, functional. The baby stopped crying, groped greedily for an erect pink nipple.

Peggy laughed shakily. "No, darling, no. I'm sorry, but the milk bar's not open for business. I'll make up a bottle for you when we get back to the ship."

"So," muttered Brasidus at last, "so it is one of *your* race."

"Yes."

"And those . . . lumps are where you fission from."

She said, "You've still a lot to learn. And now give me your tunic, will you."

"My tunic?"

"Yes. Don't just stand there, looking as though you've never seen a woman before."

Brasidus silently stripped off his upper garment, handed it to her. He expected that she would put the child back on the ground while she covered her own seminudity. But she did not. Instead, she wrapped the baby in the tunic, cooing to it softly. "There, there. You were cold, weren't you? But Mummy will keep you warm, and Mummy will see that you're fed." She straightened, then snapped in a voice of command, "Take me back to the ship, as fast as all the Odd Gods of the Galaxy will let you!"

18

SO THEY DROVE back to the ship swiftly, bypassing Kilkis—Brasidus had no desire to meet again the village corporal—taking roads that avoided all centers of population, however small. Peggy was in the back of the car, making soft, soothing noises to the querulous infant. *Achron,* thought Brasidus sullenly, *would have appreciated this display of paternal solicitude—but I do not.* And what did he feel? Jealousy, he was obliged to admit, resentment at being deprived of the Arcadian's company. Perverts the doctors in the crèche might be, but these aliens could and did exert a dangerous charm. But when it came to a showdown, as now, they had no time for mere humans, lavished their attentions only upon their own kind.

Suddenly the child was silent. The car was speeding down a straight stretch of road, so Brasidus was able to risk turning his head to see what was happening. Peggy had the stopper out of the wine flask, was dipping a corner of her handkerchief into it, then returning the soaked scrap of rag to the eager mouth of the baby. She grinned ruefully as she met Brasidus' stare. "I know it's all wrong," she said. "But I haven't a feeding bottle. Too, it will help if the brat is sound asleep when we get back to the spaceport."

"And why will it help?" demanded Brasidus, turning his attention back to the road ahead.

She said, "It's occurred to me that *we* have probably broken quite a few laws. Apart from anything else, armed assault upon the person of a police officer must be illegal."

"It is. But *you* carried out the armed assault. *We* did not."

She laughed. "Too true. But what about *our* interference with the

Exposure? It will be better for both of us if your boss doesn't know that the interference was a successful one."

"I must make my report," said Brasidus stiffly.

"Of course." Her voice was soft, caressing. "But need it be a *full* report? We got into a fight with the wolf pack—there's too much evidence littered around on the hillside for us to lie our way out of that. I've a few nasty scratches on my back and my breasts."

"So that's what they're called. I was wondering."

"Never mind that now. I've got these scratches, so it's essential that I get back on board as soon as possible for treatment by our own doctor."

"I thought that you were the ship's doctor."

"I'm not. I have a doctorate in my own field, which is not medicine. But let me finish. We had this fight with these four-legged sharks you people call wolves. I fell out of the car, and you jumped out and saved my life, although not before I was mauled a little. And that's near enough to the truth, isn't it?"

"Yes."

"Now, the child. She'll fit nicely into the hamper you brought the provisions in. The poor little tot will be in a drugged stupor by the time we get to the spaceport, so she'll be quiet enough. And with your tunic spread over her, who will know?"

"I don't like it," said Brasidus.

"That makes two of us, my dear. I don't like having to conceal the evidence of actions that, on any world but this, would bring a public commendation."

"But Diomedes will know."

"How can he know? We were there, he was not. And we don't even have to make sure that we tell the same story, exact in every detail. He can question you, but he can't question *me*."

"Don't be so sure about that, Peggy."

"Oh, he'd like to, Brasidus. He'd like to. But he knows that at all times there are sufficient officers and ratings aboard *Seeker* to handle the drive and main and secondary armaments. He knows that we could swat your gasbags out of the sky in a split second, and then raze the city in our own good time." There was a long silence. Then, "I'm sorry to have gotten you into quite a nasty mess, Brasidus, but you realize that I had no choice."

"Like calls to like," he replied with bitter flippancy.

"You could put it that way, I suppose, but you're wrong. Anyhow, I'm sure that I shall be able to persuade John—Commander Grimes—to offer you the sanctuary of our ship if you're really in a jam."

"I'm a Spartan," he said.

"With all the Spartan virtues, I suppose. Do *you* have that absurd legend about the boy who let the fox gnaw his vitals rather than cry out? No matter. Just tell Captain Diomedes the truth, but not the whole truth. Say that it was all my fault, and that you did your best to restrain me. Which you did—although it wasn't good enough. Say that you saved me from the wolves."

They drove on in silence while Brasidus pondered his course of action. What the Arcadian had said was true, what she had proposed might prevent an already unpleasant situation from becoming even more unpleasant. In saving Peggy's life, he had done no more than his duty; in helping to save the life of the deformed—deformed?—child he, an officer of the law, had become a criminal. And why had he done this? With the destruction of the laser-camera the alien had lost her only advantage.

And why had he *known,* why did he still *know* that his part in the rescue operations had been essentially *right?*

It was this strange awareness of rightness that brought him to full agreement with his companion's propositions. Until now, he had accepted without question the superior intellectual and moral stature of those holding higher rank than himself, but it was obvious that aboard *Seeker* there were officers, highly competent technicians with superbly trained men and fantastically powerful machinery at their command, whose moral code varied widely from the Spartan norm. (Come to that, what about the doctors, the top-ranking aristocrats of the planet, whose own morals were open to doubt? What about the doctors, and their perverse relations with the Arcadians?)

Peggy's voice broke into his thoughts. "She's sleeping now. Out like a light. Drunk as a fiddler's bitch. I think that we shall be able to smuggle her on board without trouble." She went on, "I appreciate this, Brasidus. I do. I wish . . ." He realized that she must be standing up in the back of the car, leaning toward him. He felt her breasts against the bare skin of his back. The contact was like nothing that he had ever imagined. He growled, "Sit down, damn you. Sit down—if you want this wagon to stay on the road!"

19

THEY ENCOUNTERED NO delays on their way back to the spaceport, but, once they were inside the main gates, it was obvious that their return had been anticipated. Diomedes, backed by six armed hoplites, was standing, glowering, outside his office. A little away from him was John Grimes—and it was not a ceremonial sword that depended from his belt but two holstered pistols. And there was another officer from the ship with him, wearing a walky-talky headset. The Commander glared at Brasidus and his companion with almost as much hostility as did Diomedes.

Diomedes raised an imperious arm. Brasidus brought the car to a halt. Grimes said something to his officer, who spoke into the mouthpiece of his headset. Brasidus, looking beyond the young man to the ship, saw that the turrets housing her armament were operational, the long barrels of weapons, fully extruded, waving slowly like the questing antennae of some giant insect.

"Brasidus." Diomedes' voice was a high-pitched squeal, a sure sign of bad temper. "I have received word from the village corporal at Kilkis. I demand your report—and *your* report, Doctor Lazenby—immediately. You will both come into my office."

"Captain Diomedes," said Grimes coldly, "you have every right to give orders to your own officers, but none whatsoever to issue commands to my personnel. Doctor Lazenby will make her report to me, aboard my ship."

"I have means of enforcing my orders, Commander Grimes."

As one man, the six hoplites drew their stun guns.

Grimes laughed. "My gunnery officer has his instructions, Captain Diomedes. He's watching us from the control room through very high-powered binoculars and, furthermore, he is hearing everything that is being said."

"And what are his instructions, Commander?"

"There's just one way for you to find out, Captain. I shouldn't advise it, though."

"All right." With a visible effort, Diomedes brought himself under control. "All right. I request, then, Commander, that you order your officer to accompany Brasidus into my office for questioning. You, and as many of your people as you wish, may be present."

Grimes obviously was giving consideration to what Diomedes had said. It was reasonable enough. Brasidus knew that, if he were in Grimes' shoes, he would have agreed. But suppose that somebody decided to investigate the contents of that food hamper on the back seat, some thirsty man hopeful that a drink of wine might remain in the flagon. Or suppose that the effects of the alcohol on the presently sleeping baby suddenly wore off.

Margaret Lazenby took charge. She stood up in the back of the car—and the extent of her dishevelment was suddenly obvious. The men stared at her, and Grimes, his fists clenched, took a threatening step toward Brasidus, growling, "You bastard."

"Stop it, John!" The Arcadian's voice was sharp. "Brasidus didn't do this."

"Then who did?"

"Damn it all! Can't you see that I want at least another shirt, as well as medical attention for these scratches? But if you must know, I made Brasidus take me to watch the Exposure."

"So the village corporal told me," put in Diomedes. "And between you, the pair of you slaughtered an entire wolf pack."

"We went too close, and they attacked us. They pulled me out of the car, but Brasidus saved me. And now, Captain Diomedes, I'd like to get back on board as soon as possible for an antibiotic shot and some fresh clothing." Before leaving the car, she stopped to lift the hamper from the back seat, handed it to Grimes' officer.

"What's in that basket?" demanded Diomedes.

"Nothing that concerns you!" she flared.

"I'll decide that," Grimes stated. "Here, Mister Taylor. Let me see."

The officer turned to face his captain, with his body hiding the hamper from Diomedes and his men. It was not intentional—*or was it?* Grimes, his face emotionless, lifted Brasidus' torn tunic from the open top of the wickerwork container. He said calmly, "One wine flagon. About six inches of gnarled sausage. The heel of a loaf of crusty bread. *You* decide, Captain, what may be brought off the ship onto your world,

I decide what may be brought from your world onto my ship. Mister Taylor, take this hamper to the biochemist so that its contents may be analyzed. And you, Doctor Lazenby, report at once to the surgeon. I'll receive your report later."

"Commander Grimes, I insist that I inspect that hamper." Three of the hoplites stepped forward, began to surround Mister Taylor.

"Captain Diomedes, if any of your men dare to lay hands upon my officer the consequences will be serious."

Diomedes laughed incredulously. "You'd open fire over a mug of wine and a couple of scraps of bread and sausage?"

"Too right I would."

Diomedes laughed again. "You aliens . . ." he said contemptuously. "All right, you can have your crumbs from the sergeants' mess. And I'd like a few words with your Doctor Lazenby as soon as she can spare me the time. And I'll have rather more than a few words with *you*, Brasidus, *now!*"

Reluctantly Brasidus got out of the car.

"And you let her threaten you with a laser weapon—and, furthermore, one that you had allowed her to carry. . . ."

Brasidus, facing Diomedes, who was lolling behind his desk, said rebelliously, "You, sir, checked her equipment. And she told me herself that the thing did function as a camera."

"All right. We'll let that pass. You allowed her to use a stun gun on the village corporal and the innkeeper, and then you drove her out to the Exposure. Why, Brasidus, did you have to stop at Kilkis, of all villages, on this day, of all days?"

"Nobody told me not to, sir. And, as you know, the dates of the Exposures are never advertised. You might have been informed, but I was not."

"So you drove her out to see the Exposure. And you got too close. And the wolves attacked you, and pulled her out of the car."

"That is correct, sir."

"Surely she could have used this famous laser-camera to defend herself."

"It was damaged, sir. She had to throw it away in a hurry. It blew up."

"Yes. I've been told that there's an area on the hillside that looks as though some sort of bomb had been exploded." He leaned back in his chair, looked up at the standing Brasidus. "You say that the wolves attacked her. Are you sure that it wasn't you?"

"And why should it have been me, sir?"

"Because it should have been. You let an alien order you around at gun point, and then you ask me why you should have attacked her! And now . . ." the words came out with explosive violence, "*What was in the hamper*?"

"Wine, sir. Bread. Sausage."

"And what was your tunic doing there?"

"I lent it to her, sir, to replace her own shirt."

"So, instead of wearing it, she put it in the hamper."

"The air was warm, sir, when we got down from the mountains. She asked me if she could have it so that the fibers from which it is woven could be analyzed by the . . . the biochemist."

"H'm. All in all, Brasidus, you did not behave with great brilliance. Were it not for the fact that these aliens—or one alien in particular—seem to like you, I should dispense with your services. As it is, you are still useful. Now, just what were this Margaret Lazenby's reactions when she learned of the Exposure?"

Lying, Brasidus knew, would be useless. The village corporal at Kilkis would have made a full report. He said, "She was shocked. She wanted to get to the site in time to rescue the deformed and defective children."

"You were not in time, of course."

"No, sir. We were not in time." He added virtuously, "I made sure of that."

"How, Brasidus?"

"I knew the way, she did not. I was able to make a detour."

The answer seemed to satisfy Diomedes. He grunted, "All right. You may sit down." For a few seconds he drummed on the desktop with his fingertips. "Meanwhile, Brasidus, the situation in the city is developing. Commander Grimes allowed his Arcadians, as well as the human members of his crew, shore leave. There was an unfortunate occurrence in the Tavern of the Three Harpies. An Arcadian, accompanied by a human spaceman, went in there. They got drinking with the other customers."

"Not the sort of place that I'd drink in by choice," Brasidus said, the other's silence seeming to call for some sort of comment.

"They were not so fortunate as to have a guide, such as yourself, to keep them out of trouble." (*You sarcastic swine*, thought Brasidus.) "Anyhow, there was the usual crowd in there. Helots of the laboring class, hoplites not fussy about the company they keep. It wouldn't have been so bad if the two spacemen had just taken one drink and then walked out, but they stayed there, drinking with the locals, and allowed themselves to be drawn into an argument. And you know how arguments in the Three Harpies usually finish."

"There was a fight, sir?"

"Brilliant, Brasidus, brilliant. There was a fight, and the human spaceman was laid out, and the Arcadian was beaten up a little, and then stripped. There was, you will understand, some curiosity as to what her body was like under her uniform."

"That was bad, sir."

"There's worse to follow. At least four hoplites had sexual intercourse with her by force."

"So it is possible, sir, in spite of the malformation."

Diomedes chuckled obscenely. "It's possible, all right. Everybody in the tavern would have had her if the other spaceman hadn't come round and started screaming for help on a little portable transceiver he wore on his wrist. A dozen men from the ship rushed in, real toughs—and I wish that my own personnel could learn *their* techniques of unarmed combat. Then the police condescended to intervene and laid everybody out with their stun guns, and then Commander Grimes, who'd heard about it somehow, came charging into my office threatening to devastate the city, and . . . and . . .

"Anyhow, you can see why I had to handle this Lazenby creature with kid gloves. Even though Grimes admits that his own crew were at fault—he had issued strict orders that no sightseeing party was to consist of fewer than six people—he was furious about the 'rape,' as he called it. You saw how he reacted when he thought that you had been doing something of the kind. He demanded that the rapists be punished most severely."

"But they were hoplites, sir, not helots. They had the right . . ."

"I know, I know. When I need instruction in the finer points of Spartan law I'll come to you. The conduct was discourteous rather than criminal. The culprits will, by this time, have been reprimanded by their commanding officer, and will, in all probability, be back in the Three Harpies, telling anybody who cares to listen what intercourse is like with an Arcadian. It is, I gather, quite an experience. Are you quite sure that you didn't . . . ?"

"Quite sure, sir."

"That's your story, and you stick to it." Again there was a pause, and the muffled drumming of Diomedes' fingers on the top of his desk. Then he went on, "Even on Sparta we have experienced occasional mutiny, infrequent rebellion. Tell me, Brasidus, what are the prime causes of mutiny?"

"Discontent, sir. Overly strict discipline. Unjust punishments . . ."

"And . . . ?"

"That's about all, sir."

"What about envy, Brasidus?"

"No, sir. We all know that if we show ability we shall become officers, with all the privileges that go with rank."

"But what if there's a privilege out of reach to everybody except a few members of one aristocratic caste?"

"I don't see what you mean, sir."

"Brasidus, Brasidus, what do you use for brains? What about that nest of Arcadians in the crèche? What do you suppose the doctors use them for?"

"I . . . I can guess."

"And so they have something that the rest of us haven't. And so"—Diomedes' voice dropped almost to a whisper—"the power that they've enjoyed for so long, for too long, may be broken."

"And *you*," said Brasidus, "envy them that power."

For long seconds the Captain glared at him across the desk. Then, "All right, I do. But it is for the good of the State that I am working against them."

Perhaps, thought Brasidus. *Perhaps.* But he said nothing.

20

CLAD IN A LABORING Helot's drab, patched tunic, his feet unshod and filthy, his face and arms liberally besmeared with the dirt of the day's toil, Brasidus sat hunched at one of the long tables in the Tavern of the Three Harpies. There were hoplites there as well as manual workers, but there was little chance that any of them would recognize him. Facial similarities were far from uncommon on Sparta.

He sat there, taking an occasional noisy gulp from his mug and listening.

One of the hoplites was holding forth to his companions. "Yes, it was on this very table that I had him. Or *it.* Good it was. You've no idea unless you've tried it yourself."

"Must've been odd. Wrong, somehow."

"It was odd, all right. But wrong nohow. This face-to-face business. And those two dirty great cushions for your chest to rest on . . ."

"Is *that* what they're for?"

"Must be. Pity the doctors can't turn out some of those creatures from their birth machine."

"But they do. Yes. They do."

Everybody turned to stare at the man who had just spoken. He was a stranger to Brasidus, but his voice and his appearance marked him for what he was. This was not the sort of inn that the nurses from the crèche usually frequented—in an establishment such as this they would run a grave risk of suffering the same fate as the unfortunate Arcadian from the ship. "They do," he repeated in his high-pitched sing-song, and looked straight at Brasidus. There was something in his manner that implied, *And* you *know, too.*

So this was the fellow agent whom Diomedes had told him that he would find in the tavern, the operative to whom he was to render assistance if necessary.

"And what do *you* know about it, dearie?" demanded the boastful hoplite.

"I'm a nurse . . ."

"That's obvious, sweetie pie."

"I'm a nurse, and I work at the crèche. We nurses aren't supposed to stray from our wards, but . . ."

"But with a snout like yours, you're bound to be nosy," said the hoplite, laughing.

The nurse stroked his overlong proboscis with his right index finger, grinned slyly. "How right you are, dearie. I admit it. I *like* to know what's going on. Oh, those doctors! They live in luxury, all right. You might think that practically all of the crèche is taken up by wards and machinery and the like, but it's not. More than half the building is *their* quarters. And the things they have! A heated swimming pool, even."

"Decadent," grunted a grizzled old sergeant.

"But nice. Especially in midwinter. Not that I've ever tried it myself. There's a disused storeroom, and this pool is on the other side of its back wall. There're some holes in the wall, where there used to be wiring or pipes or something. Big enough for a camera lens." The nurse fished a large envelope from inside the breast of his white tunic, pulled from it a sheaf of glossy photographs.

"Lemme see. Yes, those are Arcadians, all right. Topheavy, ain't they, when you see them standing up. Wonder how they can walk without falling flat on their faces."

"If they did, they'd bounce."

"Look sort of unfinished lower down, don't they?"

"Let *me* see!"

"Here, pass 'em round, can't you?"

Briefly, Brasidus had one of the prints in his possession. He was interested more in the likeness of the man standing by the pool than in that of his companion. Yes, it was Heraklion, all right, Heraklion without his robe but still, indubitably, the supercilious doctor.

"Must have come in that ship," remarked somebody.

"No," the nurse told him. "Oh, no. They've been in the crèche for *years*."

"You mean your precious doctors have *always* had them?"

"Yes. Nothing but the best for the guardians of the purity of our Spartan stock, dearie. But who are we to begrudge them their little comforts?"

"Soldiers, that's who. It's we who should be the top caste of this world, who should have the first pickings. After all, the King's a soldier."

"But the doctors *made* him, dearie. They made all of us."

"Like hell they did. They just look after the birth machine. And if there wasn't a machine, we'd manage all right, just as the animals do."

"We might have to," the nurse said. "I heard two of the doctors talking. They were saying that the people were having it too soft, that for the good of the race we should have to return to the old ways. They're thinking of shutting the machine down."

"What! How can you be a fighting man if you have to lug a child around with you?"

"But you said that we could manage all right without the doctors."

"Yes. But that's different. No, the way *I* see it is this: These doctors are getting scared of the military, but they know that if most of us are budding we shan't be much good for fighting. Oh, the cunning swine! They just want things all their way all the time instead of for only most of the time."

"But you can't do anything about it," the nurse said.

"Can't we? Who have the weapons and the training to use 'em? Not your doctors, that's for certain. With no more than the men in this tavern, we could take the crèche—and get our paws on to those Arcadians they've got stashed away there."

"More than our paws!" shouted somebody.

"You're talking mutiny and treason, hoplite," protested the elderly sergeant.

"Am I?" The man was on his feet now, swaying drunkenly. "But the King himself had one of the doctors executed. That shows how much *he* thinks of 'em!" He paused, striving for words. They came at last. "Here, on Sparta, it's fair shares for all—excepting you poor damn helots, of course. But for the rest of us, the rulers, it should be share an' share alike. Oh, I know that the colonel gets better pay, better grub an' better booze than I do—but in the field he lives the same as his men, an' all of us can become colonels ourselves if we put ourselves to it, an', come to that, generals. But the colonels an' the generals an' the admirals don't have Arcadians to keep their beds warm. Not even the King does. An' now there's some of us who know what it's like. An' there's some of us who want more of it."

"There are plenty of Arcadians aboard the spaceship," somebody suggested.

"I may be drunk, fellow, but I'm not *that* drunk. The spaceship's a battlewagon, and I've heard that the captain of her has already threatened to use his guns and missiles. No, the crèche'll be *easy* to take."

"Sit down, you fool!" ordered the elderly sergeant. "You got off light after you assaulted the Arcadian spaceman, but he was only a foreigner. Now you're inciting to riot, mutiny, and the gods alone know what else. The police will use more than stun guns on you this time."

"Will they, old-timer? Will they? And what if they do? A man can die only once. What I did to that Arcadian has done something to me, to *me*, do you hear? I have to do it again, even though I get shot for it." The man's eyes were crazy and his lips, foam-flecked. "You don't know what it was like. You'll never know, until you do it. Don't talk to me about boys, or about soft, puling nurses like our long-nosed friend here. The doctors have the best there is, the best that there can ever be, and they should be made to share it!"

"The police . . ." began the sergeant.

"Yes. The police. Now let me tell you, old-timer, that I kept my ears flapping while they had me in their barracks. Practically every man has been called out to guard the spaceport—the *spaceport*, do you hear? That alien captain's afraid that there'll be a mob coming out to take *his* pretty Arcadians by force, and fat old Captain Diomedes is afraid that the space commander'll start firing off in all directions if his ship and his little pets are menaced. By the time that the police get back to the city, every Arcadian in the crèche'll know what a *real* man is like, an' we shall all be tucked up in our cots in our quarters sleeping innocently."

"I didn't see a single policeman on my way here," contributed the nurse. "I wondered why." And then, in spurious alarm, "But you can't. You mustn't. You mustn't attack the crèche!"

"And who says I mustn't? You, you feeble imitation of a . . . a . . ."

He concluded triumphantly, "of an alien monster! Yes, that's a point. All this talk of them as alien monsters. It was only to put us off. But now we *know*. Or some of us know. Who's with me?"

The fools, thought Brasidus, *the fools!* as he listened to the crash of overturned benches, as he watched almost all the customers of the tavern, helots as well as hoplites, jump to their feet.

"The fools," he muttered aloud.

"And you would have been with them," whispered the nurse, "if I hadn't slipped a capsule into your drink." And then Brasidus saw the thin wisp of almost invisible vapor that was still trickling from the envelope in which the photographs had been packed. "I have access to certain drugs," said the man smugly, "and this one is used in our schoolrooms. It enhances the susceptibility of the students."

"Students," repeated Brasidus disgustedly.

"They have a lot to learn, Lieutenant," the nurse told him.

"And so have I. I want to see what happens."

"Your orders were to protect me."

"There's nobody here to protect you from, except that old sergeant. But why wasn't *he* affected?"

"Too old," said the nurse.

"Then you're quite safe."

Brasidus made his way from the tavern out into the street.

21

HE WOULD HAVE retreated to the safety of the inn, but he was given no opportunity to do so. A roaring torrent of men swept along the street, hoplites and helots, shouting, cursing and screaming. He was caught up by the human tide, buffeted and jostled, crying out with pain himself when a heavy, military sandal smashed down on one of his bare feet. He was sucked into the mob, made part of it, became just one tiny drop of water in the angry wave that was rearing up to smash down upon the crèche.

At first, he was fighting only to keep upright, to save himself from falling, from being trampled underfoot. And then—slowly, carefully and, at times, viciously—he began to edge out toward the fringe of the living current. At last he was able to stumble into a cross alley where he stood panting, recovering his breath, watching the rioters stream past.

Then he was able to think.

It seemed obvious to him that Diomedes must have planted his agents in more than one tavern. It was obvious, too, that Diomedes, ever the opportunist, had regarded the unfortunate incident in the Three Harpies as a heaven-sent opportunity for rabble-rousing—and as an excuse for the withdrawal of all police from the city. And that is all that it was—an excuse. It was doubtful, thought Brasidus, that Grimes had demanded protection. The spaceman was quite capable of looking after himself and his own people—and if the situation got really out of hand he could always lift ship at a second's notice.

But there were still puzzling features in the situation. The military police were under the command of General Rexenor, with the usual tally of colonels and majors subordinate to him. Diomedes was only a captain. How much power did the man wield? How much backing had he? Was he—and this seemed more than likely—answerable only to the palace?

The mob was thinning out now; there were only the stragglers half-running, stumbling over the cobblestones. And already the first of the scavengers were emerging from their hiding places, sniffing cautiously at the crumpled bodies of those who had been crushed and trampled. Brasidus fell in with the tattered rearguard, kept pace with a withered, elderly man in rough and dirty working clothes.

"Don't . . . know . . . why . . . we . . . bother . . ." grunted this individual between gasping breaths. "Bloody . . . hoplites . . . 'll . . . be . . . there . . . first. All . . . the . . . bloody . . . pickings . . . as . . . bloody . . . usual."

"What pickings?"

"Food . . . wine . . . Those . . . bloody . . . doctors . . . worse . . . 'n . . . bloody . . . soldiers. . . . Small . . . wonder . . . the . . . King . . . has . . . turned . . . against . . . 'em."

"And . . . the Arcadians?"

"Wouldn't . . . touch . . . one . . . o' . . . them . . . wi' . . . barge . . . pole. Unsightly . . . monsters."

Ahead, the roar of the mob had risen to an ugly and frightening intensity. There were flames, too, leaping high, a billowing glare in the night sky. The crowd had broken into a villa close by the crèche, the Club House of the senior nursing staff. They had dragged furniture out into the roadway and set fire to it. Some of its unfortunate owners fluttered ineffectually about the blaze and, until one of them had the sense to organize his mates into a bucket party, were treated with rough derision only. And then the crowd turned upon the firemen, beating them, even throwing three of them into the bonfire. Two of them managed to scramble clear and ran, screaming, their robes ablaze. The other just lay there, writhing and shrieking.

Brasidus was sickened. There was nothing that he could do. He was alone and unarmed—and most of the soldiers among the rioters carried their short swords and some of them were already using them, hacking down the surviving nurses who were still foolish enough to try to save their property. There was nothing at all that he could do—and he should have been in uniform, not in these rags, and armed, with a squad of men at his command, doing his utmost to quell the disorder.

Damn Diomedes! he thought. He knew, with sudden clarity, where his real loyalties lay—to the maintenance of law and order and, on a more personal level, to his friend Achron, on duty inside the crèche and soon, almost inevitably, to be treated as had been these hacked and incinerated colleagues of his.

The Andronicus warehouse . . .

Nobody noticed him as he crossed the road to that building; the main body of the rioters was attempting to force the huge door of the crèche with a battering ram improvised from a torn-down streetlamp standard. And then, looking at the massive door set in the black, featureless wall of the warehouse, he realized that he was in dire need of such an implement himself. He could, he knew, enlist the aid of men on the fringes of the crowd eager for some violence in which they, themselves, could take part—but that was the last thing that he wanted. He would enter the crèche alone, if at all.

But how?

How?

Overhead, barely audible, there was a peculiar throbbing noise, an irregular beat. He thought, *So the Navy is intervening*, then realized that the sound was not that of an airship's engines. He looked up, saw flickering, ruddy light reflected from an oval surface. And then, in a whisper that seemed to originate only an inch from his ear, a familiar voice asked, "Is that you, Brasidus?"

"Yes."

"I owe you plenty. We'll pick you up and take you clear of this mess. I had to promise not to intervene—I'm just observing and recording—but I'll always break a promise to help a friend."

"I don't want to be picked up, Peggy."

"Then what the hell do you want?"

"I want to get into this warehouse. But the door is locked, and there aren't any windows, and I haven't any explosives."

"You could get your friends to help. Or don't you want to share the loot?"

"I'm not looting. And I want to get into the crèche by myself, not with a mob."

"I wouldn't mind a look inside myself, before it's too late. Hold on, I'll be right with you." Then, in a fainter voice, she was giving orders to somebody in the flying machine. "I'm going down, George. Get the ladder over, will you? Yes, yes, I know what Commander Grimes said, but Brasidus saved my life. And you just keep stooging around in the pinnace, and be ready to come a-runnin' to pick us up when I yell for you. . . . Yes, yes. Keep the cameras and the recorders running."

"Have you a screwdriver?" asked Brasidus.

"A screwdriver?"

"If you have, bring it."

"All right."

A light, flexible ladder snaked down from the almost invisible hull. Clad in black coveralls, Peggy Lazenby was herself almost invisible as she rapidly dropped down it. As soon as she was standing on the ground the pinnace lifted, vanished into the night sky.

"What now, love?" she asked. "What now?"

"That door," Brasidus told her, pointing.

"With a *screwdriver?* Are you quite mad?"

"We shall need that later. But I was sure that you'd have one of your laser-cameras along."

"As it happens, I haven't. But I do have a laser pistol—which, on low intensity, is a quite useful electric torch." She pulled the weapon from its holster, made an adjustment, played a dim beam on the double door. "H'm. Looks like a conventional enough lock. And I don't think that your little friends will notice a very brief and discreet fireworks display."

She made another adjustment, and the beam became thread thin and blinding. There was a brief coruscation of sparks, a spatter of incandescent globules of molten metal.

"That should be it. Push, Brasidus."

Brasidus pushed. There was resistance that suddenly yielded, and the massive valves swung inwards.

Nobody noticed them enter the warehouse—the entire attention of the mob was centered on the door of the crèche, which was still holding. When they were inside, Brasidus pushed the big doors shut. Then he asked, "How did you find me?"

"I wasn't looking for you. We knew about the riot, of course, and I persuaded John to let me take one of the pinnaces so that I could observe the goings-on. Our liftoff coincided with a test firing of the auxiliary rocket drive—even your Captain Diomedes couldn't blame Commander Grimes for wanting to be all ready for a hasty getaway. And the radar lookout kept by your Navy must be very lax—although, of course, our screen was operating. Anyhow, I was using my infrared viewer, and when I saw a solitary figure slink away from the main party, I wondered what mischief *he* was up to. I focused on him, and, lo and behold, it was you. Not that I recognized you at first. I much prefer you in uniform. Now, what is all this about?"

"I wish that I knew. But the mob's trying to break into the crèche, and I've at least one friend in there whom I'd like to save. Too . . . oh, damn it all, I am a policeman, and I just can't stand by doing nothing."

"What about your precious Diomedes? What part is he playing in all this?"

"Come on," he snarled. "Come *on*. We've wasted enough time already." He found the light switch just inside the door, pressed it, then led the way to the hatch in the floor. They went through it, down into the basement, and then to the big chamber. Peggy helped him to open the door, followed him to the far insulated wall. Yes, that was the panel beyond which lay the tunnel—the slots of the screwheads glittered with betraying bright metal.

At the far end of the tunnel the door into the crèche was not secured and opened easily.

22

IT WAS QUIET in the passageway, but, dull and distant, the ominous thudding of the battering ram could be heard. And there was the sound of crying, faint and faraway, the infants in the wards screaming uncontrollably.

"Which way?" Peggy was asking. "Which way?"

"This way, I think." He set off at a run along the corridor, his bare feet noiseless on the polished floor. She followed at the same pace, her soft-soled shoes making an almost inaudible shuffle. They ran on, past the closed, numbered doors. At the first cross alleyway Brasidus turned right without hesitation—as long as he kept the clangor of forcible entry as nearly ahead as possible, he could not go far wrong.

And then one of the doors opened. From it stepped the tall, yellow-haired Arcadian whom Brasidus had encountered during his first trespass. She was dressed, this time, in a belted tunic, and her feet were shod in heavy sandals. And she carried a knife that was almost a short sword.

"Stop!" she ordered. "Stop!"

Brasidus stopped, heard Margaret Lazenby slither to a halt behind him.

"Who are you? What are you doing here?"

"Brasidus. Lieutenant, Police Battalion of the Army. Take us to whoever's in charge here."

"Oh, I recognize you—that painfully shy workman who strayed in from the warehouse . . . *But who are* you?"

"I'm from the ship."

"What I thought." The blonde stood there, juggling absently with her knife. *And she'll be able to use it*, thought Brasidus. "What I thought," repeated the woman. "So, at long last, the Police and the outworld space captain are arriving in the nick of time to save us all from a fate worse than death."

"I'm afraid not," Peggy Lazenby told her. "Our respective lords and masters have yet to delegate. We're here in our private capacities."

"But you're hung around with all sorts of interesting-looking hardware, dearie. And I can lend Brasidus a meat chopper if he wants it."

Brasidus said that he did. It was not his choice of weapons, but it was better than nothing. The Arcadian went back through the door, through which drifted the sound of excited, high-pitched voices, returned with the dull-gleaming implement. Brasidus took it. The haft fitted his right hand nicely, and the thing had a satisfying heft to it. Suddenly he felt less helpless, less naked.

"And what's your name, by the way?" the blonde Arcadian was asked.

"Lazenby. Peggy Lazenby."

"You can call me Terry. Short for Theresa, not that it matters. Come on."

With her as a guide, they found their way to the vestibule without any delays, bypassing the wards which the infants were making hideous with their screams. But the noise in this entrance hall was deafening enough; it was like being inside a lustily beaten bass drum. Furniture had been piled inside the door, but with each blow of the battering ram, some article would crash to the floor.

There were doctors there, white-faced but, so far, not at the point of panic. There were nurses there, no braver than their superiors, but no more cowardly. They were armed, all of them, after a fashion. Sharp, dangerous-looking surgical instruments gleamed in tight-clenched fists, rude clubs, legs torn from furniture, dangled from hands that had but rarely performed rougher work than changing a baby's diaper.

"Heraklion!" Terry was calling, shouting to make herself heard above the tumult. "Heraklion!"

The tall doctor turned to face her. "What are you doing here, Terry? I thought I told you women to keep out of harm's way." Then he saw Brasidus and Peggy. "Who the hell are these?" He began to advance, the scalpel in his right hand extended menacingly.

"Lieutenant Brasidus. Security."

"Looks like a helot to me," muttered somebody. "Kill the bastard!"

"Wait. Brasidus? Yes, it could be . . ."

"It is, it is!" One of the nurses broke away from his own group, ran to where Heraklion was standing. "It is. Of course, it's Brasidus!"

"Thank you, Achron. You should know. But who are you, madam?"

"Doctor Margaret Lazenby, of the starship *Seeker*."

Heraklion's eyes dwelt long and lovingly on the weapons at her belt. "And have you come to help us?"

"I let myself get talked into it."

"I knew you'd come," Achron was saying to Brasidus. "I *knew* you'd come." And Brasidus was uncomfortably aware of Peggy Lazenby's ironic regard. He said to Heraklion, more to assert himself than for any other reason, "And what is happening, Doctor?"

"*You* ask *me* that, young man? You're Security, aren't you? You're Captain Diomedes' right-hand man, I've heard. What *is* happening?"

Brasidus looked slowly around at the little band of defenders with their makeshift armament. He said, "I know what *will* happen: massacre, with ourselves at the receiving end. That door'll not hold for much longer. Is there anywhere to retreat to?"

"Retreat?" demanded Heraklion scornfully. "Retreat, from a mob of hoplites and helots?"

"They—the hoplites—have weapons, sir. And they know how to use them."

"Your Doctor Lazenby has weapons—*real* weapons."

"Perhaps I have," she said quietly. "But ethology happens to be my specialty. I've studied the behavior of mobs. A machine gun is a fine weapon to use against them—but a hand gun, no matter how deadly, only infuriates them."

"There's the birth-machine room," suggested somebody. "I've heard said that it would withstand a hydrogen-bomb blast."

"Impossible!" snapped Heraklion. "Nobody here is sterile, and to take the time to scrub up and break out robes at this time . . ."

"The birth machine won't be much use with nobody around to operate it," said Brasidus.

Heraklion pondered this statement, and while he was doing so a heavy desk crashed from the top of the pile of furniture barricading the door. Halfheartedly, three of the nurses struggled to replace it, and dislodged a table and a couple of chairs. "All right," he said suddenly. "The B-M room it is. Terry, run along and round up the other women and get them there at once. Doctor Hermes, get along there yourself with all these people."

"And what about the children?" Achron, in his agitation, was clutching Heraklion's sleeve. "What about the children?"

"H'm. Yes. I suppose that somebody had better remain on duty in each ward."

"No, Doctor," said Brasidus. "It won't do at all. Those wild animals out there hate the nurses as much as they hate you. To the hoplites, they're helots who live better than soldiers do. To the helots, they're overprivileged members of their own caste. Those nurses with the villa outside and the crèche have all been killed. I saw it happen."

"But the *children* . . ." Achron's voice was a wail.

"They'll be safe enough. They might miss a meal or a diaper change, but it won't kill 'em."

"And if there's no other way out of it," put in Peggy Lazenby, "we'll make them our personal charge." She winced as an uproar from the nearer ward almost drowned out the heavy thudding of the battering ram. "I sincerely hope that it never comes to that!"

One of the nurses screamed. The pile of furniture was tottering. The men below it tried to shore it with their bodies, but not for long. A spear probed through the widening gap between the two valves, somehow found its mark in soft human flesh. There was another scream, of pain, this time, not terror. There were other spearheads thrusting hopefully and not altogether blindly. There was a scurrying retreat from the crumbling barricade. Suddenly it collapsed, burying the wounded man, and the great valves edged slowly and jerkily inwards, all the pressure of the mob behind them, pushing aside and clearing a way through the wreckage. And through the widening aperture gusted the triumphant howling and shouting, and a great billow of acrid smoke.

The mob leaders were through, scrambling over the broken furniture, their dulled weapons at the ready. There were a half dozen common soldiers, armed with swords. There was a fat sergeant, some kind of pistol in his right hand. He fired, the report sharp in spite of the general uproar. He fired again.

Beside Brasidus, Peggy Lazenby gasped, caught hold of him with her left hand as she staggered. Then her own pistol was out, and the filament of incandescence took the sergeant full in the chest. But he came on, still he came on, still firing, the hoplites falling back to allow him passage, while the Arcadian fumbled with her gun, trying to transfer it from her right hand to her left. He came on, and Brasidus ducked uselessly as two bullets whined past his head in quick succession.

Then he fell to his knees as Achron shoved him violently to one side. The nurse's frail body jerked and shuddered as the projectiles thudded into him, but he, like the sergeant, refused to die. He lifted the table leg with which he had armed himself, brought it smashing down with all his strength onto the other's head. The wood splintered, but enough remained for a second blow, and a third. No more were necessary. The sergeant sagged to the floor, and Achron, with a tired sigh, collapsed on top of the gross body.

"He's dead," muttered Brasidus, kneeling beside his friend. "He's dead."

But mourning would have to wait. Hastily he shifted Achron's body to one side so that he could get at the sergeant's pistol. And then he saw the face of the dead man, recognizable in spite of the blood that had trickled down it.

It was Diomedes.

He got to his feet, ready to use the pistol. But he did not have to. Firing left-handed, Peggy Lazenby had shot down the other mob leaders, then used the weapon to ignite the tangle of wrecked furniture and the floor itself.

"That should hold 'em," she muttered. "Now lead us out of here, Doctor."

"But you're wounded," Brasidus cried, looking for telltale patches of wetness on the dark material of her clothing.

"Just bruised. I'm wearing my bulletproof undies. But come on, you two. Hurry!"

23

SUDDENLY THE SPRINKLERS came on, saturating the air of the vestibule with aqueous mist and choking, acrid steam. But this was a help to the retreating defenders, a hindrance to the mob. Frightened, the rioters drew back. They had been ready enough to charge barefooted through and over blazing wreckage; now (but too briefly) the automatic firefighting system instilled in them the fear of the unknown. *An acid spray*, they must have thought, *or some lethal gas*. When their shouts made it obvious that they were inside the crèche, Heraklion and his party were already halfway along the first of the lengthy corridors.

The Doctor, it was obvious, knew his way. Without him, Brasidus and Peggy Lazenby would have been hopelessly lost. He turned into cross alleyways without hesitation, finally led them up a ramp, at the head of which was a massive door. It was shut, of course. Heraklion cursed, wrestled with the hand wheel that obviously actuated the securing device. It refused to budge.

Peggy Lazenby pulled out her laser pistol. Heraklion stared at her ironically. "Sure," he said. "Go ahead—if you've all day to play around in. But long before you've made even a faint impression, you'll wish that you'd kept the charge in that weapon for something more useful."

The mob was closer now. They did not know the direction their quarry had taken, but they were spreading through the vast building, looting and smashing. Sooner or later some of them would stumble upon the ramp leading up to the room housing the birth machine. *Sooner*, thought Brasidus, *rather than later*. He examined the pistol that he had taken from Diomedes. It was a standard officers' model Vulcan. One round up the spout, four remaining in the magazine. He regretted having dropped the cleaver that Terry had found for him.

"Here they are," announced Peggy unemotionally. She fired down the ramp, a slashing beam that scarred the paint work of the walls at the foot of the incline. There was a scream, and, shockingly, here was the rapid, vicious chatter of a machine carbine. But whoever was using it was not anxious to expose himself, and the burst buried itself harmlessly in the ceiling.

"I thought that only *your* people were allowed firearms," said Heraklion bitterly to Brasidus. Brasidus said nothing. If Diomedes, armed, had been among the mob leaders, how many of his trusted lieutenants were also involved?

Still Heraklion wrestled with the hand wheel, and still Peggy and Brasidus, pistols ready, kept their watch for hostile activity. But everything was quiet, too quiet—until at last, from the alleyway that ran athwart the foot of the ramp, there came an odd shuffling, scraping sound. Slowly, slowly the source of it edged into view. It was a heavy shield mounted on a light trolley. Whoever had constructed it had known something about modern weaponry; a slab of concrete, torn up from a floor somewhere, was its main component. Of course, it could not withstand laser fire indefinitely, but long before it crumbled and disintegrated, the riflemen behind it would have disposed of the laser weapon and its user.

There was a small, ragged hole roughly in the center of the slab. Brasidus nudged Peggy, drew her attention to it. She nodded. Suddenly something metallic protruded from the aperture, something that flared and sputtered as the laser beam found it. But Brasidus, at the last moment, switched his own attention from the decoy to the rim of the shield, loosed off two hasty but accurate shots at the carbine that was briefly exposed, at the hands holding it.

Then Heraklion cried out. Under his hands the wheel had moved, was moving of its own accord. The enormously thick door was opening. The Doctor grabbed his companions, pulled them through the slowly widening gap, pushed them clear of the narrow entrance as a deadly hail of bullets splattered around it. Then he turned on the colleague who had, at last, admitted them. "Shut it! At once!" And, as the man obeyed, he demanded coldly, "You were a long time opening up. Why?"

"We had to be sure that it was you. We couldn't get the closed-circuit TV working."

"Even on this primitive planet," commented Peggy Lazenby, "one can find oneself at the mercy of a single fuse."

The little crowd of refugees, with their nervous chatter, seemed out of place in these surroundings. There was an air of mystery—of holy mystery, even—that could not be dispelled by the intrusion. Tier upon tier towered the vats, empty now, but spotlessly clean and gleaming. Mile after convoluted mile ran the piping—glittering glass, glowing plastic, bright-shining metal. Bank upon bank stood the pumps, silent now, but ready, in perfect order, awaiting the touch of a switch to carry out their functions as mechanical hearts and lungs and excretory organs.

"There's no place like womb," remarked Margaret Lazenby.

"What was that, Peggy?"

"Never mind. You're too young to understand." Then, crisply official, "Doctor Heraklion, what now?"

"I . . . I don't know, Doctor Lazenby."

"You're in charge. Or are you?"

"I . . . I suppose that I am. I'm the senior doctor present."

"And Brasidus is the senior Security officer present, and I'm the senior Interstellar Federation's Survey Service officer present. And what about you, Terry? Are you the senior anything?"

"I don't know. But the other girls usually do what I tell them to."

"So we're getting some place. But where? Where? That's the sixty-four-dollar question." She took two nervous strides forward, two nervous strides back. "I suppose that this glorified incubator is on the phone, Doctor Heraklion?"

"It is, Doctor Lazenby. Unluckily the main switchboard for the crèche is just off the vestibule."

"A pity. I was thinking that you might get through to the military. Or even to the palace itself."

"We tried that as soon as we were warned that the mob was heading our way. But we got no satisfaction. In fact, we gained the impression that the top military brass was having its own troubles."

"They could be, at that," contributed Brasidus. "That sergeant who was leading the rioters, the one with the pistol—it was Diomedes."

"What!"

Heraklion was incredulous, Margaret Lazenby was not. She said, "It makes sense, of a kind. This wouldn't be the first time that an ambitious, comparatively junior officer has organized a coup. And I think I know what makes him tick—or made him tick. There was the lust for power, of course. But, with it, there was a very deep and very real patriotism. I'm a woman, and I had to meet him officially. I could tell, each time, how much he hated me and feared me. No, not personally, but as a member of the opposite sex.

"There are some men—and he was one of them—to whom a world

like yours would be the ultimate paradise. *Men Only.* There are some men to whom this stratified social system of yours—cribbed, with improvements, from the *real* Spartans—would seem the only possible way of running a planet.

"But . . ."

"But, Doctor Heraklion, there are other men, such as you, who would find the monosexual, homosexual setup rather unsatisfying. And you, my good Doctor, were in a position to do something about it."

Heraklion smiled faintly. "It's been going on for a very long time, Doctor Lazenby. It all started long before I was born."

"All right. The doctors were able to do something about it. I still don't *know* how this birth machine of yours works, but I can guess. I suppose that all approved Spartans make contributions of sperm cells."

"That is so."

"And the most important contribution—correct me if I am wrong—will be the annual shipments made by the aptly named *Latterhaven Venus* and *Latterhaven Hera.* Venus and Hera were Greek goddesses, by the way, Brasidus. Women—like me, and like Terry and the other playmates. How did the ships get their names, Heraklion?"

"We have always suspected the Latterhaveneers of a warped sense of humor."

"I wonder what the mob is doing?" asked somebody anxiously.

"We're safe enough here," said Heraklion curtly.

Are we? thought Brasidus, suddenly apprehensive. *Are we?* It seemed to him that the floor under his bare soles had become uncomfortably warm. He shifted his stance. Yes, the floor *was* heating up. He looked down, saw a crack in the polished surface. Surely it had not been there before. And if it had been, there had not been a thin wisp of smoke trickling from it.

He was about to tell Heraklion when a device on Peggy Lazenby's wrist—it looked like a watch but obviously was not—buzzed sharply. She raised her forearm to her face. "Doctor Lazenby here."

"Captain here. What the hell are you doing? Where are you?"

"Quite safe, John. I'm holed up in the crèche, in the birth-machine room."

"The crèche is an inferno. Admiral Ajax requested my aid to evacuate the children and to restore order in the city. We're on the way now."

The floor tilted, slightly but sharply. One of the vats shattered loudly and the piping dependent from it swung, clattering and tinkling, against the vessels in the tier below, breaking them. The smell of smoke was suddenly very strong.

"Is there only one way out of this place?" demanded Peggy sharply.

"No. There's a hatch in the roof. Through the records room." Heraklion told her.

"Then that's the way that we have to go to escape from this alleged H-bombproof shelter of yours." Into her wrist transceiver she said, "You'll have to pick us off the roof, John. And while you're about it, you can send a squad of Marines down to save the firm's books. No, I'm not joking."

Luckily the hatch was clear, and luckily the ladder was readily available. Through the little room they passed—the women, the surviving nurses and doctors, then, last of all, Heraklion, Peggy and Brasidus. Brasidus had almost to pull her away from the shelves of microfilmed records, and from the glass case in which was displayed the big, flat book on the cover of which, in tarnished gold, were the words, *Log of Interstellar Colonization Ship DORIC. First Captain Deems Harris.*

They were on the roof then—the tilting, shuddering roof, swept by scorching eddies and black, billowing smoke. The night sky above them was alive with the noise of engines, and from below sounded, ever louder and more frightening, the roar of the fire. Cautiously Heraklion made his way down the listing surface to the low parapet. Brasidus followed him. The two men cautiously peered over, flinching back when a sudden gust of flame seared their faces, crisping their hair and eyebrows.

Grimes had sent down a landing party. Disciplined, uniformed men and women were handling chemical fire extinguishers, others, in a chain, were passing the children out of the blazing building. And still others had set up weapons to protect the rescuers; the rattle of heavy automatic fire was loud and insistent above the other noises.

Peggy Lazenby had joined the two men. "Intervention," she murmured. "Armed intervention. Poor John. He'll be in the soup over this. But what else could he do? He couldn't let those babies burn to death . . ."

"As we shall do," stated Heraklion grimly, "unless your captain does something about it, and fast." As he spoke the roof tilted another few degrees.

But the peculiar, irregular throbbing of the inertial drive was louder now, was deafening. Directly overhead, the glare of the fire reflected from the burnished metal of her hull, *Seeker* dropped through the vortex of smoke and sparks. Lower she sagged, and lower, until men and women cried out in fear and ran in panic to escape from the inexorably descending pads of her vaned landing gear. Lower she sagged, and lower—and from her open main airlock the boarding ramp was suddenly extruded, the lower end of it scant millimeters only from the heaving, cracking surface of the roof. Even Brasidus knew that he was privileged to watch an exhibition of superb spacemanship.

Down the extended ramp ran six men. Peggy Lazenby met them, cried, "This way!" and led them to the still open hatchway. And a vastly amplified voice was booming from the ship, "Board at once, please! Board at once!"

Heraklion hustled his people into some sort of order, got them onto the gangway, the women first. He stayed with Brasidus, making sure that the evacuation proceeded in an orderly manner. Still the two men waited, although the loudspeaker was blaring. "Get a move on, there! Get a move on!"

At last the six men and Peggy Lazenby were emerging from the hatch, she last of all. They were heavily burdened, all of them, and she, clasping it to her as tenderly as she had clasped the rescued child, carried the antique log book.

"What are you waiting here for?" she demanded of Heraklion.

He said, "We have no spaceships, but we have read books. We know of the traditions. This crèche is *my* ship, and I shall be the last to leave."

"Have it your own way," she told him.

She and Brasidus went up the ramp after the six marines. Heraklion followed them. Just as he reached the airlock, a geyser of flame erupted from the open hatch and the once flat surface of the roof cracked and billowed and, as *Seeker* hastily lifted, collapsed.

"That *was* my ship," whispered the Doctor.

"You can build another," Peggy told him.

"No," he said. "No. No longer do we have any excuse not to revert to the old ways."

"And *your* old ways," she said, "are not the old ways of Diomedes and his party. That is why he hated and feared you. But can you do it?"

"With your help," he said.

"That," she said, "is a matter for the politicians back home. But let's get out of this damned airlock and into the ship, before we fall out. It's a long way down."

Brasidus, looking at the burning building far below, shuddered and drew back hastily. It was, as she had said, a long way down.

24

THE NIGHT OF the Long Knives was over, the Night of the Long Knives and the four action packed days and nights that had followed. The power had fallen into the streets, and Admiral Ajax, warned by his own intelligence service of the scheduled assassinations of himself and his senior captains, had swooped down from the sky to pick it up. The birth machine was destroyed, the caste system had crumbled, and only the patrolling airships of the Navy kept Sparta safe from the jealous attentions of the other city-states. Cresphontes—a mere figurehead—skulked in his palace, dared make no public appearances.

Grimes and his *Seeker* had played little active part in quelling the disturbances, but always the spaceship had been there, hanging ominously in the clouds, always her pinnaces had darted from one trouble spot to another, her Marines acting as ambulance men and firemen—but ambulance men and firemen backed by threatening weaponry to ensure that they carried out their tasks unmolested.

Brasidus had rejoined his own police unit, and, to his surprise, had found that greater and greater power and responsibilities were being thrust upon him. But it made sense. He knew the spacemen, had worked with them—and it was obvious to all that, in the final analysis, they and the great Federation that they represented were the most effective striking force on the planet. They did not strike, they were careful not to fire a single gun or loose a single missile, but they were there, and where they had come from there were more and bigger ships with even heavier armaments.

The universe had come to Sparta, and the Spartans, in spite of centuries of isolationist indoctrination, had accepted the fact. Racial memory, Margaret Lazenby had said, long and deep-buried recollections of the home world, of the planet where men and women lived and worked together in amity, where the womb was part of the living female body and not a complex, inorganic machine.

And then there was the last conference in John Grimes' day cabin aboard *Seeker*. The Lieutenant Commander sat behind his paper-littered desk, making a major production of filling and lighting his pipe. Beside him was Margaret Lazenby, trim and severe in uniform. In chairs facing the desk were the rotund little Admiral Ajax, the tall, saturnine Heraklion, and Brasidus. A stewardess brought coffee, and the four men and the woman sipped it appreciatively.

Then Grimes said, "I've received my orders, Admiral. Somewhat garbled, as messages by psionic radio too often are, but definite enough. I have to hand over to the civil authorities and then get the hell out." He smiled bleakly. "I've done enough damage already. I fear that I shall have to do plenty of explaining to my lords Commissioners."

"No, Commander." Heraklion's voice was firm, definite. "You did not do the damage. The situation, thanks to Diomedes, was already highly explosive. You were only the . . . the . . ."

"The detonator," supplied Ajax.

"Just how explosive was it?" inquired Grimes. "I'd like to know. After all, I shall have a report to make." He switched on a small recorder that stood among the litter on his desk.

"Very explosive. Some of us at the crèche had decided to make women, not only for ourselves, but for every man on Sparta. We had decided to revert to the old ways. Diomedes knew of this. I still think that he was actuated by patriotism—a perverted patriotism, but patriotism nonetheless."

Peggy Lazenby laughed scornfully. "Fine words, Doctor. But what about the female baby who was exposed, the one that Brasidus and I rescued?"

"Yes, the Exposure. *That* was a custom that we intended to stamp out. But the unfortunate child, as well as being female, was mentally subnormal. She'd have been better off dead."

"So you say. But you forget that the planets of the Federation have made great strides in medical science during the centuries that you have been stagnating."

"Enough, Peggy. Enough," said Grimes tiredly. He put his pipe into a dirty ashtray, began to sort his papers. "As I told you, my orders are to hand over to the civil authorities. Who are they? The King? The Council?" The Spartans smiled scornfully. "All right. I suppose that you gentlemen will have to do. You, Doctor Heraklion, and you, Admiral Ajax, and you—just what rank *do* you hold these days? I've rather lost track, Brasidus. But before I hand over, I want to be sure that the Admiral and friend Brasidus know what it's all about. Heraklion knows, of course, but even the most honest of us is liable to bend the facts.

"This ship, as you know, is a unit of the fleet of the Federation's Survey Service. As such she carries, on microfilm, a most comprehensive library. One large section of it is devoted to colonizing ships that are missing. We're still stumbling upon what are called the Lost Colonies, and it's helpful if we have more than a vague idea as to their origin. This Sparta of yours is, of course, a Lost Colony. We've been able to piece together your history both from our own reference library and from the records salvaged from the crèche.

"So far, the history of colonization comes under three headings, the First Expansion, the Second Expansion and the Third Expansion. The First Expansion was initiated before there was a practicable FTL—faster than light—drive. The Second Expansion was carried out by vessels fitted with the rather unreliable Ehrenhaft Drive, the so-called gaussjammers. The Third Expansion made use of timejammers, ships with the almost foolproof Mannschenn Drive.

"The vessels of the First Expansion, the deep-freeze ships, went a long way in a long time, a very long time. They carried at least three full crews—captains, watch-keeping officers, maintenance engineers and the like. The colonists, men and women, were in stasis, just refrigerated cargo, in effect. The crews spent their off-duty months in stasis. But there was, of course, always one full crew on duty.

"As a result of some incredible stupidity on somebody's part, the crews of many of the early ships were all male. In the later ones, of course, the balance of the sexes was maintained. *Doric*—the ship from which this Lost Colony was founded—had an all male crew, under First Captain—he was the senior of the four masters—Deems Harris. This same Captain Harris was, probably, a misogynist, a woman hater, when the voyage started. If he were not, what happened probably turned him into one.

"Third Captain Flynn seems to have exercised little control over his officers—or, perhaps, he was the ringleader. Be that as it may, Flynn decided, or was persuaded, to alleviate the monotony of his tour of duty by reviving a dozen of the more attractive colonist girls. It seems to have been quite a party while it lasted—so much so that normal ship's routine went by the board, vitally important navigational instruments, such as the Very Long Range Radar, were untended, ignored. The odds against encountering a meteoric swarm in deep space are astronomical—but *Doric* encountered one. Whether or not she would have been able to take avoiding action is doubtful, but with some warning *something* could have been done to minimize the effects of the inevitable collision. A collision there was—and the sphere in which the female colonists were housed was badly damaged, so badly damaged that there were no survivors. I should have explained before that these deep-freeze ships didn't look anything like a vessel such as this one; they consisted of globes held together by light girders. They were assembled in orbit and were never intended to make a landing on any planetary surface.

"Anyhow, Captain Flynn aroused Captain Harris and the other masters and their officers after the damage had been done. Captain Harris, understandably, took a somewhat dim view of his junior and formed the opinion that if Flynn had not awakened those women the collision would not have occurred. Oddly enough, as his private journal indicates, he blamed the unfortunate wenches even more than he blamed Flynn. He despised Flynn for his weakness and irresponsibility—but those poor girls he *hated.* They were thrown into some sort of improvised brig.

"Meanwhile, *Doric* was far from spaceworthy. Apart from the slow leakage of precious atmosphere, much of her machinery was out of kilter, the automated 'farm,' upon which the crew depended for their food and their atmospheric regeneration, especially. Although the world that you know as Sparta was not the ship's original objective—oddly enough, long-range instrumental surveys had missed it—*Doric*'s quite excellent equipment picked it up, made it plain to Captain Harris that he could reach it before air and food and water ran out. So, putting all hands save himself and one officer back into stasis, he adjusted his trajectory and ran for this only possible haven.

"His troubles were far from over. The shuttles—relatively small rocket craft used as ferries between the big ship in orbit and the world below—had all been ruined by that meteoric shower. Nonetheless—it was a remarkable feat of spacemanship—he succeeded in getting that unhandy, unspaceworthy and unairworthy near wreck down through the atmosphere to a relatively soft landing.

"At first glance, the survivors were not too badly off. The planet was habitable. The fertilized ova of various animals—sheep, pigs, cattle, dogs and cats, even—had all been destroyed by the crash landing, but the local fauna was quite edible. And the ship had carried a large stock of seed grain. There was a decided imbalance of the sexes—the only women were Captain Flynn's hapless ones, and there were all of five thousand men—but even that would right itself in time. The ship—as did all ships of that era—carried equipment that was the prototype of your birth machine, and there were supplies of deep-frozen sperm and ova sufficient to populate a dozen worlds.

"But . . .

"Twelve women, and five thousand and forty-eight men.

"Rank, said Captain Flynn and some of the other officers, should have its privileges. It most certainly should not, said the colonists—among them, of course, the twelve men whose wives the women had been.

"There was trouble, starting off with a few isolated murders, culminating in a full-scale revolt against the officers and those loyal to them. Somehow the twelve girls were . . . eliminated. Deems Harris doesn't say as much in his journal, but I gained the impression that he was behind it.

"Now, this Deems Harris. It is hard for us in this day and age of quick passages to get inside the skins, the minds of those old-time space captains. Probably none of them was quite sane. Most of them were omnivorous, indiscriminating readers, although some of them specialized. This Deems Harris seems to have done so. In history. By this time, with his colony off to a disastrous beginning, he seems to have hankered after some sort of culture in which women played a very small part—or no part at all. One such culture was that of Sparta, one of the ancient Greek city-states back on Earth. Greek women were little more than childbearing, housekeeping machines—and the Spartan women suffered the lowest status of them all. Sparta was the state that specialized in all the so-called manly virtues—and little else. Sparta was *the* military power. Furthermore, the original Spartans were a wandering tribe called Dorians. Dorians—*Doric*—See the tie-up? And their first King was Aristodemus. Aristodemus—Deems Harris.

"The first Aristodemus, presumably, kept women in their proper place—down, well down. This latter-day Aristodemus would go one better. He would do without women at all." Grimes looked at Margaret Lazenby. "At times I think that he had something."

"He didn't have women, that's for certain. But go on."

"All right. Aristodemus—as we shall call him now—was lucky enough to command the services of like-minded biochemists. The sperm, of course, was all neatly classified—male and female being among the classifications. Soon that first birth machine was turning out a steady stream of fine, bouncing baby boys. When the adult populace started to get a bit restive, it was explained that the stock of female sperm had been destroyed in the crash. And somebody made sure that the stock *was* destroyed."

"But," Brasidus interrupted, "but we used to reproduce by fission. Our evolution from the lower animals has been worked out in detail."

"Don't believe everything you read," Peggy Lazenby told him.

"Your biology textbooks are like your history textbooks—very cunningly constructed fairy tales."

"Yes," said Grimes. "Fairy tales. Aristodemus and his supporters were able to foist an absolutely mythical history upon the rising generations. It seems fantastic, but remember that there was no home life. They—like you, Brasidus, and like you, Admiral—knew only the Spartan state as a parent. There were no fathers and mothers, no grandfathers and no grandmothers to tell them stories of how things used to be. Also, don't forget that the official history fitted the facts very neatly. It should have done—after all, it was tailor-made.

"And so it went on, for year after year, for generation after generation, until it became obvious to the doctors in charge of the birth machine that it couldn't go on for much longer. That bank of male sperm was near exhaustion. This first crisis was surmounted—ways and means were devised whereby every citizen made his contribution to the plasm bank. A centrifuge was used to separate X-chromosome-bearing sperm cells from those carrying the Y-chromosome. Then the supply of ova started to run out. But still the race was in no real danger of extinction. All that had to be done was to allow a few female children to be born. In fact, this did happen now and again by accident—but such unfortunates had always been exposed on the hillside as defective infants. Even so, the doctors of those days were reluctant to admit female serpents into this all-male paradise.

"And now Latterhaven comes into the story. I'm sorry to have to disappoint you all, but there never was a villainous Admiral Latterus. And, apart from the ill-fated *Doric*, there never were any spaceships owned by Sparta. But while Aristodemus was building his odd imitation of the original, Terran Sparta, the First Expansion ran its course. Then, with the perfection (not that it ever was perfect) of the Ehrenhaft Drive came the Second Expansion. Finally, there was the Third Expansion, and there was the star ship *Utah*, commanded by Captain Amos Latter. It was Latter and his people who founded the colony—one run on rather more orthodox lines than yours—on Latterhaven, a world only a couple of light years from this one.

"The Latterhaveneers made explorations of the sector of space around their new home. One such expedition stumbled upon Sparta. The explorers were lucky not to be slaughtered out of hand—the records indicate that they almost met such a fate—but they were not, and they dickered with the Spartan top brass, and all parties eventually signed a trade agreement. In return for the spice harvest, Latterhaven would send two ships each Spartan year with consignments of unfertilized ova.

"The situation could have continued indefinitely if we hadn't come in—or if Diomedes hadn't found out about the doctors' secret harem."

"The situation would not have continued," stated Heraklion. "As I've told you, Commander, it was our intention to introduce a reversion to the normal way of birth."

"That's your story and you stick to it. It could be true, I suppose; it would account for the way that Diomedes hated you." He refilled and relit his pipe. "The question is, what happens now?"

"What does happen?" asked Admiral Ajax.

"To begin with, I've been recalled to base. I shall have to make my report. It is possible that the Federation will replace your birth machine—although, come to that, you should be able to import materials and technicians from Latterhaven. You might even be able to build a new one for yourselves. But . . .

"But the Federation is apt to be a little intolerant of transplanted human cultures that deviate too widely from the norm. Your monosexual society, for example—and, especially, your charming custom of Exposure. This is your world and, as far as I'm concerned, you're welcome to it. I'm a firm believer in the fifth freedom—the freedom to go to hell your own way. But you've never heard a politician up on his hind legs blathering about the Holy Spirit of Man. If you want to reconstruct your society in your own way, in your own time, you'll have to fight—not necessarily with swords and spears, with guns and missiles—for the privilege.

"I advise strongly that you send a representative with us, somebody who'll be able to talk sense with my lords and masters, somebody who'll be able to take a firm line."

"There's Brasidus," said Peggy Lazenby softly, looking directly at him: *You and I have unfinished business*, her eyes said.

"Yes. There's Brasidus," agreed Grimes. "After all, he knows us."

And he'll get to know us better. The unspoken words, her unuttered thought, sounded like a caressing voice in Brasidus' mind.

"But we need him," said Heraklion.

"A first-class officer," confirmed Ajax. "He has what's left of the Police eating out of his hand."

"I think that one of *my* colleagues would be a better choice as emissary," said Heraklion.

"So," murmured Grimes. "So . . ." He looked steadily across his desk at the Spartans. "It's up to you, Lieutenant or Colonel or whatever you are. It's up to you. I'm sure that Admiral Ajax will be able to manage without you—on the other hand, I'm sure that Doctor Heraklion's friend will prove a quite suitable envoy.

"It's up to you."

It's up to me, Brasidus thought. He looked at the woman sitting beside the space commander—and suddenly he was afraid. Diomedes' words about the frightening powers wielded by this sex lingered still in his mind. But, in the final analysis, it was not fear that prompted his answer, but a strong sense of responsibility, of loyalty to his own world. He knew—as the aliens did not, could never know—how precarious still was the balance of power. He knew that, with himself in command—effective if not titular—of the ground forces, peace might be maintained, the reconstruction be commenced.

"It's up to you," said Peggy Lazenby.

He said firmly, "I'd better stay."

She laughed, and Brasidus wondered if he alone were aware of the tinkling malice that brought an angry flush to his face. "Have it your own way, sweet. But I warn you, when those tough, pistol-toting biddies of the Galactic Peace Corps get here, you'll wonder what's struck you."

"That will do, Peggy." Grimes' voice snapped with authority. "That will do. Now, gentlemen, you must excuse us. We have to see our ship secured for space. How soon can you get your envoy here, Doctor Heraklion?"

"About an hour, Commander."

"Very good. We shall lift ship as soon as he's on board." He got to his feet, shook hands with the three Spartans. "It's been a pleasure working with you. It's a great pity that it was not in pleasanter circumstances."

This was dismissal. Ajax in the lead, the three men walked out of Grimes' cabin. Brasidus, bringing up the rear, heard Peggy Lazenby say softly, "The poor bastard!"

And he heard Grimes reply, in a voice that held an unexpected bitterness, "I don't know. I don't know. He could be lucky."

For a long while Brasidus wondered what they meant, but the day came at last when he found out.

The Inheritors

For my favorite aelurophobe

1

GRIMES WAS ON the carpet—neither for the first nor the last time.

He stood stiffly in front of the vast, highly polished desk behind which sat Admiral Buring, of the Federation's Survey Service. His prominent ears were angrily flushed but his rugged face was expressionless.

The admiral's pudgy hands played with the bulky folder that was before him. His face, smooth and heavy, was as expressionless as Grimes's. His voice was flat.

He said, "Commodore Damien warned me about you when you were transferred to my command. Not that any warning was necessary. For one so young you have achieved a considerable degree of notoriety." He paused expectantly, but Grimes said nothing. Buring continued, but now with a hint of feeling in his voice. "My masters—who, incidentally, are also yours—are far from amused at your latest antics. You know—you *should* know—that interference, especially by junior officers, in the internal affairs of any world whatsoever, regardless of the cultural or technological level of the planet in question, is not tolerated. I concede that there were extenuating circumstances, and that the new rulers of Sparta speak quite highly of you. . . ." The thick eyebrows, like furry, black caterpillars, arched incredulously. "Nonetheless . . ."

The silence was so thick as to be almost tangible. Grimes decided that it was incumbent upon himself to break it.

"Sir?"

"Nonetheless, Lieutenant Commander, your continued presence at Base is something of an embarrassment, especially since a party of vips, political vips at that, is due here very shortly. Some commission or other, touring the galaxy at the taxpayer's expense. I don't want you around so that politicians can ask you silly questions—to which, I have no doubt, you would give even sillier answers.

"Furthermore, this whole Spartan affair has blown up into a minor crisis in interplanetary politics. Both the Duchy of Waldegren and the Empire of Waverley are talking loudly about spheres of influence." The admiral allowed himself the suspicion of a smile. "In any sort of crisis, Grimes, there is one thing better than presence of mind. . . ."

"And that is, sir?" asked Grimes at last.

"Absence of body. Ha. So I'm doing you a good turn, sending you out in *Seeker*, on a Lost Colony hunt. There have been persistent rumors of one out in the Argo Sector. Go and find it—or get lost yourself. I'm easy."

"Maintenance, sir . . ." said Grimes slowly. "Repairs . . . stores . . . manning. . . ."

"They're your business, Captain. No, I'm not promoting you, merely according you the courtesy title due to the commanding officer of a ship. You look after those no doubt boring details. And"—he made a major operation of looking at his watch—"I want you off Lindisfarne by sixteen-hundred hours local time tomorrow."

Grimes looked at his own watch. He had just seventeen hours, twelve minutes and forty-three seconds in which to ensure that his ship was, in all respects, ready for space. Maintenance, he knew, was well in hand. There were no crew deficiencies. Taking aboard essential stores would not occupy much time.

Even so . . .

"I'd better be getting on with it, sir," he said.

"You'd bloody well better. I'll send your orders down to you later."

Grimes put on his cap, saluted smartly and strode out of the admiral's office.

2

SHE WAS A survey ship rather than a warship, was *Seeker*. The Survey Service, in its first beginnings, had been just that—a survey service. But aliens being what they are—and humans being what *they* are—police work, on large and small scales, had tended to become more important than mere exploration and charting. The Survey Service, however, had not quite forgotten its original function. It maintained a few ships designed for peaceful rather than warlike pursuits, and *Seeker* was a member of this small squadron. Nonetheless, even she packed quite a wallop.

Lieutenant Commander John Grimes was her captain. His last assignment, during which he had stumbled upon a most peculiar Lost Colony, had been census taking. Now he had been actually sent out to *find* a Lost Colony. He suspected that *anything* might happen, and probably would. It wasn't that he was accident prone. He was just a catalyst.

Nothing had happened yet; after all, it was early in the voyage. He had lifted from Lindisfarne exactly on time, driving through the atmosphere smoothly and easily, maintaining his departure trajectory until he was clear of the Base Planet's Van Allens. Then, with the inertial drive shut down, the ship had been turned about her short axis until she was lined up, with due allowance for drift, on the target star. The Mannschenn Drive had been started, the inertial drive restarted—and passage was commenced.

Satisfied, he had filled and lit his pipe, and when it was going well had ordered, "Deep space routine, Mr. Saul." He had made his way to his quarters below and abaft the control room and then, ensconced in his easy chair, had opened the envelope containing his orders.

The first sheet of the bundle of papers had contained nothing startling. *You will proceed to the vicinity of the star Gamma Argo and conduct a preliminary survey of the planets in orbit about same, devoting especial attention to any of such bodies capable of supporting human life.* "Mphm . . ." he grunted. The rest of the page consisted of what he referred to as "the usual guff."

At the head of the next page was the sentence that brought an expression of interest to his face. *We have reason to believe that there is a humanoid—or possibly human—settlement on the fourth planet of this system. Should this settlement exist it is probable that it is a hitherto undiscovered Lost Colony. You are reminded that your duties are merely to conduct an investigation, and that you are not, repeat not, to interfere in the internal affairs of the colony.*

"Mphm," grunted Grimes again. Noninterference was all very well, but at times it was hard to maintain one's status as a mildly interested spectator.

Appended hereto are reports from our agents at Port Llangowan, on Siluria, at Port Brrooun, on Drroomoorr, at Port Mackay, on Rob Roy, at Port Forinbras, on Elsinore, at . . .

"Mphm." The Intelligence Branch seemed to be earning its keep, for a change. Grimes turned to the first report and read:

From Agent X1783 (Commander, I.B., F.S.S.)
Dated at Port Llangowan, May 5, Year 171 Silurian (17/13/57 TS)
To O.I.C. Intelligence, Federation's Survey Service, Port Woomera, Centralia, Earth.
Sir,

POSSIBLE LOST COLONY IN ARGO SECTOR

I have to report the possibility that there is a hitherto undiscovered Lost Colony in the Argo Sector, apparently on a planet in orbit about Gamma Argo.

It is my custom, whilst stationed on this world, to spend my evenings in the Red Dragon tavern, a hostelry that seems to be the favorite drinking place of whatever merchant spacemen are in port.

On the evening of May 3 several officers from the Dog Star Line's Pomeranian *were lined up at the bar, and were joined there by officers of the same company's* Corgi, *newly berthed. As was to be expected, the personnel of the two vessels were old friends or acquaintances.*

The table at which I was seated was too far from the bar for me to overhear the conversation, but I was able to make use of my Mark XVII recorder, playing the recording back later that night in the privacy of my lodgings. The spool has been sent to you under separate cover, but herewith is a suitably edited transcript of what was said, with everything of no importance—e.g. the usual friendly blasphemies, obscenities and petty company gossip—deleted.

First Mate of Pomeranian: *And where the hell have you been hiding yourselves? You should have been in before us. I suppose that you got lost.*

Second Mate of Corgi: *I never get lost.*

First Mate of Pomeranian: *Like hell you don't. I remember when you got your sums wrong when we were together in the old* Dalmation, *and we finished up off Hamlet instead of Macbeth. . . .*

But what's twenty light-years between friends?

Second Mate of Corgi: *I told you all that the computer was on the blink, but nobody would listen to me. As for this trip, we had to deviate.*

First Mate of Corgi: *Watch it, Peter!*

Second Mate of Corgi: *Why?*

First Mate of Corgi: *You know what the old man told us.*

Second Mate of Corgi: *Too bloody right I do. He's making his own report to the general manager, with copies every which way. Top Secret. For your eyes only. Destroy by fire before reading. He's wasted in the Dog Star Line. He should have been in the so-called Intelligence Branch of the clottish Survey Service.*

First Mate of Pomeranian: *What did happen?*

First Mate of Corgi: *Nothing much. Mannschenn Drive slightly on the blink, so we had to find a suitable planet on which to park our arse while we recalibrated.*

Second Mate of Corgi: *And what a planet! You know how I like sleek women. . . .*

First Mate of Corgi: *Watch it, you stupid bastard!*

Second Mate of Corgi: *Who're you calling a bastard? You can sling your rank around aboard the bloody ship, but not here. If I'd had any sense I'd'a skinned out before the bitch lifted off. Morrowvia'll do me when I retire from the Dog Star Line! Or resign . . .*

First Mate of Corgi: *Or get fired—as you will be, unless you pipe down!*

Second Mate of Corgi: *You can't tell me . . .*

First Mate of Corgi: *I can, and I bloody well am telling you! Come on, finish your drink, and then back to the ship!*

At this juncture there are sounds of a scuffle as Corgi*'s chief officer, a very big man, hustles his junior out of the Red Dragon.*

Third Mate of Pomeranian: *What the hell was all that about?*

First Mate of Pomeranian: *Search me.*

The rest of the recorded conversation consists of idle and futile speculation by Pomeranian*'s officers as to the identity of the world landed upon by* Corgi.

To date I have been unable to identify this planet myself. There is no Morrowvia listed in the catalogue, even when due allowance is made for variations in spelling. Also I have checked the Navy List, and found that the master of Corgi *is not, and never has been, an officer in the FSS Reserve. None of his officers hold a Reserve commission. It may be assumed, therefore, that the master's report on the discovery of what appears to be a Lost Colony will be made only to his owners.*

Corgi, *when she deviated, was bound from Darnstadt to Siluria. Her normal trajectory would have taken her within three light-years of Gamma Argo. The planetary system of Gamma Argo was surveyed in the early days of the Second Expansion, and no indigenous intelligent life was found on any of its worlds. . . .*

"Mphm . . ." Grimes refilled and relit his pipe. This was interesting reading.

He turned to the report from the agent at Port Brrooun. He, the shipping advisor to the Terran Consul, had been spending most of his free evenings in an establishment called the Beer Hive. Brrooun had been *Corgi's* next port of call after Llangowan. Her second officer had confined his troubles to a sympathetic Shaara drone. At Port Mackay, on Rob Roy, he had gotten fighting drunk on the local whiskey and had beaten up the chief officer and publicly abused the master. Normally such conduct would have led to his instant dismissal—but Captain Danzellan, of *Corgi*, had been most reluctant to leave the objectionable young man behind, in the hands of the civil authorities. The Intelligence Officer at Port Mackay, although knowing nothing of the Lost Colony, had been intrigued by the failure of the master to rid himself of an obvious malcontent and had wondered what was behind it. His own theories, for what they were worth, included a Hanoverian plot against the Jacobean royal house of Waverley. . . .

It was from Port Fortinbras, on Elsinore, that the next really interesting report came. The agent there was a woman, and worked as a waitress in the Poor Yorick, a tavern famous for its funereal decor. The agent, too, was famous insofar as the Intelligence Branch of the Survey Service was concerned, being known as the Bug Queen. Her specialty was recorders printed into the labels on bottles.

Transcript of conversation between Harald Larsen, owner-manager of Larsen's Repair Yard, and Peter Dalquist, owner of Dalquist's Ship Chandlery:

Dalquist: An' how are things at the yard, Harald?

Larsen: Can't complain, Pete, can't complain. Southerly Buster*'s havin' a face lift.*

Dalquist: Drongo Kane . . .

Larsen: You can say what you like about Drongo—but he always pays his bills. . . .

Dalquist: Yeah. But he drives a hard bargain first.

Larsen: You can say that again.

Dalquist: An' what is it this time? General maintenance? Survey?

Larsen: Modifications. He's havin' his cargo spaces converted into passenger accommodation—of a sort. An' you remember those two quick-firin' cannon I got off that derelict Waldegren gunboat? Drongo's havin' 'em mounted on the Buster.

Dalquist: But it ain't legal. Southerly Buster*'s a merchant ship.*

Larsen: Drongo says that it is *legal, an' that he's entitled to carry defensive armament. . . . Some o' the places he gets to, he needs it! But I checked up with me own legal eagles just to make sure that me own jets are clear. They assured me that Drongo's within his rights.*

Dalquist: But quick-firin' cannon, when every man-o'-war is armed to the teeth with laser, misguided missiles an' only the Odd Gods of the Galaxy know what else! Doesn't make sense.

Larsen: Maybe it doesn't—but Drongo's got too much sense to take on a warship.

Dalquist: What if a warship takes on him?

Larsen: That's his *worry.*

Dalquist: But he must be thinkin' of fightin' somebody. . . . Any idea who it might be?

Larsen: I haven't a clue. All that I know is that his last port, before he came here, was Brrooun, on one o' the Shaara worlds. He told me—he'd had rather too much to drink himself—that he'd fed a couple of bottles of Scotch to a talkative drone. He said that he'll buy drinks for anybody—or any thing—as long as he gets information in return. Anyhow, this drone told Drongo what he'd *been told by the drunken second mate of a Dog Star tramp. . . .*

Dalquist: Which was?

Larsen: Drongo certainly wasn't telling me, even though he'd had a skinful. He did mutter something about Lost Colonies, an' finders bein' keepers, an' about the Dog Star Line havin' to be manned by greyhounds if they wanted to get their dirty paws into this manger. . . .

Dalquist: An' was that all?

Larsen: You said it. He clammed up.

Unfortunately Captain Kane and his officers, unlike the majority of spacemen visiting Port Fortinbras, do not frequent the Poor Yorick, preferring the King Claudius. On the several occasions that I have been there as a customer, at the same times as Southerly Buster*'s personnel, I have been unable to learn anything of importance. Attempts made by myself to strike up an acquaintance with Captain Kane, his mates and his engineers have failed.*

Grimes chuckled. He wondered what the Bug Queen looked like. It seemed obvious that she owed her success as an agent to her skill with electronic gadgetry rather than to her glamour. But Kane? Where did *he* come into the picture? The man was notorious—but, to date, had always managed to stay on the right side of the law.

But it was time that he, Grimes, put his senior officers into the picture.

3

THEY WERE ALL in Grimes's day cabin—his departmental heads and his senior scientific officers. There was Saul, the first lieutenant, a huge, gentle, very black man. There was Connery, chief engineer. The two officers in charge of communications were there—Timmins, the electronicist, and Hayakawa, the psionicist. There were Doctors Tallis, Westover and Lazenby—biologist, geologist and ethologist respectively—all of whom held the rank of full commander. Forsby—physicist—had yet to gain his doctorate and was only a lieutenant. There were Lieutenant Pitcher, navigator, Lieutenant Stein, ship's surgeon and bio-chemist, and Captain Philby, officer in charge of *Seeker*'s Marines.

Grimes, trying to look and to feel fatherly, surveyed his people. He was pleased to note that the *real* spacemen—with the exception of Hayakawa—looked the part. Ethnic origins and differentiation of skin pigmentation were canceled out, as it were, by the common uniform. With the exception of Maggie Lazenby the scientists looked their part. They were, of course, all in uniform—though it wasn't what they were wearing but how they were wearing it that mattered. To them uniform was just something to cover their nakedness, the more comfortably the better. And to them beards were merely the means whereby the bother of depilation could be avoided. The growths sprouting from the faces of Tallis, Westover and Forsby contrasted shockingly with the neat hirsute adornments sported by Connery and Stein. The only one of the scientists at whom it was a pleasure to look was Doctor Lazenby—slim, auburn-haired and wearing a skirt considerably less than regulation length.

Grimes looked at her.

She snapped, "Get on with it, John." (Everybody present knew that she was a privileged person.)

"Mphm," he grunted as he carefully filled his pipe. "Help yourselves to coffee—or to something stronger from the bar, if you'd rather." He waited until everybody was holding a glass or a cup, then said, "As you all know by this time, this is a Lost Colony expedition. . . ."

Forsby raised his hand for attention. "Captain, forgive my ignorance, but I've only just joined the Survey Service. And I'm a physicist, not a historian. Just what *is* a Lost Colony?"

"Mphm," grunted Grimes again. He shot a dirty look at Maggie Lazenby as he heard her whispered *"Keep it short!"* He carefully lit his pipe. He said, "The majority of the so-called Lost Colonies date from the days of the Second Expansion, of the gaussjammers. The gaussjammers were interstellar ships that used the Ehrenhaft Drive. Cutting a long and involved story short, the Ehrenhaft generators produced a magnetic current—a current, not a field—and the ship in which they were mounted became, in effect, a huge magnetic particle, proceeding at a speed which could be regulated from a mere crawl to FTL along the 'tramlines,' the lines of magnetic force. This was all very well—but a severe magnetic storm could throw a jaussjammer lightyears off course, very often into an unexplored and uncharted sector of the galaxy. . . ."

"FTL?" demanded Forsby in a pained voice. "FTL?"

"A matter of semantics," Grimes told him airily. "You know, and I know, that faster-than-light speeds are impossible. With our Mannschenn Drive, for example, we cheat—by going astern in time as we're going ahead in space. The gaussjammers cheated too—by coexisting with themselves all along the lines of magnetic force that they were on. The main thing was—it worked. Anyhow, visualize a gaussjammer after a magnetic storm has tangled the lines of force like so much spaghetti *and* drained the micro-pile of all energy. The captain doesn't know where he is. But he has got power for his main engines."

"You said that the micro-pile was dead."

"Sure. But those ships ran to emergency generators—diesel generators. They churned out the electricity to drive the Ehrenhaft generators. The ship's biochemist knew the techniques for producing diesel fuel from whatever was available—even though it meant that all hands would be on short rations. So, for as long as she could, the ship either tried to make her way back to some known sector or to find a planet capable of being settled. . . ."

"Analogous," contributed Maggie Lazenby, "to the colonization of many Pacific islands by Polynesians in Earth's remote past. But this colony that we're supposed to be looking for, John . . ."

"Yes. I was getting around to that. It's supposed to be in the Argo Sector. It was stumbled upon by a Dog Star Line ship that made a deviation to recalibrate her Mannschenn Drive controls. It won't be a Lost Colony for much longer."

"Why not?" asked Forsby.

"To begin with, the Dog Star Line people know about it. The Shaara know about it. *We* know about it. And Drongo Kane knows about it."

"Drongo Kane?" This was Forsby again, of course. "Who's he?"

Grimes sighed. He supposed that his physicist knew his own subject, but he seemed to know very little outside it. He turned his regard to his officers, said, "Tell him."

"Drongo Kane . . ." murmured Saul in his deep, rich voice. "Smuggler, gunrunner . . ."

"Pirate . . ." contributed Timmins.

"That was never proven," Grimes told him.

"Perhaps not, sir. But I was on watch—it was when I was a junior in *Scorpio*—when *Bremerhaven*'s distress call came through."

"Mphm. As I recall it, *Bremerhaven*'s own activities at the time were somewhat dubious. . . ."

"Slaver . . ." said Saul.

"Somebody had to take the people off Ganda before the radiation from their sun fried them. Whatever ships were available had to be employed."

"But Kane was *paid* by the Duke of Waldegren for the people he carried in *Southerly Buster*."

"Just a fee," said Grimes, "or commission, or whatever, for the delivery of indentured labor."

"What about this bloody Lost Colony?" demanded Maggie Lazenby.

"We're supposed to find it." Grimes gestured toward the folder on his desk with the stem of his pipe. "I've had copies made of all the bumf that was given to me. It consists mainly of reports made by agents on quite a few worlds. Our man at Port Llangowan, on Siluria, recorded a conversation between officers of *Corgi* and *Pomeranian* in one of the local pubs. *Corgi* had found this world—which seems to be called Morrowvia—quite by chance. Our man at Port Brrooun, on Drroomoorr, recorded a conversation between the second mate of *Corgi* and a Shaara drone; once again Morrowvia was mentioned. The same young gentleman—the second mate, not the drone—got into trouble at Port Mackay on Rob Roy. Normally he'd have been emptied out there and then by *Corgi*'s master—but keeping him on board must have been the lesser of two evils."

"Why?" asked Forsby.

"Because," Grimes told him patiently, "the master of *Corgi* didn't want word of a new world that could well be included in the Dog Star

Line's economic empire spread all over the galaxy. Where was I? Yes. Our woman at Port Fortinbras, on Elsinore, recorded a conversation between the owner of a repair yard and the owner of a ship chandlery. The repair yard was doing some work on Drongo Kane's ship, *Southerly Buster*—the mounting of armament, among other things. Kane had told the owner of the yard something—not much, but something—about a Lost Colony found by a Dog Star tramp. . . ."

"And what are *we* supposed to do, Captain?" asked Forsby. "Plant the Federation's flag, or something?"

"Or something," said Maggie Lazenby. "You can rest assured of that."

Or something, thought Grimes.

4

AS FAR AS Grimes knew there was no real urgency—nonetheless he pushed *Seeker* along at her maximum safe velocity. This entailed acceleration slightly in excess of 1.5 G, with a temporal precession rate that did not quite, as Maggie Lazenby tartly put it, have all hands and the cook living backward. But Maggie had been born and reared on Arcadia, a relatively low gravity planet and, furthermore, disliked and distrusted the time-twisting Mannschenn Drive even more than the average spaceman or—woman. However, Lieutenant Brian Connery was an extremely competent engineer and well able to maintain the delicate balance between the ship's main drive units without remotely endangering either the vessel or her personnel.

Even so, Grimes suffered. *Seeker* had a mixed crew—and a ship, as Grimes was fond of saying, is not a Sunday School outing. On past voyages it had been tacitly assumed that Maggie was the captain's lady. On this voyage it was so assumed too—by everybody except one of the two people most intimately concerned. Grimes tried to play along with the assumption, but it was hopeless.

"I suppose," he said bitterly, after she had strongly resisted a quite determined pass, "that you're still hankering after that beefy lout, Brasidus or whatever his name was, on Sparta. . . ."

"No," she told him, not quite truthfully. "No. It's just that I can't possibly join in your fun and games when I feel as though I weigh about fourteen times normal."

"Only one and a half times," he corrected her.

"It *feels* fourteen times. And it's the psychological effect that inhibits me."

Grimes slumped back in his chair, extending an arm to his open liquor cabinet.

"Lay off it!" she told him sharply.

"So I can't drink now."

"You will not drink now." Her manner softened. "Don't forget, John, that you're responsible for the ship and everybody aboard her. . . ."

"Nothing can happen in deep space."

"Can't it?" Her fine eyebrows lifted slightly. "Can't it? After some of the stories I've heard, and after some of the stories you've told me yourself . . ."

"Mphm." He reached out again, but it was a half-hearted attempt.

"Things will work out, John," she said earnestly. "They always do, one way or the other. . . ."

"Suppose it's the wrong way?"

"You'll survive. I'll survive. We'll survive." She quoted, half seriously, " 'Men have died, and worms have eaten 'em—but not for love. . . .' "

"Where's that from?" he asked, interested.

"Shakespeare. You trade school boys—you're quite impossible. You know nothing—*nothing*—outside your own field."

"I resent that," said Grimes. "At the Academy we had to do a course in Twentieth Century fiction. . . ."

Again the eyebrows lifted. "You surprise me." And then she demanded incredulously, "What sort of fiction?"

"It was rather specialized. Science fiction, as a matter of fact. Some of those old buggers made very good guesses. Most of them, though, were way off the beam. Even so, it was fascinating."

"And still trade-school-oriented."

He shrugged. "Have it your way, Maggie. We're just Yahoos. But we do get our ships around." He paused, then delivered his own quotation. " 'Transportation is civilization.' "

"All right," she said at last. "Who wrote that?"

"Kipling."

"Kipling—and science fiction?"

"You should catch up on your own reading some time. . . ." The telephone buzzed sharply. He got up and went rapidly to the handset.

She remarked sweetly, "*Nothing* can happen in deep space. . . ."

"Captain here," said Grimes sharply.

Lieutenant Hayakawa's reedy voice drifted into the day cabin. "Hayakawa, Captain sir. . . ."

"Yes, Mr. Hayakawa?"

"I . . . am not certain. But I think I have detected psionic radiation—not close, but not too far distant. . . ."

"It is extremely unlikely," Grimes said, "that we are the only ship in this sector of space."

"I . . . I know, Captain. But—it is all vague, and the other telepath is maintaining a block. . . . I . . . I tried at first to push through, and he knew that I was trying. . . . Then, suddenly, I relaxed. . . ."

Psionic judo . . . thought Grimes.

"Yes. . . . You could call it that. . . . But there is somebody aboard that ship who is thinking all the time about . . . Morrowvia. . . ."

"Drongo Kane," said Grimes.

"No, Captain. Not Drongo Kane. This is a . . . young mind. Immature. . . ."

"Mphm. Anything else?"

"Yes. . . . He is thinking, too, of somebody called Tabitha. . . ."

"And who's *she* when she's up and dressed?"

"She is not dressed . . . not as *he* remembers her."

"This," stated Maggie Lazenby, "is disgusting. I thought, in my innocence, that the Rhine Institute took a very dim view of any prying by its graduates into private thoughts. I was under the impression that telepathy was to be used *only* for instantaneous communications over astronomical distances."

"If every Rhine Institute graduate who broke the Institute's rules dropped dead right now," Grimes told her, "there'd be one helluva shortage of trained telepaths. In any case, the Institute allows some latitude to those of its people who're in the employ of a recognized law enforcement agency. The Federation's Survey Service is one such. Conversely, the Institute recognizes the right of any telepath, no matter by whom employed, to put up a telepathic block."

"I still don't like it. Any of it."

"Mr. Hayakawa," said Grimes into the telephone, "you heard all that?"

"Yes, Captain."

"And what are *your* views?"

In reply came a thin chuckle, then, "I try to be loyal, sir. To the Institute, to the Service, to my shipmates, to my captain. Sometimes it is hard to be loyal to everybody at once. But, also, I try to be loyal to myself."

"Putting it briefly," said Maggie Lazenby, "you know on which side your bread is buttered."

"Butter is an animal-derived food, Miss Commander, which I never touch."

"Mr. Hayakawa," asked Grimes, "do you hear anything further from the strange ship?"

"No, Captain. The block has been reestablished."

"Let me know when you do hear anything more." He punched buttons, then spoke again into the instrument. "Captain here, Mr. Timmins. Mr. Hayakawa has reported a vessel in our vicinity, apparently heading for Morrowvia. Have *you* picked anything up?"

"Just the normal commercial traffic, sir. A Shaara freighter, *Mmoorroomm*, Rob Roy to ZZrreemm. *Empress of Scotia*, Dunedin to Darnstadt. *Cutty Sark*, Carinthia to Lorn. *Schnauzer*, Siluria to Macbeth. And, according to Sector Plot, the following ships not fitted with Carlotti equipment: *Sundowner*, Aquarius to Faraway, *Rim Eland*, Elsinore to Ultimo. . . ."

"Thank you." Then, speaking more to himself than to anybody else, "*Schnauzer* . . . Dog Star Line . . . cleared for Macbeth. . . . She might finish up there eventually. . . ."

He ignored Maggie's questioning look and went to his playmaster. As its name implied, the device provided entertainment, visual and audio—but this one, a standard fitting in the captain's quarters in all FSS ships, was also hooked up to the vessel's encyclopedia bank. "Get me Lloyd's Register," he ordered. "I want details on *Schnauzer*. Sirian ownership. Dog Star Line. . . ."

The screen lit up, displaying the facsimile of a printed page.

Schnauzer—a new ship, small, exceptionally fast for a merchantman, defensively armed. (The Dog Star Line had long insisted that its vessels were capable of conducting their own defense on some of the trade routes where piracy still persisted.)

"Mphm," he grunted. Back at the telephone he ordered Timmins to send a coded message to FSS agent at Port Llangowan, on Siluria, to ask the names of *Schnauzer*'s personnel when she cleared outward.

He strongly suspected that the master would be Captain Danzellan.

5

"MASTER, ROGER DANZELLAN," the Federation's man on Siluria replied eventually. "First mate, Oscar Eklund. Second mate, Francis Delamere. Third mate, Kathryn Daley. Chief engineer, Mannschenn Drive, Evan Jones. Chief engineer Interplanetary Drives, Ian Mackay. Juniors, H. Smith, B. Ostrog, H. Singh. Purser/catering officer, Glynis Trent . . ." The message went on to say that Captain Danzellan and Mr. Delamere had both been among *Corgi*'s complement when she had last been at Port Llangowan. The last piece of information that it contained was that Francis Delamere was the nephew of the Dog Star Line's general manager.

So, obviously, the Dog Star people were interested in Morrowvia. On receiving the report from *Corgi*'s master they had acted, and fast. A suitable ship had been shunted off her doubtlessly well-worn tramlines, and Danzellan had been transferred to her command. Probably he had not wished to have Delamere as one of his officers—but Delamere had pull. Nepotism, as Grimes well knew, existed in the Survey Service. In a privately owned shipping company the climate would be even more suitable to its flourishing.

There was only one thing for Grimes to do—to pile on the Gs and the lumes, to get to Morrowvia before Danzellan. Fortunately, the merchant vessel was not fitted with a Mass Proximity Indicator—the Dog Star Line viewed new navigational aids with suspicion and never fitted them to its ships until their value was well proven. Sooner or later—sooner, Grimes hoped—*Seeker* would pick up *Schnauzer* in her screen and, shortly thereafter, would be able accurately to extrapolate her trajectory. *Schnauzer* would know nothing of *Seeker*'s whereabouts or presence.

And Drongo Kane in his *Southerly Buster?* A coded request for information to the Bug Queen brought the news that he had lifted from Port Fortinbras, his refit completed, with a General Clearance. Such clearances were rarely issued. This one must have cost Kane plenty.

Grimes was spending more and more time in his control room. There was nothing that he could *do*—but he wanted to be on hand when *Schnauzer* was picked up. At last she was there—or *something* was there—an almost infinitesimal spark in the screen, at extreme range. Grimes watched, concealing his impatience, while his navigator, hunched over the big globe of utter darkness, delicately manipulated the controls set into the base of the screen. Slowly a glowing filament was extruded from the center of the sphere—*Seeker*'s track. And then, from that barely visible spark just within the screen's limits, another filament was extended.

"Mphm," grunted Grimes.

The display was informative. Relatively speaking, *Schnauzer* was on *Seeker*'s port beam, a little ahead of the beam actually, and steering a converging course. Morrowvia was out of range of the M.P.I., but there was little doubt that both ships were headed for the same destination.

"Have you an estimate of her speed yet, Mr. Pitcher?" asked Grimes.

"Only a rough one, sir," replied the tall, thin, almost white-haired young man. "Give me an hour, and . . ."

"Extrapolate now, if you will."

"Very good, sir."

"Two beads of light appeared, one on each filament. "Twenty-four hours," said Pitcher. The range had closed slightly but the relative bearing was almost unaltered. "Forty-eight hours." The bearing *was changing*. Seventy-two hours." *Schnauzer* was slightly, very slightly, abaft *Seeker*'s beam. "Ninety-six hours." There was no doubt about it. At the moment *Seeker* had the heels of the Dog Star ship.

Grimes was relieved. He did not want to drive his ship any faster. An almost continuous sense of *déjà vu* is an uncanny thing to have to live with. The temporal precession field had not yet reached a dangerous intensity, but it had been increased to a highly uncomfortable one. Already there was a certain confusion when orders were given and received. Had they been made? Had they been acted upon?

Grimes waited for Pitcher to answer his question, then realized that he had not yet asked it. "Assuming," he said, "that your first estimate of *Schnauzer*'s speed is correct, how much time do we have on Morrowvia before she arrives?"

"Sixty hours Standard, sir. Almost exactly two Morrowvian days."

Not long, thought Grimes. Not long at all for what he had to do. And not knowing what he had to do didn't help matters. He'd just have to make up the rules as he went along.

He said, "We'll maintain a continuous watch on the M.P.I. from now on. Let me know at once if there's any change in the situation, and if any more targets appear on the screen."

"Drongo Kane?" asked Saul.

"Yes, Mr. Saul. Drongo Kane."

The first lieutenant's eyes and teeth were very white in his black face as he smiled mirthlessly. He said, his deep voice little more than a whisper, "I hope that Drongo Kane *is* bound for Morrowvia, Captain."

"Why, Mr. Saul?" Grimes essayed a feeble jest. "Two's company, three's a crowd."

"Racial hatreds die very hard, Captain. To my people, for many, many years, 'slaver' has been an especially dirty word. Ganda, as you know, was colonized by my people. . . . And some hundreds of them, rescued by Kane's *Southerly Buster* before their sun went nova, were sold by him to the Duke of Waldegren. . . ."

"As I said before," Grimes told him, "they weren't *sold*. They entered the duke's service as indentured labor."

"Even so, sir, I would like to meet Captain Drongo Kane."

"It's just as well," said Grimes, "that he's not a reincarnation of Oliver Cromwell—if he were, Mr. Connery would be after his blood too. . . ."

He regarded his first lieutenant dubiously. He was a good man, a good officer, and Grimes liked him personally. But if *Southerly Buster* made a landing on Morrowvia he would have to be watched carefully. And—who would watch the watchman? Grimes knew that if he wished to reach flag rank in the Service he would have to curb his propensity for taking sides.

"Mphm," he grunted. Then, "I'll leave Control in your capable hands, Mr. Saul. And keep a watchful eye on the M.P.I., Mr. Pitcher. I'm going down to have a few words with Hayakawa."

Lieutenant Hayakawa was on watch—but a psionic communications officer, as any one such will tell you, is *always* on watch. He was not, however, wearing the rig of the day. His grossly obese body was inadequately covered by a short kimono, gray silk with an embroidered design of improbable looking flowers. Scrolls, beautifully inscribed with

Japanese ideographs, hung on the bulkheads, although space had been left for a single hologram, a picture of a strikingly symmetrical snow-capped mountain sharp against a blue sky. The deck was covered with a synthetic straw matting. In the air was the faint, sweet pungency of a burning joss stick.

Hayakawa got slowly and ponderously to his feet. "Captain san . . ." he murmured.

"Sit down, Mr. Hayakawa," ordered Grimes. The acceleration—now more than two Gs—was bad enough for him; it would be far, far worse for one of the telepath's build. He lowered himself to a pile of silk cushions. Not for the first time he regretted that Hayakawa had been allowed to break the regulations governing the furnishing of officers' cabins—but PCOs, trading upon their rarity, are privileged persons aboard any ship.

He settled down into a position approximating comfort—and then had to get up and shift the cushions and himself to another site. From the first one he had far too good a view of Hayakawa's psionic amplifier, the disembodied dog's brain suspended in its globe of cloudy nutrient fluid. The view of Mount Fujiyama was much more preferable.

He said, "We have *Schnauzer* on the M.P.I. now."

"I know, Captain."

"You would," remarked Grimes, but without rancor. "And you still haven't picked up any further . . . emanations from her?"

"No. Her PCO is Delwyn Hume. I have met him. He is a good man. What you called my judo technique worked just once with him. It will never work again." Then Hayakawa smiled fatly and sweetly. "But I have other news for you."

"Tell."

"*Southerly Buster*, Captain. Myra Bracegirdle is the CPO. *She* is good—but, of course, we are all good. Her screen is as tight as that maintained by Hume or myself. But . . .

"She is emotional. During moments of stress her own thoughts seep through. She hates the *Buster*'s mate. His name is Aloysius Dreebly. Now and again—often, in fact—he tries to force his attentions on her."

"Interesting," commented Grimes. He thought, *This is building up to one of those situations where everybody hates everybody. Mr. Saul hates Captain Kane, although he's never met him personally. Myra hates Aloysius. The way Maggie's been carrying on lately I'm beginning to think that she hates me. And I doubt very much if Captain Danzellan feels any great affection for Mr. Francis Delamere. . . .* He grinned. *But Frankie loves Tabbie. . . .*

He said, "And is *Southerly Buster* bound for Morrowvia?"

"I cannot say, Captain. But she is around. And just before you came in I 'heard' Myra Bracegirdle think, 'Thank the gods there're only seven more days to go before we arrive!' "

And that, Grimes told himself, *means that she gets there at the same time as us. . . .*

He clambered laboriously to his feet, went to Hayakawa's telephone. He punched, first of all, for Lieutenant Connery's quarters, but the engineering officer was not there. He called the engine room, and found him.

"Captain here, Chief. Can you squeeze out another half lume?"

"I can't." Connery's voice was sharp. "The governor's playing up, an' we're havin' to run the Drive on manual control. If I try to push her any more we'll finish up last Thursday in the middle of sweet fuck all!"

"Can't you fix the governor?"

"Not without stoppin' her an' shuttin' down. If you want to carry on, it'll have to wait until we get to Morrowvia."

"Carry on the way you're doing," said Grimes.

6

SEEKER SAW NOTHING at all of *Southerly Buster* until both vessels were in orbit about Morrowvia, just prior to landing. This was not surprising, as Drongo Kane's ship had been approaching the planet from the Shakesperian Sector, whilst Grimes had been coming in from Lindisfarne. The angle subtended by these points of origin was little short of 180°. Furthermore, once Morrowvia itself had come within MPI range the instrument, insofar as bodies of less than planetary mass were concerned, was practically useless. And radar had been useless until the shutting down of the time/space twisting interstellar drive.

There was *Seeker*, hanging in equatorial orbit three hundred miles up from the surface, and below her was Morrowvia, an Earth-type world, but unspoiled. There were blue seas and vast expanses of green prairie and forest land, yellow deserts and polar icecaps as dazzlingly white as the drifting cloud masses. There were snow-peaked mountain ranges, and long, winding rivers, on the banks of which, sparsely scattered, were what seemed to be towns and villages—but from a range of hundreds of miles, even with excellent telescopes, human habitations can look like natural formations, and natural formations like buildings, and telltale industrial smog was altogether lacking.

On the night hemisphere the evidence was more conclusive. There were clusters of lights, faint and yellowish. Said Grimes, "Where there's light there's life, intelligent life. . . ."

"Not necessarily," Maggie Lazenby told him. "There are such things as volcanoes, you know. . . ."

"On this hemisphere only? Come off it, Maggie."

"*And* there are such things as luminescent living organisms."

"So what we're seeing are glowworm colonies? And what about the reports from our agents on Siluria and Elsinore and Drroomoorr? Would either the Dog Star Line or Drongo Kane be interested in glowworms?"

"They might be," she said. "They might be."

"Yeah?"

"Yeah. It's high time, Commander Grimes, that you cured yourself of your habit of jumping to conclusions, that you adopted a scientific approach. . . ."

Grimes decided against making some cutting retort. The other officers in the control room were looking far too amused by the exchange. He grunted, then demanded of Lieutenant Saul, "Any sign yet of *Southerly Buster*, Number One?"

"No, sir. Perhaps Mr. Hayakawa . . ."

"I've already asked him. As far as his Peke's brain in aspic and he are concerned, the *Buster*'s maintaining absolute psionic silence."

"*Peke*'s brain?" asked Maggie.

"Can *you* think of any definitely *Japanese* dog at a second's notice?"

And then a voice came from the NST transceiver. It was a man's voice, harsh, yet not unpleasant, strongly accented. "*Southerly Buster* to Aero-Space Control. *Southerly Buster* to Aero-Space Control. Do you read me? Over."

"But there's not any Aero-Space Control here," announced Lieutenant Timmins. "We've already found that out."

"Kane knows that as well as we do," Grimes told him. "But, to judge by his record, he always maintains a facade of absolute legality in everything he does. This fits in."

"And I suppose," said Saul, "that he's already tried to establish communication with the local telepaths, if any, just as we did."

"Not necessarily. His PCO will have 'heard' our Mr. Hayakawa doing just that, and she'll have learned that Morrowvia is lousy with telepaths, but none of them trained. . . . Oh, they *know* we're here, in a vague sort of way. . . ."

"*Southerly Buster* to Aero-Space Control. *Southerly Buster* to Aero-Space Control. Do you read me? Over."

"There she is!" shouted Pitcher suddenly.

There she was, in the radar screen, a tiny yet bright blip. There she was, a new star lifting above the dark limb of the planet, a tiny planetoid reflecting the rays of Gamma Argo.

"If we can see her, she can see us," commented Grimes. He went to the transceiver, ordered, "Put me on to him, Mr. Timmins." He said sternly, "FSS *Seeker* to *Southerly Buster*. FSS *Seeker* to *Southerly Buster*. Come in, please, on audio-visual."

"Comin' in, *Seeker*, comin' in . . ." drawled the voice. There was a swirl of light and color in the little screen, coalescing into a clear picture. Grimes and his officers looked into a control room not unlike their own—even to a weapons control console situated as it would have been in the nerve center of a warship. And this *Southerly Buster* was a merchantman. . . . Drongo Kane calmly regarded Grimes from the screen—bleak yet not altogether humorless blue eyes under a thatch of straw colored hair, in a face that looked as though at some time it had been completely smashed and then reassembled not overcarefully. He said, "I see you, *Seeker*. Can you see me?"

"I see you," snapped Grimes.

"Identify yourself, please, *Seeker*. Can't be too careful once you're off the beaten tracks, y'know."

"Grimes," said the owner of that name at last. "Lieutenant Commander in command of FSS *Seeker*, Survey Vessel."

"Pleased to meet you, Commander Grimes. An' what, may I ask, brings you out to this neck o' the woods?"

"You mayn't ask. That's Federation business, Captain Kane."

The pale eyebrows lifted in mock surprise. "So you know me, Commander! Well, well. Such is fame."

"Or notoriety . . ." murmured Maggie Lazenby.

"Did I hear the lady behind you say somethin'?" inquired Kane.

Grimes ignored this. "What are your intentions, Captain Kane?" he demanded.

"Well, now, that all depends, Commander Grimes. Nobody owns this world 'cepting its people. I've asked if I could make a landing, but got no reply. I s'pose you heard me. But nobody's told me *not* to land. . . ."

"What are your intentions?" demanded Grimes again.

"Oh, to set the old *Buster*'s arse down onto somethin' safe an' solid. An' after that . . . Fossick around. See what we can buy or barter that's worth liftin'. There're some spacemen, Commander—an' I'm one of 'em—who have to *earn* their livin's. . . ."

"It is my duty—and the way that I earn *my* living—to afford protection to all Federation citizens in deep space, interplanetary space, in planetary atmospheres and on planetary surfaces," said Grimes, with deliberate pomposity.

"You needn't put yourself out, Commander."

"I insist, Captain. After all, as *you* said, one can't be too careful when off the beaten track."

Kane's lips moved. Grimes was no lip-reader, but he would have been willing to bet a month's salary that grave doubts were being cast upon his legitimacy—and, were this a less tolerant day and age, his morals. "Suit yourself," said Kane aloud. "But you're only wastin' your time."

"I'm the best judge of that."

"Suit yourself," growled Kane again.

Meanwhile, *Seeker*'s inertial drive had stammered into life and the ship was both slowing and lifting under the application of thrust, being driven into a powered, unnatural orbit so that *Southerly Buster* could pass beneath her.

"I thought you'd be landing first," complained Kane.

"After *you*, Captain," Grimes told him politely.

And just where would Kane be setting his ship down? If *Seeker* had arrived by herself Grimes would have adhered to orthodox Survey Service practice—a dawn landing at the terminator, with the full period of daylight for the initial exploration. And should it be considered safe to establish contact with the indigenes at once, a landing near to an obvious center of population.

Kane had never been an officer in the Survey Service, but he had done his share of exploring, had made first landings on planets upon which he had been the first man to set foot. Slowly, steadily *Southerly Buster* dropped through the atmosphere, with *Seeker* following a respectable distance astern. All *Seeker*'s armament was ready for instant use; Grimes had no doubt that the other ship was in a similar state of readiness. *Corgi*'s people had been hospitably treated on Morrowvia—but this was a large planet, probably divided among tribes or nations. Even though all its populace shared a common origin there had been time for divergence, for the generation of hostilities.

Down dropped *Southerly Buster*—down, down. Down dropped *Seeker*, her people alert for hostile action either from the ground or from the other ship. Grimes let Saul handle the pilotage; this was one of those occasions on which the captain needed to be able to look all ways at once.

Down dropped the two ships—down, down through the clear morning air. Kane's objective was becoming obvious—an expanse of level ground, clear of trees, that was almost an island, bounded to north, west and south by a winding river, to the east by a wooded hill. To north and west of it were villages, each with a sparse sprinkling of yellow lights still visible in the dawn twilight. It was the sort of landing place that Grimes would have selected for himself.

Then the viewscreen, with its high magnification, was no longer necessary, and the big binoculars on their universal mounting were no longer required. And the sun was up, at ground level, casting long shadows, pointing out all the irregularities that could make the landing of a starship hazardous.

Kane was down first, setting the *Buster* neatly into the middle of a patch of green that, from the air at least, looked perfectly smooth. Saul looked up briefly from his controls to Grimes, complaining. "The bastard's picked the best place. . . ."

"To the west of him . . ." Grimes said. "Almost on the river bank. . . . It doesn't look too bad. . . ."

"It'll have to do, Captain," murmured the first lieutenant resignedly.

It had to do—and, as Grimes had said, it wasn't too bad.

Only one recoil cylinder in the tripedal landing gear was burst when *Seeker* touched the ground, and there was no other damage.

7

THIS WAS NOT the occasion for full dress uniforms, with fore-and-aft hat, decorations, ceremonial sword and all the other trimmings. This was an occasion for comfortable shorts-and-shirt, with heavy boots and functional sidearms.

So attired, Grimes marched down *Seeker*'s ramp, followed by Captain Philby, the Marine officer, and a squad of his space soldiers. Maggie Lazenby and the other scientists had wished to accompany him, but he had issued strict orders that nobody excepting himself and the Marines was to leave the ship until such time as the situation had been clarified. And this clarification depended upon the local inhabitants as well as upon Drongo Kane. Meanwhile, Grimes had said, no foolish risks were to be taken.

As he marched toward the towering hulk of *Southerly Buster* he regretted his decision to land to the west of that ship; he had put himself at a disadvantage. The light of the still-low sun was blinding, making it difficult for his men and him to avoid the lavish scattering of quartzite boulders that protruded through the short, coarse grass. And it made it impossible to see if Drongo Kane had any weapons aimed at him and his party. Probably he had—but *Seeker*'s main armament was trained upon Kane's ship and ready to blow her off the face of the planet at the slightest provocation.

It was a little better once he and the Marines were in the shadow of the other ship. Grimes's eyes adjusted themselves and he stared upward at the blunt, metallic spire as he walked toward it. *Defensively armed!* he thought scornfully. Those two famous quick-firing cannon reported by the Bug Queen were merely an addition to what the *Buster* already had. Even so, in terms of laser and missiles, *Seeker* had the edge on her.

Southerly Buster's ramp was down. At the foot of it an officer was standing, a skeletal figure attired in gray coveralls with shoulder-boards carrying first mate's braid. The man was capless, and bald, and the wrinkled skin of his face was yellow, almost matching the long teeth that he showed when he smiled at the men from *Seeker.*

"Commander Grimes?" he asked in an overly ingratiating voice.

"Mr. Dreebly?" countered Grimes.

"Aloysius Dreebly, sir, at your service."

And so this, thought Grimes, was Aloysius Dreebly. Small wonder that Myra Bracegirdle, *Southerly Buster*'s PCO, hated him. He matched his name—as people with ugly names so very often do. They, as it were, grow to fit the labels that misguided parents bestow upon them at birth. *And this Dreebly*, Grimes continued thinking, *I wouldn't trust him behind me. He'd either kiss my arse or stab me in the back—or both.*

"And will you come aboard, Commander? Captain Kane is waiting for you."

"Certainly, Mr. Dreebly. Lead the way, please."

"Oh, sir, I'm afraid I cannot allow these other men aboard the ship. . . ."

"And I'm afraid that I can't board unless I have an escort of my own people. Captain Philby!"

"Sir!"

The young Marine officer had his pistol out, pointing at Dreebly. His sergeant and the six privates held their rifles at the ready.

"But, sir . . . what are you thinking of? This is *piracy!*"

"Hardly, Mr. Dreebly. All the way from our ship to yours we were tracked by the muzzle of one of your quick-firers. Surely you will allow us to show *our* teeth."

"Let the bastards aboard, Dreebly!" boomed Kane's voice from a loudspeaker. "But put your guns away first, Commander. I don't expect my guests to check in their pocket artillery at the door—but, on the other hand, I take a dim view if it's waved in my face."

At a word from Grimes Philby reholstered his pistol, the Marines slung their machine rifles. Dreebly shambled up the ramp to the after airlock, followed by the party from *Seeker*. Inside the compartment, Grimes looked about him curiously. He had been expecting something squalid—but, at first glance at least, this seemed to be a reasonably well-kept ship. There was a distinct absence of Survey Service spit-and-polish—but such is found only in vessels where there is a superfluity of ratings to do the spitting and polishing. There was shabbiness—but everything looked to be in excellent working order.

The elevator from the stern to the control room would accommodate only four men. Grimes decided to take Philby and one private with him, told the captain to tell his sergeant and the remaining Marines to stand guard in the airlock and at the foot of the ramp. (The Marines were apt to sulk if anybody but one of their own officers gave them a direct order.) Dreebly led the way into the cage and, as soon as the others were standing there with him, pressed a button.

She was quite a hunk of ship, this *Southerly Buster*, thought Grimes, as they slid rapidly upward, deck after deck. She had probably started life as an Interstellar Transport Commission's *Gamma Class* cargo liner but, under successive ownership, had been modified and remodified many times. A vessel this size, even with a minimal crew, would be expensive to run. Whatever Kane's activities were, they must show a profit.

The cage came to a gentle halt. "*This* way, please, gentlemen," said Dreebly. He led the way into a short alleyway, to a door with a sign, CAPTAIN, written above it. The door opened, admitting them into a spacious day cabin. Drongo Kane rose from an easy chair to greet them, but did not offer to shake hands.

He was as tall as his lanky bean pole of a mate, but there was a little more flesh on his bones. He moved with a decisive sort of grace, like an efficient hunting animal. He wasted no time on courtesies.

"Well, Commander Grimes?" he demanded.

"Captain Kane, I thought that we might combine forces. . . ."

"Did you, now? You've very kindly seen me down to the surface in one piece—not that I needed you—an' now you can go and play soldiers off by yourself, somewhere."

Grimes's prominent ears flamed. He was aware that Captain Philby and the Marine were looking at him, were thinking, *What's the old man going to say (or do) now?* Well, what *was* the old man (Grimes) going to say (or do) now?

He said, "I represent the Federation, Captain."

"An' this planet, Commander, is not a Federated World."

"Yet," said Grimes.

"If ever," said Kane.

"I was sent here by the Federation . . ." Grimes began again.

"To claim this planet—possibly against the wishes of its people?"

"To conduct a survey."

"Then conduct your survey. I'm not stoppin' you."

"But I'm responsible for your safety, and that of your ship, Captain.

You're a citizen of Austral, a Federated World, and your vessel's port of registry is Port Southern, on that planet."

"I don't need any snotty nosed Space Scouts to see me across the road."

"Maybe you don't, Captain Kane—but you're here, and I'm here, and I am obliged to carry out my duties to the best of my ability."

"Cor stiffen the bleedin' crows!" swore Kane disgustedly. Then, to somebody who had come in silently and was standing behind Grimes, "Yes, Myra?"

Grimes turned. So this was the Myra Bracegirdle of whom Hayakawa had talked. She was a tall girl, but thin rather than slender (this *Southerly Buster* must be a poor feeding ship), her face with its too prominent bones, too wide mouth and too big, dark eyes framed by silky blonde hair.

She said, "A word with you, Captain. Alone."

"Oh, don't worry about the Space Scouts, Myra. They're here to look after us. We have no secrets from *them.*"

"*They* are on the way here, Captain. They saw the ships land. They have heard about spaceships, of course, but have never seen one. . . ."

And what about Corgi? Grimes asked himself. *But she could have landed on the other side of the world from here.*

He said, "Captain Kane, do you mind if I call my ship?"

"Go ahead, Commander. This is Liberty Hall; you can spit on the mat and call the cat a bastard."

But as Grimes was raising his wrist transceiver to his mouth it buzzed sharply, then Saul's voice issued from the little instrument. "First lieutenant here, Captain. Mr. Hayakawa reports that parties of natives are approaching the landing site from both villages."

"I'll be right back," said Grimes.

"Don't let me keep you," said Kane. "Mr. Dreebly, please show these gentlemen off the premises."

"Oh, Captain," Grimes said, pausing in the doorway, "I shall take a very dim view if you act in a hostile manner toward the natives."

"And what if they act in a hostile manner toward me?"

"That," said Grimes, "will be different."

8

GRIMES DID NOT hurry back to his own ship, neither did he dawdle. He would have liked to have hurried, but was aware that Kane would be watching him. He walked at a moderately brisk pace, with Philby at his side and the other Marines marching after them.

"Sir," asked Philby, "do you think they'll be hostile?"

"*Corgi*'s crew didn't find them so, Captain Philby. But she landed on another part of the planet, among different people. We'll just have to play it by ear. . . ."

"A show of force . . ." murmured the young officer, as though he were looking forward to it.

And he was, thought Grimes. He was. He glanced at Philby's face—young, unlined, features, save for the strong chin, indeterminate. A Marine Corps recruiting poster face. . . . There was no vice in it—neither was there any sensitivity or imagination. It was the face of a man who could have written those famous lines—and without ironical intention:

Whatever happens, we have got
The Maxim gun—and they have not.

"Don't forget," said Grimes, "that this is *their* world, and that we're interlopers."

"Yes, sir, but we're civilized. Aren't we?"

"Mphm."

"And these people, out of the mainstream for so long, need to be taught the Federation's way of life. . . ."

Was Philby joking? No, Grimes decided, he was not. He said mildly, "The Federation's way of life as exemplified by whom? By the crew of *Seeker*? By Captain Drongo Kane and *his* crew? Or by Captain Danzellan and *Corgi*'s or *Schnauzer*'s people? Kane and Danzellan are Federation citizens, just as we are."

"Yes, sir. I suppose so. But . . ."

"But we have the superior fire power. Not all that superior. From what we saw aboard *Southerly Buster* I'd say she packs the wallop of a young battleship. And I should imagine that *Schnauzer* could show her teeth if she had to."

"What are your orders, sir?" asked Philby stiffly, obviously regretting having initiated the conversation.

"Just keep handy while I meet the natives. Better call another half dozen of your men down. Have your weapons ready—but not too obviously."

"With your permission, sir." Philby raised his wrist transceiver to his mouth. "Mr. Saul? Captain Philby here. Would you mind telling Corporal Smithers to detail six men for EVA? Yes, number three battle equipment. Over."

Then Grimes gave his orders. "Mr. Saul, Captain here. Do as Captain Philby says. And ask Dr. Lazenby if she'll join me at the after airlock. Yes. At once. All other officers and all ratings, with the exception of the six Marines, to remain on board. Yes, main and secondary armament to remain in a condition of readiness."

He heard the sergeant, who was a pace or two behind him, whisper something to one of the Marines about a show of force. He smiled to himself. He was not showing the force at his disposal—but it was nice to know that it was handy.

He beckoned Maggie down from the open airlock door. She walked gracefully down the ramp, despite the fact that she was hung around with all manner of equipment—cameras, recorders, even a sketch block and stylus.

She said, "We've had a good look at them through the control room telescope and binoculars. They seem to be human. . . ."

"Are they armed?"

"Some are carrying spears, and a few have longbows. . . ."

The additional marines clattered down the ramp. Grimes looked at the automatic weapons they carried and hoped that they would not be used. He was pleased to see that each man had a couple of sleep gas grenades at his belt, and that one of them was carrying extra respirators; these he handed out to Grimes, Philby and to the other members of the party that had gone to *Southerly Buster*.

There was activity just by the boarding ramp of that ship, too. Grimes borrowed Maggie's binoculars, saw that Kane, Dreebly and three more men had come outside and that a folding table had been set up. The wares spread upon it glittered in the strong sunlight. Trade goods, Grimes decided. Bright, pretty baubles. . . . And did he hope to buy a territory, a continent, a planet, even, for a string of glass beads? Why not? Things as strange had happened in Man's long history.

The first of the party of natives, that from the north, was now in sight from ground level. They moved with catlike smoothness over the grass, threading their way around the outcropping boulders. There were twenty of them—ten males and ten females. *Ten men and ten women*, Grimes corrected himself. Six men, carrying long spears, were in the lead, advancing in open order. Then came the women, eight of whom carried bows and who had quivers of arrows slung over their shoulders. This appeared to be their only clothing. The remaining four men brought up the rear.

Humans, thought Grimes, studying them through Maggie's glasses. Exceptionally handsome humans. That all of them were unclothed was no indication of their cultural level—naturism was the rule rather than the exception on several highly civilized planets, such as Arcadia. Their skins varied in color from pale gold to a dark brown, the hair of their heads and their body hair—which was normally distributed—was of a variety of colors, black, white, gray, brown, a coppery gold. . . . Grimes focused his attention on a girl. The short hair of her head was parti-colored, stripes of darker and lighter gray alternating. The effect was odd, but not unpleasing. He grunted. There was something odd about her eyes, too. But this offshoot of humanity, cut off from the main stem for generations; must have tended to grow apart from the generality of humankind.

The natives came to a halt by *Southerly Buster*'s ramp. The men stood aside to let two of the women, the two who carried no weapons, advance slowly to where Drongo Kane was standing by his table of trade goods. These two women were a little taller, a little larger than their companions, but no less graceful. They wore an air of maturity, but they were no less beautiful. They were talking to Kane and he seemed to be having no trouble understanding them, and they seemed to be having no trouble in understanding him.

"Here they come, sir," said Philby. "*Our* lot."

Grimes lowered the glasses, turned to face the visitors. This was a smaller party, only six people. Once again there was an equal division of the sexes.

Their leader, flanked by a spearman on either side of her, advanced slowly to where Grimes, with Maggie Lazenby beside him, was standing. Grimes saluted with a flourish—and a part of his mind stood back and laughed wryly at his according this courtesy to a naked savage. But a savage she was not. Savages tend to be dirty, unkempt; she was fastidiously clean. Her short hair was snowy, gleaming white, her lustrous skin was brown, the lips of her generous mouth a red that seemed natural rather than the result of applied cosmetics. The overall effect was definitely erotic. Grimes heard one of the Marines whistle, heard another whisper, "Buy that one for me, Daddy. . . ." He could not blame either of them—but felt definitely censorious when Maggie murmured, "And you can buy either—or both—of her boyfriends for me. . . ."

The two men were tall. Both were golden skinned; one had orange-colored hair, the other was black-haired. Of their essential maleness there was no doubt. Each, however, was built more on the lines of an Apollo than a Hercules, and each moved with a fluid grace as pronounced as that with which the woman walked.

To her, not at all reluctantly, Grimes returned his attention. He knew that the slow inspection that he was making was not mannerly, but he could not help himself. He told himself that it was his duty, as captain of a survey ship, to make such an inspection. Her eyes, he saw, were a peculiar greenish-yellow, and the tips of her ears were pointed. Her cheekbones were prominent, more so than the firm chin. His regard shifted slowly downward. Beneath each full but firm breast there was a rudimentary nipple. But she was human, human—even though the bare feet, which should have been long and slender, were oddly chubby.

She was human when she spoke. She said, "Welcome to Morrowvia." The accent was strange (of course) and the timbre of her voice held a quality that was hard to define.

"Thank you," replied Grimes. Then, "And whom do I have the honor of addressing?" The words, he realized as soon as he gave them utterance, were too formal, too far removed from everyday speech. But she understood them. Evidently the vocabulary had not become impoverished during the long years between first settlement and rediscovery.

She said simply, "My name is Maya. I am the queen."

So I'm saved the trouble of saying, "Take me to your leader," Grimes thought smugly. *Drongo must be doing* his *dickering with some very minor court official. . . .* He asked suavely, "And what is the name of your country, Your Majesty? Is it, too, called Morrowvia?"

Puzzle lines creased her rather broad face. And then she smiled. Her teeth were very white and looked sharp, the teeth of a carnivore rather than of an omnivore. She said, "You do not understand. The captain of the ship called *Corgi* made the same mistake when he landed at Melbourne, many kilometers from here. I have been told that he called the Queen of Melbourne 'Your Majesty.' He explained, later, that this is a title given to queens on your world, or worlds. . . ." She added modestly, yet not without a touch of pride, "I am the elected Queen of Cambridge, the town to the south of where you have landed."

"Melbourne . . ." echoed Grimes. "Cambridge . . ." But it made sense. Homesick colonists have always perpetuated the names of their home towns.

"*He*—Morrow—left us a book, a big book, in which he had written all the names that we are to use for our towns. . . ." Maya went on.

Yes, it made sense all right. It was all too probable that the people of a Lost Colony would deviate from the human norm—but if they still spoke a recognizable major Earth language, and if their centers of population were named after Earth cities, whoever rediscovered them would have no doubt as to their essential humanity.

"Then what shall I call you," asked Grimes, "if 'Your Majesty' is not correct?"

"Maya," she told him. "And I shall call you . . ."

"Commander Grimes," he said firmly. It was not that he would at all object to being on given name terms with this rather gorgeous creature—but not in front of his subordinates. "Have you a second name, Maya?" he asked.

"Yes, Commander Grimes. It is Smith."

Maya Smith, thought Grimes, a little wildly. *Maya Smith, the Queen of Cambridge. . . . And not a rag to cover her, not even any Crown Jewels. . . . And escorted by henchmen and henchwomen armed to the teeth with spears and bows and arrows. . . .*

Spears and bows and arrows . . . they could be just as lethal as more sophisticated weaponry. Grimes looked away hastily from the Queen of Cambridge to her people, saw, with relief, that there was no immediate cause for worry. The Morrowvians were not using the time-honored technique of enthusiastic fraternization, of close, ostensibly friendly contact that would make the snatching of guns from their owners' hands all too easy when the time came. There was a certain stand-offishness about them, in fact, an avoidance of too close physical proximity. Some of the Marines, to judge by the way that they were looking at the native women, would have wished it otherwise—but Philby and his sergeant were keeping a watchful eye both on their men and on the visitors.

Grimes felt free to continue his conversation with Maya. He gestured toward *Southerly Buster*, where the people from the other village were still clustered about Kane and his officers. "And your friend . . . what is she called?"

"*She* is no friend of mine. That *cat!*"

"But who is she?"

"Her name is Sabrina. She is the Queen of Oxford." The woman turned away from Grimes, stared toward Kane's vessel and the activity around her boarding ramp. She said, in a rather hurt voice, "The other ship has brought gifts for the people. Did you bring no gifts?"

"Mphm," Grimes grunted. He thought, *There must be something in my storerooms that she'd fancy. . . .* He said, "We did not know what you would like. Perhaps you would care to come on board, to take refreshments with us. Then we shall be able to discuss matters."

Maggie Lazenby snorted delicately.

"Thank you, Commander Grimes," said Maya Smith. "And my people?"

"They may come aboard too. But I must request that they leave their weapons outside."

She looked at him in some amazement. "But we never bring weapons into another person's home. They are for hunting, and for defense. There will be nothing to hunt in your ship—and surely we shall not need to defend ourselves against anything!"

You have been away from the mainstream of civilization a long time! thought Grimes.

He called the first lieutenant on his wrist transceiver to warn him to prepare to receive guests, then led the way up the ramp, into the ship.

9

THE SURVEY SERVICE has procedures laid down for practically everything, and as long as you stick to them you will not go far wrong. Grimes didn't need to consult the handbook titled *Procedures For Entertaining Alien Potentates*. He had entertained Alien Potentates before. Insofar as the milking of such beings of useful information was concerned he had conformed to the good old principle—candy is dandy, but licker is quicker. Of course, it was at times rather hard to decide what constituted either candy or liquor for some of the more exotic life forms. . . .

The majority of the natives had been shown into the wardroom, there to be entertained by the first lieutenant and—with the exception of Maggie Lazenby—the senior scientific officers. In his own day cabin Grimes had Maya Smith, the two men who constituted her bodyguard, and Maggie. He knew that it was foolish of him to feel ill at ease sitting there, making polite conversation with a naked woman and two naked men. Maggie took the situation for granted, of course—but her upbringing had been different from his. On Arcadia, the planet of her birth and upbringing, clothing was worn only when the weather was cold enough to justify the inconvenience.

"Tea, Maya?" asked Grimes. "Coffee?"

"What *is* tea?" she asked him. "What *is* coffee?"

"What do you drink usually?" he asked.

"Water, of course," she told him.

"And on special occasions?"

"Water."

"Mphm." He got up, opened his liquor cabinet. The light inside it was reflected brightly from the labels of bottles, from polished glasses.

Maya said, "How pretty!"

"Perhaps you would like to try . . . What would you like to try?"

"Angels' Tears," she said.

So she could read as well as speak Anglic. Grimes set out five liqueur glasses on the counter, uncorked the tall, beautifully proportioned bottle and filled them. He handed one to Maya, then served Maggie, then the two men. He lifted the remaining glass, said, "Here's mud in your eye!" and sipped. Maya sipped. The two men sipped. Maya spat like an angry cat. The men looked as though they would have liked to do the same, but they were too overawed by their unfamiliar surroundings.

"Firewater!" ejaculated the Morrowvian woman at last.

Grimes wondered what the distillers on Altairia would think if they could hear their most prized product so denigrated. This liqueur was almost pure alcohol—but it was smooth, smooth, and the cunning blend of spices used for flavoring could never be duplicated off the planet of its origin. Then he remembered a girl he had known on Dunsinane. He had not minded buying her expensive drinks, but he had been shocked by the way in which she misused them. The ending of what promised to be a beautiful friendship had come when she had poured Angels' Tears over a dish of ice cream. . . .

He said, "Perhaps this drink is a little strong to those who are not accustomed to it. But there is a way of making it less . . . fiery." He pressed the button, and in seconds a stewardess was in the cabin. The girl blushed furiously when she saw the nudity of the two Morrowvian men, but she tried hard to ignore their presence.

"Jennifer," said Grimes, "bring three dishes of ice cream."

"What flavor, sir?"

What flavor ice cream had that girl used for her appalling concoction? "Chocolate," said Grimes.

"Very good, sir."

She was not gone long. Grimes took the tray from her when she returned; he was afraid that she might drop it when attempting to serve the naked bodyguards. He set it down on the table, then took Maya's glass from her. He poured the contents over one of the dishes of ice cream, handed it to her. "Now try it," he said.

She ignored the spoon. She raised the dish in her two hands to mouth level. Her pink tongue flickered out. There was a very delicate slurping sound. Then she said to her bodyguards, "Thomas, William—this is *good!*"

"I'm glad you like it," said Grimes, handing their portions to the two men. Then—"The same again?"

"If I may," replied Maya politely.

Alcohol, even when mixed with ice cream, is a good lubricant of the vocal cords. Maya, after her second helping, became talkative. More than merely talkative . . . she became affectionate. She tended to rub up against Grimes whenever he gave her the opportunity. He would have found her advances far more welcome if Maggie had not been watching amusedly, if the two bodyguards had not been present. Not that the bodyguards seemed to mind what their mistress was doing; were it not for her inhibiting presence they would have behaved toward Maggie Lazenby as she, Maya, was behaving toward Grimes. . . .

"Such a long time . . ." gushed Maya. "Such a long, long time. . . . We knew we came from the stars, in a big ship. . . . Not *us*, of course, but our first fathers and mothers. . . . We hoped that some time some other ship would come from the stars. . . . But it's been a long, long time. . . .

"And then, after the ship called *Corgi* came, we thought that the next ships would land at Melbourne, and that it'd be *years* before we saw one. . . . The Queen of Melbourne, they say, now has a cold box to keep her meat and her water in, and she has books, *new* books, about all sorts of marvelous things. . . . And what are *you* giving *me*, Commander Grimes?"

I know what I'd like to give you, he thought. The close proximity of smooth, warm woman-flesh was putting ideas into his head. He said, trying to keep the conversation under control, "You have books?"

" 'Course we have books—but we can't make any new ones. Every town has a copy of The History; it was printed and printed and printed, years ago, when the machines were still working. . . ."

"The History?" asked Grimes.

"Yes. The History. All about Earth, and the first flights away from Earth, and the last voyage of the *Lode Cougar*. . . ."

"The ship that brought you here?"

"Of course. You don't suppose we *walked*, do you?"

"Hardly. But tell me, how do you get about your world? Do you walk, or ride, or fly?"

"There were machines once, for riding and flying, but they wore out. We walk now. Everywhere. The Messengers are the long walkers."

"I suppose that you have to maintain a messenger service for the business of government."

"What business?" She pulled away from Grimes, stood tall and erect. It was a pity that she spoiled the effect by wavering lightly. "What government? *I* am the government."

"But surely," Grimes persisted, "you must have some planetary authority in overall charge. Or national authorities. . . ."

"But why?" she asked. "But why? I look after the affairs of *my* town, Sabrina looks after the affairs of *her* town, and so on. Who can tell me how much meat is to be dried or salted before the onset of winter? Who can tell me how the town's children are to be brought up? *I* am the government, of my own town. What else is needed?"

"It seems to work, this system of theirs . . ." commented Maggie Lazenby.

" 'Course it works. Too many people in one town—then start new town."

"But," persisted Grimes, "there's more to government than mayoral duties—or queenly duties. Public health, for example. . . ."

"Every town has its doctor, to give medicine, set broken bones and so on. . . ."

Grimes looked appealingly at Maggie. She looked back at him, and shrugged. So he plodded on, unassisted. "But you must have a capital city. . . ."

Maya said, "We have. But it does not rule us. We rule ourselves. It is built around the landing place of the *Lode Cougar*. The machines are there, although they have not worked for *years*. There are the records—but all we need to know is in The History. . . ."

"And the name of this city?"

"Ballarat."

So Morrow—presumably he had been master of *Lode Cougar*—was an Australian. There was a Ballarat, on Earth, not far from Port Woomera.

"And how do we get to Ballarat?" asked Grimes.

"It is many, many days' walk. . . ."

"I wasn't thinking of walking."

"The exercise wouldn't do you any harm," Maggie told him.

"In my house there is a map. . . ."

The telephone buzzed sharply. Grimes answered it. Saul's deep voice came from the speaker, "Captain, our orbital spy eyes have reported the arrival of another ship. Mr. Hayakawa says that it is *Schnauzer*."

So—*Schnauzer* had arrived, earlier than expected. Presumably Captain Danzellan's PCO had picked up indications that other vessels were bound for Morrowvia. And presumably he would make his landing in the same location that he had used before, in *Corgi*. Where was it again? Melbourne. Grimes tried to remember his Australian geography. The Ballarat on Earth wasn't far from Melbourne. He hoped that this would also be the case on this planet, so that he could kill two birds with one stone.

Lieutenant Saul could look after the shop in his, Grimes's, absence. Somebody would have to keep an eye on Drongo Kane.

10

GRIMES WOULD HAVE liked to have been able to fly at once to Melbourne, to be there and waiting when *Schnauzer* arrived. But there was so much to be done first—the delegation of authority, the pinnace to be readied and stocked for an absence from the mother ship of indefinite duration and, last but not least, to determine the location of Captain Danzellan's arrival point with accuracy. The orbiting spy eyes would do this, of course—provided that *Schnauzer* was not using some device to render their data erroneous. She was not a warship—but it was safe to assume that she was fitted with electronic equipment not usually found aboard a merchantman.

So, early in the afternoon, Grimes and Maggie Lazenby accompanied Maya and her people back to their town. Fortunately their intake of fortified ice cream had slowed the Morrowvians down, otherwise Grimes would have found it hard to keep up with them. Even so, he was soon sweating in his tropical uniform, and his bare knees were scratched by the long, spiky grass that grew on the bank of the river, and he had managed to twist his right ankle quite painfully shortly after the departure from *Seeker*. . . .

Lethargic though they were, the Morrowvians made good time. Their bare skins, Grimes noted enviously seemed proof against the razor-edged grass blades—or it could be that they, somehow, avoided painful contact. And Maggie, once they were out of sight of the ship, removed her uniform shirt and gave it to Grimes to carry. She was as unself-conscious in her semi-nudity as the natives were in their complete nakedness. Grimes wished that he dare follow her example, but he did not have the advantage of her upbringing.

There was one welcome halt on the way. One of the bow-women

called out, and pointed to a swirl that broke the otherwise placid surface of the slow-flowing river. She unhitched a coil of line from the belt that encircled her slim waist, bent the end of it to a viciously barbed arrow. She let fly, the line snaking out behind the missile. When it hit there was a mad, explosive flurry as a creature about half the size of a full grown man leaped clear of the water. Two of the men dropped their spears, grabbed the line by its few remaining coils. Slowly, with odd growling grunts, they hauled it in, playing the aquatic creature like an angler playing a fish, towing it to a stretch of bank where the shore shelved gently to a sandy beach.

Grimes and Maggie watched as the thing was landed—she busy with her camera.

"Salmon," announced Maya. "It is good eating."

" '*Salmon?* thought Grimes. It was like no salmon that he had ever seen. It was, he supposed, some kind of fish, or some kind of ichthyoid, although it looked more like a scaly seal than anything else. But what it was called made sense. Long, long ago somebody—Morrow?—had said, "Give *everything* Earth names—and then, when this world is rediscovered, nobody will doubt that we're an Earth colony."

A slash from a vicious looking knife killed the beast, and it was slung from a spear and carried by two of the men. The journey continued.

They reached the town at last. It was a neat assemblage of low, adobe buildings, well spaced along dirt streets, with trees, each a vivid explosion of emerald foliage and crimson blossom, growing between the houses. Maya's house (palace?) was a little larger than the others, and atop a tall post just outside the main entrance was a gleaming five pointed star, wrought from silvery metal.

There were people in the streets, men, women and children. They were curious, but not obtrusively so. They were remarkably quiet, except for a group of youngsters playing some sort of ball game. These did not even pause in their sport as the queen and her guests passed them.

It was delightfully cool inside Maya's house. The small windows were unglazed, but those facing the sun were screened with matting, cutting out the glare while admitting the breeze. The room into which she took Grimes and Maggie was large, sparsely furnished. There was a big, solid table, a half dozen square, sturdy chairs. On one wall was a map of the planet, drawn to Mercatorial projection. The seas were tinted blue, the land masses either green or brown except in the polar regions, where they were white.

Maya walked slowly to this map. Her fingers stabbed at it. "This," she said, "is the River Thames. It flows into the Atlantic Ocean. Here, on this wide bend, is Cambridge. . . ."

"Mphm." *And this Cambridge*, thought Grimes, *is about in the middle of a continent, an island continent that straggles untidily over much of the equatorial belt, called—of all names!—England. . . . And where the hell is Melbourne?* He studied the map closely. There was a North Australia, another island continent, roughly rectangular, in the northern hemisphere. And there was a River Yarra. His right forefinger traced its winding course from the sea, from the Indian Ocean, to the contour lines that marked the foothills of the Dandenongs. Yes, here was Melbourne. And to the north of it, still on the river, was Ballarat.

He asked, "How do your people cross the seas, Maya? You said that all the machines, including the flying machines, had broken down years ago."

"There are machines *and* machines, Commander Grimes. We have the wind, and we have balloons, and we have sailing boats. The balloons can go only with the wind, of course, but the sailing boats—what is the expression?—can beat to windward. . . ." Then she said abruptly, "I am a poor hostess. You must be thirsty. . . ."

Not as thirsty as you must be, thought Grimes, *after gorging yourself on that horrid mixture. . . .*

"I could use a drink, Maya," said Maggie.

The Morrowvian woman went to the shelved cupboard where pottery, brightly and pleasingly glazed, was stacked. She took out six shallow bowls, set them on the table. Then she took down a stoppered pitcher that was hanging on the wall. This was not glazed, and its porous sides were bedewed with moisture. She poured from this into three of the bowls. The remaining vessels she filled with food from a deep dish that she extracted from the depths of a primitive refrigerator, a large unglazed earthenware box standing in a small bath of water. She used her hands to transfer cubes of white flesh from the dish to the bowls. There was no sign of any knives, forks or spoons.

She lifted her bowl of water to her mouth. She grinned and said "Here's mud in your eye!" She *lapped* the liquid, a little noisily. Grimes and Maggie drank more conventionally. The water was pleasantly cool, had a faint vegetable tang to it. Probably it was safe enough—but, in any case, all of *Seeker*'s people had been given wide spectrum antibiotic shots before landing.

Maya, using one hand only, quite delicately helped herself to food from her bowl. Without hesitation Maggie followed suit. Her fine eyebrows arched in surprised appreciation. Grimes took a cautious sample. This, he decided after the first nibble, was *good.* It reminded him of a dish that he had enjoyed during his last leave on Earth, part of which he had spent in Mexico. This had been fish—raw, but seasoned, and marinaded in the juice of freshly squeezed limes. He would have liked some more, but it would be a long time, he feared, before he would be able properly to relax and enjoy whatever social amenities this planet afforded.

Maggie, having followed Maya's example in licking her hands clean, had unslung one of her cameras, was pointing it at the map. She explained, "We have to have a copy of this, so that we can find our way to Melbourne."

"It will not be necessary. I can send a Messenger with you. But I warn you, it is a long journey, unless you go in your ship."

"We shall not go in the ship, Maya," Grimes told her. "But we shall not be walking, either. We shall use a pinnace, a relatively small flying boat."

"I have never flown," said Maya wistfully. "Not even in a balloon. Do you think that I . . . ?"

"Why not?" said Grimes. *Why not?* he thought. *She'll be able to introduce me to her sister queen in Melbourne.*

"When do we leave?" she asked him.

"In the morning, as soon after sunrise as possible." That would be a good time; Melbourne was only a degree or so west of Cambridge. The flight would be made in daylight, and arrival would be well before sunset.

She said, "You will excuse me. I must make arrangements for my deputy to run affairs during my absence."

"I must do likewise," said Grimes.

They looked at each other gravely, both monarchs of a small kingdom, both with the cares of state heavy on their shoulders. It was unkind of Maggie to spoil the effect by snickering.

"I shall send an escort with you," said Maya.

"It is not necessary. All we have to do is to follow the river."

"But wolves have been reported along the river bank. . . ."

And if the "wolves" of Morrowvia bore the same relationship to Terran wolves as did the Morrowvian "salmon" to Terran salmon, Grimes didn't want to meet them. He said so to Maya.

So he and Maggie, escorted by four spearmen and two bow-women, walked back to the ship. The members of the escort were too awe-stricken by the visitors from Outside to talk unless spoken to, and after ten minutes or so of very heavy going no attempt was made at conversation.

11

GRIMES DID NOT get much sleep that night.

He did not want to leave his ship until he was reasonably sure that the situation was under control. Drongo Kane was the main problem. Just what were his intentions? *Southerly Buster* had been kept under close observation from *Seeker*, and all the activity around her airlock had been filmed. Highly sensitive long-range microphones had been trained upon her—but Kane had set up some small noise-making machine that produced a continuous *whup, whup, whup*. . . . Hayakawa, disregarding the Rhine Institute code of ethics, had tried to pry, but Myra Bracegirdle, Kane's PCO, was maintaining an unbreakable block over the minds of all the *Buster*'s personnel. He had then tried to pick up the thoughts of the people in the town of Oxford, with little more success.

Grimes studied the film that had been made. He watched, on the screen, Kane talking amicably with Sabrina, the Queen of Oxford. He seemed to be laying on the charm with a trowel, and the Morrowvian woman was lapping it up. She smiled smugly when Drongo hung a scintillating string of synthetic diamonds about her neck, and her chubby hand went up to stroke the huge ruby that formed the pendant of the necklace, that glowed with crimson fire between her ample, golden-skinned breasts. She looked, thought Grimes, like a sleek cat that had got its nose into the cream. If it had not been for that annoying *whup, whup, whup* he would have heard her purring. It was shortly after her acceptance of this gift that Kane took her into the ship. Dreebly and two others—a little, fat man who, to judge by his braid, was the second mate and a cadaverous blonde in catering officer's uniform—remained by the table, handing out cheap jewelry, hand mirrors, pocket knives (a bad guess, thought Grimes amusedly, in this nudist culture), pairs of scissors and (always a sure way of buying goodwill) a quite good selection of children's toys. But it was the books that were in the greatest demand. The lens of one of the cameras that had been used zoomed in to a close-up of the display. Their covers were brightly-colored, eye-catching. They were, every one of them, handouts from the Tourist Bureaus of the more glamorous worlds of the galaxy.

Did Kane intend opening a travel agency on this world? It was possible, Grimes conceded. After all, the man was a shipowner. And his ship, according to the report from Elsinore, had been modified to suit her for the carriage of passengers.

"I don't like the looks of this, Captain," said the first lieutenant.

"What don't you like about it, Mr. Saul?" asked Grimes.

"I still remember what he did on Ganda."

"He can hardly do the same here. These people aren't being evacuated from their world before it's destroyed. They're quite happy here. In any case, the Gandans were skilled workmen, technicians. These people, so far as I can see, are little better than savages. *Nice* savages, I admit, but . . ."

"Forgive me for saying so, Captain, but you're very simple, aren't you?"

Grimes's prominent ears reddened. He demanded sharply, "What do you mean, Mr. Saul?"

"You've seen even more of these people than I have, sir. Have you seen an ugly man or woman?"

"No," admitted Grimes.

"And there are worlds where beautiful women are in great demand. . . ."

"And there are the quite stringent laws prohibiting the traffic in human merchandise," said Grimes.

"Kane is bound to find some loophole," insisted Saul. "Just as he did on Ganda." Then his racial bitterness found utterance. "After all, he's a *white* man."

Grimes sighed. He wished, as he had wished before, that Saul would forget the color of his skin. He said tiredly, "All right, all right—Whitey's to blame for *everything*. But, from my reading of history, I seem to remember that it was the fat black kings on the west coast of Africa who sold their own people to the white slave traders. . . ."

"Just as that fat yellow queen whom Kane entertained will sell her people to the white slave trader."

"I wouldn't call her *fat* . . ." objected Grimes, trying to bring the conversation to a lighter level.

"Just pleasantly plump, dearie," said Maggie Lazenby. "But, as you say, Drongo won't be able to pull off a coup like the Gandan effort twice running. And even if he makes a deal with some non-Federated world, *he's* still a Federation citizen and subject to Federation law."

"Yes, Commander Lazenby," agreed Saul dubiously. "But I don't trust him."

"Who does?" said Grimes. "During my absence you'll just have to watch him, Mr. Saul, like a cat watching a mouse." He added, "Like a black cat watching a white mouse."

"A white rat, you mean," grumbled Saul.

12

BEFORE SUNRISE THE pinnace was ready.

Grimes was taking with him Pitcher, the navigator, Ensign Billard who, as well as being assistant communications officer (electronic), was a qualified atmosphere pilot, and Commander Maggie Lazenby. All of them carried sidearms. The pinnace, too, was armed, being fitted with a laser cannon and two 20 mm machine guns.

Just as the sun was coming up, Grimes, Pitcher, Billard and Maggie stood outside the ship, watching as the small craft, its inertial drive muttering irritably, was eased out of its bay high on the ship's side, maneuvered down to the ground. It landed rather clumsily. Saul stepped out of the pilot's cabin and saluted with rather less than his usual snap. (He had been up, working, all night.) He said, "She's all yours, Captain."

"Thank you, Number One." Grimes looked at his watch, the one that had been adjusted to keep Morrowvian time. "Mphm. Time Maya was here."

"And here she is," said Maggie. "Enter the Queen of Cambridge, singing and dancing. . . ."

Maya was not singing and dancing, but she looked well rested, alert, and as though she were looking forward to the outing. She was escorted by a half a dozen bow-women and a like number of spearmen, two of whom were carrying a large basket between them. Curiously, Grimes looked into the basket. There were bowls of the raw fish that he had enjoyed the previous day, other bowls of what looked like dried meat. He looked away hastily. All that he had been able to manage for breakfast was a large cup of black coffee.

Maya looked with interest at the pinnace. "How does this thing fly?" she asked. "I don't see any wings or gasbag. . . ."

"Inertial drive," Grimes told her briefly. "No, I'm sorry, but I can't explain it at this hour of the morning." He turned to Saul. "All right, Number One. I'm getting the show on the road. I leave *Seeker* in your capable hands. Don't do anything you couldn't do riding a bicycle."

"What *is* a bicycle?" asked Maya.

"Remind me to bring you one some time. . . ." He visualized the tall, lush, naked woman astride such a machine and felt more than a little happier.

Pitcher and Billard clambered into the pinnace. They stood in the open doorway and took the hamper of Maya's provisions as the two Morrowvian spearmen handed it up to them. Then, Maggie, disdaining the offer of a helping hand from Grimes, mounted the short ladder into the doorway. Grimes, however, was courteously able to assist Maya to board. He glared coldly at Saul when he noticed the sardonic look on the first lieutenant's face. Then he boarded himself.

Pitcher, with a chart made from Maggie's photographs, and young Mr. Billard occupied the forward compartment. Grimes sat with Maggie and Maya in the after cabin. As soon as the women were comfortable—although Maya was sitting on the edge of her seat like a young girl at her very first party—Grimes ordered, "Take her up."

"Take her up, sir," acknowledged Billard smartly. He was little more than a boy and inclined to take himself seriously, but he was able and conscientious. The noise of the restarted inertial drive was little more, at first, than a distant whisper. The pinnace lifted so gently that there was no sense of motion; even Grimes was surprised to see the sleek hull of *Seeker* sliding past and downward beyond the viewports. She ascended vertically, and then her passengers were able to look out and down at the two ships—*Southerly Buster*'s people were sleeping in; there were no signs of life around her—at the winding river, at the little towns spaced along its banks.

Maya ran from one side to the other of the small cabin. There was rather much of her in these confined quarters. "Oh, look!" she said, pointing. "There's *Cambridge!* Doesn't it look *small* from up here! And that town on the next bend is Kingston, and there's Richmond. . . . And there's the weekly cargo wherry, there, with the sail. . . ."

Grimes could not appreciate the distant view as it was obscured by Maya's breasts, but he did not complain.

"Sir," called Pitcher, "do you want us to steer a compass course, or shall we navigate from landmark to landmark? That way we shall not put on much distance."

"From landmark to landmark," said Grimes. "We may as well enjoy the scenery."

"You look as though you're doing that right now," commented Maggie.

"Would you mind getting back to your seat, Maya?" asked Grimes. "We shall be accelerating soon, and you may lose your balance. . . ."

"Make sure you don't lose yours . . ." Maggie murmured.

The irregular beat of the inertial drive was louder now, and its vibration noticeable. The pinnace turned in a wide arc, and then the landing site was astern of them, and the two, tall ships were dwindling to the size of toys. Ahead of them, and a little to starboard, was a snowcapped mountain, Ben Nevis. Below them was a wide prairie over which surged a great herd of duncolored beasts. "Bison," said Maya, adding that these animals constituted the main meat supply of her people. She offered strips of dried flesh from her basket to Grimes and Maggie, much as a Terran woman would offer chocolates. Grimes took one and chewed it dubiously. It wasn't bad, but it would not worry him much if he never tasted any more of it.

He took a pair of binoculars from their rack and stared down at the so-called bison. From almost directly above them he could not get much of an idea of their general appearance—but he knew that the Terran animals of that name had never run to six legs, whereas these brutes did.

The gleaming peak of Ben Nevis hung in their starboard viewports for long seconds, then dropped slowly astern. The pinnace, now, was following the course of another river, the Mersey, and Maya was pointing out the towns along its meandering length. "Yes, that must be Lancaster. . . . I visited there two years ago, and I remember that thickly wooded hill just by it. . . . Most of the people living along the Mersey banks are Cordwainers. . . ."

"Cordwainers?" asked Grimes, thinking that she must be referring to some odd trade.

"It is their name, just as Smith is the name of most of us along the Thames. . . ."

"And what names, how many names, do you have on this world?" asked Maggie.

"There's Smith, of course. And Wells. And Morrow. And Cordwainer. That's all."

"Probably only four male survivors when *Lode Cougar* got here," said Grimes. "And polygamous marriages. . . ."

"Chester," announced Maya, pointing to another town. "Brighton, and the shipbuilding yards. . . . That schooner looks almost finished . . .

Manchester, *I think*. . . . Oh, this is the way to travel! It took me weeks, many weeks, when I did it by foot and by wherry!"

"And why do you travel?" asked Maggie.

"Why do *you* travel?" the other woman countered. "To . . . to see new things, new people."

"And what new things have you seen?"

"Oh, the workshops at Manchester. You must have noticed the smoke as we flew over them. They smelt metal there, after they've dug the ore from the ground. They say that for years and years, before the process was discovered, we had to use scraps of metal from the ship to tip our spears and arrows."

"And so your weapons are made from this iron—I suppose it's iron—from Manchester?" asked Maggie.

"Yes."

"And what do you buy it with? What do you barter for it?"

"The salmon are caught only in the Thames. Their pickled flesh is a great delicacy."

"And tell me," Maggie went on, "don't some of you Smiths and Morrows and Wellses and Cordwainers get the idea, sometimes, that there are other ways of getting goods besides barter?"

"There are on other ways, Commander Maggie."

"On some worlds there are. Just suppose, Maya . . . just suppose that it's been a bad year for salmon. Just suppose that you need a stock of new weapons and have nothing to give in exchange for them. Just suppose that you lead a party of spearmen and archers to, say, Oxford, to take the people by surprise and to take their bows and spears by force. . . ."

"Are you mad?" demanded Maya. "That would be impossible. It is not . . . human to intrude where one is not wanted. As for . . . *fighting* . . . that is not human either. Oh, we fight the wolves, but only to protect ourselves from them. We fight the eagles when we have to. But to fight each other . . . unthinkable!"

"But you must fight sometimes," said Maggie.

"Yes. But we are ashamed of it afterward. Our young men, perhaps, over a woman. Sometimes two women will quarrel, and use their claws. Oh, we have all read The History. We know that human beings have fought each other, and with weapons that would make our spears and bows look like toys. But we *could* not." There was a long silence, broken when she asked timidly, "And can you?"

"I'm afraid we can," Grimes told her. "And I'm afraid that we do. Your world has no soldiers or policemen, but yours is an exceptional world. . . ."

"And are *you* a soldier, Commander Grimes?"

"Don't insult me, Maya. I'm a spaceman, although I am an officer in a fighting service. I suppose that you could call me a policeman of sorts. . . ."

"The policeman's lot is not a happy one . . ." quoted Maggie solemnly.

"Mphm. Nobody press-ganged me into the Survey Service."

Then they were approaching the coast, the mouth of the river and the port town of Liverpool. North they swept, running low over the glittering sea, deviating from their course to pass close to a large schooner, deviating again to make rings around a huge, unwieldy balloon, hovering over a fleet of small fishing craft whose crews were hauling in nets alive with a silvery catch, whose men stared upward in wonder at the alien flying machine.

Pitcher called back from the pilot's cabin, "We're setting course for the mouth of the Yarra, sir—if you're agreeable."

"I'm agreeable, Mr. Pitcher. You can put her on automatic and we'll have lunch."

Maya enjoyed the chicken sandwiches that had been packed for them, and Pitcher and Billard waxed enthusiastic over the spiced fish that she handed around.

13

IT WAS AN uneventful flight northward over the ocean. They sighted no traffic save for a large schooner beating laboriously to windward; the Morrowvians, Grimes learned from Maya, were not a sea-minded people, taking to the water only from necessity and never for recreation.

As the pinnace drove steadily onward Maya, with occasional encouragement from Grimes and Maggie, talked. Once she got going she reminded Grimes of a Siamese cat he had once known, a beast even more talkative than the generality of its breed. So she talked, and Grimes and Maggie and Pitcher and Billard listened, and every so often Maggie would have to put a fresh spool in her recorder.

This Morrowvia was an odd sort of a planet—odd insofar as the population was concerned. The people were neither unintelligent nor illiterate, but they had fallen surprisingly far from the technological levels of the founders of the colony—and, even more surprisingly, the fall had been arrested at a stage well above primitive savagery. On so many worlds similarly settled the regression to Man's primitive beginnings had been horridly complete.

So there was Morrowvia, with a scattered population of ten million, give or take a few hundreds of thousands, all of them living in small towns, and all these towns with good old Terran names. There was no agriculture, save for the cultivation of herbs used medicinally and for the flavoring of food. Meat was obtained by hunting, although half-hearted attempts had been made at the domestication of the so-called bison and a few of the local flying creatures, more reptilian than anything else, the flesh and the eggs of which were palatable. The reason why more had not been done along these lines was that hunting was a way of life.

There was some industry—the mining and smelting of metals, the manufacture of weapons and such few tools as were required, shipbuilding. Should more ever be required, said Maya, the library at Ballarat would furnish full instructions for doing everything, for making anything at all.

Government? There was, said the Morrowvian woman, government of a sort. Each town was autonomous, however, and each was ruled—although "ruled" was hardly the correct word—by an elected queen. No, there were no kings. (Maya had read The History and knew what kings were.) It was only natural that women, who were in charge of their own homes, should elect a woman to be in overall charge of an assemblage of homes. It was only natural that the men should be occupied with male pursuits such as hunting and fishing—although women, the younger ones especially, enjoyed the hunt as much as the men did. And it was only natural that men should employ the spear as their main weapon, while women favored the bow.

No, there were no women engaged in heavy industry, although they did work at such trades as the manufacture of cordage and what little cloth was used. And women tended the herb gardens.

Maya confirmed that there were only four families—although "tribes" would be the better word—on Morrowvia. There were Smiths, Cordwainers, Morrows and Wellses. There was intermarriage between the tribes, and in such cases the husband took his wife's surname, which was passed on, also, to the children of such unions. It was not quite a matriarchal society, but it was not far from it.

Grimes steered the conversation on to the subject of communications. There had been radio—but many generations ago. It had never been required—"After all," said Maya reasonably enough, "if I die and my people elect a new queen it is of no real concern to anybody except themselves. There is no need for the entire planet to be informed within seconds of the event."—and transmitters and receivers had been allowed to fall into desuetude. There was a loosely organized system of postmen—men and women qualified by powers of endurance and fleetness of foot—but these carried only letters and very light articles of merchandise. Heavier articles were transported in the slow wherries, up and down the rivers—which meant that a consignment of goods would often have to be shipped along the two long sides of a triangle rather than over the short, overland side.

There was a more or less—rather less than more—regular service by schooner between the island continents. The seamen, Grimes gathered, were a race apart, males and females too incompetent to get by ashore—or, if not incompetent, too antisocial. Seafaring was a profession utterly devoid of either glamor or standing. Grimes was rather shocked when he heard this. He regarded himself as being in a direct line of descent from the seamen and explorers of Earth's past, and was of the opinion that ships, ships of any kind, were the finest flower of human civilization.

The airmen—the balloonists—were much more highly thought of, though the service they provided was even more unreliable than that rendered by the sailors. Some of the airmen, Maya said, were wanting to fit their clumsy, unmaneuverable craft with engines—but Morrow (he must have been quite a man, this Morrow, thought Grimes) had warned his people, shortly before his death, of the overuse of machinery.

He had said (Maya quoted), "I am leaving you a good world. The land, the air and the sea are clean. Your own wastes go back into the soil and render it more fertile. The wastes of the machines will pollute everything—the sky, the sea and the very ground you walk upon. Beware of the machine. It pretends to be a good servant—but the wages that it exacts are far too high."

"A machine brought you—your ancestors—here," pointed out Grimes.

"If that machine had worked properly we should not be here," said Maya. She smiled. "The breaking down of the machine was our good luck."

"Mphm." But this was a *good* world. It could be improved—and what planet could not? But would the reintroduction of machinery improve it? The reintroduction not only of machinery but of the servants of the machine, that peculiar breed of men who have sold their souls to false gods of steam and steel, of metal and burning oil, who tend, more and more, to degrade humanity to the status of slaves, to elevate the mindless automata to the status of masters.

Even so . . . what was that quotation he had used in a recent conversation with Maggie? "Transportation is civilization."

More efficient transportation, communications in general, would improve Morrowvia. He said as much. He argued, "Suppose there's some sort of natural catastrophe . . . a hurricane, say, or a fire, or a flood. . . . If you had radio again, or efficient aircraft, the survivors could call for help, almost at once, and the help would not be long in reaching them."

"But why?" Maya asked. "But why? Why should *they* call for help, and why should *we* answer? Or why should *we* call for help, and why should *they* answer? We—how shall I put it? We go our ways, all of us, with neither help or hindrance, from anybody. We . . . cope. If disaster strikes, it is *our* disaster. We should not wish any interference from outsiders."

"A passion for privacy," remarked Maggie, "carried to extremes."

"Privacy is our way of life," Maya told her. "It is a good way of life."

Grimes had been wondering how soon it would be before the pair of them clashed; now the clash had come. They glared at each other, the two handsome women, one naked, the other in her too-skimpy uniform, somehow alike—and yet very unlike each other. Claws were being unsheathed.

And then young Billard called out from the forward compartment. "Land on the radar, sir! Looks like the coastline, at four hundred kilometers!"

Rather thankfully Grimes got up and went into the pilot's cabin. He looked into the screen of the radarscope, then studied the chart that had been made from the original survey data and from Maggie's photographs of that quite accurate wall map in Maya's "palace." Yes, that looked like Port Phillip Bay, with the mighty Yarra flowing into it from the north. He thought, *North Australia*, here we come! Then, with an affection of the Terran Australian accent, *Norstrylia, here we come!*

That corruption of words rang a faint but disturbing bell in his mind—but he had, as and from now, more important things to think about.

He said to the navigator, "A very nice landfall, Mr. Pitcher," and to Billard, "Better put her back on manual. And keep her as she's going."

Maya was by his side, looking with pleased wonderment at the glowing picture in the radar screen. Grimes thought, *I wish she wouldn't rub up against me so much. Not in front of Pitcher and Billard, anyhow. And not in front of Maggie, especially.*

14

IT WAS SUMMER in the northern hemisphere, and when the pinnace arrived over Melbourne, having followed the winding course of the Yarra to the foothills of the Dandenongs, there were still half a dozen hours of daylight left. The town, as were all the towns, was a small one; Grimes estimated that its population would run to about four thousand people. As they made the approach he studied it through powerful binoculars. It was neatly laid out, and the houses seemed to be of wooden construction, with thatched roofs. Beyond the town, on a conveniently sited patch of level, tree-free ground, towered the unmistakable metal steeple of a starship. There was only one ship that it could be.

Suddenly the pinnace's transceiver came to life. "*Schnauzer* calling strange aircraft. *Schnauzer* calling strange aircraft. Do you read me?"

"I read you," replied Grimes laconically.

"Identify yourself, please."

"*Schnauzer*, this is Number One Pinnace of FSS *Seeker*. Over."

There was a silence. Then, "You may land by me, Number One Pinnace."

Grimes looked at Pitcher and Billard. They looked back at him. He raised an eyebrow sardonically. Pitcher said, "Uncommonly decent of him, sir, to give *us* permission to land. . . ."

"Mphm. I suppose he was here first—although I don't think that planting a shipping company's flag makes a territorial claim legally valid."

"They could rename this world Pomerania . . ." suggested Pitcher.

"Or Alsatia . . ." contributed Billard.

"Or New Pekin . . ." continued Pitcher. "Or some other son-of-a-bitching name. . . ."

"Or Dogpatch," said Grimes, with an air of finality. And then, into the microphone, an edge of sarcasm to his voice. "Thank you, *Schnauzer*. I am coming in."

Acting on his captain's instructions Billard brought the pinnace low over the town. People stared up at them—some in the by now familiar state of nudity, some clothed. Those who were dressed were wearing uniform, obviously personnel from the Dog Star ship. The small craft almost grazed the peaked, thatched roofs, then settled down gently fifty meters to the west of *Schnauzer*, on the side from which her boarding ramp was extended.

"Well," remarked Maggie, "we're here. I don't notice any red carpet out for us. What do we do now?"

"We disembark," Grimes told her. "There'll be no need to leave anybody aboard; the officers of major shipping companies are usually quite law-abiding people." *Usually*, he thought, *but not always*. He remembered suddenly the almost piratical exploits of one Captain Craven, the master of *Delta Orionis*, to which he, Grimes, had been an accessory.

"What about Drongo Kane?" asked Maggie.

"You can hardly call *him* a major shipping company," said Grimes.

Three men were walking slowly down the merchant ship's ramp. In the lead was a bareheaded, yellow-haired giant, heavily muscled. Following him was a tall and slender, too slender, young man. Finally—last ashore and first to board—was a portly gentleman, clothed in dignity and respectability as well as in master's uniform. All of them wore sidearms. Grimes frowned. As a naval officer he did not like to see merchant officers going about armed to the teeth—but he knew that the Dog Star Line held quite strong views on the desirability of the ability of its ships and its personnel to defend themselves.

The door of the pinnace opened and the short ladder extended itself to the grassy ground. Grimes buckled on his belt with the holstered pistol, put on his cap and, ignoring the steps, jumped out of the small craft. He turned to assist Maggie but she ignored his hand, jumped also. Maya followed her, leaping down with feline grace. Pitcher was next, then Billard, who spoiled the effect by tripping and sprawling untidily.

Schnauzer's master had taken leading place now, and was advancing slowly, with his two officers a couple of paces to the rear. Unlike them he was not wearing the comfortable, utilitarian gray shorts, shirt and stockings but a white uniform, with tunic and long trousers—but portly men look their best in clothing that conceals most of the body.

He acknowledged Grimes's salute stiffly, while his rather protuberant brown eyes flickered over the young man's insignia of rank. He said, in a rather reedy voice, "Good afternoon, Commander." Then, "You are the commanding officer of *Seeker?*"

"Yes, Captain. Lieutenant Commander Grimes. And you, sir, are Captain Roger Danzellan, and the two gentlemen with you are Mr. Oscar Eklund, chief officer, and Mr. Francis Delamere, second officer."

"How right you are, Commander. I realize that there is no need for me to introduce myself and my people. But as a mere merchant captain I do not have the resources of an Intelligence Service to draw upon. . . ."

Grimes took the hint and introduced Maggie, Maya, Pitcher and Billard.

"And now, Commander," asked Danzellan, "what can I do for you?"

"If you would, sir, you can tell me what you are doing here."

"Trade, Commander, trade. This is a competitive galaxy, although you ladies and gentlemen in the Survey Service may not find it so. My employers are not in business for the state of their health. . . ."

"Aren't they?" inquired Maggie. "I would have thought that the state of their *financial* health was their main concern."

"A point well taken, Commander Lazenby. Anyhow, the Dog Star Line is always ready and willing to expand its sphere of operations. When a Dog Star ship, *Corgi*—but I imagine that you know all about *that*—stumbled upon this world, quite by chance, the reports made by her master, myself were read with great interest by the Board of Directors. It was realized that we, as it were, have one foot well inside the door. It was decided to strike the iron while it is hot. Do you read me, Commander Grimes?"

"Loud and clear, Captain Danzellan. But tell me, what sort of trade do you hope to establish with the people of Morrowvia?"

"There are manufactured goods from a score of planets on our established routes for which there will be a demand here. For example, I have in my hold a large consignment of solar-powered refrigerators, and one of solar cookers. On the occasion of my first visit here a refrigerator was left with the, er, Queen of Melbourne. I was pleased to discover on my return that it is still working well, and even more pleased to learn that other, er, queens have seen it, and that still others have heard about it. . . ."

"You will remember, Commander Grimes," said Maya, "that I told you about the cold box."

"So even this lady, from Cambridge, many miles from here, has heard about it."

"Mphm. But how are the people going to pay the freight on these quite unnecessary luxuries—and for the luxuries themselves?"

"Unnecessary luxuries, Commander? I put it to you—would *you* be prepared to sip your pre-prandial pink gin without an ice cube to make it more potable? Do *you* enjoy lukewarm beer?"

"Frankly, no, Captain. But—the question of payment. . . ."

"These are sordid details, Commander. But I have no doubt that something will be worked out."

"No doubt at all," commented Maggie Lazenby. "When people want something badly enough they find some way of paying for it."

"In a nutshell, Commander Lazenby. In a nutshell." Danzellan beamed upon her benignly. Then, "I am sorry that I cannot ask you aboard my ship, but we are rather cramped for space. In a merchant vessel carrying capacity for money-earning cargo is of greater importance than luxurious accommodation for personnel."

"I understand," said Grimes. Such merchant vessels as he had been aboard housed their officers in far greater comfort than did the Survey Service. He went on, "Maya, here, wishes to pay her respects to her sister queen. We will accompany her."

"I'll show you the way, Commander," volunteered Mr. Delamere eagerly.

Danzellan frowned at his second officer and the young man wilted visibly. Then the captain relented. "All right," he said. "You may take the party from *Seeker* to Queen Lilian's palace." He added sternly, "See that they don't get lost."

15

DELAMERE LED THE way from the landing site to the town, walking fast. He did not pause when he took the party past a survey team from *Schnauzer*, busily engaged with tapes, rods and theodolite, working under the direction of a young woman with third officer's braid on her shoulderboards. He acknowledged her wave absently. Watching the surveyors was a large group of children, with a smaller number of adults. These people, Grimes saw, were very similar to those whom he had encountered at *Seeker*'s landing place—well formed, beautiful rather than merely handsome. He was interested to note, however, that here the rudimentary nipples below the true breasts were the exception rather than the rule, whereas among Maya's people almost every woman—as she herself—was so furnished.

The dirt roads between the houses were level and tidy. The wooden buildings were well spaced and these, unlike those in Cambridge, had glazed windows—but, probably, the winters on this continent would be relatively severe. There was an amplitude of trees and flowering shrubs in every open space.

Lilian's palace was larger than the other houses. It had, like Maya's a tall staff standing outside its main entrance, a pole surmounted by a star fabricated from glittering metal rods. Also, in the full light of the westering sun, there stood just outside the door a metallic box, mounted on small wheels. Grimes had seen such contraptions before; this was the famous sun-powered refrigerator.

A tall woman came out to meet them. Her skin was creamy; the hair of her head and body was a glowing orange color. She said to Maya, "Welcome, sister. My house is yours."

"Thank you, sister," replied Maya. Then, "We have corresponded, but I did not think that we should ever meet."

"You are . . . ?"

"Maya, from Cambridge, Lilian."

"I know of you, Maya. Now I have the pleasure of knowing you."

"Lilian . . ." said Delamere.

"Yes, Francis?"

"How is Tabitha?"

"She is well, Francis."

"Can I see her, Lilian?"

"It will be well if you do not, Francis. Unless you are willing to abide by our customs."

The young man looked desperately unhappy. His long nose quivered like that of a timid rabbit. He said, "But you know. . ."

"What do I know, Francis? Only what I am told. Only what I see with my own eyes." *(And those green eyes*, thought Grimes, *will see plenty.)*

"Lilian," Maya said, "I have brought friends with me."

"So I see." The woman was regarding the people from *Seeker* with a certain lack of enthusiasm. Her attitude seemed to be, *If you've seen one stranger from beyond the stars, you've seen them all.*

"Lilian, this is Commander Grimes, captain of the ship called *Seeker*. The lady is Commander Maggie Lazenby. The gentlemen are Lieutenant Pitcher and Ensign Billard."

Grimes saluted. Lilian Morrow inclined her head gravely, then said, "Be pleased to enter."

They followed her into the palace. Inside it was very like Maya's official residence, the big wall map being the most prominent decoration on a wall of the room into which she led them. She saw them seated, then excused herself and went back outside. While she was gone Grimes asked Delamere, "Who is Tabitha, Mr. Delamere?"

The second mate flushed angrily and snapped, "None of your business, Commander." Then, obviously regretting his display of temper, he muttered sulkily, "She's Lilian's daughter. I . . . I met her when I was here before, in *Corgi*. Now her mother won't let me see her again unless . . ."

"Unless what?" prompted Maggie. "Unless what, Francis?"

That's right, thought Grimes. *Turn on the womanly charm and sympathy.*

Delamere was about to answer when Lilian returned. She was carrying a tray on which was a rather lopsided jug of iced water, a dish of some greenish looking flesh cut into cubes, glass drinking bowls. She filled a bowl for each of them from the jug.

The water was refreshing, the meat tasted how Grimes imagined that the flesh of a snake would taste. He supposed—he hoped—that it was nonpoisonous. Maya seemed to be enjoying it.

"And now, Commander Grimes," asked Lilian, after they had all sipped and nibbled, "what do you here?"

"I represent the Federation, Lilian. . . ."

"Just as Captain Danzellan represents the Dog Star Line. Captain Danzellan hopes to make money—and Morrow warned us about *that*—for his employers and himself. And what do *you* hope to make for yourself and your employers?"

"We are here to help you, Lilian."

"Do we need any help, Commander Grimes?"

"The Survey Service, Lilian, is like a police force. You know what a police force is. You have read The History. We protect people from those who would exploit them, rob them, even."

"Have we asked for protection?"

"You may do so."

"But we have not done so."

"Yet."

"Lilian knows that she has nothing to fear from us," said Delamere, more than a little smugly.

"Indeed, Francis?" The look that she gave him drove him back into sullen silence. Then she addressed Grimes again. "Commander Grimes, the relationship established between ourselves and Captain Danzellan is, on the whole, a friendly one. Captain Danzellan, in exchange for certain concessions, will bring us goods that we cannot make for ourselves. Before anything is decided, however, it will be necessary to convene a Council of Queens. I, of course, speak only for Melbourne—but Morrow foresaw that a time would come when matters affecting the entire continent, the entire world, even, would have to be discussed. Word has gone to my sisters of Ballarat, Alice, Darwin, Sydney, Perth, Brisbane—but there is no need for me to recite to you the names of all the towns of North Australia—that decisions affecting us all must soon be made. It is fortunate that our sister of Cambridge is with us; she will be able to report to her own people on what we are doing."

"These concessions . . ." began Grimes.

"They are none of *your* business, Commander."

Grimes looked appealingly at Maggie. She was supposed to know what made people tick. She was supposed to know which button to push to get which results. She looked back at him blandly.

Damn the woman! thought Grimes. *Damn* all *women*. He floundered on, "But perhaps I should be able to advise you. . . ."

"We do not need your advice, Commander."

"Mphm." Grimes fished his battered pipe from his pocket, filled it, lit it.

"Please!" said Lilian sharply, "do not smoke that filthy thing in here!"

"So your great ancestor warned you about smoking. . . ."

"He did so. He warned us about all the vices and unpleasant habits of the men who, eventually, would make contact with us."

"Oh, well," muttered Grimes at last. Then, "I suppose that there is no objection to our visiting Ballarat, to look at your library, your records. . . ."

"That is a matter for the Queen of Ballarat."

And there isn't any radio, thought Grimes, *and there aren't any telephones, and I'm damned if I'll ask Her Majesty here to send a messenger*. He said, "Thank you for your hospitality, Lilian. And now, if you will excuse us, we'll get back to our pinnace and set up camp for the night."

She said, "You are excused. And you have my permission to sleep on the outskirts of the town."

"Shall we set up a tent for you, Maya?" Grimes asked.

"Thank you, no. Lilian and I have so much to talk about."

"Can I see Tabitha?" pleaded Delamere.

"No, Francis. You may not."

Schnauzer's second officer got reluctantly to his feet. He mumbled, "Are you ready, Commander? I'm getting back to my ship."

He led the way out of the palace and back to the landing site, although his services as a guide were hardly necessary. *Schnauzer*, dwarfing the trees that grew around the grassy field, stuck up like a sore thumb.

Back at the pinnace Grimes, Pitcher and Billard unloaded their camping gear, with Maggie watching and, at times, criticizing. The little air compresser swiftly inflated the four small sleeping tents, the larger one that would combine the functions of mess-room and galley. Then Billard went to the nearby stream for two buckets of water. A sterilizing tablet was dropped into each one, more as a matter of routine than anything else. If the broad spectrum antibiotic shots administered aboard *Seeker* had not been effective it would have been obvious by now. The battery-powered cooker was set up, and in a short time a pot of savory stew, prepared from dehydrated ingredients, was simmering and water was boiling for coffee.

The four of them sat around the collapsible table waiting until the meal was ready.

Grimes said, "What do you make of it, Maggie?"

"Make of what?" she countered.

"The whole setup."

She replied thoughtfully. "There's something *odd* about this world. In the case of Sparta there were all sorts of historical analogies to draw upon—here, there aren't. And how shall I put it? Like this, perhaps. The Morrowvians rather resent the violation of their privacy, but realize that there's nothing much that they can do about it. They certainly aren't mechanically minded, and distrust of the machine has been bred into them—but they do appreciate that the machine can contribute greatly to their comfort. I imagine that Danzellan's 'cold boxes' will be *very* popular. . . . As for their attitude toward ourselves—there's distrust again, but I think that they are prepared to like us as individuals. Maya, for example, has taken quite a shine to you. I've been expecting to see you raped at any tick of the clock. . . ."

"Mphm."

"You could do worse, I suppose—though whether or not she could is another matter. . . ."

"Ha, ha," chuckled Pitcher politely.

"Hah. Hah," growled Grimes, inhibiting any further mirth on the part of his subordinates.

"Anyhow, as far as behavior goes they do tend to deviate widely from the norm. The *human* norm, that is. . . ."

"What do you mean?" asked Grimes.

"I rather wish that I knew, myself," she told him.

16

GRIMES HAD PITCHER work out the local time of sunrise, then saw to it that everybody had his watch alarm set accordingly. Before retiring he called Saul aboard *Seeker*—his wrist transceiver was hooked up to the much more powerful set in the pinnace—and listened to his first lieutenant's report of the day's activities. Mr. Saul had little to tell him. Maya's people had made considerable inroads into the ship's supply of ice cream. Sabrina's people had been coming and going around *Southerly Buster* all day, but neither Sabrina nor Captain Kane had put in an appearance. Saul seemed to be shocked by this circumstance. Grimes shrugged. Drongo's morals—or lack of them—were none of his concern.

Or were they?

Grimes then told Saul, in detail, of his own doings of the day, of his plans for the morrow. He signed off, undressed, wriggled into his sleeping bag. Seconds after he had switched off his portable light he was soundly asleep.

The shrilling of the alarm woke him just as the almost level rays of the rising sun were striking through the translucent walls of his tent. He got up, went outside into the fresh, cool morning, sniffed appreciatively the tangy scent of dew-wet grass. Somewhere something that probably was nothing at all like a bird was sounding a series of bell-like notes. There were as yet no signs of life around *Schnauzer*, although the first thin, blue drift of smoke from cooking fires was wreathing around the thatched rooftops of Melbourne.

Grimes walked down to the river to make his toilet. He was joined there by Pitcher and Billard. The water was too cold for the three men to linger long over their ablutions, although the heat of the sun was pleasant on their naked bodies. As they were walking back to the camp Maggie passed them on her way to her own morning swim. She told them that she had made coffee.

Soon the four of them were seated round the table in the mess tent to a breakfast of reconstituted scrambled egg and more coffee. Rather surprisingly they were joined there by Maya. The Morrowvian woman put out a dainty hand and scooped up a small sample of the mess on Grimes's plate, tasted it. She complained, "I don't like this."

"Frankly, neither do I," admitted Grimes, "but it's the best we can offer." He masticated and swallowed glumly. "And what can we do for you this morning?"

She said, "I am coming with you."

"Good. Do you know the Queen of Ballarat?"

"I know of her. And Lilian has given me a letter of introduction." With her free hand she tapped the small bag of woven straw that she was carrying.

"Then let's get cracking," said Grimes.

While Maggie, with Maya assisting rather ineffectually, washed the breakfast things Grimes, with Pitcher and Billard doing most of the work, struck and stowed the sleeping tents. Then the furniture and other gear from the mess tent was loaded aboard the pinnace, and finally the mess tent itself was deflated and folded and packed with the other gear.

From the pinnace Grimes called *Seeker*, told Saul that he was getting under way. While he was doing so Billard started the inertial drive, and within seconds the small craft was lifting vertically. As she drew level with *Schnauzer*'s control room Grimes could see figures standing behind the big viewports. He picked up his binoculars for a better look. Yes, there was the portly figure of Captain Danzellan, and with him was Eklund, his mate.

"Take her south for a start, sir?" asked Pitcher. "And then, once we're out of *Schnauzer*'s sight, we can bring her round on the course for Ballarat. . . ."

"No," decided Grimes. The same idea had occurred to him—but Lilian knew his destination, and she was at least on speaking terms with Danzellan and his officers. In any case—as compared with Drongo Kane—the Dog Star people were goodies, and if anything went badly wrong they would be in a position to offer immediate help. "No," he said again. "Head straight for Ballarat."

Ballarat was different from the other towns that they had seen. It was dominated by a towering structure, a great hulk of metal, pitted and weathered yet still gleaming dully in the morning sunlight. It was like no ship that Grimes or his officers had ever seen—although they had seen pictures and models of such ships in the astronautical museum at the Academy. It was a typical gaussjammer of the days of the Second Expansion, a peg-top-shaped hull with its wide and uppermost, buttressed by flimsy looking fins. To land her here, not far from the magnetic equator, her captain must have been a spaceman of no mean order—or must have been actuated by desperation. It could well have been that his passengers and crew were so weakened by starvation that a safe landing, sliding down the vertical lines of force in the planet's solar regions, would have been safe for the ship only, not for her personnel. Only the very hardy can survive the rigors of an arctic climate.

Hard by the ship was a long, low building. As seen from the air it seemed to be mainly of wooden construction, although it was roofed with sheets of gray metal. No doubt there had been cannibalization; no doubt many nonessential bulkheads and the like were missing from the gaussjammer's internal structure.

Billard brought the pinnace in low over the town. There were people in the streets, mainly women and children. They looked upward and pointed. Some of them waved. And then, quite suddenly, a smoky fire was lit in a wide plaza to the east of the gaussjammer. It was a signal, obviously. The tall streamer of smoke rose vertically into the still air.

"That's where we land," said Grimes. "Take her down, please, Mr. Billard."

"Aye, aye, sir!"

Quietly, without any fuss or bother, they landed. Even before the door was open, even before the last mutterings of the inertial drive had faded into silence, they heard the drums, a rhythmic thud and rattle, an oddly militaristic sound.

"Mphm?" grunted Grimes dubiously. He turned to Maya. "Are you sure the natives are friendly?"

She did not catch the allusion. "Of course," she said stiffly. "*Everybody* on Morrowvia is friendly. A queen is received courteously by her sister queens wherever she may go."

"I'm not a queen," said Grimes. "I'm not a king, even. . . ."

"The way you carry on sometimes, aboard your ship, I'm inclined to doubt the validity of that last statement," remarked Maggie Lazenby.

"Open up, sir?" asked Billard.

"Mphm. Yes. But nobody is to go outside—except myself—until I give the word. And you'd better have the twenty millimeters ready for use, Mr. Pitcher."

He belted on his pistols—one projectile, one laser—then set his cap firmly on his head. Maya said, "I am coming with you."

Grimes said, "I'm not in the habit of hiding behind a woman's skirts."

"What skirts?" asked Maggie Lazenby. Then, "Don't be silly, John. Maya's obviously one of *them.* When they see her with you they'll know that you're friendly."

It made sense.

Grimes jumped down from the open door to the packed earth of the plaza, clapping each hand to a pistol butt as soon as he was on the ground. Maya followed him. They stood there, listening to the rhythmic *tap-tappity-tap* that was, with every second, louder and louder.

And then a woman—a girl—appeared from around the end of the long, low building. She was naked save for polished high boots and a crimson sash, and was carrying a flag on a staff, a black flag with a stylized great cat, in gold, rampant over a compass rose. Behind her marched the drummers, also girls, and behind them a woman with a silver sash and with a silver crown set on her silvery hair. She was followed by six men, with spears, six female archers, and by six more men, each of whom carried what was obviously an automatic rifle of archaic design.

Abruptly the drums fell silent and the drummers divided their ranks to let the queen pass through. She advanced steadily, followed by her standard bearer. Her skin was black and gleaming, but there was no hint of negroid ancestry in her regular features. Apart from the absence of rudimentary nipples she was what Grimes was coming to consider a typical Morrowvian woman.

Grimes saluted.

The standard bearer dipped her flag.

The queen smiled sweetly and said, "I, Janine Morrow, welcome you to Ballarat—the landing place of *Lode Cougar* and of our forebears. I welcome you, spaceman, and I welcome you, sister."

"Thank you," said Grimes. (Should he call this definitely regal female. "Your Majesty" or not?)

"Thank you, Janine," said Maya. "I am Maya, of Cambridge."

"Thank you, Janine," said Grimes. "I am John Grimes, of the Federation Survey Service ship *Seeker*."

17

GRIMES CALLED THE others down from the pinnace and introductions were made. Then Janine led the way to her palace, which was the long, low building hard by the ancient spaceship. In a room like the other rooms in which they had been similarly entertained there was the ritual sharing of food and water, during which the Queen of Ballarat read the letter that Maya had brought. Grimes was about to get a glimpse of it during her perusal; the paper was coarse-textured and gray rather than white, and the words had been scrawled upon it with a blunt pencil.

Janine said, "Lilian is favored. Twice she has been visited by Captain Danzellan, and now Commander Grimes is calling on her."

"Now Commander Grimes is calling on *you*," Maya pointed out.

"And so he is." Janine smiled sweetly, her teeth very white and her lips very red in her dark brown face. "And so he is. But what brings you to Ballarat, Commander Grimes? Do you have gifts for me?"

"I shall have gifts for you—but I have nothing at the moment. You will appreciate that we cannot carry much in a small craft such as my pinnace."

"That is true," agreed Janine. "But every time that Captain Danzellan has wished to look for information in the museum or the library he has brought me something." She gestured toward one of the walls where a new-looking clock, with a brightly gleaming metal case, was hanging. "That is a *good* clock—far better than the old one with its dangling weights. This one does not have a spring even—just a power cell which Captain Danzellan tells me will be good for centuries."

"From the way that you greeted us," said Grimes, "I thought that you were pleased to see visitors from the home world of your ancestors."

"But I am, I am! Too, it pleases me to try to—what is the word?—to reconstruct the old rituals. I have studied The History, as have we all. Also, I have access to records which my sisters elsewhere have not. I received you as important visitors must be received on Earth. . . ."

"Mphm."

"I am sorry that I could not fire a salute, but we have no big guns. In any case, the supply of ammunition for our rifles is limited."

"You did very nicely," said Grimes.

"Bring on the marching girls . . ." muttered Maggie.

Grimes, surreptitiously, had eased his watch off his wrist. The instrument was almost new; he had purchased it from the commissary just prior to departure from Lindisfarne. He said, "Perhaps you will accept this, Janine. It is a personal timekeeper."

"Just what I've always wanted," she said, pleased.

"I take it, then," said Grimes, "that you are the custodian of the books, the records, the . . ."

"Of everything," she told him proudly. "Perhaps, while Maya and I have a gossip, you would care to be shown around?"

"We should," said Grimes.

Their guide was the young woman who had carried the banner. Her name was Lisa Morrow. She vouchsafed the information that it was usually she who conducted visiting queens from other towns through the palace, but that it was the first time that she had been responsible for a party of outworlders. She did not seem to be greatly impressed by the honor, or even to regard it as such.

The palace was more than a palace. It was a library, and it was a museum. They were taken first of all into the Earth Room, a huge chamber devoted to Earth as it had been when *Lode Cougar* had lifted from Port Woomera on her last voyage. This had been the overcrowded planet dominated, in its northern and southern hemispheres respectively, by the short-lived Russian and Australian Empires.

Lode Cougar, concluded Grimes, had carried a lot of junk—but even in the days of the Third Expansion a ticket out to the stars was very often a one-way ticket; it was even more so in the days of the First and Second Expansions. Those first colonists had been so reluctant to break every tie with their home world.

Here, in the Earth Room, were maps and photographs, reproductions of famous works of art, even files of newspapers and magazines. These latter had been chemically treated to make the paper impervious to normal wear and tear, but now were practically unreadable—and Lisa Morrow took good care her charges did not, as they would have loved to have done, leaf through them. Grimes could make out the headlines on the front page of one of the papers, *The Australian.* "*Lode Tiger* missing, feared lost." No doubt the same paper had carried similar headlines regarding *Lode Cougar*. This had been long before the days of trained telepaths or the time-and-space-twisting Carlotti Communications System, but the established colonies had maintained a reasonably fast mail service with Earth. Grimes had read somewhere that it had taken less time for a letter to get from Port Southern, on Austral, to Sydney, in Australia, than it did to get through the post offices at either end. This state of affairs had persisted until the introduction of Carlotti radio transmission of all correspondence.

There were books, too—*real* books, properly bound, although with very thin, lightweight covers and paper. There were shelves of *How To* volumes. House building, boat building, aircraft building . . . mining, smelting, casting . . . navigation . . . surveying. . . . Useful, Grimes supposed, if you did not, as you were supposed to do, finish up at an established colony but, instead, made a forced landing on a hitherto undiscovered world.

There was fiction—but, in spite of their age, these books looked almost fresh from the printers. Grimes had suspected that the Morrowvians were oddly lacking in imagination. Anything factual—such as the famous History—they would read, or any book that would aid them to acquire necessary skills. But the products of the storyteller's art left them cold. This attitude was not uncommon, of course, but it seemed more pronounced here than elsewhere. What books had Danzellan given to Lilian on the occasion of his first visit? Grimes asked Lisa the question.

She told him, "One by a man called Blenkinshop on first aid. And one about the fisheries on a world called Atlantia. We are having copies made for the library."

"So you have a printing press?"

"Yes, Commander Grimes. It is used only when a book is almost worn out or when there is something new that has to be printed."

"Is it hand operated?"

"No. We have an engine, driven by steam. Shall I show it to you now, or would you rather see the *Lode Cougar* room?"

"The *Lode Cougar* room," Grimes told her.

This adjoined the Earth Room, but was not as large. It contained relics of the ship herself. There were cargo manifests, log books, crew and passenger lists. There was a large photograph of the *Cougar*'s officers taken at Port Woomera, presumably shortly prior to lift-off. It was typical of this sort of portraiture, whatever the day and age. The captain, his senior officers on either side of him, was seated in the front row, his arms folded across his chest (as were the arms of the others) to show the braid on his sleeves. Standing behind the row of seated seniors were the juniors. Grimes stopped to read the legend below the photograph.

The captain's name was not, as he had expected that it would be, Morrow. (But in an emergency, such as a forced landing on an unexplored world, anybody at all is liable to come to the fore.) The name of Morrow was not among those of the officers. A passenger, then? Examination of the ship's passenger list would supply the answer.

Lisa was pointing to a shelf of volumes. "And these," she was saying, "were Morrow's own books. . . ."

Grimes paused on his way to the display cases in which the ship's documents were housed. Books told one so much about their owner's makeup. His eye swept over the fiction titles. He realized, with pleased surprise, that he had read most of them, when he was a cadet at the Academy. Early Twentieth Century—and even late Nineteenth Century—science fiction aboard a starship! But it was no more absurd than to find the same science fiction required reading for future officers of a navy whose ships, even though they had yet to penetrate to The Hub, fared out to The Rim. *The Planet Buyer* . . . that had been good, as he remembered it. *The Island Of* . . .

His wrist transceiver was buzzing. He raised the instrument to his mouth. "Captain!" Saul's voice was urgent. "Captain, I would have called you before, but we've been having transmitter trouble. Drongo Kane left in his pinnace at first light this morning, heading north. He's got Sabrina with him and three of his own people, all armed."

"You heard that?" Grimes demanded of his officers.

They nodded.

"Thank you for your attention," Grimes said to Lisa, "but we must get back to our pinnace."

"Is Drongo Kane a friend of yours, that you are so eager to greet him?" she asked innocently, and looked bewildered when Grimes replied, "That'd be the sunny Friday!"

18

GRIMES PAUSED BRIEFLY in the room where Janine was still gossiping with Maya. As he entered he heard Maya ask, "And how do *you* deal with the problem of the uncontrollable adolescent?"

He said, "Excuse me, ladies. I've just received word that Drongo Kane is on his way here. . . ."

"Drongo Kane?" asked Janine, arching her silver brows.

"The captain of a ship called the *Southerly Buster*," Maya told her. "A *most* generous man."

"Goodie goodie," exclaimed her sister queen. She looked rather pointedly at Danzellan's gleaming clock on the wall, then at Grimes's watch that was strapped around her slim, brown wrist.

"Perhaps he'll give you an egg timer . . ." suggested Maggie Lazenby.

"What is that?" asked Janine.

"It's not important," said Grimes impatiently. "Excuse us, please."

He led the way out of the palace, to where his pinnace was grounded in the middle of the plaza, looking like a huge, stranded silver fish. He looked up at the clear sky. Yes—there, far to the southward, was a tiny speck, a dark dot against the blueness that expanded as he watched. Then he was aware that the two queens had followed him outside.

"Is that Drongo Kane?" asked Janine.

"I think it is," he replied.

"Then I must prepare a proper reception," she said and walked rapidly back to her palace. Maya stayed with Grimes.

She said, "Janine prides herself on doing things properly."

"If she were doing things properly," Grimes told her, "she would have a battery of ground to air missiles standing by."

"You must be joking!" she exclaimed, shocked.

"Have our own armament in readiness, sir?" asked the navigator.

"Mphm. I *was* joking, Mr. Pitcher. But it will do no harm to have the twenty millimeters cocked and ready."

Two women were building another fire in the brazier that had served Grimes for a beacon. One of them produced a large box of oversized matches from the pouch that she wore slung from her shoulder, lit the kindling. Almost immediately the column of gray smoke was climbing skyward.

Kane's pinnace was audible now as well as visible, the irregular beat of its inertial drive competing with the more rhythmic efforts of Janine's drummers, warming up behind the palace. It was coming in fast, and it seemed that it would overshoot the plaza. But Kane—presumably it was he at the controls—brought the craft to a spectacular, shuddering halt when it was almost directly over *Seeker*'s pinnace, applying maximum reverse thrust. That would not, thought Grimes disapprovingly, do his engines any good—but he, himself, had often been guilty of similar showmanship.

Oddly enough no crowd had gathered—but no crowd had gathered to greet Grimes. There were only a few deliberately uninterested bystanders, and they were mainly children. On no other world had Grimes seen such a fanatical respect for privacy.

Drongo Kane was dropping down now—not fast, yet not with extreme caution. His vertical thrust made odd patterns in the dust as the pinnace descended, not unlike those made in an accumulation of iron filings by a magnetic field. When there was little more than the thickness of a coat of paint between his landing gear and the ground he checked his descent, then cut his drive.

The door in the side of the pinnace opened. Drongo Kane stood in the opening. He was rigged up in a uniform that was like the full dress of the Survey Service—with improvements. An elaborate gold cockade ornamented his cocked hat, and his sword belt was golden, as was the scabbard. A score of decorations blazed over the left breast of his frock coat. Grimes thought he recognized the Iron Cross of Waldegren, the Golden Wings of the Hallichek Hegemony. Anybody who was highly regarded by those two governments would be *persona non grata* in decent society.

Kane jumped lightly to the ground, seemingly unhampered by his finery. He extended a hand to help Sabrina from the pinnace. Jewels glittered on her smooth, golden skin, and a coronet ablaze with emeralds was set on her head. She was inclined to teeter a little in her unaccustomed, high-heeled sandals.

"Cor stone me Aunt Fanny up a gum tree!" whispered Maggie.

"Captain Kane is *generous*," murmured Maya.

"Mphm," grunted Grimes.

Inside the pinnace two of Kane's officers—and they were dressed only in their drab working uniforms—were setting up some sort of machine, an affair of polished brass, just within the doorway. Grimes stared at it in amazement and horror.

"Captain Kane," he shouted, "I forbid you to terrorize these people!"

Kane grinned cheerfully. "Keep your hair on, Commander! Nobody's goin' to terrorize anybody. Don't you recognize a salutin' cannon when you see one? Sabrina, here, has told me that this Queen Janine is a stickler for etiquette. . . ." Then his eyes widened as, to the rattle of drums, the procession emerged from around the corner of the palace. He licked his lips as he stared at the high-stepping girl with the *Lode Cougar* flag—that sash and those boots—especially the boots—did something for her. He muttered to himself, "And you can say *that* again!"

With a last ruffle of drums Janine and her entourage came to a halt. Kane drew himself to attention and saluted grandly. "Fire one!" snapped somebody inside the pinnace. The brass cannon boomed, making a noise disproportionate to its size. "Fire two!" Again there was the gout of orange flame, the billowing of dirty white smoke. "Fire three!"

At first it looked as though the spearmen, archers and riflemen would either turn and run—or loose their weapons off against the spacemen—but Janine snapped a sharp order and, drawing herself up proudly, stood her ground.

"Fire four!" *Boom!*

"Fire five!"

Janine was enjoying the show. So was Kane. Sabrina, at his side, winced every time the gun was fired, but tried to look as though this sort of thing was an everyday occurrence. Maya whispered urgently to Grimes, "This *noise* . . . can't you make him stop it?"

"Fire nine!" *Boom!*

"Fire ten!"

Janine's bodyguard had recovered their composure now and were standing at stiff attention, and there was a certain envy evident in the expressions on the faces of the drummer girls—but the standard bearer spoiled the effect when the drifting fumes of the burning black powder sent her into a fit of sneezing.

"Fire sixteen!" *Boom!*

Surely not, thought Grimes dazedly. *Surely not. A twenty-one gun salute for somebody who, even though she is called a queen, is no more than the mayor of a small town. . . .*

"Fire twenty!" *Boom!*

"Fire twenty-one!" *Boom!*

"A lesson," remarked Maggie, "on how to win friends and influence people. . . ."

"He certainly influenced me!" said Grimes.

Kane, accompanied by Sabrina, marched to where Janine was standing. He saluted again. Janine nodded to him regally. The standard bearer, recovered from her sneezing fit, dipped her flag toward him. The spearmen and riflemen presented arms. Grimes watched all this a little enviously. He was sorry that Maya had not briefed him regarding Janine's love of ceremonial, as obviously Sabrina had briefed Kane. But it could be that Kane knew Sabrina far better than he, Grimes, knew Maya. There are more things to do in a shared bed than talking—but talking in bed is quite a common practice. . . .

"Shall I fire a burst from the twenty millimeters," asked Pitcher wistfully, "just to show that we can make a noise too?"

"No," Grimes said sternly.

"Sir," called Billard, "here comes another pinnace!"

Danzellan's arrival on the scene was anticlimactic. When he came in to a landing the queen, together with Kane, Sabrina and two of *Southerly Buster*'s officers carrying a large chest of trade goods, had returned to her palace and was staying there.

19

CAPTAIN DANZELLAN WAS in a bad temper.

He demanded, "Commander Grimes, why didn't you tell me that Drongo Kane was on this planet? I learned it, only by chance, from Lilian after you had left Melbourne—and then my radio officer monitored the conversation you had with your first lieutenant. . ."

"To begin with," said Grimes tartly, "you didn't ask me. In any case, I gained the impression that you wanted nothing at all to do with me or my people." He was warming up nicely. "Furthermore, sir, I must draw your attention to the fact that the monitoring of Survey Service signals is illegal, and that you are liable to a heavy fine, and that your radio officer may have his certificate dealt with."

Danzellan was not awed. "A space lawyer!" he sneered.

"Yes, Captain. And a space policeman."

"Then why don't you arrest Kane?"

"What for?" asked Grimes. "He has broken no laws—Federation or local. I can neither arrest him nor order him off Morrowvia."

"Commander Grimes, I am paid to look after my owners' interests. I cannot do so properly while this man Kane is running around loose, corrupting the natives. To be frank, if you were not here I should feel justified in taking the law into my hands. Since you *are* here—I appeal to you, as a citizen of the Federation, for protection."

"Captain Danzellan, Captain Kane is cooking up some sort of deal with the natives. He, like you, is a shipmaster. *You* represent your owners, Kane *is* an owner. You allege that he is corrupting the natives and imply that he is queering your pitch. Meanwhile, *I* am wondering if whatever sort of deal *you* are cooking up will corrupt the natives. . . ."

"Of course not!" snorted Danzellan. "The Dog Star Line will always have their best interests at heart!"

"And the best interests of the management and shareholders . . . ?" put in Maggie.

Danzellan smiled in a fatherly way. "Naturally, Commander Lazenby. After all, we are businessmen."

"Mphm," Grimes grunted. He said, "Kane is a businessman too."

"But I was here first, Commander Grimes."

"*Lode Cougar* was here first, Captain Danzellan. Get this straight, sir—unless or until either you or Captain Kane steps out of line I am merely here as an observer."

"Then may I suggest, sir, that you start doing some observing? That is what I intend to do. I am going to call on Janine, now, to see if I can find out what line of goods Kane is peddling."

"I'll come with you," Grimes told him. "Maggie, you'd better come too. And you, Maya, if you wouldn't mind. Mr. Pitcher and Mr. Billard—stay by the pinnace."

The two men and the two women walked across the plaza to the main entrance of the palace. Four natives were standing in the doorway, spearmen of Janine's ceremonial bodyguard. They held their weapons not threateningly but so as to bar ingress.

"Let me pass!" huffed Danzellan.

"The queen insists on privacy," said one of the men.

"But I know Janine. We are good friends."

"The queen said, sir, that she and Captain Kane and her other guests were not to be disturbed."

Grimes nodded to Maya. Possibly she would be admitted while the offworlders were not. The Morrowvian woman walked forward until her breasts were pressing against the haft of one of the spears. She said indignantly, "You know who I am. Let me in!"

The spearman grinned. His teeth were sharp and very white. He said, "I am sorry, lady, but I cannot. Janine mentioned you especially."

"And what did she say?" demanded Maya.

"Do you really want to know, lady?" The man was enjoying this.

"Yes!"

"She said, lady, 'Don't let Commander Grimes or any other foreigners in here while I am in conference. And the same applies to that cat from Cambridge.' "

"Cat from Cambridge . . ." muttered Maya indignantly. "You can tell Janine that should she ever visit *my* town she will not be received hospitably."

"Well, Commander Grimes," asked Danzellan, "what are you doing about this?"

"What can I do?" countered Grimes irritably.

"We can talk things over," suggested Maggie Lazenby.

"Talk, talk!" sneered Danzellan, "while that damned pirate is raping a planet!"

"It's all that we can do at the moment," Grimes told him. "I suggest that we return to our pinnace. And I suggest that you, sir, do some talking."

"All right," said the shipmaster at last.

"The Dog Star Line's interest in this world will bring nothing but good to the people," stated Danzellan.

"Mphm," grunted Grimes skeptically.

"But it is so, Commander. If we are allowed to run things our way the planet will remain virtually unspoiled. There will be no pollution of the air, the soil or the seas. Unless the Morrowvians so desire it—and I do not think they will—there will be no development of heavy industries. The small luxuries that we shall bring in will demand power, of course—but solar power will be ample for their requirements."

"It all sounds very nice," admitted Grimes, "but what do your employers get out of it?"

"Oh, they'll make a profit—but not from the Morrowvians."

"From whom, then?"

"From passengers. Tourists. As you know, we have been, for many years, primarily freight carriers—but there is no reason why we should not break into the passenger trade, the tourist trade specifically. Trans-Galactic Clippers have been doing very nicely at it for some years now. But TG has the game sewn up insofar as the worlds on their itinerary are concerned.

"Now we, the Dog Star Line, have a new planet of our very own. We can build our own hotels and vacation camps, we can run cruises over the tropical seas in big schooners that we shall build and man—already recruiting for their crews is being opened on Atlantia." He smiled sympathetically at Maya. "I'm afraid that's necessary, my dear. Your people aren't very sea-minded."

"And you think that this scheme will work?" asked Grimes, interested.

"Why shouldn't it work, Commander? The advertising need only be truthful. Think of the posters, the brochures with photographs of all the beautiful, naked women—and, come to that, of the equally beautiful naked men. Visit Morrowvia—and shed your clothing, your cares, your inhibitions! Why, it'll have Arcadia licked to a frazzle!"

Maggie looked very coldly at Captain Danzellan. She said, "Arcadia is not a holiday resort for the idle rich, nor does it wish to be one. Our naturism is a way of life, not an advertising gimmick."

"Are you an Arcadian, Commander Lazenby? But what you said about naturism being a way of life on Arcadia applies equally well to Morrowvia. And we, the Dog Star Line, will do nothing to destroy that way of life. I have studied history, and I know how very often a superior race, a supposedly superior race, has ruined a simple people by forcing upon them unnecessary and unsuitable clothing. We shall not make that mistake."

"No, you won't," said Maggie. "It might affect your profits."

Grimes said, "I still think, Captain Danzellan, that you will ruin this world, whether or not you force the women into Mother Hubbards and the men into shirts and trousers."

Danzellan shrugged. "There's ruin *and* ruin, Commander Grimes. Which is the lesser of two evils—a flourishing tourist trade, or the introduction of heavy industry? Come to that—will the tourist trade be an evil?"

"And the tourists will *pay?*" asked Maya. "They will bring us things like the sun-powered cold boxes, and the clocks and the watches, and jewels like the ones that Captain Kane gave to Sabrina? Not that *I* want jewels," she added virtuously, "but I should like a cold box, and a clock that does not have to have the weights wound up every night."

"Maya is talking sense," said Danzellan.

"Yes, I am talking sense. You people have so many things to make life comfortable that we cannot make for ourselves, that we should not care to go to the trouble of making for ourselves. If offworlders are willing to pay for the pleasure of breathing our air, basking in our sunshine—then let them pay!"

"And there," said Danzellan smugly, "you have the attitude of a typical Morrowvian."

"But she's so simple," expostulated Grimes. "Her people are so simple."

Before Maya could answer Maggie stepped in. She said, "Perhaps not so simple, John. Apart from anything else, they have The History and Morrow's dictums to guide them. Too, there's an odd streak in their makeup. . . . I wish I knew . . ."

"I wish I knew what Kane was up to," said Danzellan.

"Don't we all," agreed Grimes.

20

THEY SAT IN the main cabin of *Seeker*'s pinnace—talking, smoking (even Maya tried one of Maggie's cigarillos and said that she liked it) and waiting for something to happen. Danzellan was in touch with his own ship by his wrist transceiver and also, of course, with Mr. Delamere, who had piloted *Schnauzer*'s boat to Ballarat and was remaining inside the craft. Grimes used the pinnace's radio to tell Mr. Saul what had happened so far and, meanwhile, all transceivers not otherwise in use were tuned to a variety of wavebands, in the hope that Drongo Kane's messages (if any) to *Southerly Buster* could be monitored.

At last Kane's voice sounded from Maggie's transceiver. He said simply, "Blackbird." The reply was almost immediate. "Pinnace to Captain. Blackbird." Then, "Pinnace to *Southerly Buster*. Blackbird." Finally, faintly, "*Southerly Buster* to pinnace. Acknowledge Blackbird."

"Blackbird?" echoed Grimes.

"I don't like it," said Maggie. "I don't like it. That word rings some sort of a bell. . . ."

"Captain to *Seeker*," said Grimes into the microphone of the main transceiver. "Captain to *Seeker*. Do you read me?"

"Loud and clear, Captain."

"That you, Mr. Saul? Keep your eyes open for any activities around *Southerly Buster*. Kane has just sent a message to his ship. It must be a code. Just one word. Blackbird."

"Blackbird . . ." repeated Saul. Then, "Have I your permission to use force?"

"What are you talking about, Saul?"

"Operation Blackbird, Captain. Didn't you know that blackbirding was a euphemism for slave trading?"

"He's right . . ." whispered Maggie. "And there are worlds where women such as these would fetch a good price—some of the Waldegren mining colonies, for example. . . ."

Grimes was thinking rapidly. If he departed at once it would be all of seven hours before he was back aboard *Seeker*. In seven hours a lot could happen. Saul, as second in command, was in full charge of the ship until her captain's return. Saul, normally, was a most reliable officer—but could Saul, with all his racial prejudices and bitternesses, be trusted to deal with the situation that was developing? Kane would scream to high heaven if a single shot were fired at his precious *Southerly Buster*, and he would not be the first pirate to have friends in high places—although heaven would not be one of them. Even so, if Kane were about to do something illegal he would have to be stopped.

The situation, Grimes realized, was made to order for Drongo Kane. *Seeker*'s captain was hours away from his ship—and so was *Southerly Buster*'s captain, but it didn't matter. The obnoxious Mr. Dreebly could embark the passengers, quote and unquote, and then lift ship into orbit, where Kane's pinnace could rendezvous with her. And once the Morrowvians were aboard the *Buster* she would be virtually untouchable insofar as hostile action by *Seeker* was concerned.

"Mr. Saul," ordered Grimes, "do all you can to prevent the natives from boarding *Southerly Buster*. Do not use arms unless there is absolutely no alternative. I am returning at once." He turned to Danzellan. "You heard all of that, Captain?"

"Of course, Commander."

"Good. Then I'll ask you to keep an eye on Drongo Kane for me."

"I'll do that, with pleasure."

Maggie said, "I'll stay with Captain Danzellan, John. I want to have another look at *Lode Cougar*'s records—if Janine will condescend to let me back into her palace after Kane has left. I have an idea that what I find may have some bearing on this situation. If it's what I'm afraid it might be—then be careful. Be bloody careful."

"I'll try," said Grimes.

"You always do, but . . ."

She followed Danzellan as the shipmaster returned to his own pinnace. Pitcher asked, "Take her up, sir?"

"Yes, Mr. Pitcher. And flog your horses. Put her on a direct Great Circle; we've no time for sightseeing."

While the navigator busied himself with charts and instruments Billard did his best to make the pinnace behave like a guided missile.

They wasted no time, screaming southward high over the countryside, over the sea. Maya was awed, a little frightened, even, and sat there in silence. Pitcher and Billard exchanged occasional monosyllables, while Grimes stuck to the transceiver. Timmins, the senior radio officer, was at the other end. He reported, "*Southerly Buster* seems to be ready for immediate lift-off, sir. All ports, save for the main airlock, have been sealed." Then, a little later, "Two officers have left the ship and are walking toward the town of Oxford. Mr. Saul and Captain Philby have followed them, with six Marines." Later still, "Mr. Saul reports that the way was barred to him and his party by a dozen spearmen and a dozen archers. He is returning to the ship. I'll put him on to you as soon as he's here."

Grimes studied Saul's face in the tiny screen. The man was struggling to repress his smoldering fury. "Captain," he said, "these damned people don't *want* to be helped. They were there on the river bank, with the spears and bows and arrows, and some damned woman, the deputy queen she said she was, ordered me back. She said, 'We don't want you and the likes of you here. Captain Kane warned Sabrina about you.' "

"So . . ."

"So what are your instructions, Captain?"

"Get a boat out, to keep a watch over the town and to report what the people are doing. Have *Seeker* in a state of instant readiness for lift-off. . . ."

"I've already given the orders, sir. But the armament . . ."

"I've already told you not to go firing guns off indiscriminately. But . . . mphm. Have the belts for the sixty millimeters loaded with sleep gas shells. And if you use 'em—and you'll have to justify their use to me—make bloody sure that you don't *hit* anybody. Understood?"

"Understood, Captain."

"Good. Then keep me informed."

Grimes turned to Maya. "Can *you* tell me," he asked, what *is* going on?"

"I don't know. We have always kept ourselves to ourselves, Sabrina and I. We have never been close friends. We have never been friends. But Captain Kane gave many gifts to Sabrina's people. There were books, with beautiful pictures of other worlds, with accounts of other worlds. There were . . . catalogues, giving details of all the goods that may be purchased on other worlds. . . ."

"First Lieutenant to Captain." It was Saul again. "Number Three boat is in position over Oxford. We are trying to get a picture to you."

And there, on the screen, was the picture of the town as seen from the air. The boat was hanging almost directly over the central plaza and transmitting a magnified image. The two men from *Southerly Buster*, being clothed, were easily identifiable. They were busily marshaling about two hundred Morrowvians into an orderly column. Even from above it was obvious that they were all women. To one side of the plaza a half dozen light handcarts had been loaded with possessions—cushions, pieces of pottery, longbows and quivers of arrows. One of Kane's men went to inspect the cart that was loaded with weapons, called a woman to him and was obviously telling her that these would have to be left. Then whoever was in charge of the boat got a longrange microphone working.

"I'm sorry, Peggy. These will have to be left behind."

"But the girls must have them, Bill. What will they do for sport on Caribbea if they have no bows?"

Caribbea? wondered Grimes. Probably it was the most glamorous world depicted in the brochures that Kane had distributed—but Essen would be a more likely destination for this shipment of female slaves.

"You can't use bows and arrows underwater," explained the man Bill patiently. "In the seas of Caribbea they use spear guns."

"But we don't *like* water. None of us likes water. Nobody will *make* us go into the water, will they?"

There's not much water on Essen, thought Grimes. *Only enough for washing and drinking—not that those Waldegren miners wash much, and they don't believe in diluting their schnapps. . . .*

"Nobody will *make* you do anything," lied Bill.

His companion called to him. "Dump that junk, and we'll get the show on the road!"

"Our ETA, Mr. Pitcher?" asked Grimes.

"We're doing the best we can, sir, but we can't make it before nineteen-hundred Local—another four and a half hours."

"Mr. Saul, do you read me?"

"Sir?"

"Lay a barrage of sleep gas on the bank of the river as soon as that column from Oxford gets under way."

"Very good, sir."

"And be *careful*."

"Of course, sir." Saul's voice was hurt.

"Let me know as soon as you open fire, and give me a picture if you can."

"Very good sir." Grimes could almost read the first lieutenant's thoughts: *Get off my back, Whitey!*

It is not only the black races who hate slavery, thought Grimes, *and it is not only the black races who've been enslaved. But what the hell is Kane playing at? Pressing ahead with his blackbirding under the very nose of a Survey Service ship. . . . He's always prided himself on being able to keep just on the right side of the law.*

He said, "Get me Mr. Hayakawa, please."

"Yes, Captain?" asked the psionicist at last. His picture did not appear on the screen; that was being reserved for the transmissions from the lookout boat. "Yes, Captain?"

"Mr. Hayakawa, I know that your opposite number aboard the *Buster* is maintaining a block, but have you been able to pick up *anything?*"

"Yes, Captain. A few minutes ago there were stray thoughts from the mate of *Southerly Buster.* They ran like this, 'And the beauty of it is that the stupid Space Scouts can't touch us!' "

"That remains to be seen, Mr. Hayakawa," said Grimes. "That remains to be seen."

21

THE TROUBLE WITH radio as a means of communication is that anybody can listen. Grimes, in his later conversations with his ship, had employed a scrambler. He did not know whether or not *Southerly Buster* ran to a descrambling device. Apparently she did not. Dreebly appeared to be proceeding with his embarkation procedure as planned.

In an orderly march the two hundred young women streamed out of Oxford, a score of spearmen at the head of the column, another twenty male warriors bringing up the rear, behind the carts laden with small possessions. Kane's two men were in the lead. Grimes, remembering the general layout of the country, knew that once the van of the procession passed a low, tree-crowned hill it would be in the field of fire of *Seeker*'s guns. With an effort he restrained himself from taking over the fire control from Saul. He knew that a direct hit from a non-lethal gas shell can kill just as surely—and messily—as one from a high explosive projectile. But Saul was on the spot, and he was not. All he could do was to watch the marchers proceeding slowly along the bank of the winding river.

He heard Saul say quietly, "Bearing one hundred and seventy-five true. Range three thousand. Shoot."

"Bearing one hundred and seventy-five. Range three thousand. *Fire!*"

Even over the radio the hammering of the heavy automatics was deafening. Watching the screen Grimes saw a neat seam of explosions stitched across the line of advance of the Morrowvian women, saw the billowing clouds of greenish vapor pouring from each bursting shell.

"Traverse, traverse! Now—ladder!"

Nice gunnery, thought Grimes. Saul was boxing his targets in with the gas shells.

A new voice came from the transceiver. It was Dreebly's. "*Southerly Buster* to *Seeker*. What the hell are you playing at?"

"*Seeker* to *Southerly Buster*. What the hell are *you* playing at?"

Grimes decided that he had better intervene; Mr. Saul was not in a diplomatic mood. He said quietly, "Commander Grimes to *Southerly Buster*. What is the nature of your complaint, please?"

Dreebly spluttered, then, "What is the nature of my complaint, you ask? Some butterfly-brained ape aboard your ship is firing off guns. There're shells whistling past our control room."

"Routine weekly practice shoot, Mr. Dreebly," said Grimes. "Don't worry; we never hit anything unless we want to."

"But you're firing toward Oxford!"

"Are we? But our range setting is well short of the town."

"I know what you're firing at, Commander Grimes. You've a boat up, spotting for you!"

"What am I firing at, Mr. Dreebly?"

"Pah! You make me sick!" Dreebly broke off the conversation. Grimes returned his attention to the screen. The gas was slowly thinning, and through its translucent veil he could see the untidily sprawling figures of the Morrowvians—and of Kanes two officers.

Maya demanded, "You haven't killed them? You haven't killed them?"

"Of course not," Grimes told her. "They'll wake in a few hours' time, without even a headache. I've just put them to sleep, that's all. . . ."

Meanwhile Timmins had succeeded in tuning in to the conversation between Dreebly and Kane. Kane was saying, "Get them aboard, and then get off-planet! Yes, I *know* they can't walk—but you've ground cars, haven't you? And there are respirators in the stores. Pull your finger out, Dreebly, and get cracking! What do you think I pay you for?"

Saul was back on the air. "Sir, you heard all that. What do I do now?"

I could answer that question a lot more easily, thought Grimes, *if I knew that Kane was breaking Federation law. But he seems to have the idea that he is not. . . .*

"What do I do now?" repeated Saul.

"Mphm. Carry on with your practice shoot, Mr. Saul. Use H.E. Chew up the ground between *Southerly Buster* and the . . . er . . . intending emigrants."

"Emigrants! The *slaves*, you mean, Captain."

"They aren't slaves yet. Just make a mess of the terrain so that it's impassable to Kane's ground cars."

"But he's got boats, sir. He can use them."

"He has two boats—a pinnace, which is still at Ballarat, and one lifeboat. The lifeboat is just big enough for his crew. It will take it a long time to ferry two hundred people—especially as they will have to be lifted aboard it, and lifted off."

"I see, sir. . . . But what if *Southerly Buster* fires at us?"

"They won't dare, Mr. Saul. At least, I hope they won't. If they do—*if* they do—it is your duty to take every possible measure for the protection of *Seeker*."

No, he thought, *Kane won't open fire, or order his mate to do so. Apart from anything else, he's the injured, innocent citizen and I'm the big, bad, gun-toting villain. I'm not happy about things at all, at all. But I* must *stop him.*

Meanwhile, he wished that he were back aboard his ship. He *liked* guns. He knew that this was childish of him, and that it was high time that mankind outgrew its love for noisy pyrotechnics. He knew that a gun pleads to be pointed at something—and then begs to have its trigger pulled. He hoped that Saul would remain content merely to wreak havoc on the landscape.

22

SAUL WREAKED HAVOC on the landscape. Grimes, watching on his screen, thought, relishing the play on words, *He's* wrecking *the landscape*. What had been grassland was now a crater-pitted desolation over which drifted acrid fumes, and the copses had been reduced to jagged, blackened stumps.

Kane came on the air. His voice, despite the fact that it had been relayed through at least two stations, was loud and clear. He said, "Commander Grimes, this is Captain Kane. My mate tells me that your first lieutenant's runnin' amok."

"Running amok, Captain Kane? What do you mean?"

"He's shootin off his guns—*your* guns—like a madman. Wastin' the taxpayer's money. He's interferin' with the embarkation of my passengers."

"Passengers, Captain Kane?"

"Yeah. Passengers. I own me own ship, an' if I decide to go into the passenger trade, that's my business."

"I'm sure it is, Captain. I'm sorry that my arrangements clashed with yours, but we were due for a practice shoot. . . ."

"Oh, you were, were you? An' did you promulgate a warnin'?"

"Unfortunately the facilities for so doing don't exist on this planet."

"Listen, Grimes, keep your nose out of my business or you'll get it bloodied."

"I'm inclined to think, Kane, that your business is *my* business. I represent the Federation. . . ."

"An' the Federation is supposed to encourage honest trade, not interfere with it."

"*Honest* trade?"

"You heard me. Honest *and* legal."

"All right, Kane. I have your word for it—for what it's worth. Where are you taking those women?"

"It's no concern of yours, Grimes. But it's only natural that after generations of isolation they'll want to see new worlds."

"Mphm. And how are they paying their fares? You never impressed me as being a philanthropic institution."

Kane laughed. "Have you never heard of *Travel Now, Pay Later?* TG Clippers do a lot of business that way, an' so does Cluster Lines."

"But these people don't have money."

"There're more important things in life than money—not that I can think of any right now."

Grimes realized that he was being talked into a corner. He said firmly, "I have to know where you intend taking your . . . er . . . passengers."

"I've already told you that it's none of your business."

"Would it be . . . Essen?"

"I'm not sayin' that is is—but what if it is Essen?"

"All right, Captain Kane. *If* you don't mind, I'll just assume that it is Essen. There'd be a good market there for women, wouldn't there? And Federation law definitely prohibits any kind of traffic in human beings."

"Yeah. It does. I know the law as well as you do, Commander. Probably better. An' I'm tellin' you flat that I'm breakin' no laws. So I'll be greatly obliged if you'll tell your Jimmy The One to get out of *my* mate's hair."

"I'm sorry, Captain Kane, but I just can't take your word for it."

"No, you wouldn't, would you? We couldn't have a spick-an'-span Survey Service commander takin' the word of Drongo Kane, a poor, honest workin' stiff, master of a scruffy little star tramp, could we? Oh, no. But I'll tell you this. One of your own officers, that Commander Maggie Lazenby, is in Janine's palace now, an' that stuffed shirt Danzellan is with her. Janine's lettin' 'em look at the *secret* records, the ones that she showed me. I'm not kiddin' you, Grimes. She'll tell you that you can't touch me."

"That remains to be seen, Captain Kane."

"Why don't you call her now?"

"Why not?" agreed Grimes tiredly. He got on to Timmins, ordered him to arrange a hookup. After a few minutes Maggie's voice came through the speaker of the pinnace's transceiver.

"Commander Lazenby here, *Seeker*."

"Stand by, please, Commander Lazenby. I'm putting you through to the captain."

"Captain here," said Grimes.

"Yes, John?"

"I've been talking with Captain Kane. . . ."

"Yes. I know. He's just come into the Records Room."

"He assures me that whatever he's doing is quite legal, and that you'll bear him out."

"Yes, but . . . I've just unearthed some very old records. . . . And from what Captain Danzellan tells me . . ."

"She says yes," put in Kane. "An' until the law is changed, if it ever is . . ."

"I said yes, *but* . . ." insisted Maggie.

"And if Tabitha is not lying . . ." contributed Danzellan.

"She said *yes!*" snapped Kane, his customary drawl forgotten.

"Maggie!" said Grimes forcibly. "Report, at once, in detail what you have discovered."

But there was no report. Kane used his wrist transceiver to jam the signals from those worn by Maggie and Danzellan, and before either or both of them could take any action the far more powerful transceiver of Kane's pinnace blocked all further transmissions from Ballarat.

23

YES . . . *BUT*.

Yes . . . *but*.

But *what?*

Meanwhile, Mr. Saul had made the terrain between the landing site and Oxford quite impassable to any ground vehicle, and would have to be restrained before he blew away all *Seeker*'s 60 mm ammunition. Grimes told the first lieutenant to cease fire, at once.

But what loophole in Federation law had Kane discovered? What possible means of stopping that loophole had Maggie discovered? Where did Francis Delamere's local girlfriend, Tabitha, come into it?

Grimes decided that *Southerly Buster*'s lift-off from Morrowvia must be, at the very least, delayed. Could he stop the *Buster*'s boat from ferrying, a dozen or so at a time, the unconscious women to the ship? Yes, he could—but only at grave risk to the boat's passengers. Embarkation would have to be allowed to continue; by the time that it was complete he, Grimes, would be back aboard *Seeker* and would be able to take full charge.

Seeker's cannon were silent now, and *Southerly Buster*'s one remaining boat had nosed cautiously out of its bay and was flying to where the victims of the gas shell barrage were sprawled in the long grass. *Seeker*'s boat transmitted pictures of all that was going on. The small craft from the *Buster* dropped to a landing among the sleeping bodies and two men, wearing respirators, scrambled out of it. Working fast, they dragged fifteen of the women into the boat, careless of any abrasions or contusions they might inflict. They were equally careless with their two anesthetized mates—but that was no excuse. Kane's men were clothed and the risk of painful damage to their skins was so much less.

"Do I have to watch this, Captain?" the first lieutenant was raging.

"I'm afraid you have to, Mr. Saul," Grimes told him.

"Of course, if you can think of any way of stopping it without hurting any innocent people . . ."

Saul did not reply.

The first load was carried to *Southerly Buster*, the boat landing at the foot of the boarding ramp. Its passengers were dragged out and dumped on the ground, and almost immediately the boat began its return journey. Meanwhile a cargo hatch had been opened high on the side of the ship and the arm of a crane swung out. A net was lowered and the women, together with the two unconscious men, were piled into it, swiftly hoisted up an inboard. It was obvious that Kane was blessed with an efficient second-in-command.

Seeker's boat followed the one from *Southerly Buster* back to her loading site. There was a repetition of the callously efficient handling of the unknowing passengers—and then another, and then another.

But Grimes's pinnace had crossed the coastline now, was rushing inland. Grimes hoped to be back aboard *Seeker* before *Southerly Buster*'s embarkation was completed, although he could not hope to make it before sunset. Dusk was sweeping over the countryside as the two ships came into view, Kane's vessel towering brightly in the harsh glare of working lights. Saul had the hatch of the pinnace's bay open and waiting, and Billard expertly jockeyed the craft into the opening. Grimes was out through the door and running up to the control room before the pinnace had settled to her chocks. He found Saul staring sullenly out of a viewport.

"That's the last boatload," said the first lieutenant morosely. "Recall our boat, sir?"

"Do just that, Mr. Saul. I want the ship buttoned up for lift-off."

"Yes. . . ." Saul gestured toward the *Buster*. "*She's* buttoning up."

The boom of the crane was withdrawn, the cargo hatch was shut. *Southerly Buster*'s boat lifted from the ground where she had discharged her last load, nosed up the mother ship's side to her bay. The ramp folded up and inward. The airlock door slid shut. Faintly there came the clangor of starting machinery, the unmistakable broken rhythm of the inertial drive.

Grimes ordered, "Use your sixty millimeters again, Mr. Saul. Tracer, time fused. I want every shell bursting directly over her—not too close, but close enough so they can hear the shrapnel rattling around their control room."

"Aye, sir!"

The automatics rattled deafeningly, the tracer streaked out from the muzzles in a flat trajectory, the bursting shells were spectacular orange flowers briefly blossoming against the dark sky.

Not at all surprisingly Dreebly's voice came screaming from the transceiver. "Stop firing! Stop firing, you idiots, before you hurt somebody!"

"Then shut down your engines!" commanded Grimes. "I am grounding you."

"By what authority? You have no authority here. This is not a Federated world."

"Shut down your engines!"

"I refuse."

Dreebly did more than merely refuse. Winking points of blue flame appeared from a turrent on *Southerly Buster*'s side. The streams of tracer from the two ships intersected, forming a lethal arch. Freakishly there were explosions at its apex as time- and impact-fused projectiles came into violent contact with each other—but the majority of *Seeker*'s shells still burst over *Southerly Buster*, and those from the *Buster*'s guns burst directly over *Seeker*.

"The bastard's hosepiping!" exclaimed Saul.

Yes, Dreebly was hosepiping, slowly and deliberately lowering the trajectory of his stream of fire. Would he have the nerve to fire at rather than over a Federation ship? Grimes knew that *he* did not have the nerve to fire directly at *Southerly Buster*. Should he do so there would inevitably be casualties—and those casualties might well be among the *Buster*'s innocent passengers.

He said to Saul, "Cease fire."

"But, sir, I could put that turret out of action. . . ."

"I said, cease fire."

Seeker's hammering guns fell silent. There was a last burst from the *Buster*'s automatics, a last noisy rattle of shrapnel around *Seeker*'s control room. From the transceiver came Dreebly's taunting voice, "Chicken!"

"She's lifting," said Pitcher.

"She's lifting," echoed Saul disgustedly.

"Secure all," ordered Grimes, hurrying to the pilot's chair. "Secure all! There will be no further warning!"

He heard the coded shrilling of the alarms as he belted himself in. He checked the telltale lights on the control panel before him. By the time that the inertial drive was ready to lift *Seeker* clear of the ground *Southerly Buster* would be beyond pursuit range.

Was everything secure? It would be just too bad if it wasn't. The trained spacemen he could trust to obey orders promptly, the scientists were a different kettle of fish. But he couldn't afford to worry about them now, could not afford to indulge in the archaic, time-consuming, regulation ritual of the countdown.

He pushed the button for full emergency rocket power—and almost immediately tons of reaction mass exploded from the venturis in incandescent steam. The giant hand of acceleration slammed him deep down into the padding of his seat. *Seeker* was lifting. *Seeker* was up and away, shooting skyward like a shell fired from some gigantic cannon. She overtook the slow-climbing *Southerly Buster*, roared past her as though she were standing still, left her well astern.

On the console the telltale light of the inertial drive was now glowing green. Grimes cut his rockets and the ship dropped sickening until the I.D. took hold, then brought up with a jar. She shuddered in every member as Grimes applied lateral thrust, as she lurched sideways across the sky. Pitcher, who had realized what the captain was trying to do, was doing, had stationed himself by the radar. "A little more, sir," he called. "Easy, now, easy. . . ." Then, "hold her at that!"

"Hold her!" repeated Grimes.

The ship shuddered and groaned again, but he was holding her in position relative to the ground below, to the still-climbing *Southerly Buster*. Then—slowly, but not so slowly as to conceal his intentions—he reduced vertical thrust. Dreebly tried, but in vain, to wriggle past *Seeker*. Grimes anticipated every move. (Later he learned that Hayakawa had been feeding him information, that Myra Bracegirdle, loyal rather to her sex than to her ship, had worked with and not against her fellow telepath.) It seemed that he could not go wrong—and every time that Dreebly attempted a lateral shift *Southerly Buster* fell victim to the parallelogram of forces, inevitably lost altitude.

At last it was obvious to Mr. Dreebly that he had only two choices. Either he could return to the surface, or he could commit suicide by crushing his control room and everybody in it against *Seeker*'s far less vulnerable stern. He was not in a suicidal mood.

Grimes could not resist the temptation. He called for a microphone and for a hookup to the *Buster*'s transceiver. He said just one word, and that with insufferable smugness.

"Chicken!"

Slowly the two ships dropped through the night—*Southerly Buster* cowed and inferior. Apart from that one taunt there had been no exchange of signals. Slowly they dropped, the defeated Dreebly and the overconfident Grimes.

It was this overconfidence that led, at the finish, to disaster. Just before Dreebly's landing Grimes miscalculated, and his stern made brief contact with the *Buster*'s stem, doing her no great damage but throwing her off balance. With all his faults, Dreebly was a superb shiphandler. He fought to correct the topple, and had he not been inhibited by the ominous bulk of the other vessel hanging immediately above his control room he might well have done so. *Southerly Buster*'s fall was not completely catastrophic, but it was a fall, nonetheless. Visibly shuddering, she tilted, further and further, until her long axis was parallel to the ground.

It was then that Dreebly lost control, and there was a tinny crash as she dropped the last half meter.

24

IT WAS, GRIMES admitted glumly, quite a mess. Just how big a mess it was depended upon the legality or otherwise of his actions, the illegality or otherwise of Kane's operations. Legalities and illegalities notwithstanding, he was obliged to give assistance to the damaged—the wrecked—ship.

She was not a total write-off, although on a world with no repair yards it would be months before she could be made spaceworthy; she would probably have to be towed off-planet to somewhere where there were facilities. (And who would have to pay the bill? Kane would certainly take legal action against the Federation.)

Fortunately everybody aboard *Southerly Buster* had escaped serious injury, although the unfortunate women from Oxford, who had just been recovering consciousness at the time of the crash, were badly bruised and shaken. Them Grimes sent back to their town in *Seeker*'s boats.

He said to Saul, "I've done enough damage for one day. I'm turning in—for what's left of the night."

"The report to Base, sir. . . ."

Grimes told him coarsely what he could do to the report, then, "It will have to wait, Number One. I don't want to stick my neck out in writing until I have a few more facts."

"But you put down an attempt at slave trading, sir."

"Mphm. I hope so. I sincerely hope so. But I'm afraid that the bastard Drongo has some dirty big ace up his sleeve. Oh, well. Sufficient unto the day is the evil thereof. I'm getting some shut-eye. Good night, Number One."

"Good night, sir."

Grimes went up to his quarters. He paused briefly in his day cabin, poured himself a stiff drink, downed it in one swallow. He felt a little better. He went through into his bedroom, and stiffened with astonishment in the doorway, Maya was there, curled up on the bed, her back to him. She was snoring gently—and then immediately was wide awake, rolling over to face him.

"Maya . . ." he said reprovingly.

"I had to sleep somewhere, John," she told him, even more reprovingly. "And you seemed to have quite forgotten all about me."

"Of course I hadn't," he lied.

"Of course you had," she stated, without rancor. "But you had much more important things on your mind." She was off the bed now and was sagging enticingly against him. She said, in a very small voice, "And I was frightened. . . ."

The scent of her was disturbing. It was not unpleasant but it was strange—yet somehow familiar. It was most definitely female.

He said, "But you can't sleep here. . . ."

"But I have been sleeping here, John. . . ."

(So, she had begun to use his first name, too.)

She pleaded, "Let me stay. . . ."

"But . . ."

Her hands, with their strangely short fingers, were playing with the seal-seam of his shirt, opening the garment. They were soft and caressing on the skin of his back, but her nails were very sharp. The sensation was stimulating rather than painful. He could feel her erect nipples against his chest.

She pleaded again, "Let me stay. . . ."

Against his conscious will his arms went about her. He lowered his head and his lips down to hers. Oddly, at first she did not seem to understand the significance of this, and then she responded avidly. All of her body was against him, and all of his body was vividly aware of it. He walked her slowly backward toward the bed, her legs moving in time with his. Through the thin material of his shorts he could feel the heat of her thighs. She collapsed slowly, almost bonelessly, onto the nest that she had made for herself with pillows and cushions. He let her pull him down beside her, made no attempt to stop her as she removed the last of his clothing. (For a woman who had never worn a garment in her life she was learning fast.)

Their mating was short, savage—and to Grimes strangely unsatisfying. What should have been there for him was not there; the tenderness that he had come to expect on such occasions was altogether lacking. There was not even the illusion of love; this had been no more than a brief, animal coupling.

But she, he thought rather bitterly, *is not complaining*.

She was not complaining.

She, immediately after the orgasmic conclusion of the act, was drifting into sleep, snuggled up against him.

She was purring.

25

DOG TIRED, HIS nerves on edge after a sleepless night, Grimes stood in his control room and watched Drongo Kane come roaring in from the northward. He had been expecting Kane; Mr. Timmins had monitored the radio signals exchanged by Mr. Dreebly and his irate captain. He was expecting Maggie, too, but not for at least another hour. She had told him that Captain Danzellan was bringing her back to *Seeker*. She had refused to tell him what it was that she has discovered in the ancient records kept in Janine's palace, saying, "It will keep."

"Damn it all!" he had exploded, "I shall have Kane to deal with. And if what I suspect is true, legally I won't have a leg to stand on. Not unless *you* can pull a rabbit out of the hat."

"Not a rabbit," she told him. "Most definitely not a *rabbit*."

And that was all that he could get from her.

He had made use of the ship's memory bank encyclopedia facilities. In a Survey Service vessel these, of course, were continually kept up to date. He learned that although a committee was considering revisal, or even repeal, of the Non-Citizen Act this piece of legislation was still law. As far as he could see the act applied most specifically to the natives of Morrowvia—and that left him well and truly up the well known creek, without a paddle.

And here was Kane, dropping down from the morning sky, a man who knew Federation law so well that he could always bend it without actually breaking it. Here was Kane, a shipmaster *and* a shipowner who had learned that his vessel had been as good as (as bad as) wrecked by the officious actions of a relatively junior Survey Service officer. Here was Kane, more than a little annoyed about the frustration of his highly profitable activities.

Here was Kane.

Southerly Buster's pinnace slammed down alongside the parent ship in a flurry of dust and small debris. The door opened and Kane jumped out. He was no longer wearing his gaudy finery but had changed into utilitarian gray coveralls. Sabrina, still aglitter with jewelry, appeared in the doorway but Kane, irritably, motioned her back inside.

Dreebly, his head bandaged, came out of the ship. He stood there, drooping, while Kane obviously gave him a merciless dressing down. Then, slowly, the two men walked all around the crippled hulk, with the mate pointing out details of exterior damage. Grimes already knew what the damage was like inside—the Mannschenn Drive torn from its housing, the hydroponics tanks a stinking mess of shattered plastic and shredded greenery, most of the control room instruments inoperable if not completely ruined.

Saul came to stand by his captain's side. They watched as Kane and Dreebly clambered into the near-wreck through an amidships cargo hatch. The first lieutenant said happily, "You certainly put paid to *his* account, sir."

Grimes said, not so happily, "I only hope that he doesn't put paid to mine. . . ."

"But, sir, the man's a blackbirder, a slave trader! You've wrecked his ship—but that was the only way that you could stop the commission of a crime."

"Strong measures, Mr. Saul—especially if there were no crime being committed."

"But he fired on us, sir."

"At, not on. And we fired at him first."

"But he still hasn't a leg to stand on. . . ."

"Hasn't he? I've checked up on the Non-Citizen Act. I'm afraid that the Morrowvians do not qualify for citizenship. They have no rights whatsoever."

"I don't see it, sir. They're backward, I suppose—but they're as human as you or I."

"They're not," Grimes told him. "They're not, and that's the bloody trouble. What do you know of the Non-Citizen Act, Mr. Saul?"

"Not much, sir. But I can check up on it."

"Don't bother. I'll fill you in. That particular piece of legislation dates back to the bad old days when, briefly, the genetic engineers had far too much say. Although they were concerned primarily with the life sciences their outlook was that of engineers. You know, as well as I do, the peculiarities of the engineering outlook. If human beings and machines can't work together with maximum efficiency—then modify the human to suit the machine, not the other way round. A planet, like a house, is a machine for living in. If it is not suited to its intending occupants—then modify the occupants to fit. Then the generic engineers took things further. They manufactured, in their laboratories, androids—beings of synthetic flesh and blood that were, in effect, artificial men and women. Then they made 'underpeople'; the word was coined by a Twentieth Century science fiction writer called Cordwainer Smith and later, much later, used in actual fact. These underpeople were even less human than the androids, their very appearance making obvious their animal origins. They could not interbreed with true humans any more than the androids could—but they could breed, although they could not crossbreed. Put it this way—a dogman could mate with a dogwoman and fertilize her, or a catman with a catwoman. Only dogs—or ex-dogs—with dogs. Only cats—or ex-cats—with cats.

"Then there was the Android Revolt on Dancey. There was the virtual take-over of Tallis by the underpeople, although without bloodshed. The Federation Government put its foot down with a firm hand. No more androids were to be manufactured. No more underpeople were to be bred. All existing androids and underpeople were deprived of citizenship. And so on.

"It was quite some time before I realized the nature of the situation here, on Morrowvia. Kane, somehow, twigged it long before I did. But, last night, the final pieces of the jigsaw puzzle fell into place with a quite deafening *click*. I should have seen it before. There are so many clues. . . ."

"What do you mean, sir?"

"You did the science fiction course at the Academy, Mr. Saul."

"But I never cared for that wild stuff. I can't remember much of it."

"You must remember some of it. Anyhow, we all assumed that this planet was named after the captain of *Lode Cougar*. But I saw some of the records in the museum at Ballarat. Morrow was *not Lodge Cougar*'s master, neither was he one of her officers. He must have been one of the passengers—and a genetic engineer. I don't know yet how many survivors there were of *Lode Cougar*'s original complement when she landed, although Commander Lazenby will no doubt be able to tell us. I don't think that there could have been many. I don't think that there were any women of childbearing age among them. But, like all the ships of her period, she carried banks of fertilized ova—both human and animal. Perhaps the human ova had been destroyed somehow—or perhaps Morrow just didn't want to use them. Perhaps the ova of all the usual useful animals—with no exception—had been somehow destroyed—or perhaps Morrow was an aelurophile. I rather think that he was. He was also a science fiction addict—there are shelves of his books on display in the museum at Ballarat. He also had a rather warped sense of humor. The clues that he left!"

"What clues, sir?" asked Saul.

"In the names he gave—to the continent where *Lode Cougar* landed, to the four families that he . . . founded, to the planet itself. The planet of Doctor Morrow . . . the island of Doctor Moreau. . . ."

"You're way beyond me, sir."

"Mr. Saul, Mr. Saul, you should have read that Twentieth Century rubbish while you had the chance. One of Morrow's books was *The Island of Doctor Moreau*, by a writer called Wells. Wells's Doctor Moreau was a rather mad scientist who converted animals into imitation humans by crude surgical means. Morrow . . . Moreau . . . see the connection? And one of the four family names on Morrowvia is Wells, another is Morrow.

"Another book was *The Planet Buyer*, by Cordwainer Smith. It was Cordwainer Smith who invented the underpeople. One of his favorite planets—he wrote, of course, before men had landed on Earth's moon—was Old North Australia, shortened to Norstrilia. So Morrow called the continent on which he landed North Australia, and made Cordwainer and Smith the other two family names.

"Meanwhile, he was having fun. He was breeding a people to fit in with all his own pet ideas. Evidently he disapproved of the nudity taboo, just as Commander Lazenby's people do on Arcadia. His political ideas bordered on anarchism. Possibly he was an anarchist. I seem to recall from my reading of history that there was quite a powerful, or influential, Anarchist Party on Earth, in both hemispheres, at the time of the Second Expansion. It worked underground, and it contributed to the decline and fall of the Russian Empire. And we see here the results of Morrow's ideas. Utterly unselfconscious nudism, no central government, no monetary system. . . .

"It's a pity that this Lost Colony was ever discovered. Its people are more human than many who are officially so—but they have no rights whatsoever."

There was a silence, then Saul said, "We, our people, know what it was like. . . ." Grimes looked at him rather nastily so he hastily changed the subject. "But tell me, sir, what did you mean when you said that the pieces of the puzzle fell into place last night?"

"You've served in *Pathfinder*, with Captain Lewis," said Grimes. "So have I. You know his taste in pets. You know how obvious it is, once you step inboard through the airlock. . . .

"Well, since you ask, my quarters stink of *cat*."

26

MAYA JOINED THE two men in the control room. She looked as though she had slept well. She glanced incuriously through the viewports at the disabled *Southerly Buster*, then said plaintively, "I'm hungry. . . ."

Go down to the galley and see if the cook can find you some fish heads . . . thought Grimes—and then despised himself for thinking it. He said, "Mr. Saul, would you mind taking Maya to the wardroom for breakfast?"

"But what does she *eat*, sir?" asked the first lieutenant desperately.

"I'll try anything, everything," she said sweetly, "until I find something I like."

Grimes watched her as she followed Saul out of the control room. There should have been, he thought, a tail ornamenting those shapely buttocks. A nice, furry, striped tail . . . He shrugged.

The officer of the watch reported, "Sir, an unidentified craft is approaching from the north."

"That will be *Schnauzer*'s pinnace," said Grimes. He went to the transceiver, selected the most probable waveband. "Commander Grimes to Captain Danzellan. Do you read me? Over."

"Loud and clear, Commander. Danzellan here. My ETA your landing site is thirty minutes Standard, twenty-four minutes Local, from now. I have your Commander Lazenby with me. Over."

"Thank you, Captain Danzellan." Should he ask to speak with Maggie? No. She had made no attempt to speak with him. And Grimes was in a misogynistic mood. *Women! Cats!*

He returned to the viewport. He passed the time by mentally composing the sort of report—or complaint—that he would write if he were Drongo Kane.

To: Flag Officer in Charge of Lindisfarne Base
From: Drongo Kane, master and owner of s/s Southerly Buster
Subject: Piratical action by Lieutenant Commander John Grimes, Captain of ESS Seeker.
Sir,

I regret to have to report that while my vessel was proceeding on her lawful occasions she was wantonly attacked by your Seeker, under the command of your Lieutenant Commander Grimes. Commander Grimes not only used his armament to impede the embarkation of fare-paying passengers, subjecting them to a sleep gas barrage, but also fired upon Southerly Buster *herself. Later he attempted to ram my ship after she had lifted off, and only the superlative skill of my chief officer, who was in charge of the vessel at the time, averted a collision. Although contact between the two ships was avoided contact with the ground was not. As a result of this,* Southerly Buster *sustained severe structural damage. . . .*

"Pinnace in sight visually, sir," reported the O.O.W.

"Thank you, Mr. Giles."

Danzellan came in more slowly and cautiously than Kane had done, but he wasted no time, setting his craft down at the foot of *Seeker*'s ramp. Grimes watched *Schnauzer*'s master get out, then help Maggie Lazenby to the ground. He told Giles to telephone down to the airlock sentry, instructing the man to inform Captain Danzellan and Maggie that he would be waiting for them in his quarters. He went down to his day cabin, hastily shutting the door between it and his bedroom. The smell of cat was still strong.

He found and filled his foulest pipe, lit it. When Danzellan and Maggie came in he was wreathed in an acrid, blue smog.

"What a fug!" she exclaimed.

The intercom telephone buzzed. It was the O.O.W. calling. "Sir, Captain Kane and his chief officer are at the airlock. They wish to speak to you."

"Send them up," said Grimes.

"What in the universe have you been *doing*, Commander?" asked Danzellan. "Fighting a small war?"

"Or not so small," commented Maggie.

"I," Grimes told them bitterly, "was attempting to prevent the commission of a crime. Only it seems that slave trading is not a crime, insofar as this bloodly world is concerned."

"The underpeople . . ." said Maggie softly. "Underpeople—and the still unrepealed Non-Citizen Act. . . . But how did you find out? It took me hours after I was able to get my paws on the records. . . ."

"I added two and two," Grimes told her, "and came up with three point nine recurring. All the clues are so obvious. Rudimentary nipples, paw-like hands and feet, the way in which the people eat and drink, and the use of 'cat' as a term of opprobrium when, apart from the Morrowvians themselves, there isn't a single animal of Terran origin on the planet. . . ."

Danzellan grinned. "I see what you mean. I've been known to refer to particularly stupid officers as 'pathetic apes.' "

"Those same points had *me* puzzled," admitted Maggie. "But I'm surprised that *you* noticed them."

"And Morrow's books," went on Grimes. "*The Island of Doctor Moreau*. The Cordwainer Smith novels. The names of the four families—Wells, Morrow, Cordwainer and Smith. And North Australia. . . ."

"You're losing me there," admitted Maggie.

A junior officer knocked at the door. "Captain Kane to see you, sir. And Mr. Dreebly."

Kane blew into the room like the violent storm after which his ship was named. He blustered, "I'll have your stripes for this, Grimes! As soon as your bloody admiral hears my story he'll bust you right down to Spaceman Sixteenth Class—unless he decides to shoot you first!"

"Slave trading," said Grimes, "is prohibited by Federation law."

"Yeah. It is. But, Mr. Commander Grimes, such laws exist only for the protection of Federation citizens. The Morrowvians are non-citizens."

"How do you make that out?"

"How do I make that out? Because they're under-people, Commander—which means that they have the same status as androids, which means that they have no bloody status at all. They're no more than cattle—with the accent on the first syllable!" He laughed briefly at his own play on words, turned to glare at Dreebly when he essayed a snicker. "The only protection they can claim is that of the S.P.C.A.—and there's no branch of that society on Morrowvia!"

Grimes looked at Maggie appealingly. She flashed him a fleeting smile of encouragement. He looked at Danzellan. The portly shipmaster winked at him.

"Slavery," said Grimes firmly, "is still a crime, ethically if not legally."

"So is piracy, Grimes. Ethically *and* legally."

"I seem to recall past occasions in your own career. . . ."

"We're not talking about them. We're talking about *this* occasion in *your* career. The unprovoked attack upon an innocent merchantman. To begin with, Grimes, you can place your artificers at my disposal. *If* they make a good job I just might tone my report to your bosses down a little." He laughed lightly. "A stiff note on paper, instead of a stiff note on cardboard. . . ."

"Mphm," grunted Grimes thoughtfully.

"In fact, Commander," went on Kane, speaking quite quietly now, his exaggerated accent gone, "I think that you could help me considerably. . . ."

And Kane, thought Grimes, *owes his survival to the number of friends he has in high places. And Kane is an opportunist. For all he knows I might be an admiral myself one day. He's debating with himself, "Shall I put the boot in, or shall I let bygones be bygones?" Too, he's probably not quite sure if he* is *altogether in the right, legally speaking. . . .*

"Don't trust him, Commander," said Danzellan.

"Keep your nose out of this!" snarled Kane.

"*I* discovered this planet," stated Danzellan. "The Dog Star Line . . ."

". . . can go and cock its leg against a lamp post," Kane finished the sentence.

"Gentlemen," said Grimes soothingly. "Gentlemen. . . ."

"I can't see any round here," remarked Maggie.

"You shut up for a start," he told her. But he realized that her flippancy had broken the tension.

"What do you say, Commander?" persisted Kane. "You have a workshop, and skilled technicians. . . . Get the old *Buster* back into commission for me and you can write your own report to your superiors." He grinned. "After all, I'm just a semiliterate tramp skipper. Paperwork's beyond my capabilities."

"And what about me?" asked Danzellan interestedly.

"The Dog Star Line's big enough to look after itself, Captain, as I have no doubt that it will. My own activities, for quite some time, anyhow, will be confined to this continent of New England. You," he said generously, "can have North Australia."

"Thank you, Captain. I appreciate the gesture. But I feel obliged to tell you that my employers are not quite the soulless bastards that they have often been alleged to be. They would not wish to share a planet with a slaver. Not," he added, "that it will ever come to that."

"So you're pulling out?" asked Kane.

"No."

"I warn you, Captain Danzellan, that if you or your people try to make things awkward for me, I shall make things even more awkward for the Dog Star Line. They'll finish up by buying me out, at my price. It will not be a low one." He turned to Grimes. "And what do you say, Commander, to my proposition to you?"

"No," said Grimes. "No, repeat no."

"You'll be sorry. My report—and it's a damning one—has already been written. My Carlotti transmitter is quite powerful, and will be able to raise the Lindisfarne Base station with ease. You'd better have your letter of resignation ready."

He turned to go.

"Hold your horses," said Maggie sweetly. "Hold your horses, Captain Kane. I haven't said *my* party piece yet."

27

SHE SAID, "YOU'D better all sit down and make yourselves comfortable, as this is quite a long story. You, John, just read the very beginnings of it. You, Captain Kane, read enough to convince you that slaving activities, with Federation law as it stands at present, would be quite legal. And I was able to do more research than either of you.

"The story of *Lode Cougar* is not, in its early stages, an unusual one. There was the gaussjammer, lifting from Port Woomera, bound for the newly established colony on Austral—*your* home world, Captain Kane. As well as the intending colonists she carried cargo, among which was a shipment of fertilized ova. Dogs were required on Austral, and cats, to deal with the numerous indigenous vermin. There were cattle too, of course, and horses—oh, all the usual. And there were human ova, just in case the ship got thrown off course by a magnetic storm and had to start a new colony from scratch, in some utterly uncharted sector of the galaxy. Quite a number of colonies were started that way.

"*Lode Cougar* was unlucky—as so many of the old gaussjammers were. A magnetic storm threw her thousands of light-years off course. Her navigators were unable to determine her position. Her pile was dead, and her only source of power was her diesel generators. The engineers kept these running—which meant that the ship's biochemist was having to produce fuel for the jennies rather than food for the crew and passengers.

"But all they could do was to stand on and stand on, from likely star to likely star, pulling their belts ever tighter, finding that some suns had no planetary systems, that other suns had worlds in orbit about them utterly incapable of supporting any kind of life, let alone life as *we* know it.

"Almost inevitably there was a mutiny. It came about when a gang of starving passengers was caught foraging in the cargo spaces—*the refrigerated cargo spaces.* Is it cannibalism when you gorge yourself on fertilized human ova? A rather doubtful legal point. . . . Anyhow, the master of the *Cougar* decided that it was cannibalism, and ordered the offenders shot. In the consequent flareup there was rather too much shooting and then an orgy of *real* cannibalism. . . . Things went from bad to worse after that, especially since the captain, his senior officers and most of the more responsible passengers were killed. Among the survivors was a professional genetic engineer, a Dr. Edward Morrow. He wrote despairingly in his private journal, 'Will this voyage never end? Men and women are behaving like wild beasts. No, I must not say that, because my fellow passengers are worse than beasts. No decent animal could ever sink to such depths.' That passage sticks in my memory. It explains so much. Some time later he wrote that the ship was approaching yet another sun, and that Bastable, the liner's third officer, hoped that it would run to a habitable planet. 'If it does not,' Morrow wrote, 'that is the finish of us. Soon there will be only one survivor, gnawing the last shreds of human flesh from the last bone.'

"*Lode Cougar* cautiously approached the world that was still to be named. It looked to be habitable. There was a meeting of crew and passengers—what was left of them—and Bastable told them that the landing would have to be made in high magnetic latitudes, for the obvious reason. The others told Bastable that the landing would have to be made in some region with a hospitable climate; nobody was in fit condition to undertake a long trek over ice fields. Bastable acceded to their demands, after a long argument. Had he not been the only man capable of handling the ship he would have been murdered there and then.

"He got her down, as we know. He got her down, in one piece. The experience shattered him. He went to his quarters immediately after the landing, got out the bottle of alcohol that he had been jealously hoarding, and drank himself into insensibility. In his weakened condition—like all the rest he was more than half starved—it killed him. Regarding his death, Morrow made more unkind remarks in his journal about the human race.

"With the very few survivors a colony of sorts could have been started, might possibly have survived. There were ten men—nine of them, including Morrow, passengers, one of them a junior engineer. There were six women, four of them young. Morrow persuaded his companions that they would have a far better chance if they had underpeople to work for them. The only ova that had survived the trouble were those of cats—but Morrow was expert in his profession. With the aid of the engineer he was able to set up incubators and then—all that was required was in the ship's cargo—a fully equipped laboratory.

"He wrote again in his journal, 'The first batch is progressing nicely, in spite of the acceleration. I feel . . . paternal. I ask myself, why should these, my children, be *under*people? I can make them more truly human than the hairless apes that may, one day, infest this new world. . . . '

"Regarding the deaths of his fellow *Lode Cougar* survivors he says very little. One suspects that he knew more than he wrote about the food poisoning that killed Mary Little, Sarah Grant and Delia James. One wonders if Douglass Carrick fell off that cliff, or was pushed. And how did Susan Pettifer and William Hume come to get drowned in the river? It is interesting to note, too, that Mary, Sarah, Delia and Susan were the potential childbearers. And, as well as working in his laboratory, Morrow set up a still and soon had it in operation, turning out a very potent liquor from a fermented mash of berries and wild grain. The surviving men and the two remaining women didn't care much then what happened, and as Morrow had succeeded in activating a team of robots from the cargo he was independent of them. He didn't bother to kill them as his first batch of 'children' was growing to forced maturity. He just let them die—or be killed by wild animals when they went out hunting for meat."

"Yes," said Kane. "I know all that. The Morrowvians are non-citizens."

"I haven't finished yet, Captain Kane. There was something of the Pygmalion in Morrow—as there must have been in quite a few of those genetic engineers. He fell in love with one of his own creations—his Galatea. He even named her Galatea."

"Touching . . ." commented Kane.

"Yes, wasn't it? And he married her; he'd decided that his people couldn't live in a state of complete anarchy, and must have a few, necessary laws. So he made the union legal."

"Uncommonly decent of him," sneered Kane.

"But that didn't stop him from having quite a few concubines on the side. . . ."

"So the Morrowvian idol had his feet of clay."

"Don't we all, Captain, don't we all?"

"So the records prove that true humans can have sexual relations with these underpeople. I'd found that out long before I saw the precious records. Judging by the stink in here, Commander Grimes has found it out too."

"John! What have you been doing? Don't tell me that you and Maya . . ."

"I won't tell you if you tell me not to."

"So you did. I hope you enjoyed it, that's all."

Kane laughed patronizingly. "So I'll leave you people to your family squabbles, and get back to my ship and send my report off to Lindisfarne. A very good day to you all."

"Wait!" Maggie snapped sharply. "I haven't finished yet."

"I don't think that anything further you can say will change my mind. Underpeople are underpeople. Underpeople are property. Period."

"There is a ruling," said Maggie slowly, "that any people capable of fertile union with true people must, themselves, be considered true people."

"And so, to coin a phrase, what?"

"Morrow's unions were fertile."

"So he says. How many glorified tomcats were sneaking into his wife's or his popsies' beds while he was elsewhere?"

"The Morrow strain is strongest in North Australia, among the people who bear his name."

"What evidence is there?"

"The Morrows are a little more 'human' than the other Morrowvians. Very few of their women have supplementary nipples. Their general outlook is more 'human'—as you know yourself. That show you put on for Janine with the saluting cannon. . . . And the show she put on for us."

"Yeah. I grant you that. But I think the words of the ruling you mentioned are, 'a fertile, *natural* union.' Old Doc Morrow was a genetic engineer. I've heard it said that those boys could crossbreed an ant and an elephant. . . . I'm sorry. I'm really sorry for you all. You've tried hard, but by the time the Federation reaches a decision I'll have made my pile."

"I," said Danzellan, "can supply more proof for Commander Lazenby's arguments."

"You, Captain? You're no biologist, you're just a shipmaster like myself."

"Even so. . . ." The master of *Schnauzer* was obviously finding something highly amusing. "Even so. . . . You know, it's just over two hundred and twenty days that I first landed on Morrowvia—and that's about two hundred and seventy days Standard. . . ."

"I can do sums in my head as well as you can."

"I am sure you can, Captain Kane. And are you married? Have you a family?"

"No—to both questions."

"It doesn't matter. Well, on the occasion of my first visit, my second officer, Mr. Delamere, got Tabitha, the daughter of the Queen of Melbourne, into trouble, as the saying goes. The young idiot should have taken his contraceptive shots before he started playing around, of course. He's really smitten with her, and managed to get himself appointed to *Schnauzer*, rather against my wishes. Now he wants to make an honest woman of the girl—once again, as the saying goes—but Lilian, Tabitha's mother, will not allow him to marry her unless he complies with local law. This means that he will have to change his name to Morrow, which he does not want to do. He will, of course. The Dog Star Line wants a resident agent on this planet. And even though the queenships are not hereditary in theory they usually are in practice."

"What are you driveling about?" asked Kane crudely.

Danzellan flushed. He said stiffly, "Tabitha has presented young Delamere with a son."

"And how many local boyfriends has she had?" demanded Kane.

"She says that she has none. Furthermore, I have seen the baby. All the Morrowvians have short noses—except this one, who has a long nose, like his father. The resemblance is remarkable. . . ."

Kane refused to concede defeat.

"Paternity tests . . ." he mumbled.

"I can soon arrange those, Captain," Grimes told him. "Don't forget that I have my own biologists, as well as other scientists." He turned to Danzellan. "Did Mr. Delamere come with you, Captain? Call him up, and we'll wet the baby's head!"

"You can break a bottle of champagne over it!" growled Kane, pushing his way out of the day cabin, brushing past Maya who was just coming in, and complaining, "I'm *still* hungry, John. They say that all the ice cream is finished. . . ."

"Go on," said Maggie. "Do the decent thing. Buy the girl a popsicle to show her how much you love her."

"I'll have some more ice cream made, Maya," promised Grimes, looking at her with combined pity and irritation, noticing that Danzellan was regarding her with condescending amusement.

The Morrowvians, thanks to the long-dead Morrow's skill—he had even imposed the right gestation period on his people—were safe from

Drongo Kane and his like, but had no defenses against Big Business as represented by the Dog Star Line.

Or had they?

Grimes suspected that they, with their innate feline charm combined with selfishness, would not do at all badly in the years to come.